ISTANBUL WAS A FAIRY TALE

MARIO LEVI

ISTANBUL WAS A FAIRY TALE

TRANSLATED BY ENDER GÜROL

DALKEY ARCHIVE PRESS
CHAMPAIGN • DUBLIN • LONDON

Originally published in Turkish as *İstanbul Bir Masaldı* by Remzi Kitabevi, Istanbul, 1999

Library of Congress Cataloging-in-Publication Data

Levi, Mario, 1957-
[Istanbul bir masaldi. English]
Istanbul was a fairy tale / Mario Levi ; translated by Ender Gürol. -- 1st ed.
    p. cm.
ISBN 978-1-56478-712-5 (pbk. : alk. paper)
1. Jews--Turkey--Istanbul--Fiction. I. Gürol, Ender. II. Title.
PL248.L45I8813 2012
894'.3533--dc23
                        2012001866

Partially funded by a grant from the Illinois Arts Council, a state agency

This book has been supported by the Ministry of Culture and Tourism of Turkey in the framework of the TEDA project

www.dalkeyarchive.com

Cover: design and composition by Sarah French
Printed on permanent/durable acid-free paper and bound in the United States of America

to my grandfather

The contributions of Attila İlhan, Cem Mumcu, Cevat Çapan, Buket Uzuner, Süzet Levi, Yelda Karataş, and Ragnhold Berstad are gratefully acknowledged.

FOREWORD

Being some methods by which the reader may locate, unearth, and then peruse
the contents 'concealed' in the present book.

I am well aware that the accounts narrated here or the experiences that dictated themselves to me in dribs and drabs and eventually transformed themselves into a manuscript forming the contents of the present long story may be potentially disturbing for certain individuals. During the never-ending nights, I had had the impression that I was trying to understand, even to analyze—which is more important—my manuscript, looking at it from a distance, and keeping aloof from those who had endeavored to impose it on me. Those were the nights during which I had tried to find a room in my life for what I had been imparted with. This feeling, whose roots lay entrenched far back in an inheritance, had eventually made me what I am; it was a feeling that I could not rip from myself despite the fact that I did my best to convey said manuscript to the reader on a different wavelength through that voice within me, despite all those secret corners that I had access to in my breast and all the tricks I had contrived toward that end. As far as my limitations permitted, I had to conceive and tell the story of this legacy to the best of my abilities, in my vernacular description of the extent of this circumstance in my life in the city where I was born and raised. In this way, I could make headway on a shoreline familiar to me, out of harm's way and unperturbed, thanks to the strength that this conviction gave me. I could evoke this shoreline in a conventional language, clad in the garb in which other people have been accustomed to see me. This frame of mind wherein I felt at home was just one of the circumstances I preferred to hold on to; just one of the circumstances. I had heard other voices calling me during the days I was learning to swim in still waters. The fear of remaining rooted to a given spot, of living and dying confined in a well-delineated space had had its part to play in arousing in me the desire to hurl myself headlong toward other places where I could not linger or stay for long, but I lacked the heart to bring myself to act firmly on such a notion. That was the reason that prompted me to such foolish fancies. That was the reason why I became a liar. I learned to live on lies and betrayed the people I cherished. I filled my lungs with the smoke of nearly 'everything that emitted smoke' to the detriment of my asthma, except for the carbonic acid in the gas released by burning coal in the stove. That was the reason why I had evinced the desire to marry a freckled slut with hazel eyes and flaxen hair who had taught me wantonly the secret language of lovemaking during my years of apprenticeship, and who, now and then, expressed the wish to be a lecturer someday in the sociology department of a university. That was the reason why I had started reading Spinoza on the Day of Atonement. That was the reason why pandering had tickled my fancy and I had wanted to become a copywriter. That was the reason why I had developed a hatred for prudish women whose sole concern was the preparation of crisp and golden pastries and in whom the development of the dexterity required in stuffing grapevine leaves was considered to be a matter of professional pride. That was the reason why I was disgusted with women whose peroration on freedom came to naught as they merely acted out things while remaining tightly bound to their matrimonial conventions and tradition; I disliked women whose aim it was to provide themselves with more security or who gossiped about my views, trying to prove to the world at large that they were mistresses of this world, by merely defining things without living them; thus contriving a sound scientific basis to satisfy themselves. Such was my wasteland, and I disclosed to no one my confidence tricks at the time. The child within me, the child who was thought to have been abandoned, the child who always felt a compulsive desire to attract attention, had the desire to emulate living such a life. That child had never tired of making requisition for just such a person. And he was in the right. He was fully justified in his aspirations for such tomfooleries. Was I by any chance trying to retrace my steps toward that thrilling adventure of which I never ceased to imagine, of which I had the premonition of encountering frequently in the course of my life and of which I was convinced of coming upon now and then in the darkest corners of my being? That may well be the case. I think I must ask myself once more about this story I am trying to elaborate on within myself in full cognizance of the frustrations, suspicions, and betrayals I have been subject to. I know that this will submerge me in a long period of gloomy introspection. I must see whether the simmering discontent and suspicion that my confessions may provoke in some people is of the same mold as the other perceptions I hold against my will. For, what I have gone through has taught me to shut up and bury my feelings deep within my heart. After all, I was born under a climate in which it was not so easy to persuade people to view things from different angles or to frustrate them by holding a mirror up to them so that they may see in it their own image. I took refuge in the languages of that climate; those languages were my sanctuary. Despite the ordeal I had gone through when I had set out, I'd not had the slightest intention of flustering people by my presence and exposing them to the things I had in store for them. I simply had been goaded by an instinct to tell a story, just to tell it. It was the story of someone leading the life of a fiddler, of living within a story, journeying to various countries of the world . . . After all, I was a wandering Jew whose aim it was to give birth to a land of his own, to discover it and live in it. Just like any other Jew, I was a stateless person. An ordinary Jew in the sight of some people, I was a nondescript individual that people looked at with suspicion and would not rely on; I had no vernacular to speak of and happened to be an outsider. When and where had that story begun, who had initiated it, the story which I might appropriate and call 'our story'? Where, when and for whom? Was it one of those stories that involved postponement, the putting off of expectations, living, living to the bitter end, living in defiance of 'them,' showing them, or living by narration and giving birth to a brand new morning after a night that seemed to have no end. A story stuck in the past we narrated, or rather—what is more important—the past we believe we narrated; the past expressed in a given tongue, using certain words? Such issues, in a certain sense, required courage in an individual that might insidiously lead to minor homicides, to the murder of certain things for which a proper definition was lacking. It was not in vain that we had cogitated on the fact that we were exhausting ourselves for everybody every passing day; just like the traveler in love . . . Those relationships could perhaps be defined in time in terms of our solitudes. For, the words, yes, the words, were not our words after all. However, those words may well have revealed our nakedness, our very selves; yet, we had been surreptitiously eradicated from our roots by those who were overeager to lend us their own vocabulary. Can we consider ourselves now to be in a position to ask one another what exactly those words had been? Can we reclaim them from each other and remind each other of them? Can we put on their garb once again? Can we? Can we identify ourselves with ourselves?

The experiences one enjoyed in those relations were certainly nobody's fault. Not a single moment was the consequence of a chink in one's armor. There was no such thing as wrong and right anyway. All that existed was what one actually had experienced or the things one desired, now left behind; things that are experienced and then desired to be bequeathed, or, in other words . . . things that one was desirous to show to one's fellow beings in order to make oneself conscious of what one experienced, even if only for a fleeting moment.

This book can therefore be read in more than one way, if a similar approach is adopted toward what has been narrated. If he so wishes, the reader may rest content with reading the section entitled 'The Starlings,' consisting of a few pages at the beginning of the present book. Those who opt for such an alternative shall be considered to have read and gone through the entire book. To understand another person or persons, even this step may suffice. For, this did have its precedence! This much had been enough and then some. Images or visions had proved to be adequate. The choice to consume it and put it in a corner believing it shall remain unaffected was a choice that strategically positioned us in familiar places, reinstating us to our original quarters; whilst the pages that narrate the rest, my ongoing adventure, are meant for those curious about details, for inquiring minds. The trivia and forgotten languages are meant for those willing to take a few steps toward knowing another person. The reader may, from the first page to the last, move forward listening to and feeling the sound of his own footsteps; he may skip sections or follow another order he himself may choose. I am aware that this suggestion is far from being a new proposal. In different climates, in different contexts, different people prefer to follow this voice. As I dare to make this suggestion or state this reminder, oblivious to my reiterations, I have the feeling that I'm more inclined to cogitate on the orientation of my life in this manuscript, thus being indifferent to my will. It has never been easy to pluck up the courage to collate data. To place oneself in that picture and view it, I mean truly view it, when the time is ripe, calls for one's patience rather than one's mastery. To be able to see it necessitates the focusing of one's attention on the issue with dedication and spontaneity as well as zeal, enthusiasm, and commitment, just like in the case of a relationship we try to cultivate and preserve lest we lose it, forms us and shows us to ourselves in the most straightforward manner. I can't possibly foretell where this trivia may lead and there is no need to repeat again at this juncture the fact that when a person gains ground in his march toward another person, or when he advances within himself with all those ancient images inherent in him, he doubtlessly experiences his own adventure, solely his own. I created a hero who endeavored to look through another window upon the city where I was born, the briny odor of whose sea he had drawn deep into his lungs, the odor which would not abandon him at a point where I felt I had found a vital clue; it was a hero who had dared to proceed on a long walk in order to discover his language, his vernacular. On this walk, the secret of the land was inherent. This language would set the boundaries of this land. As a matter of fact, this land was language incarnated, the horizon that this language revealed, the dreams that this language evoked and conjured up, the sentiments that the said language gave rise to. The story itself was an old story. The hour mentioned in the story was the hour already spent, experienced elsewhere; for instance, the death mentioned in the story was an ordinary death; the book in the story was the book painstakingly written both to be concealed and to be made public. The male protagonist was a person who took up the manuscript that he had written then tried to narrate and fictionalize his unique land. This person was at the same time the witness, the spectator, and the hero of his tale; in other words, a person condemned to be both inside and outside the tale. The walls were also there, those walls that had drawn up the borders of the land, the walls that delineated which was more important. In fact those walls were not unfamiliar to me. They were my own walls; the walls I wanted to rediscover, the walls I was supposing to tell the story of in my vernacular. This uneasiness could be explained in this way. The fear of taking a wrong step might in fact be sought for in the history of those walls, but that fear was cancelled in them. But the fact that I was born as an outsider in the peninsula nearest to the western world was not my fault; I was not responsible for having been the hero of my life in the 'Tale of Istanbul,' for emulating certain people and the heroes of other books that made up the course of my life, or for using the words of other people indiscriminately, laboring under an old illusion, or hoping for a new journey toward liberation. My Istanbul was a fairy tale. It was a tale, my own tale. The tale was 'their' story. The tale was our story. The tale was your story. The tale was the story of those who felt themselves alien in their own city. The tale was the story of my imagination that saw the waterway of the Bosporus like a womb, despite all the experiences I had gone through. This tale was the story of the fear of the consequence of a wrong overarm stroke or paddle which would cause my engulfment, my being swept away by currents and counter-currents toward something unknown. The short and the long of it, this tale was a tale.

THE STARLINGS

The day was declining and you were smiling

I cannot distinctly recollect where, when, and under what circumstances I'd met her. Nor can I remember those who were earmarked as the ones with the brightest futures. Yet, there is no scarcity of photographs from our past—a past very different to that of other people, one which I know I can never forget or dare to show to anyone, one which I can never rid myself of—that reveals me to myself ever more clearly as time goes by. These photographs embodied our nights, the things that we failed to share and which we could disclose to no one; they also concealed the expectations which I constantly and repeatedly rehashed in total disregard of my past experiences. For instance, we had our summer nights when we watched the city in which I had been living for ages through a different window. We used to sit on the balcony. The flowering of the marvels of Peru concealed in it the solitudes of many a garden in my life. It had occurred to me at the time to touch one of those gardens once more. Mother had a glowworm in her hand. It emitted uninterrupted luminous signals in the warmth of her palm. There were other glowworms as well . . . I had tried to share my old songs with her on the balcony and in other rooms of the house. I was conscious of the fact that the songs, the songs truly experienced, would never leave us in the lurch. I could foresee that certain songs would sooner or later be transported to different spaces in time. At such times we, ourselves, became songs: the vernaculars we had mislaid could not be found anymore, the deceptions I had tried to describe in other tales led to new disappointments. This was the reason why we had preserved some of our memories and were bent on protecting them; in fact, some of these retentions were the intuitions that we projected onto our loves and which nourished our dreams.

I had also wanted to tell of how I had felt defeated and forsaken during those nights of togetherness, exchanging tactile sensations. I could put pen to paper and cling to my writing; an occupation I would never relinquish. The fact is that when we were together I used to forget other people, all my designs, aspirations, my anticipatory mental attitudes, and my procrastinations were even more important. My experience with her was a prolific death, if one may say so. A fecund death! In her touching me, in our nightlong billing and cooing that titillated my entire being, my entire mind, and sexuality, my entire childhood was contained. Yes, my entire childhood! My entire childhood . . . those memories I had lost in my childhood. Today, from that house, what I recollect most are the songs I feel compelled to speak about and share with people.

When all these things rush to my mind, I find it difficult to confess the fact that I have always remained on good terms with her and never wanted to part from her. Even at times when I endeavored to share with her the most precious words and photographs of my life, I failed to find literal expression for what I had in mind; it was a failure. I don't know why I walked the earth surrounded by these walls of mine. To what purpose, I wonder? What exactly were my expectations and anticipations? Can it be that I feared to let myself go, thus draining her to the dregs, after taking all the probabilities into consideration? Maybe . . . The same was true for the others we knew, who too were lost under the shadow of fear; we could not carry ourselves as we should have done, because we had failed to abandon ourselves body and soul to the care of one another. As a matter of fact, we had drained the lifeblood of our relationship and our passions in our endeavor to conceal, to a certain extent, our personalities . . . She knew this, I think, from the very moment of our first encounter and our dates that followed, from the time when we had decided to be close to each other and live under the same roof. Those were the times when the child within me was calling for that house, lost in memory, and wanted, in the company of his mother, to keep alive the glowworm in the palm of his hand, till the end of its life!

Those were the nights during which we had shared our sexual desires, just like the rest of humanity, when someone else would lay their hands upon things that belonged to another, things that we could not properly define . . . Those were the nights during which we had written our histories, stories that no book could possibly contain. She knew this all too well. She knew for whom I kept it alive, for something that was missing, that something which I, as time went by, understood and continued to understand better . . . It may be because she had wanted all these things for herself, for herself alone . . . that I had to remain myself and in my self.

That is why I remained attached to her and would never part with her . . . never . . . despite all my expectations, my next-of-kin, and my walls. I'm smiling, and I have started to learn how to coexist with her. I'm well aware that I cannot get rid myself of those nights and those mornings that sneaked into my room mingled with the sounds I thought I had forgotten. For, I am beginning to understand that men who love each other by injuring and harming each other, through all the shortcomings and heartaches that go with it, cannot sever themselves from each other despite all their ill-defined concepts of deception and deference.

Her name . . . Her name for me was 'Dejection' . . . Dejection . . . This was the only title I could recall in view of our long-standing attachment . . . For she kept distant from me other times she might have spared the two of us, her sentiments and her principles, and her other appellations. I can feel this; I can understand this better now after sensing the delays that those deceptions gave rise to. However, just like all other sincere and honest relationships, this relationship also called for some extra effort, effort in order to understand it better. This is the reason why we'll continue to remain together and try to give birth to other nights of faint hopes. We'll continue to stick to each other . . . whether we want to or not . . . One can't understand the sea unless one actually lives on it; neither the sea nor the *Mirabilis Jalapa*; one can't understand the scent of the lime blossom if it is not coupled with the fear of losing it; losing it in actual fact. As I keep on brooding over these things now, it seems likely that I shall be in a position to lend her other names as well, when the time comes . . . A mere snapshot will be enough for me . . . I think that I'll have to store certain photographs indelibly in my memory so that I may remain in them. Then I'll be able to smile again, but no one among the whole mass of people will understand the reason for my smiling nor the person I am smiling for . . .

Evening had set in . . . The woman looked through the window. She listened to the sounds coming from outside. "Starlings," she said, "they will be with us this year also, with voices borrowed from others . . . just like us . . . like us." Tears rushed to her eyes. She leaned her head on her husband's chest and closed her eyes. They would have their cup of tea in that garden, in their garden, once again . . . They were once more the heroes of an untold Chekhov story. The clock had once more struck the same hour . . .

Who had stayed at whose place for whom?

Olga

She had rather unconsciously drawn the boundaries of her realm in her small apartment at Şişli. She wore her diamond necklace in order to be able to remain the princess in that fairy tale which she honestly believed to be real with all its concomitant associations and aspirations. She was a woman of infatuations. Her cherished dream was to depart one day for Mexico.

Madame Roza

She had remained devoted to Greek; on no account would she ever let it be consigned to oblivion, that Greek tongue that she had imported from Thrace as a child along with the memory of a vast expanse of daisy fields. These were the keys that opened many a tabooed room for her along with the secret corners of this tale. She had observed life firmly believing in the virtues of patience and endurance. Nobody dared to say anything likely to imply a dubious relationship between her and a milliner at Yüksek Kaldırım. She had been a real haven for every member of the family.

Madame Estreya

She had preferred to beget and foster her love somewhere far from the heroes and heroines of this tale. Nobody could ever learn about her affairs in that exotic part of Istanbul. At a time when everybody was becoming scarce in their own manner, she had returned to her family as a lifeless body. Her looks were reminiscent of the sea's fathomless depths, the meaning of which could only be understood properly by one individual.

Muhittin Bey

Both Selahattin Pınar's songs and Chopin's *Polonaises* had been a source of delight for him. He preferred to remain the hero of a tale that had been unable to complete its movement. Life, for him, had been a dirty joke.

Eva

She was the daughter of a wealthy banker from Riga. The days during which she had made up her mind to marry her third cousin were weighted by a secret, a secret she would eventually disclose to her daughter. Her love affairs had always been colorful and assumed mysterious meanings. When she was obliged to leave Odessa for Alexandria, the thing that had troubled her most had been her separation from her piano.

Schwartz

Once a triumphant officer in the army of the Austro-Hungarian Empire, he figures in the present story through his identity as an amnesic hero wandering at random in the streets of Istanbul. He believed he had had a country of his own once though he could not properly describe it; however, he had a photograph of it. The memory of a farm of which he had been the owner seemed to be lingering in his mind.

Yasef

Two things interested him in particular: 'toadying' and the compilation of anecdotes. He was a firm believer in women's fickleness; toward the end of his days, he used to say he had lived longer than he should have. Had he been conscious of the fact that he had been able to transmit to his son his skill as a comedian?

Ginette

Her story was a long one; she was born at a time when the war was still raging. She was believed to have been brought up first in a convent near Paris, then in Istanbul; she was already a young girl when she found herself in Haifa. She had lost an important part of herself in another war. When she revealed herself to the narrator in Vienna at the least unexpected moment, she was grim-faced, in spite of the fact that what she had always desired most in life was to be smiling, to always wear a smiling countenance.

Enrico

He deeply felt the absence of his elder sister when he fell down that deep well.

Marcello Algrante

He had chosen a path that led him to an altogether different God. He had studied at the *Galatasaray Lycée*. Voltaire had been his favorite author.

Sedat the Arab

He had carried his double-barreled gun with pride all his life. He had been a commercial traveler, riding in his minibus that he had named 'The Detective' throughout Anatolia, selling perfumes. He had in his possession maps showing routes known to nobody. He was a skillful mimic. That small town in the proximity of Istanbul was important not only for him, but also for another person figuring briefly in the present tale.

Henry Moskowitch

He was the son of a wealthy businessman who had amassed a huge fortune under the Empire. His amorous exploits with a countess figuring in the present tale (whose name he could never discover) had marked the beginning of an end. According to rumors, he had had many other affairs with famous singers and actresses of his time. In actual fact, he had had just one fairy tale princess.

Uncle Kirkor

He had been an eavesdropper, though quite by chance. An unfortunate accident had compelled him to give up his job as a lathe operator to take up commerce. He had been Monsieur Jacques' most reliable friend. His inability to ask his wife to prepare for him a dish of mussels had had a very meaningful reason behind it.

Juliet

Her cherished hope was to be able to appear on the stage as Nora. She tried to show her rebellious tendencies through her beautiful photographs. Her intention had been to put in an appearance as a powerful feminine character in the presence of her narrator. She had performed her dances solely to the accompaniment of her own songs. She had shed tears during the funeral of her daughter.

Consul Fahri Bey

His residence at Salacak resembled a hermit's hut. He spoke of having rescued many a Turkish-Jewish prisoner from concentration camps.

Ani

She had tried to banish from her mind all thoughts of her deficiencies, investing them in men whom she easily abandoned. However, her story had not made this easy for her. There should have been other ways of getting along with her father, ways more concrete and warm.

Rosy

Reserved as she was, she had nourished deep within her great rebellious impulses. A light touch was enough to trigger a storm in her, a storm that revealed her entire soul. On the other hand, no one could ever learn whether she had experienced that touch in her life. Nevertheless, it was already too late when all these things came to light.

Berti

He had been successful in adding his long walks in Istanbul to his travels the world over. Movies had been his absorbing hobby. Among his diversions, reading *The Guardian* occupied an important place. A good many of his connections had opined that his studies at Cambridge had been a waste of time. He had to convince himself that he had been a good father.

Nora

She had mentioned the impossibility of going back in the train she was sharing with her mother. The place where she had been heading for was a place toward which everybody would like to go but had to put off. Could this have been the reason why the narrator had wished to tell all about this? Was this the reason why the narrator didn't forget her, because of that missing link? He will quite probably tell about it in another story some other time. Her name befitted her actions if one thinks on 'that play.'

İncila Hanım

Her teachers at the conservatory had seen in her a prospective Seyyan Hanım. However, she had taken risks by opting for solitude and deception, by marrying Hugo Friedman and getting lost in London. She regularly returned to her seaside residence at Kanlıca every year for the sake of the old clutter left behind; thus she remained tied to her past as she sipped her raki while watching the sea of the Bosporus.

Monsieur Robert

In his small hotel room at Sıraselviler, where he had ventured to return, were the photographs of a man of failure, of a man who left behind him a long past during which he had lived so many other lives. It had not been so easy for him to accept the fact that his actual home had been the small apartment of İncila Hanım in London. Neither could he forget the night when he had lit the cigarette of Princess Soreyya in that vast saloon in Monte Carlo. Whether he was alive or dead during the days when the present story is narrated is a mystery.

Monsieur Tahar

He was stylishly dressed and carried a cane; the dark spectacles he wore when he went out gave him the air of an old spy condemned to live in a given city rather than of a retired journalist. He believed that mysticism was a long poem, a gift to humanity, not fully understood yet. Had they known the experiences he had

had in Casablanca during his adolescence and youth, his friends in old age would have understood him better.

Monsieur Aldo

A Catholic Arab born in Beirut; a Levantine from İzmir; a resident of Thessalonika; an Istanbul Jew called Ashkenazi; all four of his identities. Some claimed that he had spent his last years in Barcelona, some in Goa. Some asserted that he had died of syphilis, while others believed that a Syrian arms dealer had stabbed him. All these were his multifarious identities and lives. Actually, he was a notorious swindler. It was said that he had connections the world over.

Lola

Thanks to her studies in music and dramatic arts in Budapest, she had been a colorful figure on the stage in Soho. She had had to pay a high price to escape from the gas chambers. Had her encounter one evening with Monsieur Robert really changed the course of her life?

Carlo

He boasted of having mastered thirteen languages in addition to Yiddish. He was a staunch believer that true love could only happen at sea. The fact that he ended up being a pilot duly qualified and licensed to navigate a ship into and out of the special waters on the Bosporus may have had its roots in this conviction. However, when he decided to remain betrothed to the sea, he had intended to persuade himself that he actually was expecting somebody, and would be waiting for that person till the bitter end.

Şükran

In her small, gloomy, and stinking apartment, she kept dreaming that one day she was sure to be heading for a sunnier aspect. Her story might be inserted in a daily paper as an ordinary incident.

Hüsnü

His failure to feel himself as adapted to Istanbul was due to his obsessive clinging to 'outlandish value judgments.' The reason for his despair, for his inability to embrace his daughter at difficult times, may have had its origin in his estrangement from the bright lights of the city. One should not forget that Bafra cigarettes never quit his fingers and that he diligently kept that newspaper till the end of his days. Going back to his hometown without having acquired a flat in the city must have played a part in this.

Anita

There was a step she wanted to speak about to her narrator. The moments they met had not been coincidental; it was a necessary consequence of the story's plot. But in order that that step might be taken forward one should believe that other flowers had also sprouted on the skirts of the mountain.

Eleni

She had not deserved to be cooped up in that house. She had reacted to this by wandering stark naked in the rooms in which she was penned up. It was rumored that a daredevil army officer had wooed her in her younger years. Pinpointing that officer might have completely changed the course of the story.

Tanaş

The taste of the sandwiches he made in his delicatessen at Perşembe Pazarı must have indelibly remained on the palates of gourmands. He was believed to have been attached to his daughter by a secret passion.

Jerry

He was believed to have drawn the entire plan of a huge rocket. When he had gone to study at Harvard University, a rumor was spread that he belonged to a secret society. At the time of penning the present story, his whereabouts are still a mystery.

Marcellina

According to some she was a real woman; while others thought that she was but a virtual image. You could run into her anywhere in the world at the least expected moment.

Harun

The compelling reason for his abandonment of guitar playing and the resignation of his managerial position in a big company in order to launch into the business of gastronomy by producing meatballs was never explained. Although he was one of the principal actors in the story, he preferred to remain always in the background.

Joseph

He had never been able to tell anyone the identity of the individual he had been looking for in that 'vast white land.' As he was returning from the island riding a phaeton toward the lights of the city, one wonders if he had finally understood that everything fitted together after all.

Niko

He claimed that he had a paramour in Thessalonika waiting for him like Penelope. If he hadn't been such a skillful tailor, everybody would have called him a vest thief. When he was deported on that ominous day of exile from Istanbul, he had entrusted the gramophone records bearing the brand His Master's Voice—dating from the epoch of Monsieur Schurr and the Geserian Brothers—to a close acquaintance, in the hope of returning to the city one day to recover them. However, the said collection vanished into thin air, the identity of the acquaintance in question remains unknown.

Yorgo

Yorgo was Niko's cat. It was claimed that it understood Greek and drank raki.

Aunt Tilda

She had been only partially successful in seeing movie stars embodied as real people. When she had had the honor to be invited to that wedding party, she firmly believed that she had made herself as handsome as Merle Oberon. Nevertheless, she had surreptitiously crossed that boundary. Both in her marriage and in all her illicit relations, she bore the traits of that long walk.

Moses

Tradition had compelled him not only to become a tailor, but also to live in a succession of cities. That watchmaker from Odessa had transmitted to him a tale he would carry with him in the years to come, and, what is more important, he retransmitted it to other people as well. The fact that he caught pneumonia in Istanbul, his last refuge, was absurd.

Henry Weizmann

He was a Spanish-Jewish communist who had taken refuge in France in the wake of the Civil War. Had he not sent 'that letter' to Monsieur Jacques, he would not have appeared in the present story. He had been to Istanbul on two occasions. His second visit must have been, in all probability, for the sake of having a role in the story's other moments that were left untold.

Rachael

She waited everywhere for Nesim, whom she loved, lived for, and whom she tried to understand. Her contemplation of life with a smile on her lips was not merely an expression of her personality. She felt a deep remorse for having forsaken her autistic brother who had lost his hold on reality, but she knew well enough that she could not tear herself from her family who was settled in another land. All these things took place before the concentration camps. Had a belief in Job's legacy had its adherents even then?

Muammer Bey

His bow tie was an integral part of his neck. His conviction that work was an impediment to living had obsessed him throughout his life. He was to assume an important role in the days of the capital tax, a role that may well have been overlooked by many.

Madame Perla

Being deprived of her sight, she had seen places no one else had ever seen and touched spots no one else had ever touched. She had never forgiven her husband for having died without giving her notice. In her later years, her son preferred to conjure up her beautiful former image, which he presented whenever they were back from Şehzadebaşı. They had a caïque of their own in which they boarded and cruised about the Golden horn.

Avram

He had been a connoisseur of the good things in life as well as a perfectionist in his profession; he meticulously mended old carpets, making them new. The days in which he and Moses (a hero of an ancient tale) were avidly waiting to see the winning numbers of the national lottery at the café Sarı Adam had been long after the conflagration. The phobia of dropping dead one day in the street may perhaps be connected with the impression that the blaze had left in him.

Mimico

He had tried to capture a whole world, the whole gamut of luminescence in his marbles. Had he been able to tour the island on his bike, a great many of his friends would have looked at him in a different light. The dishes he consumed at that restaurant in Tepebaşı may have been, for this simple reason, his most tangible meals.

Lena

She seemed to have come from a movie. She smoked with a long cigarette-holder and said that life started after midnight.

Nesim

His sincere admiration for the German language had not prevented him from being sent to the concentration camps. If one takes into consideration certain incidents from his life, one may say that he was a real Ottoman gentleman who had never broken his attachment to Istanbul. In that small city on the shore of the Atlantic Ocean, he had persuaded himself that he could be rescued from that cold road to death by taking refuge in his Turkish nationality. However, the heroes of the time were obliged more than ever to take certain particulars into consideration.

Monsieur Jacques

He was a man of contrasts who nurtured in his mind certain perceptions of mortality, as seen by different individuals. Without him, this long story could never have been penned. In his letters from Spain addressed to his parents, he proved to be a person well versed in the niceties of life. Tales, as much as beach combing in his later years, were of great importance to him. He was a skillful player of bezique. He had a special fascination with roses. All of these matters might be sufficient in describing his feelings at the seaside restaurant at Kireçburnu as he sat watching the sea traffic on the Bosporus.

TALES AND RECOLLECTIONS

Estreya's star

As the years went by, one learned how to carry, in different guises, the burden of sorrow caused by the inevitable acts of forsaking and being forsaken. In time, one discovered the charm of hiding oneself behind a façade. Upon reaching a certain stage, there came a moment in one's life when one felt like disclosing, even to one's inner voice at an irreversible moment of loneliness, what one was leaving behind and where . . . even though one might feel exposed and vulnerable despite all of one's proliferations—a feeling of nakedness despite one's rich attire. Anyway, one had to believe in the existence of a clear path in order to be able to go on living—in a certain time and space—where one's loneliness could not possibly define, in light of the facts, the influence of other people on one's journey. To express it with a string of empty platitudes in the current jargon can be constrictive because the others were there. The others . . . just like those found in traditional tales . . . in different places, in different climates, at diverse latitudes of sensations, in cities where one could never live as long as one lived in one's imagination . . . The others would be there; even though one moved away and settled elsewhere; even though they were lost to sight, they would still be visible; even though one left for somewhere else, set out for other regions of the earth carrying along one's boundaries within, they would not relinquish their grip. The play put on the stage was your play in fact, the stage for which everybody got prepared in their respective changing rooms; the changing rooms, wherein they feared intrusion into their privacy and mirrors, and were more often than not ignored; it was a play enacted by the spectators along with the players, as they could not possibly absent themselves from it. Preparations were always made by someone for someone else, for days properly generated, for nights properly reproduced through the stage, or more precisely, for nights saved.

For the weekends one spends and shares with others through short incursions to the countryside, with short sallies in measured steps . . . through a tacit understanding known to everybody that nobody dares to question by raising his voice.

In all probability, that was how it had always been in the past. After all, nothing had changed in the real sense of the word; was it ever possible? You might ponder upon victories, defeats, disappointments, remorse, and separations that would eternally come back to you through all channels. Nevertheless, in order to have a clearer picture of the longing of Monsieur Jacques (more for Olga than for anybody else) not only should one experience all these eventualities, but one should also know how to attain the height of patience required in the telling of a convoluted tale by putting up a spirited defense against the influences of retroactive experiences and future prospects and justifications.

Attaining such heights in daring to advance toward certain people, even through cautious steps . . . gingerly, to wit somewhat unmanly . . . it was not possible for me, in my capacity as a visitor who had had access up to a certain extent to those lives in my capacity as a stage actor, to guess, during those interminable nights, who exactly was or had been associated with which particular apparition, scent, or sound, and to collate the fragments into a whole in the most perfect manner to their great satisfaction, so long as those individuals lived. It had also been my desire to descend into those labyrinths. Man watches man, but yet is an obstacle despite all his attempts at understanding him. There were also certain visions and feelings that occupied other regions in people's lives. In time, I was to have an insight into the importance of these regions once I learned how to keep up with them, despite my occasional escapades. What remained to be done, under the circumstances, was to know how to unearth clues, how to discover them and how to live the stories concealed behind appearances, in unidentifiable corners, by trying to live them, or at least, by making as though one had lived them, and, by daring to go on as though one was in pursuit of an elusive image. That was the only way to go beyond a stage play meant to be enacted for other people with scenes performed or represented through dialogue. I believe I have already mentioned the magic of certain outcomes one encounters in other tales as well.

We had come together for the last time at Juliet's house to commemorate Madame Estreya, who had lived elsewhere, in a different fashion, in compliance with the requirements of the path that had led her there. She died surrounded by other people, despite having reserved her last moments for herself, for herself alone. Nobody had considered her death as an ordinary death; nobody would be left cold in her absence in the proper sense of the word. Following the funeral, we had, as tradition required, come together for a repast, the procedure of which never changed, and which all the family members were supposed to attend. This was the last duty to be performed. Nobody could usurp this experience from anyone. Nobody . . . Not even life itself . . . Not even the lives that seemed a betrayal to certain people. This togetherness was at least an opportunity to experience anew those private moments we keep inside ourselves without disclosing them to others, trying to fit them into a shorter bracket of time. During the said repast, just like in all such cases, partly because of this very fact, we were face-to-face with our recollections, petty remorse, and the memory of the deceased. Although the lives were not always our own lives, the dead were our dead. This was clear enough even during the last prayer recited to commemorate them. One should bow with respect in the presence of the family members considered, or rather believed, to have ascended to heaven. The rabbi took a roll call of the departed while the congregation chanted in unison "They are in Heaven." This was how it had been and was desired to have been over the centuries . . . At that moment the features of those deceased came from your own images, the truth which you could not always disclose just to any chance newcomer. It goes without saying that you could return to the past by recalling the people you had left behind at different times and places; you could realize this return without letting your surroundings get a hold of you, despite having seen and lived those locations. These curtailments were your own, while the stage play was being addressed to the people at large.

The funeral was conducted in a small synagogue at the cemetery. Madame Estreya had neither a large enough assembly to fill a big synagogue, nor enough money to warrant a first class funeral service. I remember her image vanishing in the din of the distant past. However, the image now looks tarnished with certain details blotted. This is the reason why I cannot communicate the legacy she must have entrusted to certain individuals whom I have not met. It seems that certain things have sunk into oblivion for good and are irretrievably lost. All the paths that had led up to her have closed, as they were meant to be. She had always been an outsider; an outsider among outsiders, condemned, if one may be allowed to qualify her as such, or maybe as someone who had chosen to be an outsider after a certain point. An outsider . . . Yet, Madame Estreya was Madame Roza's sister, the second daughter of her family, who had preferred a thorny way of life at a heavy cost, who always wanted to be considered aloof, at a distance, although not so much a castaway as Aunt Tilda. Despite the beauties of their traditions and their conservative character, there were so many cruelties that had accompanied them, so many archaic failures. Their tale was meant for those who could remain content with very few incidents as far as plot was concerned, for those who would deem that a few sentences would be more than adequate, and for those who would prefer to remain faithful to their traditions. The tale should be an ordinary tale, not deserving to be a topic of serious discussion or to be elaborated upon, rendering it totally unrecognizable.

To the best of my judgment, Madame Estreya was the most beautiful girl belonging to the family; she had deep blue eyes, possibly inherited from a distant Thracian relative. During her high school years, she had been an introverted music lover. The high school they had enrolled her in was a distinguished establishment where young girls were brought up as ladies. At the time she had taken a fancy to Dickens and had identified her brother, Monsieur Robert, with the heroes in Dickens' novels, which she read over and over again. When she was still a student at the *Galatasaray Lycée*, she had fallen in love with a young man who was also a student there. A happy coincidence must have arranged her meeting with this sensitive young man who was to figure prominently in her life, his name was Muhittin Bey. An individual who liked music, making no distinction between the songs of Salahattin Pınar and Chopin's *Polonaises*, both of which he used to listen to in rapture, and who preferred to keep his love for poetry as a secret he disclosed only to a few of his companions. What had the circumstances that had led to their fatal encounter been? I have never been able to discover; nor shall I ever be able to do so henceforth. It seemed as though there was a kind of gap between themselves and others. This was one of the reasons that brought reticence, a tabooed subject never to be referred to. However, as far as I can gather, it was one of those overwhelming love stories, an ineluctable love that had to be eventually sanctioned despite all hostile reactions and barriers, in which the parties involved vowed to each other to share their lives for better or for worse, resigning themselves to all the consequences, and, according to others, the parties involved, as castaways, were determined to lead each other toward each other's unhappiness. It looked as if they had vowed allegiance to each other with full knowledge of the fact that the whole thing was going to end up in an interminable brawl. Their domicile had been in Feriköy for a time. Then they had moved to Harem, a locality alien to them and completely removed from their families, as if they wanted to give their banishment an official identity. Harem was, at the time, a district removed from the commotion of society, where a Jew would never think of residing. As far as I know, this had been Estreya's idea. This was a choice that could be made perhaps but once in one's lifetime with a view to determining one's place in the world, in full anticipation of a bright future. For a bright future, yes, but at the same time, to impart on certain people the cry of revolt, the servitude of love, the call of a true love and the determination not to turn back, by having their bridges burned once and for all; to be able to stick to one's determination to continue on this one-way journey by taking into consideration all untoward events looming ahead, wrapped in sentiments of abandonment and the call of self-affirmation. Apparently, this change of domicile had not been easy for Muhittin Bey, as he had always considered himself part and parcel of the 'opposite coast' of Istanbul. He would never cease to convey his passionate attachment to that place by telling people how he had given refuge to a childhood friend, Apostol, at his house during the September Incidents; he would also narrate this to his six-year-old nephew during a trip to Beyoğlu, holding him by the hand, showing him the devastation and the rabble caused by the events referred to the day before, saying to him: "A sight which you will never again witness in your lifetime!" thus reaffirming to himself, this evil act, perhaps with a faint hope of returning to those days of yore, years after his love affair.

Yearnings, disappointments, simple joys . . . They had lived this love, in their confined space, learning in installments what forbidden love might bring or take away from them. Believing that they had earned their requited love at the cost of all the experiences they had had to face, in total disregard of other people, of traditions and of the suffering of those they had left behind, without hiding themselves behind other people and forsaking tradition. This determination explains why they had preferred to keep detached from their families. It goes without saying that patience was required in order to be able to properly understand their sentiments and lifestyle choices once seen in their proper places. Through the years, religious holidays had always been occasions of lost opportunity, visits home made tentatively, a timid attempt at reconciliation. Home, for them, was now different, having undergone a process of gradual transformation; such visits were approached with circumspection and suspicion. And so, they proved fruitless. Filling the void that had come about in the course of their absence had already become impossible. It was too late, the links forming the backbone had been severed at the base and the bridges had all been burned.

Madame Estreya, had, according to an unwarranted assumption, been converted to Islam, assuming the name Yıldız. However, in the long run, it became clear that this had been a monstrous lie. This might also have been a stratagem to cope with the difficulties encountered at the time from that remote realm. Moreover, such an undertaking might provide certain clues to other realities that lay in deeper strata. Nevertheless, such a decision would have to have been made solely by Madame Estreya, just like in those days when banishment was still practiced. As far as I know, Muhittin Bey was an indulgent man, a lenient and refined character who would be loath to espouse such trickery as a means to resolution, even in light of those circumstances.

After his retirement, he occasionally came to pay a visit to Monsieur Jacques. Those were the times when he had closed his little grocery store at Kadıköy Pazarı, the one that glanced from a distance at Balıkpazarı in Galatasaray with a plebeian look. I remember him from those days. I believe neither Madame Roza nor Madame Estreya knew anything of these visits. However, I must acknowledge I haven't the slightest evidence to prove this. On the other hand, I may well be mistaken in my observation and be the victim of an illusion thoroughly devoid of substance. The fact is that I just feel inclined to find credence in such an unlikely scenario in order to believe once more in this improbable story, a story which I one day hope to revisit in search of the truth. This is not so bad; after all, when one thinks of the shortcuts we dare to take for the sake of those yearnings we keep postponing and patiently waiting. To experience the passion of pursuing those scraps of expectation was necessary after all for embracing a new day, yes, the dawn of a new day.

On top of that we should also take into consideration the fiery spirit that those moments held, that lay concealed somewhere, beautiful, unsoiled, and untouched, just because they had yet to be experienced. This may have been the reason why the stories never came to fruition; they just couldn't be concluded.

As for my approach to the truth, to the things I perceived as a witness . . . Muhittin Bey was an extremist, a member of the People's Party. He often squabbled with Monsieur Jacques who was a diehard democrat. Their altercations in the shop were a way to add color to their drab existence and ignore what was going on around them. The façade of daily events, known and discussed by everybody, were in fact the shield behind which people concealed their lives. I think there was some common ground where they could reach a brittle understanding, a sentiment I could not identify or define despite all efforts. That space had, I think, been shared at times when the harshness of the world was most sharply felt, a space where they needed no additional words or expressions. The affection that attached them to each other may have been a deep one, subliminally experienced . . . During those days of occasional visits, it had been their custom to eat at the Borsa Restaurant. I had had the opportunity to be present at one or two of those luncheons, during which Monsieur Jacques used to discourse upon the changing times, human beings, and the deterioration of Istanbul's overall atmosphere. They felt that they were being gradually alienated from the city in which they lived. "Life is a dirty joke," said Muhittin Bey at one of those luncheons. Life, a dirty joke . . . These seemed, at first, to be the lyrics of a cheap song . . . Yet, when one gives some thought to platitudes one can see how easily they epitomize the lives of so many. Life, a dirty joke . . . This attitude to life was familiar to Monsieur Jacques; he could not possibly feel estranged from a human being who experienced this emotion and who knew how to confront life in this way. I'm sure that there had been, there must have been, a time when he did not consider the husband of his sister as a member of his family, not as an El Turco. This was a time, I think, that lent meaning to that place, a time deeply felt, one that cannot be truly articulated to anyone.

As far as I can infer from the altercations at the shop, Madame Estreya had also become a member of the People's Party. This was a courageous act by a Jewess who had lived under the Ismet Paşa regime. Yet, she had had many reasons for reacting against that life, against her family.

One evening, Muhittin Bey, who, while singing a song of Selahattin Pınar to the accompaniment of the lute he himself played for the woman with whom he had been living, had suddenly died, reposing his head on his lute, with a faint smile on his lips; a heart attack probably . . . This was the end of him. It was like a joke. This was perhaps Muhittin Bey's last performance, a performance that represented his attitude to life and his position in it. This is why I never forgot his maxim: "Life is a dirty joke." He had left his song unfinished. This perspective, this 'moment of eternity' suited his world well. It was Monsieur Jacques who had arranged the funeral service. To my mind this is a detail not to be overlooked.

This was the story of Muhittin Bey and Estreya. No child was born to them. Was there any particular reason for this? Pills perhaps? According to Madame Roza, there was a reason for it. According to Monsieur Jacques, this was a question that begged no explanation, a question that could not easily be explained. It was as if this had been a secret shared between two people, between him and Muhittin Bey. It was a secret of a shared life, a double-edged secret which could only have been disclosed and explained unilaterally. The secret was one of those destined to remain buried along with the departed.

Madame Estreya had not gone back to her own people after Muhittin Bey's death; she had not even shortened the intervals between her usual visits to the house she had had to abandon years before, let alone returned. The doors had been irrevocably closed. Those two lives were no longer the same. If my memory serves me well, she herself had gone the way of all flesh, broken by the thought of a life spent alone, separated from the man with whom she wished to spend it. Her body was discovered by her neighbors. Such incidents were apparently a daily occurrence in the neighborhood, in any case.

As I brood over these things now, I ask myself now and then the reason why Monsieur Robert and Aunt Tilda had treated their elder sister with such indifference. I can still remember the turn of events which always remained a mystery to me. In such a mood, I try to believe in the existence of those days and nights that I'm no nearer understanding, but yet were experienced by others. However, if a gap in the sequence of events did occur, and if such a gap was risked with all its related consequences, Madame Estreya must have been responsible for this gap. The rest was mere fancy, resignation, and despair. For, she was one of those who knew how to close one's doors at the right time. Otherwise, no meaning could have been elucidated or defended, at least none worthy to be defended for the sake of those days passed in exile.

Through her death, that repast in which we took as part of a duty, so to speak, Madame Estreya stayed in my life in this guise always at arm's length; she preferred to remain aloof and was treated with a frosty silence in general; she exercised her discretion by opting for a life at home, for a life of self-annihilation, rather than setting out on a long journey. All things considered, she abided in her feminine identity as someone whose solitude had been awarded to her, not feeling ashamed in the least, always self-satisfied and alive, and—this is particularly important—meeting all the challenges she encountered on her way bravely without the least complaint. I may, perhaps, by this addition, explain the fact that there was no one left to say farewell to nor anyone from whose underclothing she could have torn a piece from on the occasion of that modest ritual (which has always thrilled me) when she returned from the realm in which she had opted to live to the land she had abandoned, by herself, or to be precise, in the image that her body had left behind. None of her relatives lived in that house anymore: Madame Roza had died; Monsieur Robert was in London and was unable to return to Istanbul; Aunt Tilda had not responded to the calls stating that her sister's soul was in repose all alone in a synagogue with no one to pray for it. Not even the mourner's kaddish for the deceased had been recited. Those were the days when I had acquired the fundamentals by which one could view time and suffering through the window of humor. The fact that the said prayer was left unrecited meant that I had missed an exiguous performance I would have liked to have borne witness to. This was somehow different from other rituals that called for the presence of a whole congregation. People were wont to pray together in unison without having an inkling of what they uttered, over and over again, tens of thousands of times, in the tongue of a distant world, the distance of which was hardly definable for them, for the mere sake of the perpetuation of an order alien to them. I never forgot those moments. I was sure that they did not know that the prayer they recited was not even in Hebrew, but a far cry from Babylonia, from that ancient exile. However, I cannot ignore the feeling of security that the mere fact of being together gave me while praying with heterogeneous words, that inexpressible feeling of warmth that one can't help but experience, thus creating a place where one felt, by force of circumstances, the difference which one could not avoid. Leaving aside all these things, in case you wished to advance toward a world out of the ordinary, you might think that the desire that the function which prayer involved could be linked to an experience related to separation and an absolute remembrance.

The words had assumed different meanings in different worlds through beautiful associations . . . Such was the prayer that had not been recited for the soul of Madame Estreya. This was so characteristic of her, especially if one took into consideration the long struggle she had waged in the hope of being understood. She did not want to remain misunderstood by others even after she died. This was the poetic side of what had been experienced, certainly; it was merely a part of the role she played which I had assigned her. The actual truth was naturally different. The prayer had not been recited; at least ten individuals of the male sex had to be present in order that the said prayer might be properly executed. Male and female, we were eight in all, a family of eight at the service. That means the required quorum was lacking, those who were absent had failed to show up once more; they happened to be in places where they were not supposed to be. Madame Estreya had been abandoned to her destiny in every respect. Even in her fatal end. Estreya signified 'star.' But her star seemed not to have twinkled for certain people . . . for those who had opted for covenants.

To understand, to try to understand . . . This phrase must have had some relevance not only for those banished from Babylonia, but also for Monsieur Jacques who never ceased to tell me about the adventures of the prophets Abraham and Solomon and Joseph and David who are still alive in my imagination as legendary figures. Death left men face-to-face with the varying solitudes experienced in the depths of one's soul. Monsieur Jacques was, at the time, embedded in a solitude far removed from the play that was being enacted, in a loneliness unattainable by other human beings. One could infer this from his reluctance, after the recital of prayers, to sit at the table which had remained unchanged throughout the years and which had dispatched many a soul to the world without return; at the table that remained unaltered, forever unalterable; but where he ate with relish, sitting in one of the armchairs whose covers had not been removed, sipping at his raki, the contents of his plate which consisted of a few olives, a slice of white cheese, homemade aniseed-flavored toast, and, last but not least, the borekita (flaky pastry) prepared by the skillful hands of Madame Roza who knew well the proper degree of its consistency, which he devoured to crown his repast, that delicacy which I associated with those summer mornings that had been mislaid somewhere in the past. Now I can fit him in that frame once more. He had before him the tripod encrusted with mother-of-pearl on which he placed his glass of raki which he was to make a gift of to Berti and Juliet after the demise of Madame Roza, as a token of remembrance of an occasion of no great bearing yet one which was unforgettable. His fingers wandered on the designs on that tripod. Everything associated with that flaky pastry, eggplants consumed with raki, every design on that tripod set a person out on an altogether different journey, giving the clues of life, of their lives, that had been mislaid somewhere else.

Madame Roza also had gone the way of all flesh just like Olga. There was thus a place where one was condemned to abide for eternity. This was perhaps the place that essentially belonged to her, a place where she had ended up after so many vicissitudes. The time came to finally connect to the correct place for the first time, without evasion or postponements . . . This was the only way to explain the lingering of his gaze on the old pocket watch, which he eyed with a wry smile. I knew the story, or, to be precise, the stories that that silver watch concealed. There were men who had put faith at different times in different climates. These men, who conversed among themselves in a totally different tongue, converged within that timepiece, amongst the labyrinthine paths of that watch. I had been obsessed with the detailed designs on it. Only time would tell whether I would be allowed or denied access to that world. For, I might choose to stay in one of those rooms and hide there, experiencing the pleasure of my flight. No need to say that this was a risky path to take. How else would I be disposed to express my desire to see myself while gazing at those people?

The watchmaker from Odessa

It has been my desire to share with some people the fact that certain loves have no end, and continue forever and ever muffled somewhere in the course of one's life in defiance of separations, just like those relations that continue even after death, like certain words, pictures, and objects that acquire, on that long path, viability by assuming additional meanings. There are an infinite number of reasons for my believing that the said path is a long one, a very long one at that. For one reason, I may mention the watch that reminded Monsieur Jacques, with some misgiving, of Olga whenever the issue of time was brought up. Whose meaning was concealed in those modest, repressive nights. Time had passed for certain people which involved the impossibility of severance and parting. To compensate for certain inaudibility and irretrievability, it was necessary to explain certain things, whenever words failed, by an individual's access to certain alternative logic. As a matter of fact, everybody was aspiring to approach that line of horizon within himself, to search for immortality, in one way or another.

Monsieur Jacques must have had certain recollections containing certain minor details relating to the night when that ancient Ukrainian pocket watch had become part of him, memories destined to remain a secret between two individuals. Still, those caught at unwarranted times, whose glances and words betrayed and who tried to hide themselves behind these words, were able, over a course of time, to shed light on a dimly lit path, provided, of course, that fallibility was taken into consideration. The most important clue that I could discover in this story, which somehow enabled me to be transported to those distant lives, was the fact that this watch was the legacy of Olga's father, and that it had built a bridge between certain lives in ancient Odessa: those people dating from childhood who irrevocably undergo transformation as the years go by and who return to us in new guises. This tale had its origin, I think, in one of those bygone days, in a bygone time . . . expecting to add meaning to different lives with different dream fragments, in different climates, with insignificant illusions . . . I knew this feeling. Under the circumstances, my progression toward a new fantasy, toward a new mystery, was inevitable. In order that I might attain my objective, even though little by little I was, as usual, in need of certain questions, even though they might be left unanswered. Hadn't we treaded this path in order to give birth to certain tales for ourselves in total disregard of others, of the actual heroes of those tales who were far removed from us and who lived in different places with different sentiments and rules? Hadn't those tales flourished partly because of this and formed our identities? Who had been the life companion of this watchmaker, for instance? Which odors had he smelled at home? What had been his fantasies and anticipations while making a particular watch in a particular shop or workshop, which, at times, served also as his refuge? What had prompted Olga's father to make the story of that watch travel farther than Odessa? Precious words and images, transported by people during compulsory journeys to different climates; inexhaustible hours, words, and images that with their very special associations regenerated hope . . . The story had assumed a very different temporal dimension through quite a different hand at that old apartment of Olga's in Şişli. Meanings attached to journeys and points of no return had become diversified. Details unpredictably changed at the most unexpected moment; also our journeys and the course of our lives, in which we wanted to have a firm belief, cast all doubts away. It may have been a gift by a friend intended as a keepsake, in order to transform a separation into a union through a different path. All things considered, no one recognized the watchmaker from Odessa. This gave rise to a multitude of questions, probabilities, and consequently to the proliferation of rumors. For instance, that watch might not have been made for a friend, if one bears in mind the awe-inspiring character of that young woman from Riga; in this, a sentiment, expressed allusively, in a totally different way, without recourse to any verbal expression, might have been involved; just like many other similar sentiments that have failed to have been properly experienced, a sentiment that might have been waiting for a different occasion, dreaming of and nourishing another point in time. Have you never experienced or heard from others the accounts of someone taking a wrong refuge?

The watch might not have been made in Odessa, after all. Nevertheless, in this section of the story, there should be—through all accounts, despite this probability, a feeling that would attach a few people, amenable to friendship, for the sake of that line of horizon that was open to changing borders and probabilities, for the narration of a long history, of a journey—a maker who had tried to shape time according to his own whims. Yes, a maker . . . a maker with glasses, wiser than his age would account for, a maker rather reserved, a maker who told the time with his looks, postures, and words of his own.

For the time of others.

For the time of others.

For those who are obliged and will be obliged to brood over the times that cannot be redeemed.

Tick tock.

Tick tock.

Thousands of, ten thousands of, millions and billions of tick tocks.

Tick tocks like in other stories and lands and worlds of empathy.

There, in that story I have omitted something, there should have figured a watchmaker; a watchmaker who should whisper silently, or as best he can. A maker, that would have enabled us to understand better the time and what we were going through and the things that we allowed to escape in order to live, giving us fair warning by his looks and presence, although from a distance, yet compelling us to reflect on things we would let slip away, so as not to forget to set down the reasons we did, hiding himself between the lines of that story. This might well be someone removed from the stir of society, living in a derelict town, someone who had spent his life among thousands of watches and clocks, who had never left his hometown, who had reached a point no one else could reach in that small world of his, who had discovered all the minutiae, or someone positioned in one of the proud clock towers in big cities, fully conscious of those ancient clocks over a particular period of time, identifying himself as the only hero of an ancient tradition, or someone positioned at a lighthouse illumining a sea rarely frequented, during those interminable nights, interpreting time for us in a different way.

That maker should bear the name of one of my heroes, who endeavored to tell what he wanted to say only through his looks, a figure of my immortal and endless novels.

Alexandria was a tale

The Olga I knew, the Olga I want to revive in my imagination, was a girl from a wealthy family of bankers from Riga who had received a good education, but had the courage to shove away all the possibilities and probabilities that her mother had provided for her by marrying her third cousin with a view to building her own life, or, to be precise, to earning her own living, to the dismay of the people who knew her. In the life she left behind were houses, journeys, and expectations quite different from those that were to emerge later on. This fact is instrumental in revealing to us the inner workings of Olga's mind, while allowing us a glimpse into what was of significance to her in her day-to-day life. This tale can also be read as a testament to Olga's resolute march ahead on the idealistic road of revolt, as she risks everything against its consequences. A tale or merely a revolt . . . In time, one would realize that the reason for this revolt was a risky love affair of delirious posture, one of those delusions that people seem never to be conscious of. A secret that might cause a life to assume a thoroughly different aspect in the eyes of others.

As far as I can gather, Olga was one of those women who knew how to abide by her mother's testament throughout her life, nourishing it with her own values. She was fated to tell another tale with a similar disposition. This was a tale different in terms of its geography, words, voices, and bondages. A mother's shadow had remained attached to a woman for whom it would be looming over for many years. I would try to follow this vision when the appointed time came. The labyrinths I would run into would soon show me once more the difficulty of turning my back on her. However, a thoroughly different timescale was required for this tale. I knew for certain that it was calling out to me. This call was at the same time the voice of my morbid attachment to fantasies and my enthrallment by them . . . It provided me with new masks which I could borrow from others, as I could not devise my own validation from what I had experienced. What enables us to convey to others the fragments of expectations within us are stories related to the fact that we are living at different times, in different worlds, and in the company of different people.

Mornings dawned with new stories, new individuals, new expectations, and new delusions . . . To my mind, there was an interesting point to that story, narrated to me and to us by Olga, about the woman of Riga. To understand those lives, starting from this point had seemed to me a feasible option at the time. The heroine of this tale of hers was at the same time a woman, who, despite all her endeavor and courage, tried to explain every experience as refracted through an ineluctable 'Jewish destiny' that attached her to a life derived from the power of her delusion, and, according to some, just because of this delusion; persisting with it, even in her difficult moments. This attitude, this behavior adopted toward life, would exhibit itself often during those critical moments when a resolution was required to be reached or on the days when clocks struck certain hours, when living by other times necessitated some sort of self-confidence. The concept of 'belief in compelling necessity' had a towering importance in this undertaking, a concept worth arguing for. What sort of necessity could direct a young girl from Riga to choose a different path in life? Where should one be looking for that call, in which particular delusion? It's true that Olga had mentioned an illusion, but of what sort was it? What shortcomings and disappointments had nourished it? Olga could not or would not expatiate on this subject. Probably, the subject had a dark side for her as well. In other words, the woman from Riga may not have told anything to anybody about this portion of her life, neither to her daughter nor to anybody else. This was a probability not to be overlooked, especially if one thinks of the yawning gap between mothers and children. However, I'm of the opinion that at this stage, the subject assumed quite another dimension. Based on sentiments that were allowed to be intuited and that could be expressed and shared only through intuitions, I had concluded that Olga had also planted a seed of delusion in her mother, never to be forgotten or annihilated. When I tried to see the events from such an angle, I found it more amenable and reasonable to conclude that she had remained and preferred to remain reticent about certain experiences she had shared with her mother. With the passing of the years, having witnessed certain deaths, this delusion may have lost its importance to a certain extent. As time went by, one learned how to forgive and became willing to forgive many people for the sake of their deaths. However, Olga had mentioned in that tale, in her tale, the woman from Riga and her mother only *en passant*. It was as if Olga had wanted to take vengeance for certain minor details, either in full consciousness of them or quite unconsciously. This must have been mere spite or an act of defiance against her mother. Personally, I could never learn, though I tried, the reason for this cantankerousness. After all, I was not supposed to understand certain sentiments and fit them into the places they belonged. However, I knew full well that I could at least rely on my observations on a given subject, when I focused my mind on this woman who knew how to impress one by her refined manners and elegance. This conviction enables me to widen the aperture of her tale's door, left ajar by the teller. When one thinks back to the world of her childhood and adolescence, one is inclined to conclude that her greatest love had been her father; she had been, as the saying goes, her father's daughter, to the detriment of her relationship with her mother. I can keep track of Moses Bronstein easier in this way, of this self-denying but hopeless father who had tried to give everything to his daughter in order for her to make a success of her life, and who, according to some people, left behind no laudable memories. The story takes us back to a remote past full of different episodes, to the days in which we shall run across that watchmaker, in order to understand better and to attach greater value to certain moments and details . . . The year was 1905. Moses Bronstein had escaped to Alexandria together with his wife with whom he would be sharing a life of adventure, in the hope of providing his four year old son with a better future, leaving behind, much against his will, the pogroms, those monumental deaths, those long nights in which he had to deprive himself of so many things, of that district people esteemed to be of great worth, of a part of his life, a life that could instantly transform itself into a long forgotten recollection, relying on the existence of a few relatives and especially on his profession as a tailor, which, wherever he went, he could practice and thus bring in some money. He had emigrated to Alexandria, hoping that certain disasters might spawn glorious days, with a strength originating partly from what was left from 'that history' and partly from the indestructible orientalism rooted within him . . . with the acrid joy that heading for a different life provided . . . experiencing, with heartache, in some deep corner of his soul, the feeling that his exiled state inspired in him . . .

How credible was it and to what extent was what Olga had told her friends about those old days true? To give a satisfactory answer to this question is certainly impossible, just like in the case of other such questions. Yet, taking into consideration all sorts of probabilities, the tale may, if one knows how to concentrate on certain moments of it, leave in one, something indelible. A tale to stand the test of time for the sake of sharing dreamlike visions, worthy to be shared, with all the shortcomings involved, with deficiencies, untruths, and misinterpretations expecting to fit into day-to-day life . . . A tale of Alexandria . . . A tale that Olga added new meanings to with every curtailment of her journey through time, from which she occasionally returned as the years went by, and to which she felt more firmly attached as she moved further into the past. Here was concealed an unexceptional joy, a quest for a feeling of happiness . . . Therefore, the thought that the tale may have been penned differently does not interest me too much. On his deathbed, her father, who was getting prepared to set out for a journey different from his previous crossings, had, after a long protracted wait, said: "A Jew must learn to resign himself to the consequences of being a Jew." This had taken place during an evening when Odessa, Alexandria, née Istanbul was receding to a distant past. Those ancient streets in those ancient cities, once inhabited, were destined to be occupied again, in an Istanbul of quite different dimensions. Those were her father's last evenings and were to be recorded despite all difficulties. Olga was to transmit these words of her father to somebody else, years and years in the future, on the occasion of another fantasy on another night when she no longer sustained any belief in those bygone days that had assumed such significance thanks to the warmth of the heart and the sacrifices of motherhood. Certain feelings and words that give meaning to those sentiments can be understood properly and can be better placed as time goes by; usually years after, usually when it's too late, when the aftertaste of certain separations is magnified by remorse and experience. It seemed that those nights were pregnant with a variety of sentiments which Moses Bronstein believed to be in agreement in every respect with his beloved daughter, the only friend left for him in life. But I know. Olga had always kept within her heart the bitterness of the fact that those nights were delayed. Those belated nights were the expression of something missing, if one ponders upon the charm of that friendship, one can feel renewed and inspired. However, it was a time when father and daughter failed to communicate, despite their cohabitation, despite their reciprocal affection. This was in the nature of family deaths which revealed themselves in diverse fashions. However, eventually, everybody succumbed to them differently, leaving behind very precious things. If I approach the sentiment that could have been shared on those nights in this way, I can understand Olga's dejection somewhat better. Moses Bronstein's introversion could certainly be justified. Despite her crestfallen state, Olga was conscious of this fact. Otherwise, she wouldn't consider her father as a missing, kidnapped friend. It wasn't so easy. If one considered what he had suffered, one should not lose sight of the fact that her father was one of those individuals who had had affairs with a multitude of people during his life. He had been a wanderer in the first place, a tailor who could narrate the incidents that he had witnessed through his wanderings. He had lived in a variety of cities, in different worlds. As far as his profession was concerned, his fate in it might remind many of that strange feeling of absurdity. He had been a wanderer, obliged to go about nailed with that identity, which might also explain his inability to remain at a particular spot for a long time, and also his tenuous connections with people. Was this a criterion for failure? I doubt it. There were so many people not equipped with such a condition that required other people's failures to cover up their own shortcomings.

Lives, people, fantasies, and those long journeys prolonged by those fantasies. All those adventures in Alexandria were bound to remain mere dreams, a tale of vestiges, of dirty streets, exotic voices, sounds, and odors . . . Moses Bronstein had lived twelve years in Alexandria with a little woman from Riga whose skill in preparing borsch had no match, who knew how to put up with all sorts of difficulties, who never once dreamed of going back to her former life in her house smelling of onions and cabbage, not only by the power of resolution that her womanly responsibilities gave her, but also thanks to the money she gained from the German lessons she gave that enabled the family to eke out a living. There had also been days of deprivation and yearning which lent meaning to their life that involved diverse perversities about which there was no doubt. Those were the days during which sorrows were blended with acrid joys, poverty fed by hopes, by that historical journey, during which Judaism was conveyed, in a sense, through the calls to prayer of Islam. In those days, the extension of a helping hand by the wealthy cousins who had invited him to the city—just as is the case in different climates and lives expressed elsewhere in colorful details—was possible only up to a certain point. Therefore, those days, partly because of this state of affairs, had entailed, at least at the commencement, minor disappointments. However, as time went by, everything had returned to normal. In other words, that new place had gradually become familiar. Lives left behind were no longer yearned for. Lives, just like objects, clothing, and photographs could be transported in one way or another to other realms. The essential thing was to have a proper understanding of the meaning of this journey. However, as time went by, the health of Moses Bronstein declined and the doctors were unable to detect the cause of his suffering, which was sometimes excruciating. One of the aged physicians had claimed that the cause of those pains could be explained by the change in climate. The body had resisted all those years against all sorts of vicissitudes before finally yielding. To emigrate to a colder climate might be a remedy deserving consideration; to a colder or milder climate; to one deemed to be more clement. If one considers the existence of those who mystically influence certain lives, the old physician's advice might be interpreted in many ways. It was not easy to decide, to change one's abode and live in a different land and to cope, in the face of the challenge of a new life after all the struggles, with brand new problems, doubts, and, what are even more important, apprehensions. They had decided to leave for London. However, Olga's elder brother Jacob, whom she had never had the chance to set eyes upon and who was sixteen years old at the time, had expressed his confirmed opinion about his determination to stay either in Alexandria or in another country. The ordeal they had suffered—certain relations that Bronstein could not reason, despite all his efforts—had matured Jacob, as far as he could tell, before his time. One should be prepared for such hardships and separations in life. They set out altogether on different journeys. They knew this song; they had learned it and they would master it with practice. This separation must have been partly facilitated by this irresolution. One could not foresee the development of things at the start of this new journey. All they could understand was that they were expected to know how to uphold their prospects and to reassert the ineluctability of fate. The family was to reunite some time in the future. They believed, they wanted to believe in this. To cherish such hopes, to believe that life was always possible. Olga had not forgotten. During one of those nights when they had all been together enjoying their belated meeting and referring to those days in Alexandria, Jacob's father had said: "We had learned the meaning of abandonment, resistance, and deprivation." It seemed as if a poem was concealed in these words, for the sake of change, a meaningful and original path. A poem that could convey a meaning for those who had been left behind . . . The story relating to Jacob had lingered in him as a puzzle, pregnant with questions and suspicions, in addition to the poetic inspiration that the beautiful paths it had opened had brought about. This puzzle would, in time, assume an altogether different hue, on the day when the tale would have returned to him from somewhere he least expected and with a person he least thought of. The adventure of the Bronsteins had begun on a summer day . . . Those were the days when a great number of people were suffering from the consequences of war . . . Those were the days when the little woman from Riga had a tremendous desire to play the piano.

To be able to speak Yiddish in Kuledibi

Of old, travels lasted a long time; long enough to make those who resolutely set out fully conscious of the hardships involved. We can perhaps better understand that sense of adventure, the vessels that weigh anchor at their respective destinations along the course traced and bequeathed to us by those stories, by reviving in us, at our pleasure, the image that those long nights left in us, thus resuscitating those days for a redeemable world.

On his way to London, toward a new destination, Moses was to pay a short visit to his cousins in Istanbul. In all of the correspondence between him and these cousins, who had emigrated from Odessa to settle in Istanbul, a prospective reunion, on the occasion of a religious holiday celebrating faithful Jews, was often discussed. This yearning had assumed greater significance as the years went by. The incidents related to the different lands, different feelings and different lives they had diligently kept in the stores of their memories, memories that had acquired greater worth. Good times they were!

The friendly reception of Bronstein in Istanbul was sensational as it marked the beginning of a new tale, the beginning of an enthralling, amazing, poignant and, at the same time, sad story . . . For, the very first incidents at the outset indicate that the vicissitudes of the fifteen years that had elapsed in between had, according to other people's accounts, been spent quite differently. Cousin Norbert Feldman, thanks to his mastery of foreign languages, and his making optimum use of an entrepreneurial genius at the right time in international relations, had been able to sign lucrative contracts in foreign countries, and the Ottoman Empire had in return awarded him contracts in the field of road construction, thus enabling him to amass a great fortune. The convertible parked on the seashore was sufficient evidence of his wealth, nay, of his opulence. This was part of the ritual; those years lived in different places and with different people had to be displayed in one way or another. You could compensate for the suffering experienced in other circles and countries only in this way—by transforming the years of hardship into joy and self-complacency. One should not of course omit those who had been unsuccessful in their enterprises and had to watch the time pass them by. Relatives that had to stay in foreign lands knew such feelings all too well. Similar moments had been experienced in the past and would be experienced in the future. "What did you do there for so many years?" was the question to be asked. But to what extent did it question the inquirer so much as the person the question addressed? To decide on this was not so easy if one took into consideration the details involved. However, in this case, the question interested Moses in particular, who was walking on the shore of a city he was not familiar with, through streets strange and new, toward a future unknown to him. What have you been doing for such a long time? Eva, that little woman from Riga had clasped the hand of the man whom she wanted to consider the only man in her life and with whom she wanted to live. Why? Was it because she also had asked or had had to ask that question because she had felt that certain circumstances were inviting her? To tell you the truth, I can't say exactly. For, I don't want to advance toward those people whose sights I catch but a glimpse of from a distance despite my unwillingness to do so, setting out based on certain information acquired from my own sources that I had been imparted with by other people. Aside from these points and the potential feelings that they may have given rise to, all that I could know for sure is the piecemeal progression of the Bronstein family toward a city utterly alien to them. In this section of the story I would like to, partly because of this, imagine Moses casting a look at his watch in order to chart his own time in Odessa. What if Moses had already cast another look at it in that street and what if that look had shown him only his wealth, convincing him of his actual existence? One morning . . . just like at the moment of separation in Odessa . . .

Those were the years when the number of cars was scant in Istanbul (for men that had immigrated from different parts of the world had brought with them different lifestyles), the years in which a longstanding decline was witnessed in many aspects of the community, notwithstanding the persistent survival of certain customs and conventions among certain people, the years when people stared at certain events from a distance without getting involved in them. Norbert was said to have been very kind to Moses in those days. With a view to seeing his dear cousin and wife comfortably settled in that sumptuous eight-room apartment at Taksim, furnished with antiquities and valuable paintings, he had spared no colorful expense . . . there was even a radio and a framed photograph of his children.

Norbert and Moses held long talks during the days that followed . . . Long talks, *tête-à-têtes* . . . just like during their childhood and adolescence . . . It looked as if they wanted to prove to each other, for dissimilar reasons, that despite the adventures they had experienced all those years before, there had been certain things that had survived . . . Moses had spoken of Alexandria, of his prospects for the future, of his concerns about Jacob, of his ailments, of his failure in being a good father, and of his profession as a tailor; while Norbert had recounted his undertakings and successes, the Palace, the hectic days, and suggested that on such days new possibilities could be expected to dawn. He ended by reverting to the subject of the Jews in Istanbul, claiming that Yiddish was even spoken in the streets and advised Moses to remain in that city in which he had been living for years—where one could always find the means to eke out a living, where no one would ever be starving—instead of departing for London. This was, certainly, one of those moments that could quite unexpectedly change one's course in life. Actually, Norbert did not merely give him a piece of his mind during these exchanges, for, he promised to assist him in finding customers through his connections should he change his mind and open a tailor's shop, as he was supremely confident of cousin's skill in that trade. As for his ailment . . . well, physicians, who were also sent for by the Palace, were near at hand. After all, all these things were but minor details. The important thing was to seize that mood and to fill in the gaps between them. They could try to recover the atmosphere of the old days under different conditions and circumstances, hoping for better days ahead.

Leaving aside all that had gone before, he was badly in need to reconnect with someone from the past, with a family member.

Once again there was another life behind the visible objects on display . . . a life whose darkness was carried over by variegated glimmers. This exchange of ideas had taken place at a restaurant overlooking the Bosporus.

The adventure of Moses and the woman from Riga had begun, to the best of my knowledge, upon the inception of an unanticipated story at the least expected moment. They had reason to have an unshakable belief in fate during the days when they took part in this story rather hesitantly, overwhelmed by those inevitable question marks.

They had spent a short time at Norbert's house before they moved to a small apartment in Kuledibi, to a small apartment, much smaller than those of the same class, with a sigh of despair at the fact that they were once again starting everything anew . . . Moses' first shop had been somewhere near Tünel and his first customer had been a German, a factotum of Norbert's who took care of his foreign business; when he made his first sallies to Istanbul, he was believed to have known the places where he had lost certain things fairly well along with the people who had been instrumental in contributing to such losses . . . Olga was the fruit of these cold winter years. To have a child after a lapse of sixteen years had brought great satisfaction to the family despite the hardships involved. This had served as a palliative to compensate for the absence of Jacob who had been, and had to be, abandoned in Alexandria, and who, after a while, had immigrated to America in pursuit of quite a different lifestyle; a necessary consequence of the need to fill another wide gap.

The diamond necklace

I could find but a few pictures that would likely lead me to Olga's memories of childhood in Kuledibi. To the best of my knowledge, Monsieur Jacques had also been in the same predicament; even he had been in a similar predicament! To explain this blankness and to shed some light on that obscure region was not easy. This blankness, this darkness, was a story in its own right; in other words, it was likely to break ground for another tale; the contents of this darkness should be in another story which I experienced, through all the events I discovered and lived. Was Olga lonely, as lonely as she had remained in my memory? Nobody can ever know this, of course. A long time has gone by since then. All the witnesses have gone away, taking their representations of her along with them. Had there also been witnesses apart from them that might convey to me new answers or new questions? If so, I still pin my hopes on such a likelihood for the sake of a future story. Nevertheless, my recollections at this stage are but a simple and inevitable consequence of what I can discern from such a distance. Her life had always remained a puzzle in other people's eyes. How did this happen? How on earth had one gone up such a blind alley, both for her sake and for ours? Was this due to the reserve of this woman who had fascinated many people with her beauty and elegance at every turn, the details of which I highly valued, to her self-defense as though she were a fugitive, or to a diffidence buried deep within her and to her inability to act otherwise? All these things might be equally valid. Nevertheless, despite her taciturnity and elusiveness, we do know certain things in connection with her years at the French college *Notre Dame de Sion*. The memorabilia dating from those years provide us with some clues with reference to the history of that introvert, of a person whose introversion got deeper and deeper.

Can we speak, at this stage, of that relationship that is not so easy to be shared as one would wish? Different voices conjure up the past in certain people differently, with different words, with white lies associating different episodes in the mind. One can formulate an idea under such circumstances about the attitude that people adopt toward life. I must confess that I have my suspicions about the accounts that Juliet gave regarding that remote past. To my mind, in narrating the incidents of those days, she must have omitted certain passages, details and places. Monsieur Jacques remained silent; he did not speak . . . Or perhaps, he preferred to be oblivious of certain things . . . I find this quite natural and justifiable. There was also the account given by Uncle Kirkor, jack-of-all-trades and master of none, who had once served as a factotum in a shop. Because of what he narrated one could infer certain interesting clues that might give the story more sense. One had to be able to read between the lines, however . . .

To be able to read between the lines . . . to know how to listen properly . . . to take the challenge of listening and spending all due effort . . . We were accustomed to transfer to our time what different witnesses had conveyed. We had tried to bring to life once more the different witnesses with their different voices and perspectives . . . witnesses we never forgot and could never forget for the sake of our lives . . . It so happened that we had also come across such predicaments on certain days and at unexpected moments in the truly believable stories of others. All these reminded us of a story lived in missing fragments, personalized in the course of time, one which assumed meaning as time progressed; a story perpetuated despite certain people. This is the story that commenced when Olga—despite all the shortcomings of her own life, convinced that she could rely on her wildest dreams, having derived her impetus from the fascination she had created among her surroundings thanks to her excellent dissertations, and who had been praised by the nuns not only for her achievements at school, but also for being a young girl prepared to confront the problems she would encounter in future with probity and discretion—encountered Henry Moskovitch on her graduation day, at a time when she secretly considered herself already a graduate in many respects. It was one of those evenings; a harbinger of summer . . . a Rita Hayworth film was on at the Melek movie theater . . . There was a common ground for certain songs that they associated with each other; a common ground where they modulated from one key to another . . . even though that ground conjured up different worlds of sentiments, concealed in different eras. Just remember the times when you conversed with people in alien surroundings, filled with unaccustomed glances, completely indifferent to the words exchanged. At such times, you would not be conscious of the fact that another life was in your sights, one which would gradually absorb and enslave you, while you were preparing gingerly to recieve that person through intricacies that seemed insignificant to you. In general, all things experienced are exclusive to that moment, to that very touch, because, certain relationships wait for that precise moment and place. Then one starts penetrating into that magical world, often without return . . . Olga's story, whose sole richness was based on her dreams about Henry, son of Isaac Moskovitch, partner of Norbert Feldman, who had lived a life of licentiousness in all the aspects that his riches had afforded him, was indeed such a story. Some trite songs and fortuitous encounters may have marked that meeting in that spring evening . . . In the movie theater they had sat next to each other. The hall wasn't crowded. They drank lemonade. Rita Hayworth called her admirers to a distant world. The evening was crowned with a dinner at Tokatlıyan, a dinner that was to leave an indelible impression on a young girl of high expectations. They had sauntered toward Taksim square. On their way, Olga had encountered a school friend. She had felt a reserved pride upon seeing her. Henry was a man about town, tall, dark and handsome, reminiscent of Valentino who had been the idol of many a young girl and whose physical beauty matched his elegance, his refined manners and costumes, which his tailor in Beirut had made for him; not to mention his big receptions and dancing style that would stand in comparison with many a professional dancer. The next morning, Olga received a bouquet of scarlet gladioli from the renowned florist Sabunjakis which she could never forget. To have met a celebrity like Henry Moskovitch and to dream of having been in his company was certainly a thrilling experience. This naturally had triggered a sequence of events . . . To get the feeling of the realization of a dream at an unexpected moment that opened a vista never dreamt of and to be able to share a life hardly imaginable with unpredictable individuals . . . dinners and the brightly illumined clubs of the time . . . It was Olga's cherished fantasy just before going to sleep in her bed that the pale moonlight bathed, to dream of the long life she would share with Henry . . . However, Moses had some sort of an intractable presentiment of disaster; he was apprehensive about his daughter's future, fearing that the course of events might not turn out as she would have planned ever since the moment Henry had intruded into their lives. You could not possibly convince an infatuated person bewitched by a fancy in which she had absolute confidence that a thorny path of return might be looming ahead. Maybe despair or affection might determine the line of demarcation between making a comment and refraining from doing so in a given situation. Would you take the risk of ruining the dreams of someone whom you cherish at the cost of causing her weariness of spirit? This conceptual thinking must have been the reason for Moses' reservations. Time would bear out his premonition. Separation would be knocking on Olga's door within about a year from the time of their meeting in the movie theater, before spring was in Istanbul, to the detriment of all the fantasies she had woven in the meantime. For those who had their heads screwed on the right way, this space of time was long enough to remain permanently printed on one's mind. A diamond necklace bought at Diamenstein had marked the separation. She had suddenly remembered. Months ago, on one of the evenings when they were strolling arm-in-arm in Pera, they had caught sight of that necklace while looking for a brooch they would be making a gift of to a friend. "This must be meant to adorn the neck of a princess, of a heroine of a fairy tale," she said, wandering her fingers over the stones. Henry had clasped her hand upon hearing these words but had said nothing. Those were the evenings when she was as proud as a young girl strolling in Pera could be . . . The short note that accompanied the necklace said that he had to leave for Vienna and sojourn there for some time and apologized for this misfortune, he thanked her for the time they had spent together which he considered a sort of gift, confirming the image she had of herself as a real princess in a fairy tale. Years had gone by before Olga was able to become aware of this unexpected severance which had left a deep scar in her. Life would certainly continue for her in the company of different people, sharing different lives. The long years ahead would fling open the gates for a new love, for a love even more arduous. But Olga's attachment to Henry was to remain despite all the trials and tribulations she would have to undergo; it was an attachment beyond the dimensions of love. In other words, Olga's relationship with Henry never broke despite her involvement with different people and the upsurge of different expectations. It was not an end, however. It just couldn't be. It simply was placed in a different compartment of her life, a compartment that could not easily be acknowledged by other people at large. Henry was to recognize the grave error he had committed in parting with Olga years later, after having to endure irreparable losses . . . in those years, in the wake of these losses, he was to find himself immersed in great agonies and black despair . . . Actually, despite the glossy countenance of it, Henry's story was one of hopeless failure, a washout, a debacle . . . a story of being swept up by a flood; he had perceived this truth almost immediately after his severance from her. He had gone to Vienna in pursuit of a woman with whom he had been in correspondence with for quite some time but about whom nobody could give any satisfactory information. In his old age, when his behavior had become erratic, he would live with her in Istanbul; they had watched the sunset on the Pierre Loti hill and made love dreaming of a seaside resort on the Bosporus. However, the fatal day had come and the woman finally realized that she could no longer go on living like that; she became aware of the fact that she intrinsically belonged to the Vienna which she had left and went back to her husband, a man thirty years older than herself. Actually, she was a countess, a genuine one whose lifestyle matched the standing she had justifiably regained. All things considered, her love affair was a desperate business. They had set out on a wild goose chase only to realize soon after that they'd been pursuing a will o' the wisp . . . Was that the place where the storms and tempests had originated? Time tried everybody in different fashions. That Viennese woman, that ancient 'lady of the mansions,' a widow whose aspirations had been to crown her life with revelries and balls and whose songs attracted innumerable philanderers, would cause Henry's ostensibly inexhaustible wealth to be squandered in a haze of delight brought about by sham victories, paving the way in due course for loans borrowed from old friends whenever he chanced to run into them, and from his distant relatives, even from the clerks who had once been in his employ, with a view to pandering to his whims and saving himself from starvation, loans which were never to be paid back. His settlement at the old people's home at Hasköy by the good auspices of Olga, who never deserted him, coincided with the days when he was destitute. His last affair would henceforth be with a woman, a former teacher of French, to be precise, a woman who claimed to have once been a teacher and who considered speaking French as a sign of nobility, like her contemporaries, and who resolutely awaited an illusory visitor; a woman who never went out to take some fresh air in the city, flatly asserting that Istanbul was not *her* Istanbul anymore. In the midst of the fantasies of women proliferating in his imagination, each reminding him of a different defeat, he would live to fight another day in full consciousness of the fact that his flights and pretenses would lead him nowhere except to Olga. The existence of that woman, of another woman, was necessary for him to cover up his defeat. Olga was aware of this. To propagate life endlessly, to protract the climax of the stage play making sure that it does not reach its catharsis, postponing death in chambers one has taken refuge in, such illusory visions should appear normal; especially if we remember our inability to strip ourselves from the grip of fantasies, delusions and illusory expectations in an infinity of chambers. Could one explain Olga's devotion to Henry by this chimera despite all that had occurred in the meantime, in a new, completely different room, believing that she had discovered a new dimension? Or, viewed from a different angle, could one think that, such a relationship, or at least the vestiges of it, might conceal beneath all those sacrifices a latent hatred that can hardly be disclosed or acknowledged? In other words, is it possible that Olga would have ventured during her brief visits to Istanbul to witness the abandonment of a man, who had once been forsaken, not only by his acquaintances, but also by his memories, fantasies and expectations? Am I being unfair? Perhaps I am. The Olga I knew had always known how to lose, how to endure losses regardless of the prevailing circumstances. All these considerations aside, no matter what her feelings were, she had been the only person that visited him at the old people's home. It was there you could find her holding conflicting emotions with bated breath, generated by repressed and resuscitated feelings, and by the thrill that isolation and loneliness provide one with, as well as by one's resignation to one's fate in the presence of other abandoned souls. Olga was there for the long haul. There in one way or another, somewhere in the very heart of life . . . Just like in her other relationships.

This wasn't the end of the story of her devotion. If one takes into consideration certain events, one can see that Olga, not content with being there, had gone much farther and prepared the grounds for her one-time lover's tittle-tattle about the old days. Olga had been a listener . . . She listened and tried to share her experiences. She listened in order to prove to him that the days they had spent together were still valuable to her. She listened in order to enable Henry, in his last days, to be proud of himself, of his past. She had also secretly, surreptitiously put some money into the pocket of this gentleman of old who had squandered his great wealth for the sake of an incredibly illusory life. Yes, his life had been an incredibly illusory one, a life that would hardly afford them to dream of an obligation to share his last moments. Henry had told Olga that he had found some money in his pocket whose origin he could not explain. In return, Olga had told him that his wealth was inexhaustible no matter what he did. She never once desisted from telling him words such as: "You must've forgotten it or mislaid it only to find it again; you still have some money, you see? Frankly, I'd never have believed you could have spent all you had!" On the other hand, Henry felt compelled to spend even that money; after all, he was a connoisseur of the good things in life. Yet, in the world he lived and to which he was confined, Henry's insatiable greed to purchase odds and ends had been reduced to nil as there was nothing left to buy anymore. However, he occasionally thrust money into the hands of someone going on an errand, asking him to buy madeleines and liquor chocolates. The errand boys who went to Beyoğlu did not refuse him this favor; they found in him the man they themselves could never be; in their eyes, he was a prince that had emerged from an old tale; a prince that had lost his princess . . . Moreover, leaving everything else aside, Henry was generous in his tips, the only person who knew how to reward the services rendered to him. He offered people the madeleines and liquor chocolates relished by Olga. Olga never forgot his refined hospitality. Her former lover used to spruce up, putting on an appearance for the sake of the good old days . . . for the sake of the good old days . . . as though he would live those little victories anew . . . in one of the suits he had picked up among the wreckage of that long tremor, a tremor that had lasted for years. Olga hated to recall the fate of his suits sold for insignificant sums of money to any chance comer for the supply of his daily needs. When she remembered those tremors, the only thing she did was to escape and shun those specters and hallucinations, just like they used to do long ago. However, there were times when they could cling to life, in all its solidity, to a life in which they had an unshakable belief. Years of practice had trained them in this. At such times, face-to-face, they felt even more destitute than in their adolescence when they consumed madeleines secretly for fear of being caught by their parents. Henry used to set aside a couple of madeleines, trying not to attract Olga's curiosity. This was part of the game. It did not escape Olga's attention, however. By the way, she never mentioned Monsieur Jacques. Regardless of the heroes they encountered, both knew all too well the fact that they had lived each other's lives. Such acts were but deployments of their little game . . . This had turned into a kind of ritual. Everybody was familiar with it. It had become easier for Olga to face this in view of Henry's indifference and defeat, during his last years only a few people could put up with him.

I was imparted with this information through the accounts of Uncle Kirkor and partly by Olga's occasional lapses. I hope I haven't misjudged and erred in my estimations. This was one of the most important episodes in Olga's life, as far as I know. In her visit to the old people's home at Hasköy, one could witness an act of self-sacrifice and a loftiness of spirit.

What especially attracted my attention was her wearing the diamond necklace whenever she went to visit him. Was this an esoteric poem devoid of sentimental attachment, the expression of her latent feelings of vengeance difficult to be disclosed? I doubt it. To my mind, she had wanted to be the princess of a fairy tale, of her own tale. This may have been the reason why she stayed with Henry to the very end. The only person who had avowed her noble bearing had been her former lover whom had been swept from his path by an insignificant fantasy. This tale had been their spontaneous propagation. To my mind, this was the most important reason for their coexistence in each other's tales.

Uncle Kirkor's view

Uncle Kirkor had left me with the impression that he knew the answers to a good many questions about Olga. Such questions that are generally used as a starting point for certain people. Questions that we could not bring ourselves to ask . . .

The reason for this was simple. He had drawn a distinct line between knowing and making out as if he knew, while at the same time giving the impression that he knew nothing. Nobody had ever understood what exactly he did and didn't know about us. A man who had been watching his friends, for years on end, from the confined area of security he had allocated for himself . . . The meaning of these looks may have been retaliation for defeats suffered elsewhere, for defeats one could not obviate . . . This was one of the doubtless probabilities; an anticipated and expected probability . . . However, I had taken a fancy to him; I'd been looking forward to seeing and knowing such enigmatic people, particularly at such moments . . . Actually I knew, of course, the man, Uncle Kirkor, was far away, in a place none of us could ever reach . . . I reckon that this was how it should be . . . I had experienced such distances in other relationships . . . That long story was partly the product of such anxieties . . . This attitude of Uncle Kirkor's had, of course, annoyed a good many people. However, for us, for those of us who could chance upon or knew how to extort a few memories from him, it was quite a different affair. For those who had knowledge of him, he was someone who always remained still in order to see, hear and learn about ongoing events. He used to act as though he had witnessed nothing; what is still more important was that he knew how to keep silent. It was a fact that he was aware of other realities related to Olga's diamond necklace to which we did not have access. He had overheard certain telephone conversations, and certain looks had been reflected in his own guise in all probability . . . Could I arrive at certain conclusions on the relationship of Olga and Henry based on bits and pieces of evidence from those talks? I don't know for certain, nor shall I ever. However, with regard to certain relationships, I learned, over time, how to be satisfied with what had already been given in the stories of certain individuals. This also held true for people whose sorrows, expectations and memories I had shared, people to whom I had got nearer and people whom I accompanied in their journeys and with whom I breathed the same air. Having reached a given stage on our journey, we had become each other's visitors. Visitors . . . simply visitors . . . To remain and to be obliged to remain satisfied with what one has been given . . . This state of affairs now and then gave rise to deceptions. However, this place, the place that Uncle Kirkor had indicated, was once a place of refuge and somewhere where one could indulge in wild fantasies, fantasies whose boundaries could only be drawn according to the individual's own pleasure.

What Uncle Kirkor had pointed to was not simply the place in question and the individual in it. The reason why I failed to give him his due for his contemplativeness and reticence had its rationale, of course. I think I owed it to him to realize the importance of listening, of knowing how to listen. To be able to listen, to concentrate one's thoughts on a given individual, to see him effectively . . . and in so doing, to be sparing in one's words, considering that certain things, the things assumed to be right, are doomed to undergo variations more or less according to circumstances. This was the rule then, the most important rule of being a true witness. Nevertheless, Uncle Kirkor had, to the best of my knowledge, already gone beyond the identity of a witness. He was a confidant, a place of refuge for certain people. "I'm a bottomless well. The stone you throw in me is lost forever, even to yourself, mind you," he told me once. In this statement was also hidden, I think, the modest pride of being conscious of his responsibility, of having been conversant with the ins and outs of those lives to which he could not help making occasional allusions to in every conversation. I knew this. This was his most glorious success in life, especially if one remembers the inevitable defeats people suffered in battles. He seemed to have made the best of this success, especially in his later years . . . savoring it for quite a long while, reviving innumerable fantasies of his life in certain parts of his being closed to everybody else. Embedded in him was the history of a whole era. We must not forget the fact that he had been the factotum in Monsieur Jacques' shop, an old-timer, in the latter's words. At this stage, you could proceed on and play with your fantasies and discover, if you wanted to, his desire to explain the function of an organization which kept abreast with the changing business life of the day that seemed to be innate in his personality and in the impression he made on others. However, these private judgments, which failed to go beyond their individual character, could not and had not been able to explain him to us, despite all the clues it provided us with. Perceptive people had understood this.

Uncle Kirkor had unexpectedly succumbed to a heart attack; he had been one of the trustworthy friends and sole confidant of Monsieur Jacques. Was this privileged position of his a consequence of his taking the shop for his own house, his breathing space; or of his display of it as such to others; or, was it a consequence of his comprehensive knowledge of the family; of the fact that he was conversant in Spanish although he did not speak it; or of his unerring intuition that told him the exact moment when the boss wanted to be left alone; or again of his familiarity with the business, of the management of which he was prepared to immediately take over in preference to Berti? All these things may have had their parts to play in the development and perpetuation of that friendship. There were in that shop other details and bits and pieces that built up Uncle Kirkor. For instance, every morning he was the first to come to the shop and the last to depart in the evening; however, not before having emptied the ashtrays, switched off the lights, checked the faucets and the fuses; he had in his possession one of the two keys for the shop, the other being in the custody of Monsieur Jacques. He tried to satisfy the feeling of paternal authority he tasted through occasional rapprochements of Berti. He had never had the chance of going on holiday because of matrimonial troubles with Ani, his wife; he had not thought it decent to engage in such a venture, as he thought it hardly fitting of his character. Tactful and forbearing, for years he had had to tolerate the reproaches of Madame Ani, who accused him of failing to achieve success in life, he tried to tolerate her affront with the wisdom of a sage. Could one establish a link between this state of affairs and his moderate addiction to drink; with his being careless about his attire; with his occasional absences; with his excessive indulgence in candies; with his habitual absences from Sunday services; with his striking up friendships with strange people and with the slovenly attitude of a sage he occasionally displayed? The answers to these questions must be concealed in the labyrinths of that life not readily shared. These accounts I've been able to lump together, based on different witnesses at different times, seem to be sufficient to lend meaning to a certain extent to particular acts and words. For instance, being at school had always been a nuisance. He had often entertained the notion to tell his companions how foolishly they behaved in subjects to which they attached overdue importance. But he had failed to express it because of his introversion and diffidence; this had been the source of his being qualified as a layabout, an idler, among those whose blinders allowed them to see only his terseness. His failure in finding a longstanding shelter for himself in the milieu in which the bullies thought that nonconformists should be ostracized (this they considered to be their reason for existence) had resulted in his being ousted from the French college Saint-Michel where his father desired him to acquire the French language. At the time he had not even turned fourteen. Having been awarded low grades as a junior, his father had to ask the school to cancel his enrollment . . . at a time when they were short of money . . . He had certainly been annoyed at having been a failure at school. Years later, he had to recollect his school years and tell of his experiences in a compensatory humorous style, saying: "My report card was riddled with potholes!" He actually deplored the fact that he had been dismissed from school. He hadn't even learned how to play volleyball; he might have learned a lot from that friar who was well disposed toward him and when the time came his acquisitions would have enabled him to engage in a successful business life. But the fact was that life began for some people from quite a different starting point. He never forgot this, he simply couldn't. This was the most important reality that that shop offered despite all that had gone on in between. The day he had become conscious of this fact had been the day he had experienced one of the greatest deceptions in his life. He had to account for it by such words as: "Well, I had to interrupt my education. I was young. I was in a hurry to practice an art or craft as soon as possible and launch into business life with a view to avoiding being a burden on my father's shoulders," he said one morning. I had learned thus that he had frequented the college Saint-Michel for some time. He had made tea and no one had showed up yet at the shop. Nevertheless, in order to evade the past we are in need of such expressions: you had to have recourse to such words in order to facilitate your life with old memories and fantasies which you didn't want to see consigned to oblivion. To make public true defeats one had suffered in one's lifetime was never easy. It was never easy to confess defeats, real defeats, I mean. Uncle Kirkor no longer mentioned his school days anymore. (Whenever the subject of school days was mentioned, it occurred to me to think how his life or lives might have traced a different course had he imposed his alien condition on his peers. But I saw no way out. I'm aware of this fact. I'm aware that there are many people who happen to be in the wrong places, living with the wrong crowd, resigned to their ill fates when looked at from a distance, or at least when we think we are gazing at them from a distance.)

Having failed to give school life its due, he had been apprenticed to Master Barkev, a distant relative, to work at the lathe. Those were the days when poverty was raging across the country. Early in the morning we used to get up and set off for the workshop. One could observe among the crowd on the bridge fellows with patched-up trousers; even our stockings had patches on them. "I don't think you'll remember those wooden eggs we used to thrust into our socks when darning," he said once. I had said nothing in return, but merely smiled. Whatever I would have said would divert him from his cherished recollections and daydreaming. Otherwise, I remembered perfectly well the wooden egg dating from that time in my life in those ancient houses in which I had had many experiences I did not want to share with anyone. I distinctly remember the time when I had insisted on living in them and was reluctant to vacate . . . How distinct in my memory it seems to me now, that wooden egg I used as a toy. It is a nonentity now; yet, at the time, it imposed its presence on us and stood for something essential in our lives. You cannot just break your rapport with certain objects, if a certain house you inhabited outlived other houses you lived in . . . I remember well the drawer in which the wooden egg in question was kept. The interesting thing is that despite its impression on me, which I can hardly describe and am unable to define, the said egg was a constant reminder in my life nevertheless; I had a special place reserved for it. That egg had never been for me a simple and ordinary plaything. Nevertheless, that charm, that magic that attached me to that image, was, I think, concealed in this enigma. To remind Uncle Kirkor of this would be irrelevant. It was a fact that everybody revolved around his own role, or roles, and lived as his own individual character through his recollections and servitudes. There were many images that hid themselves behind scarred wounds, that seemed to have been forgotten by a multitude of worlds, each reproduced, one unlike the other . . . That may have been the reason why he had opened this window to the old days to people alien to him.

The fact was that Uncle Kirkor was apprenticed to Master Barkev, though he was reluctant to talk about his days there despite his nostalgic feelings about them, wrapping himself in the garb of an ancient man that if encountered anywhere must be regarded with sympathy. He had embarked on that venture that was to radically change the course of his life and lead him to a place completely different from the place where he could otherwise have stayed for the foreseeable future, at a time when he was somewhat more hopeful of new prospects . . . This episode I learned from Monsieur Jacques quite by chance as it had never been on our agenda. Despite our common emotional grounds, we also had islets which we mutually preferred to keep as forbidden zones. Given the wide difference of age between us, barring our respective emotional worlds that opened towards different vistas, there was, it seemed, another life. We both had eventually realized that this was a no man's land.

As far as I could gather from what Monsieur Jacques told me, during the days of his apprenticeship in that life wherein the rules were quite different from those in the classrooms, fed by small expectations and readymade dreams, everything had gone fine at the beginning. Thanks to his skill and behavior he had endeared himself not only to his master, but also to the artisans in the market, despite his accent and shyness. Master Barkev began to entrust to him the work of his favored customers, and his confidence grew with the effect that he could eventually pass his bench after so many years of labor to someone he could train himself. To have gained the confidence of his master was certainly important for someone who was but a novice. That was more than a simple trust or empathy; these epithets might be *à propos* in describing those days. It sometimes occurs to me that Master Barkev proudly exhibited to his friends in the market certain pieces made by his apprentice. "This is Kirkor's work; perhaps not so perfect, though. But he's got talent, I must allow him some time yet," he used to say with some pride and excitement which he tried to cover up. Just a sign of emotion from the master which should be taken for granted. They sometimes continued to work long after they had closed up the shop. These were invaluable times spent on the road that led from apprentice to master. Nevertheless, certain events were to take other turns, beyond one's control, making life unpredictable at unexpected moments, leading to unwarranted days for which no preparations could have been made. One day, Master Barkev had to leave the workshop to purchase materials. It was a day one wished to obliterate from memory, a day one might recall only if one so specifically wished, a day that obsessed one more and more as one tried to forget it, a day that could be explained away on the grounds that, when taken unawares, it might provoke in one the sense of the absurd. Kid Arthur was there; he was undergoing training in silver inlaying under Mr. Hrant, his master, who was notorious for his irascibility and alertness, and whom people addressed not without some diffidence. Professionals had already formed their judgment about him. It had not been two years since his engagement and he had achieved no progress; nor did he give the impression that he would do so in the near future. Had he been somebody else, that somebody else could not have remained long with Master Hrant, a devoted professional, whose work demanded admiration. Yet, because of an old, very old code that Master Hrant was keeping as a secret from everybody else, for the sake of togetherness, he abided there. "Business is slack, but, I cannot dismiss him now. You know, it's a question of responsibility. I've got to suffer the consequences of my wrongful act of the time," he told Master Barkev one day, bending his head to his breast. "To my mind he still loves you," he said. "Too late!" had been Master Hrant's answer. Uncle Kirkor was there cleaning the bench. His presence was hardly felt, although they were sure that their secret was safe with him. At his age, he had failed to properly understand what had been going on. Only much later would he be able to establish connections between the facts, long after the people involved had gone to different places and abided in remote lives. They were indeed sure that no secret would leak out. He had lived in a world wherein apprentices were not only trained on the job, but at the same time received an education to meet the future challenges of life. Master Barkev had been conscious of the merit of his apprentice. Kirkor was tight-lipped; he never spoke unless he had to. Therefore he had to remain a listener; he had to acquire as much as he could from those who supported him. Uncle Kirkor had not said anything to Kid Arthur about what he had overheard, despite the fact that he had been his closest friend in the Market. He did not consider this as a betrayal. For, he knew that Kid Arthur was an extremely sensitive boy who could not put up with certain bare facts; he was sensitive to the point of morbidity according to the judgment of those around him . . . He himself was the only person who truly loved and understood him. Kid Arthur endeavored to put up with the pranks, in their monotony—from people who tried to cover up their own failures and lack of self-confidence hidden behind a plurality of masks—by laughing at his own shortcomings, clumsiness, and, what is still more important, at his stutter, in an easygoing, yet necessary way . . . The kid that had come to visit him at the workshop was the self-same kid . . . Uncle Kirkor was at that moment in the process of fixing a piece which Master Mıgır, a Luna Park *habitué*, had fabricated by taking great pains in a chunk of a press that only he could operate, and whose repair and maintenance he himself undertook. Upon Kid Arthur's inadvertently pressing the button of the press, the cutter had sliced off Uncle Kirkor's arm, radically changing his life in the blink of an eye . . . Uncle Kirkor, who had lost consciousness following the trauma, pleaded with Kid Arthur to immediately call for help. Neighbors had rushed in to take Kirkor to the nearest hospital. It was said that so much blood had oozed from him before he was taken to hospital that if timely help had not been sent for it would have been fatal. Master Barkev was said to have acted like a father to his apprentice during his stay at the Balıklı hospital, and spared nothing at the risk of Master Vahan's likely reaction. Among his visitors at the hospital was also Master Mıgır. He had brought him a railway carriage he had fabricated in iron, whose doors could be opened and shut, promising him that other carriages and a railway engine would soon follow. Other visitors included artisans from the Market; some bringing bouquets of flowers, some candies, and some *eau de cologne*. With a view not to leave him alone during this difficult time and to try to pinch a moment of bliss from his tragedy, even for a brief period, by simply being a presence, an onlooker to this disaster . . . Everybody had endeavored to hearten him, telling him that promising days lay ahead in the Market; his reaction to this was a beatific smile. For, he already knew what awaited him, and intuited that those who tried to hearten him were also aware of this. He realized that what he foresaw became a reality on the day he was discharged from the hospital. Master Barkev seemed to hold himself somewhat aloof from him. His voice had a different inflection which could be perceived only by those who knew him well. The master did not mince his words; he told him bluntly not to come to the workshop anymore. "With a single arm you can no longer do your job, you've got to find another occupation for yourself," he said. Perhaps, financial considerations had prevailed over the affection felt for the individual. Uncle Kirkor had not reacted; he had merely said "Goodbye, Master" and avoided his gaze. A word to the wise was enough . . .

The paths of the participants involved in the incident had subsequently changed course. Master Mıgır, at the cost of ruining his family, had married a woman with whom he had been head over heels in love and who used to sing songs from the movies of old; but, unable to bear the shock of her elopement with an alcoholic, a mechanic who operated the 'tunnel of horrors' at the Luna Park, and believing that a businessman's sense of honor had been at stake from his having been in default, he had eventually put an end to his life. His next-of-kin claimed that his suicide was not related in any way to what had befallen Kirkor. On the other hand, in the face of this backdrop, of which he had been the unintentional author, Kid Arthur's already sensitive spiritual constitution suffered greatly; he lost his mental balance completely and was confined to an asylum for the rest of his days. Master Barkev refused to employ any apprentice after that and gave up his intention to train a new novice as a substitute for the victim. As for the principal actor in this play, Uncle Kirkor, as far as I could gather from certain stories from our rare *tête-à-têtes* that provided me with clues about life in general, he had borne the worries caused in him by this lack of confidence all his life in a secret corner of his being, without blaming anyone, believing, however, that some people, certain individuals from his past would be filled with remorse sooner or later; without accusing or identifying anyone in particular, in full consciousness of the fact that certain convictions were upheld and were supported by little lies or illusions . . . in order not to lose his will to struggle against his master's betrayal, which, in time, I think, was to lend itself to different interpretations. Not for nothing had he said: "provided we remain alive," one of those days when he seemed to conjure up certain notions or established a link between them and his experiences. Provided we remain alive . . . these words would come back to me years later, reported by certain members of 'that family.' This was the story of a harrowing experience that was kept ever fresh in the mind. "Actually, I might have been a good lathe operator even with a single arm. But, I'd no chance," he told me, during one of our conversations. "It was my fate . . . Here we are at the end of the road, at the end of our life . . . " It was a moment of pessimism, of resignation to one's fate, actually inconsistent with someone who had always been hopeful of what the future would bring, of the realization of his most intimate wishes, an anticipation he had never formerly given up. However, regardless of the attitude adopted toward this deception or defeat, when one observes what Uncle Kirkor had gone through in the wake of that incident, one could not help believing, in that different path, so to speak, known to some as fate. For example, could one explain the socialist side of Master Vahan? He used to make furniture for the house of the Venturas at Akmescit, and preferred to make his comments on daily life and political developments in his smattering of French, which he had acquired simply by listening to his mother speak. He could not quit smoking despite his asthmatic condition, and under the pretext that "otherwise they wouldn't appreciate my work," he refused to work for the new rich upstarts whose behavior gave him the creeps and about whose lack of culture he was positively convinced. He believed that money could buy everything despite his financial difficulties and the penury he suffered, thereby causing others to suffer alongside him. He learned from Monsieur Jacques, when he had asked him to arrange a job for his son after that unfortunate accident in order to allow him to get some practice in business, a young man who had succeeded in becoming a self-made man, who had taken over the responsibility of the family, in need of a young, industrious, and what is still more important, reliable employee. Did he realise that through this exchange of words, which, at first, seemed to be a casual dialogue, he would eventually open up the lives of two people toward a lasting togetherness? As far as Uncle Kirkor could remember, in his old age, at a time when he looked back to his past not without some prickliness, thinking that it would do him some good and would be an answer to his moroseness, loneliness, and slovenly behavior, when he was about thirty or thirty-three years of age, he had been married off, by the good offices of certain people ever present at such situations, to 'Ani the Lame,' who had an original, exotic, and strong sex appeal. I have it from Monsieur Jacques that Ani was at the time in pursuit of a 'risky objective' in order not to be obliged to return to her plebeian family from Kayseri residing at Samatya, as a woman abandoned, after having had an illicit relationship, or, according to some, having been a mistress of a married colonel, at the time she had been introduced to Uncle Kirkor. Ani was the daughter of 'Serkis the Moody,' a maker and seller of pastırma (dried, smoked beef) in his shop no bigger than a chest, somewhere in the Eminönü Market, which he opened or kept closed according to his mood that day, and who, whenever the occasion presented itself, claimed that superior quality pastırma was made not of entrecôte, as some people, deluded by its appearance, might think, but from fillet of beef. The first speculations relating to his relationship may have been indulged in during the ramblings that had their origin in that shop cubicle. Uncle Kirkor had seen himself as a rescuer of Ani, a knight-errant. Considering the reigning circumstances, Ani herself may have seen him in that garb. However, to the best of my understanding, the said identity of a savior was not of the sort that one would associate in one's mind as a unilateral act of supererogation without wanting anything in return. She had, thanks to her feminine touch, appeared to have saved Uncle Kirkor from certain things. This is not my observation, but Monsieur Jacques' . . . Kirkor, at least at the beginning, during the days immediately succeeding his matrimony, paid special attention to his attire . . . Those were the days when he could laugh to his heart's content . . . Yet, this had been the social disposition of the day . . . For, after a while, the relationship took a different course, one not easily accepted and accounted for. Everybody got the gist of the affair in due time. Despite all efforts to avoid it, the incubus was always there. Ani had considered this matrimony a shield; it was as though she wanted to point out certain inroads into her eccentric and somewhat perverse spiritual constitution. For she had wanted to compensate for the great disappointment she had suffered by sleeping with other men, in spite of her knowledge of the fact that by this act she grieved and wounded her husband who continued to love her and served as her latent conscience. Ani and Uncle Kirkor had looked on their defects, each other's defects, from very different angles, possibly from solitary ones. The relationship was the sort of alliance that both sides carried on from their respective perspectives, within the confines of their respective tricks, servitudes and lies. The scenes in the stage play had tableaux in fact, tableaux one would better understand as one penetrated them. Ani felt herself nearer to Uncle Kirkor after each escapade and the latter justified them to himself resignedly to a certain extent by the plea of her eventual return to him after her moral turpitudes. After all, the very fact that a woman, who had had in her parlor many suitors, had married him despite his disabled state gradually boosted his self-esteem, making headway toward his serenity. His crippled condition was compensated in Ani with a like defect. Actually, this had played a pivotal role that had, according to outsiders, joined them in holy matrimony. The motive power had been Ani's full breasts, her beautiful face and penetrating looks, and last but not least, her feminine charm. With her womanhood and femininity she had overcompensated for her so-called defect. One should also take into consideration the milieu she had been living in, where the saying "a lame wench has a beautiful pussy" had a wide acceptance among the public. Uncle Kirkor was well aware of all of this. Their respective conditions were not equal, in other words. This had partly played the role of the prompter. The cost to Uncle Kirkor of his journey toward serenity had been considerable. However, it was a hard fact that those who had achieved success in life and reached privileged positions were people who had paid, had chosen to pay or had been obliged to pay a heavy cost in life.

Details of a long walk that lent meaning to the word fate, much different from the widely accepted definition . . . Uncle Kirkor certainly had his own interpretation of his shop with every passing day as a home in which the role played by fate should not be overlooked . . . Life was a path that had to be trodden, or an interminable play that one could not share with others: a play like the one featuring Ani and himself, in which everybody had become familiarized with their role, despite their resistance and expectancies, and eventually it obliged them to go along with it and try to convey it through their delusions. To switch the lights in the shop on and off with certain minute rituals imperceptible to an ordinary onlooker, to have Ismail, the drunkard, grease the shutters of the shop at prescribed intervals, which he meticulously lifted and lowered every evening; to gets bits of profits out of other people's affairs, hiding in his cache cigarettes that he had stolen from packages lying about, offering them to his guests, as a token of his generosity, shifting the places of fabrics saying that "every fabric has its own season and every season its own place" of which the texture, the weave, the quality he readily identified thanks to his expert knowledge acquired throughout his apprenticeship, as though he wanted to convey the message that seasons influenced individuals' idiosyncrasies. This act was some sort of a ritual for Uncle Kirkor. I now and then saw him sweep the front of his shop, early in the morning. I used to gaze at him with a smile. He understood me. There were other people who could take care of this, of course. He certainly knew it. However, when I caught him in the act, he had ready clichés to utter in a special broken accent to justify his actions. "After all, it's our means of existence . . . You must take good care of it and not put it out of sight . . . " I don't know why, but this sentence assumed quite a different and deep significance on Uncle Kirkor's tongue. This was one of the interesting things about that little ritual. Occasionally, we spoke in French. In the rudimentary French of Uncle Kirkor—whose vocabulary hardly exceeded fifty or sixty words. Those were the days of our hijinks. In his vocabulary were also obsolete words dating from the time of his visit to his cousin in Marseilles years ago. Among his recollections of those mornings—of those early mornings—were also the impressions left on him by the visions, voices and scents of the past. Those were our concretely lived mornings. What had been left there were the realities of the places that Uncle Kirkor revived in his imagination. They were the war years that the younger generation would never be able to imagine; those were the times when, despite penury, they had never been short of margarine. I remember the day when the new buses had arrived imported from Sweden. Parsek Dikranyan, their neighbor, a devotee of all things American, had, one day, at midnight, in the company of his wife and daughter, left for New York. According to the accounts that reached us, Parsek, after having engaged in many an uphill struggle, had ended up working as a driver, and, having worked in the profession for many years, died looking back at his days in Istanbul with a certain amount of nostalgia, especially missing the odors that permeated the Spice Market. Nevertheless, rumors were spread to the effect that he had not died a natural death, but had been killed by the dagger of an Italian florist, and that his breathtakingly beautiful daughter, Ida, had become a prostitute. This was one of the stories between Uncle Kirkor and I that had left certain fleeting impressions on me. I think he had been instrumental in contributing to the development of my narrative style and my art of listening. These were my favorite stories, the ones dearest to me. He also reminded me of the cryptic messages that were played by foreign broadcasting stations on the shortwave, transmitted by the French Resistance, after the Ankara radio signed off at eleven o'clock. Among the messages he had especially remembered was one transmitted by the French Resistance Organization: Le cochon est constipé. It was a message he had never been able to decipher, a message whose mysterious meaning preoccupied him until the very end; a message that no longer held any significance. He also remembered listening to the speeches of Général Charles de Gaulle. They got a vicarious thrill from the ongoing events. "They will win . . . Europe will be liberated," his father had said. Their mother was also with them, she had not yet departed. She used to buy the daily *Le Journal d'Orient* for her husband from the newspaper stand at Tünel. This daily was the last remnant of the dailies published in French in Turkey. It too was coming to an end, almost without anyone noticing. He used to cast a glance at the paper. At times, the friar at the college Saint-Michel was revived in his memory. He also remembered the morning of the horrible devastation caused at Beyoğlu following the September Incidents, when the main streets were littered with the contents of the shops.

Uncle Kirkor was for me a valuable witness and was one of the principal actors in that long story. However, in this story there was another actor that made him a living and unforgettable hero. To understand Uncle Kirkor without having an idea about that actor was impossible. To turn a deaf ear to that actor's account would be tantamount to listening to Uncle Kirkor with only one ear. It appeared that that actor had encountered Uncle Kirkor for the first time at a very special moment of his solitude that no one had had any inkling of. How otherwise could one play that prank on others?

Niko, the Waistcoat Tailor

I know well enough by now, that, in time, certain words are liable to assume a plurality of meanings. What I don't know or am not sure about, however, is whether these words eventually hit the mark they aim at in defiance of the meanings involved. Now that I have set out to trace the path that led from Uncle Kirkor to Niko, I feel somewhat hesitant whether I should use a phrase I had been reserving for the story I have not yet penned: they had lived the poem of showing another place to another person . . . When I brood over the story in question, it seems to me that that sentence half-opens the door to another world. All the same, I can't help asking the question despite this probability. I wonder how many people and how many lives can one person live through in a lifetime? I was to learn, one day, from Olga, during a seemingly casual talk, that the incidents which had occurred on that fatal day at Pera—which was in terminal decline, gradually deteriorating into Beyoğlu—which can also be considered as an extension of that awful awakening that compelled certain people at the least expected moment to depart for places they were reluctant to reach, had created a deep sorrow in Uncle Kirkor, the origin of a growing gap within him. In that story, it seemed as though everybody was trying to tell each other, at an opportune moment, certain things that were banded together. Certain things . . . lurking in the shade, of lasting remembrance, alive, in their own voices, things not consigned to oblivion . . . Just to see to it that those stories are conveyed to posterity, to avoid mass extinction, to secure their permanence in one way or another, in memories . . . "He is after Niko," Olga said, as if disclosing a secret, with looks expressive of the fact that she had been among the material witnesses to certain situations in the past, on one of those days of Uncle Kirkor's soul-searching, when he had absconded for a short time from the shop on the pretext that he was going to "drink some soup" while his actual intention was to knock back a raki, to be in pursuit of Niko, of a lost soul, although bereft of hope, not to sink into despair, to shoulder one's past, as a sense of belonging to some place, to some person . . . Learning this from Olga (a fact that Uncle Kirkor had never mentioned during our morning talks) was for me, to be honest, a source of special grief. Situations revived and reproduced past stories even in their new places, stories that inevitably changed their makeup in someone else . . . What had exasperated me was not his reticence, the sense of alienation which I deemed to be quite natural given our relationship and the age gap between us despite the sympathy we felt toward one other, his preference was to relive the story all alone, in his own depths, far removed from his friends. However, it occurs to me now that in time we had developed a tacit understanding and begun sharing the different memories of Niko within us, as regards minor but important details, without imparting anything of significance to each other. Long after those days, years, very many years later . . . Uncle Kirkor had, I think, understood that I had come to know Niko by inference, by what I could glean from other people's observations and verses. As a matter of fact, I had tried to intimate this to him. We had spotted each other's secrecy on an extremely fine line of thought partly because of this. To carry on the story through different paths depended on us. Certain details we deemed important had already found us outside of our brief encounters and short visits. We had our shortcomings and little puzzles. The fact that we had been unable to properly tell each other of the inception and the progress of our stories relating to Niko was most probably due to our recourse to fantasy, just like in the case of many other narrations of ours. I was to experience a like feeling with certain other people who had imparted extremely long stories to me. In conclusion, we have to acknowledge that a great many people live and continue to live like the rest of us. Nevertheless, I think that this part of the story had a special attraction for us. For, we had already grown accustomed to evading certain facts, our facts. Evasions were our evasions, and the borders that we had traced were part of our lives. I could never learn, for this reason, when exactly had this story begun, and in particular, why. All that I know and can say is that Niko, introduced to me as a good drinking companion with whom one could share many a problem and dilemma, had taken part in this story through his identity as a waistcoat tailor carrying on his trade at his workshop on Aşir Efendi street. The workshop in question was a ramshackle construction whose creaking floor reminded one, at every opportunity, of its run-down condition. It had never occurred to Niko to replace the linoleum that bore on it the marks of endless stories, the footprints of a multitude of people, a linoleum, of which the color had faded away and the designs of which were wiped clean, while the torn bits and pieces caused the customers to trip. There was also a cat called Yorgo: a cat that looked as though it had been there since time began. It is said that Niko spoke to him in Greek so that the people present might not understand what he said. However, I never knew who those present were. Who may they have been? Visitors that popped in for various purposes or the customers or the other cats that now and then paid a visit, perhaps? Heaven knows! It's a bit difficult for me to answer these questions as a hero of another story who had merely been a spectator watching from a distance. However, even though such a question may have been left unanswered, it provides enough clues to enable certain people to easily observe certain aspects of life. That means to go as far as the desired location, following the clues at hand, is again within our reach . . . It is said that Yorgo also relished raki. Niko had made a point of treating his chum with his allotted portion before shutting down the shop. Apparently, the cat knew very well the amount of water that had to be added to dilute the potion; any addition or reduction to his wonted quantity of water was immediately sensed since he refused to drink it. There was another man in the shop acting as assistant to Niko by the name of Şeref from the province of Urfa, a type who was spare with his words. He stammered; a blood feud had paved his way to Istanbul. This rumor could be interpreted differently, of course: was this a search or an attempt at removing one's roots? Was this a question of a settlement of accounts or an avoidance of a reprisal? Nobody could come to a definitive conclusion. One day, this age-old visitor failed to show up. He had disappeared without giving any notice . . . Had he been disposed of? Was he going to meet his inexorable fate? Nobody knew.

These are the photographs I could gather from the collection, arranged in the order I saw fit, although I'm still at a loss to fix them in their proper places in Niko's story. It appears that the starting point had been a neighborhood relationship and that the masks—which those who had their parts to play in their respective lives knew very well how to wear—appeared to have been adapted better and better with every passing day. It seemed to indicate that several individuals, after having converged at a crossroads in their lives, had continued to live collectively. After their departure from that crossroads, it seemed that certain photographs thus reflected a collective outlook. Certain photographs were looked at casually, most probably from a communal point of view, by those sharing all the tactile feelings and delusions involved; without them being conscious of where, what and how certain particulars had been appropriated at what level. Masks had been put on, remained unidentified . . . With a view to being able to remain hidden as long as possible among other individuals. As people imbibed their teas, their conversation based on ready-made prescriptions with empty political platitudes hardly involving private interests despite differences of opinion, they proffered immaterial solutions, taking care to pay due attention in order to keep remote from certain things. This was, in a certain sense, the categorical imperative of history; the consequence of a choice related to the sentiment that a particular place imparted to certain people through the inspiration of history. The places in question had either been previously pinpointed or the individuals in question were compelled to choose them for themselves. You might sometimes show reluctance in identifying those places. Football matches had, for a length of time, caused people to forget the worries created by the monotony of life and the inevitable bondage to monetary concerns. In those little worlds, the moments were lived in small steps; the invisible moments of life were spent along with those passing glances. Ears were lent to the elderly people in their identity as aged and were deemed worth listening to, while the young people were presumed to be promising to the extent they abided by social rules. Were they among the voiceless murderers, defenders of the status quo, lost in their little dreams they told no one about? At the time nobody could provide an answer to this question. After all, the world was a place of such sentiments where even pouring out one's grievances to one's friends was vented with insipid truisms, with platitudes that conveyed only a couple of unforgotten words, a far cry, reminiscent of a muted call . . . All these things were embodied in the relations that Uncle Kirkor and Niko had got entangled with, for better or for worse. However, in my estimation, barring all these cover-ups and efforts at concealment, they had their own particular stories that were inaccessible and incomprehensible to others. The intelligence I could obtain from different quarters intimated that there was in this a desire to proceed on toward such a story. The story was of two individuals, who had endeavored to act or continued to act, in one way or another, on other people's stages, being at variance with each other or at least seeming to be at variance with each other; the story of two companions, each in search of a role for themselves that would enable them to carry the burden of those defeats and deceptions believed to be the fate of every mortal. I think these roles were performed as spontaneous acts, acts that might have been slyly masqueraded as self-defense. It seemed that they had performed on that stage their most important and successful roles. According to Olga, who had told me the story of their controversies with her own additions to, and subtractions from, the actual happenings. Uncle Kirkor, when he was in the mood on certain mornings, dressed Niko, renowned for his mastery in waistcoat tailoring, teasing him with remarks about his alleged habit of filching, imitating the local Armenian accent: "You rascal, waistcoat tailor! Tell me how many yards of fabric have you ripped off from others for your waistcoats today, you dirty infidel?" In return, Niko, in his local Greek accent, got even for this recriminatory remark by retorting: "Cad! Weren't you a *habitué* of bawdy houses that catered, at Sabri's place, in return for some consideration, to the lust of people of lewd practices?" This was, apparently, a nod toward the 'filching' of Uncle Kirkor by an allusion to a closely-guarded and shameful secret known to a very few people; to a secret dating back to an almost forgotten time, that was wished to be consigned to oblivion. The publicizing of such an offense was thus compensated for by the disclosure of other offenses. This was an intimidation tactic used for restraining both parties from further revelations. Barring all these things, that long stage play, that prank played on life, in other words that buffoonery that aimed to remain linked to the places in question necessitated the enactment and representation of those scenes. As for those offenses . . . had there been no such offenses there would have been no heroes; without them the heroes in question would not and could not even conceive that such creation had ever taken place. That moral order knew how to absorb and adapt to the said errors. The comments that have reached me from those times confirm my convictions. Thanks to the personalities of Niko and Uncle Kirkor, everybody had, after a while, found some happiness. Niko was partly justified in alluding to the bawd Sabri who had been instrumental in catering to the needs of the men of Istanbul at the time by opening the doors of perception for them, having it in mind to remind Uncle Kirkor of a time in his life which he preferred to keep secret from the general public. As a matter of fact, I had had some information about this past . . . According to the gossipers, Uncle Kirkor used to pay visits to a great many brothels on the notorious Abanoz Street. He had continued to pay his visits to the houses of ill repute, even when he had become old, when he married Madame Ani. According to some, this had a very simple, ordinary and specific explanation, although others considered it rather important. Uncle Kirkor had fallen in love with a woman there who had not only embraced his disability, but who had also taught him how to live with originality. One day, without saying anything to anyone, she left to work in a brothel in İzmir, and, according to the accounts of the residents of that notorious street, married a pharmacist's assistant much older than herself, who earned his living by measuring the blood pressure of people in the surroundings area by means of an outdated sphygmomanometer, eventually settling at Karataş. This was the whole story, at least the story that had reached our ears. We could never learn the name of his lover. No definitive understanding could be ascertained as to the truth behind this story whose origin had remained a complete mystery, and whether this was exactly how it had played out or not no one knew . . . Nor could we learn how the news of her marriage had been received by Uncle Kirkor. All that one could ascertain was the fact that Uncle Kirkor had ceased to frequent the said quarters and retreated from view. This was the moot point that Niko had been harping on about. I know for a fact that he tried to establish the links from a distance while he was treading a path in a different time frame. I may have missed certain details, of course. Yet, looked at from this angle, I cannot deny the fact that I do sense some sort of treachery in this mnemonic.

As for the revelation of Niko's petty larceny . . . I don't think he had suffered greatly from the disclosure of his secret. This singularity of his had apparently, in one way or another, been known to everybody in his circle and eventually came to be seen as a pleasant extension of collectivity. This may have been a bonus due to the fact that it cushioned the blow of the teasing. His half-drunk state even in the middle of the day and his frequent lapses of oral hygiene had made him a laughing stock. One's conscience had to be cleansed in one way or another in order to give way to other petty offenses.

Monsieur Jacques would confirm, years after my conversation with Olga that had enabled me to have an insight into the relationship between those two kindred-spirits, the reality relative to Niko's ill-gotten waistcoat trade. The backdrop was of a different time, one pregnant with meaning. Monsieur Jacques, like many people who had lived during those days, had felt the need to comment on the changing values, values that were actually being gnawed away at the roots. The number of tailors who understood the sartorial expressions exchanged between master and apprentice was ever decreasing. "For instance," he said, "here we have Niko, who, despite the fact that he is a liar and hardly keeps his promises and his shop stinks of raki, the jackets he tailors fit his customers perfectly. You can throw whatever you have, whenever you have it, into the bargain." He had a way to smooth out the fabric he tailored. He wore a wry smile on his face. He was lost in the distance beyond any boundaries I could ever imagine. "He was a bit of a filcher, but anyway . . . " he added afterwards. I had some difficulty in understanding what he meant by the word filcher. He may have used it in order not to insult a person of a time past, not to stain the memory a man had left behind. I think it was also a sort of sympathy. The same appreciation was also shared by Uncle Kirkor who happened to be there, and who had, benefiting from the opportunity, cut in, making the following remark for a friend he had lost: "The waistcoat bawd! He hardly knew how to play backgammon!" Monsieur Jacques had first cast a glance at Uncle Kirkor from above his spectacles. However, both had begun laughing at the same time at this remark. This was one of those guffaws that was deeply felt and well justified, a peel of laughter that embodied a kind of heartache. Monsieur Jacques had afterward said to Uncle Kirkor in imitation of Niko (that was my impression anyhow) something in Greek which I hadn't understood. He had a smattering of Greek like all the Jews of the time. The remark had been confirmed by a nod from Uncle Kirkor. I'd felt this. One could feel that Niko was somehow present at the time, in a place to which I could never have access . . . Moreover, one had to dwell on the significance of the phrases used by Uncle Kirkor while referring to Niko, as well as to their associations. For reasons well-known to those who live with another tongue, in addition to the so-called vernacular, he could not properly pronounce the word 'backgammon,' for instance, without provoking derisive laughter. Leaving aside all the remarks that one could allow oneself, one thing was acknowledged: namely his mastery of backgammon. Although it was said that he often cheated while playing hurriedly and manipulated the dice so that they fell as he would have wished, everybody who had played a game of backgammon with him knew how exhilarating the game was. The same exhilaration was shared by the onlookers as well. There was no doubt that he was topnotch. His most admirable characteristic was his inability to acknowledge defeat. His matches with Sedat the Arab, who teased him with swear words like "son of a bear" during their game (the bet being a cup of tea) gathered a whole crowd of onlookers.

The Joke of Sedat the Arab

I distinctly remember that Sedat the Arab was, in the first instance, a man who had sought to live the life he always imagined for himself in some other place, in such a place that people lived as if lost in a poem. He had traveled all over Anatolia in his minibus baptized 'The Detective' because of the initials 'DT' on the license plate; it was a minibus which he had to take to the service station every other day; he doted on her, even though she was already an old banger. He also took pleasure in displaying the various features of people's faces by mimicking them behind their back, in the manner of a professional. This was his hobby, and, if one considers his attitude to life, one can say that it was finesse. He was full of life. Full of it! He had lived many a life, many a path ran through him, different nights and dawns that not many people could have lived. He hadn't gone to university and had to shoulder the inferiority that this failure burdened him with everywhere he went, especially his failing to have become a doctor. He had to compensate for this frustration through his accurate diagnoses of many a disease that his friends suffered from and the therapeutic methods he recommended; and according to his own account, he had saved many lives. However, I interpreted this as a kind of joke, a joke that ought to lead us to a revision of the reality behind that failure. In my opinion, we should look for the meaning concealed in his outlook on life in those secluded and out-of-sight places where he lived. It looked as if he had spent more than half his life, or, to be more precise, of his life visible to me, on those secluded paths. When we noticed his absence, we were sure that he had set out for one of his usual journeys in Anatolia. Nobody knew what his destination was and when he would be returning—and by which particular direction. The length of his stays at the places he visited varied drastically; they were sometimes short and sometimes very long. All I can remember is that if one considers how often he engaged in such sallies, one would be inclined to conclude that he must have spent at least half the year on such voyages. This is why I think that he took his minibus not only as a companion, but also as his workshop and home, to wit his sanctuary. However, he was not the only person of this kind, for there were many people in his circle who sallied forth on such vagaries in different directions for different reasons. Yet, these were emotions which, although visible up to a certain extent, were not of the sort one could empathize with. Once they were experienced they became lost and gone forever; yet, they remained in certain people serving as repositories. In many a city and town, he knew the addresses of such places as pharmacies, post offices, hotels, cafés, unlicensed brothels, restaurants, etc. He had a vast knowledge about land routes. The road map in his mind was not the official map of the overland routes; it was exclusive to him. He liked to freak out now and then. I knew this. Those freak-outs involved other maps. We could read from the sorrowful expression on his face that he was to set off early next day. When he returned from his journeys, he stayed in Istanbul at places where he was recognized; he put in an appearance at varying locations of his choice before taking flight with a view to perpetuating his destiny, his wandering. He had no idea about when he would return. "The road tips us a wink . . . Source of livelihood, you know . . . " It was his livelihood; that much was true. This was not all, however; Sedat the Arab enjoyed an almost legendary fame through the marketing of his merchandise and his collecting of valuables. This may be a feature that made him conspicuous in the eyes of others. To treat someone in a way that is calculated to please him, that's what a decent person should do. But had he been decent himself? Perhaps not; but he had an uncanny ability to feel the pulse of his customers. There was no doubt about it; the crux of the matter lay in this. Thus, at the places he stopped, he persuaded people, posing as a refined gentleman from Istanbul, to buy his pharmaceutical products, or, if need be, as a lovable rascal, a pettifogger, whatever the circumstances warranted. He recited poems to some, while he harangued others about the country's problems. He was a leftist with the leftists and a rightist with the rightists. As far as I know, he spoke Kurdish well, although he was not a Kurd himself. He knew how to perform the prayer of the Muslims although he was not a Muslim. Thus, by giving the supplicant what he wanted, he skillfully refrained from giving what he should actually have given. This was his petty revolt. I took cognizance of this fact years later when I managed to have a distant view of it. At the time I misread the signs, and results, of what was going on. However, in order for me to pass judgment on these happenings, other people must also be considered. The number of witnesses and followers of Sedat the Arab's legendary fame was, of course, considerable. However, despite all of his renown and his modest achievements, he had been indifferent to saving money as far as I know. This stands as evidence to his other pursuits, of his goals and desires to see other places. As though this was not enough, he spent every penny he had on the treatment of his wife who was suffering from cancer. I still retain those days in my memory. The craftsmen in his circle had even collected money to subsidize his wife's treatment. Sedat the Arab had realized, especially back then, how deeply he had been attached to her. According to the accounts of his next-of-kin, his mobilization was not simply the cause of a repayment of gratitude, but also one of the greatest disgraces of his life; a disgrace or a sense of defeat one can only acknowledge with difficulty . . . or a resentment, a resentment harbored against life, against days he could not turn to good account despite all his efforts, the days he thought he had missed and failed to make the best of . . . Could one establish a relationship between this bitter resentment and his sudden death of a heart attack in a small hotel room in a town near Istanbul where he stayed on his return journey from a long eastern sales campaign to celebrate his fiftieth year? Perhaps. However, what was still more important was the place where he died, where he succeeded in dying, rather than this question mark he had left unanswered. He had died in the place he cherished most, on the road . . . He had experienced in that town an original feeling he had never felt before; a feeling that showed us an attribute, a time, a part of which we had not been conscious of until then . . . The scene we had been faced with had puzzled us for many years. It looked as though this had been the performance of the last act of a play. Or, as if the play had ended in such a way that not even its actors could have foreseen, not being prepared for such a catharsis . . . The fact is that when he died, there was a woman with him. We had been told that the woman was a sophisticated pharmacist who was in an unhappy marriage. They had spent a passionate love affair full of sound and fury that had lasted for two years. We have this information from Vedat Bey, his cousin who ran a perfume shop, and who had gone downtown to collect Sedat's remains. Vedat Bey described the lady pharmacist as a very beautiful and refined woman who knew how to listen to people. Everybody had more or less guessed what merit and character Sedat had found in her.

On my way to another place years later, my path had strayed toward that town . . . My intention was to take some rest and have a glimpse of it as long as I could, and, last but not least, to find, if I could, that pharmacist. It was a small town and the inhabitants were friendly. It did not take me long to track down the pharmacy in question. However, it turned out that the pharmacy had changed hands and was being run by another lady. The new owner was an attractive woman of about fifty. At first, she seemed cagey about what I wanted to learn, but in the end, she told me everything she knew. The lady pharmacist I had been looking for had apparently preferred not to stay any longer in that town, and felt obliged to leave, according to hearsay, to the south where she had opened a new drugstore. She had ended up marrying an old university friend who had been wooing her. She had put a certain order to her life and was back on her feet. The townsmen with whom she had been on intimate terms had heard that she had eventually found what she had been looking for in the south. As a matter of fact, she was from Iskenderun. She was nearer now to the climate of her youth which she had been missing. About the incident in that hotel room when death had overtaken him, she said that the man in question was a refined gentleman, a rich businessman. While narrating this part of the story, she had had to break off every now and then. Could she have been inventing things? I don't know; but I had the impression that I was acting in a play in which everybody in the town was taking part.

It seemed that nothing had changed; everybody looked like they had stayed right where they had been. I think the reality of the situation lay in my being pushed out or through the impression of my being ousted. As I was leaving the pharmacy, the lady shook my hands warmly and said: "It appears that the man was a refined gentleman, a real gentleman. However, he seemed to have had some serious problems." As I came out I noticed that there were people who wore meaningful smiles on their faces. There was no change of expression . . . I had to leave . . . I had realized that I had reached a dead end . . . I had no other choice but to continue my journey. Another person who continued her journey for the sake of her own story was Elisa, Sedat the Arab's wife. It had taken her two years to completely recover; she finally married a wealthy widower with two grown-up children; thus, she had had the privilege of enjoying, as best she could, the remaining part of her life living in the summer of the Princes' Islands, a thing she could never afford during her previous marriage. Years later, I ran into her on the island at an ordinary moment during an ordinary day. She seemed to be enjoying good health. She spoke to me about her husband's affairs and of their children as though they were her own. She had not mentioned the name of Sedat. His father being an Antiochian Armenian and his mother a Jewess from Gaziantep, Sedat used to boast of his mixed blood. The only certainty for him was the concrete reality of a lived day. Such an attitude was automatically reflected in many aspects of his lifestyle. The witticism he used to tease Uncle Kirkor with was in reality a projection of this attitude toward delusion. Needling him at these incendiary moments, Uncle Kirkor, whose habit it was to swear like a trooper, would simply utter: "Fuck you! Son of a bitch!" In this, there seemed to be concealed a special affection whose origin was not to be so easily detected. Whether it could be shared or not . . . This was an important issue as it was with other people. However, when one takes everything into consideration, as far as one can infer from the accounts of his contemporaries, Uncle Kirkor had shared with Niko things which he could share with no other person. Even during a game of backgammon . . . I know for a fact that there were many things they had jointly discovered and reproduced. Nevertheless, his common experiences with Niko require a totally different dimension that we ought to discover. There is a place to which only the people whom one cherishes belong, to whom one feels attached and with whom one can never break, a place that faithfully follows one everywhere . . .

Niko the Stoker

Olga had said that Uncle Kirkor had put away the backgammon board sometime after Niko's departure, never to touch it again. This did not appear strange to me; it was an act that befitted him perfectly; after all he ought to react in some way or another. This didn't happen immediately, however. The meaning of a particularity of a given experience could be perpetuated only in conjunction with the man with whom that experience was shared. A particularity of a given experience could not be re-experienced with another person, once the person, with whom the said experience had been shared, was no more. Nothing could supersede that experience. There was no other way to experience the said particularity having been immortalized for that particular person. Yes, for that particular person . . . not to soil with a new person the days lived jointly with the old. This was directly related at the same time to one's awareness of oneself, to one's self-defense—the need to find self-justification and worth. In those days when you have the perception of being sought after you might think about changing your attire once more. You might inquire how many snapshots had remained from those times of which you were proud. Under the circumstances, I believe I can understand better now why Uncle Kirkor had preferred to bury certain memories in his heart. Such tactile feelings must remain bound. Yes, those feelings must not be impaired. The snapshots must remain unaffected. That was the reason why we had made a point not to pass by 'that street' after the loss of 'that woman.' This was the reason why the finishing touches had to be put on the story of those backgammon games, so that they could be viewed from this particular angle. The witnesses were aware of this. They slammed the round pieces so strongly in the heat of the game that the pieces were frayed. Those passionate moments, the state of euphoria infected the onlookers who forcefully connected with the players' emotion, sometimes reaching such a height that the general feeling was that a brawl between the fans of both parties seemed imminent. This demonstration pointed the way toward the losing party treating the winning party to revelry in one of the taverns at Balıkpazarı, or, occasionally to a water pipe session at one of the joints under the Bridge. Sometimes a frenzy overwhelmed the bystanders. Among the onlookers there happened to be greenhorns as well. In such competitive games, the onlookers usually watched each other, or, more precisely, watched as if they were the players themselves.

The evenings passed under the Bridge were the evenings during which there usually reigned a general silence, a general reserve; the evenings during which the actors performed, or were caused to perform their parts, most probably, on a totally different stage . . . Would it be possible for someone at home picking up the scent of fried fish to suddenly be carried away to scenes seemingly sunken into oblivion, scenes poorly enacted, and trapped in the past? Perhaps.

However, regardless of what had transpired, Monsieur Jacques, who had visited the same places long after those evenings had passed, managed to reignite memories in my imagination. The memories of the open-air movie theater he had been running somewhere near Kadıköy in a block of flats, a vestige of the accounts of Toros the Cameraman, who often spoke of Sylvano Mangano in her film *Bitter Rice*, which he had copied and reproduced without having duly obtained a license during those cold winter days, in those good old days, the number of which he ignored, in a mood similar to what those rundown open-air movie theaters might have felt like during their demolition, thinking of the dilapidated state of the home he could not repair because of his destitute condition, immersed in his reflective solitude. These memories are as vivid in my mind as the impressions that a long conversation would create in reproducing the human faces lost in that refuge, the refuge the stage actors found in each other.

Uncle Kirkor and Niko had made a point of smoking a water pipe with double flexible tubes. This had a simple reason apparently. When the ember was low, someone had to manipulate it in order to keep it going. The practiced hand knew how to do this. This gave a special pleasure to the water-pipe smokers. For this reason Niko had taken charge of handling the tongs that would keep the fire blazing. Uncle Kirkor occasionally warned Niko to be vigilant and not let the fire go out. To this warning Niko retorted affectionately, saying: "By God, it won't." The same remarks were repeated every evening. It's a fact that certain clichés are *de rigueur* in rituals. One day Uncle Kirkor made the remark: "The mouthpiece fits your mouth quite well," in his broken accent. To which, Niko retorted, pointing to an angler: "Oh bother! Kirkor! Look at the fisherman, he thinks he's skilled merely because he caught a single horse mackerel!" In order to catch the meaning of such altercations one had to be familiar with the jargon used in that world, with such teasing and mutual asylum—the *Weltanschauung* that reigned there. Afterward they kept quiet for a long time as though they were far away, as though they lived in distant realms . . . Uncle Kirkor used to make occasional remarks to

Niko, saying: "Nicky, are you aware that we are drinking like fish? We are petering out." Upon which Niko stirred the ember to keep it aglow. Toros, under the impressions and observations he had, appeared to have shot the best film of his life, intending to put it on in his private movie theater which he did not want to share with anybody, keeping it solely to himself. Secluded in his corner, befitting the world of the water pipe, without giving thought to the fact that these words, these 'designs' would assume completely different meanings once reproduced and shared . . .

Uncle Kirkor's remark about drinking like fish was undoubtedly referring to the evenings spent in the pub. Those evenings remind me of Niko sticking out like a sore thumb displaying his modest superiority while selecting the appetizers with great alacrity. At such moments, with my head in the clouds, fascinated by the anecdotal legends of Istanbul, I seem to be under the influence of certain 'cut-and-dried scenes.' So what? This part of the game, if such a path was chosen, could be the source of acrid joy . . . At such times, in order that I might perpetuate this experience, I thought of their habit of reverting to knocking back a drink at a cheap joint when they were broke, although I was perfectly aware that Niko's preference was the stand-up bars. As for the conversations going on in that world of exile, closed to some, consciously or unconsciously . . . to imagine those moments is not that difficult if one takes certain liberties with the details. Henceforth, all that remained to be done for me was to compile certain tittle-tattle tales and patch up the story . . . Niko might have spoken about his wife, who had, at the most unexpected moment, abandoned him to go to Athens, and who, in spite of her visits to the aforementioned city felt like an outsider herself and therefore started an affair with a gypsy from Yedikule; about his homosexual son who had been touring the world in the company of an American TV correspondent; about that 'Casablanca legend' he could never succeed in smothering; about the possibility of making big money if he risked that journey, by putting into practice certain bright ideas hovering in his mind; and finally about achieving bliss by getting married to 'that woman' he believed to be still waiting for him in Thessaloniki.

In the hope that it would slightly dispel his feeling of loneliness, Uncle Kirkor had most probably confessed that he had not repudiated his wife despite her adulteries; he had never thought of divorcing her and never turned his back on her or accused her of cheating. Wrought as he was by the feeling of frustration for having failed to enjoy the paternity of his son, bitterly disappointed in the wake of the accident that had caused him to stray from his professional path of lathe operator by the inadvertency of Kid Arthur—the conductor of the said accident who was fated to die after spending many years in the asylum La Paix in fits of delirium, repeating his name frequently—who Uncle Kirkor felt a deep remorse for having failed to pay a visit to while he was in the throes of death. I know for a fact that every one of these incidents was a little story that might generate a new beginning. I know that these stories were of the sort that many people would have preferred to turn their back on, and might judge them 'over-stuffed.' But those who had continuously failed to realize their enchantment, during those long, interminable yarns, had many deceptions and frustrations of their own to tell about, and would have liked to recount them, in the faint hope of linking certain nights to certain mornings . . . We can call this nostalgia, lingering in certain people, of inexpressible alienations, as well as the indelible impressions of an exiled individual, who ventured to live in a different Istanbul to the one he remembered, inhaling its odors, voices, features and eventualities night and day . . .

An exile difficult to explain—wherein everybody lives their own estrangement in a different way despite sharing a common bond with those of their homeland—a tie that cannot be severed. Actually, in case one prefers to linger in that world, nourished through fantasy, it will be a long story which may enable the discovery of other lines of enquiry. Seen from this angle, despite all the accompanying adversities, it is worth suffering to the bitter end. Yet, one can't live in reality to one's heart's content. To what extent this exile had been voluntary could never be articulated; you could not even imagine it. However, it was going to turn for Niko into an exile whose boundaries could be delineated more easily as a consequence of the renewal of the residency permits for Greek nationals that allowed them to continue living in the country during the sixties. Was this the end of that Istanbul tale of which the origin was unknown, lived by two people, never to be narrated in history books, which might seem to certain people as an episode in a legend lost in the darkness of the past? Those who had the privilege to have seen those days claim that Niko had gone to Athens with a mind to one day return. Had it not been the same for those uprooted from their homeland because of ethnic considerations or professions? Hope for a homeward journey . . . in order for one to carry the burden of life and postpone the crack of doom easier . . . On one of the days on the eve of his departure when

Monsieur Jacques had visited him to buy a drinks cabinet with a mirror inside it, equipped with a mechanism that switched on a light bulb when opened—the odor of which bore witness to its use as a well-stocked treasury of drinks and a dressing table—he had said to him: "It's a legacy of my father." He had with some pride indicated to him the old phonograph records with 'His Master's Voice' on them, making the remark: "Dating from the time of Monsieur Schur and the Geserian Brothers," records he had entrusted to a friend whose name he did not mention. Monsieur Jacques had witnessed that rich collection of records that had not been inherited from his father alone, but also consisted of records he himself had bought throughout his life: Seyyan Hanım, Hafız Burhan, Münir Nuretting, Suzan Lutfullah Hanım, Neveser Hanım, tangos, Greek songs, Neapolitan songs, etc., all of these were entrusted to this anonymous individual. Taken into custody by the said person . . . with a view to returning them, of being able to return . . . with a view to seeing to it that the records might feel at home in their new location . . . However, the person they had been entrusted with, and the locality where they happened to be, have not been discovered to this day. The words exchanged between him and Uncle Kirkor at 'their last supper' also remain a mystery. All that is known is the fact that from that day on, both Olga's, and, according to various witnesses, Uncle Kirkor's introversions had somewhat intensified; on the other hand, the latter, who had not been frequenting his wonted pub for a good many years, had resumed his practice of celebrating certain days he deemed worthy to be remembered, or for smoking a water pipe clandestinely while he waited for Niko. Olga had heard him say to Monsieur Jacques one of those days, when the thought of being forsaken weighed heavy on him: "Decisions relative to the critical moments of my life have always been made by others." If one lends credence to what was being said, he was in a dejected state; lonely, in despair and lacking in self-confidence just like the moments of expectation leading to the hours of water-pipe smoking. I believe that this moping, and especially this despondency, caused him to stay away from the pub for quite a while despite all sorts of thin excuses. Although he stayed away from the pub to compensate for this defect, he had not failed in guzzling a small bottle of raki with fish he himself fried at home nearly every Sunday. This ritual seemed to be the manifestation of a memory he did his best to keep fresh in his mind which he was loath to see consigned to oblivion. This was the story of an attempt or a wish to perpetuate a recollection or a ritual among his other associations. Niko had obliterated all traces that he might have left behind, he had neither written a letter nor sent a word. This had naturally given rise to all sorts of rumors about him. According to one account, Niko, unable to bear the absence of certain individuals he cherished, after having imbibed considerable quantities of alcohol, had committed suicide, throwing himself into the sea at Piraeus, confident that his body would be cast ashore; yet, according to another report, having settled accounts with his wife, he had gone to the USA to marry a rich widow who owned oilfields and had disappeared among the billionaires. Yet another story claimed that he was brought to Monsieur Jacques by Alexis the Bartender; according to this rendering of the story Niko had gone to 'that woman' in Thessaloniki, but had been repudiated by her for his having waited too long. Having gone mad at this cool reception, which had ruined the dreams he had been embellishing all these years, he killed her and spent his remaining years in prison smoking cannabis. Had Niko been the principal actor in either of the stories mentioned above? I wonder. To the best of my knowledge, Niko had preferred to keep aloof in order to be able to put up with his yearning for a life he had been torn from against his will. Uncle Kirkor's attitude was no different. His rarer visits to the pub might be explained by his reluctance or concern about running into certain people. It was an elaborate deception. The conversation seemed to be at quite a different level of frequency. However, it seems to me that what particularly delighted Uncle Kirkor was this ritual at home, where he could turn his incarceration into a viable lifestyle, an unostentatious liberation. What remained for Uncle Kirkor was to justify this little ritual by talking about it or sharing it with certain people or reproducing it in some sense. His elaborate narration of how he had purchased the fish he fried on Sundays, how he prepared the salad and its dressing, and how he absorbed alcohol, most probably resulted from this need. He never neglected to boast about drinking a whole bottle of raki to its dregs, as if to give it its due. When I asked him when he would be kind enough to bring some stuffed mussels from home he kept silent. How could I have known that he could not possibly ask his wife for such a favor, that this might be interpreted as a silent revolt against his marriage that was harrowed with absurdities and senselessness, that he had actually been missing that 'lost taste' with an ever increasing appetite, one he had identified with his mother to whom he felt he was approaching and would have liked to be reunited with. Once, we were having dinner at Kireçburnu; it was an autumn evening. Madame Roza, Juliet and Berti were at the table; there were also two other individuals whom I do not want to mention, and who will never figure in this story from here on. Monsieur Jacques' gaze was lost in the distance, he may have been looking at those big boats coming from Russia, or perhaps from Ukraine, having weighed anchor at the Odessa harbor, whose gangways happened to be astern. He had a sad countenance. I knew why. I knew who he had in his mind. These boats carrying different passengers arrived in Istanbul from the same direction . . . Among the snacks that had been brought to the table was also a dish of stuffed mussels. "The mussels are delicious!" I said; to which Monsieur Jacques had retorted saying: "You should taste the stuffed mussels made by the Armenians; they are excellent cooks! Kirkor's mother never failed to supply us with that delicious dish whose flavor I could find nowhere else. Kirkor used to describe in detail, with great relish, how his mother prepared it. Poor Silva, alas, she wasn't fated to see the marriage of her son. That had been her greatest wish in life . . . after that unfortunate accident . . . However, during the last years of her life they had made up; they were reconciled at last. Madame Silva was a very fat woman, obese and heavy. Was it a heart attack or asthma that had put an end to her life? I don't know . . . Kirkor couldn't ask Ani to prepare stuffed mussels for him after she came to know him. That's rather strange . . . I think he thought stuffed mussels as a dish symbolized a warm home . . . Oh Bother! May she rest in peace!" These had been the words that Monsieur Jacques uttered that night; only these words, nothing else. His gaze was lost in the immensity of the sea. That was one of those nights during which nobody felt in the mood for conversation, when everybody's imagination was wandering somewhere else, when everybody knew that they would be lingering at the place their imagination had taken them. Berti asked at a late hour of the night: "Ever realized how every one of us is a child, in essence?" That was the proper sentence to best express the hours we were passing. I don't know whether this was a source of remorse or pride. To this day I cannot decide. The story of a life full of deceptions, senselessness, and, especially, of absurdities . . . This was, in a sense, the summary of Uncle Kirkor's life.

"Eat my arse, Niko" were the words he had spouted a few minutes before he died at the hospital where he was taken because of a heart attack on a cold winter morning; he had to be taken to the church to which he had never been in his life. Apart from Madame Ani, only a few individuals who worked in the shop had attended the funeral at that small church at Ferıköy. Madame Ani had said in the graveyard that she was intending to go on a world tour but had died within four months because of a diffuse cancerous growth; these were the signs that epitomized the absurdities involved in these incidents. As though these things were not enough, years later we were to be taken by another surprise. Uncle Kirkor had a brother who worked as a waiter in one of the pubs at Kumkapı. I didn't go to visit that man. I had the feeling that that place had best be kept a secret for the time being and would be made accessible in a different timeframe. I must not deny the fact that I was filled with a perverse joy whenever I came to think of it. No doubt, there was hatred, a profound hatred in that story. How else could one explain this hiding or dissimulation? Uncle Kirkor must have been greatly amused by concealing from us this significant secret. This was another aspect of the absurdity that was highly difficult to explain. Even though this may seem nonsensical, I believe I must trace the reason for his being at cross-purposes with Olga. How interesting her view of that story was from the old people's house at Hasköy! When Olga had gone there he had whispered the following remark in my ear: "She has spruced herself up, the wench; be sure she is going to visit her man!" As a matter of fact, everybody felt himself obliged to make a remark when her attire was smart, elegant and sober. At times, her elaborate coiffure was the subject of astute observation. Inclining toward my ear, he said: "I wonder what number of dye she uses? Any idea how they dye a woman's hair?" Sometimes he elaborated on his remarks and said: "You know what? She has invested a lot of money in her hairdresser!" I believe there was also a latent appreciation here. However, such an attitude cannot explain away certain facts. This seemed like a confrontation between a woman—a woman who tried to perpetuate the idea of nobility in her imagination together with her modest means, a woman who endeavored to keep Uncle Kirkor's circle at arm's length, partly for self-protection, a woman who felt herself more and more estranged from her milieu—and a man who had been obliged to carry the burden of destitution on his shoulders all his life and experienced his lack of competence in every respect and who had spent every effort to be on the up and up, something I know from first hand experience. I'd been a witness in the past to this hostility. What is regretful, however, was the blindfolded attitude of the players who had failed to realize their solitudes and common traits. Oh the number of opportunities missed! Despite their differences, Uncle Kirkor and Olga had exchanged a great many secrets. Olga had seen the reflection of Niko on Uncle Kirkor's complexion. What Uncle Kirkor knew about Olga was far richer than the vestiges of those visits to the old people's house at Hasköy. He had ventured on a new path without saying anything to anybody. This showed that he was an astute observer who knew how to keep track and infer a lot from the clues available to the extent that even detectives would be envious. Actually both of us had followed the same track. The same track . . . despite our different objectives, expectations and misconceptions . . . despite our diverging views . . . In order to be able to find out the real reason for our habit of putting up obstacles in order to protect us from those liable to injure us on this rugged path, clasping each other's hands, appearing before them with the false-hoods and illusory manifestations we agreed upon, I had once spoken, or rather tried to speak, about the fascination killing gave one. Uncle Kirkor was certainly conscious of this meditation, of the concern for self-defense. To begin with, he was a friend of Niko. They were familiar with this idea, they must have been . . . All this reminded me of Yorgo who had over the years endeared himself to Niko; Yorgo had the knack to now and then pop up rather skillfully. I believe Niko got the gist of the matter. This may have been the reason for his excessive drinking and playing the role of drunkard. The only difference was that he had seen other places. Niko was reported to have said that he had died. He must have ventured on a drinking binge somewhere else. One should be lenient toward Niko for this falsehood. We are obliged to behave with understanding. Betrayal never received the approval of anybody. Nobody had succeeded in surviving by taking refuge in lies . . . However, frankly, what Niko witnessed after the heartache of his self-betrayal could not be denied. Yorgo had done something that he had failed to do and took the required step; the step that he had to take, a step that no one had dared to take before. Did he regret it? We can never know. The most pertinent remark had come from Monsieur Jacques who had said: "The most important thing for him was the raki which should exist everywhere he went." No fertile imagination was needed for this . . . His mastery of the Turkish language was certainly a problem. Yet, I feel assured now. He must have eventually rescued himself. We all have to believe in this. One of us was going to appear on another stage. Yes, one of us was going to appear elsewhere . . . I wish I could have said this to Niko. Nevertheless, I'm still at a loss as to where I'm supposed to join that story in order that I may realize this little dream of mine.

Time to part

The detective work of Uncle Kirkor had given certain clues that allowed me now and then to keep abreast of matters in many other stories, thanks to which I had viewed those days in another perspective, not only those days, but also those places, which had enabled me both to live and refashion them. I had to grow up. Uncle Kirkor was aware of this, the other people who had been the heroes of those stories knew this as well. Everybody knew it, except me. I can't tell now whether I was sufficiently grown up to satisfy the expectations of Uncle Kirkor. I must acknowledge the fact that I had failed to prove it. I cannot say why, because I don't know what growing up exactly is . . . This fact had gained wide acceptance among them. They were sure they would be in a position to indicate the point once I had reached it. Their observations and interpretations were directed toward the spot they intended to specify . . . The meaning in their looks was directed at covering up the said place. If one took all these things into consideration, there was a writer lying in ambush, the author of certain stories acting as the conscious or unconscious agent of this automatic writing; this author who assisted me to shift from one story to another and knew how to open the doors for them. This seemed to hold true also for that story which had found Monsieur Jacques and Olga in bed together. This had been the case at least at the beginning, during the initial episodes of the story. It seems to me that that story, for Monsieur Jacques, had its inception at that small apartment of Olga's at Şişli which looked like a sanctuary, or a country to which one had defected, which had over the years acted as a hideaway remote from the temptation of his prohibitions and their grip on his life. So it seemed to me. I was to be initiated into it gradually, by approaching the problem through different avenues; the novels I borrowed from the French Cultural Centre; unforgettable songs; conversations that lasted till the early hours under candlelight, inhaling the perfumed atmosphere; a story that involved refuges taken, refashioned by various days, in different ways, in multifarious anxieties and despair; a story that many people lived or imagined to live in their own lives, representations they always wanted to see . . . . Representations tinted by those days of expectations at the French College *Notre Dame de Sion*, by those spacious living rooms in the house at the Kuledibi Jewish Quarters, and by those unheated bedrooms, long corridors, and smell of coke stoves . . . A few short bridges stretching to a lost time . . . A flawed Venetian vase with semi-obliterated designs, sweet yeast bread, cheese-toast baked in the oven, conversations exchanged in languages spoken the world over—German, Arabic, Yiddish, French—languages stripped bit by bit of their original meanings; a porcelain tea set of Czech origin with missing pieces, a small decanter with variegated hues, imitation Christofle cutlery kept especially for festive occasions, an anonymous still life the frame of which bore on its reverse side the address of a picture-framer in Pera, a bedspread, deep blue, that used to inspire Olga, when she was a young girl, to have a lie-in in the depths of the sea, a silver picture frame whose picture had been taken off and left untenanted for lack of a new photograph deserving to occupy it . . . It was certainly inevitable for these reconstructions to stir up new representations that were unexpected, just like that sinuous path that led from one story to another. One wonders how Olga could carry the burden of the wound that Henry had bequeathed to her, during those lonely nights that she tried to decorate with images in order to add some meaning to them from one room to the next. How could she carry them across into those new rooms in the company of that young girl she could not bring herself to kill despite all that she had done? What, after those long years, had brought Henry back to have a different sort of relationship and obliged him to confess that certain errors committed in the past might gain a footing all the same somewhere in his life? Her father's principle argument was: "What is important for us is what we actually produced in the past, not what we are planning to do now or what we shall be doing tomorrow," and had, after days of strenuous hardship, aided her success in imposing her tailoring skills on a restricted circle in a different climate; what should have been the words she used in order to explain the reasons for her irresistible and hasty approach to her boss, Jacques Ventura, a friend of her father's, in the workshop where she had begun to work and wherein she had succeeded, in her days of dejection, in bringing about certain things for which she could no longer find, about that togetherness she imagined that could now never be realized, about that relationship, which, thanks to her deep attachment, had assumed meanings that she had been nourishing all her life? As time went by, as she proceeded on that road within her, the only path she could tread, she had begun considering Jacques Ventura whom she had started viewing as a man of destiny, not only as a prohibited lover, a spouse accepted at all events whether the conditions favored it or not or as a reliable companion, but also as a father figure whose compassion also included some unique elements. Monsieur Jacques was younger than Moses Bronstein. Yet, one sometimes preferred to live and let live in regard to certain relationships as one would have liked to see them. Despite everything, she had begun working in the workshop soon after she had lost her father. This might explain the void she experienced; it was a different kind of solitude. I distinctly remember, Olga had ventured out one evening and took the risk of returning home the long way when she had made the decision to follow that life, or, to be precise, those lives. She was offended. Offended and injured . . . But against whom had she taken offense? Against those who had caused her to live or not to live those days, against that woman whom she kept alive inside her, that woman whom she had to accept was barring everything? She couldn't bring herself to decide on this. She had yearnings. These yearnings might well have been for those days past, irretrievable, irrecoverable, or they might be yearnings of an indescribable sort. I could understand that feeling. This was the feeling experienced by everyone who had to live removed from life, far away and abandoned. Olga felt dejected and nostalgic that evening. It's true, she felt removed from those days, but smiled all the same. Time passing causes people to forget certain days, or incites one to live in a different fashion . . . Moses had died of pneumonia . . . Yes, from pneumonia . . . as if to display to his circle once more the absurd and meaningless nature of life; in his wisdom, having left behind and transcended their expectations realized or unrealized, he allowed those men to share and discover the man left inside them all . . . Olga was smiling that evening. She had a sad countenance which she tried to conceal; a sadness that her past experiences made even more beautiful. "I'm glad I'll be meeting your mother," her father said on his deathbed, "I've missed her so much. I know Schwartz also loved her. She suffered a lot but I had always been by her side." This was a story of fidelity deeply experienced that Olga knew and understood even better as she grew older. That evening, in that room where there was someone else smiling at us from far away.

You might get lost in Istanbul

Schwartz's story in Istanbul, of which Olga has no recollection, had begun in those days when that wandering tailor was doomed to carry with him his destinies to ever new realms, with that forbearing woman from Riga who faithfully followed her husband wherever his path led, and subserved him when needed, at a time when they were getting to know and acclimatize themselves to their new surroundings. Those were the days when they, who could never have felt at home anywhere, were familiarizing themselves with their new street, house, rooms, walls and languages; those were the days that seemed new, refashioned, reclaimed—reminiscent of an incredible and inconceivable soap opera—in the hope that one of those long war stories that gave certain people new life, would be also written and carried to another plane. The time when that revolution had swept the immigrants to a completely different city, to a completely different life, where they could perpetuate their line of nobility only in their past history or within themselves; the time when the new visitors had imported into Istanbul not only their attire, but also their hairstyles, lifestyles, dialects, music, dances, and, in particular, their legends, thanks to whom the sea, the beaches, the Princes' Islands were re-discovered; certain 'jewels'—which had not previously been considered fashionable—at certain soirées; their low necklines, their gambling and prostitution customs, their traveling habits. Poverty had increased; the country was being secretly and slowly disrobed for all to see. According to the account of Moses, it was a clear and sunny winter morning, according to others, a freezing one; he was getting ready to fit the dark blue uniform on Signore Bompiani, director of one of the maritime transportation agencies who had divorced his wife with whom he had been married for twenty years and ventured to marry his secretary, that dark girl from Fındıkzade. A man passed by his small workshop at Tünel in a striking officer's uniform decorated with medals and wearing a sabre . . . So far, so good! The strolling of foreign army officers in uniform in the streets of the city was nothing out of the ordinary at the time. Nevertheless, the man, after a short while, made an about turn, and, as though he was addressing the troops under his command, shouted "Achtung!" while he made as though he was firing at an imaginary target with an imaginary weapon under his arm. Dadadadada; an officer speaking German with such awkward gestures that he looked as though he had been thinking deeply about his own thoughts, feelings or behavior; (he was not unfamiliar with such cultures and representations. He readily understood that the man had been a member of the Austro-Hungarian Empire) was this the picture of a man strayed from his path, of someone who had ventured to taste a new life in a foreign country? This question might not have crossed Moses' mind at that critical moment of their encounter. Yet, barring all that was experienced and ruminated over, one could not imagine that a man who had ventured to launch himself into alienation with all its potential snares, whether willingly or against his will, would remain indifferent to another foreigner, especially to a legendary hero that had come from the world of his childhood, to wit from his mother's lost world. Thus, he extended an invitation to this outsider, expecting to catch a glimpse of another 'moment' without the least hesitation. The outsider responded favorably to this invitation as though he had been waiting for it, behaving with composure, in due decorum, befitting a well-disciplined army officer. So they got to know each other. The fact that the name of his guest who already seemed to have been a far-flung hero of an old story was Schwartz made the situation even more interesting. For Schwartz was a Jewish name. Moses in his turn had introduced himself; as a Jew, who, although he had not had a formal education in German, had considered it his vernacular; he was another Jew who had had to part with an important phase of his life in Odessa. It was as though they had been making headway toward a certain place, indescribable and nameless. But the really interesting account began when Schwartz began by telling of his adventures. The army was visiting the city with a view to conducting certain joint tactical operations with the Allied Forces, having in mind that a war would break out sooner or later, favoring the Allies, a war that was expected to last a fairly long time. They had been stationed here for the moment for an undetermined length of time . . . Then, something had happened, and he had been 'mislaid,' while the rest of the army had long departed, going back to Vienna. (Years later a writer, a friend of mine, was to tell me that soldiers who went to a foreign land were obsessed with the fear that they might be thrown off the scent of war.) According to the account of Moses—reared by his mother who had a perfect knowledge of German, and also from his years spent in both grammar and high schools—Schwartz spoke German flawlessly but with an accent. It would be reasonable to suppose that he was a true Viennese who had received a proper education in that capital city of culture. It was quite natural therefore that he would revive in his imagination one of those dreams that had sunk into oblivion: the avenues, the cafés, the forests, the Opera, the Waltzes, the emperor Franz-Joseph, and, last but not the least, the *lieder* that his mother used to sing for him on certain evenings . . . In other words, there was more than one reason for his taking an interest in his guest under the circumstances. But the fact is that none of these subjects had been taken up. Schwartz, mislaid in Istanbul, under the effect of that dreadful shock of being forgotten, was suffering from amnesia; he had forgotten his past, or had deposited it somewhere he could not remember. Neither a place-name, nor any clue to trace his identity was available. All that he could remember was that, as he told during the following days, he had been to a different land, somewhere in Poland, in a big farm-like place. Schwartz took him to his home that day and also briefed Eva of the situation. Thus, the story was also imparted to Eva . . . with certain details added, omitted or transformed. That night was followed by a number of days, a number of days and a number of nights. Life stories were exchanged; stories of lives occasionally mislaid somewhere. Whenever Schwartz began speaking of his story he never failed to insert a new detail into the narrative flow. He seemed to be a man in search of domicile. They asked him whether he desired to return to his motherland, to Austria or Poland. But they received no response. He simply smiled at them. His gaze was at the moment fixed on the statuette of the prancing horse that Eva had brought from Riga as a young girl that stood on the tripod next to the armchair in which he was seated. He seemed to be lost in reverie, in a faraway land. "The earth had such a delectable smell those summer nights. I miss it so much," he was heard saying. In order to enable him to find his way back to his motherland, to his home and family, appeals were made to embassies. However, those appeals and attempts had all been in vain. They were told that no sufficient information was available regarding him; to be able to get in touch with certain authorities definite names and useful clues were needed which too seemed presently mislaid or sunken into oblivion.

A dead end had been the beginning of this incredible story. After some time had elapsed, it was evident that it would be inevitable for him to accept a new life, fit it somewhere between his other lives in the face of all probabilities, questions and suspicions. Schwartz would soon be proceeding on with his own story in the company of different people, in a different tale in which his past experiences and the claims made about his life would represent him like another hero of destiny deserving to be communicated and understood. This story would be jointly transmitted, its inception being forgotten, despite all likelihoods and suspicions. All the same, these measures would fail to prevent the calling into question of certain facts that might lend meaning to that meeting, and would, as a consequence of the conjectures that that meeting would have made, pave the way to completely different lives . . . How true were those accounts and to what extent did they reflect reality? For, Schwartz might well have been a wanderer, a self-exiled individual wishing to lead a life in a different country, somewhere in the exotic East, creating a lifestyle of his own. In this venture, he might have thought he would find a family who would receive him warmly and provide him with food and shelter. Our fertile imagination deprived of all boundaries may lead us anywhere. On the other hand, the story may also have been the story of an artillery lieutenant as it had actually been pronounced. In such a story, the appalling conditions of war, the deafening sound of the guns and the nights full of terror or the picture of a dying companion who communicates to you his last wish before giving up his ghost might well have been the causes of his autism. You might call it a spiritual degeneration, a mental disorder or aberration. Under the circumstances, the story may well have been the story of a soldier mislaid and relinquished, who had begun to indulge himself in eccentric acts goaded by inclinations created by the cruelties of war, causing unrest among his companions in the army division, and who, by a justifiable and confidential order from his commander, had been abandoned to his destiny in Istanbul, rather than punishing him after duly court-martialing or detaining him under strict supervision. We can also interpret it as the story of a life desired to remain detached. If there had been a constructive alternative, would a future like this have found its home in a foreign country as an attempt at vengeance? When one wanted to forget a thing or a place, to really forget it with all one's being, one usually succeeded over a course of time, no matter what the cost. However, life demonstrated, from time to time, the fact that you eventually passed the examination with flying colors. It would suffice that you did not forget the fact that you could gain acceptance in the lives of certain people in proportion to the merits you exhibited despite all your anxieties and anticipations. My thoughts having wandered in such peregrinations, it occurs to me now to imagine Schwartz as the hero of a story who had, at some point of his life in Istanbul, lampooned himself. This shows that there was in that story a life desired to be omitted and denied. Even though such a life was to be made public, at times interrogated by various methods, or imposed on that amnesiac traveler without baggage . . . It might thus be the subject of a dirty joke that involved shying away from a loved one, eschewing a betrayal; a huge, sick and cruel joke . . . We might also speak of the tragedy of a young man of a romantic disposition who revolted for the sake of an original ideal against his father of conservative views, which he interpreted as his *raison d'être*, the only alternative that had guaranteed his survival despite the centuries long exposure of his race to hardships, bitterness and injustice. In this picture, the father might come forth in the identity of a hero, as a man whose ideal had been to leave his modest textile factory that he had set up with strenuous efforts, consistent with the attitudes he adopted toward every business he handled. Could we embroider a story in which Schwartz, who, instead of accepting the lifestyle that industry proffered him, wanted to spend all his days and nights in that summer farmland to which the family took themselves once or twice a year, where they were reluctant to share the same fate with the people there and were in pursuit of worldly success. He missed those moments, those moments of brief eternal bliss . . . That hazarded, for the sake of realizing his objective, to launch a full-scale offensive against the conditions prevalent in those days and at a time when he thought he was on the brink of a victory that would pave his way to a lifestyle he thought ideal though remote from nearly all the amenities of civilization that the city would be fain to provide him with. He saw his territories occupied during the war by the enemy, irredeemably confiscated by others, by the men of another country in the name of another country, and who had not been given the chance of seeing in this picture his beloved dream of the future and the children that he expected to foster. Could the whole thing have resulted in his aspiration for a willful annihilation of the thing he thought he would be unable to give a proper definition? Why not? Given the fact that we have tried and done our best to lend meaning to the picture of that farmland within us . . . Other probabilities also occur in one's mind fancied for other heroes at other times. Under such circumstances, other questions might well open the door to other lives and indicate the path that would lead to other stories . . . I'm inclined to say that Schwartz did know the essential questions that should be asked and the real answers to them, despite all that had been seemingly mislaid. However, as far as I can gather, people had preferred in those days not to ask any questions, but to keep them to themselves. The said guest, the traveler of this long path, was doomed to stay where he was; he had figured as a hero in a story in his actual identity . . . That feeling of resignation in human nature inherited from that long history, nourished with the charm of fate, with the existence of that lost world, with expectations built up and put off for its sake . . . Oh that odor of lives heavy with patience and reproduced infinitely! I prefer to believe that no questions had been asked relative to Schwartz; for instance, where he had stayed and what he had eaten in the meantime, that is in the course of the days, the weeks, perhaps, the months that had elapsed between his being misplaced and his arrival at Moses' shop. Yet, this question was one of the key questions that would have enabled us to have access to that mystery. But they knew all too well that they owed their life there to their abstention from asking certain questions to others; let alone whether they asked them of themselves or not. One should know that every action or choice was preserved in a storehouse . . . There is another reality, a scene of life which I should like to believe to have been enacted. With reference to that scene, I'm trying to revive in my imagination what Schwartz had, most probably, after the lapse of a good many years, imparted to Moses and Eva, by the distortions he liked so much, or insinuations, that is, between the lines, if one may call them that—insignificant details containing pieces of information about what had been talked about. This occurred at a time least expected, when the tale followed its due course, when many a reality had found their proper place and became more familiar with each passing day . . . A time desired to be re-written during the lengthy and wide-ranging talks exchanged and extended in the company of cups of tea brewed on the stove until late at night. Tea, for Moses, was a secret bridge that united his past, his adolescence, with certain decisive moments in his present life . . . The tea, like his memories, had to be brewed every night anew. The cups of tea taken in that house at Kuledibi had opened the door to a different exchange of words among three people, namely Schwartz, Eva and Moses. They had realized during those long talks, after some time, why they had been and should have in fact been together . . . They had never dared to question the reason for this or speculate about it; they might have carried their experiences along with them as a native destiny; however, one thing was certain, they had understood better and better what they were supposed to understand. Olga, who remembered those nights as an onlooker, while telling this story, had wanted to draw my attention to this fact. Based on what she said, I see now that, in the spontaneity that that secret understanding provided, everybody present there had decided to contribute to this story with all his being. It is reported that a short time after his visit everybody there had literally mobilized to find for Schwartz, first a lodging and then a business which might contribute to his livelihood. There was nothing out of the ordinary in this, of course. This action was simply a token of the solidarity between two outsiders . . . A view taken from such an angle that what had been experienced makes the story actually simpler than it appears to be at first sight.

Carlo's Ships

Moses had a friend by the name of Carlo, a pilot who navigated ships into and out of the waters of the Bosporus; he boasted of speaking thirteen languages in addition to Yiddish. His breath stunk of alcohol throughout the day although no one saw him tipsy. According to reliable accounts, this somewhat different man who was convinced that real adventures and loves could only take place at sea was enamored in his youth with a girl by the name of Sylvia who was of Russian stock, like he was himself . . . His affair with her had started at a reception of which the subject was the lack of taste in matters of gastronomy of the Jews of Polish descent as compared to the Jews of Russian descent. It turned out that he and that girl had been of the same opinion. This common trait had brought them to each other. Certain companionships, or virtual images that give one the impression of grazing contacts, are always ready to flare up in the presence of a shower of sparks. It didn't take them long to consider marriage. Wedding preparations were made, mutual promises were solemnly exchanged. But, at the least expected moment, Carlo received a letter of *adieu* from her, a letter written from the bottom of her heart . . . One of those letters one hardly ever expects to receive that opens the door to disappointments that last for a lifetime. The disparate heroes of the story had had, at all events, a meeting point, where they inevitably got together, despite their being worlds apart through their different languages and times, playing the roles of the actors of small scenes of betrayal that were to be equally shared by all parties. In her letter of *adieu*, Sylvia, for reasons she could not divulge, was going, as she had been obliged to go, to Argentina. She was the only woman who could extend a helping hand to her father who had lost all his wealth and honor. Life sometimes invited people to take part in hazardous associations. This was an ordeal that an individual had to endure, at the end of which, depending on precedence, a man received an injury he had not deserved, a wound destined to remain fresh throughout his life. This may have been the reason why what was called remorse became his constant companion. Hope for pardon was the sole solace after having shared his experiences with other people . . . No sooner had Carlo got the letter, than he had rushed to her place; it was in vain. She was nowhere to be found. He could learn nothing from her neighbors. He felt that everybody knew something about her actions, but somehow preferred to remain silent. The next day, he went down to the waterfront. He walked along those streets throughout the night. He visited the places where Sylvia and he had been together. Finally he saw her in the company of her father aboard a ship about to weigh anchor. Both father and daughter were smartly dressed. They waved to each other. "Don't ever come. You won't find me in the big cities. Even if you do find me, I won't be the same," said Sylvia. While saying these words, she appeared to be concealing a deep sorrow behind them. Her father was holding her by the arm while her head was inclined down to her breast. Carlo said nothing in return. Not a single word did he utter. He was employed at the accounting department of a big maritime transportation company. He loved to watch the big vessels sailing through the waters of the Bosporus. This interest attracted him nearer and nearer to those ships. To his boss, Monsieur Lazzaro, who had been a father to him in every respect, he had confided, saying that after his separation from Sylvia he could not continue working behind a desk, that the sea called the man inside him and communicated to him his desire to become a ship navigator. He explained that as he owned a small vessel of his own, he knew the job and that it would not take him long to get accustomed to this new venture. He asked Monsieur Lazzaro, who had among his acquaintances people of some sway, to be influential in arranging this job for him. Monsieur Lazzaro thought that only this last point was correct, to be in any way convincing. He was in a position to do this for the sake of someone he loved as his own son. Yet, he was not so sure about the correctness of this decision. He had prospects of promotion in the company he was employed with. Would it be pertinent for him to venture on such conceits? Carlo insisted saying that he no longer needed much money, and that the only thing he desired henceforth was to be able to gaze at Istanbul from a different angle. They had had a somewhat lengthy discussion. Before taking the decisive step, Monsieur Lazzaro, decided to have a talk with his mother. As a matter of fact, he and she had been exchanging many confidential correspondences . . . What they had exchanged might shed light on the reasons of Monsieur Lazarro's affording protection to Carlo, who had been orphaned, including the assistance he contributed to his tuition. In the meantime, Carlo had already realized that he had to leave their presence while they were having a discussion on those private and important subjects. Carlo did this. After a long while, they came out and told him that they would be doing as he wished. The result of this was Carlo's exercising the duties of a ship pilot for a good many years to come . . .

in order to be able to stir in the wind of ships sailing towards his land from the remotest corners of the earth; in order to be the first to hail that ship that would have brought Sylvia back to him . . . However, Sylvia never showed up. Nobody knew how she lived there and under what conditions.

The apartment Schwartz inhabited was exactly like the one of his strange companion Moses. It had been a very long time since Carlo had paid a visit to the lodging in question. He preferred to sleep in his vessel. The amount of liquor he consumed kept on increasing and so he became more and more isolated. Moses kept track of him and told him aboard his vessel the error of his ways. After having remained silent for a while, he responded: "I know about passengers: Since he has come all the way here he must have had a reason." He made clear that Schwartz could stay in that apartment as long as he wished. The apartment in question was a small lodging at Yüksek Kaldırım; a derelict place sparsely furnished, displaying many details that reminded one of the accommodation of years ago, in want of some repair and maintenance. Eva took charge of this task and made the place fit for habitation in no time as if to display her feminine merits.

My farm is my identity

Everybody felt as though it was one's duty to look after Schwartz; he stirred in one's mind a feeling of assurance. Now that the lodging problem had been settled, a small job was found for him to enable him to eke out a living. This was a section of the story that—although tragic—best represented this ex-captain who had inspired confidence in many a soul thanks to his knowledge of the Yiddish language. As if duty bound, he had industriously performed the tasks entrusted to him with a smile that never quit his face. One should do well to meditate over the significance of this smile. One should imagine a path that led from the streets of Vienna, littered with culture, to a harbor in the East which had been the talk of many, to its streets with flights of stairs on which couples performed indecent acts, according to some with a background of prejudices, although purer than the acts of many so-called decent people frequenting bawdy-houses, and to pastry shops where many a tale was woven, variants of quite a different tale . . . When you think of all that has been experienced, say of past experiences, this was a silent transportation of one's exiled state that engendered one's own island in a remote city . . . just like our readiness to pay a high cost for our choices, provided that they contained challenges, revolts for the sake of a conscious and desperate struggle. However, Schwartz, despite his loneliness, his solitude and insulation that was hardly ever experienced by other people, had been, according to Olga, successful in finding for himself a family, and had nourished a warm feeling at that table, in that house, starting from the very first evening where she had come in the company of her father to tell his story. He had come to that house almost every night as though afraid to miss a ritual . . . Soberly but smartly dressed; at times dressed in his old costumes in which he knew well how to appear *comme il faut*, and neat, up until the moment, years later, he suddenly died at home.

Olga told me that the Schwartz that she had described, despite his occasional needs, had not or could not ask for anything from anybody but lived resignedly so long as the people who had received him allowed him to stay with them. We must also take into consideration another point which might give us a clue to enable us to move forward in the development of a quite different story. Olga, in a casual conversation, had spoken about a Schwartz keenly interested in neck-ties. Olga had a couple of times witnessed him asking his father, or the people with who he was familiar, with bated breath to give him one of their neckties. This obsession could not easily be explained away. It may well have been an indication of his secret preservation of certain things for the scenes of that long stage play, somewhere backstage, in his depths, despite all that had been told and represented and lived. The fact was that in trying to move ahead you left certain indistinct footprints on the backs of certain people you ran across. Certain things always got lost in some people, things wanting to be mislaid. This was another mode of viewing the fact that solitude falls short of expressing certain sentiments. To my mind, Schwartz had lived with his lack of identity in this way, yes, his lack of identity . . . in such despair, because of his inability to express himself, by such a little revolt. One should, at any rate, acknowledge the fact that reticence, or words that can be carried to another dimension, to another platform of life, became more effective in the eyes of those who felt that pain, that revolt within themselves. This strange outsider had, during his entire stay in Istanbul, never abandoned his lair, his little island and was accepted as such both by his friends and by the security officers who had held a considerable sway over people during the years of World War II. This was the most melodramatic scene of the play, I should say. Whenever Schwartz, deprived of all identity, was asked to produce papers, he showed the picture of the farm he himself had meticulously drawn in distant lands. This was but a stage play, no doubt; a play in which every player continued to act out his respective role for the sake of the part he was supposed to perform, for the sake of the variety of meanings involved, in the name of delusions or unrealized dreams. My farm is my identity . . . was this not at the same time moralizing, addressed to those who did not hide themselves behind those paths of life in which meaning lay in petty calculations related to a different kind of revolt and wherein certain groupings were reverted to as masks, including among others religion, ideology or nationalism? Moral precepts that a narrow educational system could not encompass . . . If one thinks especially of the things lost or that might have been lost in the past . . . revolts or lives worthy to be narrated to some ears . . . lives gained after a turning point, despite all the losses involved. Could one have believed in this to the bitter end? An original event or the inevitable outcomes of it reminds me once more that we might be in a position to attain many different aspects of a given reality. This is at the same time an event that prevents the establishment of certain connections. What has been lived during those long years not only explains the courage of bearing the burden of that fate, but also Schwartz's mystery of having found a place of refuge doomed to remain *terra incognita*. This guarded utterance seems to have given birth in that house to another style of expression lying in the depths, carried on by inaudible words that we are somehow conscious of. This style of expression was a dialogue that united at a given point the three individuals through their respective dilemmas, their consequential bondage and attitudes adopted toward life. The story that had brought Schwartz to Istanbul, or caused him to run against that small island within himself, seemed to have been based on an enigmatic lie, despite all its semantic content. How could anyone, like in old fictions or stage plays, be so gullible as to believe in such a whopping great lie, a lie, which, no matter how cleverly it was formed, could not escape recognition in the long run, when the actors concerned were the Bronstein family? That overstaying, that inability to depart or the reality that inevitably led to a forced coexistence seemed concealed in the few words that Moses had uttered to Olga on his deathbed. I believe that today I can interpret these words better and know how to fit them in their correct places within those lives. Eva and Schwartz had had a passionate love affair, a very deep love which had never been expressed or heightened, but experienced only by glances, fortitude and sealed lips. A love affair, between Eva and Schwartz . . . Moses also had been conscious of it. This was a sort of tacit understanding that involved afflictions known to everybody in every respect. Eva knew that Schwartz was in love with her; Schwartz knew that Eva was in love with him; both being aware of the fact that this was known to Moses. It was a love affair in which everybody had remained or seemed to have remained in his or her place, a love affair that had developed in defiance of restrictions that involved heartache, remorse and yearning for a goal totally different from its wonted aim. Under the circumstances, it was natural for Moses to remember this relationship with some gratitude and sapience years after the death of Schwartz and Eva . . .

It looked as though Schwartz had come to that house to live certain things he had not experienced before . . . Not to lose that period of his life, his time spent in that melting pot. As for Eva, vowed to her world of silence, one could read her attachment through her glances at Schwartz, as though she wanted to convey to him her tacit love by her dressy attire and delicious dishes she prepared on special occasions. She had wanted to say to him: "You know what; I actually belong to you." I can now visualize Eva, spruced up on the occasion of the birthday of her beloved. It was a small ritual; a modest and speechless ritual one wanted to experience to one's heart's content. Schwartz had no idea of his actual birthdate; how could he? This also was one of the rules of the game. For the sake of his being, a new birthday had been hypothesized. It was to be the Day of Sparkles. This day was specially selected in order to celebrate it every calendar year on a different date. The day also coincided with the ritual of kindling the wicks which had, over the course of time, become the task of Schwartz . . . "I belong to you" . . . words not uttered; words that had found no expression . . . Can a love be perpetuated in this way? There will be different answers to this question, I know. Actually, the answer that we would be prepared to provide would give a clue to our view on life. Just like in the case of those three people. "I belong to you." Even though everything may be lived or not, as one would have wished . . . In time, I came to know all sorts of other similar servitudes in the life of these people. What was decent in this tripartite relationship was that everybody had remained faithful to one another, unable to betray each other. It sometimes occurs to me to think about the fact that from the contents of the house that Eva had vacated after the death of Schwartz, she had kept only the drawing of that farm. That bronze statuette of the prancing horse had remained there as always. It wasn't easy to forget that dream of farm life despite all that had gone on in between. The map of this evasion, of this exile must have been mislaid along with Eva herself. Yes, with Eva herself . . . In a manner suiting Schwartz, befitting those dreams sunken into oblivion . . . to the bitter end . . . Otherwise, how could we ever explain such an attachment perpetrated even after death?

I am warm for the first time

Flights, exiles, meetings . . . These may have been the key words of the story of Schwartz who had lived at Kuledibi in Istanbul, unbeknownst to many. This story of Moses and Eva experienced with great boldness comes back to me, accompanied by pictures I've reconstructed based on the images and hearsay imprinted on my aural and visual memories and on the inferences drawn from data available along with some probabilities bordering on absurd. There are times when I retreat to a brown study and try to attach a meaning to all that has been lived. It was not beyond probability that Schwartz left behind a family who had never forgotten him and who was still waiting for him. It might well have been that he was assumed to have fallen in action, one of the anonymous soldiers lost in the field, and that a small party had been given there to commemorate his birthday, a small ritual held in accordance with tradition, a devotional gathering, to evoke the memory of a son, of an elder brother—who knows, perhaps of a lover—based on the logical inference that he must have been killed. Interpreting it as his last story in a realm that his people could not dream of, how could they know that Schwartz was to live for another thirty years, in a totally different time frame, indifferent to the mourning of people who may have waited for him and who may already have written his obituary. This would be an apposite aftermath to Schwartz's view of life and the world.

On the other hand, Olga, in her turn, must have, in her last days experienced a sense of absurdity. This idea was triggered in my mind by Moses' death from pneumonia. Olga had mentioned that her father used to go out without a coat during those days, impervious to the weather. Even when it snowed, he hardly put on something to keep him warm. To those who asked him if he did not feel at all chilly, he used to answer: "Are you kidding, I'm almost perspiring!" He was a man of cold climates . . . Now that he was far removed from the winters of old, what winter, what frozen street might have affected him, one is inclined to ask.

Which days and nights, what steps and glances might have been the cause of his death? The cause that made Moses perspire in the snow lay in his constitution, no doubt. Life was pregnant with funny jokes. This ailment of his was his first cold. I think that this was another indication of the fact that at times, when we feel ourselves enjoying good health, we are prone to succumb to unforeseen adversities. Why not, after all? After all, whether you wanted it to or not, a day came when you realized that you should not rely on others, even on yourself, for that matter. To fail to rely on yourself might, in truth, be interpreted as another mode of self-reliance. What is important here though is to perceive the significance of what lay in the essence of those preparations. Olga had perceived this fact and was one of the rare women who succeeded in storing this experience in some secret corner of her life. She was one of those women capable of undertaking a struggle, even a desperate struggle, at all costs. Partly because of this she had to be strong. The days during which I kept track of her behavior were an indication of this. In the wake of her father's death she had to make certain important decisions, in order to be able to withstand the storm on the horizon. As she moved from her old apartment at Kuledibi to that small lodging at Şişli, taking with her a few belongings, she had, undoubtedly lent an ear to an internal exodus. However, how long had she felt that she existed, while she took steps toward a new Istanbul, knocking on the door of a new life? Those were the days when she had entered the life of Monsieur Jacques, determined to stay there forever. The fear she felt on those lonely nights was understandable . . . Those houses, those streets, those little expectations had all been left behind to the care of those people . . . These new rooms were waiting for a new song, the song of a different and totally new relationship. That new relationship would in turn regenerate in them new dependencies . . . That would be a relationship calling for patience and self-sacrifice more closed to the established rules of morality. Had Olga perceived this? Could she have perceived it? And, what was even more important, had she been willing to do so? We had to be content with what our own answers and powers of imagination provided us with, in order that we might arrive at certain bare facts. According to the accounts of Olga, there must have been also certain events, certain words mislaid altogether, introspections, contingencies and cherished feelings within the confined space of a single room. Olga had mentioned it. In her new abode, she had to endure those long nights by reading and re-reading the books she had already read; she had also mused, not only upon her father, whom she had set eyes upon quite late in life, but also upon Henry, with whom she had shared a streaming movement toward an unknown future, and upon her elder brother whom she had never seen but who wrote about a utopian distant realm. All these were for the attention of certain people, the intention being to be able to convey all these intricacies to them. Yet, she knew well that that was impossible, simply impossible. There was no denying that those had been her men, her days; the men that she kept at arm's length from her and from each other. That obstacle that denoted a blind alley, difficult to define, demanding courage, made itself felt after a certain point, perhaps just because of this. One was in pursuit of conceiving that short byway faced with the dilemma between telling or not telling, a two-way road, a vacillation, a time of unrest that provided clues for a worldview. All this was certainly not due to despair but to self-protection and self-preservation; it was due rather to a concern about the failure to recollect words and imagery, to find in others the echo they deserved. This must have been the reason why she had confidentially kept that diary for herself, not allowing anyone to have access to it or to those letters. The texts in question were written in French. There was nothing to wonder about. French was her language of liberation; her language of hope, if one recalls the days she had spent at the French college *Notre Dame de Sion*. As a young girl the nuns had considered her likely to push the limits of a glorious life. This was the source of her self-reliance and self-consciousness, a reason for having confidence in herself and never losing hope. Do we not need to take refuge in certain successes in life although they might not bear any significance for others? Perhaps. What we should particularly dwell upon now are not the answers we can provide to this question. What we experience and are obliged to experience invites us to different places anyway, and may, in the long run, cause us to be tempted by the attraction of different people or sentiments. What concerns me particularly, what confronts us with a vacuity and what arouses in us the sense of our having missed an opportunity is the likelihood of her destroying all that she has written so far. Inconceivable! The Olga I knew attached value to her past experiences and loved to relive those moments of her past. With reference to that night of destruction, it was quite interesting to hear her say: "As I was committing them to the flames in the stove, I felt as though I was burning myself. But I felt warm for the first time in years." I never forgot those words. I made several comments on them. Why had she acted in this way? It occurs to me to think of certain events, and consequently, to imagine a story with many variants; one of which may be the following: during Henry's last days at the old people's house, he may have asked her to bury everything that connoted their cohabitation somewhere nobody would ever discover. This wish may have arisen because of a desire, while quitting this world, to leave behind as few things, as few 'graves', as possible, to convey at least to a human being near him a deception caused by defeats and disappointments experienced in this world. The fantasy of obliterating all the imprints that one left before one departs for another world . . . to depart without leaving a trace . . . even though one is believed to survive in the imaginations and minds of certain individuals. This was not a situation that one could witness every other day. One might surmise that everybody might, after all, prefer, though tacitly perhaps, to leave an imprint, however insignificant, before one departs. One should also take stock of the fact that the deception to which Henry had been subject was not of the sort one would chance to meet every day. He had experienced a deception and he had nourished despair at a great cost; he must have thought that he did not deserve such abandonment after having led such a life with those individuals. Anyway, the cost had been paid in full. The reprisals were taken for those victories and successes. But Olga was a woman who knew how to live life to the bitter end, and who proved this through action. She had seen what she wanted to see. Nobody had seen what everybody would have liked to see . . . the *auto da fé* in which all the notes had been incinerated. It was an unfortunate fact that a whole lot of details had thus been barred from our sight. Words, details, secret representations and betrayals had been saved by not being confined within the boundaries of a given text. They had vanished and been simply mislaid; for a life for two, for which a meaning was sought despite the views of others. This must have been the defense mechanism of Henry's story. Here was a person, who had, before taking up his abode in a different life that he detested, left behind years spent in a totally different existence. Our visualizing that story properly, as outsiders, was according to them, not within the realm of possibility.

Olga's white lie might have given rise to quite a different story. For instance, the burned diary and letters in question may have been purely fictive, a figment of Olga's imagination. Olga may have tried to shoulder her literary genius that she had created in her imagination, and to accompany it with a part of that identity she wrote about. It is quite natural at times that we appear in the sight of people with our shortcomings revealed, with the things that we had failed to realize . . .

We could also imagine that Olga, in addition to all these motives, aimed to invite us into this story in order to keep track of something. What makes me say this is a conviction that the letters written all those years ago with tremendous patience will, one day, after the occasion of a good many deaths, be discovered by someone and brought to light. I would like to believe this so much. I wonder if these notes and letters that are to be brought to me one day, at the least expected moment, by someone, a complete stranger to me, might change the course of this story? This may well be the case. Haven't we already observed that certain stories lead up to others and that the heroes of those stories figure solely to provide outlets for the protagonists of others?

Eva was always in Mexico City

There are inter-fated stories created at unexpected moments, for the unthought-of heroes of tales, for the sake of brand new lies and fantasies. The story that penetrated Olga's life happened to be such a story, its life took place on one of her long lonely nights, which over the course of time was transformed into a tale. Based on what I have been told and from what I could glean from the information which I had access to, the Bronstein family, after their settlement in Istanbul, continued to correspond for some time with Jacob who had stayed in Alexandria. When she recounted those scenes during which letters were read out, Olga seemed to be conjuring up certain things that she could not properly define or confront at the time . . . I knew, of course, that she was an imaginative woman living in her own dreamworld; she had also concocted other tales and legends. There had also been tales that could not cross the threshold of other lives. What had eventually come to me had been the tale of a relative going through a totally different adventure, an adventure that had been seeking its denouement somewhere totally different and was heading toward a totally different destination. A short time after settling in Istanbul, in the letters written to his son, Moses had tried to depict the new city where he had taken up his abode, reverting to all the means at his disposal—informing him of the advent of a pretty baby girl to the world, his sister, of his great remorse at having left him there, stressing the necessity of a family reunion despite all the prevailing conditions that he took for granted. In response to which, Jacob wrote back simply intimating and informing them that he missed his family very much, that he wanted very much to embrace his little sister, but that he couldn't leave Alexandria due to business commitments; because of the said obligations he had to leave for Mexico, but that he would one day come to see them and the fascinating Bosporus and the Golden Horn he had seen only in photographs at all costs. These are the types of dialogues that are carried out from a distance and are based on unbreakable ties. It seemed that in the letters there was an unsolved mystery that muffled all the small talk, and that aroused in the mind a vexed question . . . Eva's words, uttered now and then, "I'm sure he had something in his mind that he wanted to share with me, but failed to do so," had consolidated that impression. It was reported that Jacob had eventually gone to the Mexico City. We have it on the authority of the letters. The lost son, which had been the talk of the town, was nourished and sustained by those letters. The *raison d'être* of the 'outsiders,' of the 'foreigners,' was to elaborate on that dream to the extent their imagination permitted, or perhaps with a view to smothering the pain that their shortcomings and imperfections bred and to convert it, even though on a modest scale, to the anticipation of return . . . I gather that Olga had also wrought out her tale by treading this path. In his letters from Mexico City, addressed to his parents, and at times in private to his sister, Jacob had spoken of his experiences and his life there. Apparently he was dwelling in a very big mansion, reminiscent of a palace. He had a family and also a daughter . . . His time was taken up mostly by business, he couldn't write them as often as he would have liked. But he would do his best to make up for the lost time. The country he lived in was different. Even Jews could openly express their Jewish identity. Nevertheless, certain relations could cause trouble. But this was part of the game . . . Like everywhere else in the world. The way of life in the best societies was always out of the ordinary; unless one personally shared it, one could never understand it.

The correspondence exchanged between them lasted for many years, up until the moment of Eva's death in her old apartment at Kuledibi, overcome by the grief of separation from her son . . . Moses had had cups of tea more often than not those nights. Olga wanted to believe that she had left Henry in the distant past, and felt obliged to remain tight-lipped about her new and forbidden relationship saying nothing to anybody, including her father. But a time came when the letters, which had decreased in frequency, stopped altogether. Questions had remained unanswered. The thrill of anticipation had vanished in the end. The investigations that a friend of Olga's conducted at the American consulate fell through. There had undoubtedly been monkey business; something to be hushed up, something that the people in Istanbul should not know anything about. Something that would have corroborated what Olga had, by her motherly instinct, guessed. Something that the people left behind would, even though from a long distance, contribute in sharing . . . A new shortfall, an unprecedented pining, a sense of abandonment that could be shared . . . After the correspondence broke off, the name Jacob was less often heard in conversation; people had transformed him into a hero of an exotic tale while the heroes and heroines of Istanbul were in great awe of this exoticism. Olga had come upon a very sensitive crossroads. Failure in keeping a dream alive even through correspondence had occasioned a new sense of defeat in her father, or the recurrence of the feeling of remorse at a most unexpected time . . . There were times when solemn silence was preferred; when silence was converted into another sort of dialogue. To be able to be the bearer of affection to the very end was not so easy after all. Anyway, a remarkable variety of behaviors or figurations had already traced that fine line of separation in this story. Her father, during his retirement, after having closed up shop, and continued tailoring jackets at home for acquaintances, had developed the custom of stretching himself on the sofa to take a rest during which he took up the photo albums and gazed at their contents for hours. For everything was there: Odessa, Riga, Alexandria, the quays, the shops, the streets; lineaments, moments and particularities sunken into oblivion, unbeknownst to the living souls. There was also the city that had signified a new era and which had completely changed the course of his life. This city had caused him to encounter Schwartz, the limit of self-sacrifice. The dialogue he exchanged with these photographs, his most substantial conversations, was partly due to this, as was the case in such situations . . . just like the heroes that figure in the snapshots in the stories of other realms and penetrate other songs, stage plays, and film squares . . . His gaze fixed upon those photos, he used to withdraw to his inner world, and believing that he was not being observed by Olga, he sometimes smiled, sometimes wept; sometimes he spoke successively in Russian, Yiddish and sometimes in a mixture of both languages depending on the actors that figured in the snapshots he was staring at. Now and then, after his chat with those heroes, he asked his daughter to bring him a cup of tea. This custom had evolved over time into a sort of ritual; a ritual taken before setting out on a new journey . . . Olga would soon be witnessing the same anticipation in another person she was fond of. But there would be a need for more time and for other photographs. But the fact remains that certain stories might come back at the least expected moment, at the least expected place . . . One night, when she had got used to her solitude, Olga found a letter on the floor beneath her door. This letter, written in English, bore on it the stamp of Mexico City. Attached was a photograph. The young man figuring in it, in the company of a young woman, was a replica of his father in many respects; he was smiling at the holder. This wan smile seemed to conceal behind it an aura of sadness, as though he intended, simply by the expression on his face, to tell something to the viewers, to the onlookers, in the future. This was a feeling hardly definable, an inexplicable feeling, generated partly by those words, by that story, a feeling that was desired to be kept alive . . . I will never forget it. When she peered at that photograph, Olga had narrated the event as though she wanted to live that moment once again. She was overwhelmed and her voice was trembling.

Well, the photograph represented her elder brother Jacob—who she had never before set eyes on—and her niece who were living in a completely different climate. Evita was her name; as a matter of fact, the letter was written in her handwriting. She was saying that it was a much belated letter, that her father had died some two years back and that she wanted very much to see her grandfather and her aunt whom she thought of as an elder sister. Her name was Evita. This was a point that should be overlooked for those of whom who are familiar with the events of history. 'Evita' meant, 'Little Eva' . . . Jews living in their homeland named their children after their parents, so that when they were no more their memory and spirit would go on living . . . Olga never knew if her elder brother had been faithful to their tradition or religion. After what she had learned, it no longer had any importance however. She could trace the fact back to when Evita was born her mother was most probably alive. Was this a simple coincidence or another fact which might explain the reason for his stay there, another fact that people wanted to hide from her? As far as I know, Olga had also failed to find the answer to this question. She had failed to do so, but this unexpected letter had opened a door to a totally different dreamworld. The letter was not a simple correspondence but bore the characteristic of an invitation to spin out the story despite all the interruptions and separations that had taken place in the meantime, as well as the distances and losses involved. A connection had tried to be forged in a new world involving two individuals living in different countries with different languages and expectations. There was some surprise about the fact that Olga, who had always desired to create and had been capable of engendering new nights and new dawns in her dreamworld, had introduced into this story all her willingness, her past and her selfhood. So, the letters would continue to have an existence in the space of the following years despite the divergent human beings, places and nights involved. Evita had given a detailed account of her adventure. She had been married to a collector of butterflies and remained his wife for seven years before she had decided to break the matrimonial tie, as she could no longer put up with certain acts of her husband. A son was born to her who was now fourteen. She had risked establishing a new relationship and was living with a colleague of hers, an English teacher, after a lapse of four years. She felt happy. The father of her son was, according to the latest news, in pursuit of new prey in Guyana. As for her father . . . well, Jacob, the story of Jacob (for she had always addressed him as Jacob) was totally different from what they knew. It may seem unbelievable, but her father had remained faithful to his family in Istanbul. However, no human being, anywhere in the world, had had the semblance of the things, places and human beings figuring in the tale imposed on them. Jacob could live that life only in those letters . . . in order to be able to put up with the absence of his family and to familiarize himself with the idea of being a citizen of a foreign country . . . in order not to lose in his imagination a lost life on the path to a lost family . . . Firstly, he had been involved for a short while in drug trafficking in Alexandria as a consequence of his illegal dealings with certain officials, but had to give it up after being convicted and imprisoned for a term; he ran away from the gang aboard a merchant ship leaving for Mexico City, where he had worked on many an odd job, finally ending up as a sous chef in a small restaurant and marrying the daughter of the boss. Those had been the happiest days of his life. She had been the child of this marriage. Nevertheless, in time, many feelings had yielded in place of others. Her mother had declared that she no longer wanted to live the life that her husband, who was deprived of the gift of an aspiration for learning, and for higher goals, provided her with, and that she would be going to the USA to enroll in Princeton University to study anthropology, thus leaving home without any further explanation, never to return. That was the last they had heard of her. Father and daughter sat together brooding over what they should do, trying to plan out their future. After this incident, the father had given up the restaurant business and bought a second-hand typewriter, taking his place in the old square among those professionals who carried on the traditional business of writing love letters for anyone suffering from unrequited love. Her father had written thousands of love letters in his new job . . . To give some hope to others through a couple of words . . . Most probably he had to conceal his own identity in those letters, in the hope of keeping alive his love for his wife, not to lose his confidence in that love forever . . . There had been nights when he also called at some bars to have a drink or two with some people he knew . . . always in the same places and in the company of the same companions . . . Like many other travelers in other parts of the world, in the same condition, who roamed the streets at night . . . She had learned of those spots where she now and then went to pick him up. She always had a hot soup ready at home on such nights. She had never forgotten those nights. As a girl obliged to live her younger years in solitude and in a different atmosphere, to master her fears while walking those streets and to befriend the night had taken her quite some time. The experiences of the past were quite different from those of the present. Her latent fears during the day were due to the crowd and the din of the city and to its threatening character. The silence of the night brought her a kind of peace of mind she had difficulty in defining.

Jacob had lived on what he earned from this last trade he had practiced, and, according to his own words, he had "exhausted it." The story of his wealth he had written about to his family was a kind of revolt coupled with an expression of his deep affection. When he had confined himself to his house he said to his daughter, his only confidante, referring to the people he had left in Istanbul, saying that "they needed a dream; for only thus could they put up with my absence," which was true. This was a sort of a rebellion in a sense; a little revenge taken on those who had wasted so many of his days and stolen his dreams. He could get rid of the exigency of this lie only toward the end of his life. They had moved to a small house with a garden somewhat remote from the center of the town. "Henceforth, I want to live for the sake of my own reality," he said on one of those days. He had given himself to horticulture. Those were the days during which he had ceased to write, the days he could not bring himself to write; the days when he intended to obliterate all the traces he might have left behind so that he might not be traced by his family. The days he could not and would not write, the days when all the lies he could produce had been exhausted . . . Two years after he had moved to that house, one morning he had suddenly gone the way of all flesh, taking his silences with him. He had collapsed on the flowers he had meticulously grown. Heart attack had been the diagnosis. But, in actual fact—and she knew it well— the real cause was one which could never be detected by an outsider. It had to be avowed. Among the disappointments and deceptions to which he had been subjected, it had been the hope generated by this lie, the motive force that had caused her father, Jacob, whom she had never abandoned, to stay alive. After all, not only had he been obliged to be severed from his family at a critical moment of his life, but also from a woman he could never forget and without whom he could not go on living. This experience of abandonment could be endured only through such a belief . . . In her letter in which she spoke of her mother, Evita said: "I've never forgiven her, and never shall I. I don't know whether she is still alive or not. The probability that she may have died all alone in a remote corner of the world does not affect me at all." This attitude was a bit surprising and lacked credibility; an attitude that called for another notion . . . Those letters had conveyed the voice of a person who considered cheerful optimism as an integral part of her life. This was the only subject that she was ruthless and merciless about. The only subject wherein she had succeeded to achieve vehemence . . . Yes, Evita was essentially a warmhearted and excessively optimistic woman. She had spoken in her letters of her expectation to meet them one day; she had reiterated, without getting tired of her expectation, that she would either visit Istanbul, the city where her father and her family had resided, or invite her beloved aunt, the only remote relative, to where she was living. However, the realization of such a meeting required her to get her own house in order beforehand, to tidy up her life and save some money. Money for an air ticket . . . either to enable her to pay for a flight in or a flight out . . . That was how Olga had concocted her tale, and how she had lived and labored to perpetuate it through her letters, through the existence of a person in another country who would remember her in every instance. This was one of the rarer phases of her life left pure. Like every other tale . . . Like all our tales . . .

All I can gather from what has been said is that in order to carry on this correspondence she wrote innumerable letters; realistic letters, letters that aimed at comprehension and explication . . . then . . . then something had died all the same . . .

I remember now that I had, for one reason or another, lost track of this contact after a given point. It appears that there are things that I do not know, that I cannot know. I *am*, however, certain that the meeting—so anticipated—never came about. Neither in Mexico City, nor in Istanbul, nor anywhere else for that matter . . . To my mind, this fact is better suited to a credible story. It had been the aspiration of two people who had knocked on each other's door to stretch a fantasy to its boundaries in order to tell each other of their respective solitudes; this was inevitable and was to be expected . . . We have need for other people's hours in order to supplement the ones we have lost.

Madame Roza's play

I can now see more clearly the reason why I could never be indifferent to the journey of two people trapped in a fantasy despite themselves . . . There seems to be a parentage in this. A parentage difficult to define and explain; a parental relationship one feels in one's bones. Many people would be fain to consider this indulgence in fantasy, confining its preservation to one's imagination, as grim fate. The fact is, however, that after a given point one learns how to endure the realities that graze past us and which we let slip through our fingers and our isolation. One's servitude, one's enslavement by the region confined by the boundaries one has failed to trespass, becomes identified with life itself. For instance, the sentimental attachment one has established, with stories which one has related to certain objects, increases even though the said stories are not considered credible by others. One finds oneself in a position to love one's dreams more and more with every passing day; from which one makes inferences that remain exclusively in one's own possession, unknown to the heroes of one's dreams . . . For Olga, who had been waiting for her lover during those long nights in the name of real togetherness, waiting for a companion to share her life with, such was her remote bondage. In time, a great many feelings would be experienced according to their natural course after having been assigned to their proper places, out of necessity, without being converted into that togetherness capable of reproducing not only the questions but also the answers . . . Olga, Madame Roza and Monsieur Jacques . . . The path was one which the meaning was concealed in those compelling necessities for a relationship which was to be experienced, defined and considered by everybody in a different fashion according to one's respective position. On the one hand, you had Madame Roza, who descended from a large Thracian family, who had firmly grasped that knowledge relative to endurance, along with the need to be discreet and reserved in claiming the dues she had inherited from her family's tradition and history, would qualify her to be a good mother and particularly a good wife, since she knew no other way. This armor, with which she had been equipped in order to put a bold front against life, had made her into a woman who managed her family haphazardly. As the elder sister, she had endeavored to keep her brothers together and settle their differences. In time, the members of the family had dispersed, had been obliged to scatter. Like everyone else who had had to go through such experiences, she also had her share of grievances she was compelled to acknowledge. Nevertheless, despite all warnings, those brothers who had taken wrong steps and committed great errors in life, had tried to return to her, or at least intended to do so, for a brief period of time. She knew this would happen because of what she had witnessed as they grew up. She had known how to endure this situation, with pride and discretion, without offending anyone. This was a duty she had taken over from her mother at a time when she was loath to accept it, at a time when she was not prepared; a mandatory duty taken over at an unexpected moment, silently and patiently. The incidences that occurred at that time, for duty's sake, were imparted to me not by her, but by Monsieur Robert and Aunt Tilda, who always spoke of their elder sister reverently. The story was essentially one of those about self-sacrifice. The mother had died and the elder sister had suddenly found herself taking up her mantle within the family. When I consider this unexpected transition, I cannot help believing that, in time, a different feeling, a sort of hatred, must have arisen towards her mother, a feeling embedded deep in her heart. She knew the role in which she wanted to figure; to have been an elder sister, and the early maternity thrust upon her had led her to sway her authority over her father. I am inclined to interpret the way she spoke of her father reproachfully after so many years as an extension of this feeling. According to her, her father had been a gentleman of private means, who had never worked in his life, who had financed the household expenses by readily available money and was interested in appearing young. He had failed to be a successful businessman; in other words, he had never had such an aspiration in life, since the income he derived from the estates he had inherited from his father had sufficed to cover his current expenses. Whenever he was short of money, he either sold one of the estates in his possession or some gold he had stored; thus he had never been impecunious and had never borrowed money from anyone. He did have extramarital relations which might not be considered commendable, of course; but he was handsome according to the standards of the day. In addition, he knew how to look classy in his attire. His amorous exploits were partly due to the lewdness of the women around him. This weakness seemed to be a source of secret pride for her. I had sensed this when she spoke about the occasional illicit relations carried out by her father in her old age. Besides, there was something else that only her father could have done. He had contributed to the rebuilding of the synagogue at Ortaköy, which had burned down on the night of Yom Kippur; this contribution had not only been financial, but also physical, as he carried slabs to the construction site, for months on end, up until the moment it was reconsecrated and made ready for rituals. The name of her father had literally been written on those stones. She was justifiably boastful of him. This token feeling she had been harboring in her memory of that man who aspired for eternal youth was an indication of her traditionalist tendencies despite the education she had received and her conservative character on which she had based her life. She had studied at the Greek preliminary school at Çatalca where she had spent her childhood being controlled by priests, where her attire had an aura of awful sanctity. This choice had appeared to be the best stepping-stone under the prevailing circumstances at the time. Her studies in that school were to open the door to another story in which no one else would have access ever after, to a story in which a child had been killed surreptitiously in cold blood, a story beyond the imagination of a juvenile. After the family moved to Istanbul, she had continued her studies at the Alliance Israélite Universelle where the courses were given in French. Like in other schools whose curricula were in French, the language taught was a grammatically correct one, yet lacking in contemporaneity. The general impression of her generation was that the 'Alliance days' were to remain a chapter in her life she would remember as delightful. However, no one at home had ever had an inkling of the true and fanciful meaning of that period. That time spent was still vivid in her imagination; she remembered her success in mathematics which was taught by Madame Gurland, whose name was a source of mockery, and who, with her stern complexion, was notorious in that she never swerved from her principles. She had memorized La Fontaine's fables and they were still in the store of her memory as well as Victor Hugo's poems and Rousseau's ideas about the equality of all human beings. To have sat at the desks of Alliance Israelite Universelle where the Spanish language was spoken in its original accent that gave it a special flavor lent her and her schoolmates, who still organized regular meetings and played cards, a special privilege, of which they were proud. These card games had been an integral part of her way of life. Whenever she felt the need for some encouragement she recalled those meetings; those were the moments when she felt a little bit lonelier than usual, somewhat abandoned; trying to partake of the warm atmosphere of those times. All these factors had not succeeded in destroying her conservative and traditionalist tendencies; nay, they had even served her as nourishment. Such a privilege had to have a more special place than the one fostered by her traditional education. At this juncture, there was a particularity which should not go unnoticed. Having been obliged to fulfill her maternal duty at a very early age, she was obliged to leave school before completing it; had she continued her studies another year, her position as a graduate would have certainly been an asset just like it was to her other school friends who had attained high positions. This may have engendered in her an inferiority complex. The days that followed may have directed her toward the attainment of different values. I think, however, conservatism was in her veins, and provided her with energy. This attachment to socially accepted values was a consequence of the conditions of the world in which she was confined. Otherwise, she would not be so particular about religious days; nor would she stress, especially on the occasion of such holidays, that this attitude had contributed to the survival of the Jewish race, saving the whole lot of them from extermination; nor would she prepare delicious traditional cuisine she had learned from her mother, like beans with spinach, leek meatballs, squash pastry, among which was also *almodrote*; nor would she consider, not only as a token of ascendancy, but also as an assurance for rainy days, her mink coat, her diamond ring and her golden necklace of which she was proud of in terms of length and weight. All these things, these 'little lives,' had sufficed to make her a seemingly good spouse, a good mother and a good elder sister. The fact that this had earned her the nickname of 'Churchill' for her tact in handling her brothers, along with her physical resemblance to him, and the words of Monsieur Jacques, years after, in remembrance of the dead, namely, "Roza was different, she was an angel," were well grounded. Nevertheless, for me, what had made her the Madame Roza that we knew as such was Olga's entry into the scene. This ordeal was more trying than the twenty-day military service; than the days that Monsieur Jacques had mourned for Nesim; than those interminable nights during which the long-lasting illness of his elder years had given him so much pain. She had sensed at the very beginning that another woman, Olga, was no longer simply an employee working in the shop of her husband, but a woman who had sneaked into her husband's life. She had sensed it, and understood the whole affair, but had to acknowledge, after the inevitable storms that had raged in the house, that her husband belonged to her after all, and so, she had felt obliged to accept everything as normal, thanks to her husband's preference to stay at home every Friday night; thus she had connived at this illicit relationship with patience and forbearance in the hope that at the end the victory would be hers. He was well aware of the comfort that married life procured. As an individual in need not only of his wife's congeniality, conservatism and the confidence that she inspired in him—like the other heroes and heroines of insular lives—but also for her faithfulness to memories past, he could not venture to be deprived of such a comfort. The building up of a new life on the ruins of such a sanctuary was certainly out of the question. That was the concrete reality she plainly saw. However, in this struggle, wherein so much hatred had been present against all expectation, there had been a part she had been reluctant to see, to understand, and perhaps to inquire into. Barring all the appearances, had her husband really remained faithful to his family or to the woman whom he did not want a better knowledge of at closer range? This question could be answered neither by herself nor by Monsieur Jacques, nor by any other person . . . For, such a question might breed other questions; new and dangerous questions that might shatter the foundations of certain things . . . Such cross-examination may not have been indulged in, due to the failure of taking this step . . . In this testimonial project, my contribution had been to that extent only. The questions of the heroes of the story may have remained exclusive to themselves. Actually, everybody seemed to have lived this adventure within their own interior space, at their pleasure, without making any comments to anyone . . . In other words, the problem had been solved by certain shortcomings. This was another form of *de facto* perhaps. Just like in the case of the consequences that other illicit relations bring about. Just like the protection in the case of nearly all relations that assume meaning through servitude. How many people had once known somebody who had taken such steps and asked those same questions that would open brand new doors for them . . . the people who asked the questions or those who had featured in such questions? This certainly demanded courage and involved risks. This indecision would develop chronically in you and gnaw at your very foundations. Yet this cross-examination was a way out for Olga who had been caught in a dilemma, for Olga who had to put up a bold front against loneliness and had to solve all the problems that she faced in life herself. It was the curse of circumstance that had faced her. She could express herself in a different fashion from the other hero and heroine of the story, namely Madame Roza and Monsieur Jacques; this had led her to greater losses and greater gains simultaneously. Yes, to greater losses and gains . . . That was my own illusory conclusion . . . maybe a concrete reality had found expression in me as a result of my affection for her. You may call it sentiment if you want. For, Madame Roza had in the eyes of Monsieur Jacques, a spouse, a faithful spouse at that, while being a true woman at the same time, in other words, the epitome of all the merits generally required in a woman. Something one had lost or had failed to find in other women. Olga had to believe in the veracity of this. That thought, that place she had preferred to stay might eventually turn into somewhere which would enable her to provide answers to certain questions, a place to remain ostensibly intact, where she desired it to be displayed through such a character . . . Despite all defeats, destitution and deceptions . . . Aspiration for this place was perhaps the right of every one of those actors that had a role in that relationship.

Monsieur Jacques, in that world that had been presented to him, whose doors had been opened wide and gifted to him, had done his utmost, according to some, to pay his debt—his *wergild*. He had assumed all the responsibility, maintenance and care that Olga had been in need of, when she was left alone and impecunious after her father's death, in a way more generous and magnanimous than others of his ilk. What drew them to each other at the beginning was this generosity; she was a woman who knew how to listen to her feelings and knew how to convey them to others. Certain particularities had not been omitted; nothing had been spared from her. Monsieur Jacques had always acted as a gentleman when he presented her with gifts he had bought on the occasions of her birthdays, accompanied by the gentle and kind words he pronounced as he tended them to her. He had never adopted such a manner in all his life to any woman in this way, he had never looked nor could he ever look at other women like he looked at her. His was not a transitory affair; far from being transient, he looked at this affair in a different vein. There were things that were out of the ordinary in this relationship, things that had their roots in daily life. I myself had been the witness of many things that had served me to make inroads into this story. Olga, who took care of all the clients at the shop and knew all the dealings of the business, open or secret, was the only true friend and confidante Monsieur

Jacques had. Among those who had had an inkling of this circumstance was Uncle Kirkor. It occurs to me sometimes that when considering his star-crossed relationship with Olga, one should take stock of the implications of such a fact. For, Uncle Kirkor knew all too well the extent to which he had confidence in her. I attribute the impression Olga had on him to her womanhood and the special role she played, and surmise that, as I had good knowledge of her, that it deserved consideration. There was, however, a corner into which she could never have access, as it constituted a source of jealousy, the point where one had the impression that the companionship had been usurped from another. When one thinks of the potential contributions of this little defeat to the unattainability of that woman and her preference for the person in question, the problem is liable to assume a more intricate character. This confidentiality might have been generated perhaps by the inevitable preferences related to backgrounds to which Uncle Kirkor may have been blind. The fact that Olga had learned to speak Spanish and that she had succeeded in this, even though she acquired a somewhat funny accent, was noteworthy. Yet, despite all these probabilities, this confidence appears to have had another meaning, difficult to share and to express. Berti had been spared this confidence—yes, even Berti. A confidence discovered in the forbidden zone of Monsieur Jacques, a confidence loath to be deprived of and related to 'that thing' . . . Olga also had certainly taken cognizance of it. Her putting up with such a life of hardships despite all her destitution and unrealized fancies could have been possible only by such an unshakable conviction. This conviction had also led her to accept those furtive nights, those concrete nights which revived in her the hope that she could go on living her former life in Odessa separately and continue to tread a path strewn with different sentiments. The hours of separation during those nights were charged with new faces, for many years ahead . . . up until those interminable days and nights during which Madame Roza had suffered the intense agonies caused by cancer . . . "That my mother-in-law was doomed to die was as known to her as to everybody else. He had wanted to be near her in her last days. Not because of a pang of conscience, though. I think that he had understood how much he loved her, how difficult it would be to separate from her," said Juliet . . . There was some effort to protect her, I believe; an attempt at shelter and preservation; one of those stories ever recurrent, having inevitable parallels. Monsieur Jacques regarded Madame Roza on her deathbed with a sense of gratitude beyond what had been experienced in the said tripartite relationship, beyond the things that had been occasioned, the things that caused the opportunity to slip, with a sense of gratitude in a place quite different from that which one would have guessed. Experiencing such a feeling was not easy. Madame Roza, according to the information we had been imparted with, had, by her resoluteness, a guarded speech and mastery in keeping silent, having succeeded in thwarting that love, preventing it being fostered and consummated to the very end by a self-sacrifice that not many women (who had been aware of it) could bear the brunt thereafter. This had most probably been interpreted as a game, a game that both women had been privy to, but had refrained from speaking of, or alluding to, during their confidential talks. It all boiled down to a conflict of interests. A conflict that also necessitated some reserve . . . In the end, everybody had paid their share of the cost of this forbidden love in his or her own way. This situation could not possibly have brought about and nourished that feeling. This sentiment of Monsieur Jacques was one that was in the offing, at a distance from what had been experienced. His wife had looked after his mother during the last five years of her life; his mother who had to live with eyes closed to the world, not like a daughter-in-law, but like a daughter. Yes, like her own daughter; it's true, like the progeny of one's own family. By self-sacrifice, endurance, willful deprivation and joining Nesim's game wholeheartedly, careful not to let her take wind of the deceptions she had been subjected to. By that stratagem, Madame Roza had also spent some effort to come to the rescue of the house, notwithstanding her solitude, reticence and lack of means. For the sake of stories which found their repeated depths through acquired meaning in their echoes . . . Monsieur Jacques was the sort of person who believed that debts, regardless of their origin, good or bad, had to be settled in this world. Had he ever thought about this philosophy of his which so profoundly affected his life during the days he had been looking after his wife? I don't know. As far as I can remember, the frequency of visits to Olga had been reduced to a minimum. If my memory does not fail me, this had lasted for about six months. Madame Roza had died while holding the hand of Monsieur Jacques, clasping it tightly . . . her last breath, the last curtain . . . saying: "It has been difficult, hasn't it?" Monsieur Jacques was sitting by her bed not saying a word. He closed her eyelids and recited a last prayer. He continued to sit there for a long while, thinking of their life together; the very first days of their marriage; Jerry; the night of the blaze in which their house at Halıcıoğlu had burned down; his father and the first dinner they had before their nuptials. He remembered the celery in oil dressed with too little sugar and too much salt. It was not that good, yet they had eaten it. As he was telling about that moment of separation, Monsieur Jacques was especially moved when he shared the recollection of that celery. He felt as though he was re-experiencing it, a joy mingled with pain. This was a feeling to which affection and yearning added seasoning, a tragic moment turned into a nice and delightful memory after the lapse of many years. Such recollections only return to the integral part of one's life. They may even arouse in one a sort of pride. For they represent one's own true moments. For instance that recollection of the celery dish, that surmised the moment of eternity which had severed Monsieur Jacques from the woman with whom he had spent an entire life. Monsieur Jacques had long gazed at Madame Roza. He had wanted to speak a few words to her. Certain words that he expected might alleviate the burden of this separation. However, he had failed to do so. He could not bring himself to do that. It was too late. He then took up her comb from the night table and began to comb her thinning hair, comparing it to her hair when he had first seen her. He combed it meticulously and gently, in order that she might go decently to her last refuge . . . Then he had stopped. For it seemed that this sense of absurdity encapsulated the moment. Certain things, certain things that delineate your life graze past without having been experienced. "It has been difficult, hasn't it?" Madame Roza said before closing her eyes, just before her husband started combing her hair. The one that had remained behind had no choice other than to remember, while the other experienced an intense journey through time and space. A long time had been spent; lives, places, seasons heavy with different meanings and little stories had passed. These were the years that would gladden neither Monsieur Jacques nor Olga for reasons easily guessed, the years missed so to speak; what was interesting, and, if one may confess, distressing, was, Olga's sudden death one night, after having gone through a dreadful ordeal, all alone, in her bed, about six months after Madame Roza. Indeed, Olga had died about six months after Madame Roza, all alone, without a word to anybody! Yes, all alone! In the company of her tales; befitting the life she had lived . . . All of a sudden, lapsing into silence, without raising hue nor cry . . . Without having experienced that togetherness with the man she had been waiting for and to whom she had remained faithful to even in her older days, having been trespassed by no one. Was this a sort of vengeance taken by Madame Roza in such an unexpected manner, so difficult for anybody to imagine? Maybe. What was certain was Monsieur Jacques' regression and withdrawal into the solitude of himself. Monsieur Jacques, whom I'd seen at the luncheon we had had at Juliet's after the funeral service of Madame Estreya, fitted this caricature . . . Waiting was of no use, no doubt nobody would come, neither Olga, nor Roza, nor Kirkor, nor Jerry, nor any other soul . . . If so, why should one insist on looking at that old clock?

Mimico's marbles

In everybody's life there are days, nights and seasons that seem to have been left behind at different places far in the past. These are experiences and recollections that make you what you actually are, that at least expected moment cause you in your depths to meet people whom you never expected to meet, that you remember occasionally not always with compunction but sometimes with joy, and that return to you having assumed different meanings. I would never have thought in the beginning that that photograph I chanced to see in an album tossed in a corner at Juliet's would have paved the way to a story destined to be shared with certain people. It was a thick album with a green cover and black pages, an album heavy enough to befit the seriousness of certain situations. It happened to be in the cabinet of the LPs, played less and less at this stage. Lucho Gatica was there . . . Harry Bellafonte, Dean Martin, Frank Sinatra, Bing Crosby and Elvis Presley were all present. Songs kept receding into the past, one-time hits that sounded less and less familiar, songs that people no longer wanted to listen to, to preserve; among them was an album whose contents received less and less attention . . . People sometimes try to evade certain memories and recollections, certain voices, sounds and words that may remind them of certain memories . . . I had, with some hesitation, taken up that album, since this approach might also bring people together through shared memories to which one was a stranger. Juliet had observed this. She had given me a hint by her looks that I shouldn't be upset. This was not the first silent communication between us. There are more ways of exchanging information in life, through other jargons, than words and looks. Juliet's wink was a sort of little present, a sort of *laissez-passer*. She knew that I liked to head for other people's psyches, despite my uneasiness to be proceeding on and finding out the traces of other people's mislaid consciousness. Actually, it was not possible to properly reach those people figuring in the photographs; I was conscious of this. These dashed hopes were not exclusive to people whom we traced as outsiders, but the same frustrated hope held true for people with whom we had lived with over a long period of time, for people we had had contact with for one reason or another. Nevertheless, I had my own fantasies and stories to concoct despite the lack of prospects, stories that seemed never to come to an end thanks to my fancies that engendered and obliterated them, stories that helped me to take refuge in my lies once again in the face of the attacks launched by the truth. Photographs were meticulously arranged on the first few pages while seeming to have been haphazardly laid out on the ones that followed. It seemed that after a given point they had wanted to give up the idea, to renounce certain things and places, as though they had had enough of them. It looked like something that one tried to carry out as if under coercion, something that one would have liked to let go and run its course . . . Photographs loosely distributed without having been glued properly in order; photographs haphazardly inserted by the dozen among the pages. The photograph that had directed me to that story happened to be among those clusters. Its size was somewhat larger than the rest. The dimensions made it easily distinct. It seemed that in it there was one of those calls that we preferred not to define but instead chose to remain contented with through simply sensing its presence. After the lapse of such a long time I can fit that call now in its proper place. It was a place between understanding and bewilderment; a zone between comprehension and perplexity . . . For, I know more or less the unforgettable moments of that story. Having covered some distance among certain impressions, one feels compelled to penetrate the body of a different being; otherwise you feel that you will not be in a position to tell of some of your experiences. At such moments, there are realities more important than the fact that you know you cannot always disclose your feelings as you would have liked. That is the place that you should be attaching importance, in particular to those things that have given birth to them within you. I think I can explain the difference between the moment when I first glanced at that photograph and this very moment, only in this way . . . Most of the details seem to have been obliterated from my memory. What I had been beholding was, to the best of my understanding, a revelry wherein wine occupied the place of honor. There may have been a musical performance as well; a musical performance whose echoes have by now receded to such a distance in the past that the figures in the photograph and their viewers can no longer hear them. That night, more than any other, future designs must have constituted the main topic of discussion. This was not a far-fetched supposition. A wish that had remained confined to the glasses stretched in the air, hopes nourished with succinct words. Will tomorrow be more beautiful than yesterday? Who knows? Given the fact that one had come so far . . . Only the goblets replete with wine could be noticed . . . What remained were the vestiges of other stories, and views that had accompanied them. Three men smartly dressed up in dinner suits and three women wearing low-cut dresses in the fashion of the day had fixed their looks at some place in this scene of bliss they had created in the name of progress within their lives. A place they wished to magnify, and, to a certain extent, to pause, having come from different worlds, carrying those different worlds within themselves . . . I was familiar with these photographs. I had been on either side of them. That was partly the reason why I had been so inquisitive about what remained concealed behind those glances. Was it a summer night? "It was a banquet. Jenny, a cousin of Berti with whom we had lost contact was getting engaged . . . She was a close friend of mine. Formerly, we would often see each other, even before we came to know Berti. We had so many things in common; our fantasies, you know . . . Like everybody . . . Then they parted . . . the day before the wedding. Jenny seemed happy that night. She believed she had found the man of her dreams . . . Look how she laughs!" said Juliet. She pointed to a fair woman who directed her languid look into the camera. She was holding a man with glossy hair by the hand. Were you to ask if there was more to see than what was presented in the photograph, you might call this attitude not holding but hanging on . . . to hold onto someone, to desire to hold on . . . When you think of those latent fears within you, of that man you want to shun at times, you want to have perfect confidence and belief in certain happiness . . . to believe in happiness to the very end, to feel such a need, especially if your experiences and efforts have not received the attention they deserved; as if they summon you to an ineluctable solitude against your will . . . There was in that photograph something that recalled one of the prohibitions, reminding one of who had been ostracized. Had the families, whose desire it had been to show their happiness at such nights, been left outside the frame of that photograph, or had they been outside the confines of the night that brought me that photograph? Would the failure reinforce a prohibition, preserve its strength and cause such a separation? This was a probability not to be easily overlooked in the families of those involved. But I, in order to get an answer to my question, and in my hope to find another story, had chosen a new path and tried to learn if behind that smile there may have been a lover that wished to be forgotten, but with whom it had been impossible to part. How could I ever know if my question, whose origin might well have been a strange intuition, would have led me to that place I least expected it to . . . "Yes, but . . . It didn't turn out as you expected. The man had kept up his facade until the last moment. He had stuck to his guns; he had had good will and desire for another life; although he had to give it up in the end and confess everything. He had his own sexual preferences . . . There had been quite a scandal at Büyükada during those days. Jenny had loved Morris . . . Once the truth was made public, she shut herself up at home. It took some time before she returned to normal. Then, we heard one day that she had decided to go to İzmir, to her aunt. Before she left, we sat one day at a patisserie . . . She said she was going to start a new life. She had decided to become a tour guide. She spoke English and French. Her intention might well have materialized. But not a year had gone by before she was back. She changed jobs every now and then; she slept with men. She felt restless and changed places all the time. She wanted to forget and seemed to wreak vengeance on fate . . . In time, we lost contact. Much later, I heard that she had married a widower with two children from İzmir, much older than herself. She had invited no one to her wedding. She seemed to be taking refuge in evasion, as though she were afraid of something. That was the last I saw of her. Eventually she had left for İzmir for good. She never returned to Istanbul. She may have, however, although unbeknownst to us. We received a letter from her." Juliet penned in the said letter in which she spoke of her having found the happiness she had been looking for. However, she had left her sentence incomplete . . . There seemed to be something that she was shying away from, something between two people which might have changed the course of the story. She might have desired to keep a particular thing to herself she had suddenly remembered at the least expected moment. This must have been the reason for her preferring to keep silent and lending her ears to others. She had had a faint smile on her face afterward and said: "Jenny was a very beautiful girl; much more beautiful than she appears in this photograph. Sometimes she undid her hair; such flaxen hair was rarely seen. Her eyes were of amber. Her smile exposed all her teeth, which were replicas of pearls. This isn't so apparent in this photograph. She was happy all right, but that night she looked somewhat different. Had you known her, you were sure to fall head over heels in love with her." She loved to tease me now and then and to play the role of the elder sister. Despite our differing views on life and how it should be lived, this was what had endeared her to me. This approach had a dash of sex appeal seasoned with affection. On that Saturday, when we had gradually sneaked into that photograph, this affection, innate in her, was directed toward Jenny rather than toward me. It was a rainy Saturday afternoon . . . It might have occurred to Juliet to transpose Jenny for a short moment to another point in time and allow her to be shared with another person . . . "For what? For whom?" . . . Yes, for what and for whom? Was it in order to review once again, from another angle, the steps taken or not taken and the places reached over the years that had vanished in the meantime? Maybe so. Would you not be disposed now and then to retain some photographs for this purpose, to keep them in your own drawers? It had occurred to me to learn if there was somewhere else in that album Jenny had not put in an appearance with that smile of hers. I knew, however, that I couldn't ask this of those people, from the heroes of those tales. I had to acknowledge the fact that certain people who had put in an appearance for a certain term in our lives and left their imprints on us were doomed to remain confined to those photographs. What was important was to just lightly touch on those facades, making sure not to impair anything, and to learn how to touch them in this way. A light touch . . . in order to be able to place that moment somewhere never to be forgotten . . . It looked as if this was the most critical, the most sensitive point of the story. The spell should be broken on no account. Barring all sentiments and contingencies, how much could you share the photograph of that moment with the person who had experienced it, especially when so many years had already gone by? I'd felt this uneasiness when I had taken the album in my hand, and when I'd tried to touch other photographs and had dared to proceed to other periods of that history. In my intention to abandon Jenny at that moment, in that photograph, and my attempt to reanimate her with what Juliet had provided me with, there was a reason, a need for a justifiable evasion. The other hero of the story—who had experienced another evasion, a true evasion, or who had had to go through it—seemed to have the intention of speaking to me about another adventure. I could not possibly ignore the drawbacks of listening to Juliet's account—she who had stayed aloof of Morris, that eccentric man, because of his maltreatment of Jenny, who had experienced the communal spaces from which he could not tear himself away. Clues might have led me to a different aperture. Well, we could also try to overlook certain probabilities while we were trying to understand those men for the sake of the legacy of those pains left to us. I had tried to reveal this aspect of the story which gave me a thrill I tried to conceal partly because of this. Those feelings could not be disclosed easily in those places; for, from time to time you chose to hide yourself behind a different appearance. Juliet had felt that uneasiness I expected. As though caught unawares, she had taken a sip from her coffee with milk and cream and exhaled a few puffs from her cigarette. This behavior was important; for, she knew all too well how to benefit from such occasions. These were occasions when her breath smelled strongly of tobacco. This characteristic of hers excited me sexually . . . "Our contact had broken off for quite some time up until the moment I ran into her at Büyükada. We were at a café, in one of those lousy cafés. She had a man with her, a young man of fair complexion. They were at a distance of a few meters from me. I couldn't hear their words; however, it was evident that they conversed in English. From the expressions on their faces one could infer that they were discussing something serious. Now and then they stopped talking and turned their heads towards the sea. I think I was the only one to recognize her. She had changed a lot. She had grown fat and her hair had grown sparse. However, she was well dressed. Our eyes met a couple of times. She did not seem to recognize me, or preferred not to. Had I approached her, would she be disposed to talk with me? I think she would. I mean she would have liked to. Anyway, I regret now not having tried. However, something within me thwarted my intended action, I don't know exactly what; something that had to do with me, I should think. There was one other thing . . . I didn't figure there, in the picture, I mean . . . I think I'd felt this then. We'd become strangers to each other . . . " We were going through times when eccentricities recalled other eccentricities . . . "You happened to figure in other stories . . . She couldn't have done likewise. As far as I could gather, she was not given enough space. She may have desired more than what was afforded her from that experience of deception for lack of being properly understood. I'm not very far from this feeling. The affection within me was not any different from the meaning we usually attach to the word 'affection.' I'm sure of this. I think that the problem was her inability to express this affection in a way satisfactory to her friends," I said; whereupon, she said: "Yes, but she had on her countenance a sort of self-assurance which the indifference she had grown accustomed to provided her with. She seemed to have settled everything with the people who had abandoned her to her solitude, with those people of the world from which she had been estranged. Her indifference and alienation might have been partly due to this . . . Then we heard one day that she had killed herself . . . They said that she could not bear the fact that her lover had abandoned her and gone back to his own country. That day the subject they discussed might've been this . . . " she said. Speaking of avoidance, I think I had wanted to allude also to other types of evasions. I had felt it; Juliet had tried to evade not only Jenny but also Morris. To evade, feeling the need to run away from different lives to shelter in others for the sake of refuge . . . This was not being experienced for the first time, or for the last. There were so many people who based their existence on such evasions. This story would, over time, continue in a quite different fashion and pave the way to another tale. I already knew that this was going to be the case, at noon during our Saturday retreat. But I'd have to wait, or I'd have to learn how to wait. The hot toasts baked in the oven with cheese were as delicious as always. I had had a sip from the coffee with cream. She was a master in this; she knew how to create the right atmosphere. That was one of the two houses wherein I savored milk with delight. It would still take some time before I realized the importance of this characteristic. Some time . . . Once everybody had come and gone . . . I had gazed at her face in the photograph. I had thought the years had made her even more beautiful. She looked despondent, but her countenance had become more meaningful. She had grown old. Berti also had changed. Then, reverting to the couple opposite, and pointing to the man whose looks attracted attention and gave him an ostentatious appearance among the other six figures, I had remarked: "How everything eludes him; his dinner jacket, the woman beside him, you yourself, this banquet . . . " And she had said in response with a mirthless smile: "He is Mimico, his real name was Hayim, but we used to call him Mimico . . . It's a long story." She had been one of the avid listeners to the stories I told, the stories I always wanted to tell. In this, her stage experience in the past had certainly had its part to play. However, what had particularly impressed me was that power of intuition that had made her a different woman in my view. In the course of time I was to get acquainted with many women who would impress me with their intuitive power for the sake of different relationships in different ways. What made Juliet different were the efforts she made to defend herself solely by her intuitions, although she had been fully equipped with all the necessary prerequisites. This seemed to be her distinguishing feature which could be considered both developed and underdeveloped, in a certain sense. As for her wide hips and full breasts, they tended to arouse sexual desire, especially for the latent dreams of an adolescent boy, avid to touch a woman's body . . . I remember well, as we had been speaking of stories, she had cast meaningful attractive glances my way. This was one of the key moments of a storied relationship. I felt as though a closely guarded secret had been revealed. I had felt myself stark naked in front of her. As we had been sitting next to each other on the sofa, I had suddenly been conscious of that moment when her leg touched mine. This was of such a nature that it could never be experienced again, a moment intensely felt and reproduced to infinity. From the slit of her skirt one could see the entirety of her leg, a real treat . . . She leaned forward to shake out the ash of her cigarette, and trying to cover up the trembling in her voice, she had continued her story from where she had left off in order to redirect my attention to the photograph, and went on to tell the story in question that had introduced Mimico to me as a person who would always abide in me, as though I felt guilty about him. "Do not let those looks deceive you. Those were actually her happiest days. Her happiest days despite all the lies, deceptions and deceits . . . " she began as a preamble. I had asked myself once again whether you needed key witnesses in order to be able to understand certain sentiments that had been experienced in a place very distant from you. I knew the story of the people who had hidden themselves behind those appearances. I was beginning to acknowledge that I belonged to the family that those people formed, and that I would be bound to acknowledge it, years later, when I came to realize that I had learned not to feel ashamed of those shortcomings. She had continued to speak: "You should ask Berti about Mimico's youth. They had grown up together in the same district. He was a strange sort of a fellow. He was the laughingstock of the district, a timid boy," she added. And I'd said in return that laughing at people was a sort of self-defense for the weak. "It expresses the restlessness one feels at the existence of a creature different from them, the easiest way to compensate for their own shortcomings." She had smiled at my remark. She seemed to be approving of my observations. Nevertheless, it seemed that for her to speak about Mimico, to shift back to that time in the past was of greater importance. I believe this was the attempt of a person abandoned in some undesired place to free herself from her own shadow . . . To endeavor to free oneself from one's past . . . By imparting one's experiences and sharing them with others, a way of confessing things in a roundabout way . . . All I had to do was to lend an ear. Everything had assumed the air of a ritual enacted for commemorating someone . . . "Berti found the cause of it in his being orphaned. Mimico had lost his father six months after his birth; thus, he had not known paternal affection. Hard times had started for the family, who had until then made a decent living on the income derived from a small brewery and winery. Madame Victoria had to shoulder the burden of the family, acting both as mother and father to her children. The family was not that large, there were only the three of them, yet they formed a unit. She had to do something about them. A newborn infant of six months, an old mother in need of care, a new business, just like in the trash we occasionally take delight in reading in order to kill time . . . or in those cheap movies . . . these were Berti's memories from childhood days, from the days when blocks of apartments were given female names . . . When I think of Mimico I cannot help asking myself the reason why certain stories are so tragic. After all, it was not so easy to imagine oneself living a detestable life you would never have dreamt of . . . with all the responsibilities and penury . . . Madame Victoria had immediately started to work at the brewery thanks to the practical knowledge she had acquired from her husband. Scratching a living, maintaining a family . . . Monsieur Dimitro, her husband's business partner, had been of great assistance in tutoring her in the particulars of the job, just like an elder brother who had spared no effort to train her in the business. But this was at the beginning; for, later on he had harassed her. Madame Victoria, who refused to yield to his amorous inclinations, thinking that she should keep her chastity and not betray the memory of her husband, had to give in, in the end. Perhaps she had also been willing; we can never know. After all, she was a beautiful and attractive young woman. Business life, uncontrollable impulses . . . When I think of it, to be frank, there was nothing out of the ordinary in this relationship. I believe it was Mimico who had resented this and was injured at Monsieur Dimitro's frequent and long-lasting visits on the pretext of discussing business. In his crankiness, lack of confidence in people and introversion, the influence of those long nights could not be denied. Monsieur Dimitro often invited Mimico to the dinner table prepared fastidiously by Madame Victoria with appetizers, and offered him raki, telling bawdy jokes which he did not understand, wishing him to grow up and be a man. Mimico was eight or nine years of age at the time. According to the account of Berti, he felt terrified in the presence of Monsieur Dimitro during those nights and detested him . . . " As you try to imagine this scene, you might remember the age-old anecdotes in which virility is displayed in all its dimensions. In the fullness of time, I was to learn that Monsieur Dimitro, far from being an experienced gallant and an extreme dandy who had earned the admiration of women used to living with stereotyped standards, was a puny asthmatic valetudinarian who had had no extramarital affairs. Under these circumstances, Madame Victoria's choice acquired a different value. However, despite all the hustle and bustle, apocryphal stories abounded in which a web of elaborate lies were worked out for fear of being cast away, and in order to be a member of the great majority in which so many fine feelings were smothered grievously. Juliet's mindset in her stance toward those recollections had inestimable value for me. For, she happened to be one of those who had shown and taught me one of the many facets of lies . . . We had grown silent. I distinctly remember that that silence was one of those contrapuntal silences. I had thought that we could conjure up these people into whose psychologies we had gained an insight, following different devious paths to different places and possibilities after all these years; doing so in more subtle, diverse ways. To tell the truth, we lived in so many forbidden zones, with so many shadows, our own shadows . . . "Mimico was a sensitive fellow," said Juliet continuing her narrative. Acting had got her nearer to the voice that her past had given her, identifying her as a narrator. With her left hand she had stroked her hair, and after moving her hand along her neck, she diverted her looks from the photographs, assuming that feminine air I adored, casting a glance at me with a smile. Our legs touched. The timing was excellent. I felt once more as though I was stark naked . . . Then we had returned to the photograph . . . for that time, for our time, for our times . . . "The kid could not possibly understand everything by discourse or reason. Understanding aside, the fact remained that the mere sight of his mother being appropriated by another man would be enough to make him feel estranged. The boy's hopelessness in the presence of his mother's situation can easily be understood . . . Those nights must have deeply affected the boy's future attitude toward women, inflating the risk of him being seen as a cast away. Madame Victoria was reported to have been a kindhearted, loving mother. Mimico had never forgotten this. I believe that he always wanted to remain faithful to her memory. However, this period did not last long, for Monsieur Dimitro died within a few years. The brewery was sold at auction. There remained little afterward. Madame Victoria was a resolute woman; she did not resign herself to her fate stoically. She turned another of her talents to good account and began working as a tailor. She went to houses to do her job; she took Mimico with her on the days there was no school or when he was reluctant to go to school. These days apparently affected not only his own world of imagination, but also that of his friends, of his peers. Such fancies are all the more potent during adolescence. Even more so with innocence . . . perhaps because the young are not left crushed under them . . . I know this not only from the impressions of my old friends, but also from Berti. Men are somehow more innocent in the beginning as regards sexual matters. Mimico used to relate to his friends the lascivious scenes to which he had been a witness at the houses of the clients he went to with his mother, describing the women stripping in his presence—who took little heed of him at the time. Such moments were the rare instances when he enjoyed supremacy among his friends. It occurred to him however, that at times he made himself the laughingstock of his companions through his exaggeration of events. Even so, he reigned supreme during such reports. "O the things I have seen! What hips, what breasts!" He went on describing how a woman had replaced one of her large breasts that had come out from her bra back to its nest; how another woman had adjusted her panties squeezed in between her buttocks, how still another woman tactlessly exposed the tuft of pubic hair that had jutted out from the slit of her slip. Most probably he described his adventures in glowing terms. All these cock-and-bull stories may have been of his own invention, but it was undeniable that they had a powerful effect on his companions. I know this from the way Berti told me years later with great relish. Here, I must draw your attention to something of considerable significance. I doubt if you have noticed it. Mimico was shrewdly taking revenge on his companions who had ostracized him during his narrations and demonstrations. It was unkind of him perhaps, although he may be thought of as justified . . . By tickling their fancies, by arousing their jealousy, and, probably by deceiving them . . . He had at the time been robbed of a valuable story . . . His school records were far from being satisfactory . . . He had studied at the High School of Commerce; his mother could not afford to finance his tuition at colleges where European languages were taught and in which his friends studied . . . They were to learn much later what destitution was. Mimico had been faced with another disadvantage at the High School of Commerce: the inconvenience of being a Jew; he was the only Jew in the school. His companions used to call him "Dirty Jew!" Those were the days when he had been separated from Berti. During his junior years, in his adolescence, the gap widened even more. In summer, while his peers met at the square under the clock tower at Büyükada with their girlfriends and went to Dil or made the tour of the island on bicycles, he, in whom no girl paid any attention, remained with his mother and took sea baths all alone. He had to take cognizance of his alienation and lead the life of a recluse. What happened afterward, you can guess . . . The ever-increasing pain of banishment resulting from seclusion . . . As though this was not enough, he developed a phobia for riding bicycles. This seems obstinate and makes one irate . . . " She was right. It was a rather important characteristic, a very important one in fact, for a woman. In order to be acquainted with a woman, to be better acquainted with her, one need only exert extra special effort in satisfying her needs and wants. Was this characteristic a female trait? Time would tell. Yet, it was possible to lend meaning to this deception by finding room for it in those circumstances. To be obliged to go swimming all alone, to view those who journey to the beach in the company of others with envy, and, to be frank, with some jealousy, caused storms to rage within one's soul, and on top of this, to put on an air as though everything was all right . . . The fact that one could ride a bicycle had a poetic meaning difficult to express in words. At such times, one felt that such a painful experience would fail to exude from you, forever leaking inside. Then you began learning certain tricks, mastering them out of necessity. And eventually you became attached to them, up until the moment you found your match. I distinctly remember this had been one of the moments that had drawn me closer to Mimico. "Berti once told me that he had made a mistake by having left Mimico alone and that he had bitterly regretted it afterward . . . But regret does not avail, since nothing can be retrieved . . . " Juliet said at a time when I had been ruminating on the subject. She seemed to be defending Berti rather than accusing him. Her voice had the warmth of a doting mother keeping watch over her child. Her voice did not change when she spoke about Mimico. She said: "People thought that he was a borderline case, that he was retarded. I was the only one who thought differently," adding, "What was wrong with him was that he was a person who didn't know how to turn his intelligence and talent to good account, unlike his acquaintances. With a magic touch, a real woman might change everything for her man enabling him to reconnect to the world and to those who had denied him. On condition that this woman is a virtuous woman who would be willing to take care of him . . . " She had spoken without taking her eyes off the photograph; after having stared at length at the appearance that had popped up before her at that unexpected moment, returning from a far distant past. That was what one did, what one always did, to imaginatively enter into the time of a photograph, to the time of its shooting; to stare, merely to stare at it; to stare at it in order to hold onto our history more tightly, to stare at it because we cannot entrust ourselves wholly to another person. Was the fact that the continuation of our conversation was carried on, even though on a different plane, with a long interval in between, due to our failure to take cognizance of this reality at the time? Maybe. On the other hand, even though we had known this reality, we had known that we knew it; we could not explain to each other those voices produced by the silences caused by our evasions. It was evident, however, that her last sentence tried to make way for another story. This was an interim period between disclosure and concealment. I believe that this was the reason why I had suggested to her to join me in keeping the story under our hat. Personally, I also had a hand in the matter in regard to the illusion that her feminine touch created. That was why I had asked her: "What about Madame Victoria?" I had felt it. My question had generated a spark in her. She seemed to express that I had touched upon a moot point. I knew her only that much. I still entertain the same opinion. "She cherished the same opinion. She was the one who wanted her son to find a decent job and get married, during the days when his companions had either married, or were engaged to be married or had gone abroad, leaving him to live the life of a hermit. Madame Victoria had not received a proper education, but she was a clever and intelligent woman. She was honest and courageous enough to face the hard facts. Life had hardened her . . . A natural consequence of the plight of a person faced with difficulties, difficulties she had to cope with all alone, in deprivation . . . However, the fact that she was a mother was of towering importance. She could not naturally remain idle and watch her son build a wall around himself. That was why she had encouraged him to take part in the conferences and shows taking place in the *Casa d'Italia* and *Union Fran-çaise*. Those were the days when he performed the said activities, especially on weekends when he dressed in the expectation of finding a girlfriend. Yet, his behavior was eccentric and ridiculous. Well, he couldn't help it, could he? The only difference was that his circle was a community formed by individuals who were less cruel but more hypocritical. Was he conscious of having been a laughing stock? I really don't know. Those were the times when Berti and I had recently been introduced to each other. While speaking of his friends, he had also mentioned Mimico with some reservations. I'd understood. He had a secret love and reserved a special place for him. This might have been the dynamism generated by remorse. Not long after, we met at *Union Française* just before the start of a lecture. Strange! I had the impression of *déjà-vu*. It was as though I had known him for eternity. He was like a friend whom I had not seen for a very long time, or a person I had created in my imagination. I had felt nothing odd as I shook his hand. The compliments he paid to me that evening I had received from no one up until then. He was stammering. Later, much later, I learned that this was a habit of his that occurred whenever he felt emotional. I know that this may astound you, but I've got to tell it all the same. This defective utterance made him all the more attractive. This had been my impression anyhow. You may go on and predicate that I was affectionate just because I'd been exalted at the least expected moment, or that I was struggling for supremacy by attributing positive qualities to someone who had experienced shortcomings in his life, which in turn enabled me to endure my own shortcomings. I cannot deny this. Nevertheless, I had more than one reason to love Mimico as Mimico; for reasons even Berti was unaware of, reasons relating to long forgotten memories of childhood. Man learns to acknowledge certain shortcomings, to understand them, to put up with them, to feel them as part of one's being. To have to go through those experiences, both with those one loves and with those one considers alien to them, this happens to be shattering sometimes . . . Anyway . . . As the years went by, Mimico was to get rid of this shortcoming, without even being aware of it; otherwise he would have been deprived of his emotivity. Everybody had his own way of coping with problems. There were things that had to be experienced in those days. He, like everybody else, was going to experience a relationship he would never forget. Among all our relationships, a particular one is always the mark by which we determine and compare all others. Such was this relationship. His loss of emotive power came later, long after that evening . . . as a matter of fact, years later . . . when the day came and he became mute. Alas for Mimico . . . " she said. That was an apposite interjection! Now that I am able to view the whole thing cooly, in the reflection of those words and exchanges, looking from a different perspective, I believe I can better understand what Juliet had been trying to communicate to me. She had missed Mimico, she must have been concealing him in her hidden depths, very far from other people; somewhere well protected, so much so that even Mimico might have difficulty in guessing that she had. "He had praised Berti, to the point of confusing him by saying: 'She is a faithful and reliable friend and I should be extremely happy to be able to marry her and share my life with her,'" she added. A wry smile appeared on her face. There seemed to be things in her memory that she hadn't disclosed; things whose origin were in a different dimension; things that returned to her from her past, and no sooner had they been touched upon, before they were dislodged, fully revealing themselves; things that one could not define exactly. The real meaning lay concealed in those indefinable things, those hidden places, who can tell . . . "It would take some time before I could understand his intention as I got to know him better; actually he wreaked vengeance on Berti for his betrayal and abandonment; stealthily he confused and humiliated him in front of someone he cherished. It was as though he knew beforehand that this would destroy Berti. The concealment of this fact must have served him well. He had expressed his admiration in a subdued tone. With a subtlety that those who had accused him of retardation would hardly understand. This was one of his artful treacheries that might be noticed only by those who knew him well. Everybody has the right to defend himself. Under the circumstances, I dare say that he was justified in his actions. I'm sure you'd be of the same opinion," she said afterward as though waiting for my reaction. For some reason or other I had preferred not to give any answer. I don't know why but her argument of self-defense had perturbed me. There are certain moments when you hesitated to let certain people into the restricted areas you are particularly sensitive about. When one takes steps toward certain individuals, one should earn the right to do so. This might have been the reason why I opted for silence and acted as if I had had reservations about what I had been told. With reference to whether she had or tried to have frequent contact with him afterward, I did not inquire, merely for the sake of covering up this uneasiness and to avoid creating a new tension through this restlessness. "We saw him one day at Şişli with a woman on his arm," she said. It was not for nothing that certain allusions had been made and clues were given *en passant*. I had before me now a story that would likely lead me to brand new problems and create in me brand new visions. "He had married. He introduced us to his wife. She was heavily made up. We were both confused and felt out of sorts. He appeared to be happy as a lark. He made jokes. He said he was proud of his wife, of having married her and tried to prove that he was an ordinary person. They invited us to their house. We accepted the invitation and had dinner together after a few days. Mimico was in seventh heaven. The very fact of our acceptance of the invitation seemed to suggest to him that we approved of him in his new identity as a married man. He was resolute in acting as the perfect host. Lena wore a sleeveless, low-cut dress, a long emerald one. She used a cigarette-holder and interspersed her conversation with French expressions like *chez nous la vie commence après minuit*. Let me add the following remark which you may be curious about. She let Mimico light her cigarette without a second thought; she had a mink shawl around her shoulders which she took off later on. She had a beautiful body which she had wanted to exhibit. He was trying to give weight to what his wife was saying, without giving it a seal of approval, although somewhat covertly with a trembling voice. Mimico was all smiles. Lena and I had gone to the kitchen when he confessed to Berti in a subdued voice that he was 'apprehensive, very apprehensive.' The room had at that moment appeared too large for Berti; Mimico thought that even in a very small world, getting lost in the balance of probabilities was not contrary to reasonable expectation. He wanted to embrace his friend, but couldn't. The time that passed between them prevented him crossing that line, despite the fact that they had never been closer to each other. What the years had failed to achieve, was realized through a few words, though without success. Lena had approached me in the kitchen, and touching, first my waist and then my hips with both hands, had said that I had a beautiful shape but should try to dress more elegantly, like a woman. I had felt a strange sensation that I'd never experienced before; I felt hot on my breasts first and then on my face. I remember having touched my forehead with my hand. That was strange. I had felt like a small, inexperienced girl. For a very brief moment, a quite different feature of mine had been titillated. I had perceived that the woman standing facing me was a terrible woman, that wherever she touched became hot. I told Berti about my impression that very night, without making clear the reason for it. I tried to avoid going to Lena's house. Within me a different woman had been lingering, I was aware of that. A woman I'd never seen or known before, a woman for whom I'd had no inclination. Myself and Berti had been married three or four years. Why should I not experience a pleasure I had not tasted till then, just a brief encounter? I was conscious of course that this might be an invitation to an impending catastrophe. That is why I did not, could not risk it. Berti has not had an inkling of this, nor shall he ever. What was going on in that other room was more important than my experience. Just a few words, 'I'm apprehensive, very apprehensive' . . . Was this a call for help? Possibly. However, according to Berti, no matter where one happened to be in this relationship, there was no doubt that everybody was at a difficult pass. I think he felt too weak to challenge Lena. Were he to do so, he thought, Mimico's suffering would likely increase. It might well be the case that his friend whom he loved and highly valued but had failed to endear himself to had made a wrong choice. A very wrong choice at that. Nevertheless, despite all the dissatisfaction that the said choice caused, he was now with a woman, with a true woman, and according to some people with an original woman. It may be that this woman aroused apprehensions in him and made him pay dearly for the privilege; she also contributed to the realization of a dream. This woman, with all her warmth, was alive in him, in his life, in his flesh and bone. Was this not far better than loneliness, than reverting, after such a relationship, back to the old days? Under the circumstances, everything should be left to run its natural course. Sometimes I think if this attitude of Berti's, which, at first sight, appeared reasonable, might not be an attempt at disguising the fact that he wasn't in a position to help his friend. Had he once again eluded his friend and left him in the lurch? We'll never know. I think we'll never have the heart to take no for an answer. Berti, had, apparently asked Mimico; 'Is there anything that we can do for you?' Mimico having replied: 'Don't bother!' This was an important point, of course. Could it be that what he had meant by this remark was that there was no hope of return for him anymore, had he just wanted to tell me the tribulations he had undergone; and that I had better forget what he had told me? I can't tell. All I know is that this question is to remain without an answer. All that I can recollect about that night was the look in Mimico's eyes, the expression of apprehension in a boy who had lost his way, along with Lena's looks, which were inviting. In the course of time everything found its rightful place; just like in every relationship . . . Then . . . then we came together at that aforementioned dinner. Almost a year had passed. I perceived in Lena's glances at me remoteness and indifference. Could it be that she had forgotten what had happened, or wanted to insinuate that I'd lost my chance? Or was it that I had attached greater importance to certain probabilities than was necessary? I didn't dwell on it, I thought that harping on about it would be of no use; particularly at that stage . . . Mimico seemed resigned, even jovial. He had either thrown in the towel or developed his theatrical manner. Lena had been, as usual, particular about her make-up and appeared classy. She held a cigarette-holder between her lips, as was her habit, and did not fail to intersperse her conversation with French idioms and expressions. She was displaying herself once more as an attractive woman with full lips, meaningful glances, and breasts still pointed. She was warm and did not spare the guests her cheerful and radiant smile. She must've preferred to add charm to her attraction that night and introduced a new trait to her display. She may have insinuated that I had committed a grave error for having refrained from the risk of paying her that visit. Nevertheless, whatever may have been expressed or desired to be disguised, everything was in keeping with the party: everybody had come duly prepared and spruced up. Jenny was partial to Mimico. Although she was younger than him, she behaved toward him as an elder sister, even though they weren't in frequent contact. Did I tell you that they were cousins? Leaving aside this fact, they were good friends. I had that impression whenever I saw them together. Jenny was indeed a sympathetic elder sister. He had invited her to his engagement party for this reason, I think. They spoke less frequently because of Lena. I believe he tried to alleviate the qualms that lay deep within him. Everybody tried to give Mimico something sooner or later; they felt obliged to do so. Everybody was conscious of the mistake they had committed toward each other. The jokes cracked that evening were meaningful. They spoke of the good old days and glasses were raised in response to toasts proposed for the future. Everybody was hopeful that night; everybody had something to expect from life. But Lena—it must be said under the effect of the alcohol she had consumed—tried to remove herself from her surroundings, despite her endeavor to show in vain she was still present. She had drunk a lot and was still continuing to drink. However, although the effect of alcohol was apparent in her gestures, she didn't talk gibberish. Yet, there was something the matter with her. That was plain to see. You know, under such circumstances it is often difficult to take the necessary steps. You grow apprehensive. To begin with, you cannot trust your own self; you are apprehensive about the steps to take and the consequences of those steps; you are perplexed and undecided about what to say and what not to say; you feel out of sorts because you cannot communicate to your addressee what you intend to give him. Years will go by and you will realize that this was pure egoism, a kind of self-protection, which boils down to the same thing. You will again realize that there is no other way but to try to go on living with your regrets . . .

"After that night we tried to establish contact with Mimico; we did something we hadn't done before; we invited him to our house; we told him that he could come either alone or with Lena. Yet, he chose to remain remote from us. It looked as though he had lost confidence in his friends. Or he had preferred not to allow others to see the real face of the woman who was his lot in life. We were to learn all about it much later, after the lapse of some time—in other words, too late. This beautiful woman who could seduce any man by her charm, who had, I'm sure, tried a plurality of relationships, had already married twice, but both marriages had proved disastrous. The men with whom she had established matrimonial ties had been wealthy foreign businessmen. She had lived a couple of years in Lugano, a few years in Corfu and a few years in Alexandria. It was rumored that she had been the mistress of an MP. However, all these reports were based on hearsay. One felt that while she was in the company of the said MP, that it was his first attempt at dancing, drinking and enjoying a night. He was a Levantine. He spoke French and Italian as his mother tongues. He had lost all the members of his family at an early age . . . Berti had learned this, years later, from Mimico, one evening while having tea at the Park Hotel. That had been the only evening when they had been genuine friends. I feel sure that they had had better insight into their acquisitions and losses. I can't otherwise explain Berti's disclosure of his experience of that evening to me. An evening full of remorse, a remorse which he openly displayed. There were many other questions in our minds to which we had no proper answer. How did it happen that such a woman had opted for a conjugal life with a man like Mimico? According to Berti they had met at *Casa d'Italia*. The very night of the encounter, they had dined in a restaurant at Tepebaşı and had a few drinks. Mimico had, for the first time, tried to light a cigarette, which had amused Lena. Afterward, they had made a trip to the Princes' Islands, to Büyükada to be precise, where they had had a swim. Apparently they confessed to each other that, together, they had experienced the most pleasant moments of their lives. Then, at Lunapark, Lena had proposed to Mimico. She didn't have any family, as a matter of fact, there was no one to whom she was closely related. Their respective solitudes had linked them together. Eventually, their wedding was celebrated by a modest party attended by only a few neighbors and a few relatives that had cropped up from God knows where. It had occurred to no one that Lena was not a Jewess . . . However it appears that the invitees had been mystified by other facts; they must've asked themselves the same questions we ask each other after many years of marriage. What could have induced a woman like Lena to choose Mimico as a husband? Could it be the need to take refuge in someone or to have some respite, or for another reason? There was more than one possible answer hidden in the relationship. At long last, the thing that everybody had been waiting for had taken place. Two years after the shooting of this picture, Lena had abandoned Mimico without leaving a note or reason. She had gone away just as she had come, in the natural course of events. This was natural for us too; there was nothing strange in it. However, we, like everyone else, had been content with merely watching the development of this relationship from a distance without making any remark. Therefore, it was evident we might have missed a good many things. A strange presentiment, our skepticism, seemed to have quickened the coming of the final curtain. We were shattered all the same. For, we were well aware of the fact that Mimico wouldn't accept this as naturally as we had done. He had initiated himself to matrimonial life with such great expectations despite his apprehensions. This must've been the reason why he couldn't bring himself to believe that Lena could have forsaken him. He consoled himself by imagining that she must have gone somewhere with a view to solving a matter of urgency, and that she would sooner or later come back home. He went even further; he turned this fiction into concrete fact. He felt as though he had to. This was the only way that he could refresh his link with life. We tried not to leave him alone during those days. However, he wanted nothing to do with us. He did not express this openly, but the way he behaved made it apparent. He may have thought that the people whose confidence he believed he'd lost and in whom he could trust no more had no right to be privy to his troubles. It was as if he were chastising us for our belatedness and improvidence. He punished us by not allowing us to share in his grief. He needed people whom he could take to task. Now I understand it better. I think he had at the same time begun liking solitude and trying to find in this solitude another person. These were the days when he had got rid of his stammering. Nevertheless, he grew less and less talkative; he buried himself in his reticence more and more. He seemed to have chosen his own path to wisdom. After a while, our ties broke all together, under a cloak of darkness . . . Without being involved in a struggle, like before . . . Afterward, long afterward, we were denied the chance to watch the ritual of solitude even in our solemn silence, the ritual to which other people bore witness. He had become more and more introverted; that was all that we could see. During those days when he preferred to keep aloof from his former friends, when he seldom went out and looked to discard them from his life completely. I was told that now and then he frequented the restaurant where he had dined with Lena, spruced up, as though he was going to a dinner party. At the beginning, he used to make a booking for two, he had the table set accordingly, and began waiting for his wife, expecting that she, to whom he had remained faithful throughout his life, might come at any moment. Having waited for quite a while, he began eating slowly according to the rites of the ritual; he told the waiters that the woman he had been waiting for must've been delayed, that she might show up any moment; that he'd had a tacit understanding with her, according to which if either party were delayed the other party might start eating, thus asking the waiter to keep the setting of his companion intact. After the conclusion of his dinner, he got up as though there was nothing out of the ordinary, intimating to the waiters that he had enjoyed his meal, thanking them for their service and that he would call again. This habit lasted for years. In the meantime, the waiters had understood, of course, what was going on, just so much as to satisfy their curiosity. One day, by chance, when we happened to be eating at the said restaurant, Muhittin Bey, who had told others about this ritual of Mimico's and had developed it as a habit of his own, entered. He had understood his role in this play. The words used in the play were the only thing that had changed; as a matter of fact, even the words became insufficient beyond a certain point. I think Mimico had endeared himself to everybody there, through his farcical play based on an imaginary exercise. I said 'by chance,' and by chance indeed it was! After all, the world is a small place, isn't it? Muhittin Bey was an elderly gentleman, of that old Istanbulian stock; a tall man, with thick-framed glasses; he spoke slowly, articulating each word he uttered. He had an aristocratic air. He seemed to have learned how to enjoy life after years of trials and tribulations. He spoke through his looks, through looks that seemed to perceive a man's true personality. I believe he owed this to his aristocratic quality. He might have been an excellent stage actor. As a matter of fact, he had reminded me of an actor I'd seen in a film which is beyond my recollection now. All that I can remember of that man were his looks that transported one to a different realm. He seemed to have solved a good many problems in his life; he gave the impression that he made the best of every opportunity. It was an awe-inspiring and humbling demeanor; but very effective, indeed. The countenance of Muhittin Bey was not debasing. Quite the opposite in actual fact; he struck one by his gentility. He had an imposing and well-proportioned gait which commanded admiration. As we were eating, he approached and excused himself, imparting to us the fact that, given that he knew us, he should like to tell us a remembrance of his. I cannot remember having enjoyed any other story so much. It was a very long story. It was the story of a person we knew so well, to wit Mimico . . . This was how we came to know of his experiences in that restaurant, by the good graces of a person who had been more than a witness, who aided in the construction of those scenes, each of which was pregnant with a plurality of undertones . . . A friend, a very old friend that accosted us at the least expected moment. We were sitting at the same table. Muhittin Bey said that he had at last found the right people to whom to tell the story locked in the store of his memory that was desperate to see the light of day. That would apparently be his last night in that restaurant. He had worked a lot in the years gone by, had made an infinite number of acquaintances, and had finally decided to withdraw to his corner. It was as simple as that; there was nothing out of the ordinary in this. It seemed that everything was changing and was finding new breath in others. He wasn't the only one that had undergone a transformation, the recipes and the customers, the voices and the odors that made the restaurant what it actually was had also changed. This was only natural at his age. Everybody in his turn would, out of necessity, experience this. Nevertheless, being conscious of this fact didn't prevent him from feeling lonely and like a stranger at a place where he had spent so many years. Only *he* knew the stories hidden in the cracks of some of the plates; he knew how the old goblets of wine had been broken; he knew all the loving couples sitting *tête-à-tête* at the tables; he knew the story of the woman who often came to the restaurant and was later stabbed to death by her husband. But now was the time for sharing, to the extent that the possibilities and conditions involved with such a lag-in-time allowed. He was extremely happy as he planned to live night and day together with his sister, who was almost his age, in his derelict house overlooking the sea, replete with souvenirs that would abide there forever . . . He had mentioned Mimico as an old friend of his, a human being—a stranger to us as he had believed—one that he could never forget. He knew a lot of things about him, more than he professed to know. I believe that Mimico had told his story about Lena, with all its miseries, but also about his other friends and the people that had abandoned and betrayed him. He behaved as though he wanted to say that he had been expecting us, as if we were fated to meet each other sooner or later. 'Why on earth, do you think that I stayed here all this time? I'd been waiting for you,' he seemed to say; just like in those horror stories that thrilled one. 'I'd been waiting for you.' We, who had been sitting at the table, totally unaware of what was going to take place had the chance of lending our ears to the story in question. We hadn't dared to let our interlocutor know that we knew Mimico, perhaps because of our guilty complex. This seemed to us a better way of handling the situation. Mimico had been recalled to life that night as he would have liked to be, long after he had passed away. It'd been some four or five years since his demise. I can't distinctly remember now. I couldn't remember a great many events, much as I would have liked to. All that I could remember was that we had been informed of his death by a small notice that had appeared in a daily. It was a tiny announcement that would hardly engage the attention of a casual reader . . . You know what, I have the habit of scanning the obituaries every day without getting tired in the least . . . Who had placed that notice was not known; beneath the notice was written 'a friend.' The burial ceremony had been ordained. According to the wish of Mimico, the notice had been given after the service. We could never learn who that friend was.

The notice had shattered Berti . . . He took me to the Tozkoparan district, to the streets where they used to play marbles. He told me about Mimico's mastery in marble playing, as he described the old streets that kids gave an original charm to. He was matchless, unbeatable in marbles. This was one of the rare accomplishments of his life, one which he prided himself on. He devoted the major part of his leisure to this game. He dedicated the greatest part of his time to it . . . turning a deaf ear to his mother's reproaches. It was reported that he had a great number of bags replete with marbles; it was also claimed, however, that this was exaggerated. Was it possible to gather all the marbles on earth; would the power of this boy's imagination, reluctant to grow up, suffice in collecting all of the marbles within the brief span of his boyhood? To live cheek by jowl with his treasure was bliss for him. For him every marble had its own gamut of radiation. He was reminding that person, his only confidante, whose access to his forbidden zone had been allowed, of all these particulars. This was a world of its own to which marbles invited you. To be able to carry the entire burden of the world within a marble; like in a fairy tale, by giving birth to one's own tale . . . to such an extent that you would, for a while at least, be oblivious to the concrete world around you, the world you happened to inhabit . . . One evening, when school let out, he had loitered and wasted the day while playing marbles with his friends. The day was growing dark and he had not shown up. Madame Victoria was agitated; she rushed out and found her son two streets away, at that very place Berti called: 'that triangulated spot preferred for long lasting parties.' She took him by the ear and dragged him home.

"He was in the presence of his circle of friends who couldn't match him in this game and were there to witness the mastery he displayed. Right at the moment he was about to make a smart stroke. His loitering had driven her mad. He had to be subjected to a severe chastisement that evening. She was known to be a mild and kindhearted woman but when she got mad, no one could abate her wrath. This was to my estimation a kind of self-protection, as well as a measure of protection to those she loved. To be able to stand on safe ground was not so easy, after all. A desperate struggle took one to places one would be reluctant to inhabit. You see, I'm trying to understand the situation without passing any judgment on it; yet, I can't decide whether she was justified or not in venting her wrath on her son. Poor Mimico was not only humiliated in the presence of his companions, but had also lost all his marbles, as, when they were back at home, Madame Victoria had taken a hammer in her hand and broken all of them into pieces. Later on, she had confessed to my mother-in-law that what she had done was a stupid thing and that she had bitterly regretted it. Many years had passed. Everybody had grown up in their own way. What she had done was a 'little murder.' He was positive about it. He would never be able to forgive her for that. Yet, what's the use in dwelling on something that occurred years ago? As a matter of fact, Mimico had not even touched a marble after that incident; he held no marbles to the light, nor did he want to hear their clicking sound anymore. Berti thinks that this was one of the most important things that had dispirited him, the underlying cause of his moroseness. By losing his marbles he had lost his small world, his small sanctuary . . . We had been passing by Christopher's old bicycle repair shop. It was a dirty and dingy place in the basement: now tenanted by a scrap iron dealer. He didn't have to provide an explanation for it. I'd understood. I could at least imagine what must have happened. As I've told you already, many people fancied him as a backward, retarded fellow who had bats in the belfry. Many people thought him to be a timid and weak man. To my mind, he was a misfit, a person poorly adjusted to his environment; a person who had failed to make himself understood. You know the type; those who prefer to remain a member of the same flock or who cannot help being one of the herd, who find it difficult to fit in a given place with others different to them. Actually, the problem was a simple one, much simpler than one could imagine. Do you remember, I'd spoken to you once of a magic wand? Of a world liable to change by a sleight of hand? Unfortunately no one could get the hang of this; even his closest friends, even Berti, for that matter. We had no opportunity to discuss this with Jenny. She must've felt the same as me. The fact is that during those days, everybody was absorbed in their own problems, in their own human concerns. At such times, we remained aloof from other people; we tended to keep our distance . . . So distant now, so far away . . . Madame Victoria must have been conscious of this. Had it been otherwise, one could not possibly explain her desire to see her son married, to have a nice girl for himself. O, those frightful nights of sexuality! The hell that made the weekends impossible . . . Evil and cruelty dominate human relations under the circumstances . . . The existence of a reliable woman . . . the mother could discern it, although she had partly destroyed that well-protected world when she could not restrain herself from breaking his marbles. Nevertheless, men realized that after a certain point the only path left to them was in seeking mutual protection against all untoward occurrences. Barring the deceptions, the injuries received, it was not so easy to seek refuge in other people. Mimico's dilemma was his having been in pursuit of a woman who would favor his devotion to marbles. It is a pity that he could not bring himself to believe that such a woman did not exist, that he, Mimico, could not possibly have such a woman. In a nutshell, his dream was not of this world. You may come forth claiming that women are cruel and impassive in such circumstances, and I will not contradict you. Yet, one should not forget that every individual has a right to self-protection, to protect oneself or to try to do so. Madame Victoria had done everything she believed to be right for her son, but she had to succumb to an untimely death. For Mimico, this meant the loss of his most reliable sanctuary and refuge against the adversities that one was fated to encounter throughout one's lifetime. He knocked on Berti's door early one morning. To father Jacques, who had opened the door for him, he said: 'Mother has gone.' Jacques did not get what he meant by that at first; he sensed, however, that something was wrong. He awakened the house who then mobilized. They went to see what the matter was. Mimico, who opened the door and tried to explain what had happened, not with words, but by gestures that seemed to signify that his mother had gone far away. They rushed to the bedroom; Mimico's mother lay dead. They got nearer to the body. There were a couple of teardrops on her cheeks, two drops almost dried. The mother-in-law noticed this and pointed them to Berti. Had tears rushed to her eyes because she had felt a great pain before she died? It seemed that the departure hadn't been so easy. Had Madame Victoria wept because of pain or because of the fact that she was going to leave her child all alone in the world in such a vulnerable state? No one could possibly guess. However, I'm inclined to believe in the second alternative. Much as he would have wished to, Berti wanted to stay there for the day, but he could not bring himself to. He had the impression that Mimico preferred to be left alone. The same inclination had been expressed during the following days. The pouring of oil on troubled waters was necessary. Everybody was conscious of it. There had been no change in his daily routine. Mimico continued to work at the accounting department at the rabbi's office. After a while, he was engaged as a bookkeeper in a small company. After a while . . . When he needed some more money . . . He always felt the absence of his mother; he began waiting for that woman who would give him maternal affection and warmth when needed; trudging patiently on the rough paths of life . . . Then Lena popped up one day. Lena was for him a dream figure, although at the same time, a source of many worries. She might not have been a sweetheart in the proper sense of the word; she was a symbol from a dream. This must've been the reason why he didn't want to wake up. To pay the cost of the difference had been easy for no one. The latest episode was stored in Muhittin Bey's memory. The restaurant had closed shop because it had changed hands. For Mimico, this meant the severance of his vital ties to his dreamworld. This might be considered to mirror the destruction of his marbles. Yes, the loss of his marbles . . . at a time when he had after many years been deprived of his pristine energy. This development of affairs moved Mimico away from his friends; bereft of his game, life for him had lost its significance. He began building walls. Muhittin Bey was one of the rare people who had the privilege of climbing over those walls. He paid visits to him on a few occasions. One day, he went to inform him of the restaurant's inauguration. He was to be the guest of honor; a table was reserved for him. Mimico had smiled. So many years had gone by since he had last smiled. Yet, he looked prostrate. He spoke of the approach of the end . . . Muhittin Bey was with him on his last night. Just before he died, he told him that everybody had done everything that had been required of them, except for that army sergeant who had slapped his right ear, causing his deafness, whom he would never forgive. None of us knew what had befallen him during his military service. Neither Berti, nor I, nor anyone else; none of us . . . I'm sure Madame Victoria herself had not been told of it. What is more interesting still was that he had never told us (or wanted us to know) that he couldn't hear at all from his right ear. It appears that before departing he had wanted to communicate it to someone . . . that's all . . . "

We had come to the end of the narration. There was silence. After a short hiatus, Juliet had turned and said: "I wish you knew him." "Now, I do," I replied. She smiled. There were tears in her eyes. I have already tried to tell the story of egotistical behavior as best I can. I know. In similar situations there were a lot of recollections—images, and, what is still more important, attempts at evasions that assumed meanings, once they reflected on oneself . . . potentialities that had failed to materialize, that one could not enliven . . . stories that could not be conveyed despite the richness of one's imagination . . . This is the reason why I want to believe that there were many other personal attachments that that photograph concealed and that Juliet had failed to pass on in detail. For instance, what had been the reason lying behind Berti's attaching so much importance to Mimico's mastery of the game of marbles? We could also inquire into Juliet's concern about her reluctance to talk to Morris at Büyükada. Had Lena truly kept aloof from that photograph that night, as it had been claimed? In which compartment of his brain had Mimico stored the images of women changing their dresses, full of hopes and expectations? Could it not be envisioned that everything originated from people's desire that everything shown to them become material? And the fear of losing people, or actually of losing a single person, to be precise? Today I'm able to grasp better the value of the story that Juliet conveyed to me through that photograph, regardless of the fact that certain truths were kept undisclosed or distorted while being elaborated upon . . . Haven't we been told before that justice can be done even to lies after a certain point?

Actually even lies could have been exonerated; the lies, our lies . . . Otherwise, could Jenny claim in that letter that she was a happy woman and could Mimico arrange those dinner rituals, could Juliet dare to openly declare that she had popped into that restaurant at Tepebaşı without any previous intent?

Fathers, Daughters, and Mute Songs

1

When, where, and behind which window had I last seen Madame Eleni? When had I last experienced the pain of being unable to touch, simply to touch, someone from a distance? Was it yesterday, a couple of hours before? Twenty-six years ago? Or . . . It is high time now that I, after all those stories, acknowledge the fact that I feel now and then constrained to continue dreaming of those little eventualities, despite all the losses I have suffered and to go ahead and take the risk of not being able to return. I always wanted to go down to that labyrinth of death, to go down, descend to the depths . . . Whose life was it, that life that could be discovered in that immense darkness that pervaded everywhere? To whom was that victory relevant? It seemed that certain people had always been waiting for others in that realm of darkness. Certain people had been waiting in the hereafter; or at least it would seem so . . . The problem lay in that the intention never yielded progression; the step forward could not be taken; one could not believe in the existence of a coast other than his own . . . Plays continued to be enacted for other songs despite abeyances; songs continued to be sung although we knew that they were chanting untruths and were justified only by their creation . . . plays for which we could find no name and which we could not be bold enough to watch properly till the end without asking questions, to wait until the curtain fell, to make a systematic inquiry into words that we preferred not to remember, for words that remained with us in all their depths, for relationships that abided within us, relationships that seemed to have come to an end only to come to be reborn one day, for fantasies into which fresh life was breathed, for the heroes of our imagination, regardless of whether we wanted them or not. These plays, those tales of life beyond the grave that assumed meaning with that human being whom we prefer to believe alive in that labyrinth of death, having no direct connection with Madame Eleni. Perhaps by doing so I'm trying to remind myself of the lives which I could not fully live, as well as certain people and relationships which haunted my every journey toward recollection; to remind myself continuously, to be able to think that there is no genuine demarcation line between the past and the present. Am I doing this hoping that some day I will take that step? Maybe I am. As a matter of fact, I remember Madame Eleni whenever I think of that step, of that step which has not been taken as of yet. Here is the starting point of the story, I think; this place or this line of separation: a handful of photos which feed that memory, the photos that find their meaning there. At this stage I can recall, for example, the light of that old apartment which had previously opened a good many stories for me. Those who had caused the embers to glow happen to now be in different countries, in different times, living different destinies. Different countries, different times and different destinies; just like in the case with Şükran who had dared to take that step toward a brand new life in order not to breathe the air of that room which smelled of cooked food and wherein affection, hatred, disappointments and penury, even eroticism coexisted . . . Just like in the case of other people living in the margin of such lives that cannot make themselves heard as they would have liked to. They lived in an apartment that kept alive and concealed in its nooks and crannies certain peculiarities and objects which could enable me to pursue my path toward more stories. In that apartment I had lived as well; I had tried to find meanings in those voices and noises and steps according to my inclination. Those voices and sounds call me back to those lives on certain evenings. They are behind the door; their door . . . The odors of beans with spinach or of fish frying in the pan . . . That the charwoman did the chores was evident from the parquet polish; floor polish was applied using an old stocking. This meant turning an old stocking to good account. Could one associate that smell of polish with the arousal of my sexual instinct? It was possible, wasn't it? We possessed feelings which changed according to our idiosyncrasies that did not require any explanation; these feelings contributed—with what other invitations enlivened within us—to our other flights. The floor polishing had to be carried out with a dry and soft piece of cloth. Mathilda was highly pleased to see us perched on a piece of cloth, hopping on the recently polished parquet as though we were on a dance floor. The delight of Madame Floridis was no less. She wasn't content with watching our steps, but contributed also to our rhythmic movement by clapping her hands to the accompaniment of a cadence to accelerate our tempo. If I remember correctly, it was there I had learned my initial figures. The twist was not only in fashion at the time, but also suited the objective perfectly. On such evenings, Sandra looked very beautiful and Madame Floridis was full of pep, despite all her past cares. However, all these were now part of the past; they were being recalled to life and shared now in a completely different apartment, within the context of a thoroughly different story. Madame Mathilda's world, tinged by Turkish films shown on *Kervan*, by Zeki Müren's songs and by the singles which she listened to while engaged in daily chores or cooking in the kitchen, was a thoroughly different world. I can still imagine her talking through the light shaft with her neighbors. This was a preamble to her daily chores: the running films, the meals to be cooked that day and the preparations for the coming holiday were on the agenda for discussions. Film stars were, for her, members of her immediate circle. However, there were other people about whom judgments had to be passed; people at the top of her usual agenda, people that one envied, admired, sometimes victimized . . . After all, everybody had the right to defend his lifestyle or to justify it. Those images, those morning talks that added meaning to those images bring me back not only to Madame Mathilda, but also, through another window, to the faces that have become blurred now, the wry smile of Şükran who had taken the risk of living her life in another room. With her thick rimmed glasses, long wavy hair, full breasts and wide hips, Madame Mathilda commented on Şükran's glances in her vernacular, saying: "No me estan plaziendo las miadas de esta ijika" (I don't like the looks of this girl). This was not merely a derogatory remark, but there was also an allusion to a secret concern in her expression. "Ia tiene una, Un chauffeur parase" (I think she has a lover, a car driver), said Madame Chella whose remark was somewhat more disparaging. "Los vide dos vezes serka del grocery. Si los aferra el padre te cura ke la mata" (I've seen them twice at the grocery store; if her father sees them together, I'm sure that'll be the end of them). Madame Chella didn't know that he was head over heels in love with Hüsnü's daughter and that, come what may, he wouldn't let her go; despite the fact she was in a position to understand and empathize with a story of such discord, when one could not help but recall her own past experiences. Yet, she was averse to displaying such acts of good will. She was in need of proving to herself firstly the superiority of her financial power and then of her social position in comparison to thousands of other people, obliged, like Hüsnü, to live on the bare necessities of life. "At least so much was necessary," one is inclined to say, when one feels one has to go on living, and to forget about one's distress by observing those people deprived of expectations. Her long-lasting widowhood, the sorrow she felt for her unmarried daughter, already past thirty, and her attempts at covering up her exposed household must have ruined her. These must have been the factors that caused her spitefulness. This picture could be seen in nearly every climate, at all times, around the world. "Ta se lo dishe al padre," said Madame Mathilda, "Le dishe ka haga attention. Ahora te la yevan, te la kandireyan, i despues vites ke se hizo putana" (I've told her father. Be careful, I said. They may take her away any moment, deceive her, and make her a whore). Madame Mathilda was of a milder disposition. In addition, she had in her store of imagination hundreds, perhaps thousands of movie impressions; hundreds and thousands that supplied corroborative evidence to substantiate the actuality of the episodes devalued by others claiming that such actions were only seen in films. After the lapse of so many years, I can ask myself now, whether, if the conditions had been different, could I have written a scenario inspired by the woman concealed in Madame Mathilda? To imagine the feasibility of such a prospect, after the disappearance of so many scenes lost in the meantime, is beyond all possibility. What was more distressing still was the reoccurrence of that affliction to which she had had a presentiment. This undoubtedly was a foresight, one that had its origin in the storms that had been raging within her. Everybody preferred to remain a mere spectator to the fate of other families, not to let outsiders trespass the limits drawn by their own families, in order to protect the sanctity of their households. To prefer to remain aloof and keep everybody at a distance and consider it a merit; without taking stock of the fact that a man thus becomes isolated and vulnerable . . . All these things were undeniable at the time and still are at present; however, I feel I am bound to say that in the light of developing events, everybody felt himself to be at a loss. Although I'm not old enough to establish certain links between certain facts, the events themselves are still vivid in my imagination. Şükran was to launch herself on a venture, on a new exploit, with that man that Chella had seen, taking steps toward her true life . . . on a Monday morning, at a time when everybody was about to start their weekly labor . . . abandoning her family, her clothes and all that remained from her childhood, with a view to realizing her dreams . . . without taking with her anything except her own self, and leaving behind a few words in the janitor's cubicle, reminiscent of the verses of a poem . . . "I am going and won't be back. Try to forget me; I'll be doing the same." Hüsnü had carried this short note of his beloved daughter, Şükran, around with him. When he showed it to me many years had already gone by, many long years. Those few words jotted down expressed not only a rebellion, but also a deception, and a hidden apprehension. Şükran's story was one of a person being dragged along . . . of a defeat, of a drifting, as far as we could gather of course. Years had gone by before we heard anything from her. News came one day that she was working at a nightclub. Hüsnü began tracking her, making the rounds of all the nightclubs in Istanbul, denying the existence of the night lights, trying to soothe his yearning for her, replacing it with a hope, faint though it was. He had asked everybody who he believed might have had some sort of a connection with her, without fearing humiliation or becoming an object of ridicule . . . He waited for doors to open, wishing for a new salvation . . . One day we came across a piece of news in the daily. Şükran was found murdered in a hotel room along with a man who was said to be her fiancé. It was claimed that it was a *crime passionnel.* The killer was Şükran's former lover. In his deposition the man said that he was not sorry for doing it, that he had committed the crime in full consciousness. It was premeditated, in order that everybody might rest in peace . . . Such had been the account marked in police records; such was the reason why this piece of news in the papers would remain in the stores of the readers' minds. For the general reader not involved in affairs like those experienced by the characters (the true spectators of the incident) this was but stale news that had appeared in one of the pages of a daily. There was also a photo of Şükran that appeared in the column of the newspaper. She was smiling as though she wanted to cover up her grief. The picture was one of those representations in which the figures intended to show by their smile that they were happy at the moment the camera's shutter flashed . . . What remained for us was to visualize the last room, the hotel room, into which certain steps had been taken. From one room to another . . . what had changed in the meantime, what could ever change? After such a long time had elapsed in between, I'm still trying to find an answer to this question. The images that surge to my mind are the changing of bed sheets once a week, a room that had been a witness to a good many flights, erratic scenes of love and of *coitus interruptus*. A ramshackle hotel room at Sirkeci . . . That's all. Şükran's expression in the photograph was much different from that which had unnerved Madame Mathilda, those looks of a young girl who had believed that she deserved a different life. Now that I have known an infinite number of characters in my life who make love for money, I can imagine that her looks tried to express things far surpassing the expression of her eyes in that photograph, pregnant with meaning. Should we seek the gist of the matter in our failure to grasp those meanings that that expression warranted? When I go over the events I witnessed and the acts I performed, the answer seems to be positive. I'm inclined to think that Hüsnü, despite his good will and best efforts, had experienced a mental torment of his own. There was no doubt that it had been he that had perceived the meaning concealed in the eyes of his daughter who had forsaken him. There was a reality behind this affliction which he could not possibly change. This state of affairs brought him to a spot quite different from the place where other witnesses stood, where they preferred to stay and take refuge in. Actually, certain people have never been successful in building bridges. This might be interpreted as another way of putting up with life and of convincing oneself of being superior in strength. Could it be that witnesses would be transformed to mere spectators as days went by if the paths were to become thornier? The witnesses in the apartment at Şişli were to prove their status as spectators by calling on each other less frequently in the apartments into which they had moved, eventually ceasing to do so for good. Other daily lives belonged to other places, to other people . . . As long as one lived and wanted to live in other districts, streets, towns or cities with other people . . . Şükran's straying to those paths might well have been anticipated. The incident had been an ordinary one. Everybody had his own outsider within him. Everybody had an outsider within him, be he conscious of it or not, be he able to identify him or not . . . Such was the case with Hüsnü and others who brought that apartment back to life and who were obliged to live a certain period of their lives within a community. This story was an ordinary one, a trivial one much elaborated upon . . .

2

As for the other witnesses of the incident; the steps they took would show you the direction of your future path, whether you were in their company or not, you could at least decide it for yourself. Now, what had Madame Eleni, who knew the significance of the stories related to flights, felt in the presence of all these events? The answer is not so easy to find. Nay, even impossible! To begin with, at the time, Madame Eleni happened to be far away, remote from us; such had been her choice. The distance was partly our doing, I think; it was a reflection of our aloofness. To my mind, this was due to the denial of her circle, making her out as if she were denying it, to her insistence on keeping her inner world inaccessible to others, and to our failure to take that step toward her as well as to our lack of courage to do so. The story she lived and revealed to us was the story of those people, who, although close to us, preferred to keep people at arm's length, in that area which we always had difficulty in delineating its boundaries although we were in a strong position to do so, or which we could interpret, based on certain relationships, dreams and human beings . . . there were lives, moments, and contingencies we had missed. That question and what it gave rise to have always diverted me from my path; the questions I asked others and myself using different phraseologies educe me now belatedly and seem as though they can re-establish my links with certain people. When and through which particular window had I last had a glimpse of Madame Eleni, busy in that kitchen that opened to the light shaft? Was she actually naked, as she seemed to be; could it be that she had been able to strip herself naked during those evenings? When had I last tried to advance, groping in the dark, as in those stories to which I could gain no access, and which, precisely because I had failed to do so, took quite different turns from what I would have expected, were elaborated upon by hesitations, suspicions (and, most importantly), enlarged their dimensions over time, aided by our shortcomings? To try to advance in a story, groping in the dark . . . Madame Roza's gait on this path had been quite different; her steps had been quite different. Once again, she had remained behind that curtain of secrets which I have always tried to explain, and already tried to share, at other places, with other people; her finding similarities between the thunder on a stormy night and the sounds of gunfire during the Bulgarians' offensive at Çatalca of which she used to tell me when she was in the mood; her elaborating on the stories she had in her memory; her association of thunder with death; the thunder, that when she was matured, during her motherhood and grandmotherhood that appeared to her terrifying and threatening and made her feel like taking refuge in someone, just like when she was a little girl; her staying in Istanbul as an émigré; her suffering that had inevitably succeeded in permeating her former days of plenty; her grieving over her abandonment, in that small Eden, of her faithful dog who had never left her side during those horrible nights, sleeping in her house, in her room, at the head of her bedstead; her abandonment of her father who had failed to adapt himself to their new lifestyle in Istanbul and to the conditions prevailing there; her failing to pardon him for his leading us to betrayal. This woman told all these things as though she had been narrating a fairy tale; she who could not bring herself to leave the people she loved *tête-à-tête* with their own afflictions despite her own worries. She could not and would not whisper a single word about Madame Eleni's secret or her past to anybody despite our strict insistence. This discretion had been enough for me to feel lonesome once again in that story. Nevertheless, I did entertain a faint hope for years and wanted to believe that I would one day be able to discover the mystery of this story in all its elements, as I had to live other lives in all their specific details. To live other lives; by trying to bring together certain scenes with others I borrowed, lending meanings to them, without overlooking the changeability of the story beyond a certain point, like in the case of every other story that we transport to our own personal ventures . . . This seemed to be the only way, the securest way to patch up the bits and pieces. I can convey that doubt that had changed the course of the story in those days only by words which I know to have changed. The absence of answers and the fact that answers can give rise to new questions, whether one wants it to or not, lead up to the same place; the urge to go back and have access to those past experiences despite all the defeats likely to be encountered on that path . . . I had come into contact with the source, or at least thought that I had. Those scenes return to me now like an old song mislaid somewhere in the past, left to abide there for a long time, without letting it sink into oblivion. Could one attribute the taciturnity of Madame Roza to the privilege bestowed on her of being the only neighbor given the right to call now and then at Madame Eleni's for a cup of coffee, to the imposition on her circle of her superiority, to her incapacity to betray the responsibility that her past observations laid on her shoulders—it was a mysterious past and she had acquired that knowledge for the sake of her own life—or to her concealing her household secrets not only from her confidante but also from her own self, by providing answers of a general nature to my questions with trite maxims such as "well, after all, everybody has her own way of life," or "every household has its own secrets?" These were the possible explanations that presented themselves at first sight. However, outside these possibilities, each of which could lead one to a different place, there was another possibility which I thought should be considered, as I felt it nearer to me. The said opportunity made it possible for me to trace back a return, a completely different return, an opportunity that shed some light, from a different time, on the life of two people, to be precise, on their joint life . . . She had identified the hours that she had spent with Madame Eleni with a small world which she believed she had lost for good and in which she would not live ever again. In that world, there existed a sense of language which her childhood had delineated through different angles and had been abandoned in the distant past. To be able to decipher the language of one's childhood with the help of one's later experiences, to be able to return to that innocence, to that little poem, during the hours jointly reproduced by two people. The fact that Madame Roza was reluctant to allow others to cross over the borders of the island in which she led her daily life and which she tried to keep alive seems now understandable. What had prompted me to narrate these things was her almost perfect knowledge of the Greek language which might be a source of envy for many people. What she had learned in that small, cold Greek School at Çatalca (demolished during the Balkan War, but which continued to live in the memories of many people) whose teaching staff consisted of priests who created an atmosphere of terror, had made possible the reproduction of other sentiments and prepared a reliable background for sharing certain lives. It is to be noted, however, that what her father—a member of the nationalist forces who continued to shuttle between his motherland and here, during the post-war period of World War I—told about the treachery of the Greeks had left indelible traces on Madame Roza. Yet, she still had a penchant for Greeks which she could not bring herself to confess even to herself. This *terra incognita* within her remained unadulterated, unsoiled and intact. One could feel the traces of this approach in her elation while reciting the heroic Greek verses as enthusiastically as the poems of Victor Hugo and Lamartine which she had memorized at the *Alliance* in Istanbul and in her passion for sharing this enthusiasm with us. This was a return quite different from the one she had experienced while with Madame Eleni to which she tried to lend meanings in a completely different dimension. The integration of poetry was an interesting point. I believe that this made the return journey somewhat more beautiful and worthy of narration; seeking ways to resuscitate a man lost in a different time, trapped in a different body, fixed with greater yearnings . . . Those people were different. There certainly was a difference between Roza the child and Roza the mother, the spouse, the woman and the grandmother. Now, I am in a better position to appreciate the importance of those poems, of those yarns. She had not memorized any other poem since her school years; she hadn't felt the need. Nevertheless, this choice enabled her to view the world at a closer range, allowing her to attach greater and deeper meanings to those poems than their inherent significance alone. This was just one of her solitudes it seems. On the other hand, we all know the stories that solitudes engender or may engender according to one's idiosyncrasies. Is this the reason why I came to believe that Madame Eleni might fit the theme of a poem as well as the plot of a tale? Yet, this belief had not allowed me to intrude upon the boundaries of this woman who kept herself distant from her friends. This was a story involving considerable unknown elements, a story that was rewound every day. Under the circumstances it was inevitable, natural and to be expected that the incidents that had taken place in her story should persistently lead me astray. Whether we know it or not (whether we are obliged to or not) it is an undeniable fact that, not only in love affairs but in all relationships we want to possess above all else what we are liable to lose, what we are afraid to lose. However, we can derive certain conclusions from the times when Madame Roza let the cat out of the bag, although she tried to make us overlook them as though they were insignificant things. On the one hand, the rumors that many people reproduced had no relevance whatsoever to the actual facts, but were thought of as nonsense to those who tried to keep aloof from such gossip. On the other hand, certain secrets were left in the background unpronounced, with the potential for expression . . . Could this story be based on the unlikely foundation of a telltale clue? Why not? In order to understand certain stories better, like certain lives, in order to get a hold on them, was it not required to ignore the consequences of certain errors, and, more importantly, to live with these errors? Those oversights were inevitable, you couldn't, after a certain point, remain indifferent to their call, those calls which you believed capable of changing the course of a life . . . It was not possible for you to remain indifferent to the calls or to the feelings engendered by those calls . . . I must take a pause here. For, to the best of my understanding, the word 'call' had a special place in Madame Eleni's life. It was evident that she also had to forbear the consequences of the call along with all the storms that this had caused within her. Her confidential past, that had caused her to look like a lunatic who had broken all her relations with the outside world and confined her within the four walls of her house, had roused my interest especially for this reason. I had taken a few steps ahead in a story related to abandonment; in this way, I once again had the possibility to piece together the vestiges left by certain people. This was a game I could not have possibly denied myself. In this way, I should be able also to recollect the history of those dilemmas, of dreams not realized, and of defeats. This seemed to be a necessary consequence of the game. What made this game real and worth playing was this, I think. What we experienced within us was a stage play enacted more than once, the consequences of which one endured in one way or another. Otherwise, how could we put up with the existence of people we had left at a particular time of our lives, entrusting us with those certain encounters brought back to us at unexpected moments? Did the stories of other people not give us certain clues about our own which attached us to life and assumed significance by our occasional lies that took different forms as time went by? Under the circumstances, could one consider Madame Eleni's story, for instance, the story of her devotion to a man whose arrival had been awaited for a lifetime, despite all the recollections, feelings and betrayals? In addition to what we had learned from Madame Roza, there were pieces of information that certain rumors had wafted toward us. Eleni was said to have been enamored with a Turkish officer when she was in her teens. The story went that they used to meet secretly. This secrecy and the exclusion that caused it had inevitably brought them closer to each other, as the story went on. Having arrived at that critical point beyond which there was no return, they had sought the solution in escape . . . escape anywhere . . . for the sake of their love . . . in order not to lose each other further down the road . . . So far there was nothing out of the ordinary in terms of originality or precedent. In order that I might fit Madame Eleni into her place in this peculiar story, Tanaş had to intervene. He was a man who had born the grief of abandonment over many years. He had a delicatessen in Karaköy. He also was an experienced loner; he was the hero of another unique tale, and was, on top of that, Eleni's father, a man devoted to his daughter. A father devoted to his daughter . . . When you think of all that had transpired, it looks like a strange kind of love that startles one; a story of bondage, a story that shelters in it a death that only the heroes can properly define, a death deeply embedded in their secret depths, as is the case with all sorts of enslavement and passion . . . Tanaş had the premonition that his daughter, to whom he was devoted, would vanish into thin air following that escape. The only way to thwart this scheme was to keep her under lock and key; this was a kind of measure that an unrequited lover might revert to in order to hinder the elopement of his beloved with somebody else . . . This was the exact spot, the starting point of the story according to some, and, according to others, the point where the story continued under new guises. We know nothing about the details, we never shall. All that we know is that the story had begun on the night that Eleni was getting ready to elope with her captain, and that this state of affairs had lasted for many years. Eleni had been confined to the house that night. Days had dawned and the sun had set from different angles thereafter. Under the circumstances, one understands the situation better: her seclusion and the impression she created in us that made her supposedly insane—the events that, to many, may seem utter nonsense, conveyed to me by various mouths, at various times, with a view to patching them up—now meshed into a whole consisting of a succession of scenes. She had eloped taking with her the black patent leather shoes purchased for her by her officer lover for the sake of that yearning that called to her in fictions, the Bordeaux red *crepe de chine* dress, the silk *chemise*, the two scented candles she kept for Christmas Eve which she was convinced she would light one day, a couple of photographs and the small heart-shaped gold medallion that her mother had thrust into her hand as she was about to leave the house saying: "Do whatever you want to do, but make sure not to postpone beauties," or so it seemed to us now after so many years from a much different perspective. Was she really seventeen? The answer to this question was to remain a mystery to us; contributing to the formation of a persistent rumor as with all questions that remain without an answer, along with their concomitant mysteries. There are times when logical explanations fall short of the mark. The evening this question came up was such an occasion. That young girl, at an age when she should have been free, had to submit to her father's peremptory measures, despite the temptation to escape. She had experienced all possible vacillations between potential regrets and hopes, along with all their scorching effects; she must have experienced them prior to the said escape. She knew well the precious place she held in her father's heart; she should have been conscious of the fact that her departure would deprive that man, who was already subject to all sorts of erosions, of so many things. Yet, one can derive certain conclusions from certain facts she must have learned from her mother as regards the light that her feelings emitted; these things which are true for some, necessary for a life truly lived, and for others are egotistical and treacherous. If I must be frank, I feel, when I think of the different alternatives, that I am not in a position to judge the spirit directing the course of this argument. I must confess that this gives me the creeps now and then. This fear does not originate merely from my need to inquire into the matter in case I'll be subject to such a vacillation, but also from the thought that this man, whose story I'm trying to patch up based on photographs already partially torn and deprived of their gloss, might, if I were to take a wrong step, take vengeance on me, either in my dreams or in another corner of my mind where his gaze is fixed on my memory. Can this be the voice of my conscience? I doubt it. It may be a slight variant or evasion, in order not to recollect other relationships or steps not taken. Nevertheless, Eleni had dared, I should say, to experience quite a different verse within that story, at least that evening, and proved to be far more courageous compared to many other people. She had tried to at least; she had proved that she could do so. And then what? Well, this question compels us to go further into the deployment of the story. We are reminded that certain people, walking on the threshold, condemn themselves to a silent death, for the sake of their love. Eleni would be kept confined by her father who regularly went to his shop every morning; not only would she not be able to frequent her school, which had remained off the trodden path, at a place quite different to her lover's hideaway, but would not be allowed to stick her nose out of the house. Her officer would be waiting for her at the usual spot, the starting point of their elopement, of their evasion toward freedom, fed partly by their dreams. Actually, for the sake of that step, a future had already been risked. The meaning of that risk could only be grasped by those who had lived such an adventure . . . to be able to take a risk for love, whatever the consequences may have been, to jeopardize one's life for love; in the sight of those who chanced to take such a gamble, of that impression, of that adventure, Eleni, who had refrained from going to that point of encounter much against her will had exposed herself to a solitude that was to be transformed with every passing day into a labyrinth without escape . . . The pain she felt through the inability to express her unfair treatment, of knowing that she would never be able to get it across . . . the thralldom that others were reluctant to define and were often unconscious of . . . carrying on with a relationship without taking stock of things as though there was nothing to worry about . . . no, they were not for her. She had been asked to assume somebody else's identity. Her misfortune was due perhaps to her failure in observing the rules of the game . . . As far I could gather, this obligatory servitude lasted for a couple of years. She had been put in shackles in a way. The funny thing was that her officer lover had not once inquired after her despite all the afflictions felt and pains experienced. It seems that there is a break in this story; something that does not add up in light of what was experienced, something desired to be snatched from time and kept as a secret . . . When you think of those sentiments generated by those encounters, you find it difficult to think that such a love was relinquished without a fight. One is inclined to conclude that the lover must have inquired after her but failed to get in touch; it must have been so sad to fail to reach her despite one's best efforts; this must have been the incubus of the captain whose name we will never know. I wonder whether that lover had been able to remain in the army and whether he had grown sterner, merciless and implacable against life, reminiscent of the heroes in war films and novels. I wonder whether he had asked the military authorities to assign him to a duty somewhere in Anatolia, far from Istanbul, which would allow him to dream about the past during those long watch hours . . . Could it be that he had opted for another lifestyle in order to forget his grief? Could it be that he was in pursuit of a new life, a long path to consign himself to oblivion? After all, this was not a sudden disappearance, to find oneself in the middle of a desolate wasteland, victim of a betrayal difficult to explain and to express; such steps might undoubtedly conduce one to various interpretations. For some reason or other, I think about that Anatolian town, that wasteland where the lover was to entrench himself. This image often recurs to me. It is so saddening to speak about certain separations and solitudes; it was so heartrending to consider certain probabilities . . . To descry certain possibilities makes a man restless . . .

It seemed as though in the love affair between Eleni and her lover certain minor secrets had been preserved for the sake of their special value. In terms of meaning, preservation or retrieval, a photograph, a completely different photograph, must have been reconstructed with all its associations; not only to bring it back to life but to build a legacy to a life to which she attached a meaning, reserving for it a different place in her life, to her mother whom she had not seen after that morning of separation and who she kept alive within her heart like a human being worthy of tracing, to the path that her mother had left imprinted on her imagination. When one pours over that photograph, I cannot help but conclude that one could not have put up with that betrayal of values. Her refusal to go out even after the door had opened; her sporadic visits much later to her relatives at Kumkapı and to her old friend at Kurtuluş; to go out shopping for essential needs, especially on Christmas Eve, particularly mastic brioches at Yeşilköy or squid at the fish market at Galatasaray, these sorties gradually diminished in frequency however. Could all these things be linked to such a feeling? How could one explain her wandering about stark naked at home, her only sanctuary wherein she kept her dreams alive, utterly disregarding the possibility of being seen by her neighbors through the windows giving unto the light shaft, during those nights, when she had realized that certain chances had been lost, and the consequences of her ostracism had been duly acknowledged? Was this her way of proving to others that she could live a story which could never be penetrated or that she could live a life of her own which couldn't be watched from outside, a desire to live, even though for a brief space of time, that sense of freedom, believed to be alien to others? When one brooded over these things, one felt that the story had a tinge of mystery worthy to be inquired into . . . the things left or desired to be left in the dark . . . To believe in such things that were unearthed, in some way or another, at different times, is not so easy, after one's experiences over the course of the succeeding years. It was not for nothing that the curtains had been left drawn during those years of oppression, a thralldom she had contributed to by her own free will. Tanaş had locked his daughter up successively in different rooms. How had she survived in those rooms without being able to communicate with her father who loved her? So many questions need to be answered . . . This may have been the reason why I attached such great importance and tried to pay such close attention to those little paths lighted to a certain extent by suspicions, personal interpretations, and rumors (a consequence of my personal fallacies) among a multitude of other questions requiring answers. What Madame Roza had learned from Madame Eleni about the events of the night in which Tanaş had died seemed to shed some light on this narrow, but important path. Tanaş was suddenly taken ill some three years after the incarceration in question (however, in regard to the length of this time there is no consensus, it might have been three months, six months or eight years; since Eleni had mentioned several spans of time while discoursing on the subject). He was drunk, he had said to his daughter that he had an excruciating headache; he had announced that the end of his earthly career had come, that he felt it, and confessed that whatever he had done had been because of his love for his daughter whom he tried to keep away from the perils of life. He breathed out his last breath within a couple of hours after having asked her pardon in all sincerity and with some despondency. This breath reminded her of a flame that was about to go out. No word came out from his mouth during those couple of hours. Their hands clasped, they were trying to see those people whom they had prohibited from each other. Eleni lighted the two scented candles she had been keeping for Christmas Eve, which she observed were burning even more beautifully than she had expected. Then, she had put in her father's palm that small enameled golden heart-shaped locket without saying a word—she had not felt the need to speak. She had wanted to keep the meaning of that locket to herself, exclusively to herself. Tanaş had recognized the locket and held it tightly. Then he had slowly closed his eyes; the shiver observed on the lips had spread to his entire body before the final collapse . . . That was the first night that Eleni, after such a long time, could establish contact with the outside world by her own free will. That first night, if she so desired, she could have freely stepped outside and wandered through the streets for hours on end. She rang up her aunt. "Come, get my father!" she said. There wasn't the slightest trembling or a sign of sorrow in her voice. While she was telling Madame Roza about that night, she noted that she hadn't shed a single tear when her father died. What is more, she had refused to attend the funeral claiming that she was not supposed to go out of the house as this had been prohibited by her father. This may have been a sort of justifiable acquittal. One could understand and empathize with it. Just like her insertion into the dying man's hand of that locket; the primitive reprisals carried out on those who have inflicted pain on you. On the night of his death and during the following nights, her mind was preoccupied with her mother. Those were the nights when she yearned for her, for that woman who was far away; those were the nights when she could heartily weep, the nights when she felt her solitude deeply. On the nights that succeeded the demise of Tanaş, when the demarcation line progressed and regressed between thralldom and freedom, when that vacillation had been truly felt at the least expected moment. I feel inclined to consider that, along with the yearning felt for a lost mother, the said solitude seemed inexpressible and the loneliness in question must have been stored for the sake of new beginnings, in the secluded corners of her heart, taking into account the things I had been imparted with, not only by Roza but by others, people in whom I have confidence, regarding that long, intolerable father-daughter relationship. These judgments and assessments were open to various interpretations due to the inescapable delusional traits of the characters. Nevertheless, I must admit that, taking all misinterpretations into account, to know that in certain witnesses certain valuable data remained intact, aroused in me a joy of a quite different proportion, one of faint hope.

Certain things that cannot be put into words, things that are always expressed with certain missing points, things we cannot and would not call by name . . . The efforts I had been spending inserting into this story what had been recounted years later by one of the rare people who knew Tanaş relatively well, Muammer Bey, must have had its origin in that fascination that these confidential renderings had aroused in me . . . Tanaş's devotion to his daughter could be defined as an earnestness with a zeal rarely encountered. It was a strange display of affection; it might perhaps be more appropriate to call it a passion. You may call it the affection that every father feels for his daughter, but this was not the case. Muammer Bey had once sadly called it an unusual attachment, a sadness that had a touch of a smile. That description reflected some of the meanings the smile in question generated in me. "I believe that he had gone on living merely for his daughter's sake after he had been forsaken by his wife. He ran a small delicatessen somewhere in Karaköy, near Perşembe Pazarı, to the best of my knowledge. Once I myself had been a regular customer of his. Whenever my path took me there . . . many years ago, ages back . . . It seems to me that I did my utmost to shun that district of Istanbul, to obliterate it from my mind, eventually consigning it to oblivion. If I tax my memory, certain reminiscences surge in the mist of the past and I seem to visualize Tanaş who never failed to cut an unassuming figure in his shop to which he repaired every morning in the early hours . . . and then to certain corners near the subway . . . only a few details though . . . Who knows where those people of the neighborhood are now and can they even recall anything about that small delicatessen? There were a host of people who lined up to buy sandwiches at noon. The delicatessen had its regulars. As a matter fact, Tanaş knew who would buy what and when. Friday evenings were a hectic time, the time when Jewish customers called to stock up on victuals for the weekend. Salami, peppery sheep cheese, a little butter, a little anchovy, a little pastırma, a few green olives, a few slices of salted tunny, some smoked mullet, and for customers who were slightly richer, dried and smoked roe of the gray mullet called *abudaraho*. Tanaş enjoyed a refined appreciation of such subtleties. The word abudaraho had always caused laughter in me. I could not trace the origin of it. I ventured to make an inquiry as to its etymology and asked the people I knew from chance encounters and our neighbors, but to no avail. These people were not interested in such academic issues; their interests lay elsewhere, namely in tangible and factual things. The roe was delicious and went well with rye bread and was called abudaraho, that was enough, no need to inquire about it any further. This may have been a knock-on effect, or a lack of far-sightedness or of being mindful of uncertain contingencies. I had so many experiences with those people without losing track of the abudaraho. Fooleries, fun and games, pranks, sports, and larks were never lacking, these contributed to our well-being. A neighbor by the name of Moses Abudaram had a perfumery at Tahtakale where he eked out a living. He sold the *eau de cologne* he produced himself. His shop with its creaking floor and faded ceiling, a derelict building bearing signs of decay in all of its pores had a peculiar smell of its own. Whenever I called at his shop to buy *eau de cologne*, he took me to the famous meatball restaurant where he described to me in detail how he concocted his product, the ingredients and the special components making up the composition other than those known to everyone; the method of converting the pure alcohol into eighty-per-cent alcohol, the exact quantity of spirit he used, the exact time it took in letting the solution rest were narrated minutely. His description was interspersed with accounts of the happenings in other perfume shops. How, and from which sources, had he come by this documentary information? What was the origin of his meticulous, sensitive style which demanded attitude in matters of taste and of the great importance he attached to the story of his production? These questions have remained unanswered to this day. It was a mystery. He had mentioned once a paternal uncle, a talented painter, who, after spending considerable time in this profession, had become an alcoholic caused by an unrequited love and who was stabbed to death by the brother of the girl he had been in love with. His uncle had made a portrait of the girl from a distance, unbeknownst to her, drawing her image through his window whenever she passed by. He said he had the portrait in his possession and that he would show it to me one day. This was the only unifying element between them. However, the subject in question had been mentioned only once and that was the end of it. I never saw that portrait which was no doubt consigned to oblivion. You know what, I sometimes think that no matter what we do, we cannot escape our fate, nor can we succeed in attaining the things we pursue. One day, Moses was deceived into getting involved in contraband. He realized that he had bitten off more than he could chew. He barely escaped without getting caught. Having smelled a rat, he left with his family for Israel. Before leaving he said: "We are weighing anchor for an unknown destination; we are fated to assume a new identity elsewhere. Who knows what the future will bring. There may be no return, who can tell! Henceforward, everybody will get old in his own den!" A poetic expression of his thoughts, like living one's own life haphazardly in a poem . . . Notwithstanding, he did come back a couple years ago, after thirty odd years. We ran across each other at the arcade quite by chance. His speech was interspersed with Hebrew words. "Thank Heaven we're all right!" he said. He had had difficult times. He had married off his daughter with another *emigré* from Istanbul; he considered all foreign suitors ineligible. After trying his chance in freelance work, he had been engaged as a security guard in a bank, from which position he had retired and was now on a pension. I spoke to him about myself, about my collection of postcards and about the postcards that contained New Year greetings written in Armenian and sent to Paris. You may remember I had sent the same postcard to you. It had church bells on it? It was as though it had been seeking its place, its man, among the old gramophone records, padlocks and key holders displayed at the counters of Şerafettin Bey who still went to his small shop of secondhand articles at the flea market at Kadıköy, clad in his ancient costume, wearing the same old shirts and neckties he wore during his employment at the Railway Company. Actually, it was nothing special, except that the note on it was in Armenian. It had given rise to a funny feeling in me for no plausible reason. Şerafettin Bey could not remember how and when he had come by it. In fact, it was his custom to forget all that came into his shop. He did his best to forget all about the sellers of odds and ends. "Were I to remember their original owners, it would be difficult for me to dispose of them so easily," he used to say. He had to eke out a living; he worked hard in order to be able to secure better living conditions for his daughter's child who was serving a prison sentence for an intellectual offence and to add a few cents to his retirement pension. He had made me a gift of that postcard. It was a fact that we knew the story of each other's lives; we both shared accurate insights into certain things. What was written on the postcard was a mystery to him as well; he also must have had puzzling questions to which he could not provide an answer. Some people lead eccentric lives, don't they? They have their own idiosyncrasies; they have an eye for detail. However, I was determined to find out more about that inscription. So, I had recourse to Hatchik, the shoe repairer; the postcard bore on it an address in Paris. Hatchik cast a glance at it and immediately said: "It is in a woman's handwriting." The inscription was imbued with nostalgia. It read: "How cruel it is, to be obliged to celebrate Christmas without you . . . Who are the people you get together with there? I'm the same as ever; sad and dejected . . . " I remember it exactly. You must also recollect it, don't you? I'm telling it once more just because I know you'd like me to recall that memory. It also pleased Moses. He said: "The woman must've abandoned a lover in Paris. She knows that she ought to go to him but cannot afford it; pity . . . " he added: "Or it may be that the man had run away . . . to end that love affair . . . He just couldn't wait apparently. The woman may have married someone else. You think so?" After a moment's indecision he had put the following question to me: "Why on earth should a postcard sent to Paris, be in Istanbul now?" Moses was such a man, a man who would not delay in probing such mysteries. He shared with me the urge for reflecting and displaying curiosity, especially about the affairs of others. This, I think, was what had drawn us to each other; unconsciously sharing the same outlook on life and deriving pleasure from it . . . He had also asked me whether I still played the zither. He was ruminating on our revelries. "Now and then, when I'm in the mood," had been my answer. Actually, I had not touched the instrument after a certain incident. We had lost track of our positions in the conversation. Moreover, he would be dispirited to learn about it. So I had given it a miss. Sometimes, observing silence in certain matters saved the day, certain hours at least . . . We stood around making small talk. We were unwilling to part. Nevertheless, each of us had to go his own way and see certain individuals; this reality we could not shun even though it played on us. "Life has dispersed us in all directions," I said. He had grown pensive. "We've been cast away, but our spirit has remained here, all the same. We wanted to have another glimpse at our past. We could treat ourselves to a meal on the banks of the Bosporus, and see a stage play. Yet, everything seems to have undergone transformation. The old theater has burnt down and sunk into oblivion; very few things have survived to this day. Well, after all, even we have waxed and waned, haven't we?" he said. After a while, he added: "It's been five years now since Rachael passed away. I live together with a woman; but I have no intention to marry her, I took an oath not to marry again. She is not one of us anyhow. Women prattle on and on, I've had enough of idle gossip. My daughter insists that I should marry. She says that marriage will put my life in order. Life has reduced us to order already, has it not? Nothing is left that requires new arrangement. She wants me to go and live with her in her house so that the flat we live in can be relieved of our burden. That was not what we had planned at the time. Yet, that's life! Not easy to cope with! The woman with whom I'm sharing my bed at present would be only too glad to be hitched. But I'll not hear of it! No! She may leave me if she wants to. I'm not hen pecked! There's no scarcity of women in the world. We can do without them, you know! My marriage with Rachael was the outcome of a passionate love. Her family was of modest means. I'd not asked for any dowry from her family, for which my father and my uncle had reproached me. But we survived to see this very day, haven't we, Muammer?" I knew perfectly well that the dowry that a Jewish girl was expected to bring in holy wedlock was of paramount importance. Before we parted, I asked him: "Tell me, that name, abudaraho, is it in any way related to your family name?" "Idiot!" he retorted. "Had we been sellers of abudaraho, would we be in such a plight today?" Moses had his own fantasies about becoming rich like any other Jew leading a modest life. This was a confidential dream; a fantasy that converted the losers of this war into philosophers in their own right as they advanced in age. I deem the consequences of such fancies wholly justifiable . . . But enough of this, before we digress any further. Where had we been a while ago and where are we now? From the abudaraho of Tanaş to Moses Abudaram . . . I have been prattling on as usual, I know, but I wanted to introduce you to my old friend. The thing is that this little story will be of benefit to you someday, I'm certain. When we are gone . . . Now, back to the matter at hand: Tanaş! He was a wonderful talker, son of a bitch! When he was in the mood and commented on the politics of the day he exhibited a mind full of wit and wisdom. He had a rich store of anecdotes, mostly salacious. He had no self-restraint. If he felt like it, he just told it regardless of the milieu in which he happened to be and of the audience, using the exact words, without reverting to euphemisms and prevarications. He had the vice of scoffing at his customers; those that were simple souls, making sure they did not get to the bottom of it. He used to tell cock-and-bull stories about the delectable snacks he himself prepared. This always put a smile on his face and those of his friends. There were also times when he happened to be at his wits' end. We immediately realized that he preferred to be left alone at such times. His petulance must have had its origin in what was going on at home. This temper of his may have been due, not only to disagreements going on at home, but dashed hopes as well. If he confessed that he had confined Eleni, his own daughter, to home on the grounds that he could not bear to see her abandoned for a second time, the matter might have been settled. Nevertheless, Tanaş had a face he preferred to keep veiled. We could never learn exactly what had been going on at home before he died. What we were imparted with after he died can never be verified of course as the things that were supposed to have taken place did not go beyond speculation. Thus, we shall never be able to decide our position versus this narration. Funny, isn't it, not to be able to have access to the mysteries that enveloped a man so near to us? What still puzzles me is the reason why he preferred to remain so enigmatic; this sense of mystery gave him a terrific air. He gave the impression as though a deep-seated feeling within him drove him to act in this manner, a feeling whose depths we could never fathom. He passed away without disclosing his secret. Whenever we asked about Eleni, he used to say that she was all right in Greece with her mother, that she regularly wrote to him and would soon return. Basing on the contents of her imaginary letters, he used to tell stories about her. Apparently she had a life of her own there. A life concocted for our benefit, for us or for those that kept distant from her. This served to conceal her true story, of which Eleni had no inkling. The door of that house opened inward to another life; she had resigned herself to this life which she tried to carry on.

That was the evening that Muammer Bey tried to inculcate into my memory certain additional information, for the benefit of certain individuals, about things that he wanted acknowledged in relation to certain events. Among the knowledge communicated to me were nuggets of information—part of a long story narrated with words that illustrated the situation vividly—told with a wry countenance inspired by those moments as they were experienced. These words and representations would continue to impregnate certain people; ultimately joining other real life episodes in the same bed . . .

Many years went by. That small talk we had that evening, during which Eleni's story was narrated to me, was henceforth of historical interest. After such a long time, based on my impression gained from the bits of information and clues obtained, it now and then occurs to me that there might have been an incestuous relationship between father and daughter, although it is not easy to say for certain, a relationship that cannot be defined as mere passion. Those that had preferred to stay detached from it could not possibly have formulated a judgment as they had not had any access to the said relationship at close range—a relationship that gained added meaning due to the consequences of loneliness, defeat and wrath—to arrive at a conclusion where the rainbow ended. On this arduous path I had, with some dismay, to muddle through with great difficulty. The story had a magic effect that took one away to far away places not easily definable. I felt obliged to dwell on certain details that provided new insights into the matter, in support of certain gnawing doubts. I had to decipher the meaning behind every word and expression: original, ambiguous and hidden meanings; in the expectation of having a clearer insight into what might have been experienced beyond those distant boundaries. The officer that had absconded, leaving no trace behind, might have been the hero of an imaginary story of escape concocted to keep up appearances. How else could that separation have so easily been accepted into their lives? Could there be any other plausible reason for Madame Eleni's going about naked indoors? As far as I can remember, none of the people who would be in a position to provide satisfactory answers, from differing angles, are still alive. A mere vision, yes, a mere vision gives one a hint all the same, despite the lack of irrefutable proof and further excogitation. I owe this vision to Hüsnü who had made me a gift of it, when I had gone to that flat in search of missing links in certain stories I was imparted with, many years before, when a mass of people had shared innumerable relationships each of which was a story in itself. Men, streets, other lives lived elsewhere, there were so many obstacles that separated that time and space. Hüsnü had aged appropriately; his hair had turned gray, his cheeks had sunken and his voice trembled. He looked like a distant relative of that man that the residents of the block sent out on errands every other minute. I felt restless, and was on edge. I must say I was prey to apprehension; I was afraid of the person I had left behind. Hüsnü had smiled as though he had heard and saw that person. He had put his hand on my shoulder without even saying "good morning," as though I had been there only yesterday. "Come, let's have a cup of tea," he said, "there is some fresh tea in the kettle." A renewed acquaintance, a renewed familiarity . . . I was no stranger to such encounters: with the people we kept company with once or with those who were heading for those places, those who walked along in that long tale with us. The furniture had undergone no change; they were at their wonted places, the sole items of remembrance in that small apartment. They were the silent witnesses of tussles and separations. Hüsnü had described what he had witnessed to the extent time permitted. His younger daughter was married into a family living in Zonguldak and had given birth to two children;

she had to resign herself to her fate, living on the modest sum of her husband who worked in the coal mines and was filled with fear. Her companions were now of a totally different social class. Her son had gone to Germany where he had found employment, first as a student, then as an unlicensed worker before marrying a Turkish woman of German nationality from Hamburg who was older than him, with two children, whose stabbing he had served a prison sentence for. After serving his sentence, he had been involved in illicit transactions and his name had ceased to be heard of. Everyone had gone his or her own way. Hüsnü happened to be alone for a time. His wife had forsaken him as she had deemed that it would be better for him to go back home to Erzincan after all that had passed. However, he had learned how to take care of himself. As a matter of fact, he felt, at times, quite at home in his solitude. He had no expectations; life seemed dull to him. The absence of Şükran had worn him out over time and chased him away from his healthier days. He was suffering from a sort of shrinkage that he made a point of keeping a secret. He had read of his daughter's murder in the newspapers, like the rest of us; one morning, no different from any other morning that dawned on those streets, at a moment hardly expected either by us or by others, we were mere spectators of the incident. First he had paid a visit to the hotel, then had repaired to the mortuary; afterward, in the course of the following days he sought clues to the extent his means permitted, looking for witnesses who he thought should have seen the incident, for he believed there were witnesses hiding somewhere, witnesses he had not caught sight of or had failed to reach . . . He was seeking to open new doors to his daughter's murder . . . to recapture the scene in which his daughter had been stolen from him . . . to embrace his daughter more tightly than ever before. To whom could he describe the despair he experienced when he had embraced his daughter's frozen body, the heat that assailed him . . . to whom and with what words . . . with which feelings of remorse? I knew the answer to this question; as a matter of fact everybody knew. To see him was to see a specter . . . This may have been the reason why he had held his daughter's still body in his arms so tightly, so strongly, to compensate for time lost, for all that he had lost for good, for his failures in doing so in the past, during the nights they had shared . . . He was looking to hold onto her life, yet he was grasping at it. However, barring the failures and that which was unattainable, that very moment belonged to them alone, to him and his daughter. Even though it was too late to save face, the moment belonged to him and to his daughter.

Back to our story now . . . When one broods over what has been experienced, over the cherished hopes, the betrayal, the solitude and the murder, one is inclined to conclude that, after all, they were all platitudes, and the whole thing was but the story of victims dragged toward that place, to those streets and alleys lined with huge buildings, frequented by masses of people that must belong somewhere, floodlit by those alien night lights letting visions leak out from the rooms of those who had found their sanctuaries, visions released without let or hindrance in a city which may have assumed the aspect of a monster for those that had remained in her streets, in the offing; the story of a journey in which the victim shared the same fate as his executioner, in which even the executioner was transformed into a victim. The driver had actually deceived himself when he had imposed on Şükran (to whom he was devoutly attached) that dreamworld which was never to be realized. Both were bunglers in fact, they had not properly acted that play on the stage. It seemed that they pursued a utopian dream: to be able to run a boarding house in the south, in a small town, where the sun would shower its rays upon them . . . Şükran worked as a prostitute in order to be able to collect enough funds to one day live this fairy tale . . . To collect enough funds to be able to escape, to escape far, far away . . . However, just as their dream seemed to be approaching, she realized that she had been deceived; it was a deception to which she had to resign herself in order to brace herself for what life had in store for them; like taking refuge in a lie . . . They need money in order to settle the gambling debts and to pay for the drug habits of Şükran's lover, already a lost cause. They were fully mindful of this bare fact: yet this did not prevent them from continuing to build castles in the sky. There was no end to the number of people who wanted to take the road out of town . . . The play was destined to remain in its embryonic stages despite Şükran's sustained efforts and perseverance. It was enacted before it was ready to be put on stage; the protagonists had, step by step, arranged for each other's death as they journeyed toward their happy ever after. The story was, like all true love stories, a pathetic one, difficult to live with. Hüsnü had been able to see the scenes for what they were through the eyewitnesses he had contacted following his daughter's death. What he had learned had been painful enough, but he had exercised restraint. He had simply grieved for her, for his daughter: he mourned for those who had played a part in his daughter's story as well as for those who had abstained from doing so; he lamented his failure in being a better father to her. It was a feeling of delayed action rather than remorse. As he was wading around, remembering those difficult times in his daughter's life, he thought that he should've had a part to play while the play was being enacted. In those difficult times, even though he knew full well that he could not change the hard facts of life . . . Just to hold the small hands of his daughter in his own and warm up her small feet by rubbing them during those troubled nights like in the old days . . . to be able to relive those moments . . . Most likely this had been the reason for his discontent . . . This may have been the reason why he had wanted to explain away her infamous story, by reclaiming her, consigning it to oblivion. "She was my angel, my first love," he used to say with such pathos. "Were we to be blamed for it or for them? I don't know. Nor can you. Anyhow, Şükran had been the ultimate victim," he had affirmed afterward. To whom did the personal pronouns 'we' and 'them' refer? This question harps on my mind even today, after a lapse of ten years. Every time new possibilities crop up. One thing was certain though, it was a latent rebellion; but against whom? Could it be against those who had made a gift of this world to those inexperienced actors, or against those who could not afford to relinquish the world than those who desired it? Who knows? In total disregard of errors and deceptions, in spite of everything, the show had to go on. He had also said to his wife that he intended to go on living for some time yet in the den he had been occupying before going to Erzincan. He said that people's dreams had failed to materialize in this city. "All those I came to know have left to build blocks of flats here and there. I spent what I earned for my children, for their education. To no avail! It was not fated!" This sentence reflected his disillusion. I tried to have a glimpse of the faces he concealed. These words have remained in my mind to this day because of this. Hüsnü attached great importance to education. This peculiarity distinguished him from those who had emigrated to the metropolis in pursuit of other ends, at least from those I had come to know, and had an insight into. He perused the newspapers with great voracity. This habit had earned him the nickname of *fainéant*. He was aware of this, of the wrong impression he had made on the people around him. To be aware of it was one thing, to let it bother you was another. It had never occurred to him to mend his ways to satisfy the wishes of his peers. This self-assuredness had a special appeal to me. His true efforts were somewhere else, in an indefinable spot; it seemed that a lot of effort had gone into another person, into an unidentifiable person. However, the important thing for me was the comments he made on the political developments of the day, comments that no soul could ever replicate. If one takes all this into consideration, one should visualize him as a hero of fiction. But to convince people in this respect and make it acceptable as such in their eyes was well nigh impossible. So many people had been conditioned to see others only by their social front, façade or mark that an individual assumed to depict to the world at large to indicate the role they were playing in it . . . It was not so easy to imagine that someone like Hüsnü lived by those rules. The number of people who would be willing to see him in his true light would not be many. This factor may have played a part in his loss of confidence as the years went by. The Hüsnü that I encountered years later was not the same Hüsnü, the interpreter of those strange episodes. He had abandoned his quick and ready wit at perceiving and express-ing amusing points of view and of intellectually entertaining congruities and incongruities; the wit had been abandoned once and for all, buried in the places he no longer wanted to see. All that he desired now was to be able to spend the rest of his life in his village; the place that he was convinced would embrace him with all its warmth, his authentic birthplace. His native land was calling to him. The small flat where he had spent his years would accommodate other tenants. The residents of the block were being evicted as it was to be renovated and turned into a new modern building with all the amenities that such construction en-tailed, including central heating. The new landlords had asked him to vacate his flat. The other tenants were to follow suit. The residents vacated the premises in their own fashion, in order to make way for other apartments whose boundaries cannot be so easily defined, for other lives gaining meaning from expectations continually refurbished . . . "Well, we did live after all, didn't we? We are being scattered now," said Hüsnü. He thought that they had been condemned to live, that the life they led was a live history that had been sentenced to be prolonged in another part of the city. He had a store of knowledge about the residents of that block for those who cared to listen. But the Hüsnü I had seen that day ap-peared to have lost confidence in such people. Therefore he seemed willing to take that intelligence with him. This was his latent and effective rebellion . . . to be parsimonious, or to choose to be so, to transfer many aspects of people's pasts to third parties . . . Thus the impression that Hüsnü gave me that day was a feel-ing that warranted justification . . . to keep for oneself one's recollections and the recollections of other people. The same held true for Madame Eleni who stoi-cally accepted her experiences like someone conscious of her position. She remembered well the fact that one had to step over to the other side of life to be a firm believer in it. She had been the person who had seen that woman for the last time. It had been almost three years. Those were the days when she went out to work every morning as the established order required, when nobody had an inkling of the disaster, thinking that everything was as it should be and about which there was not the slightest doubt. She had knocked on her door but no answer had come. As the same undertaking had been repeated three days in succession without result, she had sent for Uncle Ibrahim, the locksmith, and the door was opened. Uncle Ibrahim was a former burglar who had had vast experience in the business over many years. He had a mine of information related to the residences in question. Telling his adventures had become a part of his life. It was his custom to steal only certain things, as he was particular and selective about his choice. He specialized in silver objects. As a matter of fact, he had stolen only silverware, of which he was proud. This had to do, I believe, with some childhood reminiscences, which, as far as I know, he had told to no one and which he could not bring himself to disclose. In the end, one day, he got caught; this was a sort of abnegation as he had been his own informer—the consequence that an association with a certain candy box had made in his mind. This had persuaded him that he had to put an end to his practice; upon which he had contrived to get caught and to be convicted to many years behind bars. During his term of imprisonment he had read many books, reading whatever he could get hold of and trying to understand their contents. He had eventually concluded that what had been of towering importance to him had been merely breaking into houses just to see their contents, to contemplate the silverware rather than to pinch it. By the time he was released, he had reached his sixtieth year. Only then did he realize that not getting married or having children had been the greatest error in his life. The first thing he wanted to do was to visit the old quarter of his childhood and to see its inhabitants, the streets that had paved the way to his illegal practices. However, he could not bring himself to fit the words to the action. He thought that it would be advisable to spend the rest of his life in a different quarter of Istanbul, in a different setting. Being conscious of his hopeless obsession to break into houses, it occurred to him to practice the trade of a locksmith. He had much experience in the trade . . . That was all he had to say. "There can be no door that can challenge my skill," claimed Uncle İbrahim. So far he had been successful in opening all the doors that people had asked him to open. As for what lay beyond the doors . . . The points that remained a mystery for the rest of us in his story had to be lived by him. That was my conviction. When I brood over what he must have felt upon breaking into houses, it seems to me that what was of particular importance to him was his experience when he was about to cross the threshold. The whole thing boiled down to a few steps . . . But these were different from normal steps. What Uncle Ibrahim told Hüsnü about what he said as he entered Madame Eleni's premises did not surprise me. The first comment Uncle İbrahim had made was: "A deathly silence!" His comment was actually corroborated by the overpowering stench. The stark reality presented itself after a few seconds. Madame Eleni, smartly dressed, was sitting motionless in her favorite armchair in the drawing-room where she had spent her entire life; her hand was supporting her temple. In her lap was a bag that contained photographs, shiny shoes, a red dress and a heart-shaped medallion. He immediately rushed to Madame Susan. They sent for a doctor who did not delay in coming; the doctor examined Madame Eleni with the utmost diligence, like an antiquarian examining an old vase, and pronounced the cause of her death: heart attack! At first, they were at a loss as to whom the incident should be reported. Nobody knew the people she visited during the latter part of her life. She struck them as someone who was utterly alone in life, a homeless person. Homelessness was Madame Eleni's home. When one goes over what had been experienced, home was the last thing to think of; yet daily life produces certain labels nonetheless. This was the *raison d'être* of one's later acquaintances. By the mediation of Madame Susan, the ecclesiastical authorities were informed, who then had assumed the service of an undertaker and the charge of vacating the premises. I had already tried to tell you about such great divides. From a story dating from the deluge I well remember the sympathies and empathies expressed by neighbors at the sight of her death. The fact that she was smartly dressed on the threshold of falling into everlasting sleep is understandable under the circumstances. The difference lay, however, in that bag on her lap. It was a sign of a person who had had many years to live, of a person that had perfect confidence in an afterlife beyond the terrestrial sphere. One wonders whether certain encounters might not occur sooner or later to those of us left behind. Should one conclude then that those passions and loves remain imperishable, that they are more often than not companions to death, that, even though they are fed by lies, a time will come when they will act as clarion calls that cannot be left unanswered? How important is this anyhow? Such questions required moral courage to inquire into what had been left behind . . . the remorse one felt for one's short-comings when one took cognizance of the delay in having taken certain steps and refrained from making certain sacrifices. I myself had experienced such shortcomings; I had been obliged to carry with me people from places I did not want to remember. This should be the reason for our desire to reproduce certain stories in ourselves while sharing them with others. The passions we were arbitrarily obliged to give up, to abase and leave unrealized, were compensated by the figment of our imagination destined in time to be turned into a hell. At such times our lies were transformed into facts, nay, into realities.

3

Falsehood and truth, solitude holding sway in depths, great depths . . . Where can we place, in the order of things we believe unassailable, the people we have abandoned to death and extinction, because of our failure in appreciating differences and in displaying the required generosity through evasion and apathy? From where do we expect them to seek us out? Madame Eleni's cloudy story, which one day I believe I'll be able to have a better insight into and narrate in a different vein, is one of those stories likely to generate such questions. We were compelled to proceed on, with greater empathy and tolerance, in order to understand the meaning certain words, colors and scents bequeathed us. Over time . . . as we came to know human beings better and better . . . by grafting the value of certain moments onto other moments . . . Can I explain my mandatory journeys to those moments, my recollection of Anita—who I want to believe is at this very moment carrying on her existence in a different country—at a time I'm ready to share with so many people so many stories, empathizing with so many different people? Perhaps I can. What I know for sure at this juncture is that it was a question of bad timing, and that a meeting had not taken place. Exactly who and what had I been shunning? What had prevented me from correctly understanding what Anita had in store for me during our brief encounters? Anita who comes to me with looks full of despair from such distant realms, as a heroine of an incredible and unacceptable father-daughter relationship, as though desiring to impart to me certain things that remained untold to that point . . . Now, I may recall that wall that other people raised between us with their defying looks, posing an insurmountable obstacle to our gaining ground toward understanding our fellow human beings . . . to describe or define that wall has never been easy . . . to offer a logical explanation as to the real causes of our avoidance of those people toward whom we were supposed to advance . . . What we appeared as afterwards was seen as a kind of egotism, but at the same time a self-defense against the scorching effect of that inferno, of our inferno; taking refuge from the world of those who knew you to be different. That was another variant of evil, certainly . . . another variant of evil . . . One cannot deny the existence of certain relationships, with all their consequences, to which one would have liked to do away with, despite your best intentions, with evasions and betrayals. You are chased by moments that make you encounter that shadow you had been trying to evade, at a spot you hardly expected. At such times you cannot even confess to yourself how and when you were involved in such relationships and who exactly was implicated; years must go by and one must have many years of experience with the people in question, having suffered the consequences and inevitable remorse entailed before one can comprehend the nature of the relationship one had and the character of the people with whom one had been involved with. These are the moments when one takes stock of the memories created in you at the least expected moment by what you had failed and not dared to experience in life. Moments of inevitable transition from one story to another, stories that one believes to be forgotten . . . The fact that I remembered the evening concerts at the Technical University—conjured up by images lingering in my mind of the two aforementioned individuals who strove to carry throughout their lifetime the burden of their oppression and solitude thanks to certain items—each of which was conducive to a new story that leaked out through visions that have become hazy, may perhaps be explained by tracking the origins of what has been left over in us from certain experiences. Those were the evenings when I was obliged to view certain relationships from a distance. Who had been the original owners of those school desks, who had listened to the lessons taught in the classrooms, who did the corridors that ran down the building belong to, the bedsteads, the Saturday evenings, the night lights? To be able to provide answers to these questions, I had the wild expectations of my imagination. Those were the evenings when I was obliged to view things from a distance . . . the evenings when I tried to find out those limited areas wherein I could take refuge and view certain individuals through false screens, in garbs they would never actually wear, vested in false regalia merely for the sake of not losing touch; the evenings I lived more passionately by postponements than I do today . . . those evenings when Aunt Tilda in her bizarre attire approached me asking how I was, when she acted out that game of bliss, when she frequented concerts for the sole purpose of breathing the atmosphere of the foyer, seen through her eyes as a genuine stage, rather than a place to listen to the performance or stare at the audience like most of the occupants of the stalls did, where she greeted everyone and pretended as if she knew everybody, where she showed off her knowledge of French, where she made as if she paid no attention or took no notice of her being taxed with the attribute of 'loony', or where I wanted more than ever to beat a hasty retreat to that island within me which was getting bigger and bigger but seemed to be so distant. I wonder whether Anita, who had emerged before me one of those evenings at the least expected moment, had also experienced this warmth and transported it to another evening. Whether those awe inspiring looks were the harbinger of a journey or of being dragged along, I was unable to figure out at the time. It was during an interval that Aunt Tilda, who in her habitual garrulousness talked to a group of people; as far as I could gather from what I overheard through the din she opined that the Polish pianist had played with remarkable agility, commenting however that his dark costume had seemed to be rather outlandish, and that he ought to have put on a frock coat, failing that, a tuxedo. The people she was addressing were a couple who gave the impression that they had been together their entire life. They were aged and seemed that they had chosen to freeze their respective lives at a spot they had decided upon. They had been successful in bringing to a conclusion a life spent in unison. Aunt Tilda was, or at least seemed to be, content despite the reactions of the individuals to whom she was talking. She was acting out. She had found her spectators to feign interest only for a brief moment . . . A faint smile flickered across their faces as though they were listening to her; their occasional evasive looks seemed to suggest that they were searching for old acquaintances fitting their status and social position. It was an evening when snow had begun falling before the start of the performance. At the end of the concert the city had assumed another aspect. The entire city was under heavy snow. It gave one the impression of being a traveler who had crossed a vast land and found himself in new territory. The crisp snow crunched as I walked through it slowly from Maçka to Şişli, absorbing the silence that was characteristic of snow. A simple joy had filled me. I was the small child who frolicked in the snow-covered fields. In addition to this magical transformation caused by the snow, Anita, who had broken in upon my life at an unexpected moment and whose looks are indelibly stored in my memory as though she had foreseen that she would leave deep traces in my mind, had her share in this feeling also. The snapshots representing that concert interval will never be forgotten and will always jog my memory, reminding me of Aunt Tilda. Aunt Tilda who still went on acting out her scenes of bliss, still stylish, and who must be wandering somewhere far removed from here, from the place where she once rambled in deserted streets with a pair of socks, wearing an old overcoat in rags, with disheveled white hair, reminding me of the days and nights when she used to share the same house with Monsieur Robert; photographs representing them together, each being the embodiment of the other . . .

Bertie and Juliet also were there . . . They were in the company of a middle-aged man and a young reserved girl with dark hair. Actually I would have preferred to greet them from a distance, but Juliet, who understood my loneliness better than anyone else, had insisted through a gesture that I join them. She seemed to imply that she was in the company of people of no great importance. That was not difficult to guess. We had a bond between us as a consequence of our converging paths, steps we shared with mutual empathy. I could not refuse her call. We had talked about our impressions of the recital, trivial loquacity, in the usual manner. We were trying to find small shields for our differing solitudes . . . Then, we had been introduced. "Anita, our sweet girl," said Juliet taking the arm of the young girl. The middle-aged man was her father. I was being introduced to friends of Juliet and Berti, whom they had never mentioned before, but who seemed to be their intimate friends. Anita had a sort of attraction that made one restless. To have known her meant taking a step in the direction of an enigmatic story that had a magical appeal, replete with mysteries. It looked as though she wanted to say, to convey, something. I am still at a loss how to exactly define my feelings at the time. I think her looks had stiffened me. I had apprehensions. I had misgivings. Anita looked like the heroine of a dream with her long wavy hair, large, dark eyes and full red lips. The magic had slowly begun to work. She had shaken my hand, squeezing it for a good while. I was to penetrate the meaning of this handshake years later. Years later when I had had the same experience with other people in different circumstances . . . There was another conversation going on in the depths beneath the words exchanged that seemed to be going nowhere. We had to revert to the question of the recital in one way or another.

There was something in Chopin's music that disquieted me despite my efforts to the contrary. There was a small detail that I could not define exactly. "You are wrong," she said with a tremulous voice, "you are unfair. He was a very unhappy person." To which I could give no answer, but had simply smiled. Those were the years when I could not naturally rid certain shortcomings of mine with spontaneity without feeling a sense of inferiority, as was the case with the handling of my indignation which I should have repressed or expressed at the right time depending on the situation.

Then we had parted to resume our seats . . . Juliet had invited me to her house as usual to which I had answered favorably. A small lie had joined us once more; it was a lie we both shared . . . The lie was in fact the correct mode of the day, the right thing to do . . . Moments that would have changed the course of our lives had not been lived as of yet. Those were the times when those steps were still a mystery to us. They were the steps that were taken within us first, the steps that would have contributed a great deal to our way of life. This is the case with the unforgettable relationships that make us what we actually are.

Chopin's works were again to be played in the second part of the program. As I gazed around, I saw Anita who happened to be two rows behind. She was looking straight at me. How could I foresee that her stare would remain fixed within me for many years to come? The years would elapse, yet her stare would remain as a vague invitation, an invitation marked with regret. Our looks crossed once more after the recital. Something had happened between us that caused alien things to be stirred within me, emerging from an unconventional place . . . This must have been the beginning of a relationship that one comes across only once in a while . . . An unexpected visitor would shake the very roots of everything . . . This was a relationship that would bring along with it death—the point of no return . . . for the sake of a life beyond death. Those looks seemed to conceal despair, hopelessness difficult to describe, a sort of liberation from life, an effort to hold on to somebody . . . to give up one life for another . . . For what reason? We were enthralled by so many relationships we could not properly experience because of the obstacles raised by the feelings that we were unable to probe into and properly define, enthralled by an anxiety which held the caption of "If only I knew" . . . In order that I could understand properly what was being conveyed to me by this cryptic and special dialogue, I needed to be able to feel the new words and sounds, and, last but not least, the audience. Did the rest consist merely of a feeling I would be nourishing in my depths and whose meanings would be lingering within me for years to come? I doubt it. The power of Anita's looks had been supplemented by an uneasiness generated by the inevitable emergence of a characteristic of hers which I had not taken notice of when we had been first introduced to each other. This was caused I think by the fact that one of her legs was shorter than the other . . . That's all I could distinguish at the time. As we went out I saw her glance at or toward me, on her father's arm, through the crowd. I had smiled in return. I believe I had tried to convey to her my desire to see her again. It was a kind of promise. She had gotten the message, I believed. Had it been otherwise I could not have carried within me the effect those looks had. Now I am trying to understand and untangle the other feelings that had caused that smile on my lips. Had I been affected, for instance, by her limping? It is easy to give a negative answer to this question and deny certain undeniable facts. To feel the need to speak about this detail after so many years reveals something I've been concealing. Those individuals and their respective distinctions that call to us . . . I had already tried to empathize once to someone the pain generated by a story that began with the aforementioned words. There were stories that paved the way to each other and stories that always reverted to the same theme . . . Some people had the talent to spin through numerous stories while certain words assumed new meanings all the time. However, you realized that in that peregrination it was yourself that you had been looking for all along. You were haunted by those visions because of this . . . This was the reason why you wished to go back to certain nights and certain breakfasts.

In Anita's story one could perceive the presence of a good many stories stored in my memory. I think I was prepared, better than most, to identify distinctions. This preparedness assisted me in understanding the path that led there, to those individuals, who were more than willing to lend an ear. This was the reason why I had the premonition that a day would come that I would see Anita once more. The episode could not have come to an end before it began. I had a fatalistic side I could not get rid of despite my best efforts, a trait which I tried to keep alive nonetheless . . . It ensured that one should wait and know how to wait.

Two years had passed before I realized that I could not leave Anita's memory there at the night of the recital, that my feelings had not misled me. I encountered her on a sad wedding night I would be fain to tell someone of when the time came, with expectations of a different sort mingled with misgivings. The wedding ceremony was taking place in the halls of a residential hotel overlooking the sea in Istanbul. Yet, there was death in the air. This death had been felt by everybody that night; they had been compelled to feel it . . . I had run into her as I was sneaking out to the lobby to avoid dancing. She wasn't surprised to see me; at least she didn't appear to be. She seemed to consider this encounter a natural occurrence. That meeting was never far away for her, as a matter of fact it had always been coming. Everything was so easy, so natural . . . Had the interval of time that had passed been so brief, or were we two old friends who had shared many incidents, visions and experiences? Why not, after all? She had not thought it fitting to ask how I was and what I had been doing over the course of the last two years. It seemed as though those two years had not existed at all. There was no other time in-between. "We've come to listen to Metin," she said with a faint smile, as if she had to justify her presence there, "he's a wonderful talent." Metin was a singer who sang oldies that nobody listened to in the nightclub of that hotel to the accompaniment of a piano he played himself; sometimes, he also played the hits of the day. Songs to remember the past and to enjoy the present, not for the mere sake of entertainment, not for those who exhibit to others that they enjoy the moment, but songs meant for those who wanted to see themselves in that fictive moment as individuals who had failed to realize their dreams. What I was observing was not the Anita from the Chopin recital. Her looks seemed to have withdrawn from the world in which she lived or seemed to have lived, while the heavy makeup of her eyes had given her a grotesque appearance. Only the looks differed. Could it be that behind the apparent naturalness there lay a concealed uneasiness, regret and the effort to cover up defeat? Only years later would I be able to provide an answer to this question . . . Certain explanations were required like in many other relationships. No sooner had you touched the story concretely than you were faced with someone who was puzzling to you. You might call this a belief, a firm belief in an answer despite all that you knew yourself to be true. This question would breed another for which I could provide no answer, a question that I was to shun ever after. This encounter might have taken place at an unexpected moment, at an undesired moment probably—a belated encounter. Had it been an ephemeral source of hopefulness for Anita, this narration of events, this utterance? Maybe. However, the answer to this must have remained in the custody of Anita forever; this fact I must acknowledge at present. All that

I can remember is the fact that I had not been in a position to say all that I had wanted to say. I had been caught unawares by someone I knew all too well would occupy an important place in my life; I was at a loss to do the right thing and I feared a confrontation, a real confrontation. Had I tried to take the necessary step, would it be to any avail? The fact that up until now I have not been able to return to that moment in my mind must explain my state of despair at the time. I believe that Anita had recognized my despair, she must have sensed it. Thus, we were following parallel tracks. There are certain relationships bound to remain prohibited and proscribed despite all probabilities and longings that cannot be materialized. This was a chance to allow one to take refuge with the help of bad timing. At the least expected moment, we had come across each other once again, shaken hands and ventured to engage in a little dialogue with an exchange of looks and words, the meaning of which we would realize years later. However, this communication was restricted to a limited number of glances and words, which I still recall. Anything more than that was not possible at the time. Before we parted, she had shaken my hand, squeezing it tightly. "Aren't they pleasant, these songs?" she commented afterward. I was to learn the real truth much later, years later, from Juliet as I was about to run away from a celebration. "Anita had been sick, very sick," Juliet said. As we continued talking, I had tried to alter the course of our conversation to reflect upon those moments, and, what is more important still, to those looks, benefiting by force of circumstance from the place where we stood in the milieu. She added: "She could not satisfy her sexual hunger. She consulted psychologists and psychiatrists but without satisfactory results. Perhaps those whom she had consulted with were not the right people. You will not believe it, but her father made the supreme sacrifice at times to find for her a male partner through remuneration . . . " I cannot express what I felt at the time even today. It was a feeling similar to a person's smothered impulse to shriek into a nightmare, it was as though one wanted to take a step back but was prevented from doing so. Anita's specter wandered through me. She had the same experience; she had the same nightmare, which she had tried to convey through her looks. We were surrounded by a crowd of people whose voices we could not hear or perceive despite their proximity because of our unwillingness to leave in the first place. Our distance from those people was due perhaps to our own deportment. Their skyline was our skyline, their remoteness our remoteness and their approach our approach. "Why didn't you say so before?" I asked her, all the original, double and hidden meanings and potentialities considered. I had tried my best not to display the shattering within me. This was a kind of bringing her to account, a sort of protest, a protest against my own self in the first place . . . Juliet had recognized it. "But you didn't ask, did you?" she said. "I knew instinctually that you'd be impressed by her. As a matter of fact, the attraction proved to be mutual. You weren't apathetic toward each other, that was evident. Her sickness was not so serious at the time. A love affair might have been a cure for her; as a matter of fact, both of you were in need of it. You knew it damn well, yet you were reluctant to take the step required." After a short silence she added: "Anyhow, you wouldn't have understood this at the time even if I had told you." "You think I can now?" I asked. "True," she said, "it's not so easy. So, we kept what secrets we had to ourselves. Not many people knew about her condition. However, if anyone should have, it should've been you!" To believe that such a life could be carried on, to resign oneself to this fate . . . In saying this, I'd wanted to put the story into words, written every day anew; the layers of loneliness that go into a story are far beyond Juliet's comprehension. One was not able to share one's despair for the sake of generating a little hope. I was to experience this in my other relationships, because of various worries that were connected in various degrees to cowardice. Nevertheless, I couldn't possibly share such feelings with Juliet at the time. In order to be able to take certain steps toward someone would need some preparation. Have I not already said that in order to be able to describe certain painful experiences one should have experienced them fully themselves? That was the reason why I had wanted to know Anita's whereabouts, I believe. I could manage to say a few words, if not everything . . . "They went to Israel some five years ago. Anita wanted to settle at a *kibbutz*," Juliet said. "When we paid a visit to them to wish them farewell she spoke with a palpitating heart of a *kibbutz* that the Rumanian Jews had set up." After a pause, she added with a voice that betrayed a longing mingled with some discomfort: "The fact is her bed-ridden mother whom she had not seen since her childhood was breathing her last breaths . . . Before she went, she had expressed a wish to see her daughter first and then her husband who had caused her so much suffering. How she managed to do this, how she managed to get in touch with them, we'll never know." It may be that Anita's father corresponded secretly with his wife behind her back. It may be that they had lied; it may be that they had recourse to lie like everybody else.

Lies, deceptions . . . resolutions, options, or letting oneself go to be swept up by the whirlwind of human relations. What could have led Anita to such a life? Was it the absence of her mother, her desire to be a mother to someone else in the absence of her own, or to take vengeance on all motherhood despite other people's opposition, by killing a part of herself gradually? Or was it her failure to carry the burden of her uncomely appearance in whose beauty she could never bring herself to believe? Whither and how far could justifications that I could conjure up in my imagination take me? It was certainly not so easy to understand certain lives and relationships properly in their true light and to fit them into our dreams of those people . . . All that I know and can say is that she was carried along within me in an unexpected night, for other nights despite Anita's absence and her disappearance in human form. After the lapse of many years I was fated to come across the piano player Metin quite by chance at a music hall and hold a conversation with him that was to last for several hours, during which he suggested to me to set out on a new journey at the break of dawn, once the night ended. He had not forgotten Anita; what's more he had reserved a special corner in his life for her. As our talk dragged on, I better understood the fact that those days had been very important to him, and so I had to navigate them with caution, on my way toward a life mislaid somewhere. A boundary had been set for me that I was not supposed to transgress. Perhaps, this is the reason why I'm now at pains to define the truths, the real truths involved in that story. The fact is that she was not ill at all. Under the circumstances I had to proceed. A young girl pimped by her father to tourists stinking of money. The young girl was helpless; she was being dragged toward a chasm. How did this happen, such a corrupt practice? Everybody would, no doubt, have their own opinion on the matter. Metin thought that they were both in need of money. That was certainly a way of putting a bold face on betrayal, a way of living and experiencing a betrayal through another. He had done his best to pull her out from this shame. But he himself could not stray beyond the boundary fixed to him. That young girl in despair who was ready to take up the invitation of a person who would truly love her concealed in her heart an evil unabated, an evil she nourished. This was a ruse which enabled her not to forget that betrayal, trying to attract people to her like a spider by putting on innocent airs. No doubt these were conflicting feelings and observations. This process of passing judgment might be the result of the efforts made to fit the remaining pieces of information into their places—making a sacrifice, declaring one's love, expressing one's deep affection, the submission to and justification of her revolt against humanity through a baser existence—on the one hand, and on the other hand, it can be seen as an evil worse than death. I had to lend an ear both to

Juliet and to Metin. The story was getting unfathomable. But which intelligence reflected the truth? What did Anita actually want to convey to me by her looks, mysterious airs, and reticence? Why had the mother gone to that distant land? Did Juliet know other things she had left unsaid, that she preferred to remain quiet about? If there was something that had to be kept secret or that required hiding, could one assume that all that had been experienced, in one way or another, have some connection to me? Could it be that that woman, consigned to memory, was a figment of one's imagination, of a dream desired to be kept fresh in one's recollection? After all, a woman—a woman who had veiled herself to me in this story—had given birth to Anita. What was of particular importance was finding out the whereabouts of that woman, and sensing her presence. A friend of mine had told me once that in many relationships, especially sexual ones, we were gratified only through delusions. He was in AA. He had been involved in the prostitution trade. He had something to say about delusions, illusions, and hallucinations, about psychedelic experiences, to anybody who wished to hear. Now that I'm trying to see and know Anita better, the Anita in my life, with my restricted means, as I remember once more the history of what has not been told and shared, I feel that what are given to us in a relationship are but illusions. She is no more, I know this; she will never show up in this vicinity, she will live henceforth only in words to be fed by fancy. All that has been experienced, the traces left indicate that we will never be able to embark on certain adventures for lack of courage and we will hurt certain individuals who have not deserved to receive such harsh treatment. We lose those people, our own people, because of this cowardice. Our trying to keep pace with the powerful, with those who seem to be winners, may, I think, be explained by the fact that we prefer not to face ourselves, the evil that is lying within us . . . evil or simply our vanity. Whenever I recall Anita, perhaps for this very reason, it occurs to me to narrate quite a different love story. However, love requires sacrifice despite occasional quarrels. I am still at a loss to give a name to what I may have felt for Anita. Those were other times, and there were things that I could not touch at those times. They say that there are certain flowers that grow only on mountains, on the heights, that there is a flower peculiar to every altitude. These are flowers which have exotic smells, flowers that I have never touched since I have never been to those mountains. I keep on promising myself that I will climb those mountains one day, knowing that they are there and will be there forever. The reason for our procrastination, and for our gradual and continual loss of those moments . . . the reason, both delusion and illusion . . . despite regeneration, is that we lose the flowers of those places, of those places dreamt of, due to the transience of nature. While someone is perpetually lost somewhere, one wishes to believe that that person stands there and will stand there forever. The sense of touch becomes that of other people and is lost to you forever as you put off your journey to the mountains. In another sense, you diminish, as you postpone your departure and set foot in a story gradually dwindling away. What remains behind is the smile of those who know those flowers. It is not for nothing that I associate the experiences I would have wished to have had with Anita with those mountains and their flora. The flower seemed to be somewhere there. To take a few steps would be sufficient . . . That's why I wanted to describe Anita as she appeared to me. The image I had of her, the image that had been imprinted on my mind . . . permeated with suspicions, regrets, and unanswered questions . . . Love requires a sacrifice, first and foremost. Leaving aside the gains and the losses, the gist of the matter lay, I think, in the fact that Anita had not encountered a true lover that could make such a sacrifice for her. I believe Metin had also understood this. There was a song among the hundreds in his registry which he had not sung, the song that he could not spare for Anita. The tears that trickled down his cheeks in referring to the past could not have been merely due to the effect of alcohol. We had run into each other at a time of regret . . . How can I otherwise explain our reluctance to meet each other again?

On the one hand there was Eleni who had evoked in me the visions of a forbidden and inaccessible realm, and on the other hand, Tanaş, resigned in his shell to a long-lasting gradual decay. Hüsnü, discontented, had had to pay in an utterly dejected state the price for his failure in complying with the requirements of the day, while Şükran had missed that shadowy flat in which she used to live during those days of horror when she approached death, perhaps the last steps taken in her struggle for life which was most probably a lost cause from the very beginning, a foregone conclusion; and there was Anita in that room of hers where her father one day left her without forewarning, leaving behind regrets, a lot of unanswered questions, and, what is more important, an uncompleted story; her father whose name I never knew and who had given me the impression that he always had other things to tell . . . fathers and daughters . . . Şükran, Eleni and Anita . . . They had their songs, songs left unfinished, not properly lived as they should have been; songs that had never been vocalized . . . It would have never occurred to them, of course, that they would one day come together in the same story. They may have guessed if one takes into consideration those paths and incidents. Nevertheless, how far could we trust those differences, if the dead ends and boundaries were to be taken into account? I must confess that during the days when it had been my intention to share my version of Madame Eleni's story, I had not expected that the events would take such a turn, that, haphazardly, I would be obliged to proceed on to other stories, and that I would have summoned those men to this story. First on the agenda was the nude figure of Eleni as seen through the window of the kitchen that opened to the shaft and the strong odor of cooking that emanated from there. The scenes of that episode—expressing despair along with revolt—would gain ground. Some people were looking for an opportunity to settle themselves in their respective places in our lives or in other people's lives just like in those songs . . . Now it is time to question whether those lives had been lived, truly lived, for the sake of a few words which would be omitted or were desired to be left with other people, at least for a period of time. Yes, for a brief period of time . . . a brief period of time . . . Those moments which direct one's course in life and leave one face-to-face with oneself . . . Where were those moments, where were they concealed in that story, the nights when Madame Eleni went around naked in her house or while she made her last preparations? Or during the pleasant moments when she was busy laying the table for Tanaş, imprinted henceforth forever in the memories of so many people? Or during one of those evenings that Şükran may have lived, at those tables, those restaurants by the seaside, in those beds, in those houses, reminiscing now and then of the house flooded by sunlight? In the games that Hüsnü used to play with his daughter whom he called my first beloved child in that small house? In Anita's dreams of conjugal nights that she believed she would realize one day through that music? In the emotion felt by Anita's father on the eve of his departure for the *kibbutz*, having said farewell to a few people he was leaving behind in the remote past for a new life ahead? One moment, a single moment, or a special, very special segment of life . . . a moment that would enable one to exist *per se* . . . In my efforts to summon people here, this was what I had been trying to find out perhaps. Have I succeeded in this? Have I? Really? I don't know, truly. What's more, all sorts of associations that this accomplishment may engender make me uneasy, and create in me a sense of the absurd, giving me the creeps. To be able to succeed . . . what did this mean, anyhow? Whose was the so-called success? What had I prevailed upon? Where were we supposed to find new words and expressions to describe those concealed figures within us? Certain shortcomings suggest to me that I still have to cover great distances. I have already said this. This seems to me like a story that will regenerate itself in time, and will be dictated to me in a different tone. If so, can it be that what has been done so far has been in vain? No, certainly not. At least, I don't want to believe that is the case, after so many steps have been taken and hopes treasured. For, I'm convinced that such feelings hold true not only with respect to stories, but also for relationships. They bring in, at every instance, a new individual, or they remove something from us along with every separation and debacle. We had been entertaining the hope that certain things might sooner or later change despite the associations they created, hadn't we? Indeed, we were expecting—we should expect in fact—that certain things would or might change. We also had to go on holding onto expectations for certain things that would enable us to look into that mirror from a different angle . . . to go on holding onto expectations . . . To enable one to make oneself believe that one did effectively live those relationships in the first place. I estimate that only by clinging to this belief can I insist upon the fact that they should not give up hope in the face of those eventualities despite the despair of the heroes of the story in question. Thus, to know that certain stories will never end like the relationships in question, that they can never be terminated, provides the justification for sticking it out to the bitter end, for clinging to life. Had not those individuals left for distant lands carrying within them that unshakable belief even when they were in the grips of despair? Had we not ventured, for this very reason, to continue our journey, our journey toward others—despite all the looks directed at us—and toward other eventualities, by our looks, by our looks of whose depths we were seldom conscious?

A hotel room at Sıraselviler

Stories for some people begin in one manner and continue in the same vein. Some objects return to us like individuals; a vision can associate in you those individuals you had been concealing in the secret corners of your heart. A day comes when the stories lingering in those images try to be conveyed through those words that were mislaid somewhere but were wished to be revived, the heroes remaining always in the same in solitude.

It's time now that I spoke out . . . whenever I recall Monsieur Robert in order to reconstruct his life, based on images lingering in my mind which I would have

liked to keep between himself and myself solely; whenever I desire to tell someone of an episode which I believe not to have been sufficiently understood by the
majority of people, for the sake of those values I would never wish to be deprived
of, I remember that small squalid hotel room at Sıraselviler and the nights spent
there in 'that room': the interlocutions and, what is more important, the fertile
poem of continually renewed hopes and deferred joys. This was the first stage
of the journey I had set out on toward regeneration, based on the visions in my
mind of the lives in other stories, those lives abandoned to their destinies. Those
words belonged to other stories, were designed to linger elsewhere and were desired to be shared with other people . . . This indicated that there were sentences
that returned to us at the most unexpected moment, inviting and compelling us
to take new paths, and to bind us with new expectations, visions associated with
these sentences, sentences we had been expecting, sentences for individuals we
had lost somewhere on our journey . . . Whenever I recall . . .

Even though what was told to me in that room cannot properly be expressed,
there had been moments delineated to me, in other words, delivered to my custody. A night commode, a bed, two old bags, costumes laden with traces of the
past, costumes providing certain clues related to the past . . . This was a picture
that enabled me to get ahead of Monsieur Robert, of the Monsieur Robert within
me. A picture that took on deeper significance as the years went by, whose details
were perceived in different guises as time progressed, a photograph one would
like to display on very special occasions, even though one feels and knows that
one cannot appear within the frame beyond a certain point, as one would have
liked to. We could add to these uncertainties the fear of touching certain visions
and details. The question here is a kind of despair. A despair generated by the
fear of the unknown in a person you would have liked to have been familiar
with, with reference to a story you had been dreaming about, simply because his
merits and demerits are unknown and are bound to remain unknown to you; a
despair generated by the likelihood of the fixation of an image in your mind; an
insignificant image liable to disintegrate at the least unexpected moment. Monsieur Robert was a man of paradoxes, if the impressions he had left with other
people are to be trusted, and also if one takes into consideration the photograph
he showed to me or those long, mandatory walks. I must say that this life, which
assumes meaning, in a way, by such conflicting elements, renders my progress
toward it difficult. That is exactly where my despair comes into play, at the very
spot where I want to conjure up this story and share it with people. Why am I so

hesitant about it, I wonder? I feel I am walking on the boundary separating the wish to tell it and the fear of telling, and I distinctly remember the reason why I had to put off the realization of certain dreams.

Monsieur Robert had left behind him the vision of an original person along with the aspects of a lifestyle lived off of the beaten path. With the gift of hindsight, it occurs to me now and then that he derived a kind of wry pleasure from leaving people with such conflicting impressions. This appeared to be the most significant rule of his legacy . . . prototypal individuals, stories generated by paradoxes and original interpretations . . . To be able to understand this it sufficed to have access to the world of the Venturas. According to Monsieur Jacques, Monsieur Robert was a man who had wasted his life on ostentations, in pursuit of the will-o'-the-wisp, by the constant lies he told himself and his acquaintances; a listless and vainglorious life. The steps he had taken had been all wrong; he had kept bad company, he had never cared about tomorrow, he had dressed in other people's clothes and had emulated others, not daring to show his true personality.

Private matters must remain private.

She had, in her capacity of an elder sister, always taken good care of him and looked after him as a protective mother should. She had firmly believed in the role she was playing . . .

Jealousies, offenses, and the covert game of fighting for superiority . . . Monsieur Robert would, one day, endure defeat through resignation in the face of the criticisms leveled against him about his life, acknowledging that he had acted wrongly, yet appearing as if he was determined to continue fighting. I understand better now this formulated intention. This was a consequence of the game's rationale. He had the capacity of perceiving the overall reality related to him, although he was a man of paradoxes and the author of errors. This was a feeling. A feeling which did not require literal explanation; a feeling which was experienced naturally, a feeling shared and desired in a different fashion. Nevertheless, leaving aside all our comments, it was not possible to see the sorrow involved in it. We tried to understand, tried as best we could. We had to venture to proceed again toward an individual in order that we might penetrate the sorrow of his long absence, with little hope of it deserving to be renewed, in full consciousness of the fact that that walk might engender within us, at the least unexpected moment, the fragments we believed we had mislaid somewhere . . . Monsieur Robert's story was in a way the story of an interminable fight that seemed never to come to an end, it seemed that one had to engage in a realm other than one's own with strangers and estrangements; the smiles of winners and losers concealing a great many sentiments and recollections. What had been experienced there had reminded me once more of this reality, of the feeling that the said reality had engendered. One is inclined to ask if that reality had any significance anymore, if any boundaries still existed for these two people fed by different hopes in different worlds. Where, how, and with whom could the boundary between the winners and the losers be traced after those steps had been taken? In other words, had this fight, if it could be called a fight at all (not by my standards), this victory, have made Monsieur Jacques happy? I doubt it. It seems to me, that after so many deaths, losses, unrealized dreams and repaid remorse, he would not feel like asking such questions. I think that from then on, one had other expectations and prospects for the days to come. There is not the slightest doubt that the path taken, ushered by those days, was a particular path of loneliness, the treading of which would involve great difficulties. In that state of omneity, of complex relations, there are moments that provide us sometimes with small clues about people's attitudes toward life. When I tackle the subject from this angle, it seems to me that Monsieur Jacques must have felt relieved for a brief period of time, if I may be excused for saying so. While facing those lives to which you prefer to be a spectator, as if looking at actors on a stage, there are certain moments when you feel like saying to yourself: "I'm thankful for being here; it's a blessing that I have not experienced what they are experiencing now." Well, mine was a similar feeling, a kind of self-consolation. Despite your dreams and performances up until that point, you could succeed better by taking refuge in the individual you would become. My integration with this sentiment, under the circumstances, was not difficult. Monsieur Jacques was a person who belonged to a world of security after all, in contradiction to Monsieur Robert, who had experienced in different guises successes and failures over the course of his business life, not to mention in his relationships with women, and the path he had taken late in life. I had seen that world; I'd never been a stranger to it. That means my words could return to me for the sake of those lives . . . Insignificant victories desired to be experienced, concealed in a world of security, considered more often than not as a sanctuary . . . even though these victories lacked security and reliability . . . petty victories, yes, petty . . . petty victories to which we all cling to, and more importantly put up with in order to be able to protect ourselves against tribulations. Was this one of the rules of our opting to be mere spectators or a consequence of having no other choice? While passing judgment on

Monsieur Robert's life, Monsieur Jacques had said: "Palo or phaeton" (Cudgel or phaeton). Later, at an opportune moment, I'd asked him the meaning of this expression; to which he had reacted by making a gesture with his hand as if to say: "Bosh!" To explain a well-established expression must have upset him; as a matter of fact there are certain words and meanings that these words conceal, that settle themselves within us without us realizing. We are used to cultivating certain words and their representations within us without having conceptualized them. We drew a lot, without questioning their origins, on certain conversations. The moment in question was one when I experienced restlessness in a way I could not define. After a short silence, during which he had sipped his tea, he said: "The first meaning refers to 'wealth or poverty,' in other words 'everything or nothing,' the second to 'cudgel or prestige.'" We both felt inclined to smile at this explanation; after which we stood silent for a while. I think we had seen, at that moment, people associated by those words that morning, in very different places in the company of very different people. "I've never been one of them; I was afraid to be," he said. "One could see the identity of the people one tried to represent better in this way." Did these words connote a boasting or regret? I couldn't tell. Could it be evasion again? There were so many people who had trodden this path for their entire life . . . mirrors reflected at times terrific images . . . Monsieur Jacques had never lived up to the adage 'cudgel or phaeton' if one considers the critical turns in his life. We had to understand this loneliness which necessitated no explanation, considering his social standing and the nature of his character. Inability to do something about it, not being able to do otherwise . . . It was not difficult for me to know and often recall this individual that Monsieur Jacques exemplified. He was one of those who could justify themselves openly, flouting all failures and errors committed. His appreciation of Monsieur Robert had been in this vein. The expression gave a full account of this adventurer. What was depressing was the fact that what had remained in the end was the 'cudgel.' However, whether you deemed it odd or not, the fact remained that the reminiscences aroused by 'cudgel' should at all events not be regarded as strange. Berti was also of the same opinion. We were faced with a fact which might pave the way to the assessment of a struggle engaged in for the sake of living, a fact which certain individuals conceal in the secret corners of themselves. That was not difficult to understand. The man who had lived in London, in another country—experiencing them in all their aspects, and who had, in the end, exhausted himself—was for Berti a hero. Indeed, the hero of an adventure that had not materialized. Whenever he recalled his uncle, he could not help remembering his years of study at Cambridge. The fact that when he had been back in Istanbul, Monsieur Robert, in his indispensable identity and façade of 'Monsieur Robert,' had found himself as someone ready to defend himself to the bitter end; this was probably due to this indispensability. "He paid no attention to what people said in the least; he lived as his conscience dictated," said Berti who tried to put into words a resentment directed both at himself and at his father. I distinctly remember that evening. It seemed as though this sentence had opened the way to a short journey back in time. This was a sentence that had enabled me to make a comment whose context was familiar to me. I had cast a glance at Juliet who was looking at Berti. Her countenance betrayed the identity of an elder sister, of a mother. I had realized then how much I loved them despite the wide divergence of opinion between us. Berti's display of secret admiration for his uncle, his mere display, had emphasized this impression still more. I'd been treading a thin boundary line, a boundary the crossing of which would take us to a more meaningful place, a deeper place than the sense of loyalty would account for. Berti had never succeeded in forsaking that individual who had been able to spend so many years in London and had turned into a hero of a lost life for that very reason. He was in need of the image of that life even after so many years; he had to persuade himself that he had not lost the power to carry on his struggle against that man in the first place, against the man bequeathed to him by his father. I could not overlook this probability; I was obliged to proceed on a path whose end I could not foresee, in the inner world of that story that was dictated to me toward that incredible life marred by anxieties. The story of those who unknowingly yield important clues about their identities through words, which seem to be insignificant, was the story lived by many with several different characters and from many walks of life. Nevertheless, I am still of the opinion that, whatever the reason was that prompted his endearment to someone forsaken, it was meaningful. This reality may not have been so important for other people, but it was of paramount importance for me. This was one of the characteristics suggestive of someone who was a good person. Yet, life was not always generous enough in the distribution of rewards. The years to come were to prove this. Berti would never be able to find this courage among his friends. Was this the recompense for the goodness generated by certain lives? Perhaps. But to be frank, I don't feel like proceeding on the path that this question may lead to. Is it because I still find it difficult to define what is 'good'? Perhaps. But what is still more important is my belief in the evil within me. The path that leads to the 'good man' has already become full of potholes for many of us.

In the family, there was another woman who had not and could not forsake Monsieur Robert. This woman, who had an important place in my life and who lived with her frenzies—this thrill-seeking character who lived in a realm of sensations completely different from those on the opposite bank—was Aunt Tilda. I hadn't had any difficulty in finding out the cause of this behavior, of this warmth. That person who had led a hectic life in London was the heroine of a tale lost, not lived. Yes, the heroine of a lost tale yet to be lived . . . even though these tales differed from one another. Her heroine was always there, she ought to be there . . . always . . . like all other heroines of the dreamworld; she knew this struggle all too well, she knew how closely it linked her to that world. She had risked so many things for the sake of those individuals, those individuals and those times that had been the cause of so many solitary walks.

These feelings were not exclusive to Aunt Tilda, of course. She knew full well that the occasional conveying of the individuals in her dreamworld, those who could not take part in her games, to the lives reproduced by lies, led one to difficult nights, to introversion. Why had Juliet been so pitiless, or chosen to be so pitiless, in the face of that return that had affected every family member in a different way? All of us had tried, to the extent our capacity allowed, to take refuge in a stranger to protect ourselves. According to her, trying to find justifications for the failure to assimilate oneself into the community of a city was not so easy. Monsieur Robert should not go back to Istanbul but should continue to live in London in full consciousness of the prevailing conditions, by not trying to assume the right to shatter that image certain people create in their minds of those who had to bear the full burden of life. The concept of responsibility was highly meaningful both for Juliet and Monsieur Jacques if one took into consideration the life of this adventurer. The incidents associated different things in our minds. The attitudes taken despite these judgments and their occasionally conflicting views indicated that no one had remained indifferent to Monsieur Robert's existence, to his experiences and to those affected by them. Which one of these was right? To answer this question was not so easy at the time. Nor is it so at present. To my mind, everybody had grasped Monsieur Robert's quiddity in their own fashion, trying to give him shape as they saw fit. This seemed to be the fate of a person who had a story to tell, who was about to set off on a journey and was directing himself to the targeted place . . . to be able to give life to a person by making him a different individual . . . It was this sentiment that supported him in his hardest times, in addition to the dreams which had already gone far beyond false expectations; to be precise, this small victory was not shared with anybody else. Now his figure emerges before me with his sad smile on his face as he was living this small victory in that hotel room. Once again in that hotel room, in that false sanctuary, trying to hold fast to those imaginary moments . . . there where breaks in time, like in certain situations . . . While preparations were being made for the celebration of Passover at the Venturas' a couple of months after he was back in Istanbul . . . as he was shaving meticulously, combing his hair and making himself smart . . . This was the time when he desired to turn the Passover evening into a real festivity, as he believed that it was not properly celebrated while he was in a different climate, remote from his family . . . with a view to collecting the fragments of the past . . . Through which open door could one peep at such people at such a time?

The Picture at Kanlıca

My attempt at getting hold of Monsieur Robert in a hotel room in the middle of the joy that such a return had occasioned had its reasons, namely to collect the fragments lingering in him within the contours of an original story that would supplement mine. To pluck up the courage to undertake that long journey which would engender once more that return, and with it, the feeling of abandonment and solitude . . . that small victory should have brought along that inevitable question . . . this lie, this sin and this lopsided smile which were surely not the first lie, first sin, nor the first lopsided smile emitted. This inevitable question was not exclusive to that Passover evening, but to many an evening and night left behind. The feelings were those generated by the room and by the steps, the steps that should have been taken. I was persuaded that I would gradually be reaching our story; then I would also be master of my own time. Leisurely . . . I had visions and dreams . . . Those sentences reminded me of a man who paced up and down the room. The man was alone as always. He felt lonely in the midst of his family which he had kept close to his heart as his last haven over the many years of his intense longing. He was lonely once again. Just like the Passover he had celebrated last year, the first Passover that he had celebrated after he had been separated from his wife of thirty-five years. He had spent that evening with two friends, one from Casablanca and the other from Istanbul who had been obliged to live the life of an exile for many years. With two friends who had not abandoned him, in whom he could rely and in whom he could find a safe haven . . . He wondered whether he had done the right thing, the fact that he had abandoned them. It was a burning question. He could have recalled those steps in the past now that he had found two individuals that would enliven his last years by their very presence, thus bringing solace to him. He knew that they were intelligent people who he had longstanding experience of on a day-to-day basis. If they wanted to they could resume their friendship as though it had never been interrupted, with the same sentiments they had entertained. Yes, they could resume their friendship as if it had never been interrupted . . . Despite the fact that it had become customary for them to lay a banquet table to celebrate even the most trivial event, their dispensing with the arrangement of a farewell party indicated that they intended to come together before too long. He hadn't been wrong in considering them true friends. He hadn't been mistaken in his conviction. For instance, he owed İncila Hanım, who, by the diversity of her behavior was a chameleon that changed its shade to meet the hue of a given situation, often reminding him of Istanbul and of a couple of unforgettable memories which he could not easily disclose to a third person, not to mention the modest sum of money he had borrowed from her when he had been in dire need. A couple of reminiscences that linked him to life and prevented him from setting off on a journey of no return; he could never compensate for these actions. At an unearthly hour of the night (or day), in a city which could swallow anyone unawares, the conviction that he could knock on the door of that small house whenever he wanted to was a boon for which he could never thank her enough. As for the money he had borrowed . . . although she had so far made no reference to it, he would recognize the debt owed to her and would certainly repay it when the time came. The attractive business offers he made to people, to his 'new people,' would sooner or later be favorably answered anyhow. As a matter of fact, the debt he owed was no more than two or three thousand pounds, which he would honorably repay . . . İncila Hanım was sure of this. The experiences of those days were still fresh in his mind. Those experiences belonged to a past, to a remote past, back to a time from which the spectators and witnesses had now been consigned to oblivion. She was not merely a true friend; but also the 'keepsake' of a friend; a keepsake from a friend: Hugo Friedman by name, who had lived his London adventure in a completely different fashion from him, in narrow rooms and with dreams far from being colorful . . . He distinctly remembered, he had corresponded with him during his stay in London and had even sat down at his table and had long talks. Hugo had been on a long and arduous sentimental journey with that girl with the beautiful voice from Kanlıca. The story of two people of different origins, two people who were believed to be someplace other than they actually were, two people fated to be the subject of discrimination wherever they went. He knew where the said prejudices took one, to places of exile. Journeys undertaken in the aftermath of certain resentments had bypassed him. That young man who could not find the family he had been searching for and that young girl who had been in pursuit of her songs on one of the most beautiful coasts of Istanbul, had already set off on their journey when they had begun corresponding. They were taking their initial steps in Istanbul, toward the life they were going to lead . . . keeping a low profile while experiencing their passions to the full. Just like in those days when his elder sister, whom he had deprived of a couple of sentences written on his soul, and his brother-in-law who had failed to find the child he had been seeking inside him, had been compelled to cross those borders. The price of it had eventually been paid off sooner or later . . . Monsieur Robert was a friend of Hugo from High School. If one takes into account their past experiences, this relationship assumed a peculiar meaning. This sentence has to be transformed in order to better define certain truths: Monsieur Robert was the only friend of that child who couldn't find his family. That child had always preferred to look at his acquaintances from a distance. There was more than one reason for this. Hugo was the child of a wealthy family who had benefited from the advantages of riches, but it was a family whose members scattered and disappeared gradually . . . The child was born into a family that had slowly prepared its own collapse at the hands of an authoritarian, womanizing, alcoholic father whose interests were limited to making money and spending it, and of a mother whose entire life was spent sitting at gambling tables. That child used to come home, dreaming that the mere stepping over of the hearth, even though for a very brief period, would provide him with warmth. He lived in a small house and ate his dinners in restaurants, clubs and snack bars. Meals cooked and served at home aided in establishing closer links with the family members during which they disclosed their big secrets. As a matter of fact, it was during one of those evenings that Hugo had disclosed the fact that he was born with one of his eyes deprived of sight. This was not distinguishable to people. He had confessed that it didn't bother him. He had been accustomed to this defect. This may have been one of the reasons why he shunned people; nevertheless, the secret resentment that this created didn't deter him from groping his way in the dark. Everybody knew of his defect, which he had experienced parallel to his mode of living; in relation to his own mode of living, to his capacity for vision . . . Nobody had drawn the boundaries of evil so far. "I must've been the product of the union of my father and mother who had been dead drunk; they still owe me an eye," said Hugo. He ascribed some importance to himself despite his 'natural' defect, perhaps with some deep-set resentment. This resentment was not against the people who had different outlooks on life, but rather against his parents who had brought him into the world with this defect. He had confessed one day with a smile that this had enabled him to take a closer account of his friends. Those were the days in which that look of his had given him access to the world of his friend, of his only friend.

Had Hugo been successful in being able to look at other people and see the individuals from whom he had been separated long ago? He could no longer recall when he had emerged to view that girl with green eyes from Kanlıca. He only remembered that the consequences that followed that encounter had forced that man who had been looking on the world, on his world, to look with different eyes on the fierce battle raging within him. These consequences were one of the connections by which the family members wished to emphasize their existences to each other . . . a price had to be paid. Their relationship involved a connection which was difficult to be acknowledged by both sides for different reasons. The experiences in question had nothing original about them in fact; they were mere platitudes. They formed the contents of a story ventured or dared to be ventured, and were expressed in different climates with different words, visions and evasions; they had also risked trespassing their boundaries and passing over the stories of their solitudes and feelings of loneliness . . . by escaping to London. He was also in London at the time. He had made the acquaintance of Lola, he was about to cross over the threshold of a new a life he could not refrain from. He also felt himself to be on the brink of a perilous adventure. They were in pursuit of a new family, of *their* family. London, which they had seen in pictures as a faraway land of dreams, had been the point where their paths converged. This expression was far from being illusory. They were to witness in the streets of the city to which they had escaped—over a course of time, while aspiring to materialize their dreams—the different dimensions their friendship would take, as their steps would lead them in different directions . . . Our innate characteristics inevitably determined our place in life. Hugo had taken his flight to a foreign land with a woman he believed to be a foreigner, in order to forget the hell he had experienced in that house at Tepebaşı, risking burning the bridges that linked him to the past. This was undoubtedly a revolt; a revolt that only a few people could understand and interpret properly. This was the biggest revolt of his life. He could not otherwise attract people's attention, the attention of the individuals he deemed to be strangers. He had set out with the intention not to see his parents again and to leave them in their own quagmire. He had been successful in avoiding his father. His mother had come to London after a few years. She had been separated from her husband after forty years of marriage. She understood her son's decision to abandon a man whose corrupt lifestyle she had to share; she felt the need to confess this fact. She had given up gambling. She had barred herself from those tables for a reason she could not affirm even to her son whom she had begun to consider her sole support and to whom she felt closer and closer. She had paid a great price for it. She had indeed given up gambling but she was still drinking heavily. Her capacity to bear the effects of alcohol was remarkable. She never became tipsy. She might have been using drugs as well. Yet not even Hugo, who had been very close to her in those days, could detect it. Those were the days when London was seen by them in a somewhat different light. Now and then they went for a drink somewhere where they could sit chatting for hours. These were moments İncila Hanım considered quite normal despite his resentment of the past. Years had gone by and everybody had forgiven everybody and begun to understand each other. Years had obliterated the pains of those tremors. Everybody tried to find the time they had lost over the course of those years, to discover and apprehend it as best as they could. Hugo's companionship, his first companionship with his mother was important in this respect, especially when one expected they would know each other better by steps deferred to be taken. The coffee houses, the cinemas, the restaurants they shared, and, in particular, their experiences during the long nights in that small house and the breakfasts taken together. Their life in London was spent in this way. She had noticed that Hugo had found the happiness he had been seeking and that he had apprehended that sadness in his soul; it had taken on an entirely different meaning. Then they had parted one day never to meet again. His mother had gone back to Istanbul after the two months, saying to Hugo, "That's it!" and passing away silently in the Balat Hospital. Hugo had received the news of her death by a short letter written by a foreign hand that had preferred to remain anonymous. The letter said that she had shared the same ward with her mother. Apparently she had felt it her duty to write that letter. The funeral had been held. The letter said that if he so desired he might do something to commemorate her in a synagogue in London. Not to call him for her funeral had been the wish of his mother. This had been her last wish lying on her deathbed shortly before she died. She had said that her son would understand the reasons for their separation. This had caused a mounting heat in Hugo's heart, a heat that had torn him from the city he loved and transported him to another place. He had not wept. He couldn't bring himself to weep. There had been a rupture in their relationship, putting an insurmountable distance and estrangement between them. However, his expectations had not been in vain. He had understood perfectly well the reason why he had not been called to Istanbul, their separation in London would have served as an appropriate parting after what had gone between them. This was one of the moments when they could truly come together even though they had spent their time in different climates. He had in fact experienced such a meeting before. His mother was close by him; she said that death "had surged up" in her. She was not sick, she had no apparent condition; yet, she felt it and heard its steps approaching . . . They had been drinking for quite some time at this stage. It was a presentiment that had to be experienced by them. He was conversing with a woman who wanted to be left alone on the brink of death; a woman who believed that people who had not entered her life until then could not induce her to recollect her past, a woman who wanted to remain by the side of strangers, by the side of people she would have known to be strangers. The path she had trodden did not permit her to think otherwise and she was reluctant to see those that had hidden themselves along that path. To have been able to come there in the company of her son had been a gain in itself. At the airport, just before she said goodbye she had given him a fifty pound note asking him to go and bet with it after she had died and to look at the faces of the gamblers, saying: "I'll be there with you!" This had been the only legacy he had inherited from this woman who had consumed her life in a totally different manner and to whom he could only approach at very rare moments . . . On the evening of the day he had received that letter he had asked

Robert to take him to a gambling house, saying: "I've got a bet to make on behalf of my mother." He had told me all these episodes, the experiences of the last moments that evening. There are stories that are written, that are desired to be written, at and for such times. Certain heroes and heroines see each other in a different light at such moments and try to find the children they have lost without paying any attention to the fact that they would become hackneyed objects . . . Hugo had indeed scrutinized the faces of the gamblers around the roulette table. He had detected the emotion they tried to conceal. "You've got to be clever to guess the lucky numbers from the way a croupier rolled the ball," said Hugo. However, Hugo had no such expectations. That night would be the first and last night he would be playing. It was a small commemorative event. He expected that his mother would be there as an onlooker, that those faces would be familiar to her, and that one of those faces might well have belonged to her. That was all. The rest belonged to those who repaid their debts and who knew how to settle a debt they owed related to worldly affairs. Amalia, who had always wanted to be called by her first name by her son's friends, Amalia, who had returned to Hugo in her identity of mother, was such a person. She was one of those people who had paid a big price for a passion, for her passion for calling bets. Only individuals like him could understand her; the fact that she gave her son that fifty pound note, her last savings, asking him to place it as a bet. Hugo had been at a remote distance from this world. This distance seemed to have determined his other steps as well. When one considers his past experiences, one can see that he had never risked playing big. His biggest bet may have been his decision to choose İncila Hanım as a companion in a completely different country. To tell you the truth he had not been alone in venturing to take this risk. Had it not been for the presence and support of his beloved, he would not have dared to engage in this risky game. Having settled in London, he had earned his living by translating the business correspondence of a big international concern, which, looking back on it, exhausted him. He might have been considered an important employee for the concern he worked for. In addition to English, he had mastered German and French. He also had a smattering of Italian. Each one of these languages was for him a symbol of other lives, of escapes to other lives . . . This, however, was his drawn boundary. There was nowhere beyond. He had possessed nothing but small fantasies, moments and letters to faraway realms, to other stories. His fantasies, moments, letters, and İncila Hanım, who had remained loyal to him even after his death, nothing else deserves mention. He had always recognized the importance that woman had had for him, she who had been his sole companion, friend and beloved, who had never let him recall anything from Istanbul. What had been presented to him as a gift was not only a token of loyalty; it was also the story of a sacrifice, when one considers their flight and the locality they had left. İncila Hanım was one of those people who knew how to devote herself passionately to love; who knew how to value the life she lived, having chosen it in all consciousness of practicality rather than from nobility of heart, in settling in a life already prepared for her . . . This was also a life of sacrifice, a story in which a man knew how to turn to good account his losses like in every story of sacrifice. Robert had been a witness to it. He was in a position to recognize the value of the things he saw, as well as to assess the experiences of these people in their true dimensions, in their multifarious aspects, because he had met such a woman, the likes of whom he had never come across in his life. His recollections of the people that had come from there had reinforced this impression in him. In order to have an insight into her journey, one had to have an idea of İncila Hanım's devotion to that romantic child who had compelled her to sacrifice a life of ease and comfort. He had not forgotten what Hugo had told him. İncila Hanım had always been the source of pride and admiration of his friends and enjoyed the reputation of being an enviable beauty in the conservatory where she had studied music. She had had many prospective suitors, not only among her friends, but also among the teachers who had imagined a blissful matrimony with her. Everybody saw in her a Seyyan Hanım. The tango world was ready to receive her with great acclaim. She remained an indelible image in the minds of people. The songs she sang at the seaside residence in Kanlıca were echoed on the opposite coast of the Bosporus. Caïques diverted their courses toward her residence to listen to her during the hours when she practiced, possibly for a prospective performance when the time came in a different life or lives. People knew well how serious and resolute she was in her practice. One wonders where those people who had listened to her in their caïques or her neighbors who had lent an ear to her melodies while bearing their own stories in their soul transported those songs? A question that İncila Hanım had asked him in their later years may have brought back certain remote experiences. She had to place her father somewhere, her father who had said that he seriously performed all that he undertook, who addressed the cognoscente saying at every instance that he withdrew to his solitude at certain prescribed hours. Şamil Şükrü Bey who had received a good education, who had made of his talent a credo to make use of his time in an optimum fashion, was a diplomat in the Foreign Service who had served in many foreign countries in the capacity of ambassador. He assessed the individuals according to their deeds and not by their promises or plans. That was the reason why he had deemed perfectionism as his philosophy in life. He had instilled this into his daughter's mind. İncila had spent her childhood and adolescence in a well-delineated discipline in a great many European cities. She had mastered English, French and Spanish; she had received her first piano lessons there. Madrid had been her favorite city. During the summer she often went to Kanlıca, at the seaside residence of her maternal grandfather who had been a *pasha*. Her mother was a painter; in the cities she lived as the wife of the ambassador general, she had not tasted the bliss she had dreamt of. She died young in her forty-eighth year. İncila was seventeen when her mother died. She had sobbed for days on end and felt as though she had been abandoned. She understood the reason why certain people did not come back despite their being missed. Those were painful days.

She had laid aside everything, work, friends, etc.: anything that would oc-cupy her in her daily life. She began to go on long walks and tried to have a better insight into her mother's paintings. İncila who knew how to exercise self-restraint was liable to be swept by a wind that suddenly rose when her deep buried feelings surged to the surface. This was a trait apparently inherited from her mother . . . A time came when this caused her to take the most important step of her life. She met Hugo at a party. They had talks and went on walks. Then they decided to merge their paths. Before she went away she had cast a last glance at her mother's paintings. She had stood for hours gazing at her self-portrait. She perceived a smile on her sad countenance which she had not noticed before. This smile was embedded in the pupils of her eyes. It was as though she told her: "Do not hesitate to go to the bitter end, that's the best thing you can do." Her looks had facilitated İncila to make her resolution to depart. She had perceived in her eyes the traces of a story that nobody could decipher. The attempts at deterring her from her resolution by her father; by her paternal uncle, an undersecretary in a government ministry; her uncle's wife whose sole concern in life was to roll out dough, stuff vegetables, embroider and who had prejudices regarding raising children; her two maternal aunts who had special-ized in keeping up appearances to persuade people that they enjoyed a perfect harmony in their marital relations; and especially her teachers who thought she was highly talented; in other words all her next-of-kin and everybody who tried to show himself or herself as a family member in those days had failed.

They had difficult times. İncila Hanım gave piano lessons in London. She sang nothing, however. Those songs, which had been left in another city, were henceforth laid to rest deep within her. As the days went by, she began sharing those old songs with the people of her immediate circle. He had heard that beautiful voice only then. This voice assumed meaning with the recollections of things abandoned in a remote life and carried over to a new one. That voice was not the voice of a person who sang beautifully, it was a voice that affected one deeply; the voice had the stain of a call. İncila Hanım was a good cook at the same time. To tell the truth she was a *cordon bleu* cook. A meal implied for her a culture, a joy of life. There were people in her circle who had lost the privilege of enjoying their hot dishes at a certain point of their lives; she was aware of this. This was one of the reasons why she lent affection to the meals she cooked . . . If only she could go now and sit together with him for a glass of wine and try to resume their relationship from where they had left off; if only she could go there for the sake of those bygone days, if only they could converse as in the old days . . . No doubt she would attire herself, wearing neat attractive clothes, as though she was dressing up for a festive occasion. It hadn't occurred to her to have her hair dyed; she had allowed her hair to grow long. She had her hair in a bun which she thought was becoming. She was meticulous about her appearance, fastidious about her accessories ranging from an insignificant hair clip to bejeweled rings that she wore to suit every occasion, each of which represented one aspect of her identity . . . for occasions lived and to be lived to the full . . . for those insignificant vainglorious occasions and concerns, not perceptible by any chance person, concerns that are beyond the grasp and understanding of ordinary people. She had many rings, both precious and cheap, each of which concealed a souvenir, a meaning of its own. Why so many rings? Why had they been of such great importance in her life? He had never asked the reason for it; he had not dared to. Every one of us has the need to furtively evade our hidden secrets, in order to be able to look on people from different angles. However, she was resolved. Despite all sorts of understandable evasions, during mealtime, however, they were sure to offer each other pleasant moments of small celebration. The poetry of a small celebration, of preparations for celebrations that lent a different meaning to our experiences mingled to a certain extent with the human requirement to take refuge in human beings . . . İncila Hanım's perpetuation of Jewish traditions after Hugo's death had enabled her to experience special moments which she had difficulty in defining properly. It seemed as though this was another form of sincere loyalty to the man she had loved all her life. At a time when she missed him terribly, she felt like having absolute conviction in this reality. As she was making preparations for that Passover evening, she had described the importance she had attached to those celebrations generated by the touch of this immortal love. She had searched and found the unleavened bread, which was a must, and prepared the leek pastry. She had asked Robert to bring along a bottle of champagne . . . Everything had happened just like in the past . . . Just to make sure that he did not forget to behave like a gentleman. She hadn't refused his gift. He had brought a French vintage wine although he was short of money. She had richly deserved it. She had the ability to appreciate this tact. He was glad that he had not been mistaken by the expression her countenance displayed at the sight of it . . . Once again they had met in a refined manner beyond the grasp of many plebeians.

Monsieur Tahar's Casablanca

Monsieur Tahar, who had been a confirmed boarder in that small apartment of İncila Hanım for years and who had always been reticent about his past, happened to be there that evening. He had also taken part in that small celebration with heartfelt sincerity; that small celebration whose true meaning lay deep in one's soul. Although they did not converse very often, they had understood each other despite their differing tastes; if one considers the relations that determined those lives, one should acknowledge the fact that they had had an insight into the meaning of friendship in their own way. They were two adventurers who had had divergent fates and polar views. Strange, but they felt this during the long hours when they sat for a game of bezique. There was no need for any clarification. Certain things had eventually found their places reserved for them even though they were not commented on. Certain feelings had been exchanged and experienced naturally. This was more than enough for those who appreciated the virtue of acknowledging their feelings, of being resigned to one's lot, of stopping in the right place on the road that led to someone else without trying to change them, and of accepting them in their true colors. Looked at from this angle, Monsieur Tahar's problem was not a complex one. One should be fair about it. What he told about his past during the time they shared together was no more than what an introvert would be disposed to disclose. He figured as a one-time Moroccan newspaperman. This past, of which a part had been preferred to be left in the dark, in the small room at Edgeware Road; a one-time Moroccan newspaperman . . . This identity was not enough in itself. She had wanted to introduce the people she lived with to his identity as a Moroccan; as a matter of fact, his trendy attire and his demeanor were deemed too fastidious when compared to many people's, the dark eyeglasses he wore when he went outside and the cane he always carried gave him the aspect of a spy exiled to a metropolis. These particularities and features were enough to make him appear a citizen of Casablanca; the legend of Casablanca was embodied in him. The wearing of dark eyeglasses might have been due to an allergy against sunlight, the use of a cane might have been the consequence of an undetectable limp; however, such unwarranted presumptions were based on mere appearances that enabled people to formulate judgments. These appearances had a backstory, as is the case with everybody. The adage that exact timings led to exact touches hadn't been hopelessly pronounced in other people's stories elsewhere. To come face-to-face with an expression which tried to appear veiled, which was unconsciously premeditated . . . You cannot possibly immediately recognize that face at such a moment . . . nor can you tell from that face whose expression had been passed to whom. All that you are able to do is to try and understand the meaning of the disguise in question a little better. After that encounter, it may take you some time before—in the company of that man whom you had assumed to be your man—you take cognizance of the fact that you discovered a new tunnel. In that new tunnel, which you have never set eyes on up to that point, and which may take you to where you want to go, you may recollect those you had lost and of whom you had been robbed. The rest of the journey would be toward the darkness . . . Monsieur Tahar's face was one of those faces that one could perceive in that darkness. Were you to ask him about it, you would be told that there had not been many people who had caught sight of it; very few people had lived with him in the days of which this consideration had been effectively paid off. This also held true for people he had left in the remote past, in a remote land. The inhabitants of distant lands . . . What images had surged in one's imagination when one took a look at that land remote from London? What individual had the city invited, London where light and darkness intermingled, where sounds and deep silences alternated almost unwittingly? Answers to these questions were not difficult to find if one took into consideration what was already known and learned. Monsieur Tahar had been the London correspondent for a newspaper, a newspaper with a high circulation according to his judgment, and had returned home upon his retirement. He had discovered the virtues of living with a modest income in a foreign city, of leading a life whose responsibility lay entirely with him . . . Meaningful coincidences difficult to explain arranged his chance encounters . . . After Hugo's departure from this world, İncila Hanım had decided to let one of her rooms, located in a quarter that gradually yielded itself to the inflow of people from whom she was being estranged more and more with every passing day, in consideration of a modest rent which would contribute to her living expenses and allow her to meet incidental costs, and to alleviate, to a certain extent, her sense of loneliness. She fastidiously selected her tenants. Not anybody could venture to occupy her premises. The woman, whose past now determined the course she was to take in the future, was obliged to follow that direction. Her first tenant had been a Brazilian anthropologist. She was an attractive, dark-skinned lady who had told her that she had received her education in a dancing school where she had specialized in the samba, but was now conducting studies on folkloric dances of other lands. She expected to obtain a scholarship from Oxford University, pending which, she pursued her studies in London. She appeared to have no regular hours as she chose to return home at any hour of the night. Dinah was her name. They had long conversations at the breakfast table during which they exchanged information about their respective countries. Almost a year after she had rented the room, she fell in love with her teacher and left for Liverpool. In a letter İncila Hanım received from her, she intimated that she had got hitched and had to interrupt her studies for the time being. She was thanking her for the talks she had had with her at the breakfast table during which she had learned a great many things which had shed light over her subsequent actions. İncila Hanım, however, could not divine what exactly she had meant by that remark. She couldn't, but that had inspired her. This was meant to be an experience congruous with her past, with her indelible past, a sheer experience. She distinctly remembered that she had corresponded with Dinah, although not very frequently. Their letters contained news about the lives they were leading . . . Two people between whom a genuine affection had developed like a mother and daughter . . . The next occupant of that room had been a reformist rabbi from New York whose name was Isaac Jacobi.

She had learned the funniest Jewish jokes and humorous anecdotes from him. İncila Hanım was going to have a better insight into the philosophy that those anecdotes contained. Isaac Jacobi had come to London to settle a problem of his paternal uncle's. For him the details were not so important; what was of significance to him was the action itself, the venture to go to another land. His dream was to be able to go to Sweden and appear in a film as a character similar to himself. He was determined to go to Stockholm one day to realize his dream. He was to stay in that room for just over a year, just like Dinah . . . "I must listen to what my father had said and start receiving lessons on the violin," he said before leaving. He was about forty years old at the time. Years later, he had imparted to her in a letter the news that he had indeed acted in a film to be distributed to a great many countries. Thus, he had fulfilled his dream. One thing he could not bring himself to do was to be married. He needed time, much time to spare for reading . . . Well, these had been the first guests of İncila Hanım.

Monsieur Tahar had come afterward. He was a discreet gentleman of refined manners and had conservative views on life; he occupied a prominent place among those who had resided in that house. He was neither curious nor inquisitive. Restraint in behavior, expression, and performance were his salient features. Even when he sat with İncila Hanım for a game of bezique and sipped cherry liqueur, he observed this restraint. In contrast with other guests, he had stayed for a long time in that room, very long indeed . . . This had to be the case, so that he could get his affairs in order. Some people needed to take innovative steps to achieve true togetherness and pause . . . That room at Edgware Road had become a sanctuary for all three of them, remote from central London. Under the circumstances, they may have been reticent about the impressions they had made during the hours they had shared with each other. They had a common ground in which they felt themselves at home and happy. To be able to breathe that atmosphere and to feel secure in it had been more than enough. This had taught them not to intrude into each other's experiences. Those days and nights had been lived as they should. They were convinced about this. This conviction had been their greatest triumph, I believe. He used to go to Casablanca at prescribed dates twice a year and stay there for a couple of weeks. He had not much to say about its streets or shores. The only remark he could make was about the weather, which was a little warmer; that was all. The rest belonged to him, solely to him . . . He had been with them during that Passover evening. He had just been back from his journey. "This time I feel really exhausted. I think I'm growing old . . . " he said. "This may have been my last trip; I told this to the people over there as well. They understood. They always do and allow me to live as I please. That's the main problem, I reckon. Their quietness was a kind of revenge they vowed to take on me through their seeming indifference. They saw to it that I remained all alone, by myself . . . " That evening he had indulged in heavy wine drinking more than was his custom. He had not had difficulty in seizing the meaning of the Festive day. The journey that dated back thousands of years; he was no stranger to that long journey to his own promised land. What was the origin of this familiarity? Despite his secular nature, he had read many books on the subject. He had been able to view certain aspects of a world through the beliefs a different land had created. His studies had given him the privilege—and precedence over İncila Hanım—of interpreting those past events which had been celebrated for centuries in different languages. It was obvious that in his childhood he had been taught the fundamentals of Judaism. He offered extremely interesting individual views likely to shatter many prejudices regarding the messages communicated by the Koran to modern man. The same held true for the Torah and the Talmud. He believed that theology was a great long elegy that enabled man to have insights into mysteries. Kabbalah had once attracted his curiosity. He had a smattering of Hebrew . . . This may have been the origin of the above-mentioned familiarity . . . However, he had tried to share with them that evening a very old anecdote of his that the wine had awakened in his mind. It was the story of a couple of eyes shedding tears. The place where these tears had been shed was the streets of Casablanca where the inhabitants had learned to coexist despite disparity of race. Some people had told him that one should be powerful in life, that one could attain God only by wrestling with one's self, with what has been given one or by trying to find out what one has been denied . . . Those were the times when people, by virtue of their self-styled authority, could pass judgment on other people's lives, when some people showed their fellow beings the paths that led to other lands . . . Did this enable in him a better understanding of his life in London? Could he make people understand Casablanca's call, and its remoteness at the same time? Monsieur Tahar had given no hint as to the possible implications of these questions. This was perhaps the most important story that he wanted to tell his 'last friends.' What had been uttered, what had been recollected belonged to those moments, to that evening. He had merely touched on certain aspects of life. After that, everybody would be treading on his words . . . This behavior, this attitude to what had been experienced befitted Monsieur Tahar. In fact, what had been desired to be concealed were those bitter days in his life. Was it not an established fact that everybody carried his own burden? These are the flights that assume different meanings according to the circumstances in the course of our lives, that determine some of our moments and that convey the meaning of our lives to us and to our fellow beings.

One might have lived those evenings

Flights and/or steps that others determine for us and occasionally lend meaning to . . . Monsieur Robert's experience of flight one evening in his sister's apartment—who was busily engaged in preparing the commemoration dinner—and the flight that he experienced a year later, widely differed in character. I had to have complete confidence in the feeling engendered by this difference, the story of a person who had come from another land somewhat belatedly made the experience of such difference inevitable. It was true that on both occasions he had been in the same room, in front of the same mirror, stylishly dressed with utmost fastidiousness, and he felt that sense of victory originating from a sense of vengeance that lay deep in his breast. The story had required the realization and experiencing of this difference; everybody felt that need, everybody that looked at that response, toward that direction from different angles. Otherwise he would not have given me those keys; otherwise I could not make headway towards him despite all the good will I had. However, the prevailing conditions necessitated that those flights take place through different corridors. The first flight brought with it renewed hope in spite of all the disappointments experienced and aspirations fulfilled, in spite of the loneliness; while the second flight implied a deepseated resentment likely to be harbored until the final days. In the first case, Madame Roza was still alive. If the place and the relations of the elder sister in the family are considered, this should be taken as an explanation. The joy of return had just been exhausted. In the second case, he would be realizing that he had already been too late for tomorrow, in other words that he would no longer be in a position to indulge in fantasies like the past, to return to the place where he had been robbed of all his toys. This was the reason why I had desired to see him again, getting prepared for that evening in front of the mirror. I want to have it clear in my mind. Monsieur Robert must have dreamt of a genuine Istanbul evening just before that first Passover night that was to be celebrated in his sister's absence. Such an evening—after so many years had elapsed in between, would be his only evening, the only one of his life. At a time when everybody was desirous to show that everything was all right, would attend, and would take a few reluctant steps forward . . . he had heard a sound; it seemed to him a call from his childhood. This journey would be the last he would be in a position to make to his family. He had called up Juliet telling her he had suddenly felt indisposed, which made his visit impossible. "I see," Juliet said, "We are always here; come whenever you feel like it." After this short telephone call he had stretched himself over the bed wandering his gaze over the room he was to vacate. He felt exhausted. This room would be the last room occupied by him in Istanbul. He heard voices outside. Voices and sounds of life that flowed away in a very different milieu; voices and sounds similar to those in other stories . . . He suddenly desired to return in the midst of that life . . . at least for these last days. The place where he happened to be was enough to indicate to what extent this aspiration was fulfilled or where it had been lingering. Yes, this room was going to be his last room in Istanbul . . . The life that had been attained, that had been thought of as having been attained and that had been interpreted differently in various instances, that made those things possible, could thus easily be lost . . . On the day we parted company, he had harangued about his feelings on that night of separation. He was full of resentment, so much so in fact, that he could not and would not impart it to anyone else. He not only resented his family, the city that had rejected him just as he had expected when he was in London, but also the individual that he had always aspired to be. Inherent in this resentment was a kind of joy that originated from his capacity to see certain realities clearly. He was conscious of the things that faced him; he felt them. He had witnessed that he had been in a position to outdistance the people who had turned a deaf ear to what he had experienced. When he had said on the telephone that he could not take part in the festivities, Juliet said: "I understand." This was an expression that had lost its force, and that had been eroded through frequent usage . . . one of those expressions that we use to justify ourselves, to dwell a little longer in the minds of other people; an expression which builds mutual confidence . . . I understand . . . then silence . . . What had Juliet exactly meant by that? He had left on her, and, consequently, on them probably, the impression that he could not put up with a Passover evening in the aftermath of his elder sister's untimely death just a few months before. That was all he could tell them to help them understand. He had suddenly felt exhilarated; it was a gaiety that a new person had generated in him. That person had approached him with mincing steps, gingerly, without making any noise, despite all expectations. Nobody could see the point he had reached anymore, or to be precise, the point he had attained. He had suddenly realized that he had outrun his rivals and that he belonged henceforth to another place. He had to have confidence in this man, to trust him as best as he could, taking into account other moments, nights and awakenings . . . in order to be able to carry better both the place he had hoped to reach and the years he had left behind. There, in the last country he knew with whom and with what he had to coexist, with what dreams in particular . . . This may have been the reason why he had recalled the Passover evening, his loneliness and the return to oneself, when he was about to set off on the true path. The associations made by what had remained in his mind from that evening summarized his life and represented it in its multifarious aspects. Those evenings also seemed to linger as a reminder of his wrong steps. He had in the store of his mind two festive evenings shrouded by a variety of masks and representations . . . two Passover evenings lived in different climates, neither of which could assume the aspect of a genuine home. What one had experienced there were different solitudes, different abandonments, different evenings, different silences and different times of reticence . . . smiles and little charades. That evening in London, Monsieur Robert tried to recapture the image of Lola he had just parted with and from whom he could not believe he was separated, İncila Hanım tried to bring back a picture of Hugo in her memory who had left with her the story of a real struggle as well as her tangos that she had never been able to sing as she would have liked to, and of Monsieur Tahar and the streets of Casablanca he remembered. They would have evoked the former Passover evenings that had left them with indelible memories. I believe that Monsieur Robert had felt better about how warmly he had been attached to the friends he tried to take along to the small hotel room in order to introduce them to me. He had begun considering them as the most reliable people in his life after the experiences he had with his family members. A warm feeling was concealed there; a feeling that would lead a person elsewhere, to somewhere one could not always describe, to a place one was always in pursuit of . . . That may have been the reason why I had wanted to present him with a little gift as a token of that night. I was at some place where I was thinking about that man concealed within me as much as about the man to whom I had given a gift, as is the case with true gifts. I should be able to describe that place, although in a different fashion, by words in which I could lend a new meaning to suit the occasion. Do gifts not generate in us our secret yearnings in addition to certain feelings, or perhaps along with certain feelings? Monsieur Robert had left behind certain barely perceptible scenes related to that night that I can describe to the extent the power of my imagination will allow. This was a source that would provide me with enough power to enable me to live according to my fancy. These were my clues. Certain items and certain words would henceforth be ours alone. A little fantasy . . . still more fantasies. What steps should we take or what keys should we make use of to enlighten our relationships and our identities in those relationships? I'm no longer upset by the thought that the place those items and words have brought me to today or may bring me to some time in the future, enabling me to live this story in all its dimensions. The contributions of people, up to a certain degree, to my becoming conscious of my 'originalities' taught me to have a reliance on my questions despite all the disadvantages involved. Paths that we took, that we succeeded in taking in others, were, in fact, paths that belonged to us, paths in which we found ourselves. All the steps we took contained ourselves; we had developed a certain attitude toward life. This was at the same time the place where stories were true, I think. We endeavored to keep track of that, sticking to our errors and the apprehensions we could not express, and eventually to lies. When I think of all of this, my conviction increases that Monsieur Robert, as a person who has committed many errors in his life and experienced misunderstandings in different ways, will not hinder my progress in reaching a different point in a story about him. And so, the gift assumes a different meaning and dimension. This is the feeling of a rebirth caused by reproduction through words. I could not possibly guess to what extent the survivors of that Passover evening in London believed, at that time of togetherness, in a rebirth after a whole lifetime spent dwelling on the past. What I knew was, if one took into consideration what Monsieur Robert had told me, the fact that Monsieur Tahar, with his profound knowledge of philosophy that was acquired and thoroughly assimilated, had spoken on slavery until the early hours, on its history and the different meanings and forms it had assumed, on the evening when liberation from slavery was being celebrated. To be liberated from slavery? To what extent was this possible? Monsieur Tahar never answered this question. No matter what we did and what we risked, we could not get rid of certain things related to us, of certain things we thought we had left behind . . . Could it be that İncila Hanım's impulse to speak that evening of Istanbul, of its sea, of that seaside residence lost in the haze of the past, the pinkish yogurt of Kanlıca, was another sort of slavery? Why not? If one agreed with the fact that it was indeed slavery, then İncila should be considered as someone who had known how to carry her slavery with optimum grace. She had singled out herself from her companions by self-imposing a return to Istanbul every year, thus imposing order on her life and transforming this habit into a little ritual . . . by re-establishing the pattern of her life every year; for, the sea called her every summer; it was a constitutional trait that had its origin in her unfathomable depths. It looked as though these mornings and evenings had forced open the doors of many a dreamworld. The true songs might have been trapped there. In a nutshell, İncila Hanım had regularly gone back to *her* Istanbul for those special moments; it had been her burning desire. The demolition of the seaside residence to yield to new construction had made no difference. In this respect, she presented a sight rather different from those proffered by the ordinary people we encounter in a good many stories, by the people we are used to seeing around us. This fact associates in us the story of an individual who looks on us and on the world at large through another window. Under the circumstances, one is inclined to imagine that the place was occupied by songs that could not be sung and could not be lived in a different climate. It seems that her El Dorado also aspired for completely new sounds and scents. It seems that the sea had flooded her imagination, facilitating her assimilation into new conditions, preserving her life in the ground floor of that new construction. The sea had literally flooded her imagination. In the early days of summer, it was her custom to put on her red, orange, and yellow streaked black swimsuit that gave her breasts a pointed appearance, and dive into the cool waters of the Bosporus. She would set the table in the evening to regale herself with delicacies while sipping at her raki, contemplating the setting sun and the vessels that glided toward the Mediterranean Sea. Years had liberated her from her bondage to houses and furniture. She must have nurtured the seaside residence in her depths somewhere. Her success in placing the shadows there in a new scene must have been an extension of her mastery at losing, losing in every sense of the word. To know how to lose . . . could you define the loss by starting from this assumption? According to Monsieur Tahar, she was a slave to the sea, to the moments and sentiments in which the sea was involved.

Why had she been so enamored with the vessels heading for the Mediterranean? Why had she chosen to go and stay in her new house, her sanctuary on the Bosporus, in those summer months as she was used to in her teenage years? The answers, the correct answers, to these questions seem to have been lost in time, buried within certain individuals. Once more, everybody had to find the right answers to their questions. Our occasional *déjà-vu* experiences involving certain individuals and certain glances had some meaning after all. I cannot deny the existence of other questions which were new and were likely to serve me as a guide in showing me a couple of little paths in certain sections of the story. For instance, where had İncila Hanım's father gone and with whom had he lived? Who had served as intermediary in selling the seaside residence, in setting it on fire and in arranging its looting, like many of its counterparts? What furniture, paintings, and objects had remained after this looting? To what extent could the remnants of the past survive in this house that confronted the Bosporus with a different face? As far as I can remember, İncila Hanım had said nothing likely to shed light on the dark corners of her life. In the restraint of Monsieur Robert one could see the traces of a like darkness. Despite all that they had shared, they were curious to know those special areas and tabooed moments. To know those tabooed moments, in other words to know the moments set apart as sacrosanct . . . in order to live . . . To resist as best one could against what they experienced . . . Now I feel I am nearer to the meaning of this attitude.

To be able to make a phone call to Lola

Late in the evening, İncila Hanım was to sing a tango, an old, unforgettable hit . . . at a time when everything was being privatized, when everybody set off on a journey in a different direction . . . It was a valediction . . . an act or instance of bidding farewell that was suited to the meaning of that night in every respect, that suited every second, every word, every color, and every perfume it evoked . . . They were immersed in a brief but profound silence. Monsieur Robert's wish to make a phone call to Lola, who lived in his former house in proximity to the house where they happened to be at the time, was thwarted. I distinctly remember it. His voice was tremulous as he was telling me what he had gone through in those moments of despair; he seemed to suffer from being unable to knock on that door. He distinctly remembered it. He experienced the same sensation on that Passover evening he had celebrated together with his family members in Istanbul . . . to make a call to Lola . . . How different everything had been years ago, how differently it had all started, had seemed and been represented! Years ago, the guests at the table had not yet met with death and had not been obliged to part with their family despite postponements. Those dreams had not yet been exhausted; those joys had not been lost at that time. At the time everybody was different, everybody looked at each other differently, everybody saw in the mirror, in their mirror, a different individual. Years ago, when he was staying at the Park Hotel with Lola, he had not felt himself a nuisance at that Passover table. They had been the subject of scrutiny for everybody. He had succeeded and would work his way up the ladder; at least it looked as though he would. He had become a legendary figure. Maybe he had wanted to make a call to Lola just to remind her of that evening. Then he had realized . . . At a moment when he was once more caught unawares by that person whom he actually wanted to forget, to shun . . . The whole thing was a stage play, what had been experienced was actually the scenes of an unwarranted play . . . Just like that evening when so many losses had been experienced . . . that evening when he had appeared to his family as a stranger . . . years ago . . . When one considers the plays enacted by the family members, plays which appeared different though they essentially remained the same, he had not even been admitted to appear in the scene, in a simple play written and enacted somewhere before with different words. He had been but a spectator, a mere visitor among them . . . To begin with, he was a person secretly envied for his successes and admired for his merits. Lands and individuals were lost because of the failures that followed . . . climates to which no return had been possible because of certain failures . . . To be looked at from different angles with different looks had been his punishment. The angle from which he was being contemplated was the place from which he had viewed his family at a distance, from the place where he had been exiled. He had once brought costly gifts to his nephews and nieces, to his elder and younger sisters. He had only memories to narrate and share with those present that evening. He had only been able to convey the image of that individual he had to abandon in a place laden with memories . . . That night belonged to him in particular. He felt himself a stranger even to those few people who had given him a helping hand, who enabled him to cope with difficulties during his hard times to the extent their means allowed. Even to those few people who succored him from different angles . . . to Roza, Tilda and Berti . . . Everybody was actually their own self; everybody empathized with the individual within themselves, the individual whose aspirations one could not materialize. By these means he possessed many sentiments which he could elaborate upon and nurture in order to enjoy his state of being a spectator as best as he could . . . all things considered, to be able to convey his memoirs to others, to share them with others was well-nigh impossible . . . Years had scattered these people over a vast area . . . He was an exile to them; exiled to such a remote realm that he could not bring himself to them even in his most difficult times. He thought himself to be beyond a mere spectator or visitor . . . An exile though he was . . . a hero of a legend built and nurtured by lies, wrong lives, wrong cities, wrong streets, and wrong houses . . . What had been lost in return was the family he sustained in London for years on end . . . a family that did not go beyond potential, beyond being but a fantasy . . .

Now I have more than one reason for remembering in detail that Passover, in order that I can insert it at a different time, into a different story . . . Once more everything was reduced to order. Madame Roza had done everything to endow the table with the delicacies it deserved. The participation of her brother in such an evening after so many years had contributed to the preparations by endowing them with original color and meaning. The large family was there again and the topics of discussion were life in general, daily political developments, the beauty of traditions, Judaism, the fate of the Jews and last but not least, the history of the chosen people and their place in the contemporary world. Monsieur Robert had taken the floor. People listened to him when he spoke, everybody kept silent and tried to express, in one way or another, their admiration for him. They had tried once more to enter into a life they knew to be unattainable through a path they decked with imagination and petty jealousies. For, this was easy . . . for little lies no great sacrifices were required. They were in the midst of a scene that had to be enacted. They had praised him for his smartness. Everybody saw in him a part of themselves, an aspect of themselves they wished they could reveal. That might have been the reason why the talks had ended in a fiasco and had failed to attain the objectives pursued. I understand this better when I recall his occasional wandering attention toward the end of the meal, his drifting far, very far away, toward the voices in his head, and moving unconsciously and gradually away from the milieu he happened to be in; this was the result of his reverie. These were brief moments, very brief moments; moments he could have fit or failed to have fit with the remnants of lives mislaid in others and fragmentary visions from alien times. You did not have to put on your thinking cap in order to understand that he had gone to a place he could not share with anyone. For instance, in the last few minutes his attention had been drawn to the glass of wine in front of him. His forefinger had wandered around its edge. The glass was of one of those sets that were used on special occasions and gingerly placed on the table. Voices and sounds happened to have been buried somewhere. Those moments were mingled with those voices and sounds . . . There was a chance that Lola had sipped her wine from this very glass. Objects which breathed in and out with us were our witnesses that concealed our secrets stealthily in their own way . . . At that very moment, he seemed to figure in a vision alien to me, and seemed destined to remain so. In a vision alien to me with individuals I would never be able to establish contact with . . . Under the circumstances, all that remained for me was to patch up the fragments of knowledge I had gleaned from other people, from Monsieur Jacques, Juliet, and Aunt Tilda. One cannot deny the fact that to wish to linger only in fragments of a whole is something in itself, after all. Those fragments that were found could find their eventual places over a course of time, leaving aside all preferences and deeds. You cannot expect me to guess at this stage where I will end up as a consequence of my efforts. All I can say is that those who try to place him somewhere within themselves often fancy that they are watching an adventure movie as they look at that distant life from outside and feel somewhat elated. The life left as a legacy to me was the remnant of a life spent gambling big in Monte Carlo, in winning and losing considerable fortunes at those tables, in being unable to go to places other than St. Moritz for skiing, in being a member of one of the reputed golf clubs in London, in going on safari in East Africa, in obtaining tickets for privileged seats at Wimbledon, in feeling the warm touch of fur coats, in staying at the ancient and illuminated hotels of Venice, in eating at the most expensive restaurants in Paris, and making innumerable trips to Kenya, Brazil, and Nigeria. It seemed as though he had earned the money for the sake of enjoying life to the full . . . It sometimes occurs to me that losing was a kind of an aristocratic privilege under the circumstances . . . But to describe this little victory as one would have liked to after so many defeats and gaps was extremely difficult . . . The life he had led was a life that the people at that Passover evening could not have lived, could not have risked; a life completely out of the ordinary, a life left in the past. To the best of my recollection, nobody had dared to ask about the origin of the fortune that had enabled him to live such an exciting life. Everybody remained content to arrive at their own conclusions. To remain a mere onlooker was easier than trying to act and understand. The person, who could not take a step forward into an individual, took that step toward himself, into his own life eventually. Monsieur Robert had mentioned a couple of times that the secret lay in the coffee trade, in being familiar with the coffee trade, and in being able to correctly interpret the fluctuations in the price of coffee. After a few mistakes he had learned that the right place to go was Brazil and Kenya for good produce and what people one should contact and how to negotiate with them. There were innumerable stories he could tell about those places. He had once told us that he could never forget the mornings when the dawn broke early, of certain trains and the railways. He had spoken about the terror that those vast lands generated. He used to speak in broken sentences . . . in sentences left unfinished. It was as though he had lived there as a different individual, an individual he could not describe or convey to us . . . This enhanced the doubt in Berti; it assumed reality. According to him, the coffee trade was just one aspect of his business. One should delve into the core of that adventure. According to his account, his maternal uncle, for whom he had great admiration, had got involved with contraband. According to Monsieur Jacques, he was a swindler who had the gift of the gab that enabled him to establish critical business relations; a swindler who succeeded in inspiring trust in foreigners through his gestures. This inspired not only a temporary reliance, but also great confidence in his future transactions. Thus he lived in his dreamworld bedecked with original visions. He had his men . . . people liable to change, speaking different tongues, with different looks and different steps that he had befriended and believed to be the most reliable people in his life after all that he had gone through with his family. It was true that his extravagance enabled him to cling to those people, but beyond that it signified the collapse of those narrow bridges. When the people in his circle caught sight of his fancies, they didn't hesitate to abandon him. When we tried to speak using the cliches which allowed other people to communicate with each other, we could see the reason for his loneliness and estrangement mirrored in his being the jack-of-all-trades and master of none. We must acknowledge, however, that his skill in finding new employment in new areas of business, his spawning of new ideas and hopes had enabled him to take different steps over the years. There was the question about what in him had caused his failure to take new steps after a certain point in time. For, he had no plans for the future that would have fixed him anywhere. This may have been the reason behind the loftiness of his ideals; ideals it would be difficult for him to pursue, to describe, to share with others. Nevertheless, he had not learned anything from these abandonments and forsakings, and had not moved away from that man within himself. It was a sad fact that what could be lived and acquired found no echo in others.

These interpretations drew boundaries he could not and would not perceive. This was the place where he encountered his next-of-kin regardless of whether he wanted to or not. One should have a better insight into Monsieur Jacques's joy that was mingled with the sadness he enjoyed there, whose origin might be traced back to his taking refuge. Berti was there, as well as those individuals that Berti had prepared the ground for, individuals like himself, individuals that he could not help seeing sprout. According to Juliet, whom I always wanted to imagine as one of the people who knew the place in question well, Monsieur Robert was a gambler who played big. His lifestyle and worldview were sufficient proof of this fact. This profession required, in the first instance, successful acting. Any individual who had the least initiation into dramatic art could easily understand that he had the remarkable capacity of creating little worlds. The journeys he had set off on to those lands were, in a way, other people's journeys. An adventurer involved in international contraband, a daydreamer who tried to endear himself to his acquaintances with lies, or an actor who endeavors to invigorate people. While people tried to attribute to Monsieur Robert lives laden with nugatory criticism, they were full of admiration for him. He was an individual, censured, kept at arm's length; someone who breathed more easily elsewhere, a relative who invited his acquaintances to partake—with their special merits and capacities— of the joy of a life that deserved to be concealed. Of all the family members only Madame Roza was persuaded that he traded in coffee, or she preferred to appear so. This conviction implied a necessity, to wit an indispensability, if one took into account the duration of that relationship. His sister needed at least one person in which to build up her trust. Life had assigned her the duty of an elder sister, the duty to protect her brother; she could not possibly leave this man who had been considered by many as the odd-man-out and treat him as a cast away to his destiny, whom she could not endear to the public. Robert, her beloved brother, might not have been conscious of this; however, if one meditated on the past, on their past, the disappearance of this sentiment somewhere between them was not so important. This sacrifice, this devotion made her happy. This made her feel that she had fulfilled her mission. She could not ask for more in this life. Moreover, not being conscious of the existence of such feelings was so much the better. She should not feel the burden of her sacrifice for someone to whom she had devoted herself. This was a critical point which was due to the fact that you assumed someone to be of your own species. Madame Roza had naturally gained considerable ground in this direction. Could one attribute the growing fatigue that she suffered (before the rest of the family) to the hardness of this undertaking which caused her to gradually loose her energy? Perhaps. Some of the family stayed in her life and some left eventually as a consequence of her situation. Here lay the reason why people wished to cling to life through relatives; the reason might also lie on both sides of a boundary which is impossible to delineate.

Now, as for Aunt Tilda . . . All these comments, opinions, and escapades had no importance at all. The refined manners of her elder brother were sufficient to make him a gentleman. The number of men that had entered her life, who had laid down a life of finesse for her had been limited. This deprivation had led Monsieur Robert to a stage from where it would be easier for him to attain the truth: his life, his philosophy of life, what he had done for Lola, and her overwhelming love for a hero made him one of the romantic heroes of old whose like is no longer to be found—the story that had paved his way to this woman and made her a slave is supportive of this view. Those were the postwar years during which masses of people had begun developing new ideals and new hopes to help them survive despite the loss of so many lives. It was in such an atmosphere that Monsieur Robert, together with Monsieur Aldo, his business partner at the time, wandered all over the cities of Europe looking for business outlets. It was an unforgettable and unique era; a time in which unforeseeable people emerged from nowhere at the most unexpected moments and intruded on our lives. "What other people saw in films, personally I'd been an eyewitness of; I led a life of madcap adventure. O those days! Nobody would believe me were I to tell them!" he said one day, referring to those times. In these words, there lay concealed not only a sense of humor, but also resentment; even solitude. I would be bearing testimony to this solitude at an opportune moment, elsewhere, in stages. In this complaint, there was also a little boasting that resisted against the past. Those moments brought along a breath from distant lands without which one would have difficulty surviving. There was a different individual . . . "You know what, I'd been sent to prison in Milan," he said, "I'd been incarcerated for four days and four nights exactly.

Had it not been for Monsieur Aldo I'd be done for. I'd have stayed there for years probably and nobody would have been aware of my absence. Aldo got me out. He had influential contacts everywhere. Big business, you know . . . " Monsieur Robert never referred to this subject afterward. He mentioned nothing about the act that had paved his way to jail. I chose to remain silent as always through such journeys in time to which I was occasionally invited. Words and questions would come to life elsewhere once again. I might have asked myself once again whether this was another story stored away in his memory, written elsewhere for other people. A recollection, an imaginary time desired to be stored and prolonged, the truth of which he could not even force himself to believe, let alone his listeners. Now that I am far removed from everybody, I can freely say it. Monsieur Robert had a knack for spreading lies. When I recollect certain circumstantial evidence, I'm inclined to surmise that he followed in the steps of an original guide, a guru, reminiscent of those legendary heroes of adventure movies, namely of Monsieur Aldo, for whom defeats and disappointments were hardly obstacles. However, I had to proceed on toward other sources. For, the traveler of that long adventure—who had cleverly lost himself in some time and space in accordance with the requirements of that little rumor that he had generated through his circle—had never taken part in our long conversations. When I try to place that past, it represents only certain details to me, I must say that certain questions had triggered in me little hope of attaining an idea of their shared past. Where had they met, how had they been introduced to each other, which dreams and journeys had been shared between them, and where, wherefore, and for whose sake had they parted ways? Who had they aspired to be at that time? All these questions are awaiting me in the dark labyrinths of that land I can never reach. In the blind alleys of dark labyrinths . . . for the sake of a few more dreams . . . for the sake of those few more steps within me . . . just as with other matters related to Monsieur Robert . . . in many of the people with whom I want to tell . . . Notwithstanding, what I have heard and with whom I could establish contact does not hinder my having a glimpse of the hero of that life even from a distance . . . Monsieur Aldo had been different people with different looks, had lived in the bodies of different people and figured in different photographs in those lives . . . He had remained in the mind of the people who had met him as a person versed in imports and who knew how to make the best of his life, and not only as someone who was a skillful poker player, a connoisseur of wines and of women. His creative talent that stunned people and which found its particular expression in trickery had earned him the reputation of being a man that opened all doors. His entourage had never doubted his mastery in fraudulent affairs. He cleared all sorts of goods at customs regardless of the regulations in effect. He was a well-known character in those surroundings. He was praised for his adage: "If you do it, so shall we." Those were words used in critical situations; the words uttered in days whose contribution to the cause was well-known in advance, the words uttered in days when settling accounts did not present any difficulties. To see things at the right time had always been effective during those days . . . He was also remembered for his disappearing at times, during which nobody could find him anywhere; sometimes he was a Catholic Arab; sometimes a native of Beirut; sometimes a Levantine from İzmir; sometimes a native of Thesallonica; and sometimes a Jew from Istanbul. These were his own stories, the identities of people who had left with him their tales, their lives. His identity changed according to the person he wanted to be as well as to the time and place in question. Partly because of this, nobody could ascertain for certain his actual origin. He had spent the last days of his life in Barcelona according to some, in Goa, according to others. According to some, he had died of syphilis, and to others, he had been stabbed to death by a Syrian arms dealer. In the said story, he was apparently in the same bed with the wife of one of the people he transacted his business with. The man was overwhelmed by a sight he didn't expect to see, and had lost control; he had deemed execution a suitable punishment. According to the account of certain people, this was a rather commendable death . . . Still, according to another version of the story, he had spent a life of luxury in a legendary manor house in Mexico City . . . This last version was, according to Monsieur Robert, the one he preferred to give credence to. He had never lost confidence in the master with whom he had collaborated once. To my mind, this was quite probably due to a connection concealed deep within himself, engendered by reasons that one need not to inquire into. Had that image in the mirror not taken us to places we didn't want to go? Had Monsieur Jacques also taken heed of this dangerous admiration? It was not for nothing that Monsieur Jacques had said with resentment, and also as though he had taken offense, about his brother-in-law for whom he had some sympathy: that the teacher whom he emulated was a bad character. It was he that had been instrumental in his being introduced to Lola. The connection had been indicated to him years ago. One day, I would tackle the story of that path . . . I was well aware that certain words called us to certain secrets. I was waiting for that moment to occur. That moment that quite often shuts out our reality and opens up to reveal a place we are quite unaware of.

At times I am inclined to believe in the power of that moment when I think of its advance toward certain individuals that reach me. It seems to me that I can better explain the coincidences and the encounters that seem inevitable . . . Coincidences and meetings that seem inevitable . . . If we rely on Monsieur Jacques, he said that everything had started during an ordinary trip to London. Monsieur Aldo had mentioned a fair lady singing in a nightclub in Soho, in addition to the affairs to be attended to and the addresses that were not written down but had to be memorized before setting off on the journey. A nightclub in Soho . . . Could it be that the adventure, that dragging had started there? Maybe. Some people desire to see, to glance at the different aspects of evasions from their respective angles . . . How else could we explain the fact that we imprison our heroes exclusively within our own delineated boundaries? That may be one of the reasons why I want to believe in those songs sung or desired to be sung, to flow into those days, to the profound depths of those people. The woman, who had sung those songs there, was said to be a woman who had come over to London to rewrite her life, trying to forget as best as she could the devastation in Hungary. She had succeeded in escaping—by a stratagem she had devised, after having lost her husband in the concentration camps where everybody had succumbed to different ends—to London with her two-year-old son whom she wanted to save from that cold breath they felt approaching, despite attempts at escape from the dark days looming ahead, despite omissions. A woman, who had started to work in such a business, trying to forget her upbringing in Budapest, her excellent background in music and dramatic arts, the splendid life she had left behind. She tried to think that it had been a dream, persuading herself, with stronger emphasis every day, that all moral values could have been omitted, if need be, believing in the fact that there were no values after all that deserved the attribute of infallibility. She had made herself a new little entourage that formed a circle around her, a circle of admirers; a woman, who made her presence felt wherever she entered; a woman who had been obliged to leave behind all that had held dear and valuable to her, just like every stranger that had gone through difficult days but had to put up with them all the same . . . Monsieur Aldo had told his student about that woman by stressing certain details. He had given him a strange warning when he handed him the address of that nightclub: "There's a song that Lola sings," he told him, "which may have a profound effect on you. Do everything with her, enjoy her in every possible fashion, but don't ever marry her." This warning gave him food for thought that aroused in him a strange feeling. This wanderer who had succeeded in acting out the role of a different person or to embody the character of a different individual in every city, who could never build up the family he aspired for, had, for some reason or other, felt the necessity to speak of marriage as an expected development, even as a perilous act, while mentioning a little adventure or the possibility of a little adventure. Could it be because he had felt that his traveling companion, his young partner, who, succumbing to the charm of his cherished dreams, might blow up his world, and, fascinated and infatuated by her charm, delude himself that he had found in Lola the woman of his dreams which would eventually lead him to a dead end without return? Could it be that he was convinced after all those years that imagination might induce one to take wrong steps that entailed the payment now and then of heavy compensations?

Was Lola's marriage with a young man like Monsieur Robert, endowed with refined manners and a tender heart, who enjoyed life to the fullest and was liable to be easily seduced by her charm, the result of her innate ability to perceive that it would be wise to join her life with a man, expecting that he would be a father to her growing son? Was she a person whom he could trust with the many things he aspired to in life, inspired by what the women he had left or had to leave in the past had provided him with? Could it be that Lola was concerned about the likelihood that she would make him unhappy after some time, this vulnerable creature often removed from actual reality, with his heart on his sleeve? All or none of these questions could be put in regard to this relationship. Any one of these questions . . . or any new questions . . . To bring forward, present, or exhibit such questions again, and even more at that, was not so difficult, given the fact that we had no possibility in hand other than what our imagination had provided us with; this was an amusing game after all that had enlivened new lives within us; an amusing game that secured our enduring attachment, causing us to take refuge in our deceptions . . . especially if you have opted for that hidden spectator who tries not to make his presence felt while watching those scenes that arouse critical points in you. In brief, to decipher Aldo's attitude toward this relationship, his viewpoint, under the dim light of memory, was not possible. This might lead us to another question. For instance, could it be that this warning had been made, in contrast with the meaning that those words explicitly conveyed, to arouse matrimonial emotions? I believe the answers to this and other questions lie hidden in his relationship with Lola. However, as far as I know, nobody has succeeded in learning anything about this relationship. In this part of the story we were face-to-face with an adventurer who knew how to keep a secret between himself and the heroes of that story. This was the hardest part he had learned to play in the long path he had trodden. His figure seems to emerge before me now, though from a distance. With whom and with which particular era of history had that man—who, with his imposing stature, was eager to veil himself behind mysteries—wanted to come to terms? Still another question that awaits an answer was the one which involved a purple-brown Cadillac that Monsieur Jacques had mentioned having seen whenever his path crossed Beyoğlu. There were incidents that joined or connected each other in various intangible and unspecified ways, and that lived more often than not for the sake of those coincidences, to wit, of those encounters . . . When I ruminate over these things, I understand better the world that Monsieur Robert had discovered or believed to have discovered in Lola. After all, everybody desired sooner or later to take steps toward the images they conceived in their dreams. The pity he felt for his fellow beings was partly self-pity. When you tried to touch a fellow being who you believe to have left behind more than one life, you thought you would have access to those lives that you had failed to live in one way or another. Stories elaborated on by yearnings, fantasies, and lies . . . There are so many reasons to knock on the door of certain prospects . . . There would be no end to embarking on quests for things that would compensate for some defect . . . A short while after that first night Lola and Monsieur Robert decided to get married during a simple ceremony without informing each other's family members, next of kin, and last but not least, Monsieur Aldo. After that first encounter, on his path toward that dearth, he would try to bring up the issue of Johann with paternal care, the child begotten by her from another man with whom she had established a marital relationship, learning of the paternity from a different source for the sake of love, of his first and only love . . .

Robert & Lola, Lola & Robert . . . the solitude of two individuals, two individuals who had been able to convince themselves of the fact that they—who had come from different worlds, whose roads would converge—could unite . . . Was that all? I don't think so. However, in order to understand the story further and to be able to retell it, I had to gain further ground. The authors of the story had desired to perpetuate this march from where they found themselves . . . When they had come back to Istanbul to celebrate the second anniversary of their marriage, the descriptions of their clothes, the nightclubs they frequented, and the room that commanded a panoramic view at the Park Hotel had dazzled his friends. That was the beginning of the legend. He had spoken about big business in London and about the life he was leading there, with the greatest delight. He had been successful in this. Even though he might not have openly said so, he had done his utmost to create in them this image. They contemplated coming to Istanbul more often, to play tennis at the Dağcılık Kulübü and swimming at the Sipahi Ocağı . . . The game had to be played by the book . . . However, these small trips were destined to be rarer and rarer as the years went by, and were to come to an end eventually. It seemed as though their trips to Istanbul had drawn a parallel with the course their relationship followed . . . dwindling to a speck. It would take Monsieur Robert thirty-five years before he could return to the city he had always wanted to abandon, for reasons he could not disclose not even to his next-of-kin, to the city where he was born and which he could not obliterate from his mind. Monsieur Robert would be known to everybody to be living in London or somewhere else in the world . . . in a distant land; the postcards, letters, and money he had sent to Aunt Tilda were proof of this. Was everything as it actually appeared? Indeed, were they exactly as they were known? Breaking with his family was his way of making headway toward the life ahead. For example, he would remain a stranger to the family, to his own small and living family, the family he had fancied to start, remaining a mere appendage despite his passionate love for Lola which the years had not eroded, notwithstanding all sorts of hardships, trials, and challenges overcome for the sake of that love, despite the affection he had shown to Johann for pity's sake. He would realize that his affection for and temporary attachment to his family were actually frustrating him; he would take cognizance of the real life reflected by the lights of the cosmopolitan city, its buses and its subway, of real life, of himself and of the different aspects of solitude. The nights that Lola and Johann held long conversations behind closed doors were, as he had told me then, the nights he felt himself very lonely, as though forsaken. Was this a sort of betrayal? Those were the nights during which he would let himself be tempted by gambling, during which he would take refuge at gambling tables that would call to him as a sanctuary; those were the nights when he would be their creator, if I may say so. This passion would last for years leading to big gains and big losses . . . sharing the fate of notorious gamblers involving huge sums of money, unforgettable critical moments, intense emotions, vivid recollections. Recklessness was his ruling passion; you could see him fly off the handle, and then suddenly transform into fits of delight the next moment. "A pit was being dug beneath my feet, but I did my best to shut my eyes to it," he told me one day. It seemed as though he tried to tell of the resentment that betrayal had engendered within him, partly blaming himself for his good will. The tergiversation had not been directed exclusively at Lola and Johann; the family he had left in Istanbul which he considered a last refuge, from which he had never wanted to part and never intended to burn bridges with, had also been involved in this treachery. He had built his life on lies for a good many years and spent many years at gambling tables. Johann would one day leave for America with his girlfriend, relying to a certain extent on the relations he had established in the world of cinema, to see if his luck as a producer would hold. Before he had set out for America, he said: "You're a very good man. But you made glaring errors in your life, very serious errors. Your biggest mistake has been to marry my mother." He answered in return: "I couldn't help it; I was head over heels in love with your mother." "I know," replied Johann, "but the fact is that my mother had experienced so many deaths in her lifetime and had lost the capacity to fall in love. She herself had told me this; she must've told you as well. That was not difficult to understand. Why haven't you seen this? Don't tell me you were blinded by your love for her. We know well that we lie flatly in the name of love; we take refuge in blatant lies, pretending to love. Both of us know this for a fact, even though we are different human beings with different personalities." Was that the moment to disclose his secret—which even those who knew him closely would place somewhere quite different from where it usually belonged, and share it with others—the secret which he had been carrying for years regarding his matrimonial tie, painstakingly, without hope? Could the talks he might hold from then on enable them to see each other in a different light, relapsing into silence? Who knows? All that he knew was that he could not put into words, despite strenuous efforts, what he actually wanted to convey. It was like the feeling that an individual would experience standing before the door of a person whom he had been yearning to see for a long time, but was incapable of knocking on. Johann would have understood him; he would have been one of the people to whom he could address, convinced that he would get to the bottom of what I would say. I can draw these conclusions because I had been imparted with the secret in question. I was the third person involved at the moment of separation, at a different time of parting. He had finally succeeded: what I had learned would enable me to look at Lola from a different angle, who had carried, throughout her life, the deaths that appeared remote and alien to everybody else. One might call this a kind of nobleness, despite all the pains it involved. One yielded to an intimately related person, to one's own hell, in the first place. The life that he had led, that he had chosen, had undoubtedly taught him this. This may have been the reason why he expected a reaction to his narrative. A reaction of which he would know nothing, and which, he would feel hidden from, a reaction of which Monsieur Aldo and his family in Istanbul would be ignorant of as well. This secrecy would one day hold true for those he would know in a different climate, as a completely different person. This was the main stipulation in our agreement. Only one question would do; one single question. A question which would take us to another coast, to somebody else's coast; the rest lying within the precincts of one's imagination . . . We might venture, for instance, to ask him about the ways he exercised his manhood in trying to understand him a little better. What were the different methods of experiencing one's virility, of favoring a woman whom one passionately loved and was attached to? Johann might desire to provide an answer to this from the outside, from a different emotional locale. However, they had preferred, like others, to keep silent or to attach meaning to their reticence in different stories. "A person in love never loses hope, without the slightest doubt," he said, after gazing for a while with a smile. He had merely said this in a murmur, bending his head toward his breast, to the individual he wanted to consider as his own son, but had to leave to tread another path. "You've done a lot for me, but I'm turning my back on you," said Johann after carefully placing the photograph album in his suitcase. Then he added: "However, our *élan vital*, the vital force that upholds us is evil, don't forget that! My mother had nothing to give to another as far as I know. What she needed was affection and love, without giving anything in return: an unrequited love. That's why I hated her." A mere smile had been his response to these words. Had his silence originated from his hopelessness or from his inability to give free rein to that suppressed and repressed anger he always tried to conceal? They had to pay dearly for this alliance; they had hung on each other with great force thereafter. That was the only moment when they had experienced friendship and affection. The moment of separation once and for all, they would not even communicate by word of mouth henceforward. Such moments had been experienced by others who knew, and had been obliged to witness, what true separation was and how to survive it. This might, in a way, be considered the call of the wild; the call of the wild that could be transported by other people to other stories by means of original feelings and visions . . . Johann had decided to set out on a path of evil that night. He had had a conversation with his girlfriend who had come to fetch him, and who looked like a fashion model with her elongated umbrella, camel hair mantle, and purple-brown scarf. This was a conversation, during which both interlocutors remained strangers to each other; one of those conversations held when one had nothing better to do; just idle talk, in other words. "America is waiting for us, ready to give us an Oscar," his girlfriend said, "we'll be back as soon as we get it." "Before we have grown old, certainly," said Johann, "before beginning to look at this city through American glasses . . . " and they had grown jocular. Yes, everybody was a stranger to everybody. What and who were they laughing at? "Write to me," said Johann before leaving. "Do write. I mean, if you feel like it." He added: "Remember me to Susan!" He wished that the Susan to whom this compliment was addressed had been Susan Hayward. A sad smile had appeared on both their faces. Once more they agreed on a common issue and were caught in an unexpected moment. "All right, old man," said Johann, "I will, if I see her." These had been his last words; the last words exchanged between them . . . This may have played a part in keeping them in his memory . . .

Could there be fragments of him left in all these words, in these wishes expected to be realized in a foreign country? Could the sentiments that accompanied this last encounter be considered among the true feelings that a father might be willing to convey to his son, despite the distance involved? Errors and human beings . . . He had returned to the stage play, to the scenes he would forever bear in mind; it looked as though he had been caught unawares by the night once again . . . He had meditated on the mistakes he had made in life; he had thought that his life resembled a poorly written play, poorly enacted, and poorly performed. He had gone outside. He had strolled aimlessly in the streets for hours on end, trying to smother those voices within him, paying no attention to the rain pouring down. This was a sight that mirrored what he had been feeling. This event was consistent with what was being experienced. Afterward, he had acted out one of the unforgettable scenes of the play . . . one of the most unforgettable and genuine . . . All alone; despite those ships, those seas, those lands . . . This was the scene in which he was trying to float the ship he had fabricated using a small piece of paper he had taken out of his pocket in that pool at Trafalgar Square. The square was almost deserted in that late hour of the night. It looked as though everybody had taken refuge somewhere. His sister had taught him how to make that ship out of a piece of paper; years ago, when everybody was a child, when Trafalgar Square was but a name in their minds . . . He had watched it drifting and dreamt of ships caught by a storm in vast oceans; the only ship he could have boarded was perhaps a ship made of paper designed to float in the pools that adorned the squares of that city. His gaze had rested quite a while on the ship that the rippling water drifted away. This scene he had also watched in one of the movies which had obsessed him, a movie in which he fancied himself as the star. The film, like all films, was lost to memory. He knew the reason why. "I'd played roulette. It was strange. I bet like mad, and the more I played the more I lost. That night my loss might equal all my losses up until then, I can't exactly tell you the amount now," he confided to me, speaking about the experiences of his lonely life. In the morning he had spoken on the phone with Lola, telling her that he intended to leave the house and that they better not see each other again. It was the morning of Johann's departure. The timing was unfortunate. He might have stayed by her side a little longer, to say the least. However, none of them was in a position to think of such a nicety. They knew all too well that they followed different paths. These were the first steps that would lead Lola, a woman who had seen hard times in other lands and who had lived as a failed hero in many stories, to a psychiatric clinic. As for him, well . . . Thirty-five years have elapsed since then. He was leaving things behind him where they belonged. He had proved to be daring enough to be able to confess to himself the incidents of that morning only later, reassessing them according to the climate in question. He was well aware of the meaning of the steps he took. This was the first and the only victory he had achieved in this relationship. Now he was hard up. He had squandered his money through gambling. He had not given up his conviction that he would continue loving Lola passionately despite all the adversities he had gone through, that a time would come when he would be pursuing her as he had done in his youth, that wherever she would go, he would be on the trail . . . Those little victories had not been in vain. This might get him nearer to the reality in the mirror. How eccentric certain people were, how versatile were their relationships, and how mercurial were the forms they assumed, quite different from their actual image. One is inclined to ask for instance who would be the person or the image one would have liked to cling to when one felt that the days one lived and one had been obliged to live were drifting away. He had asked himself this question when he had moved to a district remote from those illuminated quarters of the city; he had tried to find an answer, what image, what person? Certain places had occupied his mind in particular. During the days when everything was in order, or seemed to be, he had asked, in one of the outlying districts quite removed from where his life was spent, the illuminated life he spent had appeared to him in a completely different aspect. In the meantime, everything had changed: the nights, the streets, the odors, and the faces. There was still the possibility of glorious days. Yes, those days might still be saved. Over the course of one of those days he had found the opportunity of being engaged by prominent concerns as an adviser, as he was well informed about the world's coffee market. Yes, an adviser . . . at least temporarily, during the days when he had not severed himself completely from that life. He had to keep up appearances. His companions in the offices where he worked never knew that he lived in an outlying district. He had told them that he had been put up at the The Grosvenor Hotel. He had prepared everything. The aged receptionist by the name of Mr. Jefferson, whom everybody knew and who resembled a nobleman, whose life had been spent in manor houses, with his accent, demeanor, and poised behavior, was a close acquaintance of his. Mr. Jefferson was one of those gentlemen who knew the meaning of a life lived in resignation. In this section of the story, he had to behave assuming such an identity . . . appearing solely in this identity . . . This must have been the reason which aroused in some the desire to probe for a closer look. The game was an old one, if one considered these points. For instance, nobody should know that he had lived elsewhere in other stories. They had met at an Italian café near the hotel. It was a holiday . . . a holiday during an ordinary weekday. They were in their ordinary attire and spoke without mincing their words. They exuded warmth; years had passed since they had cemented their friendship. Mr. Jefferson had asked him why he had been absent so long from the evening teas. He had told him simply that days had elapsed, had removed him more and more to the furthest corners of the city, to a London that looked alien to him. He was no longer the same old Monsieur Robert . . . Then he had added that he had felt the need to carry on the struggle, to experience that sentiment, at least. He desired to preserve the Monsieur Robert that other people did not know, the one they could not and would not be able to perceive. Mr. Jefferson had told him that much could be done for the said Monsieur Robert, for the sake of the good old days, and that one should believe in the many ways to deal with exile. They were seated at a table in a café in the proximity of the hotel. The coffee odor mingled with the scent of fresh buns . . . It was morning . . . a morning no different from any other morning, even though certain mornings dawned reminding one of other horizons, or gave one such an impression at least . . . He had kept his promise and did his best for Monsieur Robert, who tried to refresh those mornings. Mr. Jefferson's task was to tell those who asked that Monsieur Robert was out for a meeting and wasn't expected back for a long time, and that, should they care to leave a note, he would be only too glad to deliver it to him as soon as he was back. Mr. Jefferson had also informed the night attendants of the scheme. To keep up appearances as much as possible was *de rigueur*. It may be that those moments were his last; he had desired to communicate them, to make them tangible, at least. Their encounter had taken place at least in one of the acts of the play . . . in their identities as two honest individuals . . . as two individuals who believed they had found the truth in their little lies . . . that might befit a revolt to those who could risk to rebel . . . then . . . then they were to disappear nonetheless. One day, at a time when the 'then' had a quite different meaning for me, at a time when I was trying to allot the roles my actors were to play, I went to The Grosvenor Hotel. I was led to London guided by the memory of a person who had been instrumental in making me live a night which would stay with me forever, which would gesticulate the death of a part of me. As for gambling, it was a glaring error, a suicide, let alone being a sin, throwing oneself down a chasm in all consciousness. Madame Roza's formulation of this sentence— based on a platitude, on a well-known point of view and on an understanding supplied by experience by his beloved elder sister—was the typified expression of a great many people left with diversified sentiments and a multitude of experiences. Throwing oneself headlong down a chasm . . . Was the problem related, in any way, to the storm raised at those tables, to the failure to take stock of this fall and to the connivance of it? To a secret pleasure derived from the severance with Lola's small family? He had never been willing to provide an answer to this question; he would never be able to do so.

This was one of the moments when he was confronted once again with the fact that he would not be able to tell of what he had gone through, even to his closest relations. Everybody had reserved a place for the lie relating to him. Everybody had known him to a certain extent. We had desired that some of our lies remain unshakable, to abide forever wherever they were to carry us along. Everybody had contrived a truth out of that lie. In this belated return, nobody had believed or couldn't bring himself to believe that he had been as alone as he had depicted himself to be, that he had been forsaken and had foundered. Undoubtedly the fault lay partly with him. During the days that followed his return to Istanbul, oblivious to the time when he had said to those closest to him that he had lost everything; that he had come back to Istanbul for important business affairs; that his briefcase contained valuable papers and contracts waiting to be signed; that his past experiences, the credit he enjoyed in a multitude of prominent banks across the world could solve all sorts of difficulties; that he had come from London to his birthplace that he had not visited for a very long time for a brief stay during which he purported to fix a couple of affairs and that he had effectively established contacts with otherwise inaccessible people. Yet, all his expectations had remained limited to those interviews and the topics discussed during those conversations. His attractive business prospects had not attracted due attention, they weren't clearly understood and had remained a dull, dumb show. These were the last scenes of the play enacted in Istanbul. The same had taken place when he went to the Sipahi Ocağı Club, where he hoped to say hello to a few old acquaintances, during the nights he went out to gamble, while he made business offers based on his wild imagination, even when he stayed at home or when he bought expensive gifts for Tilda, his 'little sister,' whose origin God only knew . . . The lie was being carried on in every way . . . Well, everybody was in need of such a lie. Everybody who could not disclose their darkness to people was in need of such a lie . . . everybody who was acquainted with the idea of detachment . . . everybody who wanted to see life not where he had to relive it, but at the place of his predilection. Would that morning dawn once more from somewhere new and unforeseen?

What had been experienced 'with them,' what had been desired to be collected for a new place after so many years seemed to represent the fragments of an adventure of no return . . . fragments of an adventure whose dimensions would not cease to grow in another being, accompanied by alien elements and distances. This was the moment when Monsieur Robert had cast a glance at me during the recitation of the *Hagada* on that Passover evening, all the while smiling faintly at the wine goblet before him. I thought I had caught him unawares, seeing him as a man of a completely different ilk. Then I had realized that Juliet had had a part to play in this. She was staring at us. We had arrived at that moment with diverse feelings that carried with them the memory of diverse people. Notwithstanding, we had felt that we had met somewhere removed from that old rumor, that the dinner table brought family members and families together. The words were once again incarcerated within us, they constituted obstacles that barred our way to that individual we were in pursuit of; they were our borders we could not cross, that we could not describe. What was risked was a talk that three individuals preferred to hold in their restricted and closed states, during which every contributor addressed himself in the first person; notwithstanding we had taken an important step forward in this segregated time . . . even though we were not in a position to see each other as clearly and as we ought to have done. I always wanted to believe that Monsieur Robert had made a call to Lola. New resentments could be obliterated after all those resentments. Was it possible that in that interview, a return, a return to a life to start anew had been discussed? Who knows? A man eventually learned, could not help learning, what certain returns brought and took away after a certain point in time.

It would take a long time before I could have an insight into the truth . . . a very long time . . . at a time when I was to be obliged once more to carry the results of belatedness in an individual . . . That was the first evening that Monsieur Robert had seriously considered going to London in order to get lost for good, aside from the dreams that he might have had about the prospective experience with Lola . . . to London, to that place of exile, with the intention of never returning to Istanbul . . . He had a nagging feeling which he could not define, which he could not articulate, that was tracing this path for him . . . Madame Roza's disease had not yet been diagnosed; she was not yet burdened with crippling debts; jobs prospects had not been reduced to nil . . . Those disastrous days that marked her downfall were not yet looming ahead despite the disappointments already experienced. Yet, what had been observed in that play that evening had also revealed the image of that path not yet taken. She would not be obliged to live with that individual denounced by her family, in the city where he would retrace her steps. The city where she had spent thirty-five years of her life had seemed closer to her when weighed against this sentiment. She was left there with these visions.

About a year had elapsed in the meantime . . . a year that had assumed meaning through communications that had become less and less frequent. I had often visited her at that hotel room. We used to go now and then to have a cup of tea at the Hilton Hotel. For her, it was one of the rare places, a place of refuge she doted on, and that Istanbul was endowed with, thanks to the power of the imagination of its people. She could never understand me, the fact that I did not feel myself at home there. Products of fevered imagination and elaborate deceptions had besieged us then. We had lost men elsewhere and had been looking for them elsewhere. Our history had been written in different words with missing and omitted parts; it would be written by other people or neglected altogether. Yet, there was a place where we met, where we succeeded in meeting. A place that we could not define, that we did not feel a compulsion to express, where we simply wanted to live, where we preferred to live to the fullest possible degree. A time would come when I would feel nearer. Some of us wanted to abide, to linger, sticking to certain details or to believe that we did so. We had wanted with all our heart to let ourselves be carried away by the charm of transformations, of inevitable transformations . . . Monsieur Robert had spoken to me of those years particularly in this specific corner of his; what I have collected relating to those years was mostly concealed in those tea times and to what those moments had conjured up . . . Gradually ceding the essence, the meaning and the details over to our experiences more and more . . . He was in need of a witness, of a spectator . . . What I had been looking for was a storyteller or, in other words, the missing part of my story. He had to tell his story to a third person . . . on the issue of whether I had gained some ground in the present story, we were agreed. The place we occupied in it had some bearing for both of us.

Then . . . then another year went by . . .

It was the morning of the Passover evening we had celebrated without him. He had called early in the morning. His voice on the phone was that of a dejected but resolute man. "I'm leaving for London . . . I don't intend to come back . . . " he said. "As a matter of fact, I've got the intention to pop in. Wait for me; we'll have a chat . . . " It was a Sunday. The streets were deserted . . . not a soul was stirring . . . The city was still asleep like every Sunday morning that the world had bequeathed to me. As I was passing by a bakery, I slowed down to smell the overpowering odor of the fresh bread. This stirred in my mind the image of the small restaurant I used to frequent to eat soup. The taste of that soup appeared to have made a lasting impression on me. We lose so many things and let them sink into oblivion. Could it be that our failure to reconcile ourselves with a part of our past was due to our fear of encountering the shadows we had left behind? It was a sunny and clear spring morning. A day of rest one would relish after a substantial breakfast by stretching on a sofa to peruse the dailies in the warmth of the sun's rays . . . Were such details so far removed from those people? It hadn't taken me long to get to the hotel. A room at Sıraselviler not far from the illuminated quarters of the city, although far removed from its radiation . . . Was it true that stars died without emitting any sound? Why was it that we learned of the death of a star so long after? Why so late? A room at Sıraselviler . . . a spot where a multitude of memories, and their consequent virtual representations could be shared . . . The story of that room, of the events that took place in it with their postulated meanings had begun to take shape. The authors of the story were assembling once again, in this bright morning, for a few details, words and visions . . . once again . . . for the last time . . . for diverse oaths, lights, and deaths . . . When I tapped on the door, I got it into my head that I could never get rid of this story. It may be that in knocking on that door I had reached a new ending, but the voice within me, spurred by this end, suggested that the story would be carried off to different climates as well. I had come to know this sentiment well, this little hope to which I would often return to, with other people, for other people; a sentiment which I would share with them to the best of my ability. That may well have been the reason why I had desired to alter all of those things as if they had occurred without other people knowing. Would Monsieur Robert be able to return to those days without considering his alien state? I waited; I had tried once more to wait. The hotel's corridor smelt of death like many old and derelict hotel corridors. A woman of about fifty with carefully combed white hair had just emerged from one of the rooms to hurriedly pass to the room opposite, talking to herself. Her thoughts, which she must have imagined to be quiet, would most probably continue when she entered the room. Whose room was it? What had she been looking for in the room she left, why had she quit it for another? How did she see herself, the individual who spoke ceaselessly to herself and who gave the impression that she could not get rid of that person within her? The possible answers to these questions would certainly remain a mystery to me. This event had caught me unawares, leaving me no time to face my own problems. The woman had long white hair and was wearing a transparent nightshirt which exhibited her breasts in full view . . . Monsieur Robert had opened the door as the woman entered the room. I had perceived hesitancy on her part from the sound of the steps coming from behind the door . . . the sounds of hesitancy, fatigue, expectancy, and of being led astray . . . Then we had glanced at each other. I know all too well that I shall never forget that moment. Our exchange of glances needed no further verbal expression. He had laid his palm on my shoulder. He had on his countenance that lamentable smile which would haunt me ever after. He wanted to tell me that I shouldn't be too disappointed for him; could it be that he was trying to elicit from me some encouragement on the eve of his final departure? "Yesterday evening everybody had been looking for me," I said, "I had a talk with Juliet; about your experiences. She said she was sorry for all that had happened to you," I added, holding out to him a parcel containing leftovers from the evening before: spinach rolls, leek meatballs, and two duck eggs fried after having been boiled first, as well as unleavened bread and some jam . . . The intention was to enable him to recall that warmth wherever he went . . . "She sent this to you; she said it was your portion. She'd like to have breakfast with you some day. 'I'll prepare *bimuelos* for him . . . ' she had said with a smile." Everybody knew, and had to know, that that meeting would never take place. "I can't carry more than those two bags," he said, pointing to them. I knew it; I knew that they had been witness to a multitude of different journeys. A multitude of journeys, but different journeys, journeys in a different world to the one they knew . . . At this time they happened to flank him like faithful companions . . . This reminded one of the old clothes he would no longer be in need of. "There are so many things . . . " he added afterward. To carry one's past by assuming the identity of an enduring traveler . . . in other words, to know how to carry it; to feel within one's heart the obligation to carry the burden of what remained of the past . . . This involved both living and transporting the story in a different fashion or in one single breath—to know how to stand the test of time in one single sentence; for our own sake, for the sake of that individual that we cannot dispose of; despite our best efforts . . . For other lives, for those lives that we believe we shall believe are with us forever . . . To know how to defy time in an inexhaustible sentence . . . With our acquisitions from other places, with our expectations, we will see that they are embodied within them. The paraphernalia Monsieur Robert would have required in the land he was proposing to start a new life in was rather restricted to him. His worry and discomfort was due to his indecision as to what he should take with him or not. His witnesses were there surely . . . Yet, how did he propose to go his own way, in the company of whom or in the absence of whom? To take any steps under the circumstances was disheartening, nay injurious. You might tackle the subject of life by dwindling it away, trying to share it with someone else. This had to be a feeling that would assume some meaning in the circumstances. But then again, in what esoteric words, sunken into oblivion, had that land been embedded with now? Where had you last seen such a sentiment, in which individual? In that story you wanted to write? In which unassailable castle? In a story you wanted to write and rewrite even though you had already written it?

Objects, furniture . . . Jackets, shirts, neckties, shoes, handkerchiefs, cuff links purchased for different days and different nights, different places, and different experiences . . . Business interviews, notes of paramount importance, documents, catalogues . . . Business prospects brought to Istanbul with great expectations had always been of overriding importance in his imagination. Big business opportunities, likely to change the course of a farsighted businessman's life . . . He could, for instance, set up a brokerage house which would buy and sell from the New York and Tokyo stock-exchanges. Through considerable bank credits thousands of gas masks could be imported at a very low price via India for the army, millions of syringes for state hospitals. A big coffee plantation could be bought in Brazil. One could also bid in tenders for construction projects in Nigeria benefiting from the funds offered by the World Bank. One could also be a partner in a casino. Offers were not lacking, payment facilities were sure to be obtained. Yet nobody, no one who was supposed to understand, would understand. The same thing had happened in many relationships, in the days and nights in many a country. He yearned to return to those different countries.

"Don't forget to take with you your winter wear, your overcoat . . . You know, climates change all the time. You can leave with me what you will not and cannot take with you," I told him. I had also mentioned in passing that he must not give up hope, that one day he might come back. I felt that he had a lump in his throat which prevented him from talking and that he evaded my glances. His wide imagination had narrowed. What exactly remained from the past thirty-five years of his life, from the city to which he had desired and was now obliged to leave a completely different person; from his city, of which every corner and street had something of him in it, which had left an imprint on his memory, although he felt somehow a stranger in it and considered himself a misfit there;

251

from Edgware Road; from the Arab district; from the Indian businessmen; from the elegant restaurants; from that Pakistani cloth seller in Regent Street; from that stout janitor with a husky voice; from that heavy smoker from Trinidad in that modern flat in Yorgo Street who was up-to-date with all the car models to their minutest details and histories; from that aged Jew, a collector of pipes whose name I could never learn and who used to sell newspapers in front of the underground station at Marble Arch and who gave the impression that he had had a sedate life and was known to have the skill to transform the daily spectacles he had been privy to into wisdom and sapience; from that reform-ist synagogue; from İncila Hanım whom he had frequented during his lonely hours for the sake of the good old days and in order to forget his own cares and to borrow some money; and from Victoria Casino where many of his hopes had been dashed? Which would be, do you think, the parts that would stand their ground now, in terms of the visions left behind, the moments which he believed he had lived? The words that we want to forget now and then, which we believe to have been forgotten, remind us of that song of loneliness. We ought to resume once more making headway in our questions . . . to resume once more, with pa-tience despite our vacillation. Did we ever expect that we could communicate to those people that language we tried to interpret, so that one day we could make ourselves heard? There were moments when I kept reminding myself that our clothes lived on without us, that they had to go on living despite the fact that they had been abandoned and left behind. He had long stared at his suits and jackets. He could take with him only a few of them. Then he had caught sight of his tuxedo. "I've got to take it with me," he said, "for formal gatherings, you know." Notwithstanding the fact that he knew all too well that he would never have the opportunity to put it on, that those parties had run their course, never to be resurrected. This was a bare reality for anyone who had had the desire to examine those days. However, he was in need of witnesses who knew the past well so that he might not lose confidence in those days he had lived, had been obliged to live, and had been linked to by a firm belief. He had told me a small anecdote as he was gingerly putting his tuxedo in his suitcase. It was a small yarn, a story that aptly reflected the life he built on fertile imagination, written on a background of ice. What kind of a reaction must one have experienced after having abandoned the castles of sand, built so painstakingly on the shore, left to their destiny? "O the old days, I distinctly remember, Princess Soreyya in

Monte Carlo . . . " he said. "She was standing around the roulette wheel. I'd made a fortune that night, an amount beyond my imagination. I'd gone near her. She had been losing. Having watched her for a while, I'd whispered in her ear and suggested a number. She had placed her bet on it and won. She kept on playing afterward on the same number, and swept the board each time. Then she had put a cigarette between her lips which I had lighted. She had glanced at me. She looked weary and tired. Yet, she had not lost her beauty. She held my hand and said: 'You are a real gentleman.' I was wearing my tuxedo that night . . ." Was the incident he spoke of the one I had seen that morning? Was that woman truly Princess Soreyya? Who can tell for certain? Actually, answering this question, whether true or not, was of little importance to me at all. What was consequential was the place that this recollection or fancy had occupied in my life. Princess Soreyya was the veracious heroine of a never-ending night . . . He had to take his tuxedo with him . . . that was the last I saw of him. He had preferred to go to the airport alone. He knew more or less the individuals who would be waiting for him in London. After all, he had spent thirty-five years there. He was going to get a modest retirement pension from the social insurance and live in a tenement house. The parks would be gorgeous to look at in springtime . . .

I knew well that once I left he would be gazing at his image in the mirror for a good while . . . with a forced smile on his lips . . . This, he believed, would permit him to know the person who stared back a little better . . . and enable him to get accustomed to his presence . . . an image reproduced on the canvas of the souls of those family members who could not take those forward steps had stirred Monsieur Robert in me, every time with new words, in the belief that the said steps would lead, or be expected to lead, to the materialization of certain lives, as seen through the lifetime of one man. An image that aroused in me the desire, the necessity to go forward . . . Where in that story had Princess Soreyya vanished? To whom did those nights belong? Who would be the wearers of those clothes, where would they put them on and for what purpose?

Perhaps the legend of that mirror will never come to an end. How many paths, songs, and prospects lay ahead?

A long time had elapsed in the meantime.

A bleak, dreary, and severe winter ended the year. The snow lay settled on the ground for weeks. We received no news from him. Neither a letter nor an address nor a greeting card on New Year's eve, nor a midnight call . . . However, I still believe that he must be living somewhere in London and that he will return one day with new expectations. With new prospects, as a completely different person.

I have another belief; a belief which lends meaning to what I see, that makes it possible to fit certain words, sounds, and calls within me into a place very different from where the song associated with this mode of expression leads me regardless of my wishes, and which makes me think that a day will come when I shall be in a position to relate this misinterpreted life-story to others. This was surely another way of deferring the desire to relate it, to believe in the recounting of it. However, this postponement might give me the chance to brood over a certain number of my shortcomings. For instance, I can remember at such times, Lola and Johann pitching their tent in their own darkness. As a matter of fact my ties with İncila Hanım and Tahar Bey had been broken. It seems to me that there are certain things that I cannot define, things that have been left incomplete, that I have left incomplete on purpose; things whose meaning is contained in a sort of secret joy . . . Can this be one of those expectations whose origins and boundaries have not yet been delineated and defined? Perhaps . . . Nevertheless, whatever the hidden meaning of such a question may be, I am inclined to think that in order to understand that vision of London better I will have to move on toward that darkness generated by the said shortcomings when the time comes and visit new solitudes. I must muse over İncila Hanım once again. I wonder what had this woman—who knew those journeys and that history much better than any of us—felt when she looked after Monsieur Robert in his old age? What moments had concealed what emotions? Whose nights were they? What was that which should not be lost, what could not be lost in that small flat?

What remains now is that big, thick envelope that contained "confidential information" and was meticulously sealed, that Monsieur Aldo had entrusted to Monsieur Robert long before he had set out for an unknown land. Monsieur Robert had given it to me that morning, saying: "Well, I've lived all that has been written there. What is written there can be understood only when one experiences certain feelings. The information contained therein is yours henceforth. However, you must promise me that you will open this envelope only after you have received the news of my death, or when you are convinced that I am no more." I promised him that I would do so. "There is still a long time for that," I said, and he smiled. That smile was the last smile of his I saw and I kept an image of it in my mind . . . . Then we had packed up and gone out. As he stepped out the door, he did not turn to cast a last glance at the things he had to leave behind. We did not hug each other. He had done his best not to speak more than was necessary when I helped him to put his last *impedimenta* into the taxi. It was evident that he was afraid to, lest his words leak those sentiments he preferred to keep to himself. As the taxi started to move he made a gesture with his hands as if to say: "What else could I possibly do?" waving his head to and fro. Did his looks connote a question whose answer was still pending, regret or despair? I don't know, and I never shall. Nevertheless, I kept my promise. That envelope is still in that drawer just as it had been delivered to me. It is waiting for the right moment; just like certain moments await certain people and certain people await certain moments. I know, these are two different paths, regardless of our prospects, indifference, defeats, or small victories. Both require the experience of loves deserved, affections, lives, and solitudes ... yes, the experience of loves deserved, affections, lives, and solitudes ... Little joys that those bitter experiences have made us a gift of ... to understand and to make others understand. I'm curious about the goals I will have accomplished when I feel I am ready to tear open that envelope. What can possibly be written on those pages? Can it really be a letter written by Aldo himself? ... Or else ... When I go over the relevant points one more time, I'll feel myself inclined to think of the truth in the last lies ... to believe once more in time and in poems awaiting their ages ... to believe once more in earnest ... at all events ... certain things that continue to bleed somewhere anyway ...

I must also add the fact that we had stored in us the adventures of certain people, of our heroes who had irremediably lost certain moments, but who would continually gain ground on us. You had desired to see the door that those words had prepared for you. It is true that some of the paths were long and dark. The people to whom you had turned a cold shoulder were those who could see you whether you liked it or not, the people you could never get to anymore.

Which one of these deaths would fit you, do you think?

Those faces that conceal those streets

I did my best to preserve the vividness of that image in my mind in order not to break with the tidal flow of the story. What I was in pursuit of was a text I thought I could penetrate despite my dismay in unlocking its mystery. There is no doubt that what I was to behold, once the door was unlocked and I had the courage to step in, would be much different from what I had been anticipating when I was on the other side. I could guess this; I mean this aspect of the adventure. There were feelings propagated by fears that could not be smothered as we put up a bold front against people provoking us. If we were to go back to the shadows we had left behind—in the darkness of our past, and had the boldness to touch them in the real sense of the word—we would have known each other better. I believe that was what made our march on attractive and meaningful toward those individuals. Through some people we meet, or are separated with, through those eventualities and delusions, we become the possessors of ourselves. Those are the doors which open to ourselves, to our very depths, to the history that we cannot explain. That world sucks you in so long as you don't solve its mystery. That world could be the invention of widely different fancies and lies so long as it was not truly lived. Having taken that step, you return to yourself. Back to yourself . . . to the mirror that you always wanted to hide in one of your drawers but always failed to do; back to your fear and lack of courage to reveal and confront your true face.

The image was a virtual one. An ordinary image in all probability, but one sufficient to make a man definable to others in larger dimensions, despite those visions that found different credence in different individuals. This is the reason that has induced me to commence the narration of my story with such peripheral vision. Having tried other people and other words, unfortunately it is impossible for me to be able to visualize, at this stage, my destination. It follows that I will be cutting an untimely, poor figure once again. So be it. Our deficiencies, errors, and lies that originated in our imagination contribute to our way of life, after all. We desire to remain with certain people to the bitter end until we lose all hope despite all the adversities because of our failure to solve, understand, and find answers to certain things. It was a long distance call and was supposed to be confidential; it seemed to be the peroration, the concluding part of Aunt Tilda's love affair. This finishing stroke told of a lover who, having realized his irrelevance, was intending to withdraw to his hideaway in the distance. One might call it abandonment, an abandonment whose subject could not exactly be determined; for who abandoned who, who abandoned what, and who abandoned when, were far from being explicit . . . This was one of the partings for which she was already prepared, as she had already experienced such separations before on many occasions, at different places and in a diversity of ways. The story was transferred to me from another time, and would, out of necessity, be written by me with such things in mind; it seemed to me that I had caught up with one of the most important sections of the story . . . the story by which the play was enacted; the play was about a person who had dearly paid for his eccentricity. I happened to be in a scene that featured in it, along with sorrow and fate, and the comic element as well. Associations and reminiscences overwhelmed me and I did my best to forget and recall them at the same time. What I saw had nothing to do with me, what I happened to be had nothing to do with them. In other words, what I saw there was outside my sphere and was related to me only by casual acquaintances . . . this caused my escape, my ability to escape, to be more fallacious, more unpredictable. It looked as though the reason for my desire to waste my time and effort on an impossible task was due to this. As a matter of fact, I had tried to evoke such a feeling in other scenes, in other pasts, in the slim hope that I never ceased to entertain, and in the delusions and despairs I could not confess even to myself. It occurred to me for the first time that once certain steps were taken, life was lived as a game, and certain scenes were desired to be shown to others despite human desultoriness, indecision, and love; especially loves with all their mysteries and enigmas, avid for spectators. Every love assumed new meaning thanks to the spectators it had been seeking; for every love needed at least one spectator.

Aunt Tilda stood in front of that mirror as a human being who knew how to put up a bold front to her past experiences. As she looked into it, she seemed to be after the image she had once lost. Tears rose to her eyes. All the details fitted snugly with the setting of the stage and the scene enacted. "Don't worry; our relationship isn't worth a damn!" she said to the person on the receiver as she was putting up her hair and listening with a smile to what was being spoken on the other end, occasionally nodding without any comment as though she tacitly endorsed what was being said; as though she had already seen that film. I think she was feeling herself in another world. It was as though she listened to what was being said on the phone from a foreign place with a foreign ear. Hers was an ironic and wry smile; it gave me the impression of someone looking at things from a fair distance, from a respectable distance, on one's own terms, as though one wished to call the things one set one's eyes upon and give them new names.

It looked like spring was already settled in; it was a warm afternoon, an afternoon that recalled in my mind Aunt Tilda's house at Kurtuluş which I had visited incognito, concealing my identity from everybody, especially from Madame Roza, as I could not possibly decline the persistently reiterated invitations after my successive refusals; it was a Friday in a past already consigned to oblivion associating in me the wry joy that certain visions of certain streets arouse . . . I was getting the utmost enjoyment out of an abetment. I was once more in the company of one of the tabooed and castaway groups of the family. The source of that wry joy must have been due to the experience of a transgression, the desire to transgress, let alone the associations of those Friday evenings left there and expected to be enacted on common ground for the entire family. Aunt Tilda must have been in her sixties at that stage. "It's such a pity," she said as she hung up, "you don't know what you're missing; they were going to play Mozart." She hung up gingerly as if trying not to damage something fragile. Then, she had remained immobile for a while without saying a word. Who knows what feelings, what old memories or apprehensions she had fitted into that time. This will remain a mystery. It is true that there was no scarcity of presumptive evidence that might contribute to the solution of this mystery; yet, the said presumptive evidences were my own assumptions, my own suspended judgment, nay my own solitudes.

While moving toward the kitchen, she persisted in preserving that smile on her countenance. I had preferred to keep silent and made as though I had not perceived the things I might have been inclined to witness. Both of us had to believe in this lie up to a certain extent; I knew that we could do this. Nevertheless, there was a proposed line of action independent from me. This might have been the reason why I was so anxious to be there. I had no other option but to look elsewhere to cover up my disquiet and make as though my attention had been diverted by something else. Nothing was certain; I may or may not figure in this scenario. We did in fact take a few steps toward the past, in the direction of predetermined destinations at unexpected moments; we had taken—we had wanted to take, or were compelled to take—those steps.

After a short while, she had cried out from the kitchen: "I've bought rolls for you, and white cheese to boot. Here's your cup of tea. We've things to discuss, y'know." That voice was the voice of an individual who did not give up enjoying life to the full; it was to abide within me forever and ever. As a matter of fact, she had played her part once again. She acted in the play as the leading actress. She was accustomed to converting lies into truths and living with the products of her imagination as though they were concrete realities. Now that quite some time has elapsed, I understand the invigorating effect of such behavior much better and the fact that it reinforces one's connection to life. This must have contributed to her remaining erect all these years. Yes, all these years and seasons . . . In the company of solitudes that others would have consigned to oblivion . . . Long years, long seasons . . . At least up until the moment when I saw, when I thought I was ready to see her . . . Thus it was quite natural for such a skillful individual who had always deemed life, her life, as deserving to be explored. How else can I explain her being meticulous about the white cheese—which she had made a point to see to it that it was never lacking when rolls were served? Whenever I think of it I feel elated, an elation not lacking in some sort of sadness. A sadness I had shared with many individuals who had forged a place in my heart and with whom I had planned to empathize one day during one of those tea parties that opened a diversity of paths leading to different milestones. The taste of the cheese gains special meaning when I meditate on these things. Once again I started musing over the story in the moments that assume meaning with cultivated tastes. I had tasted the sweet cake—containing mastic bought from the bakery at Kurtuluş, which came straight from the oven—for the first time in her house; the aftertaste of those peppery biscuits consumed in her small drawing-room whose furniture had seen better days still lingered long after the decline of festive occasions, mingled with the flavor of the taste of walnut cake. The same taste was certainly enjoyed by other people elsewhere. Different languages, different times, and different climates banded us together despite our deviating paths, varied work focusing us toward common grounds, efforts, and diverse places. However, what is of particular importance here is the consequences of that behavior I recalled for the sake of that woman rather than that old text to which I had access to and whose sorrow I could interpret differently according to the seasons. These tastes were small but true gifts. For Aunt Tilda had rarely been seen in the kitchen in the entire course of her life. This had never been conveyed to me within her lifetime, to be entrusted to me to be kept safe; this would have contributed to the revival of an entirely different woman; even during her lifecycle, the value of which she had to acknowledge long after and which she kept secret despite her woes and unrealized dreams; eating for her had held its charm elsewhere, in worlds beyond the boundaries of home. She had never been a housewife; she had never intended to be. For her to be a woman was to be able to realize a life of her own exclusively in the company of a man, a lover, rather than having the odors of a *ménage*. From the earliest days of her youth the actors in her life had invited her to partake in such relationships. There was a spot where dream and reality mingled, a spot whose boundaries nobody could ever draw nor wanted to draw. A handful of fantasies had enthralled her and made of her a soul dedicated to the world of dreams; one of those heroines, who, having denied all chimeras, could, with a few glances and words, deviate us from our path, leading us to the fantastic world of imagery just like in stories, novels, songs, and films. That was the reason why that cake and those biscuits were precious to me. What would she not dream up in that kitchen, toward which day and night would she be silently heading, guided by associations and fantasies that she would not risk to transport once again to a possible tomorrow, to another fantasy? I'm certainly not in a position to answer all these questions. However, all the clues I know of may well have been produced during those small talks. I feel it incumbent upon me to recall, as best as I can, all those pieces of information and patch them together. I think I need some time for this; time likely to enable me to confront the images in those mirrors, time in which the due is given and lived as required. For stories whose many aspects are desired to be written and lived . . .

Nevertheless, it occurs to me now that, save for those that had been reproduced over and over again for the sake of special occasions, what had precisely been rendered during those small talks that was wonderfully vivid in my imagination was the inimitable taste of the tea served. The light tea with lemon I had had in her house had had a special flavor for me, and has, ever since, remained indelible on my palate. There were certain refined tastes and scents that one enjoyed only at certain moments, which exclusively belonged to those moments and adhered to them alone. Could this be one of those little blissful states that one discovered later in life and kept intact? Why not, after all? She was humming a tune that seemed familiar to me as she was busy preparing the tea, a far-off air that may have remained in the store of my memory from an old movie. Then, she had emerged from the kitchen, a tray in her hand, walking with a swaying movement as though she were putting in an appearance in a scene from a stage play. She had a wry smile on her face; a smile that drew us even closer to one another. Certain details became clearer in the daylight, as soon as the sun's rays fell upon the room. She wore a long bluish-violet velvet dress; her hair was in a bun and dyed crimson. The dark red nail polish fitted in with her traditionally feminine image. She was sitting opposite me. A small, rather elevated coffee table stood between us. We were near the window. The hullabaloo of children playing football came in from outside, to which were added the voices of street peddlers and a woman calling out for her neighbor. A dog was barking, a boy kept on ringing the bell of his bicycle. The flow of things underwent no interruption; everything followed its own course. We were sitting by the window, the window which was an eyewitness to so many things. By the window that was to cause different people to experience different thoughts and feelings, just like all other windows in which we believe, or want to believe, open in time to other lives, eras, and eventualities that have cast anchor in our life or are subject to change . . . "We were supposed to attend a concert tonight; they were going to play Mozart's concerto No. 21," she said, her eyes riveted on the tray. "Fool!" she rejoined, "he wouldn't let her go, eh? To risk one's life at such an age! Afraid to be the talk of the town . . . Oh, I see, desecrating the memory of his wife! They're going to confine him in an asylum for the elderly, is that it? Fool! Fool!" This was a summarized account of the telephone conversation I had overheard. There must have been things that she exclusively reserved for herself from what had been bequeathed to her from her past experiences with that man with whom she had pleasantly shared some time. In fact, he was one of the many partners she had had. As she returned to the place which she had judged to be the right spot for her, she had taken along with her that little hope she had snatched from her relationship with him. That man was a type who had created in her an image which caused a sense of *déjà-vu* that she had tried to push into oblivion. Nevertheless, things that were to be named at different times, by different individuals, in different ways had to be spared. The struggle we wage in order to remain alive necessitates our protection, our safeguarding of those parts within us that have so far remained untouched by alien glances. It may be because of this that that relationship would be lingering there, that evening. We would no longer revert to the story of this separation. It would take years before I came to understand the fact that the experiences with that man killed, or seemed to have, killed her. Within the space of a couple of sentences, I could see the beginning of the end. What had drawn us to each other over the course of our long past was, I believe, the things that we had failed to see at the time and our inevitable feelings of remorse. Perhaps we drew nearer to the person concealed within us at such moments. A deficiency we could not define seemed to call us back to our darkness. I'm at a loss as to pin down the feeling we experienced as we took those steps, the feeling we could not help taking stock of.

She had served tea in that antique Chinese set. This set had, as is the case of every object which had a history behind it, a voice or sound concealed in it which could be heard only by certain people. In fact, this voice or sound had, quite probably, often taken him to that small apartment at Asmalımescit. She had shared that apartment with a man she had met late in life about whom she could not speak to anybody. For outside observers the marriage she had left buried there had been a sham, steeped in false faces and misguided streets. For those who had crossed the threshold, one could speak of the sedulous growth of deficiency. That growth of deficiency could only be measured in that china set which had gradually dwindled through the breakage of each item that eventually constituted the entire collection; just like him, as is the case with those people who cannot do otherwise. Yet, every breakage, every slippage had opened the door to stronger connections with the visions left in some corner of the mirror. What had been the image that had made you experience that betrayal the most? What had been the shape that had caused you to relive your loneliness, your abandonment, those things that you had desired to tell but could not do so, and what had been the object you couldn't dispose of or get rid of despite all that you had gone through? I knew all this; she, on the other hand, was conscious of the fact that I had empathized with them. We had viewed the same memories from different angles. We had converged on the same spot from different paths and points of view. The only difference was that my story had been embellished by products of my imagination, while her story was streaked with lies. Could this be the reason why I had failed to learn the true story of this chinaware which silently sheltered certain things in its innermost depths? There was no end to the stories concocted by Aunt Tilda in connection with this set, with those which had deserted her being labeled as a load of bullshit; but the stories were her stories . . . They were her realities, although they may have had no truth in them . . . They subsumed not only the dissipated warmth of a broken marriage but also the disparate things that had been stuffed inside the world of that small apartment. A secret agent who was supposed to be a senior civil servant in the U.S. Embassy, a tradesman from Beirut, the son of an Ottoman Sultan: these had been the respective inhabitants of that said world. The set had in fact been a gift from these people. They had all been gentlemen and spoke more than one language. They were *bon vivants* and loved to spruce up and dance. They had been her men; men she had mislaid, had to mislay somewhere, irretrievably. To be an elegant gentleman and an active member of the community had been *de rigueur* for them. However, none of these so-called gentlemen lovers had had a concrete existence; what she had been expressing were but the figments of her imagination. They had been mere figures and nostalgic expectations that populated her imagination, figures that had to be infused with life to the very end; those stories were, just like those songs, concocted lies, meant to fit that world; lies that made life easier to live, even though they left a bitter aftertaste and in a way were more amenable to expression, regardless of whether other people discerned what was told or not. All these parlor games gave one the clues of a colorful and distant world of fantasies as well. This was an imaginary world which had broken Aunt Tilda loose from her family, from those supposed to be by her side and from those she knew to be different, enriched at different times, visions and talks drawing their boundaries gradually, inextricably cutting deep grooves into the ground. It must have been the attraction and call of this imaginary world that indulged them in those movies and concerts. That was the place where she lived and believed herself to be living and she was convinced of its beauties.

That day both of us had desired to remain where we were, resolved not to cross over the threshold. A short time after, she had settled in her armchair. "Well!" she said with her winning smile, "Aren't you going to pour the tea for me like a perfect gentleman?" as though she was reproaching me. I knew what lay behind this subtle hint. She was in need of assistance at this stage of the ritual. Her hands were trembling out of control; it was getting worse; to hold objects was becoming more and more difficult. The diagnoses made by the doctors she had consulted had widely differed and the treatments they had respectively suggested had served no purpose. Everybody had his own way to deal with the problem. Was there an effective remedy available for her illness at the time? We had gone through difficult times over the course of which we had experienced despair and indefinable apprehensions, without even venturing to suggest an answer to this question. Once I had witnessed the following scene: during the days when Roza was in pursuit of a hopeful prognosis, she had addressed her elder sister, who had been trying to endear herself to her despite the distance that separated them, saying: "No sea che esto pagando por mis pekados Roza" (Roza dear, d'you think that this may be atonement for my sins?) and had grown silent for a while. A window which had insistently kept closed to those days had partly opened quite unexpectedly. It was a Friday morning and preparations were being made for the

Sabbath. *Éperlan aux prunes jaunes* was to be served at dinner. The shopping was done by the maid as usual. Her husband was a long-standing customer favored by the well-known fishmonger from İzmir in the Eminönü Market who always put aside the fresh catch for him, usually eight pieces, weighing about one kilogram . . . The usual dish that followed this entrée was generally stewed meat served with eggplant purée . . . and, at times, a flaky pastry. This flaky pastry, the dough of which was kneaded with dexterous hands, was served during the Sabbath breakfast that brought the entire family together; the casual visitors from the neighborhood also partook, the taste tickling their palates for a long time. She had preferred to observe silence at a time when all the steps were taken or seemed to have been taken in the name of life and solidarity. This was the beginning of an era of sadness for both of them. While one of the sisters lived her own lie, the other was at a place far removed from the very spot she would have preferred to be, despite her despair. Whose fault was it? In whose world did it lie? In their little world, they could not possibly have heard such questions put forth by others in different climates from other stories, using other words. Even though from differing angles, some doors led to the same questions and feelings associated with each other. Some might call this a state of thralldom, some a blind alley and some just a simple trick. One could not easily allay the apprehensions it created and escape the nightmares it caused; consequently, one found himself committed. When one considers all these points, Madame Roza's taciturnity might be interpreted as a sort of brooding which gave others cause to ruminate. The gap created by the silence gave way to contrapuntal flashes and recollections. One of those windows appeared to be hidden in the darkness of these recollections. Aunt Tilda's question gave the impression of an escape from a remorse which seemed to contain some other death; death or a secret and inarticulate crime that one could not possibly disclose to a stranger. Madame Roza, through her introspection, may have desired to leave her sister once more in the lurch on her way to this bitter experience of the past. It was time for her to cook in the house she never had, nor ever would abandon, on any account. This was not merely an inexorable fate, exclusive to her. A woman, who could peep into the kitchen, even though through a window, was sure to find a part of herself in Madame Roza. The plays had been staged for this purpose and the stories had been reproduced to that end. As for those who had gone or had been dragged to other places . . . Well, the warmth of those houses was in fact partly due to this close observation, despite or because of the errors committed. After a short silence, she had said: "De ti para tit e keates estos penserios. Zavali di madre ya se merikiyava muncho por ti." (You yourself are the author of your own problems. Poor mother, how she used to worry about you. She was afraid that you would turn out like Aunt Fortune. This concern had caused her end.) This talk had taken place when Monsieur Jacques had not yet shown up. Monsieur Jacques had an antipathy for Aunt Tilda, which he tried to keep concealed as best as he could; he believed that she was possessed, that the devil was nestled in her. Can it be that these impressions held their sway at the time of their encounter, during their coexistence in the midst of the 'new family'? Who can tell! Glances that could not exactly be defined transformed so many feelings in that stream and eroded so many expectations gradually and stealthily . . . One could speak of a controversy between two individuals with an unshakable belief in what they considered to be their truths; their fantasies prevented them from seeing certain bare facts, and obliterated their need to understand. One day, Monsieur Jacques told Madame Roza that Aunt Tilda might come when he himself happened to be out. Could there be in the controversy another reason hidden in the depths that nobody dared to reveal or pass judgment on? Perhaps there was. However, the venue was not the correct place where one could delve into such a matter. A matter of such consequence may well have been one of those affects subsumed into the category of the flotsam and jetsam seen overboard. Partly due to this, I felt I was not in a position to inquire into the contents of those drawers and rooms. The doors were, in a sense, our doors; because of this, they should remain closed . . . in order that I might keep my visions alive . . . The person who constantly invited me to come back to that point was that aunt called *Fortuné*. One wonders who might have been the companions of this woman who had been so close to Aunt Tilda in the eyes of her mother, and to what places she must have been to in the past. Who had drawn the boundaries of this prohibition? How had she proceeded to it, after which episodes? Which abyss lay in the origin of that fear? Madame Roza had preferred to evade the issue. What Monsieur Jacques knew about this misplaced woman, forsaken and omitted, about this relative, seemed to have been padded out with wild fancies and interpretations. According to the visitors to the house, Aunt Fortuné used to wander the streets of the Princes' Islands in her shabby attire, at times giving off the impression of a woman beside herself with rage, speaking loudly to herself, other times elated, humming a song, as though she wanted to draw the attention of the people to something beautiful that might have escaped their attention. Her hair was buzz cut. This styling had become for her a 'barbering ritual.' In this, she was assisted by an apprentice of about thirteen or fourteen-years-old from Alexandria, brought up in an orphanage who had never set his eyes on his parents and whose hobby it was to catch fish for cats. No sooner did she cry out "Boy!" than he dropped by her dilapidated house situated in the hinterland of the island, replete with articles of a nondescript nature, and cut her hair with electric clippers. And then . . . Well, there was no end to the gossip. According to one of the rumors, she was particular about the dishes she prepared only on days when she received visitors. The odors that emanated from the house were mouth-watering, although one could not exactly tell what she was cooking. According to another account, once the hair trimming process was over, she used to pull down the boy's trousers and gave him a blowjob before having it inserted between her thighs. Who had invented this story, who had heard it from whom, nobody knew. As a matter of fact, no one thought it worthwhile to trace its origin. What had been revealed were simply events that had taken place there, for the sake of that scene. She had been mislaid, if one may say so; this strange aunt that the family members wanted to consign to oblivion had stayed there for an interminable number of years. It was said that she preferred to roam the deserted streets during the winter months, in the cold and damp and that she kept indoors during the summer, when she used to receive visitors. I had not deemed it difficult to guess the reason for this; I mean her settlement there on the island. Had it been her option to settle there? Or had she been compelled to go there by forces beyond her control? Where had she been before she had begun to scuttle across the streets, what lives had she been living; what expectations had linked her to her loved ones, the ones she truly loved? Had there ever been dawns in which she had had perfect confidence? Had there been flowerpots bedecking windowsills in which she grew plants and flowers, taking meticulous care of them? Answers to these questions reached me through fragmentary recollections and visions awaiting expression. All that I could decipher was that her lawyer husband contributed to the newspaper El Tiempo with articles he wrote after work in the evenings and weekends; he had always aspired to embark upon a career in journalism, as he had failed to work his way up the ladder in jurisprudence; he had forsaken his wife and gone to live with another woman without offering any plausible explanation; this experience of abandonment was compounded even more by her son, who had left on the pretext that he had enlisted in the army, but who had actually departed for Havana for mysterious reasons and decided never to return home; and, what is more important still, was the fact that they had left no traces of themselves behind which might give a clue as to their whereabouts. According to one account, the son who had once sworn on oath that he would never leave his mother and who alternately exhibited an extroverted jovial attitude and an introverted sorrowful countenance, had, after his father's desertion, indeed enlisted, but for some reason or another, his experiences in the army had compelled him to leave for Havana. All this had been so sudden that he had had no time to inform any of his next-of-kin of his venture; just like the heroes of fictions whose fantasies invite them to travel to distant realms. What fell to those left behind was to go on living their own fantasies; fantasies and adventures that remained undisclosed in Fortuné's case for want or means of expression. As the years went by, during the days she spent in her small house at Kadıköy, when she had not yet committed the bric-a-brac in her garden to the flames, she said to the people around her that she stayed tuned to the radio news as she received coded messages related to her husband and son, and that she had to repair the island in order for them to return, time was against her, and that the plum tree seen from her bedroom window kept drawing nearer, threatening her life. According to this legend her husband had gone to Thessalonica for state affairs of paramount importance, while her son, having an eye for business, had engaged in the emerald trade and become rich. How far one could trust in the truth of these stories I cannot tell for sure; just like many stories the truth of which I cannot vouch for, and which I hesitate to tell to others, being destitute of any unimpeachable certitude for fear of being accused of stretching the truth. To the best of our knowledge Fortuné had last seen her son leave home rather apprehensively with his buzz cut. Could one trace the origin of this hairstyle which she had been wearing for years now as her latent rebellion against abandonment? Perhaps. It was an established fact that certain messages were conveyed through devious paths. I am not urged to utter this merely by the outward appearance of things, but also based on another detail which Monsieur Jacques had mentioned *en passant*. Fortuné wore an old fur coat during her wanderings on the island in the dead of winter. The funny thing was that she wore it inside out, the fur tightly wrapping her, the lining exposed to the cold air. What could be the plausible explanation for this? To give an indication of the fact that she had been ousted and consigned to oblivion? I'm aware of the fact that I can produce many answers to the same questions. However, whatever these answers may be, it seems to me that there is something very important concealed in this. It looked as though certain things had been overlooked in people's haste to find something curious, the haste of those who were in a position to see the truth. Here was a call that would enable us to get to the heart of the matter. Had that illness originated from within the family, from a family she could not sever herself from and who haunted this poor woman to whom everybody attributed the epithet of 'unfortunate'? Had her husband and son abandoned her because of her mental derangement or had she gone nuts after she had been forsaken by them? To the best of my knowledge, everybody preferred to leave this question unanswered. Nobody that I know of was in a position to perceive that boundary. Somebody had to be cruelly sacrificed to live such a life, condemned by individuals conscious of their own irrelevance. In order to survive one had to identify oneself with those in power and conspire alongside them. Fortuné's body was reported to have been fished out by fishermen long after her eyes had been eaten by the fish. She had either thrown herself into the sea from a cliff or was murdered. It was Madame Eudoxia who had informed Madame Roza's mother of the incident; Madame Eudoxia was the only person who was on intimate terms with the family, and she said at every opportunity that Fortuné had never strayed from the island throughout her time on this earth.

Aunt Tilda had never passed comments about her aunt. Never had she whispered a word about her. Yet, these images had indelibly remained in her darkness that she kept shunning. I distinctly remember her footsteps; they seem to be more audible to my ears than ever before. The disease had progressed insidiously. Despite her efforts, she had never been able to control the shaking of her hands which she guessed to be the omen of a serious and foreboding end. However, it was not altogether impossible to find ways of escape in brief, periodic moments which might beautify the passing time in a figurative sense, if one considered one's predilections in life, the means of escape or the inexhaustible and endless variability of the remnants of the imaginary world despite all that had been experienced in the meantime . . . even though certain hidden causes may have illuminated certain details differently over a course of time. This may have been the reason for her asking me—as I had been serving her like a gentleman by pouring tea in her cup—if I knew Rita Hayworth. "She was Orson Welles' Lady from

Shanghai" to which she had added "Gilda." "She is still vivid in my imagination, her pulling off her gloves as she sang Put the blame on me boy . . . " she added. "That was life, you know!"

That was life . . . These words expressed regret, despair, and separation . . . Yes, that was life. "Which movie theater was it, Saray or Melek? Melek it was, I believe. Yes Melek . . . Josy had spoken about Monsieur Saltiel, about the days when his father used to pay a visit to his father's workshop to have costumes made to order. Monsieur Saltiel was the former owner of the movie theater. It was one of the rare evenings when Josy had been talkative and jovial. Later that evening we had gone to a dancehall. We had reminded each other that the movie theater in question had once been the Skating Palace. Well I remember the song that Rita sang: Put the blame on me boy . . . Josy had a pallid expression. He knew he was sick. He was to disclose it to me in a couple of days. That was the last time we had gone to a movie theater . . . " One lived one's life by shaping one's own image over the course of time, by fitting and adjusting the images that assigned meaning to one's life to their proper places. You recall the story of the superimposed imagery, especially at such moments of flight, when you return to your inevitable solitude. Stories and secret chambers keep haunting you. Do you think you could open those doors once more after the lapse of so many years for the sake of those moments and individuals? Would you be able to abandon those glances and touches freely, even though you were to experience other such encounters? One enlivened, or tried to enliven, one's imagery according to one's own whims . . . to the extent one's own boundaries and recollections permitted . . . Had it not been your desire to keep a part of yourself whole, notwithstanding your losses, for the sake of certain stories? This held true also for those words that delineated the boundaries of those images within us of certain people, didn't it? Had we not tried to protect our words by secretly coming to terms with 'that man' we thought to abide within us forever, although we tried to wean him from our thoughts and attribute meaning to the words within our own sphere of action? I wonder to what extent could one vouch for the vernacularism of the French words spoken in a completely different climate in the piecemeal narration of a story. Which of these words can be considered reanimated for whom and for where? Which of these words are rewritten, are desired to be rewritten? Our talks that were interspersed with Aunt Tilda's occasional monologues could be found there once upon a time, and have returned. How many of these words remained over time, how many of them found a new life here? I'm aware that such questions may take me to a new story in the future and compel me to write an entirely new variant of this story. Nevertheless I feel myself obliged to believe in that world those words depicted. There were times when we had access to the new meanings that certain images had assumed. We had left behind a song to gain access to a life mislaid somewhere. In fact we were busy at that time writing our own script. We felt at home in our own film. Those shadows were our shadows, those voices our voices. Aunt Tilda's monologues contained so many stories that invoked sadness in me. The movie theaters and the films she faithfully kept in the store of her memory, the man who had once been her husband, the skating arena where she had skated as a little girl, her resentments, regrets, and the images left unrealized were all there. "It's true we hadn't had another chance to go to a movie theater . . . That evening had been the last. The beginnings weren't any different though. We had never had the chance of visiting those places as I would have liked. I think I had always expected an end. It looked as though in each of us there was an end. A diversity of ends, so many ends . . . We cannot deny that we had seen all those films; we had not missed a single one of them. Yet, as I've already said, none of our *sorties* had been as I would have liked. I would have preferred to be there half an hour before the program started so that I could meet a few acquaintances and exchange a few words with them, all the while not failing to show off my new costume. This should be the *raison d'être* of the movie theater . . . Josy was misanthropic, he shunned people . . . The movie theater Melek . . . *Only Angels Have Wings* with Rita Hayworth had been shown there I believe. Can it be that my memory is failing me? Or could it be that the film was running at Gloria? I don't think so, no. That was a long time ago, however . . . " It was high time now that certain images had to be consigned to oblivion. This was a process rather difficult to define. Had she been resenting her betrayal or was hers a sense of escape from the place to which she knew she would never go back? It may be that betrayal had been embedded in her memory, or perhaps it originated from one of the judgments in which she wished to have perfect confidence in and hoped to build a bridge between. To escape, to be a fugitive in the places she preferred to consign to obscurity . . . Were those words borrowed from a film's soundtrack, those words duly preserved, those costumes no longer worn yet not discarded, and those recollections rewritten and regenerated during a nightmare so that clues to those regrets and to the reason for a bondage to a certain path could be extracted?

It took me years to follow that trail with similar questions. This woman, whose story I believed I was able to tell succinctly, to a few people whose interest I hoped to arouse, had an all-consuming passion for movies for which she reserved a special place in her heart. In fact, she had come to me escorted by those images that had guided her life, since, to be frank, despite disappointments she had lived with her attachments, with trivia she could not give up. I was about to share a secret. Quite the reverse of what Monsieur Jacques and all of the Venturas and the Tarantos, whom I encountered quite unexpectedly, had thought, Aunt Tilda had remained faithful to her husband Joseph Rothman, the tailor. She loved with a love whose extent was to be discovered much later. She referred to him as Josy, which gave the impression that she was recalling him from a distant past. Solitudes, silences, unanswered questions that originated from the inability to part with a dearly loved one, whoever this may have been . . . Misunderstandings, misinterpretations . . . Life's fragments, scenes failed to be enacted were for Aunt Tilda concealed in the movie theater, in that eternal screen of delusions. Now I feel I will be in a stronger position to maintain and conceal what has been conveyed to me regarding that place amid the pages of another book. Rita Hayworth and the elation she had caused when she had pulled off her gloves in that famous scene, the brightly lit splendor of the movie theater Melek, alias Emek, its new appellation, the dazzling beauty of Joan Crawford in costly fur coats, fated to be identified as "Miss Pepsi Cola," the unforgettable Ingrid Bergman in the role of Anastasia and her tragic end, the scene in which she appeared divine which skillfully created the atmosphere of the Grande Duchesse, expected to be seated on a throne without subjects and her typical cough, Bette Davis' eyes, Paul Muni's laudable artistry, Edward G. Robinson as a gangster, Humphrey Bogart's noble love, the fact that even those who played a minor role in that film were prominent actors and how she had sobbed at that scene in which La Marsellaise was sung, the lunches at the Atlantik, the pastry of the Lebon, the hats and the orchids, and the supermarket Au Lion d'Or . . . We had tried to relive the past on that boundary line that separated the past from the present, in full consciousness of the fact that we were no longer in a position to express and give utterance to our merriments and the insidious sadness and restlessness they contained, to the extent our recollections, locution, and remoteness permitted, taking into consideration all eventualities. Fragments had been deposited to different people at different times . . . This could be the reason why one had desired to live that imaginary scene to the bitter end. It may have been that those fragments had been shot in a different chiaroscuro in a different movie. With a view to raising the wall of that movie theater by placing its bricks carefully one on top of the other . . . aiming at discovering and finding that place in which we expected to rediscover ourselves in addition to those we had failed to see properly and had lost by now in some place or another, in the time we were destined to live. This may have been one of those stories that those who are content with ready-made solutions or those who enjoy stories of people nostalgic about the old days, damn with faint praise as soon as they have a cursory look at the introductory chapter. Such an attitude could do nothing more than cause such purveyors of hindsight to relive, quite against their own wishes, feelings of abandonment and betrayal. We were living at the time with our reformed faces that we were compelled to change . . . to be multiplied as a crowd. Where was it exactly, the spot where solitude began; can you remember when you had became conscious of your own solitude for the first time, after which glance and which touch? I'm inclined to believe that this is the way to get to the heart of the individual, the individual we try to conceal within us . . . If one broods over that dark path, certain encounters become nightmares. However, this was conceivably the only way to reach Aunt Tilda, the true Aunt Tilda. Her story had never been a story of nostalgia. The truth that transformed her into a lunatic, who should preferably be visited more often than not, in the eyes of those nearest to her should be sought in the dead end of the person she inhabited who could not observe her surroundings and times as others could. She had been one of those who had gone through streets, doors, and rooms by unexpected transitions and means, who had shifted from one time to the next as she pleased, who had tried to live in more than one time simultaneously, by giving them all their due, who listened to the voices in her head despite the losses and defeats she had suffered, not merely remaining an onlooker but being an acting agent as well, who had taken the risk to follow the dictates of those voices, who had been compelled to live her life by her own proclivities. What have acquainted us with these facts have been Monsieur Jacques' sayings and Madame Roza's reports and the confirmed rumors that swept over the town. This had been the same experience she had had during her youth when she had sensed in a transport of delight the inebriation caused by life, and during the days she spent with Joseph Rothman, in their short matrimony. The fragments of the past mislaid in others brought her back to me as a woman, a licentious woman who had known more than one man in her life. It appears that she had played a leading role in the days gone by, in big receptions and on weekend trips. Her irresponsible behavior had naturally disconcerted the conservative milieu around her, proud of their established customs. There was nothing incomprehensible in this. Those who had based their lives on the established order would, out of necessity, find it difficult to acknowledge the existence of people lost in reverie, imagining things they could never materialize in life. During those secret sessions, the family members had come to the conclusion among themselves that this girl, who had strayed from the right path and disrupted their fixed order, had succumbed to a serious malignancy, and thought that a marriage might, in the grand scheme of things, restore her health. Such was the power of conformity . . . Putting such a resolution into action might be considered a convincing victory for the people who were obliged to agree upon the correctness of the lifestyle they had adopted. There were a plurality of ways to cover up humiliating defeats, silently, surreptitiously as though one did not experience loneliness or betrayal, just like in several other climates, histories, and cultures in the world . . . One ought to take care not to feel that repressed turbulence, and what is more important still, not to let other people sense it.

It seems that the tailor Joseph Rothman had appeared on life's stage right at this moment. Joseph was reported to have taken Aunt Tilda to the Lebon pastry shop the very day of their encounter. She had experienced her first disappointment there. You may call it disappointment or a sense of indifference if you like . . . That young girl who had had a marginal life had apparently expected to be taken to a music hall or a pub by the man who was to be her prospective husband, to a nightclub where they could dance till the early hours of the morning. Thus, the photograph would find its way into the album, among the other heroes of fiction. Could it be that she had dreamt of starring in a film, having as her co-star Robert Taylor, resting on a deck chair in the lounge while crossing the Atlantic?

Beyond the boundary Line

This preamble and the probabilities that I have reproduced based partly on hearsay and partly through my own logic have inevitably brought me to the verge of a conventional world of sentimentalism, emptied of its contents. On this threshold,

I find myself faced with an apprehension of defeat which I find difficult to relate to others. After getting so close to this woman—who I always found to be different, and believed to be different—I cannot help but asking: "It's all very well, but what was it that held this difference that was exposed to our view?" What had engendered that difference; what had caused Aunt Tilda to break loose from her circle among a multitude of words that were consumed and soiled? There are photographs sent to you by individuals, ones lost and ones desired to be lost, at unexpected moments in places unknown to you so that you can never trace the sender. This will remind you once more of the 'road story.' You will see in that particular frame of film millions of living people suggesting to you the idea that millions of people live on millions of fantasies, each unlike the other, connecting endless stories. Then you will venture to find places to fit in them the aspects of those individuals and relationships that had always been left in the shade . . . a new moment of disappearance, silence, and counterstatement . . . I wonder whether all that has been lived would assist in converging in you a few similarities with them, contrary to your expectations. Now, I am trying to see through such factors that make me uneasy, through probabilities that keep gnawing at my mind. Who possessed the said difference, where was it exactly, in which particular glance was it contained? Something—whose exact location, color, sound, and odor were not necessarily known—that led to Aunt Tilda or that originated in her, was quite probably hidden somewhere in this story. I don't think I'll ever find this something in my story or be able to trace it. Well, I don't care. I feel safe in the knowledge that at least I know how to march ahead and disappear, despite all the defeats I have suffered . . . As for the boundaries of that world of sentiments soiled and denuded of its contents, I may take a few steps forward now. Aunt Tilda had lived naturally and idiosyncratically with what lay beyond that boundary. She had to move forward silently to the place where she wanted to live. Truths, your own truths, might well return to you when you considered the meaning of this forward march. You might like to have a new insight into the place where you had come face-to-face with your own realities, with the people you confronted, and the time that this had taken place in reference to your acquisitions from that solitude. This was a small but original legacy; a legacy that one should like to preserve secretly somewhere in one's life. The extension of this legacy within me enables me to understand better the impression that Joseph Rothman had left on her despite the disappointments at the pastry shop. He had explained to Aunt Tilda that the profession of tailoring had been passed on to him by his father and that he had been trying to carry it on, that what made this profession particularly enticing was his observation that the bits and pieces of learning he had acquired could be gradually transformed into tangible things through the clothes he was making. The meaning inherent in it, which had to be unfolded and disclosed, was being gradually composed in this way, but what was being built up in that workshop no longer gave him satisfaction. He had taken a fancy to set off on a polar expedition about which he had resolutely made up his mind to carry out some day having already made all the preparations necessary for it in his mind, based on what he had studied in the books he had skimmed through. He even drew the tracks he was to follow, hoping he would eventually be able to set foot on that cold, vast, and deserted white realm even though the venture might be beset by disastrous incidences and marred by untoward events. Nevertheless, disenchanted as he was with his current lifestyle, this was the journey he had been patiently yearning for ever since he was a boy. He couldn't tolerate those who could not realize the full seriousness of his dream. Among them, his father was in the lead, the figure whose confidence he had been trying to gain. His father and master who had instructed him in the trade was no longer what he used to be. He had lost his sight a couple of years ago; the light, which he had been endowed with and to which he had been accustomed throughout his life had failed him. He did, however, endeavor to go on working as he had nothing else to cling to in life. He came to the workshop with great difficulty for the mere sake of smelling its odor . . . of inhaling that odor and experiencing those touches . . . a habit he had developed over many years . . . He saw the workshop as a place of refuge rather than a prison . . . The touching of things restored to him the necessary energy he needed. Joesph had established an original connection between himself and the clothes he used in his room—an empathy difficult to explain. He had developed the habit of conversing with them for long periods of time when left alone. What he uttered was mostly devoid of sense; it was meaningless, things that left some people alienated; those clothes were his own conglomeration of people, his ultimate coterie . . . One must acknowledge the fact, however, that he still designed impeccable clothing. Nevertheless, he hardly spoke with his acquaintances unless he was compelled to by circumstance. Nor did he communicate with himself anymore. If ever he could . . . This had adversely affected Aunt Tilda. This lapse must have come as something of a surprise to her, coming from a man who had fought his way to her through other people's steps. A fall quite different from the one he had experienced when he had taken cognizance of the importance of that fantasy that gripped his imagination of that cold, vast, and deserted white realm. That pastry shop, remote from the illuminated nightclubs, housed a hope beyond all nostalgic yearnings, deprivations, and extraneousness . . . a hope that made abandonment easier to face. There was a joy in it that sorrow enriched; a joy that originated from conveying a part of oneself to a fellow human being, or from finding that part of oneself in someone else. In that moment, in which certain feelings were observed from a different angle, one was faced to look inward. What he had grasped at such a terminal point would, I believe, shed light on a quite different path. Regrets experienced due to his delayed actions would be gnawing at him, at the man he tried to hold onto in the midst of the mass of people who would deprive him from the streets he walked, the lights, the colors he saw, and the odors he smelled . . . To root one's fantasies in a vast, white, and deserted imaginary realm . . . That was the sole fantasy that Joseph had indulged in throughout his life, the one he had been seeking to justify. The traveler she had seen, the man that fate had presented to her, reminded her of the travelers she had seen in films. On the other hand, what Joseph had found in Tilda was a woman, who, for probably the first time in his life, lent an ear to him. The moment they met was one that gave credence to those who had an unshakable belief in first encounters. What they had both seen, what each of them saw in the other, was what he or she had wanted to see.

To be able to love somebody and be conscious of it . . . represents, I think, the insidious approach of the darkness you cannot penetrate, which is populated by those you have abandoned . . . to be able to see someone else as a human being . . . Nevertheless, these two capabilities had sufficed to enable them to clasp onto each other during those days . . . Nobody could guess what the future had in store for them . . . That was not easily predicted. They had a vast imagination that went beyond the grasp of those who knew them. An imagination they both found themselves lost in, adrift amid the new days and nights . . . Could it be the place where the defeats, the real defeats were experienced?

What remains of a marriage?

Not long after that moment during which Aunt Tilda and Joseph had mutually failed to give a true picture of themselves, they got married. Could this step taken toward another fallacy be helped? Could it be that that step had found its veracity in that misapprehension? Frankly I can make no headway with such irrelevant questions at the present time, which take on new meanings through omission. As far as I can gather, they lived the meaningful years of their marriage in that small apartment at Asmalımescit, during which they frequented the movie theaters and nightclubs that Aunt Tilda adored. In those nightclubs, luminescent and radiant, finding themselves among people who preferred to lead a life similar to theirs—lost in the night, believing in certain things unreservedly in the company of their inner voices—which allowed them to live in their own pristine state, to the fullest extent possible, in the days following their marriage. This state had previously been experienced in different places by different people, although expressed through different words. The tributaries of certain rivers never change . . . Nevertheless, Joseph gradually became morose and incommunicative. He complied with all the wishes that his wife expressed without comment and preferred to be a spectator to his own experiences. What had been the origin of this resignation? Where and when had it stemmed from, consequent upon what visions? Did it have its roots in his journey toward his inner self? Or was it Aunt Tilda's behavior, inviting everybody she knew to be a part of her life, to partake in life's inebriation, although this seemed to many to be comparatively daunting? Or was it her demeanor that terrified people? Was it possible for him to see this woman, who had departed and moved further and further away from him as a stranger, like any other woman; would this be within the boundaries of possibility and logic? I am convinced that I will not be able to remain impartial in my assessments and judgments, as always, since I cannot help consolidating my shortcomings, aspirations, and resentments. The questions and responses that I've unearthed for the individuals beyond my reach may seem once more profuse and grotesque. It must be because of this that I exercise my discretion and remain content simply to graze certain truths; it may also be partly due to my lack of confidence. Could it be that somebody had considered this game of life as a game of hopscotch? Who knows? Everybody was either in the process of flight or motivated by a desire to flee . . . From my actual vantage point what I can see now is that the behavior of the man she had chosen to join in holy matrimony had gradually led Aunt Tilda to sharp disappointments. I intend to insert into the present story certain aspects of a memory from the past I had been entrusted with. It is an unforgettable recollection dating from the said period regarding this woman who had a desperate yearning for an 'outdoor' life; it is an incident related to this man with whom she was compelled to share the same room. One evening he had quite unexpectedly brought in a Sierra radio gramophone and meticulously placed it in a corner of the room. Not long after, he had gone out on a mad shopping spree and purchased an infinite number of gramophone records. Joseph's absorbing hobby quickly progressed and soon he was tuning into radio stations from around the world till late at night. After that evening, in that apartment, in which a blissful heartfelt scene was not to be witnessed for years (as was the case with similar cohabitations) there was a growing collection of peaceful polar imagery accompanied by songs of merriment, even if only for a brief period of time. Such changes were destined to wax and wane, coming to a close on that unusual evening which was to remain fixed in my memory ever after. The windows that were closed, which were believed to have been closed for good, gave out a view replete with delusions . . .

Aunt Tilda, who, as a young girl, had displayed a flirtatious character, had not cheated on her husband despite her vast vivid sexual imagination. Her family and friends, who had been instrumental in uniting them as husband and wife, wondered how wise their decision had been after seeing their actual home in that small apartment at Asmalımescit. She could tell no one the resentment she had experienced that evening. "I couldn't find a way out," she told me years later. "I was trying to deceive myself. The spectators kept commenting on our seemingly peaceful life in laudable terms. I had a grim sense of foreboding . . . " She seemed to indicate that everybody tried to dodge the issue. Certain individuals reverted to clichés in which they did not believe . . . "I couldn't find a way out" . . . These were her own words; words that kept haunting me for years. At the time she had spoken to them, I wondered whether she had found a way of speaking that would rescue her from the shadows of that time. When I brood over the visions that survive in my imagination, I believe I am now in a better position to comment on them. The path she had been seeking may or may not have been discovered by her. In the case of her not having done so, it would not be difficult to depict the experiences she had gone through for the sake of solitude and the things she had dodged. Had the reverse been the case, I would have some difficulty in retracing the steps taken. I'm about to reach a boundary beyond which the process of keeping track becomes difficult; the path to be followed will be clearer only after certain deaths and losses have taken place. It is a harrowing experience. Beyond this seems to be a terra incognita that assumes some meaning only when coupled with those voices I would have liked to have heard, but which I cannot decipher. So exciting is this wasteland! It seems that the days spent at Asmalımescit had been precious for Joseph. In all probability, certain things, desired to be conveyed through certain stories, using different expressions, under different appellations, gradually sank into oblivion during the course of this cohabitation. The matter can be explained as the resentment of a person who was unable to communicate, as he would have liked to, despite all his expectations and efforts. Had Aunt Tilda taken cognizance of this and had she had proper access into the imagination of this man who had tried to open a new door despite her retrogression? I doubt it. A relationship thrives in protean dawns; had it been otherwise, one would have been presented with it accordingly. To inhale the same night, the same night in the same place over and over, was no obstacle to a silent and steady progression toward desolation . . . remote desolation. Was this just fate or one's predilection for thralldom? Was this the source of inspiration for so many songs, had ears been lent to certain people because of this, had so many poems haunted certain people because of this, had so many stories been left unfinished awaiting their opportune time, place, and heroes?

Probing questions . . . I can hear that voice now once again . . . once again, with echoes, associations, and terror-ridden fantasies . . . That is why I'm striving to keep aloof from certain questions besieging me. I say to myself that I can postpone my departure to that place for the moment. Nevertheless, I deem it mandatory to speak of another testimony in connection to this. If my memory serves me well, to take a peek at someone on the outside, or to prefer to do so and try to close all one's shutters to the outside world had already assisted certain relationships in many respects, hadn't they? Aunt Tilda had read a great number of books during those long nights, *Les Pardaillans*, *La dame aux camélias*, The Count of Monte Cristo's exciting adventures, among others. Joseph had yielded with grace to this solitude without diverting her attention elsewhere, without making any conscious fuss in the manner of those who know they are resigned to their lot; keeping a dignified silence with weary resignation and becoming physically depleted . . . all the while trying to differentiate the changing colors of the sky, up until the very first moment the dawn began to break . . . Aunt Tilda had all her books on her night table, transporting them into her own imagination, into her own films; without seeing that man who was gingerly retreating into himself . . . Was this homicide?

Frankly I did not dare to consider this matter at length. A few steps, even a few small steps forward undoubtedly meant some progress toward the interpretation of a few words and glances. It is true; one had one's own comfort zone in which one had perfect confidence and into which others could never be admitted. Under the circumstances, we had to remain content with putting forth questions without expecting any answers . . . without waiting for any. There are words to which looks, guarded utterances, and smiles lend meaning through tactile sensations; words that are prone to proliferation, words that may not have been mentioned during talks or that may have been mentioned out of context. A different language was spoken in the place in question; that place belonged to those who wanted to expand the boundaries of a different language and move toward certain people.

I had witnessed the homicide here, in the associations these sentences evoked. It seemed to have marked a life kept as a secret between two varied individuals (at least at a given period) and to have attributed to it a subjective meaning . . . Those days had been embellished with little hopes, little problems, and little promenades; with little hopes, little snags, and great solitudes that gradually grew in depths that were difficult to mention; just like in the lives of those people who lived on the voices emanating from sedentariness and whose journey to that place is barred; just like in the case of relationships endeavored to be kept alive through objects and daily successes . . . up until the day when Joseph's illness had been diagnosed as tuberculosis as if to deride Aunt Tilda's imaginary world fed by fictions . . . This was probably the only condition that fitted that man who resolved to defend the boundaries of his realm despite certain transgressions. Under the circumstances, there had certainly been people who had failed to conceal their smiles, sorrows, and revolts . . . It is so difficult to speculate as to the confines of iniquity without having previously experienced certain things in life . . . The doctors had advised that a salubrious climate would do him good and that the sanatorium on the island of Heybeliada would be the right spot to cure his illness. However, after a second thought, they came to the conclusion that they would be reluctant to be confined to a hospital, they considered as an alternative the island of Büyükada, next to Heybeliada, which they often visited in summer. As a matter of fact, the former must have had completely different connotations to the latter. They ended up renting a house redolent with the odor of pines overlooking the sea, the city, and her distant lights. However, to have moved into that house meant proceeding toward a new solitude. Films would continue to be projected on the silver screen in movie theaters. "This is unfair," said Aunt Tilda to her elder sister who had paid her a visit. She had referred to her connubial loneliness and had had fragmentary recollections of different places. "Tilda had scared me stiff. She was capable of committing all manner of foolish acts," Madame Roza said while reminiscing on the past. It wasn't difficult to understand her. In those long winter nights when dogs gave a mournful howl, when lights glimmered in the distance, when the wind rattled the window panes, Aunt Tilda must have felt as if she was again in one of those scenes in which she would have wished to appear. She felt like the victim of a betrayal. She had thought during those nights that she could not put up with this betrayal, a betrayal she would never be able to forgive. The nights in question were the first spent on the island. She felt she had been uprooted from somewhere once again. She might well have inquired now what would death (long since expected) actually change?

It was their first night on the island. It seemed to her that another door had been closed on those lights from the city . . . Although, in a short while her life was to change in a manner nobody would have expected. Aunt Tilda had told me about this development during an evening talk at a time we felt much closer to each other. It was as though she had let her story slip at a remote distance. What was distant for her was essentially the very spot where we narrowed the gap between us. However, only after many years would I be in a position to gain an insight into the meaning of this sensational slip after having seen many places and experienced many solitudes, abandonments, and evasions; just like in relationships that build us up and remind us that we'll never be ready for anything else. Now it seems to me all the more convincing that she had mislaid a highly significant part of herself on the island. During one of those evenings we had tried to experience the rhythm of those long winter nights from several angles. The magic had worked; the time was ripe to disclose what that magic had formed. This fascinating experience was the experience of another coastal area beyond Istanbul. It was during those days of bitter experiences that she had realized how deeply she was in love with the man whose hand she walked with in life. This realization had had a great share in her aspiration for being a hospital nurse, despite her being a complete novice. This had played a major part in her standoffish approach to her man, her hardly giving utterance to her love for him . . . For, from that point on they had things to be exchanged beyond comprehension and expression . . . Indeed, beyond expression . . . although we cannot do without the use of words in life. Those footsteps were also heard by Joseph, because he too claimed those moments for himself. I had tried to hear them. That was a place where I thought I happened to be or believed I was in the proximity of. The thought that I might be nearer, even in my capacity as a spectator, to those days which had remained exclusive to two individuals, by combining what remained from the reports related to them with the products of my imagination, had replenished in me the hope that I would have the privilege of getting an insight into the profound significance of this story. It seemed to me that I had winnowed out certain facts, certain moments which one could not possibly extract, from those moments despite all the probable encounters and lies exchanged between two individuals wherein love had revealed itself; yes, certain moments, with a view to reaffirming the perpetuity of life beyond death. It was reported that Joseph, on one of the nights during which he had spoken of the France of Monte Cristo, had mentioned the splendor of illuminated salons, of the opera, of interminable nights, of dances, and of the wonderful experience of wearing fancy attire. A dream was intended to be reproduced by its rich imagery. This was a true dream in which turning the clock backward reflected a true reversion. Those nights had indeed been lived somewhere to be reproduced and abandoned eventually. The fact that they had been recollected at different locations, in different climates, indicated that, despite the desolation and withdrawal experienced in the meantime, the path taken had not reached a dead end—such a prospect being far from coveted. Was this an invitation, an effort to describe just before setting off for another destination, a world left unshared? It seems to me that all these questions conceal in them stories as different as apples and oranges, poems left unfinished. The sense of deficiency that the failure to provide answers for them had left in me could only be endured in this way; this hope that this deficiency bestowed on me, with reference to this part of the story, might perhaps enable me to stand before people. However, regardless of my role in the story, I'm obliged to disclose the fact that the thing that should be preserved was Joseph's resentment. They must have been aware of the fact that they had been heading toward the end, from probabilities and postponements, on their path far removed from the one most trodden. What had been unearthed because of the expression of this resentment and the discovery of an unknown aspect of such an individual reminds me once more of the stories that tell of the bitter experience of postponements. Aunt Tilda had asked the reason why he had not said any-thing about his life in the nightclubs. Joseph had retorted by saying that this had never been asked of him and added the following remark: "Our film had been a simple and short one, although replete with meaning"; indeed, simple and short and replete with meaning . . . Who was the original author of this sentence that Aunt Tilda reported to have been uttered by Joseph? Who was capable of being saddled with such a sentence, to be lost in the first place, trapped in places he ab-horred and through which he could not free himself? It was as though the inten-tion had been to stir up certain things whose designations would be likely to vary according to the individual and be capable of transcending any specific point in time, thus brushing us aside. This may have been the reason why Aunt Tilda had desired to perpetuate and preserve her experiences on the island. This must have been the reason why she occasionally avoided the visions that harassed her and was unable to remember certain nights in particular. Her inability to remember explained the reason why she avoided snapshots, as this represented her way of taking refuge in herself. Different individuals, whose recollections are nestled in the same body, may, at certain moments, belie each other, and prefer to consign them to oblivion. I knew this game. This expressed, in a way, the desire to eter-nally hear the voice of those they had abandoned. She kept those nights fresh in her memory by recalling them in different guises and conveying them to people in different fashions like many others that had taken part in that play. Under the circumstances, I could not possibly have had access to the actual words and expressions of Joseph on whom I had never set eyes; notwithstanding the fact that the individuals in question had been pattering in jargons that were already obsolete. The French they spoke interspersed with words of a Spanish origin was the language of communication between people whose number had considerably dwindled over time. However, I think I'll have to quote one day a monologue (of whose truth I am doubtful) within the context of that story. On the other hand, I sincerely doubt whether I'll be able to rid myself of the vocabulary of the time. "The wall between us, me and Tilda, remained impregnable. This must've been the reason for our abiding like two strangers despite our propinquity, this fear of surrender. Oh, how I wished that you shared with me the nights of your dreams that you spent with those individuals, without skipping over our platitudes and ignominies, hardly fitting the decency of our imagination. The film was a short one but one that reflected the actual truth, a film different from those we had seen, a film that emerged from the womb of our own life. The fault lay in your trying to see in me somebody else's garb, while I patiently waited and waited . . . Now, it is too late, too late for everything. I'm feeling so chilly now . . . " The words might have been very different; another expression, another cant may have been used for such a reproachful remark. I shall be recalling this speech when I take up my pen to include this incident in my story, using perhaps certain words different in sum and substance.

At this juncture, there is a point I arrive at as if groping along blindly based on what Aunt Tilda had said and in which I should like to have perfect confidence; only thus can I make headway in examining that life. I keep on telling myself that this had been the conclusion of the drift of that march and that the rationale of the story and its purport could not have been otherwise. This enables me to take a few more steps; a few steps forward, small ones though, but they are likely to take on new meanings which will enable me to provide new definitions. Aunt Tilda had moved into another territory which seemed to have had a serious effect on her life. This territory had been denoted by Joseph when least expected, after a long time spent lingering. Who was the inhabitant of that climate, beyond that boundary? What had been the reason for this long delay and anticipation? What had compelled Joseph to wait for so long? Why had he preferred to remain aloof as an onlooker amid the turmoil raging in his heart? Had this been due to his strong attachment to his wife, his one true woman, who had dominated his imagination so much as to not allow any room for the emergence of new imagery and caused his reluctance to see in the photographs the images of those individuals he wanted to shun so much against his will? Had the clues of such an expectation not been revealed during those Asmalimescit nights? I think I have a better insight into this mystery at present. To seek answers to these questions I go back to a sentence which finds more and more credence in me from day-to-day in connection with this part of the story. Aunt Tilda and Joseph had lived in a climate where they had spent their most pleasant days, removed from others for the first time, during which time dreams and realities were woven together, when they had snatched themselves from them in order to live their own life. Thus, they had closed their doors to their distant dreams . . . In the said climate, both of them had been mere kids. In that stream of time, during which they had tried to explore each other, they may have failed to exercise their discretion regarding the steps they were supposed to take; that may have been the reason why those days had come back to me in different guises and garbs. A special point, amid all these clumsy behaviors, shows once more how the path of love is clear once the door is opened. Aunt Tilda had, after the conversation that night, done something she had never done before, even under the effect of alcohol, and put her head on Joseph's chest and fallen asleep. In her dream she had seen herself in the company of Joseph in a nightclub to which she had never been before, dancing to the accompaniment of a song that stirred her to the depths of her soul. "We'll be dancing forever and ever, Tilda, until eternity," Joseph kept whispering in her ear, " . . . until eternity; a journey with no return! Yes, until eternity; till we collapse exhausted on the dance floor; till we exhale our last breaths toward each other . . . " Then, due perhaps to the effect of these words, she had suddenly regained consciousness. It was midnight. A strong wind clattered the windowpanes. Joseph was awake. "Take me to Asmalımescit," he said to Tilda, "I'm fed up with this place." They packed up early in the morning and left. Their personal effects could be counted on one hand. Certain dresses were to be worn only in particular places; they had to be put on for those places, reserved for those places only. Emotions associated with certain objects gradually died down in the depths of experiences. "We'll come back in July," said Tilda, "when the weather gets warmer." To which Joseph had answered with a mild smile saying: "For the first time in my life the month of July seems to be so distant."

It was a cold day in March. They felt like stretching their legs and had started to stroll down the island's alley when they saw a phaeton pass by, which they had both hailed at the same time. They traveled in the horse-drawn carriage up until the boat station, their ears full of the echoes of distant voices and sounds. Joseph said to her that as a child he had been motivated by the desire to sit next to the coachman. It appeared that Tilda also had the same burning desire. This had provoked in her the desire to tell him about her youth. This desire was the kind of joy that a good many people had lost in the process of concealing their childhood; however, it had so happened that this desire was called to be unearthed at this juncture. The phaeton was a proof of this, it had emerged out of the blue on a cold day of March: It was a day when trees, deceived by glimmering sunlight, bloomed as though in defiance of the approaching spell of cold air and storms . . .

Aboard the ship, Joseph had remained silent. He had a wan expression. He had suddenly stood up, telling her that he wanted to get some fresh air; and up on the deck he stood for a long while contemplating the wake of the ship. Could it be that the white foam from the top of the waves stirred in his mind childhood reminiscences? As she scrutinized this man who was gliding away from her, Aunt Tilda had wanted to sneak into this memory emerging from the store of his imagination and hold the hand of that child aboard the ship. She had failed to do so and realized that the boundary built on the island had been the last step and could not be trespassed. There was a place where two people heading for each other had to stop, a place which associated in one a lack of resonance, a sense of abandonment; it was a concrete fact, the meaning of which lay hidden in the dark and more often than not remained a mystery to us.

Joseph had broken into the apartment at Asmalımescit as a visitor, as a stranger; he had not turned on the radio, nor put a disc on the gramophone. For days, he found himself absorbed in a book which he had covered with a thick white paper with a view to keeping it at a safe distance from Tilda's scrutiny, dozing off now and then. These were their silent hours which did not prevent them, however, from eating sparingly. At the table, they told each other their childhood memories which they had not brought out into the open with any other person until then. Joseph had developed the habit of getting up early in the day to sit by the window and listen to "the voices and sounds of the dawning day," as he referred to it. The voices and the sounds redolent with odors of their own, exclusively belonging to those streets; to the streets laden with expectations for some, and conducive to regeneration and postponement for others. That book Joseph had been perusing may well have been described as absolute seclusion. With great patience Joseph moved about without a fixed course, aim, or goal through the pages he browsed, closing his eyelids now and then, as though repeating in *sotto voce* what he had read a while ago. It seems that this had been the only way to lead him there in the end. Joseph had wended his way through the pages of the book silently, furtively, until his body was discovered one morning when the streets, laden with expectations, dawned for some. As far as I could deduce from his dying expression he happened to be on his last legs in any case. He appeared to be sleeping soundly. The book he had been reading was lying on his chest and the index finger he had inserted in it indicated that he had finished reading it. His smiling face displayed serenity. Aunt Tilda had taken the book and put a mark where his finger had been pointing. She had cast a glance at the place marked by an asterisk only after the conclusion of the seventh day after his death. The book was about Amundsen's reaching the South Pole for the first time, and the mark was exactly at the point of arrival of this explorer from the North, in that white, silent and deserted expanse. This had reminded Aunt Tilda of her dialogue with Joseph at the Patisserie Lebon. That night she had browsed the book trying to pick out the hidden images among its pages. She had perused it like a stranger breaking into a house, trying not to make a noise for fear of waking the inhabitants. She had stopped at certain places hoping to come across Joseph. She had closed her eyes trying to visualize those people heading for the horizon of that godforsaken realm. When she had finished reading, the first rays of the morning were filtering into the drawing-room. She suddenly realized that the armchair in which she was sitting was the very armchair Joseph had been sitting in. The hours were the same, the voices and sounds were the same for those who could not have had proper access; and the disconnectedness was the same for those whose station at the window never changed. Aunt Tilda was swamped by a sense of desolation, a sense of desertion that she could describe only to those who had already had a similar experience . . . It was a morning in the month of July and a light breeze was wafting in from the sea. She seemed to have heard the hooting of a steamboat. Who, she wondered, would have it in mind to set off on a voyage at such a time? Who were these wandering and shelter-seeking souls that the island embraced? To whom did the smell of the pine trees belong, the lingering warmth of the shoreline on a summer evening, the cats seeking shelter in the streets, the houses that the sea watched over, the language spoken by the orthodox Greek minority, the tables smelling of anis? And then . . . and then, for the first time in her life, she felt as if death had touched her. For the first time in her life she felt truly alone; for the first time in her life she began sobbing, remote from whatever had been weighing upon her and the maddening crowd. This was a scene the like of which she had never seen in any movie; a touching scene without an audience . . . She had never seen herself like this, stripped of every garment . . . She had never seen anyone stark naked. Despite all the adventures and love scenes she had seen in films, she had never come so near to that person lost forever in that white expanse. It was a day that had eventually found its audience after many long years. The story had by now assumed a new garb, an emphatic new character that could be conveyed to others and shared by others. Thus, I had opted to remain on this side of the incident. There had been no disagreement as to the cast of characters. I wondered whether everything had been in due order; I'm still at a loss to say anything definite about this. The reason was that something was lurking in the shadows and preoccupying me. Now, what or who was the person Aunt Tilda had shed tears for that morning when she had felt detached from everything? Considering the funereal imagery, could one venture to suggest that she had been mourning for her own death? Could we intimate that our weeping was for our own transience as the participants in the ceremony seemed to suggest? This presumption has found no support thus far. I might just as well retract my steps to the ceremony held at the time as such an attempt seems to waft a scent to where I'm standing now. I don't know why, but I feel I am supposed to keep silent. I must take into account the fact that no one that I know of has broken with the experience of those mornings as one would have liked to. With reference to her recent past with Joseph, it seems as though Aunt Tilda had also concocted stories; stories of which the leading actress was not herself but others, although she had appropriated those roles herself. She had a tale to which nobody taking a view from outside could have access. The tale had been composed based on illusions and delusions. In it, imagination, viz. the area of defense, had been gradually widened. What she told me during one of our last meetings corroborates this. "Don't believe what I told you! Most of it was downright lies!" she said that evening. That was another time . . . especially when one considers what I have experienced now compared to what I had experienced then. Whereupon, I had spoken about the need we feel for stories that feed upon lies. I was intending to share this feeling at other places, at other times, and with other people. She had firmly squeezed my hand. She looked despondent, exhausted, and lackadaisical. What was more important still was that she viewed the world with an original discriminating judgment. She believed that she hadn't deserved to live the days she had been compelled to live. "One can never escape them," she said, "nor shall one ever be able to." "Who knows for certain?" I retorted. However, to be honest, I had not grasped exactly what 'them' had meant. Did it mean moments, voices, sounds, or visions? I can provide no answer to this question even now. "Perhaps some day," I say to myself. Some day, perhaps . . . But then, when that day comes, shall I be disposed to disclose 'them,' the visions that struck my fancy? I had told Tilda "Who knows for certain?" Both of us were in a position to finish the sentence as it suited us best. A wry smile had appeared on her face. By thinking back on that wry smile, I know today how to find the proper answer to that question.

All of this had been experienced during one of our last meetings. I felt I was being dragged within myself toward voices, looks, and moments I could never get rid of. We had done our best to share our story, our stories, with due patience, while risking getting lost somewhere along the way. All those moments were probably my enigmas which I'd never be able to convey. That evening when we were relishing our fresh rolls purchased from that baker at Kurtuluş, sipping on the light tea we savored while talking about Rita Hayworth, we were so far removed from that great moment of solitude when Aunt Tilda had been abandoned by her husband. Those would be cursed days for both of us.

Sentimental journey

"I'm tired . . . exhausted . . . I'm growing old. The concerts continue to take place but the movie theaters are closing their doors. The movie theaters Gloria, Konak, Elhamra, Alkazar, and Melek are no more, alas, the movie business seems to be at its lowest ebb. Where are those stars now?" Aunt Tilda said after having taken a sip from her cup of tea. I ventured to observe that everybody was still enduring the particular individuals inside them and that they continued to remember and live through their own movies and characters. This was a story lived by innumerable people, with innumerable details in special places and times which would never lose their warmth. This was the reason why we believed, why we wanted to believe, that those visions had entered our lives. It was certainly true that those individuals had got lost somewhere and at times we felt the need to call them back to a new dawn. Nevertheless, as we felt a deep longing for them, we yearned for them in the here and now, to a certain extent, for a part of ourselves no longer alive, for the individual who we believed to be living somewhere inside of us. We were those individuals at that time and space, the individuals whom we wanted to leave in our past for good. We were those people who had been yearning for those individuals who had gotten lost and who had preferred to get lost there. Certain corners, harbors or shores exclusively belonged to particular seasons. Did their reserve imply the seasons that could not be transported to another time, seasons that reanimated our withdrawal within ourselves, that moved us away from each other or off the shores wherein we had enjoyed our marches which we had imposed on our deaths and postponements? This question would bounce back to us more than once when least expected, clad in different covers. The shores were our shores; everybody had his own shore where he sought the warmth of a touch, his own steps that he had not risked to take; steps that he could not take forward, steps that had grown in size just because they had remained confined within him. These steps concealed our history which we desired to recount, to recount at least once in our lifetime, a history we would like to share with somebody. These were solitudes tried and tested, to be consigned to oblivion. However, despite my convictions regarding them, I feel compelled to remind you of this fact—that was a different time. The delusions had a property that linked one to life. We had taken these delusions for granted, without inquiring into them and not caring one whit. I believe that Aunt Tilda was both delighted and displeased with her brother's return to Istanbul. "Robert is back," she said, "I'll tell him to come here; the hotel room must've got under his skin." She made as though she was unaffected by this sudden abandonment, despite the love she had experienced from the relationship. Her giving utterance to her exhaustion, her yearning and recollections for those movies, and her desire to cling to someone, to her elder brother on whose affection she could rely, must have been due to this. Those solitary nights seemed to be more frightful compared to other people's nights. One should also pay attention to another aspect of the truth. Her wish to see her brother at her place implied the settlement of a long-standing debt she owed to him. When one considers what that return had wrought in that individual who had gone through those experiences, one could not imagine a better arrangement. Let alone being a necessity, it was simply good timing. Aunt Tilda had taken another step toward her family, back toward the days she had missed. London, and the lifestyle that had turned her brother into a hero in her family's eyes, was now far away, henceforth unattainable, inaccessible, and invisible. The magic had proved to be unsuccessful. The hero was now but an ordinary person, who was made to feel that his presence in a household where he desired to abide forever was unwanted. An ordinary individual doomed to carry the burden of his faults on his own shoulders, like a stranger. No doubt it had occurred to him to ask a question to someone that many would have liked to ask during those days. In other words, whose outstanding debt was he expected to settle? Who attempted to get what during those evenings in which proper room was made for that return? "What have you done so far in your life?" Monsieur Jacques asked his unexpected visitor. His voice seemed to display indignation, reproach, and a tinge of superiority. Monsieur Robert had appreciated what lay behind that question. After all those skirmishes, to guess the meaning of certain words was not so difficult. Guided by the light of this call, complying with the directives of other actors, in spite of other scenes he should act accordingly. He was certainly not a stranger to playing such a role. That is why he said: "Mere ostentation" with a husky voice, without trying to clear his throat beforehand, "Mere ostentation!" It was a Sunday evening, a Sunday evening when rooms seemed to dwindle, to be getting colder, and devoid of veneer. One of the fragments that memory roused in me had found its pertinent place on that Sunday evening . . . Until recently, the lights were those of another city. The stage was also different; a stage which covered up delusions, lies, and distances. He had tried to find himself once more in those visions. Not to sever his ties with that life, but to acknowledge and prove to himself that he was resolved to prolong his age-old habits. He had put on his cashmere sweater that had been a wedding present— which he had made a point of preserving intact up until recently, and which he intended to leave in London when the time came—and left to keep his rendez-vous with the five o'clock tea service at the Grosvenor Hotel. He spent that Sunday evening there all alone. The rooms seemed to have diminished; their lights had lost their luster in that Istanbul evening and were occupied by other people. To have been obliged to cast a glance from such a vantage point fascinated the man as if a magic spell had been cast on him that was difficult to describe. However, what was difficult to bear was the transformation of those people that one had known, and would have liked to regard as, one's next-of-kin, into strangers. "Ostentation! Mere ostentation!" This was a sentence that those who happened to be there, and who had insidiously envied him during the good old days would have liked to hear. The price had been paid. Those who had been on the other side of the boundary line had seen what they wanted to see. Those who were on the other side certainly had their own shores and an area beyond which one could outline and guard. The fact that our cities gained meaning with the city walls within us had already been given utterance by other individuals at other times. The stories in which those boundaries had been mere quirks of fate were waiting to be put into new words for this very reason. Aunt Tilda was not one of the heroes, she should not figure in this story. Her boundary line I had to seek among the fragments that had remained lost to others. This remoteness acted as a badge of intimacy with those who were kept at arm's length like her elder brother . . . a film star that embodied certain sentiments and was capable of conveying them to his fellow beings. A hero who had his own theme song like all other heroes, a figure of fantasy, but one who appeared to be all too real, relating to, based on, or concerned with objectively existent things in the physical world. The film star in question was Clark Gable, who she wished to see only for herself, and whose smile would abide forever; a Clark Gable, who she expected to tell her that those films were not simple fictional realities. This fantasy, like all similar wild dreams, brought with it transports of delight, a fantasy that had to entrench itself as a sanctuary. However, in this relationship, if certain inevitable boundaries were to be forced, certain concealed sentiments might have to be traced on a completely different course in a totally different story. Do you think that in tracing this sentiment one could detect an indefinable profound relationship whose characteristics one preferred to keep undisclosed? In the face of our observations and the available clues and implications, our access to such data was beyond possibility, at least for the moment. What remained behind were but the visions of a silent past, incapable of impairing this relationship. The said past intercepted postcards mailed from distant cities and unexpected telephone calls, decoding their encryptions. Aunt Tilda retained the memory of the small money orders her brother had sent through banks with which he performed lucrative business transactions whenever she was short of money, as though they had been very close, as well as of that memorable London visit during which a privately hired Rolls Royce with a private driver had been put to her disposal, of the music halls and operas, of the shopping at Harrods, the Queen's shopping center, where she had tried on ancient costumes, fashionable hairpieces, and, last but not least, of the restaurant where waiters "as refined as lords" had served her. It was an old film for which she could find no designation and was reluctant to find any name for. An ever-fresh, old film that never lost its authenticity, a film, every frame of which she lived to the core in all its colors, a film to remain stamped on her memory. She had literally run into David Niven on the bend of a street; something had driven her to knock on the door of Mr. Higgins in *My Fair Lady*; when she had posed for a snapshot at the gate of Buckingham Palace next to the royal guard she had felt that she was actually in a land of fairy tales, it never occurring to her that other individuals might also have their own dreamworld, a sanctuary for those who felt out of sorts in their humdrum daily life. In such a distant realm, she unconsciously perpetuated a fate, an attitude to life that directed her course of living. That might have been the reason why she had set too high a value on certain representations more than any ordinary individual. She distinctly remembered that through the window of the five star hotel where she had stayed, she had observed that the car hired by her elder brother used to arrive exactly ten minutes before its appointed time. The driver parked it and glanced at his watch, reporting at a regularly predictable time schedule without any unexpected deviation—typical British punctuality. The whole week she had been in a dreamworld; it was a week destined to remain stored in her memory for the rest of her life. Under the circumstances, she could not possibly have known that her elder brother had been immersed in a quagmire of debt and that he had serious marital problems. Behind that radiant world, there lay concealed quite different solitude and decline. Nobody expected to experience the consequences of a wrong step. It was a time when fantasies had not yet been frustrated or shattered, when belief still persisted in offering a beacon of hope despite setbacks and obligatory detachments. Her elder brother had gained her affections even more so after she was informed of this fact. She had found the opportunity to express this deep-rooted sentiment which had evolved and silently expanded within her as the years went by, which she had tried to enliven somewhere outside the reach of strangers. She was resolved to invite him to her house. She had a modest income, a recurrent revenue from the rent of two shops, a family legacy at Mahmutpaşa; the income was low, it was true, but it was better than nothing; a regular monthly allowance according to which she arranged her budget. One of her tenants was an old mender of worn-out fur coats, she was one of his long-standing customers; the other was a seller of clothes whose assets were dwindling. Everybody tried to live up to their own standards after all and carried their burden to the best of their ability. Factually, the brothers and sisters had equal share in the shops. However, an agreement was made for understandable reasons. Regardless of all contingencies, the shops were to remain and should remain in Tilda's possession. This bequest of Madame Roza, who had in the prime of her life taken charge as the matron of the entire family, had, to the best of my knowledge, been the consequence of a will secretly drawn up by Monsieur Jacques shortly before his death. A word given or taken under such a circumstance has sometimes greater validity than a piece of written evidence. What interested me in particular at the time, was, I believe, not that secret contract liable to varying interpretations, but rather Aunt Tilda's capital gain from the lease she took out on the shops. Had she so willed, she might have indulged in a more commercially lucrative venture. As a matter of fact, Monsieur Jacques had taken her to task more than once for failing to take such a step. Yet, I gather that such a preference had given rise to another sentiment; a sentiment devoid of all possible associations, but capable of stirring certain feelings dormant in certain people who prefer to turn a deaf ear to them; a sentiment likely to find echoes somewhere; a sentiment which was the result of an empathy even though the people were far apart, between her and the tenants of those shops trying to put up a bold front against the hardships of life. The income was modest enough, but there were other gains involved. Aunt Tilda must have felt it when she invited her elder brother. The rent she received would be enough to cover her running expenses, including incidentals like movie tickets, concerts, etc. There was nothing else she desired anyhow. However, something new had emerged that would shatter the family to its very foundations. Madame Roza, the woman who had been trying to keep the family members closely linked together, who knit friendships and who knew how to keep secrets, was fated to recede gradually from the individuals to whom she had held out a helping hand in their difficult times.

My daisy sea

Everybody had grown old in their own fashion at the place where they had always been; everybody was resigned to listen to the resonance of the sounds and voices that arose from within their own depths. For, there were moments when certain latent representations passed judgment on people and established close links between them. Lily complained of recurrent dreams marred with nightmares which frightened her to death. Madame Estreya had remained pent up in her confined and distant world of sentiment. Her visits to those who had silently denied her once had, despite the changing conditions, grown less and less frequent. Monsieur Jacques, withdrawn to his autistic world at home, was in pursuit of absolute stillness. The woman with whom he had shared a long life of innumerable devastating storms and meaningful reserve and sacrifices, lay ill, and was getting prepared for a journey quite different from those she had undertaken so far. Madame Roza was well aware of all these developments, of the facts which could not have been given utterance; it was as though she lent an ear to them trying to hear sounds of a different kind. After she had encountered the hard fact that had induced her to blurt out "Why me?" she had found herself engaged in a new and fierce battle of existence in her capacity as the matron of the family. It was the last pitched battle to be fought; she would no longer receive any further wounds on the battleground. She had made a point of not exposing her grievances to view. Yet, her throes increased. She could not help watching her body waste away with every passing day. She retired to her room on certain evenings saying that she needed some rest. This was new for her; never before had she reverted to such an expedient. Did this mean that she was suffering from a budding illness, a sort of solitude difficult to describe, one to be endured through storms that were raging in one's heart? Was this a new bone of contention between her and her ineluctable fate? When I take a look, at present, at what has been experienced retrospectively, I can plainly see that she had been virtually abandoned; she might, at a pitch, resign herself to such a state of abandonment, of depletion and prostration, had she not been faced with the difficulty of displaying to her loved ones, to those whom she had been devoted to for all those years with a deep sense of responsibility, certain scenes from her last battle which she would have preferred not to divulge. It looked as though she retired to her chamber in search of sanctuary. The mastectomy she had had last year had failed to solve the problem. The results showed that there had been metastases; the disease was spreading to other parts of the body. The medical profession had proved to be inefficient once more. Doctors were silent about the number of days she had left. "Chemotherapy and radiotherapy would no longer help her, all that we can do is to soothe her pain," said the doctors.

The image of Madame Roza from those days is still fresh in my mind. A TV set had just been purchased. This object, which, in time, would have revolutionary effects on the domestic lives of the great majority of people, had, for the moment, created for the privileged class a new diversion, and had been an important factor in bringing together the family members who were clustering in drawing-rooms to watch the black-and-white transmissions on a single channel on certain days of the week. I had been a regular visitor during those hours, especially to watch the general knowledge quiz. Monsieur Jacques who had been reluctant about this 'box,' which he deemed to be a token of wealth, and who would find nothing of interest in it for a good many years to come, used to react against this new contraption by dozing off, even though he kept denying this fact. Minor altercations involving ridicule were not rare among the family members. Berti had managed to get in some good shots on his father who had been roused from his sleep when the flash had gone off. "What's that? What impertinence!" he said as though he wanted to rebuke him. But, having witnessed the mildly humorous atmosphere, the laughter caused by the good-natured joke, he would reply to his son by bellowing "Goof." Amid the contrasting bitterness, that evening was to remain fixed on people's memories. I wonder why certain incidents, though dull and insipid in themselves, occupy important places in people's minds? Why certain moments give rise to indelible impressions. The relevant matter here was the phenomenon of reunion; a reunion anticipated without any set purpose, one that had occurred naturally. However, there seemed to be something lurking behind this reunion, something vague that was likely to remain doomed to obscurity forever. What on earth could it be, the thing that reminds us of certain aspects of our life regardless of our predispositions? This question, though transient, struck a chord in me that would re-emerge every now and then. What has remained in my memory from that evening are but pieces of information; certain moments that I can recall refer back to the snapshots in hand, to my wish to recollect the incidents of that evening, and to my nostalgic regard for them; those are recollections I find hard to give voice to at any given moment.

Yes, the quiz shows, they were forms of entertainment often found on the TV at the time in which members of a panel competed answering questions. Madame Roza was pleased to see me giving correct answers to puzzling questions. And when I failed to provide answers, she, far from reproaching me, remarked that such programs were meant essentially to instruct people, in addition to their being a form of entertainment, telling me about the *quitte ou double* program on Radio Monte Carlo she had once listened to at a family gathering. She had so many things to say about those programs. Here was another instance of an adoption of one memory for the sake of another. She remembered once a contestant that had carried the day, answering all the questions put to him, winning the sweepstakes; but what had caused a stir was not the prize he was awarded but the comment he had made after the applause had ceased. The question was: "Who was the Prima Donna at the premiere of the opera put on at La Scala?" to which the contester answered: "Maria Callas." However, when the cheers subsided, he added that he had given that answer on purpose as it was what everybody had expected him to say; otherwise the right answer should be "Leyla Gencer." This had created considerable uproar among the audience. The subsequent investigation had proved that the claim was in fact correct. This incident had wide repercussions all over France and had eventually found its written expression in Paris Match. Madame Roza could not quote the exact wording of the gentleman's remark, unlike other key moments she could convey to people which she kept in the store of her memory. She might have missed the gist of the joke and the crux of the incident was likely to have gone through alterations over time because the years that had elapsed in the meantime may have superimposed neologisms and novel features to the report. Yet, the essential thing was the existence of those moments, of the places filled by those moments laden with meaningful recollections. This exercise of memory had brought tears to her eyes. Madame Roza attached great importance to erudition. Her erudition far surpassed her husband's or her brother's. This was probably the reason for her father's reliance on her, in whom he took great pride. Such had been the sneak previews of the TV quizzes in that house . . . A few snapshots and a couple of tidbits . . . to show people the fact that somewhere in the past certain things had been enacted, thus giving oneself a grounding in order to bear what one had to go through more easily. In other words, those evenings had varied moments, touching moments. Everybody who lived and who was obliged to live in that long, blind alley felt the need to probe deeply into themselves. This is the reason why I have always wanted to lend credence to the importance of those brief moments when Madame Roza was peeping through her little window at what she had left behind for me. This act that occurred during the evening paved the way for the emergence of a joy which I can express only now despite my grieving. On my way to that little house I was unaware of the closeness I would share with the others. I'm inclined to believe that a day will come when I'll be able to define the nature of this joy more clearly, and be able to take new steps forward toward the person hidden within me. The only thing that had not lost its character was, I think, the taste of that specially prepared white coffee. The fact the memory of that white coffee still lingers on my palate despite the lapse of a decade is testament to my desire to reclaim what is lost to that distant past at all costs. There are moments in one's life when one connects to an aftertaste or scent that abides in one's memory, of which we do not want to be denied and which we cannot rid ourselves of. There were impressions that lingered, concealed behind seemingly ordinary and all too familiar representations. Regardless of the associations that this gush of enthusiasm might lead me to, this distinctive taste, which even caused me to take delight in milk, was attributable to a special concoction, the flavor of which I could find nowhere else. I'd heard the word 'chicory' for the first time in my life there; however, it would take me years to have an insight into the exact meaning of the word thanks to the research I carried out. Chicory was a thick-rooted, usually blue-flowered, perennial herb native to Europe, it is widely grown for its young leaves which are used as salad greens while the dried ground roasted root of it are used to flavor coffee. How relevant is this information at this juncture? I really don't know, nor shall I ever be able to find the right place for it. What seems of vital concern to me is the magic of this key word that carries me back to those days, along the path I am supposed to tread. Madame Roza used to dissolve the chicory tablets she bought at the Çankaya Food Market at Şişli in hot water—the properties of which had an overwhelming effect on me at the time—which she continually refer to as 'Neagora,' its former nomenclature. She diluted the solution in coffee as was necessary, preserving it in a large infusion bottle—the origin of which she made a point of keeping a secret—which she then placed in the refrigerator, mixing it gingerly with milk when it was to be served. The portion of the additive admitted during the process remained constant. The chicory is beyond my reach now. So much the better, in a way . . . I realize now that certain truths exclusively belong to particular places, and should do so, in fact. My finding delight in milk undoubtedly had latent meanings which lay deep within me. I was to experience the same delight years later after tasting Juliet's white coffee. However, my overall experience with milk had failed to prompt a love for it in me, and, what is more, a love for people who liked it. It seemed to me that that love concealed an ill; an illness I have always found difficult to define. I had come to this conclusion through a warning given to me. Lineaments, scents, and words are all mingled now. Had I been afraid of probing into certain truths? Perhaps I had. However, these are particularities that can find their true balances in other stories and places. What I want to stress here is the fact that Madame Roza continued to concoct her white coffee even during the days when she had finally resigned herself to her fate. During this process she appeared to be in a sort of trance; her stare lost in the distance, not uttering a word. So far, she had never settled accounts with Monsieur Jacques. It looked as though certain words had failed to find their place in certain instances. One wonders if the true words had lingered there. There are certain women whose fighting style and manner of love-making one cannot imagine. I figured Madame Roza was such a woman. I could not imagine who or what she might have been staring at (her looks were diverted into the distance), nor what time and space she had been regarding. Once she had mentioned a person she had recalled from her childhood days. It was an old man, a vagrant with tousled white hair, begging for a drink. They called him 'Bohor el Mintirozo' (Bohor the liar), as he was a notorious gossip. Among the accounts he gave were unexpected deaths, women cheating on their husbands, buried treasures unearthed, houses deliberately set on fire, etc. Despite his untoward reputation, he somehow managed to find people to believe him. Although they doubted the veracity of his accounts, people who were either gullible enough to be duped or people who allowed themselves to be duped for the mere pleasure of having something to believe in. To live on imaginary truths had become Bohor's philosophy in life. He was not only the village idiot, but also its storyteller. The local people had a need for such a figure. One day, he said that he was going to Istanbul to see a woman he had been in love with while in his teens for the last time. Nobody believed him; as they had interpreted this as another product of his fevered imagination, giving rise to another false effusion. However, no one saw him thereafter. Had this been the only truth he ever offered? Madame Roza was concerned about this as she realized that Bohor would be one of the people she would feel nostalgic about whenever she chose to revisit the past. She was resolved to find him before she reached her final destination and ask him: "Do we not all need to make sure that certain legends buried within us remain safe and sound in our confrontation with the truth?"

When her stare was lost in the distance, I pictured her imagining the vast green meadows and the fields of daisies that stretched far and wide. Panting, she was heading for one of her islands; she had difficulty breathing and felt a sense of constriction in her chest as she was often subject to fits of coughing. These symptoms reminded me of the asthma attacks I had as a child. I wasn't the only one who suffered those never-ending nights of silence.

That little lie

These are the photographs dating from the days of Aunt Tilda's brother's stay at her home; snapshots I can never forget. Monsieur Robert, deeply touched by his sister's hospitality, had warmly embraced his little sister and was reduced to tears. He disregarded the risk he ran to distort his legendary image because of a moment of vulnerability. At the time, the hotel room in which we had long talks and the tea hours we shared that enabled us to coexist despite our differences was not yet there. We had not yet seen each other; we had not yet felt the need to mutually open those doors. Aunt Tilda was to tell me about that emotional scene years later, when she eventually believed that I had familiarized myself with her brother. During that time, during which she had invited and received him with all his encumbrances and without reservations, she merely told me the story she had been keeping in her breast, her emotional experiences and joy; communicating to me in Istanbul the virtual image of the London adventure. No one else but Aunt Tilda could depict the flotsam and jetsam of that tale. It was a day when her elder brother was out to strike important deals. We were alone, the two of us . . . As she displayed to me the costumes, shirts, and under-wear meticulously arranged in the wardrobe in the room she had tidied up for her new guest with the charm of a naughty girl who was not without a some-what demure demeanor, she had made the following remark: "As you may well see, they're all premium products." She seemed to be vindicating something, to cast away all doubts, more than ever. She had gone into the kitchen to prepare her first meal in many years . . . after so many years . . . to make her guest feel at home. Despite all her efforts, her stoic stance, and her endeavor to clad the days in a different garb, her joy, nay her exuberance, would be short lived; like all strong emotions, this experience would also run itself out naturally. Within six months of his moving into his sister's place, Monsieur Robert would one day pack up without any pretext or desire to account for his sudden decision and said with an apologetic tone that it would be better for him to live elsewhere. The hotel room at Sıraselviler would be a later growth. Aunt Tilda had at first reproached herself for having failed to have been a perfect hostess, blotting out all other postulations. All she had done had been to express her sadness at his departure, observing that she had done everything to provide for his comfort. Whereupon her brother had tapped her on her shoulder and said that the world they lived in was corrupt and that all the habiliments, illuminations, and dark nights had but one purpose: to cover up the raging depravity. What was going on in the world could no longer be grasped by those who had preserved their pristine chastity . . . Well, this world was calling him. That was all he could say. He felt that the only advice he, who considered himself to have failed to give his little sister what was expected from an elder brother, could offer was to suggest to her to keep her childhood innocence despite all the untoward events likely to beset her. The world was in dire need of people with the hearts of children; more than ever . . . regardless of whether the world was aware of this fact or not. Aunt Tilda had reacted to her brother's comment with an eerie silence; she had presumed that her brother was quite probably handling important business deals that required an irregular schedule. After all, serious business made one pay through the nose. Her dejection had been compensated, however, as she felt a sort of pride mixed with disappointment; she had thought of film stars constantly in direct confrontation with death . . . She had, in fact, lived many years in their company. This had offered her a crumb of comfort and facilitated her alleviation of this sense of defeat. The truth lay elsewhere; of which she would be confronted much later, when she was to learn that her brother had gone to London without any intention to return home. The fact was this man whom she had idealized was burdened with a crippling gambling debt and was facing ferocious clashes with the creditors who threatened his life. Being afraid that his sister might also be involved in this dirty affair, he had decided to beat them at their own game by roaming elsewhere.

Aunt Tilda was sick with disappointment when she learned this secret from her elder sister years later. This had made her feel like a castaway. The resentment she felt seemed to linger in her when she, after a lapse of many years, had decided to impart it to me. The fact was that she thought she could do something after so many years, in the face of his magnanimity of purpose and action, despite his lack of confidence . . . Had he so desired, she could do something, at least she could try to, if the whole matter was a question of money. Yet his voice, the voice he had wanted to make heard in different places with different accents had become unfamiliar to her; he was used to living amidst a tumult of voices among which he could not make himself heard; he had been beyond the reach of her, she who had become a stranger to it.

A sharp bend in the road

When she learned about her brother's plight, Aunt Tilda decided to sell the two shops at Mahmutpaşa. Everybody connected in some way or other with these shops had pulled a long face, as each of them had his or her own memories of them. Aunt Tilda saw to it that Monsieur Jacques knew nothing about it despite the reiterated protests of Madame Roza. Her aim was most probably to achieve something on her own for the first time in her life and to experience the joy of breaking with the past, with the things to which they attributed some value. I think it is easier at present to believe that such considerations had not been taken into account by the family at the time. This may have been the reason for the inconceivable reality hidden behind the eccentric behavior of the problem child, Tilda. So long as we didn't take the risk of inquiring into the real problems, we could not go beyond a certain boundary. This seemed to be a legacy dating from ages ago, which featured, among others, thousands of marches and hundreds of thousands of words. We had been accustomed to carrying this legacy with great patience. It may be because of our attachment to this heavy, onerous burden that we often ignored our encounters with apathy. The real mystery surrounding Aunt Tilda's unaccounted for decision to sell those shops was never unraveled. The only explanation, ventured as a result of investigations conducted by Monsieur Jacques, was that in this resolution a rogue of advanced years by the name of Bedros, notorious for his handling of intricate solutions to certain problems, through his influential connections, had been instrumental in the precipitate sale of the shops in question at prices much lower than their actual value in no time. It seemed that Aunt Tilda had paid a great price for her need to seek refuge in people to compensate for her solitude in which she had been confined in the wake of her brother's unannounced voluntary exile. The matter was not cleared up.

The incident was surely not without precedence for Aunt Tilda; she had already experienced such desertions. It has never been easy to have access to people's idiosyncrasies at certain given moments of our predilection. This had to do with the steps we are supposed to take toward both our fellow man and ourselves at a chosen place marked by those idiosyncrasies. The boundaries may undergo changes because of words and representations that were believed to have been mislaid at unexpected moments but were not, just like our own inner islands; this fact makes it easier to recognize ourselves. To reach the boundaries of Aunt Tilda had never been easy for anyone. My intuition, along with my efforts to patch up certain fragments enabled me to make a landing. From this vantage point I can visualize the commencement of the split that evening. Aunt Tilda would be experiencing henceforth a series of separations in the wake of that original severance. However, a fatal incident had paved the way to it; its bearing involved not only Tilda but the entire family; for Madame Roza died. This would cause the other family members to share this separation each in his or her own way.

The picture will become clearer in your mind if you think of the great distress felt by the crowd of people at Madame Roza's funeral and the associations involved. The deceased was a woman who had done her best all her life to hold together everybody who had won her affection. The fact that she was considered an elder sister, a superwoman to whom one could revert for the solution of problems even though they were insignificant and she was compelled to keep other people's secrets, must have been due to these efforts. Her death had left a huge gap in the family that nothing could fill; a gap to be interpreted, defined, and clarified differently by each of them. Her absence would induce everybody to take cognizance of and experience the unbridgeable gap that had been insidiously brought about between her and the rest of the family members. It wasn't for nothing that Monsieur Robert, staring at the death notice in the paper, had commented that: "The best of the family alas is no more . . . Now, everybody is on their own . . . " Henceforth every member would be experiencing his or her own rupture and withdrawing to their own silence. This held true for Monsieur Jacques, Monsieur Robert, and Aunt Tilda as well as Madame Estreya who had years ago outlined her solitude. This death had caused Monsieur Jacques to withdraw within himself more often; Monsieur Robert to set off on a one-way trip to London; Aunt Tilda to feel estranged in that house where she used to reveal her private concerns to the family members present; and Madame Estreya to abandon the place where she had spent her childhood and adolescence, consigning to oblivion even the traditional religious holidays. Henceforth, everybody would live through Madame Roza in his or her own way, in his or her world in the midst of his or her reversals of fortune, regrets, and little victories.

Aunt Tilda had mentioned a series of mishaps over the course of the days that had led to the death of her elder sister. She had faced an attempted rape by a man at night in the street; she had found the corpse of the cat of the retired ambassador Sinan Bey, her neighbor, at her home; a plainclothes police officer had, one night, knocked on her door and conducted a search of her premises, the search warrant he had produced intimated that intelligence was received to the effect that prostitution was practiced in the house. Who were those people hidden behind dreams, who were the heroes of certain nights and solitudes? Such a question could only be answered in proportion to our proximity to those dreams, of course. However, we were far removed from those dreams during those days. The dreams that those days had made viable to a certain extent were related to another story which seems lost to me at present. This was her last story, the last beautiful story deserving to be told. It was about a neighbor of hers. The hero of the story was an elderly Russian gentleman. He spoke German, Italian, and French perfectly. He recited poems by Lamartine, Victor Hugo, and Alfred de Vigny. A lover of music, he played the violin. He was an enthusiastic devotee of the romantics. It seemed that he was distantly related to Oistrach, the great violinist. They might go and see him whenever they wanted to. They might attend a performance at the Moscow opera. However, the man was notorious for his opposition to the regime in power. Such a visit might involve risks, not to mention the problems that would await them on their return to Istanbul. To begin with, the landlord had filed a court case against his friend to evict her. They were firmly resolved to put up an effective defense. Czerny, the lawyer, was planned to be appointed as counsel; but she doubted if her declining means would suffice to cover the consultancy fee. She could no longer purchase gifts for her friends on their birthdays like in the old days. It would never occur to an outsider to consider these points deserving of attention. Only those who knew her could perceive the bitterness the situation gave rise to. She had made a point to add some flavor to her insipid life by such trifles. She never forgot a single birthday of her friends. Even though the people involved might have no recollection of their own birthday, Aunt Tilda would never fail to remind them of this. Her last gift to me was given on the eve of her withdrawing into the seclusion in which she was compelled to live in the company of the voices and sounds she could not divulge to anyone. It was an evening during which she had brought a couple of silver candlesticks from home, something that she desired to transport from the past to the present. She had begun to distribute pieces from her past among her acquaintances . . . She had let herself be swept up by the tidal wave and grown careless of her attire; she no longer put up her hair, let alone had it dyed. What was happening was so different from the exciting episodes we shared during those hours at tea. Aunt Tilda had given up taking care of herself and had no longer any claim to picture postcard prettiness. She set before the eyes of some family members, with great difficulty, her actual accoutrements and companions in order that they might understand the new dreamworld she inhabited, a scene at odds with her former appearance. It was a scene in which no one would have liked to appear or play a role. The stage was one on which she played the leading part in her life, a stage likely to lead to the valley of the shadow of death with a grim sense of foreboding. The spectators shared this grim sense of foreboding. However, there was a climactic moment during which reigned a deathly silence that hung over the entire audience; no one among the anxious spectators knew for sure whose end had come.

What we had been watching were but the visual representations of a decline, of a downward trend that made itself more conspicuous from day-to-day. It may be that what we had been watching so far and had been witnessing varied considerably among the audience who had been, in one way or another, off-stage. She no longer invited me to her place as often as she had before. The hours of tea were shorter. Occasionally she asked me to tell her about what I had been writing; she wanted me to get married and spoke of marriageable wallflowers; the prospective brides were girls that had attracted her attention during picnics and who exhibited a feminine charm that was difficult not to be tempted by, especially in springtime; some played the harp with great dexterity, some were ballerinas, some were plumpish with a fine voice, and some desperately lonely; in a nutshell, those were the girls of her past she wanted to transpose to the present. They were her acting partners on stage. She suggested that she would be pleased to talk with them if I so wanted. I, on my part, taking care not to offend her on any pretext, used to respond somewhat favorably to her suggestions with such phrases as: "Why not?" "If you like." "Not a bad idea at all!" "But the question remains where and how?" she used to giggle, covering her mouth with her hand, with a mischievous air, blushing with shame like a young girl who starts to recognize her femininity for the first time; those were moments when she laughed heartily. After such bouts of laughter she suddenly grew silent, a smile lingering on her lips as though she continued to converse with the invisible presence of certain people. At such moments I realized that it was time for me to leave; to depart, leaving her in communion with her imaginary beings, despite the fact that I knew that she would remain seated in that position behind closed doors for hours on end.

She ended up being called the fool of the district; it was her ineluctable fate; a fate of which certain people had had a premonition.

Her image has remained indelible in my mind; as she wandered through the streets with her disheveled white hair, wearing an old man's overcoat and dark stockings, she looked as if she had completely resigned herself to her fate. The streets were not the streets she was familiar with, and the people she bumped into on the road were those with whom she had not even a passing acquaintance. It was rumored that she invited men, especially young apprentices, to her home and gave them sexual satisfaction. We could never learn how far these malicious rumors flying about were substantiated. I believe implicitly that she had reached a point far beyond that of ordinary rebellion. She was wrecking a terrible vengeance on those who had stigmatized her as hysterical during her youth, when she looked on life optimistically and went through a period marked by uninhibited gaiety, self-indulgence, and dissipation. This had the semblance of a long process of death, a chronic suicide. What had been the factors that had paved the way to her actual plight, the nights and people who didn't show up? Her love for Joseph, who had never ceased to show affection for her, was not extinct; she took up the cause of enslaved men and seemed resolved to unfasten their handcuffs and remove their shackles. In other words, she was able to pinpoint people who happened to be where they were supposed to be. As for her . . . Did the problem lie in her inability to find answers to her case? Given the fact that the rumors were indeed true, I wonder if Aunt Tilda, in her solitude, had ever reached a climax and found inner peace in her relations with those callow errand boys and apprentices of artisans and greengrocers whose sexual desire was repressed or suppressed. I doubt it, I sincerely doubt it. I wish I could find convincing proof of this. I wish I could join her in that climate of immorality out of spite for those who had cast aspersion on her character and reputation. I wish I could rediscover her there. It seemed that in my capacity as spectator, this wish invited me to another deep silence; another deep silence in which one could truly hear his own voice, a silence that kept aloof from our everyday experiences. This silence might be pregnant with brand new problems, however. I might be questioned there about the reason why, and for whom, I had asked that question. Truly, why had I overestimated those moments in my capacity as a spectator and felt the necessity to put this question to myself and to another person? The reason must have been my desire to delve into the roots of another unstated experience . . . There, in those rooms which were wearing away to be consigned to oblivion with every passing day and whose bridges with reality were being blown up, a covert life continued to throb. Leaving aside all these considerations and my divergent thoughts, these speculations indicate that I am trying to open a new door for Aunt Tilda as a heroine of a story that pens itself in dribs and drabs. Human beings that get lost in each other and whose mutual boundaries coalesce generate new individuals, new individuals of whom the extent of their reality remains a mystery. No doubt there was a sort of escape in this; a faith which led to the demise of certain hopes in certain people who were reminiscing about the behavior adopted toward Aunt Tilda by her family. There seemed to exist things that could no longer be amenable to regeneration . . .

The sea was another road

To fail to take the turn at the right moment or to choose not to take it at all because of one's apprehensions and the things that one, in full knowledge of the
enslavement involved, would prefer not to lose . . . Although Aunt Tilda was 'his
old' aunt, the fact that she had not been invited to the wedding of Rosy, the introverted, kind, affectionate and unlucky stepchild of Monsieur Jacques, sufficed to
show the extent of the preference involved. Rosy had come upon this fact only on
the wedding night and had retorted reproachfully to Juliet, saying: "How very
treacherous of you! You should at least respect my beloved grandmother's memory!" This voice contained a wrath that seemed to conceal other revolts she dared
not put into words. This voice was the voice of an extremely sensitive, tender
heart, according to the judgment of her friends. Tears rose to her eyes. Berti had
let his head sink to his chest; he had a faint smile on his face. He felt he was in an
intermediate state between confusion and pride. He was the best person there to
understand this touch . . . Juliet was staring at me. I could not exactly tell what she
was trying to bring to the fore, but I noticed that she also looked somewhat confused . . . Monsieur Jacques was not there; he hadn't heard the words exchanged;
he looked to have gone off reminiscing to a far spot, somewhere in the distance.
When one considers what had been left for other people in other stories and what
had to be recollected, this was only too natural. We happened to be at the seaside.
Another person in another story had desired to speak of the streets of Istanbul
that led up to the sea. The sea they mentioned might well imply a larger road, into
which innumerable roads flowed, a road that reached different boundaries in different stories with differing yearnings, capable of propagating different songs.
Rosy and I, we had failed to knit together a friendship over the entire course of
our lives. She seemed to prefer to keep aloof from her acquaintances. But the fact
was that to be able to understand that distance, to have a proper insight into it,
was not possible despite what other separations had intimated to us. It seemed as
though she was fated to remain distant. Now that I can think more clearly, with a
lucid mind, I'll try to have a fresh insight into my own remoteness. I'm convinced
that I'll be able to think of a more logical explanation, at least on my account. It
looked as though Rosy had appeared to others as being unfeminine in character,
despite her impeccably clear and ivory skin, blue eyes, fair and thick wavy hair,
and full breasts that were likely to engage the attention of men. Was this one of
the reasons for our failure in closing up the gap between us? I distinctly remember

that I had felt a pang of guilt for not having established a proper connection with her, when I reflected on this incident. Whenever I visualize what we had experienced there, I can't help thinking that I won't be able to dispose of this crisis of conscience. At such times I think of the helplessness of people who are the victims of delayed reaction, while a voice from the past, from a past long ago, starts narrating to me the story of people who have failed to convey their dreams to others. I lapse into silence and reconsider the hopes associated with certain songs. I hold my tongue and take refuge in another lie to avoid encountering myself lurking around the corner. I make a quick getaway for the sake of that line of verse I did not touch and whose hideaway was a mystery for me, but, resolved as I am, I have pledged my word that I will some day find that hero I had lost in one of those streets. There was nothing original about Rosy's marriage. She had married one day like all the others in her class. She would one day bring a child into the world that in no stage of her life would she be able to attune herself to. Furthermore, she would, some day, do something she shouldn't; take a step she should not take; a step that would cost her a high price; a step that was to continue to rise in value, greater than what was originally paid. It was a special step, a step exclusive to her, a step *sui generis* . . . This might be a surmise on my part, however. Nonetheless, it was a fact that it had been my wish to consider it in this guise, to believe it as such, in order to understand certain steps better and fit them into their proper places. However, it would take some time before the accomplishment of all these things would be within my reach. From its commencement, the marriage was an ordinary affair. İzzet, who had been formally introduced to her, had been the first, and the last man of Rosy's life, who, more than likely, had but a marginal interest in her. Rumors were flying about; rumors open to finding solid ground in people's minds, to be imprinted on the brain as an image or an inflexible idea, likely to acquire the aftertaste of a fiction. İzzet had had an affair fraught with danger with the wife of a high official in the Japanese embassy. He had cultivated his friendship with her after he had most probably been introduced to her at one of the receptions at the Japanese embassy; as a matter of fact, he had been operating a business that imported goods from Japan. When information about their affair seemed to leak out, the woman, to avoid scandal, had persuaded her husband to get an appointment in another country. However, the talk of the town also implicated certain dark dealings by the said tripartite camarilla. There were allegations that this dealing was a part of a wider shady scheme. Naturally, no definite proof could be produced. It was obvious that the outward aspect of things and the audible chicanery did not reflect the true state of affairs. Nonetheless, those who claimed to be an authority on the hush-hush subject said that the woman had absconded right after the first hint of a rumor, never to return. To be frank, this was the best thing for everybody. Anyway, İzzet had escaped unscathed from this misfortune as sooner or later all problems brought along their own specific remedies. The yackety-yak died down, with all the pending probabilities and intractable problems involved, as is the result of immoderate indulgence in objects of rumor. He could repair to a sanctuary that nobody would have any inkling of; there would surely be places waiting to receive individuals like himself. Yet, he remained where he was; he seemed to have no prospects in mind. Could the reason simply have been fear, ineptitude, or the indifference that had manifested itself in a good many of his affairs to this day? The answer to these questions was bound to remain a mystery and the data related to this affair, the clues, had become inaccessible by now. As far as we could learn, nobody had dared ask İzzet about the plausibility of the right answer he would be proffering. This gap was to remain unbridgeable even after the terrible incident that was to occur a couple of years down the line. İzzet had been able to keep his family at arm's length and felt rather secure in himself. Could this be another stage play, in which everybody had resumed his or her role? Or a stage play in which the participants failed to give their respective parts their due as they had already been cast in other roles? Rosy and İzzet had become acquainted at a New Year's party lacking in fun. Both had attended the party reluctantly, upon the insistence of certain people. Rosy had been expecting more than what İzzet could willingly afford. The reaction he had to the omission of Aunt Tilda's name on the list of invitees to his wedding had caused great surprise in us. This, for him, was a most unforgettable moment. The said experience held true also for Monsieur Jacques, who had come by this knowledge only later, as far as I'm aware. Rosy bore the name of her mother for whom he still felt a great yearning. Just like her grandmother, she had resolutely taken up this affair that she deemed to be an injustice and tried to lend a helping hand to an individual abandoned to her destiny. This had taught a lesson to everybody, who should be ashamed of the behavior they exhibited in the face of injustice.

The venue for the wedding party was one of those candlelit restaurants overlooking the Bosporus. Juliet was very beautiful that evening; she looked like a model who had popped out of a fashion magazine. She had evaded my looks, possibly because she had guessed the impressions that this little betrayal might engender within me. However, it was Monsieur Robert, forced to experience a different solitude in a different country that had regretted this. He had come by this knowledge one way or another and made a phone call to me expressing his disappointment. He gave the impression that he had been injured, hurt, and displaced. He said that families were being disintegrated the world over; that families were grounded on lies, that they were but fabricated structures. Every member, bedecked with little hopes, expectations, and dreams were wasting away, gradually falling into an everlasting sleep. I was perfectly aware that such generalizations were made to cover up the bitterness lying deep within one's heart. In other words, I thought I was in a position to guess where he was heading for. I was not kept waiting for long. His family had become tantamount to death . . . death which he could no longer share with someone from a family already extinct. He wanted to go back to Istanbul, to lay his feelings bare, and to clasp Tilda in a strong embrace, fully aware of her loneliness . . . Yet, he was in no position to materialize this desire. Life had removed from him a good many of his dreams. Nature had left many of his aspirations unfulfilled. I don't remember now exactly when these telephone conversations had taken place; how many evenings had gone by in the meantime since he had settled in London? Was it his first or last evening in London? How many solitudes had he tasted? Solitudes he wanted to share from afar with someone? How had he learned of this miles and miles away? Could this be a sign of the ties with Istanbul he could not loosen? What was the meaning of this telephone call after so many years? Who was this call for, considering that there was no one left to share this death that his family had engendered in him? Why had he called someone other than Tilda, the sister he wanted so much to embrace? I could not bring myself to put these questions to him during that conversation because they might have led to unpredictable disputes. I had preferred to remain tuned in to what was being said; for fear of my likely disclosing of things I would have preferred to remain secret. I had merely mentioned that he should thank his god for having failed to set eyes upon Aunt Tilda before the horrid events. He seemed to have understood me; he appeared to have at least. I hadn't omitted the fact that her health had not been undermined following the incident. The rest was unpredictable, as nature would follow its course, as it is obliged to do.

I had lied to him for the last time. For, I had sneaked away that night unnoticed.

To describe my situation better, or perhaps to atone for my shortcomings, I had knocked on the door with certain misgivings. She had turned a deaf ear to my rap. She was at home; I heard her footsteps. It was apparent that she wanted to speak to no one . . . no one . . . whoever the visitor may be. I plucked up the courage to return after a few months had elapsed. In the meantime I had received a postcard sending seasons' greetings from Monsieur Robert. The postcard was quite different from the previous ones he had sent to me; it had on it a superb view of the African forest. "I hope you will have a better future than mine," was written on it. He added that I should pay a visit to Aunt Tilda as she did not deserve such isolation.

I had visited Aunt Tilda on a spring day. She said she was sorry she could not offer me something. Although she seemed somewhat better, her manner of conversation had changed. In the course of our conversation she fell into long brooding silences, during which she stared into space through the window. "I've lost everything, whatever I possessed, including my movies that linked me to my past; the past I fear I'll forget altogether. Everything . . . So few people have survived . . . Where are we now? Who were those people we loved, where are they now?" Having spoken thus, she had lapsed into silence. Then she had asked me to speak and I had tried to find subjects that might arouse her interest; I had spoken about the films of Claude Sautet; Romy Schneider, Bergman, Buñuel, and Saura . . . I was asking myself what and who had I seen in the *Hour of the Wolf* with Max von Sydow. I wondered what had that adolescent from the Far East shown to Catherine Deneuve in the box, I was curious about the reason why the loneliness of that child had affected me so much. The looks of that child and the tune that he hummed were still in my mind. I distinctly remember Catherine Deneuve stretched on the bed in her underwear through which her pubic hair was visible; Liv Ullmann's penetrating looks and the scene in which she said that two people who live together over a long period of time end up resembling each other. Then it was the turn of Isabelle Adjani. I had also mentioned *The Tenant* by Polanski. But I had to stop in the end. Everybody lived in a movie of his or her own after all. How could we otherwise explain our momentary silences? I might open and close the brackets and go back to where I had left off. An action was needed, an action or a word . . . I had looked for that world during a stroll. "According to the weather forecast, we'll have snow in a short while . . . Do you remember? It was years ago . . . We had met at a Chopin recital . . . Berti and

Juliet were also there . . . So was Anita, to whom you have not been introduced. I'll tell you about her some day. Yes, some day . . . when I find enough courage to tell you about my experiences there," I said. She sat in complete silence. She hadn't reacted to my words. She was simply staring through the window. There were children playing soccer, peddlers selling yogurt and rolls, and neighbors exchanging witty remarks outside on the streets like everywhere else. However, I don't think she saw or heard anything. The glow of the setting sun was on her face. She looked very old. "Films have changed, haven't they?" she said after a while, the words were uttered in a whisper.

Then she had given me a wedding gift for Rosy. A gift clumsily wrapped that gave the impression that it was preserved with care. It was a bedcover of the blue satin of old that seemed to have seen better days. It was a blue that reminded one of a lost sea, a sea that was reminiscent of one seen in an adventure film set on the other side of the world. A dream of infinity . . . "I'm sure Rosy will take delight in this," I said, "She had grieved so much over your absence at the wedding." This made her smile for the first time. "I wasn't that disappointed," she rejoined, "but I deplored the fact that I'd missed the opportunity of having my hair dyed and putting on my red dress which I've not worn for ages. If I had put in an appearance at the reception hall all the stares would have been directed at me. I would've looked as beautiful as Merle Oberon. They've robbed me of my dreams. It's deplorable, isn't it?" To have missed the opportunity of cutting a dashing figure like Merle Oberon's . . . She grew bitter and resentful . . . That's the image I still keep of her.

That was our last encounter.

I was abroad when she died. Juliet had been at her bedside and had washed her just before she passed away.

Rosy was thankful for the cover as I had guessed, but I think she failed to assign to it its true value.

Berti was among the chief mourners.

Monsieur Jacques reacted to the news saying: "May God pardon her transgressions. Well, it'll be our turn soon. No escape from it."

Once I had asked Juliet if she had said something to be relayed to me. "No," had been her reply. "She said nothing about you . . . except . . . except . . . 'Well, it's snowing heavily, isn't it? The earth is already shrouded in white . . .'" She had pronounced these words in July . . . For some life had changed its course, once again.

The codicil she had prepared to bequeath to me was that antique tea set; that tea set, witness of the hours I'll never forget; the set that in my difficult moments reminds me of the guests that attended those tea parties; of the movies, of that screen of dreams more real than reality, in which I find solace. The tea set is, at present, among the objects I value most, objects that are waiting to figure in a special story in the future.

The fact that I have referred to her in the present book as 'Aunt Tilda' requires some explanation, since I was not related to her by blood; yet, I cannot actually remember when and where I had first used that appellation. However, my mode of address must have pleased her; I'm positive about this. This was a stage play in which the actors brilliantly performed their respective roles. Old people need a young person who will appear to understand them while young men need an aged auntie with whom they can confer things they could not express openly and in whom they could try to see their future reflected. The success of the play would depend on this tacit reciprocal understanding. I must have called her Tilda then and not Aunt Tilda. It seemed as though the words uttered, the visual impact, and the verbal exchange of ideas had called for such an invocation. I must keep in mind this point when I take up my pen to write down her story. On top of the identity of 'aunt' another identity had to be superimposed. This path must have been one of those that most of us would like to keep secret yet intact forever. There was a path that opened out to darkness, to our darkness . . . I wonder if I can touch it now. I seem to hear a voice from afar . . . A voice . . . How have we come that far?

You were in the blue of a song

I ventured to play a little trick on Berti somewhere in the story I intended to write about him. To this end I had to arrange an encounter between himself and that woman—who still seemed impossible for me to describe to a third person and who had made a gift to me of one of the most beautiful corners of this city; the balcony of the small apartment overlooking the Bosporus. This woman had diverted my attention to books and the contents of their pages, which paved the way to that sense of loneliness aroused by those steps that had failed to be taken, as well as to a great number of contingencies, unanticipated joys, and, more importantly, to the deferment of expectations. The encounter would be a meeting which would find itself recorded against a backdrop of associations already pregnant with meaning from one of the photographs in my possession. It was a cool summer evening and the lights of the city had begun twinkling as the color of the sky was borrowing the hues of pink and dark blue from the sea . . . a summer evening resolute in keeping distant from the din of the city and its odors that trace the course of our daily lives . . . This had brought about a lyrical atmosphere from the very beginning.

I might begin by mentioning the associations that a ship in transit might inspire, a ship sailing from remote realms, which, in her passage through the Bosporus, would not be in a position to take up an acquaintance with its on-lookers, destined herself to be terra incognita to those she passed. This remark had served my purposes elsewhere, at other times. The settings in question also included passenger ships that carried people across the seas, from one end of the world to the other. For people living on the coastline of certain realms such views created in their imagination legendary representations, legends that fed on old languages, different words, and disparate dawns. Unless you experienced those touches, felt your way in those rooms and lived through those thralldoms you could not have an inkling of this, of course. What made a legend a legend was precisely this inexpressible darkness, our own darkness. I had felt this when I was groping my way through other people's dusk . . . as I was searching for my-self . . . You could always sense the steps of others whom you never anticipated. To be heading for it in the real sense of the word also meant running the risk of being confronted with a new solitude. Taking into consideration the experiences we had to go through with all our deficiencies, certain things released emotions, whose origin was a mystery within us.

The house I would choose as a setting for Berti's story should have a history with its inhabitants; a house that, in defiance of other houses, should have a his-tory behind it, a house that breathed simultaneously with its dwellers, a legacy to that woman from her family, with its souvenirs, voices, latent scents, and shad-ows; a house that cannot yield itself so easily to other people or be sold *in toto* to a third person. Berti, with his cream-colored trousers, claret red Italian shoes of fine leather, royal blue mohair sweater concealing a red silk shirt, Pathek Philippe wrist watch, and enamel Dupont lighter, might take on the appearance of the figure that he would have liked to play in a stage play. The woman, on the other hand, might be imagined to wear a transparent dress that highlighted her curves, a band around her neck to which would be affixed a dark red gem and a few silver bracelets on her wrists. The band around her neck with the dark red gem had the aim of cutting a dashing figure, separating her from all possible rivals and to give the impression that it had a legend behind it. He could now start sipping his raki on the rocks; it was a summer night, wasn't it? He could set the table and decorate it with food from the delicatessen amongst which melon, plums, white cheese, and pistachio should figure. Could one imagine a better odor than the smell of the sea mingled with alcohol? The woman could drink more than Berti; after all she was a writer . . . Being a woman and an author who led a solitary life, she had to make a display of her spiritual agony and let out her breath in a sigh . . . Music would be *de rigueur* under the circumstances, music that sometimes provoked sexual desire; however, the volume should be turned down, suiting the sonority of the voices, and allowing, at times, the parties of the dialogue to lend an ear to what is being played. Among the possible old hits one might think of Billie Holliday, Aretha Franklin, or Ella Fitzgerald. Elvis Presley would not be a bad choice, one of his lyrical pieces, instead of all the hits of his past. Are you lonesome tonight? would, for instance, be the right tune to listen to, if I may say so; as is the norm with such moments we try to steal away to those we have an insight into from time to time. However, we must be careful not to impair the unity of the whole; Elvis may well sing other songs toward the early hours of the morning. A surfeit of his songs may induce us to put on an LP of Leonard Cohen on the record player, for the sake of Suzanne and Bird on a Wire . . . Were she to speak of her new novel she was working on; of a writer friend who she wanted to talk about; of the wall clock, a witness to so many things; of the disputes going on between Berti and his daughter; of the years of study in Cambridge; of her increased yearning for her brother despite the lapse of such a long time and the events that took place in between; of the burning interest she took in antique objects; of the stumbling blocks she was confronted with in the office; and of the snapshots she took in the course of her travels, one could find a new narrow path to probe. My knocking at her door would coincide with her lucubration . . . in the hope that I would be allowed to have access to her haunt . . . with full knowledge of the fact that just like everybody else in times of solitude she would be absorbed in meditation in the pursuit of her own self, trying to breathe fresh life into her life from a different time; my reason for knocking on the door was not only to find a new story but also to cause my hero and heroine to experience that sense of surprise by being caught unawares . . . May I remind my readers that a play was being enacted whose denouement and conclusion was unpredictable? I would have achieved my objective; Berti's countenance would reflect uneasiness caused by the revelation of his secret; the woman, taken unawares by my unexpected presence in the kitchen as an intruder in the story, would, while being engaged in the preparation of drinks, try to share her feelings *sotto voce* with me. I had gone back on the agreement; how could I ever tell her story under such circumstances? All probabilities were based on the narration of that sentimental relationship between, on the one hand—a woman who had already covered a considerable distance in her life and had retired to her solitude, having put the finishing touches on her writings and experiences—and on the other hand a young author trying to write the sixty-year history of one family. The woman and the young author would be discussing in this atmospheric house, in the background of other works of fiction and in the light of other similar works, those traits that had come to the fore during the process of penning their stories. In other words, the work would be written piecemeal, in installments . . . with patience and dogged perseverance . . . with a view to touching certain corners of life. Our words, invocations, and secret conversations were, like all relationships (like love for that matter), desired to be reinstated intricately, since new words and invocations did not come unless those secret conversations were held. Now, I'd taken up my pen to commit to paper a story unique in its genre despite all the preparations and the promises made and honored to others. To write such a bad work would be an act of betrayal. I was to realize that I couldn't make headway beyond a certain point, beyond the wrong I had committed in doing so. The whole tale had an aspect that lacked credibility. This aspect would come to the fore only after a lapse of considerable time . . . or after certain vain expectations fell short of realization. Her feminine intuition sensed this. What she had left behind seemed to prompt in her certain things, things likely to be conceived only after risking certain losses. I was resolved not to be garrulous; I would merely say that I had simply tried my hand in setting a play on the stage. Then we would be going back to the balcony as though nothing had been discussed. Thus we, as abettors, would find ourselves on common ground. That would be the end of our intricate relationship. We would have to mislay the idea of co-authorship in the kitchen. Her intention had been to punish me by sparing herself from me. This was the feminine aspect she reflected. I would be suffering from the consequences of this abandonment and solitude years later. I had thought we might once again think of an assignation for the sake of that text; but I could not get rid of that sense of deficiency brought about by the encounters that I had had, having experienced other places, individuals, and words. However, even though after the lapse of so many years, the said encounter *had* taken place. What is more, it had taken place under circumstances much more favorable when compared to our former meetings, and we had somehow drawn nearer to each other; it looked as though we had returned to each other with a part of ourselves restored, a part that we had mislaid somewhere and had thought been consigned to oblivion forever. It may be that somewhere in-between we had been reduced still further. This deficiency was fated to someone else. We were that selfsame deficiency; the place we could not make the most of and wherein we could not materialize our dreams. We were, in fact, residing in the places we felt out of place, we could not bring ourselves to take pleasure in those places. And yet we were so near our heroes and heroines, our men whose hands we could grasp if only we were to take a few steps forward. Under the spell of our existence on that balcony we would end up being each other's spectators. Berti would find himself breathing in the evening, and consequently the present text, while the woman would cast furtive glances at me to check my progress with my writing; I, for my part, would try tacitly, merely by glancing, to insinuate my wish to carry on the play, in due consideration of all the inevitable consequences facing me. Berti had to experience this fascinating tabooed relationship. His past, that was in my custody, deserved this small gift of mine. In my capacity as author, I felt obliged to provide him with such an evening. Berti had to experience this banned relationship upon the background of his dreams and boundaries.

Photographs live

When we left the shop together in the evening, on the pretext that community taxis were not always available at Nişantaşı, we were to walk down to Karaköy where we were to take the miniature subway, the smallest in the world, and arrive in Beyoğlu. There we were to saunter along the main street, stopping in front of shop windows displaying women's clothes. Berti would ask my opinion about the items displayed in the window. I had understood his veiled insinuations, but acted as though I was totally ignorant of his seemingly disinterested observations and so communicated my impressions to him. This was how the play should be acted . . . All these scenes were for Berti's sake. I wanted him to rediscover his Lost Paradise after so many years, despite my limited means and capacities. As I was playing my role, making headway in the story, I had to have perfect confidence in myself. This may be the reason why, despite all my efforts, I took cognizance of the fact that I could not proceed (as I would have liked to) any further and had to acknowledge that the whole thing had been but the consequence of a weird idea. My rationale would be corroborated by that woman once again, by a wan smile emerging from her hidden self, from that special corner of ours, just like in her former stories that were in my custody. Did my despair lie in the boundaries that separated me from those individuals? I don't think I'll ever find an answer to this query. For the time being, I was resolved to leave those questions unanswered, to ignore the history that that woman and I had once shared, to make as if I had not heard them. To give utterance to our solitudes, dilemmas, and secret yearnings had never been easy. Leaving aside all these things, when I thought of the future stories I was planning to write, I ran the risk of encountering many new obstacles I would never be able to surmount. Such a relationship might bear resemblance to the relationship of Monsieur Jacques and Olga. It was certainly possible that people, despite their diversity, shared similar fates. Possible, all right, but certain stories could not contain certain reiterations no matter what the circumstances. Certain stories also failed to persuade us to acknowledge certain echoes that would bring us back to the same point of departure, just like with those loves that enslaved us. This may have been the reason for my restlessness. Despite all my various episodes, words, and losses, I could not shake off that individual whose stare never left me, who was peeping from somewhere that I could not pinpoint as much as I wanted to. Solitude was freedom in its own way, a sort of self-observation, I knew that. Nonetheless, true solitude or segregation was for those individuals that had never been recognized by others as they had dreamt of themselves. Was it then those walls that smothered our dreams and fantasies, killing us leisurely one by one? My keeping Berti above ground in this story for so long was becoming more and more difficult were one to consider these flights . . . more difficult from day-to-day . . . It may be due to the women I had known that I could not bring myself to imagine that woman of my dreams befriending a man like Berti, unless she thought she was likely to find a safe refuge in him from a tragedy she was trying to flee. There had certainly been misfortunes, but she was a special woman. She might have a better insight than most into the injuries that certain individuals received: exactly where, when, and by whom. I knew that the course taken in human relationships could not be predicted, and that the soul's adventure gained meaning through unforeseen harbors and unpredictable storms. Nonetheless, she had, to my mind, a very special place in a totally different story. She was expecting to hear me utter a brand new sentence, expressed or written by no one before . . . For, I still preserved that warmth she had left in me. If one took account of the *sequelae* of daily concerns, given the fact that she could not be considered, on the whole, to be of a certain age and was still attractive, there was no reason for her to be making enormous sacrifices to make claims upon a man and try to prove herself to be a model of virtue. To cut a long story short, there was some truth in what she had said in the kitchen. Ours would be henceforth what lay beyond that point. We spent, in fact, many an evening on that balcony afterward . . . *tête-à-tête* . . . exactly as it had been fancied at the beginning. We discussed the novel I was intending to write. Berti seemed to be nearer to her then . . . After all, dreams were easier lived than actualities . . . I'm inclined to believe that the story written during those days had been the result of automatic writing in a way; a story that otherwise could never be written since I never had the courage to see it exposed so frankly to the public. Nonetheless, there still is a sentence shared by both of us which has not appeared so far in black-and-white, as I have kept it veiled, asking myself if certain words could not be fitted in their right places eventually. The same point puzzles me even today, but seems to be left unanswered for the moment. However, I have not lost confidence in time; for the sake of those protractions, of my delusions, barefaced lies, evasions, and introversions which make up whatever I'm supposed to be. This was one of the major reasons for my reliance on Berti's friendship. He had come across my mind at a most unexpected moment on one of those evenings. A visitor on one of those evenings . . . Yet, I had preferred to keep silent and take the risk of betrayal. The story showed resistance. Berti's self-distrust that had decided his course of action in life had dawned upon me. He seemed to have lost that little paradise or exigency years ago, during his time at Cambridge. That city together with what had been invested therein had been epitomized in my mind by an unforgettable room, a room to remain indelible on my memory forever, a room which could not be transported elsewhere despite all the distant associations it engendered and the memories confined in it. In order to be able to have an idea of this room, one had to have an inkling of its past. This was one of the reasons why he had told very few people about his former days. Yes, that was one of the reasons. In order to go back there, to that room at rare intervals, hoping to avoid settling old scores, making a strategic withdrawal . . . I mustn't forget to mention our walks from Tünel to Taksim; walks which I visualize at present beyond the boundaries of many tales; a place where a very special path is kept alive beyond all the fantastic tales nestled within our breast, even though this path may have now been repaved using different stones, and looks at us as though we were strangers; even though we have remained on different shores, in different rooms, in different sentences. I wonder now where, in whom, and with what voice has that past lingered and abided? To judge by his observations and the attitudes he adopted toward me, I seem to be one of the rare people likely to understand him. This confidence was to take me to an open-ended story, preserved in a secret drawer for many years; a story that enslaved you and generated in you woeful imagery. I had realized this during one of our long walks. He had never wanted to let go of his story despite the wrongs he had committed, despite his faults and deficiencies. He had a firm belief that he had left an important part of his life there. He desired to tell it to someone and feel himself as a hero of that story. To tell someone and to receive visitors in his old room, even though it was now situated in a different realm. To tell, to be able to tell . . . even though he could not find the right words on such an occasion. In fact, he had been able to perceive only a part of his story. The other part, the part that had been communicated to me quite unexpectedly at some other time and place, by some other person, would remain my secret forever. The contents of this parenthesis I had come by would never be disclosed to him. Why had I acted in this way? Why had I preferred to keep from him a reality that would likely open a door to the story? Was it because I did not believe and did not want to believe in the things that had been imparted to me by a casual visitor after so many years, which I deemed to be irrelevant? Perhaps it was. However, it is my confirmed opinion that by this betrayal of our friendship my intention had been to rescue that souvenir. I don't regret it. It is to be noted that to have been on the margin of events suited both our dispositions perfectly.

Loving one's own morning

There are places that invite certain people into unavoidable lives, rooms, and pictures; this reminds you of the story of clouds chasing each other for rain; such moments emerge from different times and spaces only to merge one day. Having graduated from the English High School, Berti had decided to continue his studies at Cambridge where he intended to read political science. According to his own account, what had played a major role in his decision was the philosophy teacher of leftist tendencies, Mr. Page, whose forum On Life had generated a high level of notice and endeared him to a wide audience. The image of Mr. Page imprinted on my memory represents him as a robust and corpulent man with a scarlet complexion, a hard drinker—for instance, one winter day, for a bet, after having consumed forty-two cans of beer at a party, he had jumped into the ice cold waters of the Bosporus and swum for quite a while—whose aim it had been to inspire in his students an interest in cricket which he tried to make attractive to them by the anecdotes he told about his years of professional play as a young man. He had taken into consideration one day to play Elgar on a record player during class. He had resided in Istanbul for a good many years. One evening, while he was dining with a couple of students at Çiçek Pazarı, half-inebriated, he had told them that throughout his life only once had he fallen in love with a woman. They had forewarned Mr. Page that the next day there would be an exam; to which he had retorted that they could prepare themselves for it while they were dining at the table. What he had said had come true; for, they had discussed their subject at the table and been successful at their exam. Well, they had seen him in the company of that woman at Nişantaşı. As far as they could gather, the woman lived in London and came to Istanbul two or three times a year to sojourn no longer than a few days. Much later, they had come by the following information at another dinner table to celebrate their graduation. The woman was apparently married to a prominent politician, a member of the Working Party. Their affair had been going on for years and seemed to continue in this way, trying to experience the continued secrecy in a diverse, volatile, and mercurial atmosphere despite their waning energy that they persisted in trying to reinvigorate; by experiencing the thrill of evasion . . . the thrill that they explored under different climates and diverse cities. Only in this way could they perpetuate this prohibited love they could not exhaust. He had decided to leave Istanbul for another city. He needed this emigration. He was in need of another city, of another sanctuary, in need of a different kind of bondage. Mr. Page had submitted his resignation a few days after this confession on the grounds that he had been appointed to a job in Sri Lanka. He was going to set off on a long journey, once again, involving a new language and new surroundings. Life would be beautified with such new ventures.

He had another hope; he would be nearer to Nepal and Tibet, places he wanted to see so much for some special reasons he could not disclose. Upon hearing this, his students had remained silent; trying not to create obstacles that would likely hamper their teacher's headway in his imaginary pilgrimage. They couldn't bring themselves to believe in the adventure he was to embark on. According to them, this gentleman who had taught them how to read and recite poetry and how to live one's life as a poem was sure to go back to London and settle there. His place of solitary confinement should be London and his vernacular should remain his ultimate means of communication. That was destined to be the last evening they would meet; the last of a series of encounters spanning many years, encounters which had grown less and less frequent as time went by. I wonder if Mr. Page had observed that suspicion lurking in his students' eyes, that inquiring look. After all that he had gone through, all the tribulations endured and all the risks taken for the realization of such an effectual dream, for all the thought and planning that went into making this long journey, he was to be as remote as possible from that woman. They were fully conscious of the fact that taking certain steps forward and having an insight into them was not always possible; they knew that every-body was in need of a last city, town, or village where they could take refuge, but Mr. Page's fantasy of Sri Lanka had seemed to them a hopeless expedition.

This episode had taken Berti back to a far distant past. We had been on one of our long walks. We had had a couple of hot sandwiches and a pint of beer. It was a sunny afternoon. The shop had been the scene of a long-standing dispute that was hardly ever seen by an ordinary person in his lifetime. The words had even-tually been given utterance. We were to haunt the place a couple of times more to share our woes with our fellow beings. I was to taste draught beer for the first time and savor the rich sauce made with walnuts, bread, garlic, olive oil, and vin-egar. Berti had settled himself at a table near the exit in order that he could leave immediately when he felt like it. I thought I had understood his reason for this. There were certain places that he was reluctant to touch, to see . . . Those tables were to burn to ashes one day, to leave different images in the minds of those who had been witnesses to the event. When we were back there after a couple of years, new tables seemed to invite new customers. Berti had mentioned for the first time the lobster he had eaten at Christopher's place. It was plain he had already been there several times in the company of Jerry. This had been the first and last time we spoke about it.

Berti's glitzy image of Mr. Page contained many ordinary things; a student's making headway toward his teacher, with all the conceivable associations . . . In the meantime, he was lured into new whims, reluctant to dwell on this characteristic of the relationship he glossed over. Seen in this context, the relationship was nothing out of the ordinary. All that had been experienced at the time was in fact run-of-the-mill performances that were similar to many other episodes. What had been witnessed in that house prior to the Cambridge adventure, of which I was to bear testimony, was actually more or less identical to the commonplace incidents of everyday life for the passive spectator. The initial reaction of Monsieur Jacques to the decision of his son who wanted to pursue his studies abroad was ordinary, as were the words uttered by Berti in return, yet there seemed to be certain truths that lay behind this ordinariness or seeming ordinariness which could not be expressed so easily. In order that we might perceive those truths, we needed, usually, additional details which would enable us to transgress certain barriers. These details seemed to be embedded in those days when father and son were experiencing their first true encounter; they had dared to take the risk of seeing each other, treading warily in feelings to which they were strangers, feelings for which they were not prepared, accepting the full consequences of their behavior. They were touching at a soft spot, one they thought would remain untouched forever. However, one could deny of course that certain storms were going to rage inevitably. This seemed to be the common unchanging fate of those who were pent up in their respective worlds. Today, I must admit that I can grasp, not without great difficulty, the meaning of the whole when ruminating over the fragments that reach me piecemeal. Monsieur Jacques' adverse reaction to his son's decision was only too natural if one takes into consideration what he had been planning for his future. One had to face the inevitability of certain things under the circumstances. The ongoing business had to be passed on to someone enjoying a privileged position in the family. This was only logical and there was nothing surprising in it. Actually, according to Monsieur Jacques, his son's desire to pursue his studies abroad was a normal course to take. He was prepared to make the necessary arrangements. The problem lay in part with the area of study Berti selected. It was Monsieur Jacques' opinion that he should not be opting for an impractical subject which he would never be able to pursue in life. He might, for instance, study textile engineering, which would secure him a bright future. There seemed to be renowned educational establishments in this line both in

England and in Belgium. In the meantime, he advised his son to take stock of his decision by looking at it in a historical context. To what kind of a future would his study of political science pave a path toward? Diplomacy? An academic career? Moreover, one should also keep in mind the fact that the implications that his name carried would come as a disadvantage if he were fostering a hope for a future political career. Being a Cambridge graduate would change nothing. His name was Berti Ventura. For him the path he would tread was predetermined in this country wherein he belonged to an ethnic minority. While discussing this question with his son, Monsieur Jacques believed that his arguments were perfectly logical. He was sincere, without affectation. A considerable part of his existence, past experiences, and *Weltanschauung* were owed to those who had lent him such a sound logic. One might call it conviction perhaps. This conviction roused a high-pitched resentment in him that was not easily expressed verbally. Madame Roza had stretched her protective wings over Berti at the time. "Why not indulge his whim," she told Monsieur Jacques. "Let him go; every young man must have his fling, after all; he will come back sooner or later."

This made perfect sense of course. She would have hated to see her son as a diplomat. She had made herself hospitable to her husband's point of view by ceding to his arguments. One should not forget the hardships caused by the tax on wealth and earnings that was leveled in 1942. He was not expected to know, of course, anything about the bakery at Sütlüce. Leaving all things aside, the very idea of studying abroad gave her food for thought. After all, to be in a strange land, all alone, without any monitor to guide him might cause him to indulge in unwanted practices with undesirable people; unpredictable new horizons might seem attractive to him. Her anxiety, therefore, should be understandable concerning a son living out of her reach in a foreign country; the concerns of someone who had been living for so long in a country reeling from so many human tragedies and deaths; all these things were to the point and had to be taken with equanimity. Notwithstanding all these facts, Madame Roza had been prescient and contributed to the solution of the problem without any serious aftershocks thanks to her motherly affection. She had sensed her son's determination to leave home for a period of time during which he would create for himself his future prospects. He might have used other expressions to convey his thoughts on the matter. Yet, in essence, mother and son had a great affinity for one another. Madame Roza was a mother who knew her boundaries all too well; this held true not only with regard to her relations with her son, but also with her husband, brothers, and sisters. The reason why every family member held her in such high esteem and sought refuge in her must be down to this warmth . . . . to know one's limitations and curb one's excesses . . . to know the boundaries of people and never transgress . . . to know how far one can go with certain individuals . . . How could one ignore the power of intuition in such situations? Madame Roza's exercise of her intuitive power on her next-of-kin implied an esoteric ascendancy hard to define. She was one of those who held sway over people without making them conscious of it. This command may have exercised no significant influence over certain developments in her life; yet, she had an unshakable confidence in time. This firm belief had shed light on her most difficult times.

Berti had overheard his parents arguing in their chamber over his desire to leave from his bedroom; he listened silently without making his presence felt. This verbal strife usually took place at night when certain effects were believed to be carried more easily. Madame Roza's sway had been tested during those nights, and was revealed more tangibly. Berti had found a guardian angel in his mother once again, at the least expected moment, in the midst of a wrangle that had caught him unawares. Not long after, the path was clear; the path that had been trodden by many different people, in many different manners, and which reminded him of many different anecdotes and associations. The said dispute that had taken place between him and his parents had been his first serious miscalculation. He would have to face many other quarrels at other times in the future. These were to open the door to certain adversities, resentments, introspections, and hard feelings rather than being conducive to new hopes. However, in order to experience these feelings, they first had to be harbored somewhere. During his first major argument, Berti was imagining that he could take steps toward a thoroughly different place. This was actually a story fancied to have taken place at other times whose heroes were strangers, an ordinary story in which every hero lived his own delusions and carried his own deficiency without having an inkling of it in the least. The expectations of an individual under those circumstances, I could perceive reflected on the countenance of others. What Berti told me about those days was nothing new for us, in fact. One desired to be conscious of the originality of whatever one had left behind somewhere. One felt the need to tell anybody willing to listen about this originality. I was familiar with this need. That is why as I listened to the narration of this story I had the impression of listening to a familiar voice. This had allowed me to empathize with the incidents that had taken place in those days. I happened to be on the stage. The history was an old one. Berti was convinced that he was being guided by hope. The year was 1954. Jerry was but fourteen years old. He was as happy as a lark when he had heard the news. He had been the person that Berti had missed the most while in Cambridge.

Berti's Cambridge seemed to be a small town, a relic from a fairy tale; a town resolved to make its presence felt throughout history, not letting the unforgettable episodes from an exciting past sink into oblivion . . . Now that I am in the mood, I'm prepared to write the stories of those who carried with them their tales relating to the cities that have remained indelible in their memories. Odessa, Alexandria, New York, Istanbul, Vienna, Paris, Colombo, Rio, London, etc. . . . Those individuals had memories relating to those cities which they kept undisclosed to the end of their lives. These memories were their respective treasures that should be revealed and resurrected for their own sake. The leisurely strolls that Berti and I used to take in the city seem rather hazy now; I feel myself in no position to tell what particular images of Cambridge are buried in those meaningful memories. All that I can assert at present is that those recollections invite us to a common ground, the only difference being that each of us has access to it from opposite directions. I must say that in order for one to have an inkling of that, one has to have certain facts in perspective. The tale that Berti had transported from Cambridge to Istanbul was one whose origins went back to a secret disappointment. The tale in question spoke about a youth who was taking steps toward a city in which he hoped to realize his ambitions and aspirations. We had wandered through the streets silently, furtively, sub rosa. He had arrived in the town on an autumn day after a relatively short train journey. The first thing he had done was to put up at a small hotel. The hotel was run by an eccentric individual with an accent that betrayed his Scottish origin. What was particularly interesting about him was his true vocation; he had been a poorly appreciated Professor of astrophysics. On the third day after his arrival at the hotel he had invited him to his room, which contained a powerful telescope. The large cardboard hanging on the walls contained intricate figures and formulae. "I'll discover one day the remotest star in the universe, the star that nobody has ever set eyes upon," he used to repeat every now and then. To be able to see the remotest star nobody has ever set eyes upon . . . This unreal fancy existing only as the product of a wild and unrestrained imagination was sheer poetry, a proem to a poem. Can one ever posit that such a chimerical conception might have a potential truth in it? The question had been left unanswered. As a matter of fact, he had been to the Professor's room once more, long after he had settled in the halls of residence at his college. The door was opened by an attractive young woman who told him that the man had transferred the hotel to her and had not left any address. All that she knew was that he had packed up and left for Scotland, as from there, on higher ground, he believed he could have a clearer view of the universe. That was the last of him: by the way she also had an accent similar to the Professor's.

After a brief sojourn at the hotel, Berti had moved to his lodging at the residence hall of the college. It was a rather large one, well lit with a fireplace. It would not take him long to learn to kindle the fire. The delight in watching the flames and listening to the cracking noise that the burning logs emitted during the cold winter nights would remain fixed in his memory. He was to spend long, interminable nights in this room, nights of growing expectations, self-analyses, self-criticism, and solitudes. It was the city's desire that those who intended to reside so long in such rooms should undertake the examination and observation of one's own mental and emotional processes; it looked as though such rooms and voices were for the shadows destined to abide in inner recesses. There were scenes that certain stage plays had indelibly imprinted on the minds of certain people, standing the test of time. Had it occurred to Berti to inquire about the former tenants of the room, into the life stories of those that had preceded his occupation? This question had never arisen in my mind before. In those days, different touches brought about different needs—gaining meaning and taking shape according to those needs. The same might hold true for the bicycle Berti had bought from a secondhand dealer for taking long trips a few days after he had arrived in the town. However, I was then in pursuit of other photographs which I believed were dated from those days; I had the misconception that I could have access to those things that were concealed in the photographs in question. All that I can infer now from the data available was that the bicycle had aroused in him the desire to be heading for freedom . . . a symbol of liberty; just like the way that thousands of people in other corners of the world conceive it. Those narrow paths that this conviction had guided us into had perfectly suited our ends in those days. We resembled those people who failed to find their desired places and were continually in search of them. The delusions were the same delusions; the deceptions were the same deceptions; the fabricated expectations postponed to facilitate the living of the present were the same expectations. The only difference lay, I think, in our pursuit of other towns at other times, in our desire to retire to other towns . . . to take flight, to abscond . . . to make a break for a life amenable to transformation, a new life to be reborn . . . To dispel the darkness one finds himself surrounded by, even if only for a brief time, to go back to the light, to be reconciled with certain people, to be able to have been reconciled with them . . . to be at large, to be always at large . . . This must have been the aspiration of those people at the time, the aspirations toward a real life to be unfolded and elucidated. To flee, simply to flee . . . as though there was another life; hoping to find other ways to live elsewhere, other colors, other odors and breaths in other nights. There had been so many souls that had given credence to this utopia at the time and during the days that followed, to this chimera . . . just like Berti who had wanted to step into the lives he imagined to be different, while carrying his solitude laden with fresh hopes. To be in pursuit of nonconformity was perhaps a way to free oneself and get out of the clutches of that contrapuntal death that stands ingrained and latent in one's breast; one had to consider also that in order to understand the fact that the extrinsic streets that assumed meaning with differing linguistic worlds did not, and could not, lead to that world; one should be aware of the short life of butterflies, shorter than generally presumed.

I wonder if one could surmise that Marcellina, from Mexico City, who had come over to Cambridge to study English, might have been conscious of this fact. The prevailing circumstances would take, in time, the protagonists of that adventure to a diversity of destinations. The answer to this problem had remained anchored there; it was embedded in those travelers whose place of abode gradually killed them. Berti had encountered Marcellina for the first time at an open-air pub frequented by a mass of students. Was this the exact moment when the story had begun? Was this place the very spot where they had run into each other? For instance, what particular sentences or words, during a time long forgotten, had preceded which particular sentences or words; for instance which particular glance had been eclipsed by which darkness; to which particular glance did those voices belong, the voices that had failed to reach their ears? Here is the right time to mention the fact that the bridge called 'The Mill' was the venue where students got together. Why not recollect those places where certain lines crossed over in total disregard of what had occurred there. There was a stream flowing underneath the pub. That was what set it apart from conventional drinking places, especially in odd and whimsical ways. Their initial encounter had been through the exchange of furtive glances . . . of sidelong glances . . . of flickering glances . . . of covert glances . . . Glances cast imperceptibly through clusters of people, at the most unexpected moments. In my capacity as a spectator to this story, I must say I could stand to experience such glances myself. Berti had tried to conceal his identity as usual while he narrated this story to me years later. Marcellina had cut a dashing figure with a warm smile in her eyes, which added to those glances, prolonging those moments. Those moments, with their fleeting glances, had managed to catch them off-guard. There was no scarcity of other people and other voices trying to be heard at the time; at a time when those present were all strangers. Then, one day, they did meet. They happened to be at the same pub over the same stream. They had beer and talked about their respective countries and about their expectations from the town into which they had wandered. It was a Thursday evening. This may have been the reason why Berti had attached a special value to Thursdays. This may have been the reason why we were wont to do our Istanbul walks on Thursdays. Whenever I think on this, I feel sad. It occurs to me now that most of the steps we had taken on the said path had been quite unconscious. Had it not been so, the path might well have led us to other shrouded parts of the story. When he had learned that Marcellina was Mexican, he had tried a new way of verbal communication with her in his adulterated vernacular, Spanish. This new way would assume even greater meaning when I gave myself the task of remembering more vividly the remaining imagery of an old story. I understand better now the warmth that Berti must have felt in the use of that broken language. The first step was then taken in that confidentiality of parlance. What followed was but platitudes although every relationship produced its own poem *sui generis*. The first thing they did had been to go on long walks, roaming the streets of the town—its *purlieus*. And one day their hands had clasped each other. One wonders the reason why all these recollections that had made their way through a crowd of reminiscences and were carefully preserved in a secret corner were of such great pith and resonance? Why had the adolescent who had transported these images to an unpredictable future not been relinquished? What stories, what heroes that had generated these questions in me, had the protagonist of the story been chasing? Who was Berti, anyhow? Who was I? Who were we? And who were the people in those photographs dating from our childhood? I'm perfectly aware that these questions must remain unanswered, that certain questions already contain the answers in their privacy. Now, I must recall a dream at this juncture. Having come from different corners of the earth, they had brought about a passion they would prefer to perceive as original. After all, everybody ought to have a story he might be disposed to tell to a third person, sometime in their life. Certain foreign cities might aspire to such experiences. Certain foreign cities might aspire to such sentiments. After all, it was not always easy to make a guess about the reality of this irrelevance and the meaning that one attributed to it. It was terra incognita in a way, a kind of intuition that prohibited all transgressions which indicated a flight that had the ultimate aim of self-discovery. Those who had lingered in different episodes or interludes of the story were once again in pursuit of a chimera not easily shared, with a view to forgetting their deficiencies, even though for a fleeting moment. The aftereffects of this chimera might well pave the way to the poem we jealously keep deep within ourselves and are reluctant to divulge to others. This may have been the reason why I couldn't forget what has been transferred to me. They had forged the habit to meet two or three times a week in order to understand this empathy better, viz. this love. Could one interpret these meetings as a sort of predilection having no precedence due to undecipherable parameters? The essence of passion connotes effort—some time spent shaping the course of the actually lived time, directed at recapturing the past or inserting a different timeframe into a given period; or perhaps this is simply delusional. This delusion might well mislead one to live the day at night and the night in broad daylight; while this, in turn, might bring about new fallacies altogether. How would you explain then living according to a plan or customary ritual with reference to a particular past and the walls that surrounded it? Marcellina's justification was that she had to work hard; while Berti had had no objection to this course of action, in fact it had never occurred to him to thwart her design. There seemed to be a kind of puerility in this, a puerility indestructible, a puerility that one would like to prolong forever. They would thus strive to seize each other's paths and appropriate them; leading a life unmindful of the nature of their sentiments and of what they had hoarded in their depths. Berti was to make ground in understanding Marcellina's Spanish. Marcellina would borrow expressions from Berti's. It was as though it was imperative that they stood fast in the warmth of this language and used it to communicate their feelings to each other, saying that they lived and wanted to live for each other from now on. English would prove inadequate to express their feelings; English was their second language. They had recourse to it when they fought, when they preferred to exercise restraint.

To the best of my knowledge, this was partly due to one's experience with relationships one came to know over the course of one's life. Berti had never kept it a secret that he had faced many ordeals in his life. His puerility, honesty, and magnanimity were ingrained in this attitude. I sometimes feel like crying about certain things I cannot define whenever I view this relationship from this angle. Actually I know why and for whom I cry, why, for whom, and when . . . At such moments I prefer to keep silent . . . to lapse into silence, for my own sake, in full cognizance of the fact that certain silences are in essence contrapuntal. I wonder whether Marcellina respected these points in their relationship. An individual I chanced to meet years later would be in a position to give me a hint to this effect. However, I had so many reasons to keep my door shut to the realities I was not capable of facing at the time. To breathe fresh life into certain representations despite all the deceptions that they implied was important and preferable to me in this relationship. One should not expect a different reaction from a person who was of the opinion that certain stories would be highlighted by certain little poems and who was obsessed by this idea. What Berti had told me during our walks, in the hope that a given time might be perpetuated forever in another, for reasons I could understand, were important for me for this very reason. Among the snapshots he had brought for me, there were also souvenirs of visits abroad. Their modest dreams had taken them to Venice on vacation where they had the chance to gaze at pigeons, cats, and the waterways. They had also traveled to Amsterdam where they had seen the canals; to Belgium where they crossed over the bridges of Bruges. These trips concealed an important point of which Berti was unaware, one which was beyond the capacity of his perception. Had he been perceptive enough he would have noticed that all these lands contained inland waterways. I wonder if such premises can get me anywhere. One thing is certain though; I do not feel prepared to provide an answer to the point in question, especially now that I'm far removed from the heroes of the story. Under the circumstances all I can do is to have confidence in another day; thus, I can better fit myself into those picture frames. The British lifestyle and philosophy had become a diversion for them, a source of light entertainment. At such moments they felt more attracted to each other. They were seeing people whom they considered strangers that belonged to somewhere else. Their consigning to oblivion each other's uniqueness in such a haven was a natural consequence of their flights. The fact was that both their dreams had been living outside London, in a small town removed from the stir of society. Berti's dream had been a long one, kept fresh up until the day of his graduation. In the history of flights, everybody was left to their own devices; there was no escape from this fact.

Was Mr. Dyson a mere tutor?

In that little town far removed from the people that Berti considered his family—from those people he considered his next-of-kin, cut off from their rooms and their mutual glances and words, where he tried to discover the more tangible boundaries to his freedom and where he went for long-distance bicycle rides through its meandering paths on cool and clear mornings, which aroused in one the impression as though one was going on foot in another town—he had gone through a successful term of studies in addition to a passionate love affair. Mr. Dyson who was not only a tutor, a lecturer who guided his individual studies, but also a mentor who tried to guide Berti through the arduous journey ahead of him, he had a piece of advice for his apprentice during those last days when he had to carry the burden of all the consequences of separation which could be fathomed only after many years had lapsed: "try to forget whatever experiences you may have gone through up until now along with your hopes and aspirations for the future. This is not the end of your studies. You must be prepared for further discoveries." In this advice there seemed to be concealed a subtle hint about a long-lasting prospective education. One wonders why Mr. Dyson had desired that his pupil be equipped with different outlooks on life when he was going back to Istanbul. In order that he might have an insight into the wisdom hidden in progressive education? The reason for this desire had never been discovered by Berti even when he felt he was about to seize it. This was not difficult to understand. Every step taken, or failed to be taken, conduced further steps. He was of middling talent. In the face of this offer—interesting enough in itself, but, whose meaning could not be sufficiently elucidated, being affect-ridden under the circumstances prevailing at the time—he had owned that he felt obliged to solve the problems relating to Istanbul first of all despite the available means and potential opportunities. He intended to go back home and make the necessary preparations for a life to be shared with Marcellina. He was aware that he had to take up the challenge of a new life struggle, a new and desperate struggle involving other responsibilities. He knew and could foresee what waited him in the country of his birth where he had developed all the representations, dilemmas, and obsessions of his childhood and adolescence. The power was still in the hands of others despite his successes and ostensible superiorities. The problem had to do with this power, in fact, with the relationships created or killed by this power. Mr. Dyson was well aware of this. Those who had had the ingenuity to put up a struggle in a diversity of countries, where disparate tongues were spoken and where those who had been imprisoned in their books at different periods of time undoubtedly had a word to say. The gist of the matter lay in whether this struggle carried conviction or not. They had to consider these and never forget them. Berti felt obliged to discover the real drive that had compelled him to return. Was he risking a new subjection caused by a new fallacy rather than taking up the challenge of a new struggle? He may have been dodging certain things, the definition of which seemed abstruse. Mr. Dyson had found his pupil's relationship with Marcellina to be a mistake. It seemed as though in his relationship with Marcellina there were tracks of another invisible path which had to be discovered. He was persuaded that he would reveal this secret one day. It was too late however. Until then he would merely say that he felt he was at a dead end. The prevailing circumstances called once more for brooding silences. He was aware at least of the fact that it was too risky to transport and revive his cohabitation with Marcellina in another city. The life they contemplated together would never materialize. The best thing to do would be to just leave what one had gone through where it belonged, safe with all its riddles in case he might try to delve into the recesses of his suspicious mind. One thing was certain: he was not going to leave for another city. The story of the hero who couldn't tear himself from his streets must already have been committed to paper. This was an old story; a man's quest for re-discovery, a man figuring in some memories he had long forgotten. Those who had an insight into the story, who could empathize with it, would be those who would sooner or later have understood his desire. Berti had failed to understand the advice of his tutor at the time; for four years he had been sharing his expectations, merriments, and long-term prospects with Marcellina. It was as though he had discovered a completely new color; his confidence in women had been restored. Although their encounters had not been very frequent, they had taken full advantage of their situation, sharing the moments they had spent together. Unlike his friends, he had not had many love affairs. Marcellina had satisfied his needs, she had been successful in opening a door in him. Something no one had ever achieved before. What he needed was to be understood, for someone to attempt to understand him despite his concealed contingencies and dashed hopes. His efforts to sustain himself in a foreign land should not be underestimated. It was evident that his means were limited. His skills for having insights into men's psychology and generating warmth in them were far from matching his success in academic terms. Now I understand Berti's position much better *vis-à-vis* this relationship. Dilemmas often lead men to a diversity of antipodal points . . . We must note, however, that, while he brooded over these things, he was trying to enjoy a sort of superiority at the same time. Things that were desired to be seen, things that were desired to be displayed should take fresh roots in a different altitude, taking into consideration the point already reached. Berti's sole concern about those days had its origin in Marcellina's attempt at interpreting her lack of success in her academic work by reverting to conflicting statements and prevarications, at least to the best of my understanding. Having completed a two-year language course, she had first tried chemical engineering, then biology; however, her attempts had proved to be in vain. The underlying reasons were her experiences and the choices she had made in life, the motivation for which she was at a loss to explain. To be able to convey something or to get to the bottom of it? To perceive or to cause others to perceive? To touch or not to touch? Had Berti pondered the fact that certain sentiments in certain relationships had barely perceptible boundaries? I can't possibly hazard a guess. All that I can remember from those days is the story of an unfulfilled expectation. I can view it from quite a different angle from that of Mr. Dyson. Circumstances that were dictated in a completely different timeframe associated a completely different man in my mind, one inevitably transformed by his predilections. Berti had exhibited to his tutor a persona alien to me, a persona about which I can make bare assumptions. It was quite probable that this man was someone who could not have had access to the exact meaning of those words. This may have been the reason why Mr. Dyson had felt it incumbent upon himself to state that their talk would quite probably be the last talk they would ever have. Just before they parted, as he shook his student's hand, he had touched Berti's shoulder with his other hand, trying to inspire in him the beauty of having complete confidence in somebody. He had not failed to state that he would be very pleased to see him back and that he would never forget his responsibility in that respect. Both would cherish the memory of that day. It's true that no such return had ever taken place, but the connection would never be severed. They had kept up a correspondence even though it was on a sporadic basis. It's true that certain relationships were confined to letters, yet these letters, considering the words they contained, gave life to those relationships, to relationships that became more lively than tangible ones and were well worth speaking about. The past portended this; our books and legends had highlighted it in order that we could have a better insight into it. Words in somebody's ear, casual observations on life . . . Just to make it intelligible how he lived. Mr. Dyson was a homosexual. However, he had never made a cynosure of it; he had nevertheless felt obliged to make people feel that due to his inversion he had to adopt a different attitude, which alienated him from a good many of his friends. He had had the opportunity to state on different occasions that everybody came to this world with a purpose in life. The amplitude of this mission was difficult to define. With time, man seized the meaning of certain niceties, sometimes when it was too late. Should Mr. Dyson's invocation be interpreted differently, perhaps? Probably. Even upon receipt of the last letter, it had not occurred to Berti to ask about the foundation stone lying at the base of a good many relations and to secure a safe balance on it. Therefore, there had been vast penumbras in his relationship with his tutor which still maintained their importance and were recalled now and then. He, for his part, had failed to grasp the meaning of this insistence; he could never understand the reason why such a suspicion was entertained about Marcellina, the reason why he had had the courage to tell so much about himself to others. Could it be that the said penumbras, the area containing things of obscure classification, had been charted on purpose by Mr. Dyson, who knew his student so well? If one considered its reverberations through me, this likelihood might well have been taken into account and ignored. Nevertheless, barring the past considerations and judgments, I feel myself obliged to say that Berti's relationship with his tutor had been transported to a distant future just because of these shadows. Marcellina's place had been fixed during those talks. It was fated that they would never meet again upon his return in spite of their expectations, passion, and the common past they shared. It may well be that both had foreseen this. Yet, introspection was not a simple process. To go on living one's delusions seemed to be far easier sometimes, just because of those times. Berti had been able to detect his place in that delusion and find the sovereign remedy for his irrelevant life, but only after a good many years had gone by. That was the place he had failed to see despite all his efforts, the place Marcellina wanted to occupy. What sort of a place was it? Was there such a place? How come they had been resigned to their silences so easily after the separation? These were Berti's usual questions, doomed to remain unanswered, but which cropped up at the least expected moment. One could not deny of course the flights that were inherent in this. The enigmas left unsolved and the willful omissions of certain points were probably due to this. Those mysterious homicides had been committed in this very way in these stories. Those silent deaths and those silent births had coexisted with these solitudes and were preserved as such. Yet, time caused people to grow old regardless of the place they occupied. Berti had one day received a short letter. The sender was a stranger. He informed Berti of the death of Mr. Dyson from a heart attack. They had stayed in each other's memories across widely distant lands for many years through an exchange of questions they occasionally remembered. To the letter was attached a photograph, a spectacular photograph touched-up and well presented with excellent developing. Lines and shadows had focused on the porch of a house by the side of a dimly semi-lighted path, illuminated by a red glow. The letter stated that the photograph was attached for Berti's attention. A couple of days prior to his passing he was reported to have said: "I finally got it, after many years of expectation." The undersigned said that he was a "very close friend" of Mr. Dyson. Apparently, he had spent his last years in union with this man. No need to say anything further. Notwithstanding this closeness, he confessed that he could not make head nor tail of the mysteries that this photograph concealed and the words uttered. He was but a messenger. A man having the mission to carry messages, a person appointed by a testator to execute his will and to see its provisions carried out after his death. There were other words to be transmitted as well, ambiguous words uttered before departing. "This photograph belongs to him . . . Just send it to him . . . He'll understand . . . " said Mr. Dyson for his student whom he could never forget. After pronouncing these words he had stopped for a brief moment before continuing: "I hope he will." These words must have had some meaning exclusively for the two people involved . . . A letter was again looking for its place in the story.

Berti was deeply distressed by Mr. Dyson's death; for him this was the end of a beautiful friendship. It was the death of a friend whom one was always in need of . . . even though he was far away . . . Berti had surely asked himself then why he did not dare return to London although he had already been there on two previous occasions. On the other hand, he might well find out the reasons for this little betrayal had he so wished. However, regardless of our claim of sanctuary because of certain ostensible motives, one was faced with the lack of something in the wake of death. There might also be a sense of remorse inherent in this absence, which might serve us in transmitting some of our feelings . . . Berti had expected that Mr. Dyson, in that distant god-forsaken, but truly genuine place of his, would never go the way of all flesh. There was nothing extraordinary in our anticipation of immortality for our friends whom we had, strategically, and perhaps unconsciously, assigned a place in our lives regardless of their hyperborean location. To know that those people would be always there might account for our need for our little zones of security. The question here was to believe in the certainty of one's knowledge rather than simply knowing a fact. They could perhaps explain their reluctance or failure in seeing each other once more due to the fact that there would be no meaning in it. This relationship which could not be terminated, but which they could not properly define despite their best efforts had to stand the test of time through their correspondence. Would a certain number of words be enough to explain everything? Who knows? All things considered, there were an infinite number of ways to make a present of oneself to a given individual. Anyway, one could not possibly get rid of one's regrets and deficiencies. In the long run, Berti and Mr. Dyson must have reached certain objectives in their letters. However, this long walk had failed to provide a clue as to the mystery that that photograph concealed. The critical bond could not be established, in other words. To be frank, I was no better. Pieces would be patched up only after the lapse of many years. People had been waiting elsewhere for the right time to reemerge. I cannot forget that moment when I felt I had been engulfed in the mystery. One day I was fated to be conjured up to take my place at the twilight of the story. However, this invocation would take place without Berti's knowledge. I would thus have volunteered once more to assume the role of an accomplice. This was not my first instance of dodging a person whose story I intended to write. I now feel blessed with contentment for the fact that I have kept this secret, in other words, to have spared the pieces of information that he was supposed to know by the instigation of that visitor coming from a past long ago. I will certainly seek an answer for the action within myself one day. However, my rationale may undergo a change in the meantime. All that I can say now is that man takes pleasure in lying. Beyond that one must focus on the efforts related to self-protection through those voices. It may occur to you to know the time in the dead of the night, the real time. Do you think you can convey your feelings to a third person as you would wish? Would your apprehensions not raise barriers between you and them?

The Bridge

Despite the long time passed in between, the hours he had spent in the company of Marcellina were still fresh in Berti's memory. They had just paid another visit to the pub on the Mill Bridge. They must have wanted to relive the previous experience they had had on the day of their first encounter, to give birth to each other anew. The river ran as usual while the *habitués* had changed. Berti had held Marcellina's hand. They had stared at the town that stretched outward for a long time without uttering a word. They had promised each other that they would keep track of each other, regardless of their station upon the earth. Berti had said that he would come back soon, while Marcellina would be going to London. There was no relative left in her country who would be interested in her return, no one expected her there . . . As for the individual she had been looking to become, she expected she would show up one day . . . Once settled in London, she would inform him of her address. In the meantime, she might also pay a visit to Istanbul. Keeping track of each other seemed to be indispensable. In Cambridge, at the end of the road they had walked together, he said: "Life follows a completely different course for certain people. You'll understand this well when the time comes." They happened to be standing in front of the bus stop to which they had been turning a blind eye and which they had been trying to ignore the whole time. The bus was taking Berti to London. He should try to familiarize himself with the path that led him to that point, a point to which he was predestined; he should be capable of taking stock of his situation so that he could prepare himself to better deal with his predicament. They had melted into each other's embrace. When the bus had started off, the love they had been experiencing for each other had made itself felt even more strongly. One of the heroes of this love story was on his way back while the other stood motionless . . . she was simply there; as though tied, doomed to remain tied by expectations. Through the window of the bus he had seen Marcellina smile as though she said: "Well, this is the end then; we'll never see each other again." The bus was running and the windows were closed; no sound could be heard.

On board the plane that was taking him to Istanbul he was to recall once more the image he had retained of her. He wondered whether he could ever believe what he had been through. He had promised to the people he had left behind four years ago that he would be back soon. Well, this return would now be for good. He knew and felt that those people had opened new paths for him in his life; namely, Marcellina, Mr. Dyson his tutor, and Gordon Lucas, his roommate, a schoolfellow with whom he had shared a desk and whose view of life was quite different from his.

In whom had you lost that paradise?

After an absence of two whole years, Berti's welcoming ceremony in Istanbul had been rather modest. It seemed to him that he had told people about those days, about the wry joy of the past to a different person every time. Those were the individuals he had abandoned there and in whom he now wanted to take refuge. He yearned for them and tried to unearth them on certain nights. Who had not fancied themselves to have been a completely different person in a different story, a completely different person born to live a completely different life! Berti had believed himself as always forsaken in this odyssey. People who pave the way for our downfall are those who have no access to us, those who have always turned a deaf ear to our achievements and outcries despite their mindfulness of our presence . . . It was only Juliet who had empathized with him in his secluded state and proved to be a woman of great insight . . . Those solitudes for which nothing could be voiced that would give satisfaction. The real causes of this affinity would gradually unfold over time, time marred by deceptions, disappointments, and delusions . . . in dribs and drabs, as I saw my place in the story in a clearer light. I tried to discover the different aspects of Berti in relation to that said place, to be precise with the accretions of that place thanks to those words. Where had we been, in what time did we happen to be? At present I am no longer in a position to remember all of this in minute detail. At times, I saw myself strolling in his company; seated at a table in a pastry shop, watching a movie. I was confronted with a fragmented past. I wanted to patch it up into a whole, as I saw fit, in order to better understand the experiences we had gone through. This wholeness might be a completely different totality. On the other hand, it might not be a totality after all, and Berti's fragmentary episodes might conceal a new meaning that he wanted to get across. It is a fact that a person can see from his angle of vision what he truly wants to pick out. All that he had wanted to find in me had been a reliable friend, a confidant, one to whom secrets could be confided or entrusted during our nomadic lifestyle. Could it be that we had intended to bury our differing solitudes in each other's loneliness? Could it be that those long walks we had in the streets of our city from which we could not tear ourselves had drawn us to each other, despite all those fantasies we had indulged in? A time will come when I'll take up my pen and write what that journey meant to me. Those long walks were our burden, our way of carrying our deficiencies and yearnings. When I go over these meanings that the path we have trodden together has generated in me, it occurs to me now and then to ask myself if I'm betraying a confidence, the beliefs, principles, and ideals related to the sanctity of friendship, by communicating to others what had been entrusted to me. This might hold true for anybody who felt like sharing with people, at least with the right person, with just one single true person, a story in which he had perfect confidence in its veracity, with a view to justifying, or, exposing his experiences. In one's recounting his past history there were surely little betrayals in addition to self-delusions and efforts to deceive others. No one could perceive such subtle betrayals except those involved. However, in order to be able to better understand the reason behind our betrayals, we had to acknowledge the fact that while risking those betrayals we concealed ourselves in those individuals at the same time, so that we betrayed ourselves while betraying the individuals in question. It was our intention to hold the mirror up to ourselves while trying to hold it up to those other individuals as well. However, to be able to express this fact, we had to find the exact meaning of certain words; when I happen to be confronted with what I have gone through, with what I have been compelled to experience, I want to refresh my belief in making inroads toward, and having access to, those meanings. But I am at a loss to hazard a guess if communicating information and trying to bandy words would have any meaning after all. Any conjecture about this issue is surely beyond my reach at this juncture now that I am striving to penetrate and see through the different guises of my disappearance in those individuals. I feel sure that different facets may at the least expected moments associate in me faces I had never anticipated. I wonder if those people who preferred to remain hooked together with well-known lineaments ever had the same apprehension. They may well have had. Notwithstanding all the confidential information I am in possession of, I would rather hold my ground. One must not forget the fact that a secret did indeed protect one against threats while constituting an obstacle at the same time. To see through the meaning of the capability or the inability of taking real steps toward a person was so difficult and nerve-wracking.

One cannot deny that the celebration of Berti's return home was not totally deprived of sincerity. Madame Roza had spent hours in the kitchen to prepare the favorite dishes of her son. Regardless of the predicaments both were in, there was a certain undeniable mutual attraction between mother and son. Under the circumstances, I tried to remain a passive spectator, a spectator who tried to keep his deficiencies and resentments in the recesses of his darkness. This scene that Berti had depicted to me during one of our walks had penetrated me with all the voices and scents that accompanied it. The value of certain toys destroyed, left intact, or stolen by some culprits was highly appreciated when one bided one's time. That evening he was asked to speak about his experiences and adventures in England—in Cambridge and London. He had told them what he could recall on the spur of the moment while at the table. He had spoken about Gordon Lucas and Mr. Dyson, of the well-stocked library, not forgetting to mention his bicycle which he used to park by the public mail box in front of a house, of the chilly rooms which could not be sufficiently heated by the embers in the fireplace during the cold nights, of the crowded streets of London and of the large luxurious sedans. Uncle Robert had attended the graduation ceremony in the company of his wife. Their trendiness and elegance had not passed unnoticed. He looked fine. He had said that he had missed Istanbul and his family so much. He desired to see everybody and everything he had in the store of his mind again . . . . However, he had so many things to do first . . . He was extremely busy. He was on the eve of establishing very important business relationships with people all around the world . . . This news had enormously pleased his mother. It appeared that what he had written in his letters and what the gossips said were true. His young brother was far away, but happy; he had realized his dreams at least. He could boastfully say at present to his next-of-kin that he had in London a brother who lived like a lord. If one considers his period of matronship he was justified, one can say, in feeling proud of his own achievements and his success in life.

Now it was Marcellina's turn . . . Marcellina, about whom he could say nothing during the first visit, despite the great passion he felt for her and the possibilities ahead . . . He had said that he wanted to marry her in London or in Istanbul.

His blunt avowal had soured the atmosphere. *"Ya lo yori yo esto. Ya lo pensi ke te ivaz a kayer un dia de muchoz"* (I knew it! I had been expecting to hear of such a stupidity! I was heavy with suspicion!) said his father while his mother tried to calm him down, and had, in her usual charming reconciliatory behavior made the following comment: *"Jak, estate kayado! Deshalo ke avle ki e ezbafe!"* (Come on, Jacques, let him speak out and his tension be eased!) This fact which had bounced back after so many years had seemed to have found its former place within me. I believed I knew these people; these people who were arguing about things they could not openly disclose in the presence of others, about the evasions concealed behind those words. It seemed that they were groping for their places in this long story. Berti had desired to convey to me the exact words exchanged hoping to faithfully reflect the atmosphere. Those words seemed to have no substitute in any other language. What was the exact vernacular native to a region, the real language under the circumstances? Whose language was it? Whose loneliness and whose exile? I still entertain the hope of being able to share my experiences one day. I'm inclined to believe that there are people in a given climate subjected to the conditions of other climates and histories. I'm convinced that most of us are in need of such encounters in order to kill our executioners and phantoms, to deal a deathblow to them. However, in order for this to became reality, those same walls also have to be taken into consideration. "I can recall their lineaments. I had committed a grievous offense; I had been the bearer of the news of a murder; I felt like having been contaminated by a stranger with a mortal malady." His resentment was reflected in his voice. I had understood; his resentment was not simply due to the fact that he failed to accept Marcellina in her own right, it had its origins in the fact that they had turned a deaf ear to her even in the prevailing difficult circumstances. They had had experiences with similar extraneousness in the past; they had been compelled to. But Marcellina's case was important. Up until then no one had taken on such overriding importance. This is why he had dared to talk about her, not turning a blind eye to the disadvantages and the inevitable immeasurable latitudes involved.

Suddenly, he had looked his mother in the eye; he had felt in his bones her recalling the individuals who had played an important role in her life, the inevitable exiles and the errors committed by her next-of-kin. Where all these things would lead to sooner or later and who would be implicated in the long run was evident. However, everybody had to face this problem through his or her own perspective, according to his or her own fashion. It hadn't been for nothing that Madame Roza had to intervene in the dispute between her son and Monsieur Jacques. They happened to be on a line of demarcation where they had to make up their mind between either one of two things offered to them in the given situation where taking one entailed rejecting the other. To this you could also add the fear of understanding, of empathizing with the problem of one's interlocutor. Expecting that her son's self-purification would bring about a satisfying release of tension in him, Madame Roza might have anticipated relieving her own tension by finding out what was actually the matter. After all, the act of knowing also entailed attempts at solving other problems as well as lending credence to them. Notwithstanding this relevant fact, was it at all possible to know? I'm inclined to surmise that it must not have occurred to Madame Roza to consider this eventuality. However, she at least knew how to keep a tight hold on certain people and restrain them from crossing the boundary. She was resolved to lend an ear to her son's outpouring till he reached that boundary. Berti, on the other hand, had realized that this restricted area was the only arena in which he could make himself heard. Once again they were to tread a thorny path. To unburden oneself meant bringing something into the open, defying all dead ends; it also meant revealing one's desire for vengeance. This feeling could be understood by no one but himself, or by someone who had a deficiency like the one he had. He unburdened himself to his heart's content and tried to make vivid that secret passion. He had told of the hours he had spent in the company of Marcellina, of the promises they had exchanged for the sake of their future lives and about how their way to view the world had changed. He had told of the countries with inland waterways they had visited and the manner in which they had acquired their languages leisurely. He had withheld certain details, preferring to use them as raw material for his fantasies.

Monsieur Jacques had done his best never to mention this issue again after that evening. Underneath this behavior there undoubtedly lay a dodging of realities and a dogged insistence on his own opinion. This was not his first guarded utterance. Egotism and dread may have been concealed in this reserve. He persevered in his resolution; regardless of all sorts of eventualities, no one could persuade him that this nuptial bond with a stranger could be blissful to the end. To marry a foreign woman meant to be off-track. He had witnessed so many broken miscegenations despite overwhelming and passionate love and good will between the partners that had experienced this alienation . . . His mother was of the same opinion. The scene was one of those stage plays enacted in different countries in foreign languages. Madame Roza had once again shown her motherly and traditional protectiveness in order not to lose her son and had done her best to solve the matter. We could not assert that she had understood all that had been expressed. Considering her past experiences and what was supplied to her by others, she could not claim to be perceptive. Her trial had been the uphill struggle of a supplicant, ignorant of warfare. Her campaign was unwarranted according to the majority of people if one took into consideration the prevailing conditions; it was a lame contention gradually losing (and which was doomed to lose) its relevance, tenor, and rationale in the wake of skirmishes. She had been unable and unwilling to keep silent and dodge the issue like her husband, her lifelong consort, who had tried to exercise his paternity over their children through a puerile approach, in total disregard of realities liable to undergo change, to wear away in time or to perpetuate its vitality forever. She was firmly convinced of the existence of good grounds for her struggle in defiance of the declarations of her son and of those who led a life similar to his. Mother and son had engaged in interminable dialogues throughout those nights replete with problems; they had sat up late into the night and drank large cups of coffee and tried to go back to their far distant past. The image of the fig tree in the garden of their house on the island, whose plentiful yield every other year warranted their generous distribution of figs to the people of the neighborhood; of the worms that ate away the figs fallen to the ground; of the bathroom with the marble basin heated every Friday morning by a wood stove; of their going cycling; of Mimico; of those hot pastries that Madame Victoria used to send them now and then and of the pastelicos; although so long ago, still fresh in the store of his memory. All these incidents had taken place on an island, on *the* island; the point at hand was the expression of wistfulness; a wistfulness more or less familiar to everybody which ran alongside everybody's life; a wistfulness that everybody would wish to share with someone. His mother was no exception; she had told so much about her past, about the prehistory of the house they lived in . . . That fig tree, the odors that emanated from the garden, those nights each had its respective past laden with reminiscences. He had to be considerate and show tact in his relationship with his father. Such marriages that interfered with the 'natural' order of life never proved to be successful. Everybody was doomed to be consumed in the darkness of his fate. He should bear in mind the case of his maternal aunt Estreya. Where had she gone? To the other extremity of Istanbul, she had to sever all contact with everybody, even with her next-of-kin. Yet, she was the most beautiful girl of the family. Had she so desired she might have been among the elite of society. Had she seen the light? No one could hazard a guess, no one, even Estreya herself. However, regardless of any plausible answer we cannot deny the fact that there are moments in everybody's life when one feels that it is too late. He should have his wits about him and be careful not to forget this; for, to forget often meant dodging one's own reality; was their decision to go to the other extremity of Istanbul not an attempt at escape? They hadn't even had a baby; they were well aware that they were 'poles apart.' People they had carried over from their past to their present and had stayed true to them had convinced them of—nay inculcated them with—the fact that they were a mismatched couple. People had exposed this to them. He might well beget children from a foreign woman; but then . . . He didn't want to think that there was the chance of his child being a boy; oh no, no circumcision . . . a creature whose origin would remain a mystery; could he shoulder such a responsibility? What could he transmit to this child that would give meaning to their existence from their recorded history marred by trials and tribulations? Had their unending Sisyphean ordeal been pointless? How far could this woman, who had not had any experience of being estranged, comprehend all these things? The fact that marriage had nothing to do with love and that cohabitation changed the parties to the point of estrangement from each other had become a platitude. Supposing that the woman agreed to come over to Istanbul, would her consent be long lasting? She was a stranger after all. She might well disavow her earlier declaration and desire to return home. What then? Would he be disposed to follow in her footsteps to a land to which he was not familiar? He was expected to stay where he was, in his hometown where he was familiar with every nook and cranny. He was blessed with contentment; or at least he should be. He had attended a very good school; he had found true love. That was all very well, but everything had an end, an inevitable return to one's roots. Everybody had responsibilities that devolved; so decisions were to be taken nearer to the people they would affect; responsibilities that one could not shirk, evade, or avoid. He would have parental responsibilities like in all other families and communities. He was the eldest of the family. He was supposed to take over the flag and carry it to a predetermined spot as in a relay race. Life was as simple as that after all.

People who complicated things blinded themselves to such realities. Madame Roza herself was an elder sister who had her matronly duties and shouldered this obligation all too well. Even from the time of her adolescence, she had done her best to hold the family members united and had had to assume diverse frames of reference over the course of time; there had been dropouts certainly either due to demise or willful separation. Yet this did not prevent her from undertaking this responsibility. Her fate was sealed. She had to resign herself to it.

Three or four months had gone by. Berti had been fooling around, frequenting his old chums, watching movies, browsing books, and carrying on his research work. During his secluded meditations in his chamber on his experiences and on what he had left behind, he was beginning to comprehend better the ineluctable fate of which his mother used to speak so much. He was haunted by the voices of his past. His experiences in Cambridge had been permanently settled in his memory, inaccessible to anyone but himself. Was it a fear that gripped him that was caused by the fact that he was being persecuted by the idea that barred his way back to those places? On the one hand, there was an immediate past which could be transformed into a future heavily laden with rich fantasies, and on the other hand a past more realistic than his distant past, his distant history lived or left unlived had gradually built up and he was becoming more and more conscious of its ineluctability as time went by. Whose future would it be, whose past, in truth? Long were the days. It appeared to him at the time that his father came back home in the evening from another world. They had failed to share and brood over those days, making comments as they might have done. Years had to pass and other losses had to be suffered before they could do so. This was his struggle against other extraneous things, against other languages, beliefs, and silences . . . Not an easy job . . . I could understand this. To the extent my imagination and my vocabulary allowed, I would have a better insight into the fact that a back and forth struggle against extrinsic things could not possibly be waged without receiving serious wounds. Long days they were . . . But those days also had their nights for Berti, nights during which he conversed with Jerry and with whom he believed he shared certain things. Berti would speak to me of those nights with some despondency; a despondence tinged with remorse; a remorse which I was to account for later upon discovering a clue. Jerry had never felt at home in his school, which he was obliged to finish in one way or another. He was industrious enough but had to face the strict discipline of the friars. He smoked and had almost become an alcoholic. When, under another climate he had found himself hedged in by different prevailing conditions, he had felt he had already covered a good distance; he was grown up and experienced what loneliness was. He spoke of Nietzsche and was engrossed in mythology; American sedans and existentialism were subjects of his day-to-day talk, while his dream at the time was to become a singer. He had learned how to play the guitar; he was dabbling in musical compositions and writing poetry. Were these a new version of his childish fantasies? He spoke of Claudette, his biology teacher who exuded sex appeal; she was young and burgeoning, disposed to encounter dangers and risks and to cope with the new and unknown. She had even invited him to her home a few times. However, all these fanciful stories had proved to be unfounded, as became clear during his interrogation before the disciplinary committee of the school. The plaintiff was the teacher of biology. One day Jerry had brought a frog to school and requested his teacher to demonstrate her assertion that the anatomy of the animal was similar to the anatomy of a human being. The poor woman who had observed it leaping onto the table could not help losing consciousness. The administration had convened the concerned to make a deposition regarding the case. Whereupon Berti, being qualified to give evidence regarding the matter under inquiry had reported to the board in the company of his mother. He had the opportunity to interpret the incident in its true colors. The teacher had been a woman content with her store of generally accepted patterns of knowledge who tried to suppress her drive by overcompensation. Caught unawares, he had had difficulty in restraining himself from laughing at this unexpected incident. Nonetheless the case was serious. Jerry was facing expulsion. However, Berti, thanks to the refined manners of a British gentleman he had acquired as a consequence of his education and upbringing, had succeeded in settling the matter amicably. What had been the cause of all these things, of these lies, of these little tricks? Jerry's contention was that she hated the smart-alecks that besieged him. He had shut up and remained silent and inhaled sharply the smoke of his cigarette before blurting out: "It seems we are fated to be at cross purposes with it." Did he mean the school board by 'it'? Days were to show that words had a plurality of meanings. One could not always clearly and explicitly understand the figurative and double meanings of words. These words were exchanged between him and Jerry in their rooms. "Had I been in your place, I would have left," said Jerry. Who could have vouched for the fact that he had a completely different future in mind? "Why not go and ask Aunt Estreya's opinion?" he said. Berti had suddenly become aware that it had been years now since he had last seen her. He felt confused. To forsake or to deny must not have been so easy. To consign people to oblivion, to see that they abide in their proper climate must not have been so easy. He used to listen to Elgar's music at the time . . . He remembered Mr. Page who had covered his tracks . . . He should have been a witness to these moments . . . He should have been able to converse with him now . . . . Madame Estreya had not been an auricular witness to the conversation that had taken place during those nights. Everybody in his own climate was in pursuit of his own self. Berti had felt the pang of having failed to pay a visit to his Aunt Estreya at the time. His pangs of guilt resulted from the feeling that he would no longer be able to see a place he had left far away. However, he realized, when he recalled those days, that the matter of regret, far deeper than the bitter experiences he would have afterward, was particularly due to his having forsaken his beloved while he was carrying on with his life in Istanbul. This was a stage play well-known to me, in which I had had a role and of which I had also been a spectator. Therefore, the regret in question might not have been made explicit. This was one of those sentiments innate in your heart to which you should give their due only when you had paid a price for them; one of those sentiments which I could never obliterate once I had supplanted Berti in his original place in his adventures with his companions. In one of the days following his return to Istanbul, as someone who had failed to find what he had been looking for, burdened with questions without answers, his father had broken the silence reigning in the house with his soft voice and said: "This has been dragging on too long now. It's high time that you made your choice between 'her,' 'them,' and 'us.'" This must have been the climax of the dispute. It was evident that the personal pronoun 'her' was not limited to Marcellina alone, and 'us' did not merely signify 'our' family. It was whether he should choose the path that would lead him stripped naked straight to love with all its effects, or remain in his actual haven. Berti happened to be facing a bifurcation, he had to make up his mind and opt for either of the two alternatives. He had thus made his decision in defiance of those people, the words that they had inculcated in his mind and of all the eventualities involved. Having opted for security, he had partially been the author of his own lost paradise. Only a few steps would have sufficed to touch that paradise. The magic was concealed in those steps. However, there was no other way but to set off into the twilight. Logic and deduction would enable you to guess how the story would unfold as dictated by its heroes and heroines. Here was hidden a history of slavery; was it exclusive to Berti?

What had happened there at that time had dragged Monsieur Jacques, who had brought the issues to a climax, to a secret alcove. It was as though a sentiment, preferred to be left in the dark, had been given utterance through a completely different means, clothed in silence or hidden behind a laconic expression. Had Berti exercised his discretion in opting for the opposite coast, viz. beyond the wall, his life might have undergone a radical transformation and demonstrated to him how his past steps had been disastrous and devoid of all meaning. One of the important pawns in the game had been moved somewhat cautiously. However, it had to be admitted that over many years he had developed his skill in the game and had acquired considerable foresight in moving the pieces with great shrewdness. Father and son had run into each other unexpectedly at a crossroads, to be precise at a blind alley, at each other's dead end. One could describe this game as a silent death bound to remain hidden only in glances. The stories recounted in other lives, books, and pictures had been the previous witnesses of this death. Olga, just like Marcellina, had been a mere onlooker who watched and was compelled to watch the parties move their pieces in this game of death, the parties who approached each other for the sake of their secret. What was even sadder was the fact that even in such mawkishness, a true aspect of the father and son relationship had remained eclipsed and barren. *Piece touchée piece jouée* was *de rigueur*. This rule had to be applied to the letter. They were the protagonists of a story in which certain burning questions had to be veiled; it was a protracted meeting in the distant past through years and years at a time when a loss could be risked after a series of demises. This was due to the necessity of paying respect to death tolls . . . just like the figures acting in the same play for the same objectives. This was the price of living in a sanctuary, of the saving of one's life in due conformity with one's own criteria.

Berti's other problem, similar to the problem of many of his kind who could not do otherwise, had its origins in the fact that he was blind to the inferno behind that paradise which he believed he had lost, to real life in other words. According to him that was a place where he thought himself happier than in the overpopulated city, in that city where he was compelled to live. He had been incapable of taking stock of the reality there, of this essential element; either then or any time thereafter; if the reverse had been the case, he could have had an insight into its reflection in distorted mirrors, which would have enabled him to endure life, at least the daily difficulties, more easily. But the fact was that he had grown accustomed to this lie. Could this be another means of clinging to a branch without feeling the obligation to define what it was attached to? By the way, did we not have a similar feeling at times for the people nearest to us, whom we thought to be nearest to us? Was not our inferno concealed in those steps of ours we could not properly explain? Had we not been looking for ages now for our paradise in the glow of another age whose appellation had long been a thing of the past? The story of this dull, persistent, and sometimes throbbing pain which accompanied the experiences we had gone through lasted in certain hearts for years, intermittently in different guises up until that magical moment of which we suddenly had a glimpse into the fullness of time. That precipitation which one could observe in love-at-first-sight had its exact foil when one falls out of love. However, in order that we could understand all this we had to be sufficiently bold, brave, and courageous to lend an ear to the voices in those secret alcoves in the chambers of our heart. This was the moment when we were disposed to be familiarized with those foreign words, when we could protect ourselves, having been masters of ourselves in the background of a long and common past. I'm ignorant of the fact whether Berti had come upon these questions or eventualities when he returned to his past in the course of his introspective odyssey, heading for this relationship he had had to leave behind in the hope of consigning it to oblivion, but which he could never hope to achieve—at least by my expectations—since he could not help but objectify it. At the time we happened to be poles apart. I realize the distance that separated us more effectively now that I am trying to lend credence to what we had gone through. I have a feeling that I'm channeling a secret of his, inaccessible I think to many people, for all practical purposes. The path that led to that secret was strewn with gravel not to be displaced. After that separation, Berti had not set eyes again on Marcellina, who had ushered in his life a completely new era and kindled an inextinguishable fire. Not to be able to come into contact with those familiar objects anymore like in the old days . . . postulating that his beloved continued to live in one of those lives in one of those worlds, especially during his solitary hours . . . swept by a series of questions involving such words as where and how. He had in the past had access to representations that had nourished this feeling which was to continue to be fed so long as those deficiencies lasted. I had tried to visualize those representations; at the locations where those things took me I seemed to detect the traces of blissful moments which could not be relived or recaptured. Where were those bicycle rides now? That conceptual thinking that linked him to his former tutors and fellow companions in the name of an unshattered and different world. Where was the river that the boat rides on? In which nooks and crannies of these photographs had they hidden themselves? Did words succeed in bringing about stealth as well as explicitness? I might entertain the hope of attaining such targets had other *quodlibets* been offered for argument. Regardless of what these photographs concealed, it was obvious that certain things had been left behind for good in the distant past, certain things with changing terminology and affects over time. Berti might be chastising himself against a backdrop of that eventuality he had lost forever in the past. During his meditations in those evening hours he had ended up by committing himself to the idea that he had to remain faithful to this separation and accept the road ahead as it was paved and resign himself to that fact. He couldn't help thinking this way. Once stowed in one's memory, nothing could be deleted. So long as you were in a position to recollect those photographic memories, you were sure to feel yourself indebted to those you had left behind through the looking glass. It might so happen that you would discern the smiling faces of the figures behind that mirror. Could one interpret those as being the moments you felt to be nearest the target?

We were partly our photographs

How could you have foreseen during those nights which song, which word, or which representation was destined to set you off on that journey you had been putting off for so many years? You could never give a proper depiction of those nights. Only your own imagination could prepare you for that journey . . . equipped with the memories of old fictions or films which you would like to communicate to certain people . . . as you are in the process of consigning the former masked visages of your old imagination to oblivion . . . Berti had succeeded in going to Cambridge several years after, after a tide of about twenty years. We were not yet coeval with this event. All I knew about this journey had been communicated to me afterward; it was the seventies. It was evening. I was perfectly aware of the fact that certain representations, whose true meanings and idioms lay concealed in esoteric recesses, came to light when a story desired to be narrated often underwent alterations and changes of identity. This is the reason why I attempted to convey certain thoughts and reflections of certain representations in a garb one would have liked to identify himself with. Cambridge reminded me of that person, of his memories and the journey he took, not of a town he was familiar with. He had visited that town on and off for business purposes spending no longer than a couple of hours there; which particular business led him there he would not be in a position to say now . . . Upon his arrival there by bus he had thought that the town had been considerably altered, but, contrary to his expectations, he had not been moved in the slightest degree by what was before him. It appeared not to be the same city in which he had once roamed on sunny afternoons. He found himself staring at the river. A group of young people were training for the boat race. A girl passed by riding a bicycle. He thought about the fact that this girl would not have been born at the time of his love affair. He was feeling estranged from his surroundings; it looked as though he was faced with the shadow of a person unknown to him in those streets where he once knew the diverse features of both the day and night so well. He had understood that the town had closed its doors to him in order that he may atone for his transgression. He had felt the immediate presence of Marcellina close by, although she was to remain invisible, inaccessible, and untouchable. This was the ransom he was asked to pay. He had expressed the desire to prove that he had succeeded in coming back in one way or another. This may have been the exact spot where that sentiment he tried to perpetuate for love's sake assumed a true meaning. Beyond what had been lost, there continued to linger that aftertaste of those fantasies and recollections. The only thing that was beautiful to behold there was Berti's image of Marcellina that still lingered unchanged in his imagination. Time had come to a standstill, far removed from so many realities, from any future prospects and eventualities. It was a fact that a person continued his routine existence in another realm. This was a retributive action on the part of the young dead who wreaked vengeance on those who survived them. Berti was thus sharing a similar fate with a good many heroes of varying backgrounds. Marcellina's likeness had remained captured in those photographs. Despite the fact that she went on living with other people at other places she said nothing herself; nor did she ask Berti to speak about what had befallen him after parting company with her . . . These were my impressions, my expectations and experiences in the story in question. I may, however, not have drawn the line of demarcation between us properly. As he spoke about his experiences that afternoon, frankly I cannot think of any other way to interpret his words: "As I was staring at the river, it dawned on me that I had lost her forever . . . The funny thing was that my intention to narrate my vicissitudes to someone was greater than my actual desire to resume our relationship . . . " As a matter of fact, the demarcation line between us gained meaning through this realization. We would never be able to learn who had been lingering where and who was aspiring to make headway through the darkness lit by which particular words. We might be in search of the source of the fantasies we had been weaving through the unknown; those fantasies we used to indulge in, which every so often charted our course in life. Can it be that while we are, in the darkness of the night, impatiently waiting for the day to break, reciting memorable poems and uttering words from times past, the sudden appearance of a glimmer of light from one of the houses across from us, wrapped in darkness, provokes in us a wry joy? Could a hope be based on a circumstantial event?

On which night had Marcellina tarried?

I can't exactly remember which story it was in which I had attempted to introduce that glimmer of light. Who were those figures and unshared fantasies of another age, deprived of the mode of expression concealed in this call? Such issues had confronted me with the shattering aspects of the imagery within me, which I had always wished to unfold to people. That unearthly glimmer of light represented a chamber barring access. In the story narrated to me by Berti there seemed to be such a light; this light would also convey to me the memory of a photo we had mislaid somewhere during our long walk. Berti would not figure in this photograph that had popped up unexpectedly and was evoked by a few moments that had encapsulated me during the course of that night. The *chiaroscuro* was exclusive to those moments; it had to be left there to endure. The use of marked light and shade contrasts for decorative and dramatic effect had added to the town in which I was living—effects I could not bring myself to familiarize myself with—the features of a life which I believed I could only come across in movies or fictions. This aspect kept wandering among the images within me. I'm striving to penetrate into the meaning of things that happened in the distant past and into the incidents likely to occur in the future; and, last but not least, I nurse the ambition to bring myself to believe in what I am intending to relate. I realize that similar gripping stories are embroidered in different climates and lands, in books whose sales are among the highest of their genre and which set fire to the popular imagination. Why then this intense greed to relate, this overestimation of what is expected to be related? Am I intending to regale myself with the grievance of a third person? It certainly isn't so easy to provide an answer to this question. Thus, I must try once again to screen myself from explicitness and use words to that end, notwithstanding the impression I now have that—regardless of the suspicions to be generated in me by what I shall be trying to perform and by the experiences that shall revisit me—the properties, presented to me as that past and that life, will develop insidiously in the years ahead like a disease deep within me which I shall never be able to diagnose or define. This photograph was the same one that Mr. Dyson had spent years tracking down and which he is believed to have come into contact with before the end of his life. It was Gordon Lucas who had showed me this photograph, the other side of the story, that visitor who had occupied a special place within me, who had come over to Istanbul on business quite different to Berti's. I knew for a fact that Gordon was one of the crucial witnesses to Berti's business practices there. During our long walks he had become much more to me than merely a roommate. Life had thrust them in opposite directions, just like in other similar stories, but details relating to the ties that remained between them, insignificant to others, had been deemed deserving of preservation for years. Gordon figured in the photographs where he came across as an individual bent upon living all his passions to the bitter end, who preferred to be outdoors rather than cooped up within the four walls of a room, watching the street, the activity going on in a nightclub, the yachts with billowing sails cruising in the immensity of the ocean, or a train excursion in a faraway land fraught with dangers . . . During a stopover in Istanbul, he had traced the whereabouts of Berti, as they had been corresponding for sometime now, and gave him a call, informing him of his short stay in the city, suggesting to him that they meet for a couple of hours if he was willing as this would please him greatly. He had put up at the Hilton Hotel. After so many years a closer place could not be imagined. The meeting itself depended on Berti. In answer to this witty proposal, indicative of his British humor, Berti had not thought it proper to conceal his enthusiasm. He had also said some things which I could not make out but which had provoked laughter on both sides. Their conversation seemed to have continued even after they stopped talking. He said he would be there as soon as possible. In my capacity as a storyteller I happened to be there at the time. It was Berti's idea that I should accompany him. I had felt that I was nearing a critical point of the story. I had to acquiesce. I was glad to be one of the heroes. What was more important was that I was going to have access to a confidential communication, though I could not reveal this to Berti. Actually, our objectives had been different; our intentions varied. The same story invited us to share different fates. So off we went and hailed a taxi to take us to Şişli. Berti wanted to drop by his barber Stellio and have his beard and hair trimmed. He had preferred not to speak during his trim. Thereafter we had repaired to the Hilton Hotel by taxi. He was well acquainted with the taxi fares that changed according to the distances traveled, as he commuted often in the city. But he had paid more than the actual cost to both drivers that day. Personally I had not opened my mouth during these short trips. I sensed that his entire performance that day was a kind of initiation to me. To be sure of this it would have been necessary to scrutinize every movement of his body; under the circumstances there was no need for such certitudes. There appeared to be an unavoidable estrangement in the meeting that took place at the hotel; likewise, there was no need to interpret this bitterness. As a matter of fact, if one bears in mind the aftereffects of those old movies and stage plays, all the ill feelings and associations felt at the time were more than enough to instill in you the sense of despondency that this meeting inspired. In order that I might hide my true identity I was content with remaining a mere spectator; a spectator, despite Gordon's suspicious looks. Gordon spoke articulately and looked smartly dressed in a well-tailored suit. The start of the conversation consisted of remembrances of the good old days, recalling long-forgotten experiences and incidents. However, Gordon had been more of a listener than a talker; he proved to be self-contained and a good listener. He did not miss the chance to cast furtive glances at me in the meantime. Our glances had met a couple of times; such encounters seemed to be attempts at a different sort of dialogue, moments during which both sides tried to catch the opponent unawares. Both of us appeared to have sensed, that we were, in this part of the story, essentially different people than what we purported, people who concealed within them things they were reluctant to disclose. This privacy seemed to make both parties ill at ease. This was the uneasiness of a person conscious of being peeped at through the keyhole of a door, whereas mine was of a person knowingly peeping through the keyhole conscious of being partially obscured from view. Under the circumstances, we were to recklessly exchange clues about ourselves with laconic expressions.

Now the turn of their actual business had come. "Skip it. Does not deserve mention; rubbish," said Berti, while Gordon had said: "I'll tell you later; perhaps some other day." This comment had caused a joyful but wry expression on him. It was a joy that resulted from the fact that they had failed to share what they had been going through, about their discontentment with their lifestyles. No yarn was being spun boastfully of one's adventures, as is normally the case with a person returning home from a long journey. Both had already made their choices in their respective countries; both had their secrets which they could not transport to their past. Berti felt as if he had arrived at a small oasis in a vast desert. He was not in a position to feel that there were diverse reasons for not divulging their experiences. We saw what we came to see which threw a lifeline to our past. Behind his outer features, Gordon undoubtedly concealed a bitterness. I saw before me an individual who had been compelled to endure, with the patience of a sage, a completely different lifestyle than the one he professed. Such a person could not be left out of the frame of this story. Our glances had met silently on a few occasions. Both of us had tried to make the other feel that our origins had been marred by differing solitudes. What I witnessed that evening would remain fixed in my mind thereafter, despite the fact that my original intention had been to remain as a mere spectator. There were times when wishes, the realms of fantasy created by wishes, to be precise, yielded their place to certain obligations and servitudes. This leads me to brood once more on the meaning that fate has left to me. I like to consider what I have been going through as fatality. In this story I also had an ineluctable fate. Within the framework of those intimate associations, I would quite possibly be bound to remain as a stranger to my fate and the words spoken. Regardless of the things bound to remain a mystery to me, I know for a fact that the place I was being motioned toward was exactly the spot where I would feel sure to discover men in their true garb, stripped of their clothing. The venue that Gordon invited me to was such a place; a place wherein men would appear translucent; a vantage point from which I could have a better view of my despair and my efforts to try to transform myself into other personages figuring in new stories; in a nutshell, of my own nakedness. Berti had asked to be excused as he was going to answer the call of nature. A pair of heroes who hardly knew each other until a short time before, who knew that they would never meet again, but who were convinced that the chance to was always there, had remained in their respective shells. Could we have benefited from the opportunity to deliver a part of ourselves to the other? I, on my part, would turn this little opportunity to good account by re-living Marcellina's story—having learned the truth, which would take me to a completely different place. I wondered if the future I had acquired in the face of this truth was a more tangible one. Despite all those years that had gone by in the meantime, I was in no position to give a proper answer to this question. A suspicion was gnawing at my heart. When I reconsider what I have come by in the meantime and the words that force themselves to be given utterance, I have the impression that certain people must have committed an error, a fallacy of judgment. Whose error could this be, whose truth, whose reality? I'm aware that such questions would lead to further inquiry unless they were answered first. Had these been the impediments that had hindered the merging of stories because of the similarities of which I thought I was in a position to explain as I had become capable of deciphering the clues concealed? Gordon had asked me if I knew Marcellina. "Only to the extent that she would provide enough material for a long story which would entail suspicions, interrogations, and introspection," had been my answer. "Well," he retorted, "So far, so good. Time is pressing. Therefore let me tell you something of crucial importance regarding her. I feel that what I know must be communicated to someone who knows Berti well. I know Berti; since you've come together, he must have trusted you," he said. I had caught a glimpse of another aspect of Gordon's furtive looks. He must be trying to detect the identity of this new acquaintance to the best of his ability. It seemed to me that he had been expecting to hear me utter a sentence, a little sentence that would reveal that identity. But I had preferred to remain silent and express what I felt through my glances. I believe I had apprehensions about things that seemed to me both indefinable and unidentifiable . . . This was understandable. Reticence sometimes gives a person the possibility to have access to things which have to do with other people. In the meantime I had chosen my place. Both of us seemed to have trained ourselves against each other's games, so much as time allowed. Beyond that it was his domain, exclusively his. This soliloquy had the nature of those long monologues we usually come across in fiction. The timespan was his exclusive possession. The past returned with the last person I expected to see. "You must give me your word that what I'm going to tell you now shall not be communicated to Berti. Can I rely on you?" Gordon said. I had learned what attitude I should adopt in the face of such questions from books—the attitude of a confidant, of an author. I knew how. I had tried to give that pledge through my looks. My position required that I give that pledge in some way or other. "The thing that he never realized, strange to say, was the fact that Marcellina had assumed the guise of a person quite different from the generally accepted image of his lover, of a woman who for most of us is an extremely original woman of the world. This woman, her countenance to be precise, was according to some the very image of the devil, while according to others it was the embodiment of revolt, and still for others a drift. If we associate in our mind our restricted sphere of action and our ignorance of life's tribulations, she was a woman who had taught us how to live off the fat of the land in the face of prohibitions . . . She was a professional prostitute! You didn't expect this, did you? To be frank, this had been a surprise for us all, though we tried to preserve the established order by striving to conceal the secret *de polichinelle*. When the time came we saw the lay of the land only after all the tricks had been performed . . . after experiencing the separations. Well life runs away with such dirty jokes. This woman who had inspired each of us with her different methods of observation and self-concealment had for some reason or another chosen Cambridge over so many capital cities. Her assertion was that she wanted to study there. Could this be one of the lies she had concocted to be able to live till eternity, as she put it, in that city? Could it be that she had told whopping great lies to other people in other cities? This we shall never know. All that I can say is that the story she told had seemed plausible and compelling to us. We had lent credence to it and we believed that we could find an important place for it in the future we had been planning. We couldn't possibly know what the future would bring. Marcellina had cut a poor figure in our story; she appeared to be from humble origins. She had said that she had made a covenant with the devil in order to stand the test of time in the world of the rich. She tried to abide by the covenant with a deep-seated resentment that was not without a sense of revolt, in the garb of an impudent individual who felt no shame for what she had done. 'This is my vindication, my vow of vengeance on what has been given to me and what has been withheld from me, on the gifts presented and kept from me. This was my gradual resurrection in a different body to match my gradual dying,' she once said. Her penetrating looks bewitched me. It was as though I was sleeping with a new woman each time we had sex. To have sex with her was an ecstatic experience. It would take years before I learned that she had caused the same rapture for many other individuals. The game had long been played. Each one of us thought that he had been the only privileged subject that had tasted this delight; each one of us had had his part to play. There were four of us in fact; four comrades that fate had brought together only to disperse them afterwards as quickly as they gathered. We were thoroughly and closely interconnected, interrelated and interwoven, and were in the immediate position to tell each other our private relationships. To believe in the veracity of this proximity was essential for us. Yet, we had kept Marcellina off the record and said nothing about her to each other. Why had we acted in this way? It may have been due to that strange blissful state, not without a bit of regret, of our prohibited escapades. This was a kind of veiled fight for superiority. But then we had to relate to each other our respective experiences when Marcellina had left Cambridge for an unknown corner of London. The four of us had drained bumpers till we became dead drunk. Berti had gone back home. We knew that he would never return; at least we sensed it. I had told my friends that I wanted to make a confession and disclosed my affair with Marcellina. My revelation was succeeded by the revelations of the others. All of us had had some sort of an affair with her, each of which differed enormously. I don't think I have to tell about these affairs since you are not acquainted with them. We must own that every one of them gave voice to a different fantasy. That night we had raised our glasses to that woman who had seemed to us unparalleled. I said we were dead drunk; but we were not dead, as an important part of our life had lingered in her. She was peerless. It may seem to you somewhat unbelievable but I ran into her after many years at a reception at the Argentine embassy. I often used to attend such receptions since my function at the Ministry of Foreign Affairs demanded it of me. She appeared to be even more beautiful and was the focus of everybody's attention. I didn't mince words and paid her the compliment she deserved, to which she responded with a wry smile. 'Life is full of unexpected events and meetings, isn't it?' 'Well,' I replied, 'I think we were prepared for this, from the very start.' She gave another smile. Her continuously radiant countenance looked just as she wished it to. I suddenly realized that she had consumed a great quantity of alcohol. 'However, I cannot say when we will speak again,' she added. I was silent. She may have waited for an answer from me. But the fact was that I had nothing to say at the time. Then she asked about Berti; she knew our intimacy. I told her that we corresponded every once in a while, but that it had been years since I had last seen him. To sooth her cracking voice, she took another sip from her drink. 'Good old boy! Gawky youth!' she remarked, then continued: 'Someone unaware of the extent of his innocence.'

"It appeared that we both missed him. Both of us seemed to feel uneasy for having been incapable of acknowledging this. Yet, our yearning for him was evident. We wanted to hug him, each of us having different intentions in mind. Now it occurs to me to think that Marcellina was in search for the child she had lost in that relationship when she said that he had been 'a good old boy.' It was a fact; she had lost a child when she had severed her relationship with Berti. Children undoubtedly differed among themselves, having many diverse characteristics and features; but one could not deny the fact that all of them had one common trait; namely, being children. Marcellina's affair with Berti was quite unlike those experienced by the rest of us. Her intention had been, I think, to undertake the lengthy process of ripening that adolescent into a man, shouldering the adversity that accompanied it. This relationship seemed to contain a beauty fed by deceptions and self-delusions, a beauty deserving of exploration, discovery, and definition . . . to be able to live one's fantasies, even for a brief period of time. To my mind, this behavior displayed a humane aspect of the woman who had accepted the progress of evil as a fatality deserving of respect. Berti had turned a blind eye to what happened outside himself, he failed to see the others; he didn't even try. He had raised a wall of bliss around his experiences with Marcellina. This wall protected her against outside assailants; it imprisoned them and barred access to them. This may have scared me off trying to find out the truth, despite the fact that we had had the opportunity to talk over every vital problem that life presented to us. I don't regret it, however. I could not possibly deny him this delusion, whatever the consequences. Marcellina must have thought like me, giving fantasy its due. There was something beyond love in their relationship. Otherwise this feeling could not have lasted for so long, challenging so many storms that raged in the meantime. This conviction may have contributed to my keeping this secret for so many years. Now I feel compelled to share my experiences. I can put an end to my story at this point. However, before I do, let me touch on a point which may have aroused your curiosity. No, I did not see Marcellina after that night. Long after, I thought I had felt her presence in Buenos Aires where I happened to be on duty. She had apparently broken with that senior officer with whom she had been sharing her life, and lived all alone in a small modest apartment, while a close watch was kept over her. That was all I could learn. She had become unattainable to me. I had no other choice but to acknowledge this fact. I wondered if she occasionally dreamt of the days she and Berti had spent together. Life was a stage play that gained meaning through unexpected developments and funny jokes. However, certain actors, for one reason or another, despite all these jokes and the fact that the play was drawn-out, never met again. If this was the joke, I must say it fell a bit flat. If we were a little more daring or willing, perhaps we could provide an answer for such questions. As a matter of fact, we were not simply the actors of the play but also its author. We wrote our own plays piecemeal in others. Some of us got older quicker in this gamesmanship through losses, while those who succeeded remained in a more childlike state. This was, I think, the essential difference among us. As I keep on brooding over these things now, it occurs to me that Marcellina, who must now be leading a completely different life in Buenos Aires in the company of new acquaintances, is most likely feeling nostalgic about her past life in Cambridge. This scene of the play to which we are the spectators seems to meet all expectations. I guess we'll no longer come across each other in the coming scenes. Under the circumstances, the penning of the play will quite probably be carried on by us, as before, in our respective corners; each one of us writing it for his immediate neighbor, in his own words, seeing to it that what he writes with close mutual empathy is not articulated. However, you have also been involved in this now; you are one of the bearers of this secret. You're not going to communicate this to Berti. He is still convinced that he happens to be the bearer of an immaculate soul; uncorrupted by life. In truth, this may be. After all . . . " Suddenly Berti had come back, interrupting our conversation at the very moment when I was going to be entrusted with another secret. Gordon had his head screwed on in the right way. Conscious of the changed atmosphere, he had altered the course of our discussion. He knew well how to steer the conversation away. "And London is no longer the same London. I believe she pays the price for her atrocities in the colonies. We are but the children or grandchildren of those colonialists; this is unfair, is it not?" Berti had cut in and added: "He is my chum all right, but a bloody leftist all the same; beware of expressing your points of view so openly." This comment had made us laugh; we had forced ourselves to laugh, in fact. What we had laughed at was the diversity of people acting in a variety of ways, in the face of the range of the sentiments nestled in human beings. This had not restrained us from raising our glasses by proposing a toast to the cads, to those dirty leftists. A few minutes silence had followed. I could openly assert the reason for my muteness; I wonder if they could do the same. Could they openly declare in which photographs they still lingered, could they openly say which photographs had accompanied their upbringing? I may provide an answer for this question when I succeed in penetrating certain dark corners of this story. Gordon had broken the silence. "You haven't been late enough," he said. He stared at me with a smile like a teacher who had caught his student's indulgence. "Your friend and I had a chat. To be precise, he has been the one who was kind enough to patiently listen to me. However our long talk couldn't possibly be squeezed in during the time you were absent. In other words, the writer who would wish to commit it to paper would have a hard time of it," he added. It seemed as though Gordon knew beforehand that a conversation destined to be put into black and white would change its color under the influence of other conversations which would cause it to be interspersed with their fragmentary contents. We could not possibly have guessed after a given point which conversation had been fed by which talks, what we had added to other people's talks which we transmitted to others. This meant that reported talks also underwent changes . . . live talks, just like plain truths. The fact that all these things were within the compass of his store of knowledge, the fact that he was familiar with them by direct experience, the fact that he had beheld and otherwise had personal knowledge of them had displeased me. This had led me to interpret the smile on his face as the condescending gesture of a teacher. However, what had made me restive was, in the main, the unexpected revelation of my identity, my identity in the story. I had already felt the vulnerability of the past; it possessed a kind of seductiveness; it connoted an unsatisfied sexual drive: an unfulfilled desire for sexual outlet and gratification. These words had made me blush, an indefinable shame, defying all description. I had tried to pull myself together and said: "Then, we could see to it that Berti will feel slightly off color for a little while; a colic, for instance, which will keep him in the WC for some time. The cause of this uneasiness might be our hero's compulsion to regress to past experiences. However, he was not supposed to disclose this. When he comes back he will say: 'I wanted you two to chat for a while, to get to know each other better.' Thus, the seal of secrecy relating to things desired to be unsaid will be kept unbroken, and suspicion will thus be avoided." Gordon's reply had been: "Not too bad . . . Berti could do it." "I thought so," I said, whereupon Gordon added: "Let me go out and get some fresh air." This had caused us to chuckle once again. Gordon had not allowed us to benefit from the momentary silence and said: "Well, time to part!" After all he had not come to Istanbul for fun. We had to excuse him. In fact, he said he would be back in Istanbul again in a short while, under different conditions; when life would permit him to live as his conscience would dictate. He accompanied us leaving the hotel. He kept his eyes peeled to his surroundings with the reserve and undivided attention of a restless individual intent on getting acquainted with the neighborhood. He gave the impression of some-one who had been in search of someone he had been anticipating. Berti had asked his friend—whose bond had been refreshed after so many years even for a very brief period of time—what sort of business he was engaged in. This was an issue not touched upon during our long talk. After some consideration, with his two arms spread on our shoulders, gently smiling, he whispered, as if confiding a se-cret: "International business, y'know!"

Then he had waved his hand and parted after saying: "As I've said; I'll come back, even though it may be in a distant future . . . I'll be with you in my new guise . . . for life's sake; rigged out with a little joke." A little joke . . . These words would, in time, fit Gordon among the figures of that photograph which I have the habit of ignoring. For life's sake, a little joke . . . Could this be linked with Marcellina, in one way or another? There were stories which we refrained from disclosing to certain people; which we found extremely arduous to take the lid off of . . . Gordon and I, we had exchanged meaningful glances for the last time, at least as far as this story is concerned. My glances were supposed to confirm the pledge I had given him to keep his secret. At the same time, this marked the last moment of the dialogue we had dared to engage in, which we had tried to carry within ourselves to quite another arena. We were henceforth doomed to stay within the enclosure of this secret, which would trigger my very return to the secret time and time again. The serenity that Gordon's face reflected, the serenity which I had anticipated to observe, sparked off a special meaning generated by our shared fate. The story unfolded elsewhere, of a woman who lived far away and led a life unconscious of my existence. Who knows, I might one day decide to set off in a cloud of dust and follow the path that would lead me to her. I'm trying to convince myself that I have finally succeeded in causing the individual toward whom I had been called to share a similar destiny to empathize with this sentiment. What I had experienced reminded me of a completely different story I had entrusted to other totally different people in a completely different place, although under different circumstances. Could this be a play in which we were obliged to act, in which we would be mere spectators on different stages, whose secret bonds between the acts and scenes we could discern only when we moved far from the actual episodes? What energy had crossed the paths of Marcellina and Anita, on a shared ground of destiny? Could this be that feeling of revolt lying in our depths which I am convinced I'll be able to disclose as I see fit one day? Shall I ever be able to put in an appearance before an audience equipped with what I have been bequeathed by these people? I wonder where or with whom I'll be carrying on my existence or in whose story I would like to continue to live? Shall I be able to make these stories credible enough? I haven't found the opportunity to discuss these details with anyone. There was another detail from whose boundary we returned, from which we had to return. A detail from whose boundary we were compelled to return that we failed to insert into our story, a detail concealed which could not have been unearthed except through Berti, in view of his past experiences. How was one supposed to complete that excavation? Which photograph was that detail concealed in, and in whose custody did it lay? To this day I have failed to find an answer to this question. The answer is still important for some people, I know. Yet, at this juncture, there is no way to proceed other than to nurture some hope that a new anticipation or eventuality may appear, despite all that I know, or, to be precise, despite all that I feel. It was not for nothing that Gordon mentioned that he would return to Istanbul when the time came in the guise of an individual who had undergone a transformation . . . to return to a new city in the garb of a new man . . . these words must have been analogous somewhere in the future . . . to return to a new city in the garb of a new man . . . What we had tried to communicate to each other may have been that hope.

Gordon would, in the meantime, remain stranded.

Then, in another solitude, we would proceed, traveling on a beaten path toward a house familiar to us . . . on toward a familiar house, in stereotypical steps. Having left behind the self-same individual in differing solitudes with different associations, we were heading for Nişantaşı, in our capacity as heroes of a story being written in bits and pieces, trying to find our true locations and to remain therein to the bitter end, and, what is more important still, striving to understand and express ourselves better. I had tried once more to place Berti somewhere between my fantasies and errors. This was my way of dealing with something I liked to carry around with me: my play, my solitude. "He cuts the figure of an intelligence officer . . . I mean . . . Well, skip it!" he said after a long hiatus. At such awkward moments speech failed him and he became charming. "You heard him, he is internationally engaged; what more do you want!" I rejoined. We had continued to walk. I believe we were in need of different fictions and words. We had preferred to keep silent; to cover up certain feelings that rose in us and made us feel like discussing other people's lives. "What did he tell you in my absence?" he asked. "He told me about Marcellina. He told me that she was a formidable woman." This had made him smile. Far from being a wry smile, it was like the smile of a boy who had just learned that he had come off an exam with flying colors . . . I knew the boy hidden behind that smile.

Spring reminds me of separations

There are certain times in your life when you feel that you are being swept off toward an ineluctable fate by which your actual personality, or the person you would like to be, is carried away. These are the moments when you realize that you are inexorably linked to yourself despite all your illusions. You lapse into silence, and find yourself speechless. You don't want to open your mouth; for you have things that you would prefer would remain undisclosed. I think that these moments were, for me, the moments that revealed my inner child during my lonely walk. Gordon could not have dodged the issue. A bolt from the blue, an unexpected encounter would put us off track, adding color to our wandering . . . Well, it was a sunny evening in which everybody was making preparations for the new season. On such evenings, one perceives the scent of those future summer evenings, harbinger of more radiant days ahead. That scent stealthily attracts you towards it, and you find yourself proceeding with cautious steps lest other people may get a hint of your action. There are times when I ask myself why on earth we keep looking back to the days we have left behind instead of those ahead, despite all that we have gone through in the past. At such times it occurs to me to think of returns, of all kinds of returns, of which there have been some that had enslaved me. I ruminate on wrong steps taken and on ill-matched couples. There I come across songs and delusions that shatter my personality. What is the love that faces you at the least expected moments in a garb you hardly anticipated? I have vague recollections . . . I happened to be in a state which would prompt me to put such questions to myself; to the person I have been on familiar terms with for a long time. It was a sunny evening in Istanbul, a time when the deceptive image of Bodrum was not yet visible and had not been offered to abuse the population. "I'm planning to go to the island earlier this year. I told Juliet. I told her that we had a house there and the weather was fine . . . She told me that my father was getting on in years and that we had to take him with us this summer; she added that the weather was fine all right but not enough to warm up his bones as of yet. When stillness reigns on the island time has a special attraction for him. We all seem to be somewhat out of sorts these days . . . More about this later however . . . This will not last forever, will it? How about taking the ferry on weekends and carrying out repairs at home or tending the garden . . . In summer you'll be my guest. You didn't show up once last year. You know well that our door is always open for you. You'll come, won't you?" Berti said. "I will, don't worry. Last year was different. We were all shaken by what had happened. That summer had taken from each of us a part of ourselves never to be recovered." We had arrived at a critical point beyond which there should be no trespassing; we might make an allowance for a limited number of associations. The matter should rest at the point where it had already reached and not be elaborated further. I saw that he had empathized with the resentment I bore within me as a true friend who felt helpless. However, despite the sentiments that were provoked by that reality we had been poorly conscious of, and had failed to perceive, by that reality which we were unsuccessful in communicating to each other, he, like me, had opined not to trespass that prohibited zone. Time might be propitious to allow us to cross over certain boundaries. The discussion of the bitter experiences we had gone through might be held off for years, by which time other painful suffering may have compounded them. Both of us were conscious of this fact; conscious too were the people who had willingly or otherwise been involved during those days. We needed time. It had not been for nothing that we had shouldered the burden of those relationships that entertained receding hopes in us and were caught up in frantic struggles. We needed time; time which would enable us to use our wits only after being deeply wounded; time which would enable us to indicate in due course the importance of certain touches; time which would allow us to perpetuate our self-reliance. Under the circumstances how far could we depend on the words that told us about our place in life, on words that drew us near to, and moved us away from others? We did have words that had served to communicate our experiences and our aspirations to our distant relatives, while at the same time severing the man within us away from those countries, sentencing us to a sorrowful exile. I'm well aware that there had been a break in Berti's flow of communication. Here, I perceived a missing link difficult to explain. This was the first time this happened to me. I'm not trying to share it with any of the spectators of my fantasy. I'm obliged to share the same destiny with those who had inseminated my mind with a great variety of stories. At present I feel like I'll be able to tread that path one day, that true path for the sake of those people. For, certain conversations lead you to your true place as you move forward. Certain talks across the table gain permanence only for you and embody vital forces. You are inclined to believe in magic . . . to deliver yourself up to that magical influence and let yourself be carried off by it . . . even though you may realize that the words uttered by a speaker are transformed over many years into the words of the listener. Berti had told me that evening that springtime redeemed separations from oblivion. He had always sought an opportunity to have a confidential chat with me. We were in pursuit of a voice, a voice that we knew very well. I'd done my best to devote my attention to it. There was a reason for it, to lend an ear, to show him that my listening had become a secret pleasure, far beyond my sense of responsibility. I took pleasure in playing the role of a spectator who occasionally chose to take part in the performance. This was another method of dealing with pain more easily by watching the bitter experiences of other people. I felt at home at the place I had chosen, I had found out the mystery that this section of my past contained, and I had adhered to this belief; I had been able to do that. To believe, to be able to believe, even though superficiality was tantamount to feeling that you were attached to certain things. What I had opted for was undoubtedly evil; an evil I, now and then, took notice of during my reminiscing. But I had no other choice at the time. Eventually everybody was doomed to live with what he deserved. "My separations from Marcellina and Ginette had coincided with such occasions. Those days and those women had been different. But seasons look alike . . . " he added. There was no doubt that those days indeed brought new things. As for women, had they been really different in their manifestations? If one considered femininity and the meanings attributed to it, were women really at odds with each other? That evening I had been pursuing a woman with whom I was in love, enamored with more fervently then ever, who now seems to be gradually vanishing from my mind. This was a woman whose traits escaped me but whose presence behind a screen was indisputable, whose taboo would one day be revealed to me, I was sure of it. Was this a dream, a movie in which a comedy was being enacted? Was this dream no different than the songs we lend an ear to only to forget shortly after? I am asking these questions without seeking an answer. Answers can only be provided by those who still imagine themselves listening to that song at night in the company of that woman. I may have felt compelled to say, "Juliet was not so bad after all," to involve our women in our journeys, even though each of us had different inclinations. The place which had been left vacant by those women who had formerly fled but were presently trying to put in an appearance on the scene, was occupied by another woman . . . In reply to my suggestion Berti said: "You're perfectly right there. Juliet is a nice woman. I'm much indebted to her." He had resumed his boyish air. "How about coming to us tonight? Give a call to your people and tell them you'll be late. You don't want to remain outdoors for long, crowds upset you; you rush back to your den to lock yourself in like a misanthropist. The timing couldn't be better! Come, let's have dinner together for a change: Juliet will be preparing a delicious meal; the *entrée* will likely consist of duck with lime sauce served with artichoke bottoms filled with baby carrots plus leeks baked in Caerphilly sauce! On our way home we'll buy some salami, a spread made with fish roe, snacks from the delicatessen; anything you want." A silence had ensued, after which he added with a plaintive voice: "Believe me, Juliet has missed you so much! Only the other day we were speaking of you. She said: 'He used to visit us more often and didn't spare me his compliments. Well, we are still up and about. Tell the good old boy that our relationship had not been so cheap! If he expects to be my lover, let him behave decently!'" He was no longer the boy of before; he was a hero of a spy movie that shuttled between adolescence and estranged adulthood . . . It was evident that his intention was to drag our relationship back to the former warmth that the three of us had created. In this affiliation the key person should be Juliet without a doubt. His words took on that shape. I should deem Berti's call only too natural considering what we had been through. He had already crossed over certain boundaries despite our dodging and hiding. The time we had grasped by both hands was likely to upset certain people and make them envious. The time in question comprises certain things in our very depths far beyond the love that I could not and did not define; certain things that deserve the attribute 'original,' very different, if we consider our boundaries. On one of those nights when we had gathered together our shortcomings, dreams, and resentments about ourselves and others, I had told them an anecdote from my childhood and made them laugh. I had a train which looked almost exactly like a real one. The train fell over a bridge I had built between two chairs. Among its passengers were a mother and a small boy. During a series of accidents the mother and the boy were killed alternately. Our house had a big garden. I used to fill the pool with water and tried to make my train float but could not help seeing it swallowed by the ocean. I was all alone when I did this. All the details are still fresh in my mind except for the final destination, the train is now lost. A day came when I realized that the train had left my life for good. Having heard this, Juliet, with her matronly behavior had approached, not without a traditionally feminine poise, and sat in my lap putting her arms around me and whispered: "You know what; you are a stout-hearted fellow! Why don't you kidnap me! I'm ready to elope wherever you take me. We could perhaps unearth that train after all . . . and once we spot it we can board it and away we go! You'll have rescued me from this dreary life." "Wait! Not so fast! It's alright with me; so much the better in fact. I'll be freed from this yoke! But beware! I like you. I'd hate to see you seduced! The woman you set your eyes upon is not the woman you imagine her to be; she will mortify you! Understand?" said Berti. This short 'sex play' was enacted in that house on many an occasion in improvised versions. Roles were cast as follows: Juliet would be the woman always ready to leave her husband and throw herself into the arms of the man who would offer her a life of exciting sexual adventure; Berti would cut the figure of a despondent man ready to sacrifice everything to get rid of the woman with whom he had been with for so long. The play might well have been staged just to arouse certain latent feelings, as it had, to my mind, an informative character as well. We were free to go beyond certain boundaries: when we felt drawn to each other, we were free to take the required steps. A touch of prostration must have been concealed in our smiles. What we were after was to strengthen our belief in ourselves rather than to represent the experiences we tried to communicate to our spectators. I think I had the greatest need for this as someone who had not yet established his role and who had recourse to return to his store of fantasies in the hope that this would give a cue to what he was supposed to recite. In that section of the play Juliet had gone near Berti and turning to me had pressed her body on the man whom she loved and said: "That's the reason why I love this guy, just because he's not wise enough to love me and fully appreciate my value. Well, such are women, my dear! The time will come when you'll see it for yourself." Those scenes went on taking place in this fashion.

At present I happen to be somewhere quite removed from those representations, where the story has called me. The new places I was supposed to see and explore greatly contributed to my understanding of the places from which I had moved away. One could have an overall view of disparate things and juxtapose them in new and unexpected combinations. There were instances which justified Juliet's behavior. There had been times when I thought I had had an insight into Berti's motive for undertaking those long walks, times when I felt lonely and remorseful, times I couldn't possibly talk about to anyone. Those were the times when I deemed myself justified in my actions and wished that this self-assurance be embedded in me. That was my time. New places had caused me to take stock of certain things which I had failed to see before. Berti and Juliet happened to be cast in that truth they desired to represent to me in that little play they enacted, a truth expressed through mimicry. I had shared different secrets with them at different times. These secrets were pregnant with surprising, enigmatic stories and heroes. In other words, the secrets shared were from a different time, a fact they knew all too well. What they did not know, and preferred not to learn, were the details and the extent to which they unmasked them by reflecting their images in the mirror. They had reserved a place for me in their life as a man who knew how to lend an ear to them and keep their secrets. The strange thing was that the other family members had also adopted the same attitude. Under the circumstances, I had to learn how to play that role as best I could with the touch of a hero destined to narrate the story of certain people, that long story, which reminded me now and then of other fictions. Berti's invitation to his place after all that had happened carried a special meaning. We had to protect what we had experienced from sinking into oblivion, what had truly been lived. Under the circumstances Juliet's womanliness had occupied a place of its own, despite certain reservations. The truths were the truths that we whispered into each other's ears in a different tone and impressed upon each other accordingly. She had grasped the meaning of this expectation as much as I had. Her contours that evening reminded one of a woman who was immersed in the process of forgetting. They fitted her identity as an ex-player quite well. "All right, I'll come," I said, "But, we must buy some flowers somewhere; I know that Juliet loves flowers." "Indeed! There is in fact a flower shop nearby," he observed. The flower shop happened to be right there, aiding us with our story. I had bought a bouquet of gillyflowers disregarding all the likely blunders arising from this choice. It was my intention to return to that house with the scents I was once fond of. As we stepped out from the shop the poem produced by those small images crossed my mind once again. The poem represented our efforts to get used to the little deceptions that stemmed from that time, allowing us to cling to something. The poem was our renewed lie . . . Life was being penned for others in totally different versions, with totally different expectations. The same might hold true for a few words inscribed in a language we were not familiar with on a stone tablet. Have we been knocking on the door of the same house over all these centuries? We had taken a few steps when Berti said: "Nora has left." His voice was tremulous like the voice of an agitated man that betrayed his inner struggle, that had been lying concealed and had not yet found expression, about a truth he would have liked to disclose but was unable to do so. He was staring fixedly in front of him. He seemed to be looking within himself for a fault. There was something wrong in all these things. But what exactly? He looked like the harbinger of bad news; of bad news intended for a dear friend. Under the circumstances everybody would be living once more in their own solitude as though they wanted to experience the same words and feelings, reminding them of other heroes of other stories relating to the same figures. "I've been intending to tell this to you for quite some time now . . . It was a terrible shock for Juliet; she said bitter words and had to face scathing retorts; she felt that all she had done for her daughter had proved to be ill spent. Well, as a mother, she had her failings. I tried to tell her, to make her understand that what we thought we had been doing for Nora was actually performed to gratify our own egos." "After all," I said, "Nora has done what you would have done yourself. She chose her own life. The only thing that differs would be the way you'd choose to arrive at the same end. You're two sheep of the same flock." He said: "She would not hear of my admonition. Rosy wept a lot . . . Poor thing . . . She felt helpless . . . She's always been a poor thing, you know . . . 'Enough!' she yelled, 'Stop trying to humiliate each other! You're not going to be pulled asunder, are you?' But her voice was hardly audible in the din they made. That evening she was with her fiancé. She looked happy. Personally, he has not impressed me. But what can we do? It's kismet, as they say. My father is of the same opinion but looks resigned. 'Never mind! Leave it to time!' he says. You know him. Juliet, on the other hand, has something on her mind, of which she does not speak. To my mind she has not given too much thought to it, not as much as she should have done. She had a preference for Nora and she never tried to conceal it. This is the reason why I exercise my discretion for Rosy. Yet, I think I cannot accentuate my devotion as I ought to. I tried to have a talk with her. 'You know, dear, you can tell me, if you feel out of sorts for some reason or other. Come on, let's have a heart-to-heart talk together.' I told her. 'I'm fine daddy, don't worry about me!' Well, she's trying to make her own path. So, we're by ourselves tonight, just the three of us. Just like in the old days, in the good old days . . . " Yes, just like in the good old days. These words . . . had they been the lyrics of those old songs that invited us to partake in those deceptions and delusions that had lulled us? Just like in the good old days . . . We were perfectly conscious of the fact that the past was past and no past experience could be resuscitated no matter what one did. No word, no talk, no look, no touch could henceforth be the same . . . No night, no dawn, no summer evening would be the same . . .

We were passing by the movie theater Konak. I had a memory connected with this structure. Berti didn't know what this memory had generated and kept alive within me, which was more important still. This episode was exclusively my secret, and was bound to remain so, forever apparently. There, in the dark stood a boy who had experienced an aberration he could never forget, which was deeply engraved on the recesses of his mind. Our stares had been simultaneously directed at the poster, but most probably from different angles. Certain details still lingered in my memory. A French movie entitled *Gifle* was on. I heard the name of Isabella Adjani for the first time. The film was about the problems encountered in the relationship between a father and his young girl who had just come of age. Days one had lived during one's adolescence were generally forgotten by the time one reached adulthood. The image of the father slapping the face of his daughter was to be forever imprinted on the minds of the cinemagoers. It was a moment of confrontation between father and daughter; an unanticipated meeting, as though it was the moment when they first touched each other. The actor that played the part was Lino Ventura. Berti had a passion for movies; a trait inherited from his maternal aunt. He made no distinctions between films; he tried not to miss any of the movies running in his neighborhood. What was more important for him was the movie theater rather than the movie itself, this was an integral part of his life; the same passion was shared by Aunt Tilda. What puzzled me and was an object of regret was that despite the fact they both were aware of each other's passion, they had never lived under the same roof for any period of time. It may be that they were afraid of each other's fervid imaginations, or perhaps they wanted to shun each other's company for that very reason. They may have been afraid of each other's imaginative power, or preferred to give vent to their own stretch of imagination, each in his or her own world, as they were aware they could not possibly share with anybody what they felt and experienced within their respective zones of security. I believe we also had the same experience in our cinematic adventure and lived in the same isolation with one voluntary difference. Our divergent looks converged on the same poster through different angles. "I wonder where he is these days!" said Berti. To further enhance my puzzlement as I stood baffled, he added: "I don't think I've told you, have I? Lino Ventura happens to be a distant relative of mine." My amazement had generated a faintly malicious smile on his face. It was a smile that seemed to betray the apparently huge joke that his cynical, humorous behavior had exhibited. Was this the manifestation of a secret crossing of the family members, a confidential matter kept secret from me? Berti appeared to be pleased to see me struck dumb. I once had the idea to play a trick which I thought would boggle Berti's mind. The proposed line of action would be the following: Berti would be sitting on the balcony of a villa overlooking the Bosporus in the company of an attractive woman—an authoress with whom I conjectured to discuss the outlines of the plan in question—sipping at his drink while listening to a catchy song. The script would contain an echo of our long walks. To bring such actions—a product of our fantasies, undertaken by both of us in turn—into a state of equilibrium and stability should be considered normal. However, the real meaning of the actions in question would reveal itself to me years later, when I dared to look into the hidden aspects of certain words. On the day I read of the death of Lino Ventura in the daily, I had called him to give my condolences. In the meantime, we had given up going on our walks together. We were living on borrowed time; despite our best efforts and all those things that we had shared in the past, we belonged to other places henceforth; it was as though we took care not to let our voices be heard by each other except on rare occasions during infrequent telephone calls and casual encounters. Some people, regardless of their mutual intimacy, discover that their paths converge. Whatever has been experienced in the past, regardless of the shared days and nights, this common point of destination happens to be the spot wherein all other contingencies seem to be exhausted. One realizes that all efforts have been in vain. The good will, the wishes and the procrastinations fall short of filling the gap that has been formed. Separation guides the relationship to its natural floodplain and transports it to a union in antipodal latitudes. Our relations were to continue to be cultivated at the opposite side of the earth. Upon my imparting him with the sad news, he had lapsed into a momentary silence before he observed with what sounded like a wry smile: "Confound it! We hadn't been in contact lately." The trick had quite unexpectedly achieved the desired effect. I had immensely enjoyed the result. I want to believe more than ever that we had indeed relished this experience during that telephone conversation for the sake of those bygone days.

To my mind, at present, what has actually remained from that evening is neither Berti's experience at the time, nor his latent identification with Lino Ventura, nor the common impression that this little trick had generated. As far as I'm concerned, what has remained with me from that night was the movie theater I miss. The movie theater in question, alas no more, had connotations that went well beyond that dark moment within me. This movie theater with its spacious flight of steps and walls carved in high relief must still be fresh in the memory of the moviegoers. Konak was the name of the movie theater which had not been demolished; the bookshop too was spared a few yards away. I'm aware that all these reminiscences have nothing original about them, in that they can be observed nearly everywhere in the world, in any climate. The fact was that certain corners and landmarks of the city continued their functions elsewhere for certain individuals. The solitude that remained would still be the same solitude; no hope, no evasion, no truancy brought it change. I would realize this better in another movie theater while watching a spin-off about yet another movie theater. Man could not easily accept being deprived of certain things he had been accustomed to. One had to learn about dying in order to be able to live with death. This may have been the reason why that boy afraid to lose his toys kept surging in my imagination.

We stood before the bookshop, scanning the titles displayed in the window, "I read a story a couple of days ago," said Berti. It had been Berti's custom to buy British newspapers and take them home with special diligence; he took great pleasure in carrying them with such pride. As far as I can remember *The Guardian* was his favorite paper. I don't know if this choice was the reason why he preferred to keep it rolled up. What I was sure about was that he never read it. He was a bit of a show-off, you know. To act the showman, to adopt extravagant and willfully conspicuous behavior, to seek to attract attention to things he wished not to be consigned to oblivion were, I think, among his distinctive traits. Could it be that in sharing the story he was said to have read, he was displaying similar mannerisms? Maybe. In think I can understand his concern. "The story itself has nothing extraordinary about it; it is one of those stories that we come across sometime, somewhere, quite unexpectedly. Claptrap eloquence, you know. However, I have it enshrined in my memory; never have been able to forget it, in fact."

His words had reminded me of an evening in the past. Berti continued: "The hero has a Brazilian lover whom he had met during his years of study in Paris. The woman is married. But the love that has kindled seems to be genuine. Strong are the ties between them. Notwithstanding their mutual passion, they are obliged to return to their respective homes; the man back to Istanbul, the woman to Rio. Their correspondence regularly continues up until it gradually peters out. Life had pulled them asunder. After the lapse of a good many years, the man sees her one night in his dream and tries to communicate with her (and to other people besides) the grief he had felt over his failure to accompany her to Rio; to the city of his beloved. He complains about his frustration concerning his attempts at leaving Istanbul and about being cooped up in the house keeping his elderly maternal aunt, obsessed with a Paris she had never seen, company; trying to draw an analogy between her dreams and his own fantasies of cities he embellishes in his imagination, doomed to remain ever inaccessible to him. Inaccessible cities, lives spent to no purpose, loves thwarted . . . A hit-and-miss story, marked by a lack of a definite plan or method, a sustained purpose; there are too many 'ands,' 'ifs,' and 'buts' all right! I've got it at home; I may give it to you just to browse through at your leisure. You may well guess why it affected me. Sometimes one is surprised to see the uncanny similarity between certain lives," he concluded. He looked a bit absentminded and tired. I didn't have to mull over the fact that this had nothing to do with the effect of the season upon us which we could not ignore and which all of us had to resign had its influences. "All right, I'll read it; I'm sure I can spare some time for it," I said. He had patted me on the shoulder with a broad smile. This smile seemed to cover up a modest victory, another aspect of that joke; years had to go by before I had an inkling of it.

At the delicatessen we had purchased two bottles of wine, some Italian salami, a few slices of ham, and Gruyere. Salt bonito should be done justice to, but the shopkeeper said that he had not any left of which he would be proud to offer me. This was his conventional way of handling so-called privileged customers. The public took delight in receiving preferential treatment. To be considered someone, to be a person of considerable influence or prestige was the cherished ideal of everyone; this meant catching special treatment at the least expected moment. Berti could not possibly ignore the absurdity inherent in the idea; nevertheless, he had liked being treated in this way.

It was a September morning

As we drew nearer home the artichoke dish that Juliet must have prepared presented itself once more to our imagination. It was supposed to be served as an *entrée* cooked with lemon and sugar in the proper consistency. This might be taken for a starting point, an important event not to be overlooked. However, there was another point deserving attention. Berti had, by these comments, wanted to guide me to a new reality. Passover was being held and there was only unleavened bread available. I might have been disillusioned, but I was obliged to conform to the prevailing customs, to a future at least. What had been uttered during our walk undoubtedly had a certain nicety. However, to be frank, these words had not only served as an introduction but also provided clues betraying his view on life and his attitude toward Juliet. These words seemed to be shedding some light on certain points; namely, on what steps had been taken, or not taken, and to whom they were directed in that spacious drawing-room at Nişantaşı leaving lasting imprints on me, properly expressed or unexpressed. The clues were hidden between the lines. The meaning he attached to the Feast of Passover, the way he conceived it, the way he was associated with it looked like the expression of an attitude. He often criticized the blind submission of religious fanatics to preset rules, which, he thought to be the greatest obstacle to modernization. He scoffed at the problematic nature of edible things. Pork cutlets titillated his palate. In restaurants that served alcohol he took delight in sardonically criticizing his mother who had never tasted crustaceans in her life saying: "Tu no comes estos guzanos porche no lo tinenez visto en la casa del papa!" (I'm sure you won't touch these crabs, lobsters, and shrimps as you failed to savor them in the paternal house). At such times he happened to be hanging out with his father, who could also be interpreted as being an accomplice in the fraud. Strange to say, such occasions were the rare moments in which father and son were close to each other. The prohibition of eating leavened bread during the Feast of Passover did not apply, for him, to lunch taken at the office. 'Home' and 'outdoors' should be discerned. It was understandable to conform to traditions at home, to a reasonable extent. He was one of the faithful who paid a visit to the synagogue for religious worship, to attend a funeral service, or to celebrate a feast day or wedding. Only on such occasions he felt he ought to take part in the congregation and observe the ritual. He never failed to put on his Sunday clothes on such occasions. He attached great importance to the image he left in the imagination of the public. He fasted on the Day of Atonement and paid a visit to the synagogue when the time of breaking the fast drew near, in order to feel refreshed. He had told me once that he was fascinated by the chants that must have reminded him that the Day was drawing to a close, that it was about time to return home and break the fast in the presence of all the members of the family and that his sins were about to be forgiven. However, no one could be sure about the exactitude of this interpretation, especially coming from a person who had lost his faith somewhere during the course of his life. This chant had united a community scattered the world over, one facing language barriers that God had contrived upon the ambition of Babel, who had strived over the course of ravages to unite and worship the same God. The faithful had followed the path that had been indicated in the book and would continue to do so till the end of time. All these things considered, Berti was certainly not alone. It might be that this common faith and shared past made him happy and content. This might be an easy way to satisfy oneself as to one's religion. A comment like, "Personally, I'm not devout, but I honor my obligations; as you know old habits die hard, following them gives a man peace of mind" might express the attitude of a person who had found the true path. Berti might have taken this path in order to avoid the vicissitudes of the human condition. He had to keep up appearances . . . keeping up appearances, yes. This sentence would uphold forever the validity of the adage for people who lived like him, who had taken the same path. Certain sayings remained ever fresh for certain people. To what extent were the visions and the representations true? This question had not been answered by anyone who had contributed to the making of this artificial sanctuary. No changes loomed ahead thereafter. Silence had its voice; silence was a kind of talk within those walls. No one had put that question to Berti, no one ever tried. What I saw was Berti's predilection for remaining penned within the said vision like everybody who had opted wholeheartedly for a lifestyle similar to his, with a view to doing away with that unprecedented shadow that followed him on his heels. If anyone asked for the meaning of the adverb 'wholeheartedly,' a new interpretation might be tried for. However, like everywhere else, in order to be able to ask such a question, we were obliged not to ignore some of our fantasies. Otherwise, for those who would be reluctant to put forward that question, the visual impact would be of a conservative representation with well-defined traits that would vouch for the smooth running of everything. What was required of him was to be a human being; a human being that everybody knew could survive and breathe freely in those climates. The human being required had been provided in return for a security—like being under an umbrella. Agreement foresaw consideration . . . In such agreements you could beat a retreat and toss your grievances into some backyard to be irremediably lost forever. This pursuit of an irretrievable loss of memory would be the subject of a story in due time. This was the time of hushed betrayal; the time of betrayal that man nourished within himself and did not communicate to others. I had a deep affection for Berti, especially during his periods of introversion when he had taken cognizance of this betrayal or at least when I came to realize that he knew it was there. However, he never understood the fact that I liked him because of this very character trait he tried to conceal, to be precise, because of this resentment. I had shared with him my introspective dialogue which had not found utterance as of yet and with which I had a choice of different words to voice its expression. This may have been the reason why we could never part in the proper sense of the word.

Could it be that Berti had lied 'to his people,' along with himself, the man he had been asked to be? Answering this question has never been easy for me. This was a zone in which truth and lies could not be identified properly unless you rose to the challenge of following a certain path; you could not distinguish between what was true and false; you could not have an inkling of what fortitude was. I had been ignorant myself of these things at the time, even thereafter. There was no end to the questions; they came back upon you whether you liked it or not. Questions were never lacking . . . We had in our possession the things that we had been carrying along with those men, our nightmares, and our erroneous touches. Frankly, I had reached a stage where I gave credence to what was both true and false. What should have been of importance was not of consequence in contrast to abiding by the laws of a tradition—there being innumerable people who have succeeded in living this attachment in due coherence—the essential thing was the enactment of a play, the desire to put it on the stage, Berti's incapacity to truly believe in that sentiment he said he lent credence to. He had not even discussed it with himself; he could not bring himself to discuss it. To duly observe traditions, to make a show of this observance, was one of the easiest ways to hide oneself in this lifestyle. He was, like those who had taken part in such a play, but a spectator of his experiences, of his own self . . . Could it be that Berti had this experience on the path he had taken that he expected to lead to Juliet?

To be frank, I never wanted to witness this aspect of the relationship of two individuals I loved so much and with whom I had formed a link laden with a multitude of hope. Because, through this relationship they had chosen, for the sake of my, of our story, to appear like individuals who had failed to cross over the boundaries of my dilemmas, of things I would one day try to make heard through my tales. I owed them the possibility of belonging to a different time. Nevertheless, whether I wanted to or not, my experiences with them induced me to ask this question. In addition, to what I saw and what I could see, there were also supplemented memories. The factor that had initiated their relationship was a usual meeting that may have occurred between any two people. The meeting had been arranged by a mutual friend. This friend was someone who had made deep impressions on numerous people, according to Juliet. The venue had been Regence, the renowned Russian restaurant in Istanbul, where stories from Belarus were recounted, where Russian literature was discussed to the extent it was within the ken of the participants, and, last but not least, communism. Berti had told of his life in Cambridge while Juliet reminisced about her stage experience. The dinner at Regence was followed by a visit to the nightclub Kervansaray. Among the topics of discussion were fashion, one-time revelries, their inclinations and thoughts based on instinct and desire, as well as the places they would like to visit. They agreed that Crete was their common modest utopia; one had to consider the distance involved. This moment had apparently been the very first instant of which they had truly been intimate with each other. He had accompanied Juliet to her home at Şişli. It was raining and they had preferred to walk in the rain. As they strolled along in the darkness of the night, Juliet's body accidentally touched Berti's a couple of times. This incident, the memory of which was kept secret by both parties, was mutually revealed years later. During the days that followed they visited the nooks and crannies of Istanbul. During a bicycle tour of Büyükada, Berti had proposed to Juliet. This engagement happened only a few months after their dinner at the Regence. Juliet had been anticipating this as the natural course of events. The timing was perfect, especially when one considers the pressure put on by their parents. As the fatal time drew near, the greatest pressure related to the final decision of Madame Roza—who fully backed the arrangement. As a matter of fact, she used to anxiously await her son's return from his sallies, and was fond of learning of his expeditions straight from the horse's mouth. They had a cup of coffee and talked about the old days, of the vicissitudes of life and had a cozy *tête-à-tête*, turning a blind eye to their estrangement. Madame Roza reiterated the same call with different words. What remained with Berti from that dialogue were the following words: "She is a Jewess of a good family. Don't play the false lover with her. Marry her and bring comfort to your life." Had her sentence concealed a latent resentment, was she thus venting the malevolence she had never been able to articulate? I can provide an answer to this question only by taking both alternatives in consideration. Berti chose to take his mother's words with a warm feeling and affection, despite his underlying rebellious tendencies. His opinion commands respect. This attitude of mine may clash with certain inconsistencies I should like to avoid. Nonetheless, the emotions of an individual I would like to represent may gain the upper hand over the adverse sentiments likely to occur during the course of my narration. The essential responsibility lies, I think, in being able to express these emotions. It was a fact that Madame Roza had approached all her children's problems with maternal tenderness and self-sacrifice, as a person who had an unshakable belief in her own judgment, a person resolved to fight her way through anything, never deviating from the path of truth, a woman who proved her worth through such actions. I think Berti had been able to define this better, hiding it away for many years, until the days when his beloved daughter Rosy was making preparations for her wedding. Life would play a little trick on her. She would meet the person whom she had always wanted to avoid, namely Berti. I can visualize that person better now as she tried to endure in that place. I can also understand the rationale of my retracing steps. Options and attitudes to life generate experiences that one should enjoy with all spontaneity. This may have been the reason for our avoidance of one another. Options sometimes meant enslavement, even though this bondage may have been contrary to the spirit of those choices. The same must have held true during the days when Juliet and Berti had wanted to start a new life. Options contained the voice of certain necessities and indispensable truths. In Berti's own words this was the time when those who should be in the lead preferred to remain as silent spectators. It was apparent that certain people had relieved certain people of their roles. The fault lay with the people who had let their role be snatched away. Berti had no need at the time for sharing his experiences on the stage in question. I was well acquainted with the story; and I knew both the spectators and those who had had their roles stolen. The faces of the spectators in the mirror bore secret traits that were difficult to describe. The dowry discussions had taken place at Juliet and Berti's house on a Saturday night, during which Juliet's father had communicated, while sipping at his coffee, his opinion on the subject. According to Madame Roza's account, Monsieur Jacques had declared his approval by declaring "Besimantov!" blessing the future union. "Well," he continued, "the essential thing was the families' getting to know each other, anyhow; considering that the parties have already made up their minds." For him, it was most probably a time to forget all past victories and defeats . . . especially when the places occupied by Olga and Jerry were taken into consideration . . . as he had been able to prove to certain people that he had a family and was a free-handed father not lacking in generosity or kindness, allotting, and distributing. This 'Besimantov,' which was of Hebrew origin, was used the world over where a plurality of languages were spoken by people furtively fed by that common artery, it concealed the pride of those who had trodden the path and who anticipated their children's future favorably, although not without some resignation. A wish for a boy was made at the same time. All that had been suffered previously had been for that sanctuary, to be able to look back with a feeling of wry mirth. Following this solemn event, Juliet had served the guests liqueur chocolates from the silver candy bowl she had brought in for the occasion; it was the family's antique object. The liqueur chocolates had been bought at Baylan, the renowned pastry shop. The engagement had not lasted long. Madame Roza had narrated that eventful day of engagement as faithfully as possible. It had been a September evening straight out of a fairy tale. It was pouring rain. We were in the drawing-room. I was asked to turn on the radio. The music-hour was about to commence. Madame Roza had a special liking for Turkish music. Nora was at the piano in the next room doing her exercises. I believe I have tried to describe this scene, the story of that tune heard from afar, somewhere else. Different were the men, different were the words, different were the hours and the meanings attached. Different were the recollections, especially of the preparations for that evening. Yet, the story was the same despite all the differences. The sentiment was the same, so was the solitude. Yearnings were no different. I wanted to attain an abstraction from empirical reality and the embodiment into a unified conceptual scheme of assumed validity, but failed to do so. The truth was concrete enough, and unimpressive. I think the piano served me in compensating for this lack of execution; the balance was to remain stored, pent up in a little room; it was as though this lack of attainment was tantamount to effecting a melody, a catchy tune to accompany that woman and I to eternity. I have a bare recollection of the piece played on the piano in the next hall; was it one of Chopin's Polonaises? It must've been, in fact it was. All that one went through was essentially a prelude to what one was going to be experiencing one day, what one would most likely be faced with. Madame Roza, who happened to be in the drawing-room, didn't hear that tune; within her was a tune that obsessed her during those days, which none of us could capture. It was raining outside, a rain that could transport us to other evenings, other mornings, and other days we had experienced before. It was a September evening. That evening belonged to a woman who had mothered many children, to be precise to a woman who strove to become her own child. It was one of those evenings she was among us. The music-hour was about to start. Her melody, the melody in her head was certainly different. "This will be the last September I'll ever be able to witness," she said. After a momentary silence she had begun to recount another rainy September day as though from a tale. It had been a Sunday. A September morning . . . a bright, happy morning at the synagogue Zulfaris, where Berti and Juliet's wedding was being celebrated. The bride had in due conformity and custom ascended the stairs on the right and made her entrance to the synagogue, she then descended following the conclusion of the ritual using the stairs on the left, thus setting a foot in her new life. Everybody should follow the path deemed right for them and tread that path without deviating from it. I am still preserving that picture, a picture that we keep on reconstructing according to our respective idiosyncrasies in our own walks of life . . . It was a rainy September morning . . . rain fell gloomily over gloomy stories.

Who did you invite to the wedding banquet?

A voice was concealed that evening and the morning that followed, a voice which would give the meaning of rain a stronger resonance in my memory. My recollections of Berti and Juliet's wedding day had left within me the traces of an unfinished story. Those traces can still lead me to a few distant people . . . the individuals of that Sunday morning had been conducted to me at different times— different people to figure in that play. What are left to me now are my words, simply my words. Voices get mingled. Certain visions remain fixed in the visions conjured up. I suddenly realize that I could be, and I in fact had been, an actor among the figures on the stage of which I was called to be a spectator. We had words that concealed our lies, faults, deceptions, and delusions. We had words whose origins we ignored and tried to avoid . . . words foreign to us, mute strangers to our own words . . . words were our solitudes . . . then . . . then there were those scenes . . . similar to that Sunday morning.

Following the wedding, the guests had proceeded to the house of Monsieur Jacques at Şişli and a banquet was held attended by two experienced hovering waiters who served the dishes fastidiously prepared by Niko and Tanaş from Facio, one of the most renowned fish restaurants in Istanbul, overlooking the Bosporus. Mr. Panayotides, the owner, had done his best to make everything impeccable. Not only was Monsieur Jacques a *habitué* of the place, but also a friend in need. There was a confidential matter between them that accounts for this homage being paid. A secret we could not find out, a secret he knew we could never have access to. This was one of the traits that made Monsieur Jacques who he was. The same was true of his relationships with Monsieur Yorgo, Muhittin Bey, and Niko. Secrets were his secrets; they should be kept secret. It was sufficient for us to know that Panayotidis was grateful to him for some reason or other. Little secrets had to remain as such. I am inclined to believe now that a distance was also felt by other relatives who were custodians of this secret. This belief makes the relationships in question more meaningful and deserving to be reconsidered, retold, and re-shared. That secret inspired certain deficiencies in us that gradually returned; deficiencies were part of our history.

Juliet's mother, who was aware that her feuding brothers would be among the guests, was flustered at first during the days that preceded, and especially so during the exit from the synagogue. However, Madame Roza had been prescient and taken this delicate situation into consideration and arranged the seats accordingly. The situation was accepted with good grace and the problem was solved. Trying to forget was another sort of protraction, of self-evasion; for, had the situation been otherwise, problems with oneself and with others would create insurmountable difficulties. Those that had been witness to the incidents of that morning must have experienced like situations in other stories involving both themselves and others. She had invited the guests to the table with such words as "Today is the day on which the members of our families will have to take up with each other; having this point in mind, I have arranged the seating arrangement accordingly; the seats will thus be occupied alternately, a given member of one family sitting next to a member of the other family." The success she achieved in arraying the guests had earned her the admiration of the invitees as a perfect hostess. The atmosphere had cooled down. Everybody who had been eyeing everybody else with suspicion had suddenly assumed a lenient countenance. This was the general picture, at least. A single vision had covered up the worries of that morning that others had established.

Madame Roza's invitations had been in Spanish; she could have done it in French as well. But the fact that she had preferred to address people in Spanish rather than French, which the present audience had but a broken knowledge of, was because she thought that speaking in the vernacular would make her less presumptuous and self-effacing. This behavior would enhance her respectability. Spanish, she thought, would be the right medium that would warm the atmosphere. Moreover, she could not tell for sure whether all the guests spoke French. Cordiality and fellow feeling had to be promoted, especially between certain individuals. All these things, generated by other experiences and other cordial ties, had happened in the wink of an eye and had not been premeditated. That moment was like a silent uncertain touch to a chance spot.

But for that touch she might have had reason to keep certain reminiscences she believed to have left locked up safe and sound. Madame Roza's particular attention to this fact did not surprise me. I knew that she possessed a wealth of experience which few people could match. This characteristic of hers would one day give birth to a few particularities she would never be able to forget. Partly because of these lost traces, I had tried to discover the true hidden or disguised character of the story. Madame Roza was a woman of certain particulars which might be generally ignored. She was marked by a meticulous, sensitive, and demanding nature, intent upon niceties which one could ignore, but which, in the long run, might covertly alter the course of our lives, without making a show of her diligence. The invitation to the table that day addressed to the families should also be considered from this point of view. The words spoken had been translated into French for those whose origins had not been in Spain, namely for the Ashkenazim who lived in the Rhineland valley and in neighboring France before their migration eastward to Slavic lands. Old hatreds, resentments, and envious rivalries were henceforth consigned to oblivion, quarreling factions were reconciled . . . As time went by everybody learned to accept each other without question or objection, notwithstanding some bickering and altercations between certain people.

Another characteristic of this banquet was the encounter of Juliet's four paternal uncles and two maternal aunts at the same table. Such an encounter had never taken place, before or since. It is to be noted, however, that there had been family members who had not shown up for various reasons. Ginette was one; she was in Israel leading a totally different life. There was another woman whose absence had been deeply felt, at least by a particular person: it was Olga. Olga's fate had obliged her to experience her loneliness and abandonment once more that morning. In particular, Monsieur Jacques must not have been able to rid himself of that feeling that was prompted by the steps he had failed to take that day. That failure had made itself felt despite all efforts. There was another person suffering from the same fate. Madame Roza was not a mere spectator at the place she had chosen or was obliged to be. This fact was known to everybody acquainted with the true story, everybody who had been able to understand it. Everybody had done their duty up to a certain point, everybody . . . Perhaps that was the reason why Monsieur Jacques had tried so often to dodge those various people within him. It so happened that those voices called him to secret mysterious lives at the least expected moment.

Assorted people, esoteric lives; voices which make you believe that you can wake up as a person with different values, opinions, backgrounds, and odors in defiance of all your fantasies, transformed into songs, imbued with the garb of slavery. Words . . . letters . . . words . . . letters . . . sentences left incomplete, sentences mixed together, sentences that always lead up to the same solitude, sentences that compel you to regress to a former state and build up your defenses. Was your decision in taking those people, your people, as your own, and conveying them to others in your own words, your own words exclusively, related in any way to your evasion? Had it not been you yourself, the person within you, who had been eager to tell of it? To tell it, to hold on to somewhere, to belong somewhere . . . who was that person to whom you were so desirous to communicate it but had failed? Who was that person to whom you failed to communicate it, the person whom you tried to protect by putting off your story? Such questions and the impressions that they bring with them seem to me to be more necessary than in a great many stories narrated to me by others relating to that morning. That morning there was another person whose absence was deeply felt. It was Jerry, whose absence caused his family to yearn for him even more poignantly, the youngest brother who was to opt for a quite different isolation and who was to be transformed into a hero of fiction, a figure in those photographs I secretly kept before me, a fiction whose identity came more and more to the fore. Calls were made to Jerry that evening by the people close to him which had differing vibes and questions. Everybody had become proportionally situated with his or her closeness to him. Desire was something different. There were times when desire meant injustice, there were other times when it meant regret, and other times unbearable despair. To be content with what one was allowed to say about the story that would likely be accepted by the audience was much easier; to wit what Madame Roza had revealed, or had preferred to reveal and what the listeners were disposed to accept. The main character of that fiction had been settled in his proper place that morning by the people present there. This was a place where truth and lies could not properly be defined. He was preparing for the difficult graduation exams at Harvard where he had been studying economics. He was a brilliant student; a promising future awaited him. However, just as is the case with all similar prospects, a price had to be paid for real success in life. They had to understand this; as a family they did have experience in this respect. They had learned how to look ahead with hope and fortitude. To be able to appreciate the dawning of the day one had to experience the preceding darkness of the night. Jerry had indeed desired to attend his elder brother's wedding ceremony, but he thought his traveling such a long distance for such a brief sojourn might impair his studies. This had saddened the family who nevertheless understood his excuse. It would have been a blessing to see him there. Leaving all these things aside, there was no doubt that time was changing. One should understand the ways of young people . . . whether we liked it or not their lifestyle would necessarily be different from ours. Madame Roza had acted with subtleness and wisely intervened. Furthermore, the good old boy of Harvard had quite unexpectedly become the hero of the table. One of the Polish bridesmaids had shared her impressions in French, rolling the r's in her own fashion. One of the maternal uncles had looked at her with a condescending smile. According to him, she stuck out like a sore thumb despite the gestures of goodwill being expressed by all. One could not deny that certain feelings were being betrayed by certain looks despite all efforts to conceal them. It might well be that that man had returned to his old ways. The marriage that his brother had contracted with such a woman, with a stranger, had given rise to a lasting habitual error. Nevertheless, one could not possibly deny that the Polish bride was beautiful and attractive. Yes, a beautiful and attractive woman she certainly was! It had been this natural virtue of hers that had caused all the trouble. His eyes had been fixed on her protruding breasts that her low cut dress made still more prominent. Under the circumstances, where exactly did the problem lie? Where did those feelings come from, those drives that never before found means of expression? Juliet was to tell me an anecdote one day about her uncle. We had read the story of a man who had been forced into marriage at a least expected moment with someone he had never anticipated. Despite the short lapse of time, the man, fretting the long years of marital life ahead, had to admit that he could not get accustomed to this marriage of convenience. To what extent and purpose would being a mere spectator to other people's loves make any difference? The story seemed to induce the listener to seek answers to this question. "So what had been Uncle Victor's fate," said Juliet after a long silence. "He never loved the woman he was forced to marry; nobody ever had an inkling of his gentle soul. He used to recite a good many poems by Victor Hugo. He spent his last years in utter loneliness. He had experienced an aching black void upon the death of his wife. This experience was due, in my mind, to an incident that he recollected of his younger days. He distinctly remembered it. There was a young Austrian girl who had taught him games in a language he could not understand at the house where they spent the summer. At the eleventh hour, the memory of those times was reawakened vividly. The girl had suddenly left for Madrid. Her father was employed at the consulate. After that fatal day they never saw each other again. Nonetheless, for several years thereafter Uncle Victor had continued to repair to that residence on Heybeliada every summer . . . " Could it be that the man whose eyes had remained riveted on the bride was that same uncle? It is up to us to establish the connection between the two incidents. We should be mindful of the fact that stories lie hidden in different places for different people until their time to be told is due, they revive hope in us, even a faint one, in addition to a wry joy. Hope gains meaning through stories, even though they might lack originality; stories believed to be different all the same. This conviction, the appearance of this belief, is strong enough to foster in me a line of thought which presumes that during that day spent at that table there had been more than one story being held with bated breath. Another maternal uncle, who stood out among the guests as being dressed up to the nines, the one who enjoyed the repute of being a banker, had remarked—as though he intended to share a secret with the husband of Madame Roza's cousin who had made a name for himself as a stamp collector whose collection had earned the admiration of connoisseurs and who was always busy in his shop where he sold electrical goods—that he had greatly appreciated Monsieur Jacques for the lavish generosity he displayed for his sons' education. Behind this laudatory remark lay, I dare say, the anticipation of a disclosure about the actual amount of money spent to this end. However, this was not the right person to ask such a question. Yet, it must be deemed worthy of our attention that despite all our flaws we cannot break ourselves of our age-old habit of poking our nose into other people's private business. This may partly be due to our efforts to get rid of the hell we cannot expose to others ourselves. If it were otherwise, how could we ever put up with the burden of having skeletons in our closet and endure the sense of loneliness that this brought about? Madame Roza's words about Jerry had affected Monsieur Jacques and Berti, in particular. Different impressions had generated different meanings, different yearnings and different regrets. A wry smile had appeared on their faces; a smile whose true meaning indicated a concealed sorrow and confusion. Juliet, who had recounted to me the wedding ceremony in the synagogue, Berti's awkwardness during the ceremony, his clumsiness, the details of the dinner party as though she tried to represent them on a stage, knew all too well what those smiles concealed. These were the very first moments when she felt she was in touch with that family, with her new family. They had met halfway on the road to an agony difficult to disclose and divulge. They had become confidants; they shared a secret that would be kept undisclosed for years. This compelled all parties to remain bound to each other. Nobody could unfold the secrets of his soul to another human being. Was this disassociation a fragmentation in other people in whom one found a shared fate, a continuous recomposition of the same song?

To find one's reflected image in one's solitude

I had already tried somewhere else to describe the indignation of those whose paths converged and who had to choke back the words they felt in the process of regurgitating. In actual fact everybody was imprisoned in their own sentences, engaged in introspection. However, the said sentences had paved the way to others; we had presumed that we could bring other people to life in those sentences through a process of resuscitation. I think I understand better now the reason why I keep on going back to certain facts which seem to form a sort of unbreakable bond. The same feelings, or at least the associations these might produce, had their origins in other people and places. If one bore in mind the effects created over time by the combined words of Madame Roza, Juliet, Berti, and Monsieur Jacques about Jerry, the said origins shared a common sore spot that seemed to be very far from the actual location of where the words were uttered. Now I feel myself very close to it. A man who learned how to penetrate the darkness of other people gained a vantage point from which he had a better view of himself. On that account, Berti's experiences that day, that morning, are highly relevant to me. He had—even on that day which was one of his most memorable—experienced a place toward which Jerry's extremely original associations had directed him in a completely different fashion. That place was to form an important turning point at the time, clad in a garb that should be considered the most significant of his life. When he tried to narrate it, long after Juliet's account of the story, he gave me quite a different picture than the one Juliet had provided me with. He painted a completely different picture in order to justify himself. He appeared to be somewhat dejected, although he tried to conceal it as best as he could. He was resolved to convince himself that he had acquired the mental and emotional qualities considered normal for an adult and a well adjusted human being, although his shortcomings oozed out at times, despite the fact that all he wanted to do was to communicate and show himself so that he might attract attention and admiration.

I was well acquainted with that desire. I had tried to preserve some of my stories and keep them to myself for the sake of that yearning; or maybe I had simply played someone false. He had felt himself to be the odd-man-out during that banquet honoring his marriage. Had he been the decision maker he would have preferred a limited number of guests around a modestly laid table; a table in a secluded corner of the city, distant from strangers who took such a vitriolic joy in exposing their pretensions and their hypocrisy. He would have preferred to arrange a clandestine marriage with Juliet and merely show the parents the photographs of the wedding, risking all the resulting consequences that would be in store for them. However, he had submitted to the will of others on the way that led to the nuptial chamber. It was plain, however, that interpreting this as a form of emotional indulgence would be unfair if one considered the preceding incidents. One should not forget that he had submitted to this ordeal to avoid an additional injury to the one Jerry had already caused his parents. They could hardly endure the effects of a new grief. His duty toward the family, a duty he considered preordained, could not allow him to think otherwise. He imagined himself the hero of a play whose fate it was to face his ordeal defying all the adversities this involved. I was familiar with this play. To this play Juliet's contribution had not been negligible as far as I could see; this play in which we had taken part in different ways, with different sentimental approaches. The shelter was one whose surrounding walls had been raised by others in perseverance, envisaging varying objectives. Juliet knew of these walls. She had observed at the time, through her well-developed intuitive power, the existence of these walls and Berti's need for them. This modest discovery of hers would secure her a steady progress toward his new family through cautious steps. It had been Berti's perennial aspiration to find a woman who would guide and advise him in his actions and prospective undertakings. She had understood it in the course of their initial relations when they had first truly touched one another. It looked as though she was going to take over a duty, a transfer of duty that the other female members of his family, of his extended family had cultivated the habit of, a duty undertaken after much consideration. She was going to take over this duty from Madame Roza. This experience had enabled her to realize the boundaries of his zone of security better. This was one of the ways to find peace: to lose one's serenity in places where rules hardly underwent changes. Juliet had never said a word about this; she didn't even try to share with me (even when we had been very close to each other) her impression of those days. I come to this conclusion based on the development within me and of Berti's legacy. Therefore, it is quite likely that I have been led astray as well. Hadn't we already observed that what we have consigned to oblivion guided us imperceptibly and would never cease to do so even at times when we have profound belief in our own truths, when we need to lend credence to them? This was a kind of awareness, after all. An awareness that would remind one once more of the fact that truths and wrongs are steeped in our shadows at times. This awareness had caused me to experience that old play once more. Juliet knew these scenes all too well, the very words to be recited, and the figure she would cut in the spotlight that shone upon her face. She appeared on the stage in the part that her history had cast her in. The role she played was the most truthful and convincing role of her life, defying her eccentricity and nonconformity. The play was the embodiment of a sorrow of resignation dated from the days of yore. Women who shared a similar fate to hers felt the drive to expose this anguish. This sorrow had been sublimated and transformed into poetry. Deaths, those silent deaths, could be consigned to oblivion through other people's mortalities. Juliet would not miss this opportunity. But first, other evenings and other expectations had to be lived. Feelings found their proper places only after divesting a man gradually of his assets. As far as I was aware this was the true state of affairs, and so, I tried to preserve it. I could not possibly ignore that evening I had been trying to prepare myself for Berti's story, armed with patience, despite my alienated state and my own misconceptions. My admission this time had been from a different angle. I was being guided by Berti. The former visions would gain further meanings with new revelations. They had popped in for a drink at the nightclub Kervansaray on one of the days preceding the celebration of their engagement. There he had spoken about Marcellina and spoken of the particulars of their relationship to the best of his memory. This indiscretion was aimed at gaining a solid footing for the prospective lifelong union. The goodwill of this intention could not possibly be ignored. If Berti's account of that evening is to be trusted, Juliet had listened to the yarn spun with a smiling countenance, in a graceful and friendly manner. She had not said a word nor made any comment. Now that I am an impartial observer far removed from the actual event, I'm inclined to believe that this silence, which seemed to imply a question mark, concealed a desire to understand. Here was a person waiting to be understood. This candid confession of Berti's, this attempt at pouring out his grievances, betrayed the modest self-glorification of a man who had lost his confidence in many respects. Juliet had a great deal of tact in this matter. Barring all her faults, there existed in her a second woman who could instantaneously notice the significance of such details. It seemed that she was also the author of the implausibility and the glumness of life. Was she the kind of woman who had preferred to keep silent while listening to the episodes narrated during the early hours of that evening, to transpose them to another time? In order to be able to uncover this mystery one must have the courage to get closer to that moment. To the best of my knowledge, Juliet had not trusted in any of the platitudes expressed during such situations. She said to the man who wanted to proceed on in unison (with a past he could not forget) with a matter-of-fact voice which was at the same time smooth and velvety: "Time now to go dining! We might go from there to a nightclub to dance. We must drive our dull cares away tonight." Suiting word to action they had dined somewhere where they had discoursed on other peoples' lives and on attitudes, thoughts, and judgments permeated or prompted by feelings and frittered away the time roaming the streets already abandoned by people. In the meantime suggestions were made to which ears had duly been lent. This scene would remain fixed in their memories as a natural phenomenon both that night and the nights that were to follow. The actual players on the stage and the guest stars were known. At a time when they were lulled into the magic of the night, Juliet had said to the man who was heading back toward her with caution's steps: "We are burying Marcellina tonight . . . for your sake and mine; in fact, for the sake of us both." This call, this voice should not go unnoticed; this voice and what it invited. The lover that had been abandoned would remain so forever, a topic never to be touched on again. It appeared that that night was that night in which Berti had felt nearest to his new woman. At the place from which the voice came there was a new sanctuary; his intuitive faculty was driving him toward that sanctuary. However, one cannot deny that the sanctuary, despite its warmth and security, had also been the cause of an inevitable crack, of a silent crack not openly affirmed. One wondered to whom had those footsteps been taken. From whom those footsteps grew fainter? It is true that they had succeeded in burying Marcellina there, nervously obeying that voice's command. But this had left behind a void that would remain as such; yes, a void; a void whose obscurity and inaudibility was vulnerable to expansion and to be elaborated on in other stories. This void was due to the fact that each of them had interred Marcellina in different sepulchers without letting each other know. Certain breaks, in conjunction with certain concomitant agents, went deep, very deep. Certain families took shelter in those refuges only thanks to these breaks. This option entailed the interment of certain things with their concurrent aspirations and expectations, whose mixed designations were subject to variations depending on the human beings involved, to the time and the feeling in question. The divinities of those lives were tabooed; so were the rituals. Everybody was supposed to know for himself exclusively where exactly he lived, what or whom he lived for. To imagine a night or day cloaked differently would be tantamount to finding one's reflection in one's own solitude. The story had to be lived by someone, or had, at least, to have been told or tried to have been told to someone by someone else. However, no matter what had been witnessed and experienced that evening, one thing was certain; and that was Berti's great affection for Juliet. It appears that Juliet had expressed that night to Berti that she had the feeling that Marcellina had left behind no serious impact. Notwithstanding this observation, it was plain that she also had a clandestine 'ritual' buried in her breast. It was as though she also had tried to bury an experience somewhere, a loss, a missing something. I could never make out whether Berti had even realized this. All I knew was the fact that this nagging suspicion, this doubt, a figment of my imagination, just like in my multifarious relations, had effectively increased the attraction I felt for Juliet. She had made me a gift of a new question for which I should be grateful. I had to remind myself that certain women were reborn by virtue of certain questions, or, to put it differently, certain questions that remained unanswered could never be launched into eternity. This was the reason why I had attached special importance to Marcellina who was nestled somewhere in Berti. This led me to the conclusion that Berti could never entomb Marcellina as Juliet would have liked. Notwithstanding, Berti, despite the question mark that Marcellina had left in him, had succeeded in reserving an important place for Juliet in his life. One should not forget that she displayed the merit of a chef in her preparation of artichoke dishes. How could I ever forget the taste! That was the reason why that evening in which all time-worn controversies, solitary confinements, as well as vague expectations and fervent hopes that we continue to entertain, had seemed such a real tonic to me. We had not seen each other for a long time, almost two years. When one considers what we had experienced in the meantime and our previous dialogues, the time-lag should be deemed considerable, an interval of time long enough to generate a desperate longing that would be hard to imagine. But there it was! We could not forestall whatever had been destined for us. We had learned to live through ordeal. When she had suddenly seen me, she had rushed to hug me tightly without uttering a single word, not a word . . . We were locked in a tender embrace for a long time, as though we were trying to recapture what we had missed over the course of two years. We had tried to give this longing its due, feeling each other's presence, remaining in each other's arms, even though for a brief moment. I believe that she had, like me, recalled the poetry of beginnings and renewed relationships. I think she had also showed the desire to know if so much bitterness had been necessary for joy, for an unanticipated moment of rejoicing. I had caught sight of Berti whose eyes were full of tears. He was trying to smile. His smile expressed a wry joy. "I knew it you bitch! I knew you'd be coming back sooner or later. But why on earth did you tarry so long! Why did you have to subject us to such an ordeal? You didn't think that we'd kicked the bucket, did you! I'm here as you can see, body and soul, and still belong to you!" Juliet said. This effusive demonstration of feelings caused us to laugh. We had to force ourselves to laugh, in other words. It was one of the rare moments of my life when tears and smiles mingled . . . I felt myself as a person holding a position of higher standing in a hierarchy of ranks. I had better understood life just as death opened the door to the birth of an unexpected sensation at an unexpected moment. That poem that had inspired me with the idea that all birthdays legislated new laws would in time find a place reserved for him after many a summer.

Another detail, deserving attention in the meantime, which a great many people may let go unnoticed, was the fact that Juliet had not prepared artichoke, her specialty, that evening. The table was strewn with the ordinary Passover dishes— leek pastry, spinach pastry, boiled eggs, chicken and lettuce. Despite my frustration, the evening would stay in my memory as a memorable event. We were but three around the table, only three, like in the old days. As I was serving wine, I had been careful to abide by the requirement of the ancient tradition. It was a memorable night, a memorable night indeed! Once again we were experiencing the melancholy of swapped identities. A memorable night, a night to be a source of inspiration for the composition of a memorable song! The only witness to our cause was our story, which we could never get rid of.

Could you play the role of Nora?

Our somewhat fortuitous preparations over the course of those two years, during which we stood separated, without anyone knowing, certainly had their part to play in the enjoyment of that night, making it an event that would stay with us forever. To be prepared for such a night you had to have perfect confidence in what you believed you could share with others and were capable of getting back in return, even though from a distance, with two individuals whom you believed existed solely for you: that was the kind of night that was arising . . . However, it seemed as though in this waiting there lay concealed a deadly sentiment, the boundaries of which could not always be tested. It was your waiting that was involved, your own waiting. The waiting that carried the traces of nightmares which you could not avoid in spite of your efforts to the contrary, those nightmares laden with those things that the words had withheld from you, those nightmares with the traces of the suppressed cries they contained that you could not bring yourself to disclose to anyone. The waiting was your pursuit of sleep in that bed on those nights; the waiting was your escape from the sun on those mornings. It was, in a way, your fresh pursuit of yourself that you had lost in a story. The pursuit was injurious; it might remind you of once gathering blackberries on a deserted side road. Under the circumstances, the bitterness one had suffered and the scarring it had left would make the waiting worthwhile. The waiting justified all these episodes. Such were the episodes I felt disposed to narrate, to share with those two people whom I have held in such high esteem throughout my life. Contingencies had once again breathed life into expectations. Expectations had once again been tempting fate; beyond this was an ordinary and dull life that anyone was free to enjoy; a dull, flat, inane and vapid life not worth being told. The points at hand, the real points, belonged to others.

Two years had elapsed in the meantime . . . two years . . . or was it longer? Was it? The fact was that I needed those two years in order to retrieve that separation more clearly from my imagination. Anyway, this is no longer possible; I can no longer recollect them! A man forgets what he wants to forget in the long run. All that remains is but residue; a residue . . . in which, now and then, we hunt for the past; when we pluck up the courage to do so. There are times when we desire to return from where we have wandered, while at the same time we feel a need to stay. We suddenly find ourselves desirous to return to the place we had always coveted and for which we had been waiting; even though we are unable to define the places we have abided; even though we could not clearly define, as we would have liked, the meaning of our arrival or departure. I'm being guided to that night once again by that woman who occupied Juliet's body, for my sake, for our sake. That woman was brought to life that night, through her smile, through the legends carried by her voice. It was plain that we could not escape what had been fated to us by the bitterness this had caused. However, the price of the said bitterness had already been paid and had been welcomed with a gratification that would enable us to look at life with renewed vigor. We had understood once again that our mutual sentiments were destined to remain unchanged. We were carrying the scarred wounds of the days we had left behind. All things considered, events had evolved and come to a head within and without us at the same time. We had to understand this sentiment and try to place it in its proper place in our lives. Reprisals would take place on different nights in different rooms . . . on several nights in separate rooms . . . with a view to being enraptured once again with the dawning of the day . . . with a view to imagining once more the splendor of the vermilion of the aurora, the resurgent sea, the balcony of a perdurable house, or a long, very long walk. Reprisals implied nakedness. We were aware of that. To be treading on this thorny path was something with which we were familiar; we had tried it before in defiance of our diffidence. What we had been conscious of would, in the first place, draw us closer to ourselves . . . closer to ourselves to begin with . . . to ourselves and to our solitudes. However, in order that we could do so, I suppose we were in need of some well-deserved victories that would make room for us in the same snapshot alongside those we were likely to meet along the road. Just a number of victories . . . even though this aspiration may seem too irrelevant, futile, and meaningless to others . . .

Juliet had played her favorite hits on the record player. I can still hear them now. "Tonight," she announced, leaving the dinner table, "is my night, my program; no listeners' choices; you've got to put up with the hits I'm going to play!" Among the records she had put on were "Strangers in the Night," "Killing Me Softly," and "Green Fields" by Johnny Guitar. Among the other hits played were songs which failed to revive scenes from other movies in the imagination . . . those moments were pregnant with memories that seemed to have been consigned to oblivion by Berti. He also had participated in that wry rejoicing that marched with a deep bitterness within us.

Afterward we had parted, although only briefly. I had gone to have a look at the records. The covers of the LPs brought me back to the world I had created for myself in those days. Even today their images are still fresh in my mind. I happened to be immersed in those songs in that brief separation from those whom I had abandoned at the table. Berti, a goblet of wine in his hand, with a blank look in his eyes, was saying something in a low voice imperceptible to me. Juliet was smiling. I had realized. They happened to be in a different time; a time they desired to close off from the outside world and keep closed, which seemed to be something more real, something they considered making a part of them. That very moment, in defiance of our supposed civility, of our shared songs, I had felt like retiring to my chamber whose walls and darkness were familiar to me. I was asking myself what I had been doing there. How did it happen that I'd been taken by these people for a friend, for a guest, nay for a confidant with whom they could share their inebriation, the smell of a gillyflower, the warmth of a palm in perspiration, or a song abandoned somewhere? Even today I am at a loss to understand it. The adage "You reap what you have sown" occupied my mind. As a matter of fact I, for my part, had given those individuals certain things that were a part of the constitutive elements of the story we were obliged to share. One thing was certain, whatever my contributions were, they were not known to anybody outside our triad. Certain little secrets had the guardianship and the charge of protecting not only others but also the timid people within us. We had to learn how to live in the company of our errors. This was the only way to lead us progressively to find happiness.

At present, we happen to be in different places . . . I seem to see Berti smile at those words. I am doing the same, trying to smile. Then a silence ensues. I can almost see the silence. I inquire into the reasons for this; I keep doing so . . . waiting for an answer that never comes . . . I keep on waiting . . . waiting . . . and then . . . then . . . then I give it up.

Juliet, with the wine goblet in her hand, had danced by herself to the accompaniment of the music she had forced upon us. "I'd wanted to dance that night all by myself in the very heart of the songs. Dancing drunk, partnered by the years, to and fro with the days and nights. I think I had, or ought to have had realized it." She was obliged to display certain scenes to us from her moments of loneliness. We had done our bit and put on the appropriate garb. We were three people who had acquired the mastery to touch each other, to play the game according to its rules; we had been doing so for the last three years, playing the same role on the same stage and sharing the same concerns behind the scenes during the intermissions. Juliet had taken to her part in this scene; but the scene was a short one, lasting only for a few minutes; it didn't run on until the early hours of the morning like in the fairy tales. We were world-weary at the time, far removed from any such fairy tales. Now that I relive the past, a smile appears on my lips. There would be endless nights to follow for us to forget our fatigue . . . Juliet had suddenly stopped short in the middle of her performance at a time when we were being swept away by the fascination she had aroused in us, and, out of the blue she had uttered to herself: "What a splendid performance I had put on in Pirandello!" Who knows, perhaps what she was trying to share with us was a limitation she suffered from, her greatest woe. She was recalling her school years when she took part in dramatic plays. The audience scrutinized her closely. And there was a second figure that shared the same stage in a great many of these dramas.

Those were the days during which plays were performed more accurately. They were a couple of young girls—two girls that were making headway and had bright futures. Their teacher of literature was well versed in the dramatic arts and had advised them enthusiastically to choose an acting career. "Leave everything else aside and do everything you can to become dramatic artists," she said. Juliet had told me all these things one night at the conclusion of a stage play we had watched while Berti was on a business trip to Italy he had extended in order to take pictures. There was a joint at Elmadağ . . . I popped in for the first time that night; I was, however, to pay many a visit there later on in the company of other people, sharing passionate moments. We took our seats at a table near the window. It was my choice. We were exposed to the view of passersby. A funny feeling had come over me; I wanted people—whom I had avoided up until then—to see me sipping at my drink in the company of Juliet. That was undoubtedly a new delusion I had invented; a deception to which I was trying to cling. Deceptions apart, here I was, sipping a drink in the company of a woman for the first time. I tasted lemon mixed with vodka for the first time; it had been Juliet's choice. Now, whenever I drink vodka and lemon, the image of Juliet surges before me despite the lapse of innumerable years in between. The vodka and lemon was among my methods of time travel; yes, time travel . . . just like in my other texts . . . my other works . . . Juliet had ordered roasted chickpeas; she thought that chickpeas were the best snack to go with vodka, and she was right. Those days were also marked by my compulsive and uncontrolled cigarette smoking; the first cigarette I smoked was Harman. I had chain-smoked that evening in defiance of my previous self-imposed abstinence. The image of Sait Faik, the poet, who lived on the island and was a frequent passenger on board the ferryboats plying between Istanbul and the Princes' Islands, must have prompted me to emulate him. I had the custom to sit on the deck in the dead of winter and drink a cup of hot tea. I distinctly remember the small open-air café under the huge plane tree and the raindrops pattering on the windowpanes. Life was full of paradoxes. Paradoxes and roads that seemed to be different from what had been indicated to me . . . We had been to see a play by Eugene O'Neill. Juliet knew by her prescience that O'Neill would suit my taste. Years would confirm her foresight. However, all I had experienced that night was mere appreciation, nay, admiration for the performance. The same feeling I was to experience elsewhere at some other time, at a time when we were, and wanted to be, always together with other people. The illumination of the bar and the atmosphere in which I had found myself had greatly contributed to Juliet's beauty, no doubt. The traces of an old sorrow seemed to linger in her features; an old sorrow which could not be shared with anyone, or which was fastidiously kept concealed. I was to bear witness to these traces not only that night, that night which we had spent drinking till the early hours of the morning, but also later during our times of return. These were testimonies that opened up, or could have opened up to different places. Different places had not ceased to follow us during our periods of longing. There had been a couple of friends who had been chasing rainbows, behind the same scenes, hoping to perform the same roles . . . The stage could be expanded with those chimeras, while at the same time revealing its grim reality. Beyond, were betrayals and wanderers, players destined to lose their bearings with a smothered sound. It was not the stage that was expanding, but rather an illusion caused by those who had exited, resigned to their fate. The cost involved, however, did not deserve mention. Certain stories had already been emptied of their contents. Her companion at school had followed the advice of her teachers and become an accomplished, well-known player. Who was this celebrated actress? Juliet had not revealed her identity during our talks. "I'll give you a clue to her identity. For the moment, you'll have to content yourself with this piece of information. Her fame and seaside mansion on the Bosporus consume her colleagues with envy. You can make a hero out of her in one of your stories. She is a writer as well. You may picture her as an author in your tale," she said once. Why had she thought it advisable not to reveal the name of her companion? Was it because she was reluctant to see her as having a share in her celebrity, or because she thought that the path she had chosen was not a commendable one? Could it be that that individual whom she had abandoned halfway along the road had been dragged by fame to a destination hardly creditable, far beyond what one could qualify with the attribute 'good'? Could it be a jealousy difficult to acknowledge or a deep-seated resentment which had not found an outlet for expression? Or else, could it be that such a companion had not existed at all? Could we not infer from this that she had had recourse to concoct such a tall tale to compensate for her failure to achieve the success she would have liked to achieve on the stage and make a show of it to people? Under the circumstances could I conclude that I had been taken for a ride? Juliet had loved the plays which she considered part and parcel of her life. It looked as though a deep-seated sorrow lay behind it. This sorrow was her fate; it was the necessary outcome of an inescapable preference, of a point of view, of an attitude whose source was rooted in the past. Yet, it was precisely this point of view, this attitude and the solitude lurking behind the plays that had endeared her to me. It was a harrowing experience, but one warm and full of life . . . To take Juliet for a friend, to acknowledge her as such was easy for certain people yet difficult for others. I had detected in her a gifted player whose accomplishments I found difficult to avow to myself. She had given me something from her womanhood which I could not properly define or exemplify. At present, I'm not so sure if I'll ever be able to reveal to certain people the perspective of that companionship I have gained from her; moreover, I doubt if I'll have the capability to do it at all. All that I know and can say is that if there was any achievement on my part in this relationship, it was my stroke of genius in winning her confidence. Thanks to this I was able to penetrate into her secret chambers and learn secrets that even Berti did not know. Nevertheless, despite all the confidentiality and special privilege I enjoyed, she refused to give me clues relating to that companion of hers; she preferred not to. Now, who on earth could that woman have been? She was most probably a well-known part of the intelligentsia interested in culture, literature, and drama. I have perfect confidence that a day will come when I'll have an insight into her identity. When the day comes or when I feel ready to take on other lives as well . . . When the day comes and I can visualize Juliet in other lives and other stories . . . To cut a long story short, I want to give credence to the existence of that woman. A voice within me whispers that in that woman are stored private things related to Juliet. These secrets happened to stand behind the scene. As for her acting . . . well, she had performed in a few plays that were staged by the Jewish association and the audience had always given her a round of applause. Not only had she acted, but she had also assumed the charge of training talented young people. *The Rosenbergs Should Not Die*, *The Price*, *Death of a Salesman*, and *Andorra* were among the plays they put on stage. Then . . . then we witnessed her as a cultured and trendy lady who was also a perfect cook. Everything had a price; therefore her confidentiality also required a charge. While discussing her remarkable performance in Pirandello's play several years later, Juliet did not merely cut a dashing figure of a young talented lady, but she also wanted to express the fact that she had had to abandon her expectations, her life somewhere, somehow along the way. "I very much deplore the fact that I missed the opportunity to appear in the role of Nora. Certain things had gone wrong; utterly wrong," she said later. *A Doll's House* . . . She had missed a role she could not bring herself to forget; especially when she presumed the impression the play could create in certain people. I might well empathize with her regret, this sense of defeat she had experienced. This regret, this defeat needs an outlet for expression. The paths might well guide one to other spectators. The paths were known; they were not beyond one's ken. The nights and their baggage should not be ignored; illusions that only the night could effect; nightmares and hallucinations that obsessed us. However, what was essential was not finding the paths, but the reflection of her deficiency in her life, and the direction toward which it guided her. She was resolved to name her daughter after her lost heroine. In my mind these efforts were not in vain. If one considers traditional restraint, this was a modest revolt. Two days after the birth of her daughter, she had announced to Berti that she intended to name her Nora, disregarding the general custom and what one acknowledged as normal. The suggestion was met with some diffidence and a hint of questioning. The reaction was to be expected; it had shown understanding. Everybody knew; it was axiomatic; the second child was named after her grandfather or grandmother. However, Juliet had said that this was a token of recognition to an old promise that had been made during her life. This revelation was followed by the account of an incident she had withheld until then. The episode in question went far back to her adolescence, her coming of age that involved pains, apprehensions and expectations. The period in question contained memories that seemed to merge with reality; Nora was the name of her best friend. A fatal illness had shattered her; she was heading for an inescapable death. Juliet had been by her deathbed until she died. It had been Nora's last wish that her memory be preserved, at least by a few people. So, she had given her word. "Nora will rise again one day, believe me!" she said. "The thing I deplore most is that I've not been able to give birth to a child," said Nora. To which she had retorted by saying: "Your dream will come true one day, never doubt it, it's a promise!" Nora smiled and said "I'm on my way to the womb of a new mother!" These were her own words. Unforgettable words, destined to stay permanently inscribed on her memory . . . The story was a melodramatic one likely to affect many a listener. This episode contained a promise made not only to one person but to life itself. Under the circumstances, the decision had some justification. But to what extent was what had been recounted true? Had Juliet chosen to hide behind this story to impose her choice? I know for a fact that this might well be a kind of skill enacted for the sake of others. As far as I can guess, she had confidence in this skill. To hold on to her dreams to the bitter end, to be reluctant to share them with anyone, to convince them of a lie and a dream they would fail to understand; were these things to be treated lightly? She could avenge herself on those who had pooh-poohed her acting by returning to it, her potent and most offensive weapon. To be frank, I don't know how this idea, this possibility, came to my mind. It is natural to project one's own merits on other individuals. To externalize and regard as objective or outside oneself sensations, images, and emotions is an action we often have recourse to. Under such circumstances, the attainment of reality gets more and more difficult. However, after our talks, I believe I had come to know Juliet to the extent that I should be allowed to invite such suspicions. If we force our mind, I think, we could easily recall those places that our suspicions led us to, and which caused us to stray from our path and to lose track of one another, now and then. It wasn't for nothing that the importance of personal and private histories had been stressed with special emphasis. Finding the truth and erring were equal possibilities. Whether I was justified in my suspicion or not could only be decided by the hero of the said suspicion. Under the circumstances, I saw no other way than believing in the future at this juncture. I, for my part, have always thought that this choice was closely related to the hero of that revolt and thus promoted the nurturing of hope within me. Juliet had an outstanding account with her father that had not been settled. Were one to consider on many occasions and in various different instances (especially with regard to the acting profession which fired her imagination) her mother had become for her the symbol of death and murder. The timing was perfect! Madame Beki's name would exclusively and eternally be kept alive in at least one of her relatives. A gift, considered valuable by some, which would have been withheld if not for this secret deed: they would be all square to a certain extent; they would have to be. I believe Madame Beki had, as a mother, understood the meaning of those little silent murders. As far as I could learn, she had not reacted to this decision, and, preferring not to speak out about it, had contented herself with a few words saying: "It's the choice of our children; it befits us to spare our words and acquiesce." Her facial expressions were apparently quite unflattering. She seemed to be somewhat disillusioned, but stood dormant, something hardly to be expected from her cantankerous nature. These were Berti's impressions of those days; or maybe he had just preferred to relate them in this fashion. When he had listened to his wife's account of Nora, who had to depart this world for another for which she was not prepared, without having experienced many a pleasant episode, he had pledged his support to her. He had taken part in her revolt in other words. Nora was raising her voice in mutiny once more from another realm with completely different sentiments. Nora was returning to find herself in an alien community with a different vocabulary. The play had been enacted, eventually! However, the play had been instrumental in leaving the house wide-open to a new altercation. What the consequences of it would be could not be foreseen at the time by anybody. The cast would learn gradually how they were expected to act. The curtain was being raised. The scenery was being set up and rambling monologues were being rehearsed. A piano had to be hunted down; a piano on which a few tunes were to be played before being suddenly muffled. The piano would have been borrowed from another story for a very brief space of time.

I had the privilege of bearing witness to the continuation of the story. Juliet had become a slave of the order she herself had established according to her values. The training of Nora implied the gradual nourishment of revolt. In the hatching of this conspiracy, there lurked a cooperative effort about whose justification there was no suspicion. While Nora exercised on the piano, Juliet stood by her resolutely, patiently. It was the same determination she had shown during lectures and during their attendance of stage plays they could not stand missing. Juliet's connection to her daughter allowed her to visualize the haunting presence of her old friend Nora. This also implied singing in unison in order to infuse fresh blood into her old companion's legacy, finding a new name for a new color. This was something that she had not given to Rosy, her other daughter, as she was so absorbed in her self-centered memories. Why on earth had this never occurred to her? Why? Who was she tutoring and placing under her stewardship? Who was Nora? Her daughter? Herself or somebody else? A time would come when I would venture to find answers to these questions, through both herself and Nora. Then we would have our stories at different venues and times populated by our heroes and heroines. This issue would be a bone of contention between these two women and be injurious to both of them. Nevertheless, for my own part, despite all the incidents we had to go through, I am setting aside what Juliet had said while dancing in front of us during a separate and extremely private narrative. Juliet's tragedy was not due solely to her compulsive visualization of that individual she had abandoned in her past. What was important for her was the fact that she had not had the opportunity to appear in the role of Nora, whom she held as her idol, with all the connotations and conclusions that would imply. To have missed the opportunity to play Nora's part . . . This sentence had a deep meaning for those who knew her closely.

I had stayed there overnight. Plays in whose cast we had failed to figure assailed my mind. "They are playing *The Seagull* on the Taksim stage; we might go to see it this weekend if you like," Juliet said while spreading the snow white bed sheets like in the old days.

You walked into the darkness

It is evident that certain promises were made at points where time was gradually consumed through different postponements, for the sake of different people, for different calls and different expectations. We had not gone to see *The Seagull* that weekend. In fact, to go and see a play simply not to miss it was not worthwhile. Implicit in her suggestion to go and see *The Seagull* were two nagging aches in Juliet's heart which she wanted to intimate into my mind at that juncture of our relationship; two aches directed toward an uncertain future. "What we've experienced belongs to the past; our friendship continues unimpaired, at least for me. What's more, what we've left behind has gained a special meaning after all that has passed between us. I wish you had been entertaining the same feelings; I wish we could meet once again at a common juncture. My emotion, the hope I've been entertaining for that dream is as fresh as ever despite your expectations to the contrary," Juliet would have liked to say. However, these reflections were my invention all the same. But Juliet was one of my heroines who had opened new doors to new stories for me and with whose character I was supposedly acquainted. Juliet I thought I knew, Juliet I wanted to see, Juliet whom I had to reveal these things to one day, had to speak thus that night; there was no other way for her. No other way unless we were resolved to part company. We were perfectly aware that our space was confined. We both knew that I could not prepare the scene of parting she would have wished to act, nor could I smother the player within her. I think I was somewhat more aware of the fact that because of what had gone between us we could not be enemies. This was another kind of despair, I reckon. I would never be able to put in an appearance as the 'bad person.' I just could not part with certain people. My despondency, my fear of being left all alone, my tribulation played a role in this. I was determined not to lie at least in this case; I would try not to be evasive.

In trying to intimate to me the thrill she felt for the stage through a different channel, using the medium of one of our privileged spaces, Juliet might have diverted my attention to an absurdity which we took for granted. Nora might well have returned that night arrayed with that sense of absurdity generally associated with insurrectional activity. Our actions and preferences might rouse in us again that sense of absurdity. "This is absurd! The height of nonsense! Just like in the majority of our relationships," Juliet might have said. An absurdity . . . This word which might take us back, quite unexpectedly, to a diversity of photographs of certain episodes in which Nora and I had been the actors. A series of absurdities . . . to express the bitterness and the resentment I felt for myself; with a view to protecting myself . . . in the hope of finding a way to perform an injustice to that relationship . . . yes, to protecting myself . . . By the way, when exactly had the story begun and how had it come to an end, following which words? However, I was not so sure it had ended in every respect; I cannot be sure of this; I cannot be emphatic on that account. The same thing held true for our loves, or for our relationships we tried to carry along with our dilemmas and deceptions. We had been attracted as though by time immemorial. Over the border, there were phantoms within us; there was that shadow that we contained . . . We were striving to doggedly and secretly protect what we had left behind. Actually, we could not vouch for the certainty of the steps we had taken, were they even our own? Then, we lapsed into silence, to continue conversing with ourselves in the company of our dreams and private visions . . . those private visions we could disclose to no one. When I think of my projections onto others, I feel reluctant now to tell of what Nora and I experienced or failed to experience. The fact is that I am perfectly aware that the story will be written one day from a completely different angle. This is my professed belief, a formulated belief beyond perception. I am inclined to believe not in the relationship as such, not in the eventualities that potentially exist within me, but in its narrative. At least I have my dreams and the accompanying lies to cherish . . . my fantasies and plays . . . my plays and passions which I no longer want to dispose of . . . even though these plays and passions remind me now and then of that absurdity . . . It looks as though to set off when the time comes will not be difficult at all. In this traveling, I can visualize myself or Nora seated by the window of a bus at night traveling from one city to another.

That night might well transport different passengers and the bus might arrive at the terminal in the early hours of the morning or at the break of dawn . . . But let us not put the cart before the horse . . . years will have to elapse before the heroes and heroines of this story are considered ready for such twilight. What had been mislaid somewhere was a heartbreaking love story, after all. The tale of a sad love we could try to embellish with songs, *tête-à-tête* breakfasts, deserted streets, and telephone booths . . . in other words, there was nothing original about it, just like all other love affairs. What was original, however, were the words that had been uttered and their relevant usage. Nonetheless, I do not expect that this would truly attract the attention of those who have not had similar experiences. At the time, Nora was only seventeen. An exchange of a couple of phrases had drawn us to each other at the least expected moment and at the least imagined venue. She had said The Seducer, and I had said The Most Beautiful Arabia . . . She had said that she would set off on an expedition on one of those moonlit nights without letting anyone know and I had spoken of the shaded face of the moon. Both of us had left behind a bitter experience which we had been carrying deep within ourselves. This experience was due to our failure in finding ourselves among the family members, or to be precise, to being lost among them. Having trodden those paths, I believed we had come to the same realization; certain paths happened to cross each other over time. Our times certainly differed; words that linked us to those fantasies differed; different were our toys, songs, and the places we wanted to touch. But we had reached the same conclusion somewhat inevitably despite all these things. We had felt that loneliness and sense of abandonment within us once more. I don't think I can express this sentiment that had been aroused in me in the wake of all I do not know of people I am unfamiliar with. One thing I was certain of was the solitude, that unique solitude that could not be verbally communicated to anyone. One could not choose to be alone, nor could one communicate it to others. This inevitability generated a pleasant sensation; to feel exposed to it or make others feel it caused a funny sensation of warmth spreading within me. I had felt as if I had set off on my journey at the exact moment that Juliet had taken cognizance of the fact that she wanted to fill the gap between the fantasy she had had to leave buried in the past and the new path she wanted to travel with her daughter, Nora. This was, without a doubt, one of those narratives that was set in a different climate and at different periods of history; a narrative whose component parts varied considerably; a narrative which more often than not paved the way in other families to mysterious deaths for which no inquest could be presented. Nobody had asked Nora whether she fancied playing the piano . . . They had been accustomed to living with their shortcomings. They had no need to take stock of their shortcomings, nor any desire to speak about them to a third person. Those fantasies had perhaps been imposed because of this very reason on many young children who found themselves aged suddenly without having been asked if they deserved to be cherished. At the same time here was an occasion that deserved to be shared with someone, by a spectator like me. I was one of the few people who could have a proper insight into the stages that had brought Berti and Juliet to part with their daughter. I knew how they had reached that point. Those were the steps of individuals I knew and with whom I had shared many experiences through the years. The war of fantasies, the war that broke out because of the failure of those fantasies to co-exist with each other, in that small world . . . those small worlds . . . and of finding a foothold there. But a day came, in other words, when the term was due, when contracts were signed. War and Peace . . . How had they signed the peace treaty, after which unnameable defeats? What had these defeats been, whose defeats had they been? Answers to these questions could only be given by those involved. In this I have gained absolute confidence. The enigma lay in those defeats, in the things that had accompanied them, or perhaps in those things that were never discussed during peace negotiations. It was most probable that Berti and Juliet had only realized what they had lost in that peace process by consulting a third person. Here was a section of the story we more often than not find in books. What changed were mere appearances, and what made them meaningful were words. Here we might inquire into that drive that attracts us to those stories and prevents us from breaking with them. Words and appearances were mere keys. Only with those keys could we open the doors. It was for this reason perhaps that we had marched and would continue to march with hopes we continually refreshed despite the fact that we knew that those stories would never change but continue to be repeated. Certain stories would belong to different tongues; they would be read in different tongues by their native speakers. The play was a play of power, after all. The opposition saw one day that they had come to power. One should know how to stand still when power was attained . . . then . . . then you could hide within yourself. Families were but small countries; prisons whose iron bars were barred to sight, the lives spent there were the lives of those near death, if one chose to look through such a window. Families were small prisons, resistant to demolition, doomed to be born in other families through deficient nights and false dawns. Families were cells that every single person reproduced according to his or her own idiosyncrasies; in which they lived to the extent they deserved . . . Just like the cities that do not abandon their children elsewhere; like countries that give their citizens only the image of freedom. Under the circumstances, I had no choice but to opt either for the explanation that Berti and Juliet would not be capable of recognizing this play of power, or that they had preferred to turn a blind eye to it. This would enable them to endure their despair and the pains they tried to cover up. This was the reason why I had not talked to them about what needed to be talked about. This was perhaps a mode of living that friendship caused to sprout. However, in opting for this discretion, I believe I had been afraid to face the facts. Our talks could well prove to be background for the development of this story in a different vein. Our talks could well take us to unpredictable places just like in the case of similar settlings of outstanding accounts. This invitation might require alterations to what I had written, what I would like to have written about them. In other words, it was not beyond reason that I might have missed a detail on the road which might bring about the narration of those nights from a different viewpoint, driven by completely different impulses. I had tried to dodge that settlement for the sake of preserving my own truths, the truths I wanted to keep unimpaired because of my play for power. The price was to live with that suspicion, the loneliness that that suspicion engendered, the abandonment. The price was the fear of occasionally returning to myself.

What had guided our relations had been fear, simply fear, fear of oneself, of one's dreams, of no return. But I could not possibly disclose all these to Nora at the time. I happened to be stranded somewhere I had never been before or had any idea of. On the one hand were my confidants who had dared to give to my custody the wrongs they had done, who had tried to open for me the secret corners of their hearts, and who had burdened me with their stories; on the other hand, there was a heroine whose influence was beginning to weigh heavy on me and to whom I wanted to justify my private acts. The said heroine originated naturally from an old story that had never been lived. I was supposed to create this heroine within my own boundaries and conceptions. Actually, these were the simple facts which I was to run into frequently in other people's worlds and to the consequence I was therefore submitted to. However, I could not speak of this truth at the time. In order that I could reach the boundary of this truth I would have to live other stories.

Berti and Juliet had brought me that heroine at the least expected moment. At the time, we were not conscious of this. My only concern at the time, when I was reviewing our secrets and could not avoid asking myself once more who had stayed in whom and how, was my reluctance to betray them. As a matter of fact, I may not have known or I may not have wanted to know, at the time, what I had actually been protecting or what I had been trying to protect. It is only now that I can understand the fact that my reticence and my keeping of my feelings from Nora, my sincere feelings, was actually an act of betrayal. What has been aroused by certain things kept secret and left undisclosed are carried with the greatest difficulty. Yet, I think a considerable time must elapse before I can tell of these and settle my accounts with the consequences of this betrayal. In fact, every one of us betrayed certain things which we could but define long after we had suffered losses. Betrayal was an integral part of our secret history which we could never rid ourselves of; it was the history of our own selves embedded in others; betrayal was our solitude . . . Through the obscurity of those stories we had all betrayed Nora. The person we had betrayed was a real person who groped her way in the darkness, a person who, like anybody else, was in search of her voice. What had differed between us had been that gap that separated her from us, from the bare fact. We had all seen her as a heroine; we had succeeded in seeing her as such. To put it another way, we had become her spectator; we had succeeded in becoming her spectator. Our spectatorship was the judgment that had been passed by those judges that we had wanted to kill in other lives. Some of us had called this our conflict with the individuals within ourselves, those individuals we wanted to forget, while others had called this our fate. There were other places and contingencies, different sentiments under different names, which had dragged us to different fields, and would continue dragging us perhaps. However, after a certain point, despite all these various fields, at places which we thought new or at old places we refreshed, we would gradually waste away despite appearances we had recently been conscious of. Had this been so just because we did not know and could not learn how to fight, to really fight, our feelings, justified resentments, and indignation? The answer to this question lay deep within us. We had to look for it within us, in those fears we could not get rid of. To this question we could provide different answers, in different periods of our life, to different individuals. Nonetheless, these answers were more often than not provided by those individuals resigned to their fate. Nora, the Nora of this story, would be among those who had no other choice but to depart. Nora, then, would have the courage to take that step and succeed in turning into a heroine of another story. She would be able to live up to the meaning behind her name; she would have the courage to face that challenge during the days I'd known her. For us, she would be an embodied regret; a bitter experience embalmed, impossible to annihilate. A twinge of remorse . . . Nora . . . remorse. Because she had had the guts to live her own story with utter disregard for the pain of other individuals whom she would have ripped from her tale. She had to secure her freedom as a heroine. The boundaries of this narrative that had its origins somewhere in Istanbul years ago had to be crossed. I was sure of that; everybody knew this, everybody who had an insight into the tale and believed that other words had been lived and preserved beyond this boundary. The truth, the essential truth lay perhaps in the fact that a person not only had to know how to understand and to try to understand this, but also how to embrace both sides of the said boundary. But the boundary encompassed not only hopes but also devastations experienced by everybody differently, with different dreads and disappointments. Beyond the boundary meant, according to certain maps, no return, and according to others it meant the acknowledgment of that girl's expulsion. For, certain sympathies showed themselves with flying colors, or at least seemed to. What was known was the fact that her adventures could not have been encompassed by those moments and those relationships; adventures of old which had sought their differing means of expression in different compartments and realms. Each one of us would narrate her adventures by our own account of them, or at least would show the desire to share it with somebody. A stare, a mere stare was able to make us ruminate over the old days. A limited number of moments I now and then conjure up from Nora's past seem to invite me somewhere else. I had been given the hint of a departure on that Saturday which today seems to have been lost in the mist of the past . . . It was an afternoon when Juliet and Berti were away from home . . . It looked as if it was going to rain. Nora was exercising on the piano; she was working on a piece I frequently encountered in a good many stories; she was to take part in a contest of young successful virtuosos. I had silently sneaked into the room. She had sensed my presence but had made as though I was not there, or as if she desired not to interrupt her performance. Who was seated on that stool before the piano? What was that thing that had driven me to sketch out this section of the speech, of our speech, and convey it to others? Under the circumstances, I might have preferred not to provide any answer to this question and prepare the path for the consequences caused by the absence of any response. Yet, I knew where I happened to be, or where I had returned. As I crossed the threshold of that room, I was perfectly aware that I was going back to that story and wished to re-enter it. Considering what I had experienced before, I must say I had never been so near to that piano. So near each other we were . . . even though our stares were directed in different directions . . . near each other . . . because we had been led into the same melody regardless of our differing places in time. This meant we were to write a poem on the same theme and live it. I thought I had a renewed faith in a deception. This deception was my contrivance; it was a part of that photograph that held me tight on the days I had lived by representing its differing shadows according to the place in time. In other words, they were what came within my sphere of vision. To have taken a woman, a woman I could have potentially loved, as a heroine had been my error. It seemed as though one of those colors, one of the colors we had lost, was concealed in it. Those days without words and sentences that were the consequence of this error opened with mornings deserving to be re-lived. You might, for instance, while waiting for the ferryboat which would take you from the island to the din of the city, ask yourself about the time of that illusory experience you had associated with the taste of a fish-scented savory roll covered with sesame seeds; or, you might take delight in having yourself served tea in a glass not properly washed; you might suddenly feel like smoking a hand-rolled cigarette; you might get a cheap thrill in concocting a story about the passage of a carriage at a phenomenal time. But this was my illusion; I was in the grip of it; I found myself always in a state of preparation, always busy with preparations. Nora was unaware of this. Nor did she know anything of her having been cast in such a story as a heroine. However, I was seated next to her. She continued to play. It was as though I had been watching her hands and fingers for the first time. I had the presentiment of a transformation; the room was being transmuted into music, reminiscent of tunes that echoed in those stories, of tunes lost in the distance. I seemed to recall the voice from which the said melody was originating. We were in the midst of a concerto which could not bring two people in unison at a critical point in a story. It was Mozart. Mozart, who had failed to endear himself to me, who was assuming a new identity with this improvised little poem. I'd been laboring under a misapprehension once more; I had become aware that I had placed an individual in the wrong place because of other people who had been left there to vegetate. It was Mozart's vengeance. Mozart was wreaking vengeance on me. This reaction at the moment of encounter (which I was hardly expecting) was undoubtedly a retaliation for my pitiful deafness. This was like touching that melody by passing through that history, through the secret history I was hearing. Mozart's well-known laughter which created different impressions in different individuals echoed across the room . . . She had suddenly stopped playing and grasped my hand. Her eyes were fixed on the keys. "It's as if something is being ripped from within me," she said in an almost imperceptible whisper. We were silent. I was staring at the keys of the piano. After a moment's silence, she added: "There'll be no recital . . . I won't play for them, never . . ." Her voice betrayed resentment as well as fright. I had squeezed her hand: it had the warm presence of a young girl on the threshold of womanhood. I felt something oozing into me from that fright; something that could not be blocked, intangible, ineffable . . . Our lips were united. I felt a void, a void that dragged us to that union. That void was me, myself, at that very moment; or it was her; or perhaps both of us at that fleeting moment. It may be that that void was perhaps the most difficult step that would take us to that path for which we had been preparing unawares. That void might well be tantamount to our encrypted name or names. Yet, at this very moment I cannot properly recollect that void. All that I can remember is the scent of the chewing gum in her mouth, communicated to me by her tongue which twirled around my mouth. Our desire was roused through the displacement of erotic and libidinal interest and was accompanied by irregular heartbeats. I wanted to put faith once more in a desire that lust could not consume. My lips had grazed the contours of her lips and wandered about her cheeks and neck. Then we were locked in a tender embrace. "I don't think I really wanted it," she said afterward. This had severed us from each other. We had lapsed into a silence, shunning each other's eyes. I wonder if we had been in pursuit of our childhood at that moment. The tune that lingered on the keys of the piano was a tune I could no longer describe or define. We were still avoiding each other's eyes. In that split second, I had vaguely recollected those moments lived only once and abandoned somewhere to remain uppermost in my thoughts. I wonder if those moments were a part of these moments. "We are turning inward and undergoing a steady process of dissolution," I said. "Many people will think I'm on the wrong path . . . but I'll keep a stiff upper lip and feel myself refreshed with a new vigor," she remarked. I had observed that everybody went their own way; that that way had inexorably been traced by the people themselves and that it behooved the narrator of a given life to separate the wheat from the chaff, picking out what had, or had not, been risked for the sake of the journey. Certain visions had surged in my imagination: I'd witnessed random visions from other people's lives . . . These visions were populated with figures whose lives were in one way or another interwoven with Nora's. The figures in question had appeared to her from different angles with different voices. I felt compelled to avow that I had been heading for a long story. It looked as though certain steps were being taken to prove that they were capable of being taken and that they still would in future. Yet, those steps might not always be our own. However, to be able to proceed, or to entertain the hope of being capable of it were tantamount to having faith in one's ongoing existence. We were the slaves of a handful of expressions or sentences we appropriated after having nourished them with our imagination. The cold fact was that everybody became extinct to somebody else when a certain day came. Everybody died somewhere, sometimes along one's own path. But the number of people who could find his own characters was not great. I was heading for that long story in the hope of finding the things I expected to find beyond the border. On my way to that destination, many a stranger would be keeping me company. She had understood . . . "I shan't be what you're expecting me to be," she rejoined. I had tried to insert this insurrectional behavior somewhere in the story. The time that elapsed in the meantime proved her unshakable faith in the path she had chosen. She had never been as I had wished her to be; she gave nothing of herself to those who wanted her for their own causes. That is how she behaved. The meaning of the path she took should be sought here, through this withholding, in this effort of keeping away from everything. The path was in fact being drawn gradually through resolution . . . in the hope of coming across to another individual . . . without being aware of the fact that in the coming pages of that long story she would secure a place not easily forgotten, reminiscent of a relative of hers who was as proud and as resolute as she had been, although she had rose to the challenge of being treated as a castaway. Nora had stepped out of the story one day, leaving it unfinished at a moment least expected by those who were not prepared for such a contingency and who expected her to be heading for a life proscribed by the community. Can this be the reason why I've made the necessary arrangements to enable her to live elsewhere as if I could not do otherwise? Perhaps. Actually, she had been of those who had been the author of certain contingencies within me. Through her choice, for the sake of life, she had caused a deep-seated feeling of resurgence in Berti and Juliet. It looked as though certain things had streamed out of their control . . . certain things that they were reluctant to disclose, and which they preferred to be kept secret in their private worlds through different guises. Nora was that thing they could never be, the person they had both left behind. They should be proud of her. However, the grievance engendered by their despair and that sense of deficiency had had the upper hand and they found themselves overwhelmed, suppressing all the pleasure they would be fain to enjoy. A day would come when we would pluck up the courage to discuss this feeling and try to disclose to each other what was in our souls. To this end we had to attend other funerals vested in different garbs . . . As for what remained of those we had tried to kill in full knowledge of the fact, daring to undertake an act of complicity by the exchange of furtive glances, silences . . . she had had a story within me which she had failed to dictate to me as I would have wished her to. I don't know if I could have set out on such a journey at the time and plucked up the courage required for a prospective alteration of the story. There is no sense in providing an answer to this question, in trying to make as though I had done so and to expect a transformation once more. Haven't we finally reached our final destination, the place that we deserve? Our journey's end, unalterable henceforth; the place removed from people contrary to our expectations, the place harboring refuge. At present, I can better appreciate the inveteracy of this sentiment. She was the heroine of another story . . . the heroine of a story with different boundaries, protected by people that I kept alive through my dilemmas and apprehensions. This may have been the reason for our failure to see each other in those days. This may have been the reason for my fear of being swept up by the storm, ripping me from my grip and tossing me toward infinity. This may have been the reason why I had been trying to cling to my solitude. These were the inevitable consequences of indignation, of an indignation that could not be expressed to one's heart's content. Nora's journey there was not merely in order to discover her voice. I was going to see in all its nakedness the realities of this, there was no escape from it. It was evening and we had gone to our café at Bebek to have a cup of sage tea; it was there we had tasted it for the first time . . . As we were gazing at the yachts anchored along the edge of the Bosporus, she had said something about the invitation of a picture. I had said nothing in return. I couldn't bring myself to say anything. This had marked the end of a long relationship; it would take quite a long time before we would see each other again. Having said goodbye to our café, we had walked hand in hand to Aşiyan. On our way, as we were passing by Bebek bay, I had reminded her of the paddle boat we had hired once to go angling. She had put her arms around me and said: "Please forgive me . . . I know it's not so easy. But try to forgive me." That was the moment she had truly yielded herself to me. That was the last time we had been together. Nora was not even twenty at that stage.

I could never fix a place for Nora, the Nora of my imagination, in the story she preferred to be heading toward. Actually, the most important reason for my desire to play a little trick from the place in which I was peeping at her was because of this lack of acknowledgement. This was the trick of an urchin who tried to suppress his resentment. An urchin feeling lonely once more. His favorite toy which he would not part with and had once again been snatched away from his grasp. He would not be able to complain to anyone when he went home. According to my will, in this play Nora would have to be the heroine of a story hardly fitting her and in which she would never feel comfortable. There was no other way for me to carry her in the course of those days when I felt distant from her. That was the only way I could hold her within the limited space of a few words and sentences. I had been lured once more by the attraction of covering distances within the sphere of a lie that nobody suspected me of. This was a method I'd already used, a method that had aroused confidence in me once again in the day about to break. In this contemplated story, Nora, having let herself be swept by the pathos of a soul in mutiny and who had lived with somebody somewhere for a time, would finally realize her error, recognize the limits of her boundaries, and taking full cognizance of her incapacity to proceed on, would go back to her family in the hope of clinging even more firmly to the fragments of the life she had dispensed with to the extent they were still attainable. Knowing full well that this was an unconditional surrender, and, with a view to convincing those she had left behind of that fact, she would marry a yuppie, an owner of a large plastics factory who during his leisure hours did nothing else other than dilly-dally on his PC, who had not developed the habit of reading and who purchased stereo sets for the mere sake of showing off the technical accoutrements in his possession, being utterly devoid of any musical or cultural background, a man who was a connoisseur of well-known brands, who took special pleasure in displaying his *Mont Blanc* fountain pen and *Davidoff* cigars, who frequented the stylish restaurants for the mere sake of their names and whose hobbies were skiing, motorcycling, and reckless driving. I would ask her a couple of days prior to the wedding how come she had decided to marry such a man. She would incline her head toward her chest and say: "I'm looking for peace." As a topic of discussion I might opt for the café at Bebek. Then, we would come to a stop. We would play hide and seek and make as if we had turned a blind eye to each other. This play would go on for years on end. Based on the words she had uttered while we were at the café and during our encounters, I would conclude that she was implying certain things she had wished to convey to me. At that moment I would call to mind the preferences of other men in other worlds. In one of those stories I remember having mislaid a fragment which kept recurring in my mind; a fragment of mine ever appearing . . . Despite all that we had gone through and the moments and contingencies that were waiting to be reproduced over and over again, I would be seated at a place in the synagogue in her field of vision. During the service, our eyes would meet quite casually. I would smile. That moment would be a decisive moment for me in which a victory would be won, a little victory I had been waiting for with great patience. I would be among the last guests to congratulate her on her marriage. I would try to express my pleasure in the victory I had achieved in a manner she would understand while shaking her hand. Her hand would squeeze mine as though she would not let it go, to confirm the impression I had tried to convey to her. We would be conscious of the fact that she had taken a wrong path. The said path would then be simultaneously noticed by both of us. We would then seek to clasp our hands, a gesture in which we both would have absolute confidence. This would be the last scene of the story. However, before long I would realize that the person who had been treading that path was no other but myself and that I could find no one, including myself, gullible enough to believe in the truth of this story despite the literary style and rhetoric I had adopted. Nora once again had stood up against me and proved that she was capable of demolishing that wall. These scenes of ritual were from another story, a story whose heroes and heroines were elsewhere and were to stay elsewhere. When I go back to the past and delve into my memories, this probability reminds me of Rosy, Nora's poor elder sister, that submissive, benevolent and introverted "lady spinster" as she had been referred to by people at the time. Her own way to marriage and her behavior during the wedding ceremony would be abnormal. I would notice her because of her reaction upon learning that Aunt Tilda had not been invited to the sumptuous banquet given at that restaurant in Tarabya. The Neve Synagogue was overcrowded that day. Every one of the guests was supposed to wear a beatific smile in token of his or her contribution to the general mirth. Every one of the guests was supposed to make a proof of their emotion commensurate with their age, just like at all wedding ceremonies. I'm sure that Monsieur Jacques would have felt the absence of a few members of the family in the distant lands beyond his reach. Berti seemed agitated; his lips were trembling. It was his habit; his lips trembled when he felt restless and worried. His son-in-law had failed to endear himself to him. One day, during the wedding preparations, he had made the following observation concerning this 'new guest' whose entrances to the house had become more and more frequent: "The guy has something I can't put my finger on that displeases me," but added at the same time that such a funny feeling on the part of the father of the bride should be a natural phenomenon. Like all the other family members, he knew well that he had to put up with such ingresses. Juliet had begun sprucing up; however, I do not feel inclined to make any further observations regarding her in relation to that day. Nora was staring at her elder sister affectionately. Her stare occasionally diverted from the object of her attention. It was as though this movement was the indication of a break, of an unavoidable break. I would have an insight into the meaning of this break much later while experiencing separation. It may be that Nora had a presentiment about her fate. On that day, most of those present could feel her absence, betraying their smiles in the photographs. These made a history of endearing words, of silent betrayals remaining concealed forever, of unsettled debts, of fronts hiding certain sorrows, and of lives postponed. The crowd had not dispersed. The rejoicings, the rejoicings that did justice to the occasion were there. Nobody, no one among the guests could have guesed that they would be visiting the synagogue about five years later, this time for Rosy; yet, Rosy had taken a fancy to Nedim who had put in a dramatic appearance in the life of the Venturas during some dark spots in his past. There was more than one reason for her choice of Nedim as her husband. On the other hand, Nedim, in his turn, seemed to have found the woman of his dreams. Everything seemed alright, in other words; for many, their relationship seemed to lead to the home one should long for and kindle in one's imagination. They were comfortably settled in a spacious and luxurious apartment in Erenköy. It was one of those high-rise apartments which had nothing original about it except for its being devoid of all traits and qualities distinguishing individuality. The dwellers of this apartment might well be surrogates from any class of society. This was the result of contemporary mass production. To describe them you needed to have recourse to a few sentences which are patent lies but with which everybody is familiar and which are expected to be uttered all the same. What a fine apartment you have! Gorgeous, isn't it! However, what one requires in the first place is peace of mind. Missing things can be bought in time, there's no hurry! Isn't it nicer to purchase things gradually? I seem to remember it better now. It was a Saturday night. I had gone to Erenköy to pay a visit to their new home. It had never been my custom to pay such a visit. But frankly, Rosy had aroused considerable sympathy in me after that wedding. I think I wanted to give expression to that feeling of regret that remoteness had aroused in me. I had made her a gift of a silver picture-frame. I know that this present had no originality, or any value for that matter. But if one retraced our past it seemed to fit in with our existing routine. This had been a token of my crystallized emotion. Moreover, I had attached a special meaning to it. We had been seeking new ways of thinking in order that we could rely more firmly on our doubts, on our little deceptions, on ourselves . . . Rosy was surprised that my visit brought a gift; her bewilderment had suddenly transformed her into a childish woman. To have been a contributing factor to a little delight had made a place for me in that house, a place I could never forget. "I brought this to you so that you may place in it all the people we have abandoned to their fates," I said as I gave the picture frame to her. The meaning was implied in that encrypted phrase. I'd aimed at arriving on stage through these words. She had understood the drift of this. I noticed some tears in her eyes. This was my second moment of togetherness with her. She had thanked me with a tremulous voice and said: "It will stay in my safekeeping forever."

This was how my penetration into the house had been effected. The rest does not deserve to be narrated in detail. We had dinner, drank, listened to music, and discussed truisms. Nedim had spoken of the *Lamborghini* of his dreams, of Japan, of elegant restaurants in Istanbul likely to fascinate gourmands. All that had been discussed might be judged entertaining if the atmosphere of that evening and the man I wanted to figure in that atmosphere are considered. I knew where all these talks would lead. I hadn't found it difficult to discover the characteristics of Rosy's 'man of her dreams.' This seemed to be one of the other facets of culture. It might come to the rescue of a person in the least expected moment, which might contribute to the opening of new avenues. Notwithstanding, I believe I had been able to perceive Nedim's imperceptible merits that lay in his depths. What exactly was lying in those depths? It occurred to me that it might have something to do with his relations with that Japanese woman, or to be more precise, what we had been told about them in general. Rumors circulated that had been given credence by many people. I might well have remained under their influence. There was no doubt that the mentioning of Japan as a country deserving to be known, understood, and experienced, which seemed to have been casually referred to *en passant*, was significant. It had aroused in me a sense of doubt. I was familiar with this doubt. I would never betray the grooves that that doubt had carved within me. I was a slave to those stories. I had the opportunity to see Rosy once again at a time when I, couched in reticence, made as if I were listening to what was being narrated about Nedim's private world, in the belief that he was sharing some of its aspects with me. He also made as if he were listening to what was being told. He was seated close by, but his stare was fixed on a certain spot, which gave the impression that he was lost in the distance. He kept fidgeting with the tassels of the armchair in which he was seated. He chain-smoked and extinguished his cigarettes before they ended. Every now and then he sallied to the kitchen to empty the ashtrays. He seemed to be seeking a sort of hold in that house. That was my point of view, which might be wrong of course. We felt ourselves in different times, every one of us. Once our eyes met; I had the impression that he was being caught in the act. Had my impression been true, what sort of a crime could he have committed, I wondered. Could 'deafness' be considered a crime, a murder? Were such criminal acts perpetrated solely in those prohibited zones? I am certain I'll be evading such questions, interminably, for years to come. This evasion will remind me of a betrayal whose burden I shall have to carry to the bitter end. I know that in order to be able to take a few steps forward, to be able to get into a few individuals, one should not be bothered or at least act as such. That was our third meeting since our adventure on that wedding night, since that event we had all shared. Rosy had expressed herself in this fashion, as she was incapable of doing it in any other way; which suited the impression she had of me, or wanted to have of me; by clinging to that fragile thing to the bitter end, as long as her strength allowed; hoping to smother that scream in her depths. It's a pity that I can see all these things from my actual vantage point. To move away . . . It appears that I had to move away in order to better understand things from a distance. The funny thing was that as one moved away one inevitably drew nearer. Under the circumstances, I feel better now that I can follow the train of thought related to the happenings of that night and of the following nights . . . Rosy had preferred to give utterance to what she intended to say at close quarters. There was a place to which she felt she did not belong. It appeared that she had already felt before that the place where she had been obliged to live did not belong to her. One was witness to the case of a woman who had failed to obliterate her extraneousness in a story. Beyond that remained that boundary we failed to define. We were to meet twice in different venues after that evening. However, our discourse had come to an end in that house, with that look. I believe we were cognizant of this fact. Our distances and boundaries dragged us elsewhere. Among that crowd of people, we were to figure no more. I didn't know what the matter was. To be able to know the answer to this question and the consequences that it gave rise to, I would have to wait for many years. All I knew was that the long silence had been desired to be perpetuated. Everybody felt it necessary to hold onto that long silence according to their own quirks, for their own sake. This may have been the reason why that question had never been asked by those spectators. It was incumbent upon one to contribute to become attuned to the setting of the play being enacted so as to figure in it and be one of the players called upon to act. On weekends well-known restaurants and nightclubs were frequented and package tours were embarked upon. A girl was born to the family in the second year of their marriage, a girl to be brought up in the best possible way by the mothers of both parties. In such marriages, families on both sides were often engaged. There were times when real feelings and sentiments disappeared; people desired to see them disappear somewhere in their line of vision. Those times had to be lived. Everybody lived those times for the adventure latent in one's heart. To my mind, the tragic element in the story of Rosy was concealed in this vision. The vision in question was in part our own image; that image in which she was hidden and had to hide herself. It was about this time, one morning three years after the birth of her daughter that the world, the world as we knew it, would appear to Rosy's eyes for the last time, for she was to lose her balance while wiping the window panes on the eighth floor of her building and fall down, down into her last void. An aura of mystery had surrounded the incident that had occurred there at quite an unexpected moment. Questions, probing questions would be asked once again by individuals despite communal interests and the union of both families. Were the lives of certain people to continue to be hushed and hackneyed despite all expectations, postponements, betrayals, and lies? Sometimes a given moment, a sentence, or a few words sufficed to end a life. A single moment, a single step was all it took to put an end to a life. The incident had shattered everybody; the family was most affected because they were unprepared. To be caught unawares was a grim fate certainly. To believe in fortuitous events was another way of enduring the suffering. However, everybody was aware of the fact that that moment and that step were the natural consequence of a bitter prelude, as anyone who had had introspective experience would readily acknowledge. This inner voice may have been the reason for the crowded attendance at the funeral. Among the attendees were not only relatives, friends, and people who sincerely desired to share the pain, but also certain individuals who had not been seen for years. In other words, in addition to the close friends, those present were the belated, the remorseful, and the mere spectators. Condolences were expressed to Juliet and Berti. Juliet had hardly spoken a word. I had accosted her with some apprehension, as though I happened to be an accomplice of the crime. I always felt culpable at such unexpected deaths, a psychology difficult to describe. We were locked in a passionate embrace. "She is now somewhere else, in a place she had always wanted to be. I'm sure that she is very happy, far happier than she would have been among us. I know we'll see her no more, this is a fact. We cannot prove the correctness of our feelings because we have no evidence. Yet, we must trust in our intuition and lend an ear to our inner voice. You should know that she would have liked us to believe that the place where she has gone is far more fascinating than the place she has left behind. The blue horizon beyond belongs to us who knew how to love her truly. There is no other beyond. We mustn't rely on any other beyond," I said. Juliet had been nodding yes. She had squeezed my arm and not uttered a word. It appeared that she preferred to keep silent, to contain her voice within herself, and not let it be heard by others. Were she to talk, were she to hear that voice, she would surely be sobbing wildly. However, there would be other hours for weeping to the point of being oblivious of everything. Those were the hours when other people had become dream figures, the hours when an unexpected visitor would be tapping on the windowpane of the room, the hours when an object reminded one of its songs and when a place communed with itself . . . Those hours were the hours that matured within us. We were aware of this. I believe we knew and had sensed that we would be experiencing this recycling more than once; we knew that we would be sharing this. As she had to receive courtesy visits while seated silently on her couch dressed in black, gazing at the cotton wick dipped in olive oil contained in a glass bowl, she had appeared to me as though she were waiting for other visitors. Once again we were together. Once again . . . in a way nobody could fathom, one that we could not describe to anyone. I caught sight of Berti; he was smiling. It looked as though what I had said and tried to convey had aroused some joy in him. He seemed to say that this too would pass. Some people solemnly moved by winding their way through the alleys of our soul to the accompaniment of their voices. Some people marched on to the places beyond on our behalf. We were obliged to believe in this presentiment. We had to convince ourselves of the fact that we could walk away from the things we would be able to recall, far removed from those places that contained them; heading for other places. We would be treading new paths. Actually, we had known each other during those strolls; it had been our intention to speak to each other about them. He was silent. "You're welcome to our club," he said. "Welcome to our club," that was all. Our conversation had been concluded by these few words. Yet, for those who knew our shared past, these few words were already too many. Nora was also there, naturally. She had come over to Istanbul as soon as she had heard the news of her elder sister's death. Was she also one of the belated? Was she also among those who had heard the voice of regret within herself with reference to the days she would no longer be able to touch, the voice to describe to someone the lingering images of that chamber? Well, I don't think I'll be ever able to know. However, the very act of putting forth those questions, the fact that I felt obliged to ask them, signifies that I wanted to see her at the time. This conviction of mine is corroborated by the fact that she, after the end of the seven day mourning period, had decided to leave Istanbul by taking off the dark costume she had been wearing and to leave for where she knew she could find no one to share the burden of the days she had lived. To depart within such a brief period of time, following the traditional seven day mourning, meant for me an escape from something, from something hardly definable by everyday vocabulary. This escape connoted escape from that story, from our story. That was a different time; we had to put off making other mistakes for the time being. An exchange of looks between us had served because of this, perhaps. It is true that we looked at each other, and had remained contented. We felt obliged to remain pent up within our solitudes, within our words. Other people were but our shadows once more. They kept us within themselves. To remain attached to this feeling during those days, to be aware of our attachment to it, had aroused in me a fresh hope. Our story was pregnant with another. To entertain such a hope had given rise to a feeling in me I would describe as a wry joy, which I would be in a better position to define with time.

Fears, expectations of returns, and the renewed hope of marching on at a new time despite all that had been lost . . . We had gone through all these experiences or had tried to do so once more for Rosy; the experiences we had enjoyed without taking stock of them. We had been asked to find the individuals we had mislaid somewhere. This peremptory call was for those who were invited to find for themselves a new and precise place relating to a past lived imperfectly. We did hear the call; actually we would never be able to do away with it. Miraculously, after so many years, Juliet was to remember those seven days of mourning Nora had spent in Istanbul. Seven long days and seven long nights spent, during which mother and daughter had been inextricably close to one another, although in a different dimension in which motherhood and daughterhood had coalesced. Retaliations and frank talks had indeed been embarked upon despite fears, faults, and evasions. The term had been but a short one, if past experiences were to be considered; yet, the time was real despite those dreams doomed to remain inexplicable and unshared to the very end; a real and 'lived' time, a time whose due had been given; a correct time recorded in history to remain stamped on one's memory. The term was not so important under the circumstances; what was important was to rediscover the years lost, to add meaning to them and to find a room for that sentiment. Why had they tarried so long, why had they had to wait so long? Had their steps been taken with a view to avoiding a new death, a new void, a new deficiency and regression? Had those steps been taken toward a different future? What future was it? Whose future deserved to be carried forward? To provide answers to these questions, to take up this challenge may be impossible for a great many people. It may be that these questions are better ignored like a good many lives and stories. Otherwise, the history of those who had failed and would fail to catch time by the hands, the history of those that has not been told and that has slipped through one's fingers would not come back to us as a gaping wound during those nights. All things considered, I cannot help feeling that Juliet and Nora had had the courage to enter each other's solitude. This probability arouses in me the hope of the breaking of a new dawn. I feel that I'm gradually, stealthily approaching those people whose stories I will be able to disclose and believe I'll be capable of telling. I know that this experience is the warmth of self-reliance; the warmth of a self-reliance I cannot discover embedded in words. I might choose to come to a standstill here and to abide at this very spot, but a lot of questions crowd in on me. For instance, what had been the topics of discussion, what recollections had accompanied them to the darkness? What had drawn them to each other so closely? Was it the deep grief occasioned by the death of a loved one, or their meeting over the feeling of regret that the loss had engendered in them which would enable them to cling to one another? I might consider these possibilities and search diligently for the exact words required. Frankly, to try to explain this approach based only on these causes seems to me a time honored way of dealing with things, commendable by a good many spectators and heroes. Something was missing . . . something . . . an addition of great importance although modest in appearance. This was the exclusivity of Juliet and Nora. This was partly due to the despair, my despair, expressed in the story. This section then would be lived and was actually lived in this fashion by other people. Narration was a new missing link for which I had to find a place; a missing link that enabled me to have a fresh look one morning. There is only one thing that seems meaningful to me about those days, something Juliet had told me. On the night of the sixth day, after they had seen off the guests, mother and daughter had gone out for a long walk. A deadly silence hung over the town. The magic of the night penetrated into one's very marrow. They walked on for some time hand in hand without uttering a word. Then they were engulfed by a shower which did not prevent them from continuing their march. They seemed to have traversed that place where words failed yet found their true meanings. The shower was their shower; the rain they had failed to live, the rain they had mislaid somewhere, the rain they had withheld from each other. As they approached the house, Juliet had asked; "Will you return?" To which Nora retorted:

"Never!" Then they had lapsed into silence and restored their own voices. It appeared that this was the moment when they had best understood each other. Then Nora left the next evening as she had her own people in a different place.

Nobody had cried for Rosy, or if they did, they had preferred not to make a show of it. There was a time for crying, a time for conversing, and for feeling the need to carry on a real dialogue. We were preserving the posterity of petty details; we had learned how to do so. Other discourses, other subjects of dispute, and other suspended judgments and systematic doubts had been imposed. The subjects of dispute and the suspended judgments occupied mostly the minds of the guests, to wit, the spectators. We, in our turn, were supposed to remain passive and content, simply lending an ear to what was being told. Keeping silent and listening . . . these indicated our interest in those voices and the fact that we were desirous to coexist with them. Those subjects of dispute and the suspended judgments and systematic doubts had prompted a new absurdity within me. I knew, nevertheless, that every absurdity, every sentence that appeared simple, had a spot to which someone might sooner or later be drawn. My return to those voices was inevitable for the narration of the story. One of the questions propounded had to do with having a better insight into Rosy's last moment. How come a woman so well-off had not hired a charwoman who would clean the panes but instead decided to do it herself? Was it merely an accident? The probability of suicide was not a far-fetched assumption for those who inquired into the incident. Had this shared assumption had any plausibility, one would meditate on the cause that drove a woman with a three-year-old child to suicide. Then endless court cases . . . the person who would suffer the most would be the little child of course. The man, with such wealth, would certainly remarry. Had this ever occurred to her? It would not be difficult to provide an answer to this question at that stage. That was the reason Rosy had figured in that story as a woman who was not conscious of her responsibilities. This was obviously one of the ways to dispose of the grief that Rosy's tragic death had caused. Thus, histories would assume new meanings. All the heroes of that story, every one of them, knew that girl in his or her own fashion. Recollections had not been preserved for nothing. The girl was an original type, composed and reserved. One might well have seen her fall into the darkness. The case might be closed as far as its witnesses were concerned. Nevertheless, I, for my part, have never ceased to believe that another interpretation, far beyond the suggested ones, should be sought. I never questioned the way she died; yet, what had driven her to it nobody could imagine. This moot point might lead us to a Rosy different from the Rosy we used to know, a Rosy we had failed to picture during her lifetime. This point I have carried with me for years. No need to say that this supposition had no rationale on which I could base my assumption. It was a hunch, a mere hunch, a strong intuitive feeling hard to express in words. The story would, in time, gradually exclude its other heroes. I knew for a fact that the hope was not a new one, a hope that loomed ahead somewhere. It seemed that we were doomed to repair to our respective abodes. However, I'm no longer eager to seek new interpretations; in the meantime, in this connection I must not forget to mention that this conviction of mine has opened new doors to me. At the place I had expected to reach were memories related to other hours embedded in preserved emotions. It would take some years before it would finally seem as though I had come close to the real cause.

We had raised a toast to the memory of Rosy that evening

It was a summer evening and the city seemed deserted once again. I felt that this evening would be experienced differently by others, as an evening deserved to be truly lived. Something drove me to that tavern which I had not visited for quite a while. To be frank, I'd had no taste for taverns and drinking sprees. Notwithstanding this lack of enthusiasm in me, my steps took me to that tavern by the seaside. The sea was blue, as blue as could be. In a small secluded borough of that metropolis called Istanbul which I couldn't leave that summer, it had occurred to me to experience for a couple of hours the delight of contemplating the beautiful scenery which I had been missing for ages. My fate seemed to be sealed; this longing would open the way for me to certain experiences in defiance of the disadvantageous consequences these might entail. I had had a premonition; it was as if I had been dragged there by that man. This was inevitable; it was a question of the revelation of a secret which had tempted me. I must have already mentioned somewhere before: I feel myself related by blood to such stories, like a dream wanderer walking along a long story. My visit to that tavern was earlier than the wonted hours. At one of the tables by the seaside sat two women and two men who looked as though they had been waiting for someone. That play seemed to have been displaced to another scene with new words. New words, new looks . . . New looks and new moments meant different souvenirs and different solitudes; you might also speak of these as different seas and different deaths. Maybe it was because of this that they sat in an unusual silence. They had put the lid on or had already exhausted what they had wanted to disclose to each other. However, there were at times a few exchanges of words, after which they lapsed into silence once again, and as if they were at a loss as to what to do, they turned their gazes to the sea and stared at it, musing. Their reticence and their eyes that transfixed each other reminded one of horror films. They looked as if they had been waiting for someone for years. They stared at the tables with familiar looks and so the tables observed them in return with the same familiarity. They seemed to have resolutely decided to stay. No, they would stand their ground. This plot had occurred to me right there at that round counter. Had I ventured to pursue my line of thought perhaps I might have run into something more expected. Yet, I had suddenly realized that the man who was seated opposite me and whose looks were fixed on me gave me the overriding sensation that I had seen him before, as if I remembered the contours of someone I had left somewhere in the past. I had felt his presence right at the moment when I was busy bringing together a couple of new words in a couple of new sentences for a story I was going to write in which other people would figure. His looks seemed to conceal, to conjure up, and expose certain things that had a meaning of their own. Well, my glances had reciprocated his. He smiled and looked as though he had been awaiting my reaction. Leaving his chair, he approached me. The individual that was drawing near me was no stranger; he wasn't a hero of a fiction or play who had relinquished his place in somebody else's story in order to intrude into mine. I had been the custodian of a little but valuable souvenir. A souvenir which I had had some difficulty mentioning to date, but one that I recognized, one I'd been keeping in a distant night of mine. The gap in my memory, even though for a fleeting moment, had vexed me. Nonetheless, I had eventually been able to recall him. He was the person who had left a strong impression on me that night which I'd paid a visit to Rosy to give her the silver picture frame, with the songs he had sung to the accompaniment of a guitar he played himself, reeking of alcohol. He had said that he had a wide repertoire. He was a professional musician who had performed for many years in nightclubs. He prided himself on being able to sing in fourteen languages. He remembered that he had proposed to sing in Arabic, Hebrew, and Armenian. That night, as a finale, he had sung an Armenian song. I am not of course in a position to judge how perfect his accent had been and the degree of veracity of that Armenian song. All that I knew was the song was quite different from the other songs that he had sung. Having finished it, he paused and said: "You know what, my late mother used to love that song. Today is her anniversary. As she lay dying, she spoke in a delirium of her childhood days in Van. I've never been to Van myself . . . " A silence had ensued, an almost absolute silence. At first we all delved into our respective silences. Some had gone back to their prior birthday celebrations, some to their occasions of mourning which had united us in the verses of that song. The silence we had fallen into was then broken by our warm applause. Music had seemed even more beautiful that night, the songs that expressed once again our tissue of lies, our photographs classified in our chests of drawers. The person who had performed those songs had taken us by storm without a doubt; yet, what we truly applauded were other beings, namely those individuals whom we were reluctant to unearth. We were but a limited number of people that night in that house who would stand the test of time nestled in those songs. Rosy had listened in rapture to this friend of hers who seemed not to stand on ceremony during his frequent visits to the house. The last song sung had brought tears to her eyes, as it did for all of us. The man no longer worked in nightclubs. He had worked hard and become a prominent figure in the business world where he thought he had found himself at home. Eventually, he had reaped the fruit of his labors and was promoted to the position of executive in an industrial concern. He looked overly tired, but his position was rewarded with a generous salary. He had witnessed the pride that his father, a retired general, had felt for him. I did remember him! He stood nearer to me now. As though he had read my mind he had said: "Indeed! Just as you have remembered . . . " His black hair and beard had turned grey. "Except for this sprinkling of grey," he added. Observing my shudder, he had placed his hand on my shoulder and ordered the waiter to fill up our glasses. This was a theatrical show, no doubt, a cameo. I was supposed to know that he was well-known in those surroundings, according to the story. We were both served raki which we had diluted with water. The white cheese and the melon, the *sine qua non* snack of raki, were on the table and it was a summer evening. The tables were being honored by the presence of the regular customers. The people seated at the other table who appeared as though they were expecting someone were still there: the person they had been looking forward to seeing had not shown up yet. The streetlights were being lit and the sea seemed to flow bluer than ever. It was time for many individuals to call to mind Bodrum. The man seemed to sing in an undertone, uttering barely audible words that ran something like this: "Hi! You've called me, haven't you? Well, here I am . . . Who are you with now? Are you alone there? Or are you breathing for somebody else?"

We clinked our glasses and without uttering a single word we continued to sip at our raki. "Nice song . . . It's been ages since I've been touched by a song . . . " he said. "We are ever ready to hear such songs . . . Haven't we left somewhere on our way our dear ones to whom we were deeply attached?" I rejoined. No answer came from him; he had merely nodded in approval. "What wind has swept you here?" he asked afterward. "I really don't know; but, I may have heard your voice calling me here," I observed. He smiled at this. "You should make use of it in a story," he suggested. "I certainly will," I answered, to which he reacted once more with a smile. "What have you been doing lately?" he inquired then. "Well," I rejoined, "I'm spinning a long story of which I cannot fathom the end . . . Some of us have gone very far," I said laconically. He added nothing to this. His looks bespoke the realization of my words. "What about you?" I inquired. There was no answer. The silence was compensated for by our sipping at the raki. I had wished to know of his exploits since I had lost sight of him for a good while. "Yes; how about you? What have you been doing in the meantime?" I asked. The question begged an answer, evidently. His smiling face betrayed a secret to which he seemed proud, similar to the guilty secret of an urchin. "You'd not believe it!" he said. "Don't say you have resumed your former trade as a musician?" I dared to suggest. With a furtive glance he had made a gesture of hand as though denying the suggestion. Then he said bluntly: "I have a meatball restaurant." At my bewildered expression, he continued, saying: "You're surprised, aren't you? As a matter of fact it was a shock for everybody. However, believe it or not, I'm as happy as a clam. What's important for me is the conviction that I've found what I've been looking for. It was two years ago, I had to make a snap decision. Up until then I had been working in that plant; I was listless; I believed that my life had found security; I was entitled to a pension. I didn't have to work to the point of exhaustion; thus I led a carefree life. One day, just as I was about to quit work and call it a day, I received a file from the general manager. I was asked to study and give a detailed report on it the following morning. I was to stay on the premises until late at night. I had had other experiences of the sort, but that evening I had other fish to fry. Had it not been so, I would have acquiesced to it. The woman whom I knew solely through her voice on the phone and whom I'd been trying to persuade to go out to dinner with me had at last yielded to my entreaties. I hadn't actually seen her; I'd known her through our telephone conversations. Like in fiction, isn't it? As a matter of fact, we had been living as heroes and heroines of a fiction during those days. A pure coincidence had brought us into contact, a newspaper notice. One Sunday morning, as I was browsing the dailies just to kill time, I had come across a small notice; a woman was offering her services to those who wanted to learn the Ottoman language. Suppose you felt out of sorts and wanted to find a hobby like stamp collecting, painting, woodworking, gardening, that is outside one's regular occupation, something you find particularly interesting and enjoy doing in a nonprofessional way as a source of relaxation, wouldn't you be tempted to dial her up? Without a further thought, I called her up. The speaker at the other end of the line might well have been an elderly lady, one of those ladies of old from Istanbul. However, the velvety voice on the telephone seemed to belong to a young woman; it was like a voice I had been in pursuit of all my life, a voice which had been waiting for me. My initial intention had been to hang up after having learning of her situation. It was not an every day occurrence; a woman was offering her services as a teacher. Well, our conversation lasted for about two hours; what we discussed covered a vast gamut of topics, at the conclusion of which I had the sagacity of giving her my telephone number. I received a call from her the very next day. We talked and talked and recited poems to each other. Not many people know that I love reciting poems. My mother had imported from the East, from *her* East, an infinite number of poems which she used to read to me on certain nights. Mountains, running water, and small hamlets were often the themes worked upon. Terrors and deaths lurked during those nights. The verses she recited were the verses of forgotten songs. Dirges they were, songs expressing grief and a solemn sense of loss. She used to recite them to me especially during the nights in which she seemed to miss certain things and felt lonely. She used to express her estrangement from Istanbul in this way. I fancied I was nearest to her on such nights. Those verses had inspired in me not only a different solitude, but brought on solitude itself. That's why I was particularly fond of those verses. This had unearthed my own poems, or caused me to believe that I'd discovered them. The verses I had recited to her on the telephone were exactly the poems that were part and parcel of my being. Her verses, on the other hand, were in a different vein. Our topics of discussion were not poems, of course. We elaborated on life's major issues, on people we had lost or imaginary lives that we indulged in. It was as though we had desired to pull down the wall between us. We didn't expect to see each other. I had even sung songs to her. For the first time in ages, I thought I was singing warmly. Three or four months went by in this fashion, engaging in internal talks. One step remained; just one step which we believed was a decisive one, but which we continued to put off. She must've been aware, as I was, that this step would be far from easy. At long last I blurted out that we had to see each other. She seemed to be reluctant at first, for fear of disappointment. The disappointment might not be unilateral, she said. She was right perhaps. Ours had been a purely magical experience; the spell might be broken. Yet I was insistent; I asserted that the words we'd exchanged had been in need of a concrete touch, and the worst that we could expect might perhaps be our avoidance of each other's glances. She understood; she couldn't do otherwise anyhow. A short time after, as I was speaking about a TV series, she expressed that she would assent to my wish and was ready to face all possible untoward events. I was getting prepared to meet her and was wondering whether the dream I'd had for many years would finally come true. The venue was a restaurant at Kandilli, by the sea of the Bosporus. The story would come to an end on an autumn evening. The hero was coming, having experienced a death whose effects would linger in him for quite some time to come. The death was the death of other human beings; many a life would fade away in oblivion. It may be because of this that the hero had imagined the venue to be an island; having perused the story I'd concluded that actually I was not very far removed from the idea of an island; of an island within us in which I would be seeking refuge. I'd already told her about this story. That restaurant might well have belonged to us. When the report from management was given to me on my desk, I had plainly seen the reality which I then wanted to shun. I felt that it was the end of my career there. Without informing anybody of my actions and being forgetful of all the petty things which I had been dealing with cheek by jowl for so many years, I made myself scarce, leaving all of it behind. On the report I just inscribed in capital letters: 'DAMN ALL OF YOU!' I thus repudiated with a sleight of hand the labor of ten long years. They sent for me and begged me to go back to work as I could not possibly leave everything up in the air. But I'd done it, once and for all.

What I'd left behind no longer belonged to me. I declined all their calls. I had to face the opprobrium of my colleagues; they failed to lure me back to my desk as I was resolute and firm in my decision. I couldn't convince them of my opinion and the course of action I had decided upon; I never tried to, anyway. I couldn't resist the lure of the table I was going to share that night in the company of that mysterious woman. You won't believe it, but I proposed to her right away, without standing on ceremony. And she accepted. It's been three years now since we've been married. We have opened a small joint where she prepares meatballs. There are no more Sisyphean chores. Colleagues pop in now and then; they say in admiration that I had been right in my decision; the very people who had held me in contempt. I told them that I'd eventually found a place that belonged to me; a place where I belonged together with those I believed belonged to me," he concluded. "You might just as well say: I'm with individuals who I think belong to me, who I would like to think belong to me. I'm just fine, and yet I'm here!" I observed. He inclined his head toward his breast as if trying to cover up his confusion and took a sip from his drink. "I wish we had met before," I remarked. "Indeed!" he said and added: "There should be someone willing to write our story, our stories, in fact." "Are we not the authors of our stories, of our own stories, at least?" I inquired. "You're right there," he answered, "we'd like to return to those days to see how we trod such a path." We had stopped. Silence was the venue where we had stopped; the individuals that our silence embraced in protection, our hours during which we had forgotten each other, of whose disappearance we had taken stock. Our taciturnity buried our regrets, our desire to recapture the moments when we had died hoping to be resurrected and to return like people who had had the experience of death more than once, as heroes. "Were I to tell all these things, I don't think I would ever be able to find ears willing to listen to your adventure; they would think I had concocted it," I added afterward. "Maybe we are lonely just because of this," he rejoined as though corroborating my observation. "There are so many stories we cannot give voice to; so many episodes we have experienced, the truth of which we cannot convince others of. We are the slaves of these stories . . . " I continued. A silence had seemed necessary at this moment and we filled the gap by sipping at our drinks. The scent of anise mixed with the odor of the melon associated in us a very long story. There were people who enjoyed this subtlety with discrimination and appreciation. Just like in the case of the discriminating invitation of certain people to certain houses. "Rosy's episode was for me one of those stories of bondage. One of those stories I couldn't get rid of for years, stories that I couldn't bring myself to convey to others . . . " he said. To which I added: "As a matter of fact, I had always believed that this episode would come back to me, and, what is far more important, that it would bring me face-to-face with a person who has been waiting for me in an old photograph." His comment had been: "The story you are going to narrate may well begin with these words." There was irony in his voice, the irony of a wise man. It was as though he had already come across similar stories elsewhere. This was a sense of nakedness that I had once experienced. I was confused. "If I ever have the skill and the opportunity, of course," I said bashfully. His smile suggested sincerity. "Well, aren't we here for that?" he rejoined. We were two people who knew how to resign themselves to their fate, how to endure such an experience. We were acquainted with this sadness. As a matter of fact, this sadness had held us united despite our difference in character. We could henceforward be heading for that photograph. "You know what," he continued, "Rosy's tragic death wasn't a coincidence, it's just not the case, it couldn't be." He then began telling the story with the voice of someone who had come to knock on his friend's door late at night; it was the story which he had kept to himself and could not bring himself to share, even with his wife. He had seen her on more than one occasion, years ago in a café in Moda, seated at a table with a stranger. He had succeeded in hiding himself from her view. Apparently Rosy, who sat composed at the table, kept nodding yes. From that distance he could not possibly guess the words they exchanged. The man seemed to be insisting on something without any apparent hope. Who was that stranger, that guest who had intruded upon her life uninvited? The answer could not be guessed. But that man must have had a role in Rosy's death. However, this did not go beyond an intuitive presumption. A presumption, but one in which he had had an unshakable confidence. My story of Rosy had ended up at an entirely different anchorage following this unexpected development. There was concealed in that place things unutterable that conjured up death. After so many years that place seemed to have become a secret alcove, a tabooed sanctuary. One should demand nothing more from the past. This land of the unknown could be appropriated by us once more; however, it was a land on which we could lay claim, a land in which we could find shelter. We raised our glasses to Rosy, to those to whom we had not been generous enough in terms of affection. After all, we drank in order to be able to find ourselves. "We'll no longer be able to see each other; nothing can henceforth contrive for our paths to cross." He seemed to confirm this. After all, who had stayed there and who was capable of what was evident. "Both of us know the reason," he said. We certainly knew the reason why we had preferred to assent to this mandatory separation. We knew more things that we couldn't divulge. These should be the crowning words under the circumstances. The tavern had become replete with clients. Other tables, other times . . . And the people that were seated at those tables were still there. The man's name was Harun. That was the last time I was to see him. He hadn't mentioned the whereabouts of his steakhouse.

Nora had embarked on her own odyssey

Rosy's story to me, to be precise the story that I had access to in those days, was one such story. Henceforth all that I would remember would be a real loneliness that had left behind a few unanswered questions; it had a betrayal in its past, just like in the case of all lives similarly lived. At this juncture, I recall certain sentences that I had run into somewhere else at another time. Once again, it had been my wish to forget all about it. Yes, to forget, to try to forget . . . that was one of those evasions which found its rightful place after having sojourned to a distant land for a good many years. But, every attempt to get rid of it on the way was a morsel that was difficult to swallow. That morsel was your ghosts, the perennially perpetuated images of the leftovers from the dreams you had been trying to conceal. The world was the world of the rotten, of the obnoxious . . . yes, the obnoxious. Perhaps this was the reason why those were Nora's days despite all the injustices perpetrated and offenses committed in that house. Actually, those things hardly interested Nora, she had embarked on her own odyssey. She had shut her ears to the outside world and preferred to hear only her own voice. The path she had taken had reminded me of regret for this very reason. Today I think I am able to give easier expression to that regret. She was one of those to whom the view of the life beyond had been exposed. In fact, the light of that place had been her guide on the path she took. (Was the meaning attributed to this journey getting lost in her pursuit of new illusory hopes or in her unconscious building of her prison, her sanctuary?) When she had left, she was barely twenty. She had chosen Bodrum as her new terra firma. Her man, the companion to whom she had given her whole being, was a painter of about forty years, far older than herself, whose artistic merits had not received the due acclaim he hoped for and who had always been an outcast among the intelligentsia; he was the type of man who carried within him the spirit of revolt, as though he was a stranger. She was to stay there for several years; she would resist the temptation of succumbing to the call of Istanbul despite the deaths that had taken place in the meantime. The family was aware of her resistance and recalcitrance. There was no misunderstanding but a resistance against a fallacy. Thus, Nora's story was the story of fate. She led a life far away in the distance, removed from her family against their wishes, having chosen to learn of the wrongs she had committed away from home. Her originality was found in her preference to be, or to remain, lackadaisical. This characteristic was also one of her elder sister's traits. That was the only common thing between them. What was sad about the whole affair, of her departure to that place, was they were not like two sisters but like two strangers, and that they were unconscious of this fact. She had given birth to two children. Could this be interpreted as another example of her preference of getting lost in that solitude of no return, in that life?

Quake

The matter was old, long exiled possibly, not properly explained to others. The bitterness that Nora had caused because of her departure, because she had chosen to live at a great distance rather than close to her family was just one of the seeds of affliction with which the house was already familiar. Everybody had had an inkling of this, everybody who had taken part in that history. Setting off on journeys, castles in the sky stood like squares of films; these squares framed some unforgettable lineaments despite the separation of the figures in them. Jerry was there. Jerry had left for there years ago, to those squares of solitude, in the hope of finding the end of his road and exploring what lay beyond it. There had been no change to his attitude. The yearning had quite probably given birth to the same place again. It had nourished the same emotion with the same hope. The difference was due to the conditions that assigned identity to the time in which he sought refuge. However, I was of the opinion that there was a common ground where they, the inhabitants of the house, met silently in defiance of their severance without uttering, without being able to utter, a single word. That ground was for Jerry the expression of distance. This was the major reason for my failure in having an insight into his character, as is the case with every writer of a long story like mine. All I had at my disposal was a modest heap of words, and their projection on me. Everyone had preferred to stick to his or her own personal vision of Jerry. This was an issue which I preferred not to tackle because of Monsieur Jacques and the atmosphere that reigned over the family. I wondered in which dark cranny those words had remained concealed. Could I proceed despite those words and the reigning darkness? Could I rely on the words I had attained so long as I was able to keep this probability fresh? At that juncture, I had no other chance but to have confidence once more in time, in the fact that my march through time would lead me to a person I had no presentiment of encountering in some corner I would never have imagined. Berti had brought Jerry to me via detached phrases during those walks. The secret conjunction of those phrases happened to inhabit somebody else's world. This is why I attached such importance to them and guiding them to me. Fantasies might have led me to a different sort of hero. However, what I was beholding was but myself, or somebody else within me. This was just one other example of being unable to properly define our solitudes to others. I had recollected. I had to. That game of speechlessness was a game that involved a variety of sentences related to a variety of people. I feel as though I ought to write once again that stage play inspired by Berti's sentences. What I have before me now is the story of a misfit who had had to cope with problems ever since his school days. The first image of his that surges before me now is of a misbehaving boy who was always in trouble with the school authorities at the Saint-Joseph French *lyceum* run by the friars whose strict discipline was well-known. That discipline groped blindly, it seemed, to enable the students to aspire to different paths and to fend for themselves in the life ahead of them. If the champions of the said discipline are to be given credence, Jerry was an overactive boy trying to find a place for himself in that narrow pass. He used to pester his teachers by asking them awkward questions. Had the inquirer of such pointed questions been somebody else, that somebody would surely be expelled. Yet, being an industrious and good-natured boy, always at the head of his class, his manners were tolerated and condoned. He devoured books and studied his courses at his leisure. His preference was for books of philosophy and history. Another of his hobbies was solving puzzling mathematical problems. He had dabbled once in designing a rocket and to this end he had supplied all the necessary material and carried out all the drawings and calculations. However, his father, getting wind of his clandestine work, had vociferated: "You'll blow us all up, rascal!" Whereupon he had been obliged to shelve his project, that shelf was to carry heavier loads as time went by. He had been a lonely, introverted character; in the garden of the house in Büyükada he used to play for hours on end all by himself. Once he had witnessed a cat devouring a sparrow whose wings were broken. This had induced him to torture cats to avenge the poor sparrow. He used to tie a can to the cat's tail or thrust its head into a paper bag, or indeed cut its whiskers. When he came home, he would be covered with scratches. On the other hand, his insular character aroused the wrath of the kids of the district who often abused him. He showed no reaction to the violent behavior of his peers and gave no account of what had been inflicted upon him. All these incidents were certainly far from being commendable behavior. Yet despite this, he was doted on. Madame Roza had a predilection for her problem child whom she pampered, on the grounds that he needed help. Berti, who had imparted me with this state of affairs with detached phrases, was aware of this fact. He had even found a validation in this injustice; he had tried to plead the case to his mother who had been partial to his brother and to whom he had always been partial in return, showing affection for his elder. Madame Roza's sentimental attachment to Jerry might be interpreted as having been due to the fact that he was named after her father whom she had lost when she was only ten and for whom she had great admiration and whose absence she often felt. She had identified him with her father, finding certain parts of her father in her son. It was as simple as that. As for Monsieur Jacques . . . he must have thought that his son, being naughty and overactive, displayed a remarkable intelligence and would likely prove to be able to face up to life's adversities. I think I am now a better judge of the circumstances. Certain people or the results of the preferences you have made on their behalf, enable you, as time goes by, to see new places and evaluate certain values in a different fashion. However, in addition to what I had beheld, I had also observed Berti's resentment. This resentment had arrested the development of the child in him. This child had lived to see his hopes realized, as recorded in his old diary. However, that diary had to be deposited in its usual place, known to everybody, and which everyone tried to enliven. The diary in question was at the same time a journal of transgressions that could not be put into words or given proper expression. The established order was not the sort one could easily disrupt. To the best of my recollection, there had not been one single transgressor. There had been, nonetheless, one single event that had broken the reigning silence. Was it the day on which Berti had appeared grown up, on which he had seen that child within him matured? I'm not inclined to answer this question in the affirmative. All that I can say is that was an unforgettable day in the history of that shop. That was years ago . . . The shop was that old shop that I have always wanted to speak about. Monsieur Jacques continued to be the only master of the house. Uncle Kirkor had not yet died. Niko had gone to the place he had to go. Olga was still an attractive woman despite the eroding effect of the passing years. On that day, father and son became involved in an altercation for no reason; old deeds were brought up and dormant resentments were rekindled. This 'quake' would indelibly remain in my memory. It looked as though Berti had ventured to rebel after a long interval of postponement for the sake of all those individuals he had left in his past and felt obliged to kill. The inquisitive mind was inquiring about the mystery of fate, life seemed to be a burden to be carried whether one wanted to or not; it was imposed on man. A new page was being opened for Monsieur Jacques, after what had been divulged. There were moments that transformed us into that man from whom we thought we had moved away for good, into that man whom we were obliged to recognize and coexist with. This was a moment to settle our affairs with ourselves. A moment of settling that reminded one of those scenes in a stage play. Those scenes were also present that day. They had experienced the deferred settlement of affairs to the place they belonged. Berti was henceforth obliged to speak out and had to get it off his chest and address to his father as to his own realities. Monsieur Jacques ought to have listened fleetingly to what he had to say, without any reaction to his scathing exclamation. He had never come to terms with his elder son who had to endure many a sacrifice for his sake. As a father, this had been his greatest fault. He had always asked him to perform a job: to take over the responsibility of the shop and of the family in the days to come; to keep watch over his brother, and to maintain silence; silence, above all else. What a flat, dull, and trite story! Where had they mislaid the sporting chance of living in the skin of another man? To whom did the opportunity of being different belong, the right to give birth to a new man, of choosing one's own truth and of living it? Had he, as a father, ever lent him an ear with fatherly affection, had it ever occurred to him to inquire into his son's aspirations? Were these shelters in the name of which sacrifices would be made so important? Should certain fantasies be doomed forever and not have the right to survive in someone's imagination? How long could one shoulder a truth in solitude without giving it expression, without sharing it? Did this mean remaining quiet at all times, denying and abolishing? Why on earth those sacrifices were not acknowledged in appreciation of the benefits received, and why, in that restricted space, did everybody, though quite unaware of the fact, become each other's predator? To keep silent and remain mute . . . to be allowed to speak only to yourself, to carry on an interior monologue . . . Well, here was the very spot where Berti's words got mixed with mine, the spot where words coalesced. I had attempted to shoulder those solitudes in consideration of others. The solitude of those individuals was my solitude in a way. Otherwise, we could not succeed in remaining where we happened to be, being committed to the same story. It was not for nothing that certain feelings called forth heroes in sentences whose words kept changing without any difference in meaning; that certain repressions were fated in terms of our daily lives, should we care to consider the date. Jerry's return from where he had been was impossible under the circumstances. Jerry had wanted to be born to another family. This may have been the most important reality which Berti wanted to add to his revolt and explain to his father with whom he had been at cross-purposes for so many years. Jerry was absent henceforth. No lie could bring him back anymore. It may well have been the case that having eventually found the truth he had been seeking, he had got lost in another lie. The truth was destined to remain elusive; a suspicion would linger. Jerry was absent. He had never abided within the boundaries drawn according to his pleasure. The funny thing was that despite all his aspirations, he had been close to them even at times when he felt beyond the blue horizon. He was as present as ever, as a son in the shadows who had gone nowhere in the proper sense of the word and who wasn't going to go anywhere. Monsieur Jacques stood silent. There were tears in Olga's eyes. Upon this controversy Uncle Kirkor had closed the shop earlier than usual saying, "Let's call it a day!" suggesting that those present should better be getting home.

Of which religious order had Jerry become a member?

I had already observed that certain encounters eventually opened the door to those places put off *ad libitum*, and that, whether we wanted to or not, by following those encounters we found ourselves obliged to go on living. This already associates in me the blurred and the silent, and, at the same time, the indelible image of individuals who had been waiting for me in those places. The remaining heroes of our story—whom we understood better and better with every passing day by smothering certain things in our darkness which we could not reveal to anyone, thus having an insight into their essence, discovering their enigmatic labyrinths—had penetrated other individuals for the sake of this waiting. Essentially we owed our growth to those details we learned in those unanticipated moments. Those unanticipated moments moved us back to ourselves. Monsieur Jacques' visits to the shop grew less and less frequent after that 'quake.' These were the first days of his introversion during which he seemed to be in search of a new man. Indulging in the rediscovery of the truer days of a creed, he would, in the course of those days, aspire to embrace the magic of this creed, of an arcane language. He had realized that Jerry was dead, dead as a doornail, and would never come back to the land where he was born and raised. This was an important fact. One ought to review once again all that had been experienced. Certain things had to be enshrined in one's memory. Time was needed in order to have access to what certain individuals had left within us. Jerry had informed us years ago of his intention not to return; he desired that people would consider him to be dead and gone. That weak boy needing protection had found a shelter in that place, in the world he had been looking for. To shoulder this reality was not so easy. The expectations of the future had opened up a large gap. One could understand, under the circumstances, his desire to be considered nonexistent. This was just what happened, or to be precise, how he decided to find his own place in life. Monsieur Jacques had been obliged to embark on a venture and to prepare for a fight with his past, with the man he had nourished within him. The similarity of his story with the separations and settings of other lives lived elsewhere had shed some light on his path. The heroes of the past had left in his custody a great many photographs related to this sad affair which was to remain forever inscribed on his memory. However, what had been divorced from this time, from those deaths and separations that seemed interminable, were things his real family had been trying to build up. The beginning of the fight, or resistance, started at the point where people became conscious of this reality. One might speak of similar feelings in relation to Madame Roza's experiences. However, she had never lost hope, and kept trying to find a point that had escaped the notice of those who had had to shoulder that secret and of those who had preferred to turn a blind eye to it as she had a profound belief in the prospective return of her son. The most concrete expression of this fact was her fervent prayer every morning and night; that their son might be happy in their prosperous home one day. This firm faith should be given the credit it deserved; it had to thrive despite all that had gone on before. Jerry was alive. He simply lived elsewhere and led a different life. He was under the watch of her God; boosted by this conviction, she thought that she served to promote the betterment, welfare, and effectiveness of her son, even from afar. This was the visible aspect of the impressions created by Monsieur Jacques and Madame Roza. On the other hand, there was still the hidden face of the moon, a subject often treated by poets. Yes, the hidden face of the moon or those inaccessible experiences. The face not capable of being reached, viewed, or approached. Nonetheless, what seemed damaging was this desperation, but it was also a source of inspiration at the same time for the poetic imagination. As for Berti, I believe he was a person who had a natural talent for understanding Jerry, unlike the rest of the family members, who hadn't a mind to do so. He had never been able to wipe out that brotherly affection for him despite the lack of gratitude to which he had often been subjected. This affection was nourished by a secret yearning for him. It was a yearning I could never ignore, a yearning that had always been present throughout this long tale. This yearning might have been but the leftovers of a sentiment emptied of its contents and ripped of its true meaning, if one considers the fact that others make us what we actually are with all our deficiencies, inescapable solitudes, and exiles. We had no other choice but to go on living with these leftovers. We had no other choice but to learn how to carry on with our lives despite these leftovers, to transform our passions, resentments, and self-reproaches into new experiences and to lose them in new individuals. These leftovers were the remnants of great upheavals which had assumed meaning in their homeward journey, a meaning that had been concealed. Solitude, absolute solitude had never been our lot. Berti, being the faithful custodian of bitterness, had chosen irony to alleviate his yearning. With reference to his brother's life in the wake of that letter from America—to his brother whose years of youth he had provided me with ample information in a laconic style—he told me he had gone there to study economics at Harvard, gotten married, and become a Mormon. We had taken our shelter once again in that irony that gave one resolution to carry on one's life with heartache to the bitter end. I was one of the participants in the sensation created and boosted by this irony. To what extent was what had already been told correct? What had been the beginning and the end of that thing called truth? Berti's reserve in discussing this connection was understandable; on which I was not in a position to make any comment. Reserve should be considered a defense, a resolution to stay stranded on one's island. I had to have recourse to Juliet's account of the story in order that I might fill in the gaps related to the parts left in the shadows. I had not lost confidence in Jerry, I didn't want to. However, he was for me nothing other than a prospective hero in a story, a dramatic hero, an outsider, capable of reminding one of happiness attainable through deceptions. A couple of details could easily transform him into a ponderable and accessible individual. I had confidence in my instincts. The image suggested by words subject to transformation over time was calling me to a new chamber. Now, I wonder if, by what I could glean along my path after my contact with so many people, I have been transposed to the right and reliable place. I feel a shudder run down my spine. All I can find in the sentences which I have access to now is ultimately muteness and desolation, of which I have a fair knowledge. It seems to me as though I have crossed the border that Berti had delineated through his words and protective coloring. However, this may have been his intention. What he did not want was to be the narrator of this aspect of his life. The Harvard episode was not a secret to be kept inside. Having graduated from Saint Joseph's French college, he had shown signs of his intention to depart to a completely different place and atmosphere, namely America. This was a delayed reaction provoked by his schoolfellows, and especially by the strict discipline of the friars who had been instrumental in showing him the darker side of life. His first letters had been overenthusiastic. This was followed by a long hiatus. To know the reality of life and its diverse aspects came at a price. After all, great work demanded sacrifice and anguish. The long silence that followed his first letters was broken by an unexpected letter in which he intimated that he had gotten married, that he was happy, and ultimately had a family. Monsieur Jacques, in great perplexity, had sent Berti to America. Berti, who had spent a couple of weeks with his brother, had come back with a short account of the whole story. Jerry had married a widow twelve years his senior who had three children. He was happy, or seemed to be so at least. He was living in the countryside on a ranch. Istanbul for him seemed a long way off for various reasons. This marriage had seemed to the members of the family as a tie that was sooner or later destined to be broken. Monsieur Jacques, to whom this alliance had seemed a betrayal, could not help making the following comment: "The Rogue!" he vociferated, "He did it with the wind in his teeth!" In this human cry was concealed a defeat rather than anger. Following this, Monsieur Jacques had once more found himself incarnated as a version of himself temperamentally disinclined to talk; of a Monsieur Jacques who was conscious of the things that he had lost. On the other hand, Madame Roza had concluded that a spell had been cast upon her son and had devised a plan to break it. In her venturesome efforts, she had put more weight than had been her custom on prayers for her son in that distant land. She had rummaged through the cabinet drawers of her son in the hope of discovering things that had escaped her notice before. She had not neglected seeking aid from a sorcerer Berti used to refer to. Her reverting to such an expedient was of course kept secret over the years that passed. Madame Roza never revealed the identity or the whereabouts of that sorcerer. Only once had she mentioned that she was a master of levitation and conversed in cant. Under the circumstances, there should be no doubt that a spell had indeed been cast over Jerry. The breaking of this spell, the communication with a voice 'beyond' might take years. Under the circumstances, the rest of the family members were obliged to consolidate their old links and form a united front. In this front, everybody should choose the part he or she was supposed to play. The key to the mystery was to be found out one day; the spot where it was kept hidden would be discovered. Every progression had its course to run, inexorably changing a person's life. Berti had listened to all of this, with looks expressive of his preference to remain outside this controversy. Monsieur Jacques had responded with a curt saying: "Io no me creyo en estas vaziyuras" (I don't believe in such nonsense!) Madame Roza had to endure in secret, the resentment she felt for having been left in the lurch on this long and arduous path, and she struggled with her son's 'spell' till the end of her life.

It looked as though everybody had eventually protected or tried to protect Jerry, that they were conscious of the fact that he had deposited a part of himself in his new surroundings and that he valued his marriage. Under the circumstances, one had to consider, through a different perspective, the identity of the person to be protected. However, when I recall what Juliet had told me about it at the time, I cannot help thinking, barring all these options and the possible consequences thereof, that I'm almost capable at present of establishing a connection (which may be deemed to be due to a rather simple reason) between this and the fact that one could not probe into the heart of the matter, or, to put it otherwise, the fact that the reality of what had happened had been preferred to be kept undivulged. Monsieur Jacques had, in the course of that secret meeting that had brought the family members together, said: "We're bound to keep this ruined state of ours within the family." I can understand the feeling that this short sentence may have given rise to. When the right time came, people who stood wide apart would have to face this hushed ruin. Once more, heartache was being put off; mourning was being tried to be made more bearable through postponement. Nevertheless, I must not forget to note that those days were pregnant with another coming marriage, namely, the marriage of Berti and Juliet. What had remained with me revealed some other important images. Based on these remains, I can attain another image that seems to cover up both a new hope and a new mourning. Those must have been the days when wedding preparations had been carried out as they should. I feel bound to say that I had run into a traditional play at the point I had arrived. I had tried to observe from different angles the looks that attributed meaning to it. There were moments when our identity as spectators got mixed with our identity as performers; moments when we took up our identity as performers instead of filling our identity as spectators; and there were other moments which we wanted to perceive but were intertwined and lost in one another. Those looks dictated the story of those who wanted to abide in their satisfaction with those small victories. The identity of that person whose mystery of unreality was an enigma was destined to remain unsolved. The fact that a hat or a dress worn or a little gift presented in the synagogue had been the cause of so much talk for such a long time, or, which is more important, the existence of eyes that can perceive certain details properly were of more consequence. It was precisely for this reason that sorrow had tried to be buried in a play about happiness. It may be for this reason that other lives in other lands were built up wrapped in a secret melancholy in defiance of those realities. Madame Roza, on one of those days when the wedding dress was being tried on, was reported to have said, addressing the people who had told her that they were sure that the wedding party promised would be flawless, that she, as a mother, hoped that Jerry's turn would come next. This was the most concrete evidence of her unwillingness to acknowledge his other life in another place. Jerry's actual marriage could not be considered to have been consummated legitimately. It should be appraised as a passing fancy like the Cambridge affair of her first born. An ordinary affair, a fancy which would pave the way to a man's proper matrimony that was meant to last a lifetime. This was, in a way, a cry addressed to himself in his own silence in a foreign language, expressing his wish to believe, and to convince himself of the correctness of what he had undertaken. Immersed in his own silence, to cry, to try to cry despite all the extraneous circumstances surrounding him . . . Apprehensions that were attempted to be hidden gave a different depth to this silence. She feared that Jerry might have fathered a child. Another mother meant another child, and, what is more important still, another world. To be able to trace the genealogy of the family was getting more and more difficult. Even so, she felt obliged to try to withstand it to the bitter end . . . A child might create difficulties for his return to the family. No return, no reunion was impossible. But what was appalling were the lacerations inflicted that never scarred. To dispel his mother's apprehensions, Berti had said to her with a smile that she should not worry on that account. To begin with, there had been no child so far, and that most probably there never would be. Such a child was unimaginable in a land where a boy had taken refuge to escape from his past and where his intention had been to lose himself. Berti's smile concealed a truth to which Madame Roza would never have access. When one thought of the location Jerry was in, one could do nothing but smile. There was no end to the smiles that expressed endless nuances of despair. Madame Roza had had no other question to ask. She felt her question had already been provided with an answer; yes, the answer she had been anticipating was given. By the way, there was a sentence which could have ambiguous meaning. Notwithstanding all the contingencies that could lead us to different stopovers in the light of a diversity of meanings, this sentence caused Madame Roza to remain outside its reality. All this I had learned from Juliet years later, on one of the days when the family had been shattered because of that serious dissension. According to her, Berti had withheld from his mother a very important fact about Jerry; a fact far more important than a prospective child, who, if he was ever to exist, would likely imply to her a secret which would sweep her off her feet . . . a secret imparted solely to Monsieur Jacques. This comparatively insignificant, but all the more important secret, capable of describing an entire life could not possibly be borne by a single individual who wore his heart on his sleeve. Those who had had similar experiences, who had had the daring to face them, could easily understand this. However, this step was not far from being conceivable if one recalled the things that those relations had deprived them of, although it required further clarification. Berti, who might have felt a secret wry joy in communicating to his father the reality about Jerry, had attempted to get even with his father and retaliate against the wall of impediments which he had once raised before him. There was no way of doing away with certain evils; this had been a perennial reality. Perhaps this was the reason for our inability to smother the shadows that loomed within us.

Through these sentences Juliet had once again surged before me and showed her face which had left an indelible impression on my imagination despite the distance separating us. The words, expressing a different color caught over the course of ongoing relationships, were hardly expressible but should be taken at face value. Henceforth, she was disposed to evaluate the 'Marcellina affair' more composedly, not as a woman, but as a mother. I thought that Berti occupied a true place. I felt I ought to describe my account of the affair one day. I had imagined I would be able to revive that hope once more in that chamber, which I would ap-propriate and assess as being an integral part of me. However, one's fancy some-times led one to lose certain people. That detail which Berti had wished to share only with his father was destined to remain a mystery to us. There were still things that we would be imparted with and that we would have the privilege to see. Nonetheless, it had been our decision to nurture that secret in our own way . . .

The milliner at Yüksekkaldırım

In his last letter, Jerry had entrusted his family with a legend, if one may be permitted to qualify it as such. In the origin of that legend, which had induced people to create in their minds their respective heroes, was a wound that was associated, much against their will, with that memory. The images had evoked in me the vocabulary of others. The intervals between Jerry's letters had grown larger and larger and their contents had grown smaller and smaller until they transformed into mere postcards before drying up altogether. Did this with-drawal into silence, this retrogression mean that the separation was to be ev-erlasting, to be eventually transformed by death? As a matter of fact, there had come a day when even those brief phrases had also been spared. The silence that separated them must have be a quietude whose true meaning would reveal itself only gradually. All of a sudden, at the least expected moment, a letter had arrived; a letter whose aim appeared to be to impart the fact that the silence should be interpreted as having existed because of different points of view and different expectations as though echoing the voice of a third person. Jerry, in his letter, went on to say that the things that he had left in his homeland meant nothing to him anymore, that he was at present leading a life they could never imagine and that he would not come back to Istanbul, that it didn't even occur to him to think about it. These lines connoted a definite separation. Jerry wished they would forget about him, as though death had separated him from them. He no longer expected any money transfers from Istanbul, nor letters, nor any messages or visitors. He had better be left alone as he preferred to deal with the challenges of life and their consequences by himself. They would do well not to ask him for an explanation as he was not disposed to give one in any shape whatsoever, and supposing he did, they would not understand it. He expressed that he was at peace such as he had never been before. They had no other choice but to believe the truth of what he said. This conviction might appease their grief. He, for his part, believed that he would be able to forgive their transgressions. It became clear that nothing could be learned about the things that happened to Jerry after the receipt of this letter; what he did, what kind of a life he led, for whose sake he lived, and last but not least, whether he was alive or dead. Everyone who knew him had to endure his or her heartache silently, trying to cover it up deep inside themselves. It must be noted that very few people had been imparted with this scanty information; among others, Aunt Tilda and Monsieur Robert, in the belief that they had a right to know, had been informed thereof. This attitude might perhaps be interpreted as an avoidance of certain fortuitous consequences.

There happened to be another individual who, according to Berti, knew more than enough about this matter. This individual was a Greek milliner who ran a little quaint shop somewhere in the district of Yüksekkaldırım. Madame Roza was an old customer of the shop. As a matter of fact, she felt a deep affection for that woman, an affection similar to the one she had felt for Madame Eleni . . . to speak Greek, or, to live with the Greek language, even though for a very brief period of time . . . Could one imagine it possible to revive the ancient past and the lost children gathered together in a different destiny within this small bracket of time? His mother had had access to this magic through the door of this shop; it was quite probable that in the call of that sorcerer woman there was mixed the voice of this woman as well. Her frequent visits, for different reasons, to her during the wedding preparations undoubtedly had another meaning as well. Returning home from one of her visits, she had said that she had had a talk with Jerry. She had good news to impart to us. She said she had perceived warmth, peace, and affection in her son's voice. It was the voice of someone who had attained his goal. One wonders if that virtual image reflected a sexual perversity. The intimacy of, and the friendship between, Madame Roza and the milliner had continued over several years . . . Their dialogues or seances had taken place in that shop. Their chattering or prevaricating had not leaked out. Different were the places and the individuals toward which despair guided men.

Children of that sea

Despair and the seeking of shelter that despair makes inevitable leads some men toward fevered pursuits. I've learned by now that from such premises I can have access to many a photograph of our lives. We had also attempted to live in different stories and individuals through the words and images that made up our personalities. In the first place, we were but strangers, visitors who were trying to understand, to feel, and to see. Then we had grown accustomed to our condition; when we found the real words in each other's existence, we had made our voices better heard to outsiders and carried those people, in whom we had taken refuge, to others more easily. The story of this refuge was a long story, a hard row to hoe, a dramatic and gripping tale. My recollection of this story was consequential. A casual observer, an actor in the play, would attach, at this juncture, quite different meanings to all the presumed sentences uttered in the course of those days. There surges before me once again that old image, which, lending an ear to the voice of my dreams, I had forced the boundaries of my memory in order to be able to see. They had tried to survive in each other's existence, in spite of themselves. The experience, the narration and the penning of their refuge was a difficult story indeed! In my endeavor to cast this observer and Monsieur Jacques in roles suitable to them, I have once again come across a new sentence or a sentence in whose novelty I should like to be deceived. That observer was no other than Olga herself, Olga the embodiment of solitude and unquenchable longing. That land had also concealed the hope of two individuals who had tried to take shelter in themselves. It is as though the heroes and heroines of that story were approaching nights I had not seen before, in search of that particular hope. Monsieur Jacques speaks and tries to describe his loss and the irredeemable things that Jerry took along with him. Olga pricks her ears again and even goes beyond listening. This mode of address was undoubtedly the most correct one. Under the circumstances, she couldn't be 'that woman,' that good woman who knew like always how to listen and who inspired confidence while listening; she could also detect certain fleeting feelings in an individual who had born witness to a similar adventure from the opposite front. The details differed; they should differ anyhow. However, there were times when certain stories flowed into each other at the least expected moments despite the separation of individuals by time and distance. This was a miracle; a miracle that betokened the invariability of steps taken by certain people; their being doomed to take such steps. The sense of repetition meant, at all events, enslavement, a sort of predestination, a return to the past. Olga had, most probably, described or tried to describe Schwartz, the man whom she revered and who had shed a faint light on her solitude, on his overnight stays in winter, with whom she had an illicit relationship despite her resentment and in whose earnestness she continued to believe to the bitter end. This may have been the voice that had been a source of inspiration for Monsieur Jacques, which had contributed to his clinging to life almost to the very end of his days, an inspiration which had led him to the conviction that Jerry was alive and leading some kind of life somewhere else. It was as though a few moments and a few escapes had built up his strength anew. Now that I'm at it, I feel like reviving the picture of that togetherness within me and delving into the mystery hidden in it and conveying it to others. I feel like embracing those moments never to be forgotten, destined to abide somewhere forever. These moments inspire in me the idea that Olga had achieved domination over Monsieur Jacques, particularly through Jerry and his story. One cannot deny the fact that the sweet scent of Olga's femininity and all its associations had their part to play in this. However, in order to explain such a long relationship under the prevailing conditions, one should look for other cogent reasons. One wonders if the spell had been broken after that serious wrangle in the shop. To provide an affirmative answer to this issue would be doing an injustice to Olga. I'm not disposed to perform such an injustice even though I may be inclined to do so. I feel I'm compelled to see the light about the transformations that occurred in me. To ignore or to obliterate those from the store of my memory are beyond the bounds of possibility. Monsieur Jacques would, after that fatal day, undergo a dramatic transformation that would wind his way toward wordlessness, toward his silent world and make himself feel nearer to his own death after experiencing so many others. Had the women to whom he had remained attached over the course of those days, with mixed sentiments, resentments, hopes, and regrets, latched him onto life? Could one devise other steps, steps invisible to everyone but Monsieur Jacques, to gain admittance to Jerry's story? I think I might venture certain answers; even though the answers that I might try to suggest might be out of the ordinary; while doing so, I might indulge myself in other truths. Yet, what was consequential for me during those days was his determination to ponder over his lost son. In time, certain tales were given wide interpretations. He had told me once that the days when he would be well disposed to have a lengthy talk with his father were not far away. It appeared that he had a lot to say about his fragmented family which he had been trying to integrate. He would feel then as though he had returned from a long journey. He would narrate all his adventures. It would be so comforting and soothing . . . I distinctly remember . . . we happened to be in the shop . . . It was an ordinary evening, having nothing uncommon or exceptional about it; an evening like any other. Having gazed for a long time at the photograph hanging on the wall behind his desk, he said, "the old man seems to have missed us." Then he had stood up and, unhooking it from the wall, he had removed its dust and wrapped it up tightly. The portrait represented a typical Ottoman gentleman wearing a fez, equipped with a cane and an upturned mustache. It had been taken before he had set out in the dead of winter for a tour of Budapest and Vienna. It should be noted however that this would not be his last colloquium with the photograph. The unhooking of it from the wall was a sign of a parting of ways, of a retreat. Only Olga and Uncle Kirkor could have had an insight into this fact. I had no means of learning later what Olga had said to her four walls during her nights of solitude. The boundaries of the story I was supposed to write barred me from this. However, the words uttered by Uncle Kirkor are still in my memory: "We can still keep body and soul together!"

Monsieur Jacques' visits to the shop would go on, although there was one change: he would no longer have a say in the management of the company. Olga and Uncle Gregor's presence there would, as representatives of history and the custodians of secrets, perpetuate an old and unrelinquished memory. There were certain figures in it that still clung to him and breathed raggedly. He needed this feeling for his own sake, to have faith in those deceptions and be ignorant of his delusion. The words "We can still keep body and soul together" reflected a deep-seated affection, a sense of togetherness. There were recollections that could never be consigned to oblivion; they were to remain perennially indestructible. A few days after he had uttered these words, Uncle Kirkor was to pass away silently in his home. I believe I had a fresh view then of the elements that guided one's life. I wondered where exactly the boundaries of absurdity started. In the wake of which resentments and disappointments and who was involved in them at the time. There was no need to assume the identity of the person who had been most grieved by this death—it was Monsieur Jacques. This meant the burial of a togetherness that had lasted for over half a century in a sepulcher where no one would have access to it. Now there was another plausible reason to stay away from the shop. He had stepped onto a path in which he hoped to have a better insight into himself, to know and rediscover himself. In the history of the stiff resistance he had mounted one might encounter the traces of old legends. These legends could be found in books in languages of the ancient past. To resist resolutely, strenuously, was one of the ways of surviving on in other people's bodies despite their reluctance to accept this. All of us had tried and interpreted this legacy. But the path he had chosen was the way of loneliness despite the existence of his women; loneliness or a path of return to the source of a track one had lost. On this path he felt he was getting nearer to himself and consequently to his God. This sort of sentiment had become rekindled in the return of many people whom I knew, whom we knew. But the impression that this attitude of Monsieur Jacques' had left on me was overwhelming. I was to superimpose another meaning to this walk of his. His efforts might have subsumed a steady and silent journey that headed for Jerry or a deep, indestructible groove within him. Not for nothing had he said when he got up on certain mornings from his bed: "I saw Jerry in my dream last night. He fared well. I must go to light a candle today at the synagogue." This ritual was aimed at wishing him a long life. The history of it was recorded in various languages, in different climates, and in the world of sentiment in which it prospered. The oil that burned also established links with other lives. The children of that sea would quite probably never forget this feeling. Monsieur Jacques' progress toward his origin was not limited to these steps, absorbed as he was in books on religion. To speak to other people about the contents of these books aroused a childish enthusiasm in him. The words had endless associations. Yes, the words had endless associations. Was there simply any other way to postpone death or ignore it?

Heading for another summer

There were times when certain wrangles, bitter wrangles, anticipated with bated breath, opened new doors of possibility despite the injuries caused. Those steps taken by Monsieur Jacques were taken, to my mind, toward a solitude likely to generate a rebirth in him. One attained the voice of one's depths by not losing sight of the great distance involved. When I consider the incidents of those days in light of such a point of view, I can say that Berti was getting closer to a new persona. Berti, whom I'd observed during those moments that followed that big wrangle and who seemed to be prepared for all sorts of losses and separations, had said that he had mixed feelings, that he hoped to be able to put them in order though it might take some time, stressing the fact that he did not regret any of his actions despite the injuries that such actions had caused in him. He seemed to feel proud of the individual in revolt within him. He had finally been able to find an outlet to express his feelings of resentment that he had been nourishing along with other resentments that he kept so far confidential. This was a handsome victory, even though a belated one, which comprised defeats as well, but which required belief in a new day, a new street, a new chamber, and a new touch. He was not wrong. Those moments were for him like morning dew despite so many deaths and departures. I must describe him walking, lost in reverie, on his way home from Taksim Square toward Nişantaşı. The attractions of the shop windows and the wan smiles he saw should also be mentioned. The recollections that associated wild fantasies in his mind prompted new steps; those recollections were the food of fantasy and those fantasies were pregnant with new memories.

I should like to see Berti now after all these years in the same street that comprised his dwelling in that small area of Istanbul where quite another thralldom was concealed. I might hide myself in a corner, and thus disguised, watch him trying to recall the people related to him while he ambled: his parents, Juliet, Nora, Rosy, Gordon, Mr. Dyson, Mr. Page, Jerry, Ginette, and Marcellina who would be projected through his bearing. It would be a spring day, a spring day which would inspire in one the desire to take a ferry boat to the islands . . . just like in the days of yore. He would be wearing pants of gabardine, a beige tweed jacket, mauve Italian patent leather shoes to match his pants, a cream shirt, and sage green hand knit necktie. I can visualize him at present as somewhat lackadaisical but well disposed. He was fed by dreams; certain sentiments were enhanced to be felt more concretely; loves were but delusions, which served him to convey his deficiencies to another human being. It may be that the essential problem lay in his wish to perceive illusory images as realities. Then, an image of Marcellina brushing her teeth in the morning would surge before him. Some people left suddenly without informing anybody of their departures in order to get lost somewhere. Some people preferred different places and dates to suit such ends. Whose step was the best and the most appropriate, which step of his had remained in whom? There was no need to know the answer to this! Because, when you awoke one morning you suddenly realized that those realities and truths had lost their former energies. Truths were nullified by other truths or lies. What remained were certain probabilities and the residue of our failure to live. Probabilities and solitudes were but the expression of our fate. Berti would perhaps be asking himself if he would not have preferred to live in a flat overlooking the Bosporus with another woman in a new relationship and if he would dare venture into such a new experience. A muffled voice would give birth once more to new contours. Personally I would prefer to remain hidden in my quiet corner, remote from other people's eyes. I knew how the play was staged. I knew the answer to the question. In spite of all this, I would prefer muteness. Berti would never know what I knew. This was the only way for me to keep it secret in the present story.

The savor of that coffee

"This is my hangout. I pop in mostly in the evening . . . to have a cup of coffee, to browse papers and to spend some time thinking . . . although it is a bit off the beaten track," Ginette said. She looked weary. A sentence had suddenly emerged in my mind, a sentence in which I wanted to place my implicit trust. It would be the opening sentence of our story. Words were liable to undergo changes just like emotions and expectations. The words of other people might get nearer to you after certain deaths. You might appropriate those words; you might prefer to abide in those words in order to declare that you had deserved what you had gone through and suffered justifiably for your losses, for what you had experienced and for experiences you could not bring yourself to enjoy. "Never mind! There is a price to pay for the struggle we put up with to be able to catch those moments. We have to be fully conscious of this price. In nearly every story the important thing is to discover the right place and to know how to abide in that place and in the right individual . . . " I said. She smiled. She sensed that we had been covering distances in a story whose path we had taken and now couldn't stray from even if we wanted to. "But who on earth is he that has created a truth or showed it as though it is alive? Where do we happen to be in actual fact? To which lie are we enslaved; which is that lie that we have never been able to discover? In whose garb do we happen to be; who usurps from us our true emotions and in whose skin are we melting away and eventually dying?" she asked. To remember at the least expected moment the remains of our solitudes, of what we have left behind while entering them, and the things that we had to forego to get rid of them seemed to be preordained. We had to generate time by evasions and apprehensions. We had spent efforts in order to tell others about that time within us. Because of this we have been late in keeping up with those we have loved and because we have failed to find the right answers to these questions. There were nights that seemed to us interminable, as if there would never be a fresh dawn. I have been entertaining this feeling for quite a long time now; it has haunted me in a good many of my stories, in different guises. We had asked ourselves for whose sake and for the love of what expression in us had we tried to revitalize those words. From whom had we hidden ourselves behind those words and remained hidden in the early hours of the morning? She had held me by my hand; her look betrayed the compassion of an elder sister; a love still fresh, preserved, defying the years that had gone by. Were we in a position to describe to each other the time we had spent elsewhere for other people's sake? She had been a person who resolutely tackled her problems and made the best of her time. She should be garbed in the identity of such a hero in my story. I felt I should refresh my confidence in men. I had felt the need to trust a human being, to be the recipient of a new viable image to be formed through new expectations. Was I letting myself be deceived once again since I preferred to be duped by appearances instead of taking up the challenge to face realities? I don't think I'll be inclined to answer this question. I know by now that to try to protect someone means to protect yourself. Ginette was for me a heroine I could not relinquish. I had met her at that hangout for the sake of that story that had been obsessing me. She had said that there she heard her inner voice much better and was disposed to lend an ear to it more attentively. These moments, or in other words, this walk toward her depths had a meaning hidden in an unattainable fissure of her being. I had to mention somewhere in my story that the *raison d'être* of that hangout was to find other cafés and snugs. That day I believe Ginette had a wry countenance. I distinctly remember the sorrow and joy that seemed to be shared on her face. I wonder if this expression could be defined by words in order to be properly described. Could one interpret it as being in the right place at the right time? This had reminded me of the story of those people whom we had met in other lands at different moments. I had recalled the history of my failure to listen and to make other people listen. I had grown mute, saying to myself I could at least smile. I had smiled accordingly. We had been severed by other lives that had thwarted our reunion and by a break during which people had led different lives that they shared with others. We were aware of the fact that we were different. We were also aware that we had to preserve that which carried us to other people so that we could faithfully play it safe. It looked as though the things that had transformed this encounter into a mutual attraction consisted of certain trivia taken from the past; petty details, vestiges of the past that were fossilized; petty details dealt with and unnoticed by outsiders. It was certainly not possible for me to hazard a guess about Ginette's frame of mind at the time. However, I entertained the belief that what we had left at different places for different people was closely related to the history of our moments, of the moments inside us in that brief space of time. I had ordered strudel, which I had already tasted in several cafés in other cities, but the reason why I had asked for it had been to see it as more tangibly under the effect of that little legend I had in mind. In the meantime, in that café in whose nooks and crannies histories were concealed, which awoke in me once again a history comprised of other people's words, I had ventured to set out on the discovery of certain trifles, of my own trivia, which would be transformed one day into a story. Most of the tables were not taken. It appeared that in the off-peak hours the café was not crowded. At a little distance from me there sat an elderly gentleman absorbed in the study of his newspaper who appeared to be seeking a meaning for the war of days gone by; while two women in their forties, oblivious of their surroundings, were engaged in an animated conversation. The luster of the candelabras seemed to conceal an infinite number of recollections of an infinite number of people in which laughter was mixed with grief. "I think I feel better now despite the belated returns and the belated meetings," I said. She had understood what I had meant. "I knew that you'd love this place," she had remarked with an attractive look and smiled. "I think my comment was flat, dull, and trite. Many a story starts with those words, don't they? Sorry to intrude . . . But I couldn't help it. I'm impulsive; forgive my insistence. This is not the first time, I know. Now, you're addled, I'm sure, and hardly know where to place me and to place what I've just told you," she added afterward. "Never mind! Nobody is perfect! I've learned to take people for what they're worth. Don't worry! I'm no longer interested in trying to change people and have them fit my standards," I replied. We had mutually smiled. The sphere of our smiles also embraced our past and the people we had left behind. "This is indeed a miracle!" I avowed to myself; it was a miracle which was to reinforce the belief I entertained in the power of fate, or in meaningful coincidences at least! Our experiences and the distances that had separated us reminded me of that spell. We had within ourselves other steps that carried us to one another. My words had quite probably awakened in her certain old visions, blurred by now. There were tears in her eyes; her voice was trembling; she seemed to convey to me an affection that seemed to have remained almost intact all this time. "Oh, you were so young . . . It was quite a surprise for me to see your name and picture in the paper. It was incredible! 'Is this that gentle, angelic boy?' I said to myself. I had to take a closer look at your photograph. It was you! Yourself! You had changed a lot, but it was you all the same. You've become a writer, have you?" she asked. "This isn't generally acknowledged, mind you! You know what, when I think of that long story I'm supposed to write, nay to live, I feel downcast that I have not even begun to live it yet. And I feel suspicious whether I'm doing the correct thing or just fooling around. On the other hand, I'm well aware of the fact that there's neither truth nor falsehood *per se*. Regardless of the identity of the people we become, now and then we long to hear the sounds of the steps we take toward ourselves. To indulge in fantasy is one thing, to be able to perceive reality and to know how to live or to resign oneself to it is quite another. 'We just live' are everyday words that you can hear in ordinary films and songs . . . " She had made as though she had not listened to or heard my remarks. We had arrived at a critical moment which was supposed to have been anticipated by both of us. In full consciousness of the fact that I was reluctant to lose and that I was doing the impossible, I had tried to catch a glimpse of that elder sister's affection in her which I had been longing for. I would be better able to define this feeling in time. All that I could determine and experience during that moment was the considerable change brought on by the years in her features which I had been keeping in certain compartments of my mind to which I was deeply attached. I do not know whether my recollections had contributed to this impression or if the recollections that I wanted to bring back had. What did I care whether I recalled them or not in my desperation or in my unpreparedness! Just like emotions, words eventually found their place after certain losses, true losses. Just because of this bare fact, these moments were among those that I wanted to carry over to another time. The fact that, in that particular phase of our conversation, she said: "I was personally involved in that talk; naturally you missed me, you were supposed not to catch sight of me. Notwithstanding this fact, the person who had taken cover was not me, but you. I'd felt this. You had retreated just like you used to do in your youth, and had withdrawn into yourself. Your countenance betrayed your defenselessness . . . " referring to those moments. Everybody played his or her own part to the extent their respective histrionic skills allowed; they had to, anyway. Yet I had felt confused in hearing these words. This meant in a sense that I had been caught naked, unawares. It hadn't occurred to me to think that I could live the story in this way as well. There was no such chapter; such a chapter couldn't have been boldly devised during the days when I had a firmer belief in beginnings. The woman that a coincidence had brought to me, after the various touches of the years gone by, was a woman with a better power of intuition and foresight than any woman I had ever met. My so-called nakedness might have redeemed me from oblivion in a lost paradise and the wetness of the night's failures. My confidence in beginnings had remained that night. I was asking myself the reason for my affectionate feelings for a woman whom I had not seen for years, and whom, to be frank, I did not know too well. The answer to this question must be concealed somewhere far beyond the need I had felt for that night. I'm aware that for some years now I had been preparing for the narration of a story. One of the heroes of that story had advanced toward the days I was living in through a dent of words and images which found their places and meanings gradually. In the course of my heading for myself, I had imagined, I think, I was sharing an old complicity, and was desirous to appear before people with my lies, fantasies, and past experiences; desirous of being able to see those people and live through their writing. We owed our days to the women from whom we'd first drawn the breath of life, the women who'd raised us in that place. They gave birth to us in those dawns for the sake of the history of all deceptions. As for the details . . . "To be frank, it hadn't occurred to me to commence my story in this way. I felt myself compelled to narrate your story starting from the day when you had come to Monsieur Jacques' shop as a little girl from the background of the visions transmitted to me of your parents. In other words, I had been seeking ways to live and work through other people's voices. In order to explain the contributions of those voices to this work and to my work, I had to find different expressions, namely my own words. The work contained me; in other words, I should be able to understand better to what extent which part of me I had alienated from you. For whom was that work written? I feel sort of stranded by these questions. However, the places that move me away from you and from myself, whether I like it or not (you may call them what you like), would never have occurred to me as I began to write these first lines of the story, had I been sitting with you at a table in this café listening to your remarks about me. You had become the individual of another place and another time. Having penned this long story, at least a considerable portion of it, I would run into you during one of my strolls on a street in Tel Aviv. We would have difficulty in recognizing each other. Then, you would take me to your home and tell me about your past experiences; the fact that you were married to two men; that with your first husband you had a long marriage but an unhappy life and that you had had two sons from him; that you had got a divorce once your sons had grown; that you continued to live by yourself for a while; that in the meantime you tried to get to know yourself better; that you had ended up by marrying your second husband who was an uninhibited madcap devoted to theater and that you had shared with him a belated happiness; a belated but all the more valuable happiness. Then, you would be teaching French at some school; your profession would seem attractive to you. And then . . . " It was as though I had come to an end. I was silent. She was smiling. It was a winning smile but one that seemed to conceal a sadness. It was as if her story had been a fairy tale, written by somebody else in a distant corner of the earth, for another time. I was resolved to write all these experiences of mine, one day, along with my lies and presumptions. In my cautious passage were also figures that I might have hidden in various nooks and crannies, as my efforts also aimed at showing myself off to my heroes and heroines whom I desired to see again. I was wondering to what extent I would be getting rid of such showers of emotion. Who would be waiting for me in those showers and to what purpose? In the perplexed state in which I happened to be, I could not speak of the evil things to which such questions might lead me. My words had brought us to the threshold of a new silence which could be filled up with other fantasies. It looked as though neither of us was expected to take a step forward. That step, as a necessary consequence of my narration, would be taken by her. "I must say you are wrong in many respects. I don't know in which part of your story you could insert this, or how you can manage it, but my reality is somewhat different from your account of it. For instance, had you been to Israel sometime before the date you mentioned, we might have accidentally run into each other in a street; however, this encounter would likely be not in Tel Aviv but in Haifa. As a matter of fact, I spent some time there on a scholarship; I was doing some research. I'm still there; it's been a year and a half. I did marry, not twice, once only. And I've not been divorced. My husband is a dabbler in art, all right; however, he's not a theater fan; he is a violinist; he plays in the Haifa Philharmonic and often goes on world tours. He is of Polish extraction and has a past quite similar to mine. As a matter of fact, what had brought us together was this similarity. Both of us had experienced losses in our youth which had hampered our growth. I have two children; you were correct; however, one is a boy and the other is a girl. Well . . . We'll talk this over later . . . " she added. It looked as though the clues of a story I could not possibly fantasize of were concealed in her words. Maybe there were things that were desired to be expressed but which found no outlet; things that were withheld right at the moment of their expression; things that were regurgitated; things preferred to be kept in the shadows of the past. We had had this experience before in different climates and in different sentences. This was just one of the emotions that had brought us to the riverbank of the individuals to whom we were inextricably bonded; we could not obliterate their images from our memories. I tried to change the subject; I started talking about the image and the legend of Vienna, where we happened to be, which might be the point of departure to a new and spontaneous story. I happened to be a tourist interested in the buildings and rooms seen on a sightseeing tour. It would be the story of being in pursuit of hopes fed by trivia and wry joys, wonderful in that they were not yet shared. Somewhere there was an image of an adventure, of a little legend. This city which I was resolved to know the ins and outs of by following the tracks of some old photographs, some airs and words which set off the salient characteristics of it, this city which I was resolved to penetrate, might perhaps lead me to experience certain indefinable things not imagined so far which would light the way to the unforeseen labyrinths of a new story. Fantasies and cities . . . I felt compelled to gain access to the meaning of this togetherness, of this lingering hope. A voice was calling us from afar . . . I could describe those visions. The streets I wasn't familiar with had led me once more to one of the squares of the city. I was at the spot where the city met with strangers. The cathedral rose before me in all its splendor. I distinctly remember it. A long and old text which I had tried to enrich with lies, each different from the other, a text which I had been trying to enliven had once consumed me with its light when I had been under the effect of such a vision. The words did not belong to me; the visions and the hopes they contained belonged to other people. All the words I tried to find in those visions for other rooms and shelters belonged to other people. Under the circumstances, I was to enter with that old countenance of mine, with that face of a tourist I was being estranged from. I was standing mute. Those voices I could hear had remained outside the text I had been imagining; once more I had been compelled to converse with people far removed from me. That was the light I wanted to leave in another city, to believe that I had left it in another city. Thus I would not be in a position to touch those colors in the pictures of years gone by. What had changed? What differed after those numerous steps in numerous foreign temples? An emotion wasting away within me was smothering me. Right at this moment, I saw that woman when I was having this experience, the woman who was dragging me toward another faint hope. Before her were strewn hundreds of candles lit for hidden wishes which could be renewed ever after just because they were hidden. Silence reigned there for years on end. Tens of thousands of voices were heard in that silence, in that tunnel of silence, intoned in different places for different worlds. She had also lit a wish candle. On her face there flickered the light of other candles. This was for me one of those little rituals that was performed with all their prerequisites, duly observed despite any deficiencies. It was one of those elaborate rituals frequently practiced throughout the years with patience for the postponement of death. Whose voice was it? To whom was it addressed, for whose life? I was asking my fantasies once more whether I could trust them to show me the way to those stories. Where was I to be heading as an outsider, toward the individual I had lost or had failed to experience? Which different individual would I be trying to become, oblivious to all probabilities? All these questions were doomed to remain unanswered in the depths of that moment. Those questions meant our abandonment, our irredeemable abandonment, our hopelessness we failed to convey to the people we chose. Those questions were our history, our floral scents we could not share, our night walks, our morning cafés whose bedewed tables could not be touched. What had stopped me at that moment, or made me stand stock-still at that spot where these questions had brought me? It was as though there was an invisible wall before that voice which made its presence felt against my will. I had watched that woman from my lair, in her darkness, in such a mood. I could take a few steps forward, merely a few. Both of us were abiding in our respective solitudes, in our zones of security. She seemed to have in her eyes the traces of an inexhaustible longing despite the long separation. The war had ended years ago. The actors in that war had already buried with their dead what they had failed to live. Yet, she was still waiting for that person. It may have been because of this that she came to light a candle there always at the same hour. A candle . . . only one candle . . . in the hope of meeting him . . . Once this had been realized, progress would be easier. However, it was so far so good. Certain stories waited for a real presence just as is the case with those people and their relationships. After all, I had satisfied my need for an unforgettable detail to establish the permanence of the cathedral within me. The said detail should, at that particular instant, remain preserved for other moments. Otherwise, all the appearances there would gradually disappear in the outlines which I could not fit in anywhere in my life and could not account for properly—a construction in the process of moving away from me. The photograph had been shot, like all true photographs for perpetuity, for eternity and permanence. Although that woman had remained here at the said moment, there was another woman who was hailing me from my past. I had first run into her in the lobby of the small hotel which I considered an integral part of my pilgrimage in this city. She hadn't noticed me. She appeared as though she preferred to remain oblivious to her surroundings and her furtive glances seemed to avoid all the figures alien to her, making sure they didn't come into contact with any stranger or hotel guest. I could understand her. Those who closed the borders of a new world had wandered silently through my stories. However, what was important and should be considered from all angles was the reason why I attached such a great importance to the said borders and those beyond them, and the reason why I couldn't restrain myself from speaking about them. The answer, the true answer was hidden somewhere, I knew. In order that

I might understand the reason for this I had to take the risk of making further progress in my journey toward the darkness within me. It was not for nothing they had said that the future was already in the past. The remoteness of that woman to me felt at the same time like her closeness; it was like a stirring that had been awaiting words but failed expression. Before long I came by the knowledge that she happened to be the mother of that man who appeared to have shouldered all the burden of management for the hotel. That man seemed to be one of those heroes who had learned how to endure solitude, who called one to take part in a sad, mysterious, and at the same time, appalling stage play, whose true stories were destined to remain untold, a play that fed upon our fantasies, and what is still more important, upon our fears. He had a gash on his neck. It looked to be a deep wound that had become scarred years ago. Having checked me in in a fastidious and gingerly fashion, he had tended to me my key, saying: "I'm giving you a room that receives plenty of sunlight in the morning; if you think this might disturb you I suggest that you draw the curtains before going to bed." For which I had thanked him as I was particular about it. "In case you feel like having a cup of coffee, I may send it up to relieve the weariness that your journey may have caused," he added as I was heading for my room. My reaction to this suggestion had been quite positive. Not ten minutes had lapsed before he had appeared at my door with a tray which had the appearance of having been rescued from an ancient derelict house about to collapse. I had suddenly felt the need to touch, even though for a brief moment, a memory and to approach it. I had placed a couple of books on the table. A couple of books I intended to experience and read again in a different city. Among the said books was *The World of Yesterday*. As he was placing the tray on the table, the man said: "Welcome to Vienna!" These words must've meant something, for, after a short silence, he added: "You are a writer, I see?" I could answer his question with a question. What had revealed my identity, I wondered; what particular clue might have given him this idea? Which characteristic of a man who had been trying to wade about on a path that many people would envy to be treading? My answer would be met with a sad smile . . . for a moment to be relived and narrated some day . . . A person could attain certain truths only through one's intuitions. "You wouldn't guess it; I haven't read a single book for years now," said the man. "Many a hero that have had an impact on my path thus far have been consigned to oblivion and the new heroes do not recognize me . . . And yet . . . during those nights of apprehension . . . during those days when war had ripped men from this city . . . " he continued, but had to cut it short, leaving the words that had failed him to another time. This was the fate of sentences that were to remain without having had the chance of being transmitted to other people, but to be layered elsewhere at other times and to be resuscitated. Certain texts belonged exclusively to us. "I'm perfectly aware of the consequences that people who are deported are exposed to; regardless of the reasons involved. I've witnessed the same bitter experience in my country as well," I said. He had nodded his approval with a smile, before making for the door. Just as he was about to close the door, he said: "By the way, don't let my mother disturb you. She is a habitual sleeper; as a matter of fact, she is asleep in her room right now. Presently she'll rise and walk through the corridors before settling in her armchair opposite the reception desk only to doze off again. I couldn't part with her." This last sentence had reminded me of an individual I had abandoned somewhere in my story whose trace I had lost. This fact might trigger within me the power of imagination which would lead me to make use of my own sentences. Otherwise, I had no chance of escaping that sleep, that long sleep. I had seen her as I was leaving the premises. She was just like her son had described. She was peacefully asleep in the armchair facing the reception desk. Had she been round the corridors, I wonder; for, I had dozed off for two hours. When I came to, I thought I ought to take up the hotel story where I had left it. Well, the woman was smartly dressed as though she were to attend a formal meeting. She wore a dark blue two-piece suit on whose lapel was a white line. Around her neck was wound a silk scarf with red and black spots; a couple of pearl earrings completed her outfit. Throughout my stay in the hotel she would be wearing the same dress and accessories. A special outfit appeared to have been decided upon for a particular stay. Certain people were attached to their habits of which they could not rid themselves. A like sleep I had witnessed elsewhere. There had been groundings there, a hope that could not be killed off despite all those preparations and belatedness. I had desired to experience to the bitter end once again a moment which seemed to have been mislaid somewhere within me. I had desired to live a certain moment, a precise moment yet again. To shuttle between different times was far from easy. To live the different moments in the same vision called for the transportation of voices that had to be kept muffled to the ears of others. I was striving to be as silent as possible and to keep away all traces of fear. However, the man said: "Don't bother, she won't hear your steps; as a matter of fact, she hears nothing anymore." So, she did not hear anybody; perhaps having witnessed so many lives and deaths, she did not want to see anybody. She looked as though she had lived more than one time in one place where she would have been reluctant to be even a spectator of the incidents around her. The place where I had put up would hardly be qualified as a hotel. It was a sort of boarding house squeezed into a single flat or an old apartment. Thus, the woman's wandering through the corridors at particular hours of the day became more meaningful. As a matter of fact, I was to run into her in one of those corridors one afternoon. I felt tired; I was going back to my room; I felt myself in surroundings from which I was estranged and whose borders I could not trace. The strange thing was that I had had the impression that the woman had come out of my room; that she had momentarily been wandering through the objects that made the room inhabitable. This seemed to be an integral part of my resistance against all that had been experienced and lost. This was a ritual; a desire to walk endlessly using one's own steps in one's own time. I had felt a shudder run down my spine. She was walking slowly, shuffling. She was hunchbacked. She seemed to have difficulty in carrying the burden of her years on her shoulders. She appeared not to have noticed me. As she ran into me in the corridor, I had to move aside, letting her pass. She cast a glance at me; big blue eyes were offset against her wrinkled face. She had her long white hair in a bun. I wondered if I was to remember her features elsewhere. I felt as though I was being charmed by the photograph of an ancient life far away from the city where I happened to be. We had been the spectators of the days we had actually been living from an indefinite time hard to be shared. This was the only communication I had dared to engage her with. She had thanked me and shuffled through the corridor without casting another look. That was the last exchange of words between us. I had not thought it realistic to expect anything further from this relationship. Once more I had preferred to remain aloof from that boundary. There, I thought I would be closer to my falsehoods. I had preferred not to talk with that woman in the cathedral as the writer or the hero of a possible tale in the hope of safeguarding this boundary. I had to leave them in their own stories for my own sake, for the sake of my own tale. Was this another sort of escape? Perhaps. However, a language I was not familiar with, which I found strange, kept me removed not only from the people of a different time but also from the city which I was trying to discover. I had to live the adventure of being a spectator on my journey. I had had a similar experience when I had caught that special particular moment at the opera house. I still remember the torso of Mahler. The mirror behind the torso was contained in other mirrors and the reflection of the crystal candelabra dragged me once again toward the visions that that inexpressible symphony conjured up in me. This was a moment lost on many a visitor. Referring to the owner of that torso, our guide had made the following comment: "He had been the director of this opera house for many years. He was one of our great composers," in total disregard of the blank looks of the tourists to whom I had grown accustomed. I wondered whether a single sentence, void of contents, memorized and recited over and over again, could express that time accurately. If so, for whom had that time been waiting; at whom had those voices been aimed so that they might enable them to forget or delay which deaths? When we had gone down to the orchestra pit, what I had been told had generated a simple history of splendors in me. I had realized that I had severed myself from the group. I seemed to have fallen into a labyrinth replete with new pictures, candelabras, and mirrors. A gentle soul had been instrumental in guiding me through this labyrinth toward the exit. He was tall, with opaque eyes and white skin. He had been following me with his eyes; it was as though he had been there to catch me when I felt lost in this maze. His impressive low tone of voice belonged to someone who was afraid to disturb someone. He gave the impression of a fugitive, trying to escape notice, someone who was not wanted anymore at the place where he belonged, as well as of a security officer who knew the ins and outs of the building long forgotten by the other tenants of the house; a security officer condemned to protect the place. Under the circumstances, how was I supposed to describe and understand who it was? That man might have been a musician, a technician in charge of the lighting of the stage, or a designer who had experienced the true moments of the stage I had been dreaming of a while ago, who wanted to break with the place but couldn't do so. Under the dazzling illumination that lit the stage many different characters and features could figure. Then . . . well . . . then the rest was, I think, a question of experiencing, to the extent our capacities allowed, that brief moment of encounter, as one often comes across in such stories. After all, this was the encounter between a person who would like to express his impressions of the spot he knew so well *sotto voce* through his glances, a person who imagined he saw an old idol in an ancient building. In this meeting were two heroes trying to find their places in this reunion, two heroes looking for their places to settle into. We had gone through corridors our usher had not guided us through in order to reach the exit. Was this a part of the game? The man had said that at the exit everybody ran into the door he deserved. Every door we saw, we succeeded in seeing a vision of ourselves as a new man, a new man we were prepared to transform into. However, in order to continue the path we had trodden, we had to risk the possibility of getting lost when the time came, and of being faced with the impossibility of return from where we had ended up. For a second, my glances had turned outside looking for an answer; but, no sooner had I turned back, then I found myself all alone, abandoned. The man had vanished into thin air in one of those corridors. There remained one thing for me to do: to take that step forward. At the place where I had popped my head out were objects displayed for tourists; in that land where people returned and could not help returning, where odds and ends were sold which they intended to take back to the people they had left behind. There was no end to the number of small torsos shaped in the same mold. Mahler had the same smile as the one in the mirror . . . It was a fact, everybody had his own door he ran into and ventured to open. Darkness was descending over the city, which was preparing itself for a new night. I suddenly noticed that I was walking in the same streets that Stefan Zweig had walked and from which he could not tear himself. A poem had been killed off by other people. Memories had been ransacked by people who would never be able to have an inkling of this poem. I strived to grasp and live that poem through my own words and for my own sake. To linger in fantasies was easier than risking certain truths less injurious to man. Yet a man could not always dally in fantasies. Well, it was destined that I should experience my second disappointment in this city, in this world I had created for myself and of whose reliability I was in need. At the end of that dialogue, I had the opportunity to have a short discussion with two young girls studying at the Faculty of Letters in the University of Vienna about our legacies and the possible legacies of some writers. One could acquire clues about the personalities of those people from the books they read or the songs they considered their favorites. This was a little test, probation for those who saw each other for the first time. Among those figuring on my list was Stefan Zweig, naturally. I came to realize that a writer who had made us a gift of the world's past had been mislaid and consigned to oblivion in that 'eternal yesterday' by our contemporary, fashionable appreciation. Whom had he wanted to convey through the stories of so many lives? Had certain figures had to pay the price of their exile for nothing? Mahler and Zweig's paths converged toward a terminal point, toward a crossroads. We were nearing the end of the twentieth century in Vienna . . . I might go farther, but I had given up. There were many ways of giving birth to solitude.

There was no doubt those photographs had considerably contributed to the long-whispered conversation Ginette and I had held in that café. To what extent had I been able to convey to her the feelings I had been carrying for her, which of these details that had returned to me had succeeded in being transmitted? I don't think that I'm in a position to provide answers to these questions. I distinctly remember, however, at this juncture, that after a long silence she had said: "I think that you are exaggerating, the importance that this country attaches to her past can hardly be compared to other countries' attitudes toward theirs." "Exactly," I rejoined, "we can't get rid of the 'culture' which we tirelessly try to keep alive as 'reported speech'; it appears that we don't want to see it vanish into thin air despite all probabilities. We're trying to perpetuate those cities by feeding them with our lies. Perhaps we are in need of such lies at a time when we are gradually killing off our expectations through our realities and we are getting more and more disabled as we proceed on toward our fellow beings. We are reluctant to lose our countries. These may be experienced by anybody conscious of these restrictions. No one can appropriate anything anymore to the bitter end; we remain content by mere pretensions." "I see . . . but, still Zweig seems to be more indispensable compared to Reşat Nuri," she returned with a smile. I was surprised. I saw that she had derived an impish pleasure from my surprise. One, of course, might throw doubt on the truth of her statement. But what was interesting was that she remembered Reşat Nuri after so many years. She was conscious of this, I'm sure. What was attaching her to Istanbul were Reşat Nuri, and his novel *Shedding of Leaves*, in particular. I believe she had been successful in transposing the city in which she had spent the greater part of her adolescence and youth to her other lives thanks to a few specific details. In time I would have closer access to the meaning of these details. She had been able to manifest a resistance along with her attachment to the old values. I was recalling another characteristic of hers; she would never acknowledge defeat. This attitude was only too natural if one considered what she had left behind, taking her past experiences into account. This was the main reason why I had nodded in agreement to her statements without uttering a word. Furthermore, I was well acquainted with the concern of people who were by nature reluctant to acknowledge defeat. You could not shun your image in the mirror. Therefore, why on earth should I make things difficult for her? In this way I can explain the reason for my silent resignation and avoidance in taking stock of her characteristics. I had to know how to get ready for a possible conflict and be convinced of the fact that one day I could say "I'm ready for the challenge" and be armed with the necessary equipment. All I could do for now was to guess what she might be thinking. Based on my past experience, I had thought it practical to remind her of one of the visions of her past. It was up to her to dwell on it or not; she might go back and try to visualize how she saw that little girl from her adolescence, either disclosing it or keeping it to herself. That was all I could do. Regardless we were the co-authors of the story. We were in Vienna. But I had not yet seen that violinist in the Kartner Strasse. "Something within me suggests that you'll be writing about this city," she said. "'Maybe,' I replied, "but later, much later . . . I've got other books in mind at the moment." Certain incidents led us to very different destinations. "I'm going to write about your parents and sisters, first of all. Pay no attention to what I say, though . . . It's true, this café, this city, our *causerie* may in fact serve as an excellent introduction." I added. She had not felt like covering up her emotion and had held me by the hand. She was aware that we had set out together in pursuit of a new story.

Throwing one's fez into the sea

I am firmly convinced now that the moment which had attached me to Ginette at that café was the moment at which I had touched upon that long story. It was as though all those expectations were heading toward that fascinating moment. Different individuals had left within us differing paths for the sake of different fantasies. Differing paths were, in a sense, differing solitudes; it was, perhaps, an effort to rediscover different shadows and eventualities. To communicate something was to expose, to understand and to know how to perceive things. All these were realities we already knew; they were realities we took cognizance of on our way to finding other people. But to what extent could having knowledge of something serve a purpose in a new relationship? Who had been the lucky minority who had been rescued from those shadows by the instrumentality of knowledge? In order that we could shoulder this story, we ought to take into consideration the necessity of putting up a fierce struggle, of setting off on a long return journey, and of following a new trail. Would we be able to carry each other during this building process and hold each other by the hand just like we had done at other moments? A coincidence, a mere coincidence had been instrumental in arranging our encounter in a city where this story would be blessed with a new commencement. Vienna proved to be a new beginning which had been long put off. I had to persuade myself about the truth of this moment just at the time when I had touched upon that story. According to the account given by Monsieur Jacques about his elder brother and about the father of the woman now seated opposite me, Vienna had had a great part to play in this story. It was a night in a bygone era . . . "Nesim had told me how much he loved Rachael on a day now long since passed," said Monsieur Jacques, "although he seemed to have no intention of returning to Istanbul. It was as though a design was hidden in his words which associated another Istanbul in our minds, one that we could describe. Well, one Sunday evening, the entire family was gathered around the TV. It was one of those evenings when we used to have dinner at Madame Roza's place during which she served cold dishes. Oh the good old days! It was a delight to collaborate in the setting of the table. The plates were fastidiously garnished with salami, peppery kosher, sardines, roza leaves, peach, apple, orange jams, olives, spread made with fish roe, and dried and smoked roe of grey mullet crowned with brewed stewed tea which was served in tiny tea glasses. Berti, Juliet, Rosy, and Nora, all of us were there on that Sunday evening." I don't know what had urged Monsieur Jacques to mention Nesim. We could never have access to that mystery. The mystery belonged to the darkness; in that darkness it ought to find its meaning. That darkness in the text was quite another call . . . It seems to me now more than ever that I'll be able to transform my text to consist of the accounts of lives transmitted to me over the course of many years by men I'll eventually, I hope, be able to patch up using all the fragments of their stories entrusted to me despite all the missing elements and prospective imperfections and hiatuses. Because I can now try to visualize what might have occurred there in my identity as a person who is acquainted with the venue. That sentence could also be interpreted as follows: "Nesim would be able to realize better in Vienna, how much he had loved Rachael, that he could not live without Rachael or forego a life with her and that he could not temp fate." As for the moments lived in Vienna, in that city where he had desired to be able to forget everything, in that city of liberty and dreams which had been for him the symbol of a new life . . . in that city of waltzes reminiscent of the splendor of the Austro-Hungarian Empire, enlivened by visions transmitted to us through a chain of witnesses . . . it was Nesim's second or third year in the city. Monsieur Jacques was not quite sure about the exact date. What he remembered was the receipt, one day, of a postcard, somewhat different from those they usually received. It was long since expected. Nesim wrote that he was to return to Istanbul soon to fix something he could not, for the moment, disclose the nature of. On the postcard was the picture of a phaeton . . . According to Monsieur Jacques, this picture made all the difference; in other words, Nesim must have concealed what he intended to say in this photograph. The picture of a phaeton . . . On the postcards he had sent before there were only typical views of Vienna. To the best of my understanding this picture aimed at reminding his brother of their common cant; it was the conscious subjective aspect of an emotion the brothers shared. One of them had refrained from giving it an explicit shape, while the other had not solicitously inquired into it. Words for the attention of the general public had no meaning as the two brothers had reconnected in the depths of the illustration. However, what was important was what that return projected. Rachael also had begun to wait for his return. This was the good news she had been anticipating. She would make use of the impetus that this piece of news gave her later on. Yet, in those days, this delay seemed to be far removed from everybody. Nobody was in a position to foresee the complete transformations that were likely to take place in the world. The World War was still raging. His study at the Austrian High School, as it is called at present and which had been once the Austro-Hungarian High School, had been instrumental in attaching him, in contrast to his brother's attitude, to the German language and the world of the Germanophile. This attachment had extended its influence over certain details he wrote on the postcards addressed to his relatives in Istanbul. This strong attachment could be witnessed by his use of his second name, which he rarely used, originally written as 'Moşe,' to be spelled as 'Mosche.' This attachment was the reason why he had, having graduated from the high school, left for the capital of the Austro-Hungarian Empire, with the intention to stay there for good. The natural consequence of this immigration, without any intention to go back to the land of one's birth, was the compelling necessity to dispose of some of the things that lingered in one's soul from his country of origin. When I go over his extravaganzas, I think, Nesim could not help setting off on his journeys throughout his life with such intentions. This was fate, it seems; a fate that made him the inveterate traveler of great expeditions despite his short-comings. As a matter of fact, great expeditions were conducive to nostalgic separations, breaking off relations without the possibility of a return. Great expeditions also implied breaks of towering importance, and losses of life defying narration. This state of affairs led one to a new question generated by the wildest dreams one entertained and proliferated through endless expectations. Which of your dreams that you had fostered in that city of your birth, where you had spent your youth, your miserable experiences you are doomed to bear the traces of, could you obliterate from your memory? Nesim, according to the account of Monsieur Jacques, presented an introverted character bordering on autism. Hardly any information was heard from him apart from the fact that the Opera House was gorgeous, that the pastry was delicious, that the people were elegant, etc., which everybody knew already. He had once mentioned a deserted street, quaint decrepit buildings, and a retired, old, or ageless neighbor of his who had been abandoned by all his next-of-kin, relatives, and friends. He was a man who had taught philosophy at the University of Vienna for many years, crowned with the title of Professor, whose courses had attracted a large audience although his works had failed to enable him to establish a link with the general public. He had been imparted with the news about his neighbor, whom he occasionally visited, by his other neighbors. During his visits, the man usually dwelt upon something far removed from his old days and experiences; he discoursed on the Talmud, which he was taught in his youth. The instruction he had received had opened the way to philosophy for him, philosophy which was far beyond the boundaries of religious education. It was this instruction that had contributed to his insight into the spirit of the word, to a clearer thinking, and to a better expression of his ideas. This instruction had served him to correctly interpret many philosophical texts of secular origin, and to achieve mastery in German. I cannot formulate a judgment as to the possible rationale behind the account of his narration of all this to me. On the other hand, how could one account for the interest that Nesim had shown in philosophy? It occurs to me to conjecture that in that city to which he had gone to deal in the trade of carpets, he must often have felt lonely at night and sought to gain affection through the past experiences of that neighbor. However, what was more striking was the expression of the last wishes of that man who said that his end was not very far off. To pontificate about the Talmud implied the narration of a life whose track had been lost. New roots had taken root in a new land. Yet, in the land where he was to remain throughout his lifetime, appalling dangers were looming ahead for the Jews. Many a life was doomed to perish in this territory. Europe had no inkling of the day after tomorrow. Nevertheless he could see the disasters awaiting them reflected in the countenances of his next-of-kin and Nesim. His warnings had at the time fallen on deaf ears. When the time came for Nesim to repair to Istanbul, those cities seemed to be heading for a completely different future. I think I can understand the reasons lying behind the reluctance of those people to see the light after so many years. I am well aware how difficult it is to define truth, or what is believed to be the truth, and to look at it from outside through a different point in time. In other words, the interpretations I'll make will be the expression of myself rather than the description of those people. Therefore, I do not intend to proceed any further at this juncture. Yet, all things considered, I cannot help being obsessed by a question, a key question likely to contribute to my solving it; whether that return, that unexpected return, had been Rachael's doing, or was this love but a mere side-note? Had those who had been eyewitnesses to this incident wished, in defiance of those days, to observe the commotion that this love had caused among the family members? It is doubtful if Monsieur Jacques himself had an inkling of the answer to this question. Nobody could provide a satisfactory explanation for the reasons conducive to Nesim's sudden departure from Vienna, nor to the exact role of the Professor in his life. Now, as for the gossips and rumors that ran after his arrival in Istanbul . . . No sooner was he in Istanbul then he had gotten engaged to Rachael, and a short while after that he had been enlisted in the army. First the return home from Vienna, then the engagement, and to crown it all off the enrollment . . . These vital decisions likely to direct one's path in life had been taken rapidly, more quickly than anticipated. Why the rush? Those were the days in which everyone heading for a different target had high hopes for the future and felt on the eve of a new era. The city was striving to preserve her traditional territory and looked askance at the adventurers. As an enlisted man, Nesim was assigned to a post at the Customs House in Sirkeci, where he had established important links with Indian officers from His Majesty's army. Had he a plan of action in mind that involved a possible post-war re-establishment of relations with the West that he had to forego because of his irrevocable departure for Europe? Upon this unexpected inquiry of mine addressed to Monsieur Jacques, the latter had retorted, not without some unaccountable resentment, saying in a veiled style that every house had its secrets and that appearances should not be deceiving. I had surmised that I had opened up after many years a subject preferred to be kept buried. I had realized once again that I had been barred and could not cross over the boundary delineated by the past of other people; if I still insisted on forcing my way beyond said boundary I would be left in the lurch and what steps I ventured to take would quite possibly lead me to the wrong destination. This was one of the rare questions I would have liked to ask about that man from the distant past. In this long odyssey of mine I had decided to wait and see the fragments patch up slowly over the course of time. I had perfect confidence in the place I had chosen for myself. This was the only perspective through which I could observe those men; they could show me their insularity only in this way. There was no other way for me to keep track of their steps. Everybody needed a listener, after all. We could not escape this fact in the history we tried to write. We would not and could not possibly kill our witnesses and spectators. Every one of us was waiting for a listener ready to lend an ear in earnest. The point at stake might be lying in our inability to listen properly or cause other people to do so. Perceiving the boundaries drawn between us meant our prevention from crossing over them, thus injuring each other. That is why it was of great importance to recount the exact times when questioned. You could not possibly have an idea of the things people would be disposed to divulge, of the anxieties and perplexities they would face. Monsieur Jacques might have been reticent about the real reasons for his elder brother's second departure. After having welcomed innumerable illicit relations, Vienna might have barred the way to her own reality. Different languages might have opened new paths for different people. All these eventualities could be predicted and considered worthy to be taken into consideration. The stories of adventurers lost in foreign lands that had shaped lost people would be recorded as little legends. There would be no end to the stories and fantasies; they were inexhaustible so long as the power of imagination existed. However, when the venture was making headway toward those countries or to the new age, these eventualities could only be taken into consideration up to a certain extent in the case of Nesim. For, the spot where days had dawned for some and waned for others never to be reborn was the exact spot where he had transmuted into a real tragic hero. To have a clearer insight into this I would have to have recourse once more to the testimony of Monsieur Jacques. Under the circumstances, all of us were compelled to understand or at least try to understand the situation, which was one of the paramount requirements of our responsibility, to understand and to discover oneself in the texture of the story and to express it. According to Nesim he was a typical Ottoman. This attachment had turned him into another day's and another man's fight. There was no mystery in this experience. The collapse of an empire was tantamount to the destruction of a country and of its cultural values. Upon the declaration of the republic, Nesim had felt himself an exile in his own fatherland. This implied the obligation to live in a foreign land. These days coincided with the days of the disintegration of the Austro-Hungarian Empire. A history was being consigned to oblivion by others. Those were the days of destruction, the days of devastation which heralded the gradual abandonment of the earth not only of an era but of a world of conception. This desolation pointed to a betrayal and apprehension of failure to find one's compass in an uncertain future. There and then, more than one person would be enjoying this experience. How could one dismiss a world built on ruins while at the same look to preserve identity and values? Nesim would be reluctant to recognize this world and would decide to depart for another in the company of Rachael, heading for new hopes and expectations. A country postulated to be indestructible would gradually gain a new meaning in this journey to those expectancies. On the other hand, no one who fed those hopes with delusions could foresee that this journey would insidiously prepare the ground for a collapse. From the deck of the ship weighing anchor for Marseille, Nesim had waved both his hands as though he wished to express that "that was the end of it all." That was the end of it all! Had his sign been an indication of such a presupposition? If so, the end of what? What was that thing he presumed to have ended, or felt would eventually come to an end? Was Nesim, who was gesticulating on the deck of the vessel, intending to convey to his parents that he had left something on the quay of which he had a premonition? Had he described his destination already? Some desire to contribute to the life of certain people they feel affection for through a different meaning, by their own dreams and wild imagination. The sign may have been pointing to this suspicion. Monsieur Jacques had brought this suspicion to attention for the first time, as far as I can surmise. There was an interval of about twenty years. Monsieur Jacques would turn out to be a believer in fate and consequently in the correctness of this suspicion.

Bound for Marseille at a date when the new country was less than a year old, Nesim seemed to be dejected although full of expectations.

Carpet smuggling

Nesim and Rachael's choice of France as their new home rather than Vienna must be considered natural. In order to be able to perceive the emotional dimensions of this choice, it would suffice to remember the fact that Vienna was, at the time, on the brink of another collapse. The boundary was not clearly perceptible or well-defined; one could not easily trade the time spent in the streets of one country for those of another; Vienna would certainly not undergo changes to the extent that she would allow other cities to replace her, even for a brief period of time. Nesim was adherent to his lies, not being truly conscious that they were actual lies. Despite his estrangement, he had felt affection for his deceits like all his fellow beings . . . Under the circumstances, France was a country yet untouched. Rachael spoke French; she would surely have felt herself half at home there. Paris, on the other hand, was the only city in Europe, other than Vienna, that would be disposed to offer business possibilities for the son of Avram. Considering all the different aspects and contingencies in life it appeared that all the roads ended up in that city, whose legends survived thanks to her language spoken in the other countries of the world. The few years that followed seemed to me to be pointing toward a gloomy era lost in the darkness of the past. All that I could learn through his father's relations was that he had been engaged in the carpet trade, and that he lived in a suburban area with his wife and newborn daughter. At this juncture, we can dwell on certain points which may be fitted in their proper places sometime in the future. Just as in the case of his recounting certain reminiscences about his brother, Monsieur Jacques seemed prudent and wary not to leak anything susceptible to misinterpretation to a third person. What was the reason for this circumspection? Was it to jealously protect Nesim or his failure in having settled his long outstanding accounts with him? Something within me suggests that I will come round to this question and tackle it differently. I believe that certain incidents transmitted to me as 'reported speech' may serve to contribute to the clarification of certain points left in the dark. Nesim had been shuttling between Paris and London, dealing with the sales of certain antique carpets smuggled by his friends in Vienna during the war years from mosques and churches in Serbia, under the pretext of keeping them 'in custody,' thereby making considerable sums of money. Monsieur Jacques seemed to boast of his brother's transactions not without some discomfort. The discomfort to remain unveiled forever was, to my mind, just the tip of the iceberg. Certain emotions remained latent in the dark unless they were touched. After recounting the incidents he had waved his hand and said: "Confound it! None of these rumors have any solid foundation!" On the other hand, the expression "His friends in Vienna" must not be overlooked in the context of the long path I had taken. Was it possible that these so-called friends had been the cause of Nesim's unexpected departure from Vienna? Escape or complicity may well have been the cause. Why not look into the matter from a different angle? Either one of these alternatives might have been the answer, however we cannot go beyond speculations. Monsieur Jacques had not been very articulate in his speech; he had been skillful in erecting barriers before the paths that might lead up to forbidden zones. To be boastful and trigger people's imagination were tactics often reverted to by such individuals.

You had transported the country you loved to that little city

Regardless of the solitude involved, taking refuge in another person's last moment sometimes meant to cling like ivy to one's own life. When I venture to look at the incidents of those days from this window of reality, I realize that I had shared with Nesim's brother a common fate, despite our differences. When one deliberates upon the history of the gales smothered in a woman's soul, one can see that they had played a great part in the life of those two brothers. A voice coming up from the depths into whose source I had been reluctant to delve may have led me to formulate this judgment. In other words, I cannot decide where I am supposed to be in this predicament to which I have been exposed all these years. Cowardice seems to oblige one to seek shelter in reticence. I think we all know by now, the price of reticence and the fact that it robs certain people of their potential. In addition to the inhibitions, restraints, emotions, and hopes generated through the silence shown by the women in the life of the two brothers, there were interior dialogues that seemed never to come to an end. Olga and Madame Roza had penned Monsieur Jacques within the walls of two interrelated and inseparable stories which were integral to each other. As far as I can deduce from what I have been imparted with, a like situation existed in the relationship of Rachael and Nesim. Rachael cut a figure of a woman in pursuit of inner peace and tranquility. This inner peace was concealed by her smiling countenance. Her smile connoted a certain view, a struggle for survival. She was a woman whose taciturnity had a special attraction. I had the aptitude to perceive her finesse. I might strive to listen to the voice of such a silence. I can understand the departure of Nesim, of an introverted person, during a night of loneliness, heading for a woman in whom he had absolute confidence. As far as I can judge, Rachael, who was a tenacious woman, had confidence in her future. Her attitude toward life reflected the inclinations of Madame Roza who had had to undergo severe tribulations; it was difficult to define or describe her frame of mind to others so that they might understand; its origins might be traced to her idea of fate, which extended far beyond land, climate, even time. For example, they could recognize Eve, whom they had never set eyes upon, and who lived in a completely different time bracket, should they ever run into her in any part of this story. This proximity was due to a voice that came from a far distance. This voice was the driving force that perpetuated life's everlasting journeys. Rachael had known the multifarious facets of these journeys. They accounted for the unforgettable days of the past and triggered hopes for a different future. This reminded us of the fact that endurance was an integral part of womanhood. This I infer, out of necessity, from what I have learned to this day. Even during the days when Rachael courageously faced the challenge of a new conflict in Biarritz in the name of this 'togetherness' as she was seeing Nesim off to Vienna, she was firmly convinced that he would return one day, displaying this womanly virtue brilliantly. Subsequent to his dealings in the carpet trade, Nesim, who had figured out that he could no longer be firmly established in Paris, had settled in a small town on the Atlantic coast and continued his life, removed from the stir of society, with the woman who had been faithful to him. This was the farthest point to the West. This point must be given due attention as it marks an important characteristic in the man who was always on the go, a man of fugitive disposition. However, his relinquishing the carpet trade was as important as this characteristic because it connoted the estrangement of his relations with Istanbul. Nesim had actually stepped into a different land then for the first time. Nevertheless, at this juncture, certain details seem to have been lost forever. We run into darkness here, reminiscent of the years he had spent in Paris. I must not omit the letters kept in one of those rooms, letters that Nesim had written to his brother during the initial years of his new life. Monsieur Jacques had said that he had hidden those letters somewhere but could not remember exactly where he put them, and so were lost in the meantime. Where was that place? What sort of a place was it? What fears and solitudes had they carried over to Istanbul? For whom had they been considered as skeletons in the closet? All these questions might seem awkward to the eyewitnesses. One could explain this oblivion through deteriorated mental health over the course of many years, characterized by a marked decline from the individual's former intellectual level and often by emotional apathy. We could wink at Monsieur Jacques' usual remark "well kept, ill searched" and explain it away in relation to these letters. We could justify the lie or at least claim its indispensability. There were situations where lies hit the intended targeted and were transformed into palpable truths. Based on such an assumption, I assume that Monsieur Jacques might have reserved certain things for himself in the wake of his tragic death. To hide or to be hidden was another instance of the effort spent in preserving the days already lived, attributing new meaning to them . . . It followed that certain souvenirs should not be entrusted to the hands of strangers. Those snapshot years that froze at fixed points and at certain moments might not be suitable to be exposed to the eyes of outsiders. One cannot deny or ignore, of course, the meaning and the history of self-exposure. In similar situations, photographs may push us, as well as strangers, toward other episodes. What is of special importance is the illusory effect of those photographs, the dreams which we wish to continue. On the other hand, the snapshots, which we prefer to keep exclusively to ourselves, breed a latent resentment. You may think that you will not be able to express your feelings, your true feelings to another person despite all your goodwill. Reticence is an obligatory choice, a desire to be understood, therefore a kind of revolt. Reticence requires effort in order to appreciate others in a different light; it leads one to listen to oneself better and to open the way to a better self-understanding on the path one has taken. This reticence targets the protection of oneself, the defense of oneself. It was a choice in whose indispensability I wanted to believe. I think I appreciate better now, after so many years, through the phraseology of Monsieur Jacques, that angelic woman who had, throughout her life, resignedly put up a bold front against adversities without a complaint to anybody. It appears not to be so difficult now to find the light I need that would take me to the reality in question, a reality that would allow me to see the features of those years spent in Biarritz. In order to strike roots in that small town by the ocean, it appeared that a fierce battle had to be fought. I wonder if an escape was implied by this journey from Paris in search of a new life. The answer to this question is doomed to remain a mystery to me. It will remain as such during the entire length of my story, a question likely to suggest our occasional disconsolateness in the presence of other people. Results seem certain; one cannot possibly attain wherever he intends to go; speechlessness is another answer to this . . . Nevertheless, we cannot refrain from asking such questions when the right moment comes. The odyssey of our imperfections and of things we could not realize in life calls us back to ourselves. We set out to find that place that has made us 'the other.' I had tried, for instance, to detect a sense of escape in Nesim's sally from Paris to that small town. The travelers of those days might not have experienced this. Nonetheless, I was after a poem, first to find the inspiration for it and then to put it on paper. It was a poem I wanted to see, hear, and live . . . A poem . . . about my imperfections, about the things I could not realize in life and about my regrets . . . A poem . . . even though I know I will be deluding myself as I am looking for myself, as a person . . . Were I to acknowledge Monsieur Jacques' accounts as the only source available, I must say that Nesim had gone to Biarritz, to that centre of tourism, after abandoning the carpet trade, having a new occupation in mind. It was the beginning of the thirties. Nesim tried opening a hosiery shop somewhere near the coastline entitled "Les bas Nisso." Difficulties encountered in isolation must have engendered in him the sadness associated with a new start in life. Paulette was seven and Anette, born in Paris, was but two years old. Those were the days when Rachael acted as a jack-of-all-trades, trying to inspire hope in Nesim by her forbearance and smile, reminiscent of the days of expectation in Istanbul. In such days, just like in the case of people jointly taking up a challenge in the face of adversities, one of the couple ought to be more optimistic and more powerful. The gestures might take hold in the mind of the other individual. On the one hand, she had to shoulder the responsibility of two little girls, on the other, she had the burden of a husband who had gradually become introverted and retired to his solitude, absorbed for hours in papers that arrived from Germany. The children had to be mollycoddled, protected, and cared for with affection and kindness. To be the mother of a family . . . this was one of the periods when she reminded herself of the days in Istanbul, the time that she had spent in that house at Tepebaşı; she looked to turn her new house into a sanctuary, into a warm home for her loved ones. Life was trying once more. In the rounds she made calling at various cafés to pass out the publicity leaflets they had printed for the promotion of their newly opened shop, she had, at times, received interesting offers. These unforgettable moments, to which she was not accustomed, the offers she had received had left in her strange impressions which could be the subject matter of a long story of self-sacrifice. To devote her life entirely to her children in total disregard of all eventualities, to try and find her way in life following such a path was a necessary consequence of settling down in such a place. Nobody was obliged to inquire into the source of this feeling. What was important was to put up with the consequences of that responsibility. To abide there, to abide there forever came at a price. Nesim had payed this price before too many other people had experienced it. It gained meaning through deficiency, a little regret he had had to carry over by chance to his new life, to his new boundaries, enabling me to see him at a special and particular point in time. In the meantime, in addition to her understandable difficulties, Rachael had also suffered because of her insane brother Enrico whom she was obliged to leave in Istanbul, and whom she believed to have lost forever. Enrico had been attached to his elder sister, to the world he saw, with which he tried to familiarize himself. Apparently, after this inevitable separation, he withdrew into himself all the more; he hardly ever spoke, spending the greater part of his time in his own room, going out only to eat or at night when everybody had gone to sleep; he kept reciting the prayers his elder sister had taught him to which he added words of his own invention whose meaning escaped him or to which new meanings had been attributed; he was reluctant to see other people or to become close with them. Nevertheless, to know the real meaning of those prayers, of those supplications, dating from hundreds of years ago, meant almost nothing to Rachael. What was vital for her was the peace of mind her brother found through the words he added to them which associated valuable and singular connotations in him. This was a kind of language entirely severed from the world of reality. At such moments they used to join hands. Rachael had made her brother a gift of a breviary with a silver jacket to enable him to carry on this wonted practice. This gift was like a testament, a kiss of goodbye. Enrico was going to decipher Hebrew in an unconventional way. Could clinging to such an idea be interpreted as an escape? Escapes contained remarkable feats that individuals propagated. Thus, such escapes remained fixed on the reverse side of history in this sense. Nonetheless, this feat to which we frequently returned with a view to knowing ourselves better, would be gaining a special meaning in this tale over time.

Marcel, Rachael's atheist older brother, who prided himself on having remained faithful to the codes of the *Galatasaray Lycée*, and who, after many years of practice as a pharmacist had retired to devote his time to the reading of books of philosophy, had given me when I was enrolled in the French High School, among the books of Voltaire—which, to his mind, would contribute to my French—that breviary with a silver jacket as a 'precious family relic,' saying: "This book is important in that it was my brother's bedside book; my brother who had died in agony. The contents may not interest you but it had served its purpose." At the time I had no idea about the meaning of the word 'atheist,' although I had a vague idea that it connoted something blameworthy. Marcel Algrante was a person who commanded respect thanks to his erudition and life experience. However, this manifestation of respect had kept him somewhat aloof from the usual currents of the day, perhaps due to his aberrant views. Could this be interpreted as a sort of betrayal never openly expressed and doomed to remain dormant? I cannot say for sure whether Madame Roza's remark at seeing this book had shed a ray of light to his remoteness; Madame Roza, who had recalled a school teacher's comments: "It's a pity I cannot bring myself to believe in God, in your God, which grieves me so much," saying: "Atheism brings endless anguish to man, I'm afraid. However, everybody has in him an innate religious sentiment. Hadn't I told you that no one could be an atheist against one's better judgment?" All that I know is the affection I entertained for this quirky individual at a time when I was trying to re-establish the connection in contrast to the attitude of the family members. I had succeeded in expressing this sentiment by saying, when we had met, that I would be giving the book its due, at a time when he spoke of developing his talents, of a 'brotherhood temple,' the meaning of which was far from clear to me, and with which I was far from familiar. To believe in a probability to the bitter end . . . This probability found its true meaning in the impression that that book made on us. It was as though this gift would serve to perpetuate one's life in another. I think I had understood what Marcel Alagrante had meant by 'another God.' These little touches were responsible for that little affection and solidarity between us. These touches would, in time, be responsible for my considerable progress toward that individual. The time would come when I would be attaching the great value that that book deserved. However, for this, I had to fit in their places in my story, the anecdotes that Monsieur Jacques was to transmit to me upon his return from his visit to that small town to see his elder brother and nieces. What had been transmitted were 'their days there,' their apparitions. Biarritz was a city that experienced the bewitching beauty of the ocean. The coastal habitation of Rachael and Nesim was a flat above their shop. The brine that clung to the shop window necessitated wiping every morning. The English tourists used to climb the heights to have a view of the huge billows, some measuring more than a few meters. The sight was overwhelming especially in stormy weather. He had been among its regular spectators. He recalled the sea of his youth when he used to accompany his mother to the swimming complex for women at the Golden Horn. He hadn't acquired mastery in swimming and so he dared not go far from the shore. The sight of the billows scared him even from afar; he associated them with death. The town was near the border. They often crossed over the border and visited the Basque Provinces. He had acquired a smattering of Spanish. To observe that his vernacular had some currency in a foreign country had pleased him. The warm feeling that this had engendered in him was to survive over many years, coupled with its lies and delusions. The two brothers had strolled along the beach at Biarritz recalling the experiences of their youth. Nesim appeared to be content with his actual life; he looked happy. He loved his wife and children. He no longer missed Istanbul. It hadn't been so easy at the beginning, but he had got used to this sort of life. He had succeeded once again to feel at home in a foreign land. He did miss a few things and a few flavors. However, what made life worth living was yearning and longing for the things one loved, the rest should be considered mere residue of experience. Every departure and separation came at a price. What was important was his discovery of a new life in a small town on a distant coast. He had turned his back on the cities that had attracted him through their legends long ago. No, he wouldn't go back, he just couldn't. He had new surroundings, new acquaintances, a new family, and a new language. His squat figure had earned him the nickname 'Le petit Turc.' That was his identity there. When he thought of the struggle he had put up in settling there, he felt happiness mingled with some trepidation. Now and then he gave recitals to his neighbors just like he used to do in Vienna and sang old Spanish songs and romances. He was loved and respected. The incidents in Germany, whose language was his vernacular, upset him in a way. However, he had decided not to speak his mind. "Tomorrow will be another day," he said, "a day will come when even 'they themselves' cannot but avow the devastation they would cause." Who would have guessed that those billows would rise and fall at such a distance?

Enrico was about to fall into a well

Among the things that Monsieur Jacques had imported from Biarritz were also the memories of long nocturnal *tête-à-têtes* with Rachael. Those were the nights when Nesim retired to his chamber with his dailies and magazines. The main topic of discussion was Enrico. Rachael had recounted what she had done for her brother, to be precise, what she wanted, but failed to do for him, mentioning that she would never forget how they held each other's hands so tightly. She had held him, a wounded boy, by the hand trying to cross the border of that little world. She had wanted to be the elder sister of a person doomed to remain a boy. That was another world that others could not understand so easily. In that small town she seemed happy in her own way; there were people around her whose hands she grasped with different feelings and expectations. She felt he was living in his own reality among her family members whom she could no longer abandon. She thanked God every night before going to bed for having blessed her with such a life, although she was filled with regret when she thought of Enrico whom she had abandoned within those borders. In her daily prayers she asked to be pardoned for this transgression. Certain nights seemed interminable to her; she was unable to sleep, and when she dozed off, she had nightmares. In one of those nightmares she had seen her brother with that book in his hand stammering incomprehensibly. She took it to be a favorable sign. Whatever the past experiences may have been it was not too late for certain new 'exploits.' This was a way of inquiring into the state in which Enrico may have been. He had understood this. Notwithstanding, he had withheld certain important things from Rachael; he had merely stated that life had dispersed the members of the family and even the nearest relatives failed to communicate with each other. He could not bring himself to tell her that Enrico, after having stammered incomprehensible syllables in his room one night, had stretched himself on his bed, and, in a lethargic manner, had said "Rahelicas, me esto cayendo al pozo" (Rachael dear, I'm falling into a well, hold my hand tight!) before expiring. He had promised Marcel Algrante, who had described these hours in their minutest detail, that he would not disclose them to anybody. He didn't doubt that through this lie he had discovered a truth, the truth of that day. Rachael would never be ready for the storm that this truth might provoke.

This death was not the only death that he would keep secret. Different deaths at different places would have to be kept quiet.

Rachael was to hear of Enrico's death much later. I don't know to what extent this stratagem had been successful. To the best of my knowledge, Monsieur Jacques was in no better position to know. Notwithstanding, Rachael, despite the fact that she tried to convince herself that everything seemed to be alright, her intuitive power was making her restless. Toward the end of that night she said: "I cannot forget what I did to him." In this sentence there was concealed not only her wish to preserve her disloyalty in her memory, but also her desire for it to be consigned to oblivion. She could not have expressed this any better. This recollection would remain indelibly stamped on her mind. He had taken in his arms this woman whose self-sacrifice had made many a soul more than happy; she had sought happiness in the eyes of those she loved. She had made a vow: what she had done for her brother would be known and acknowledged by everybody one day.

To forecast a brewing storm

The Biarritz days would be the last days in which Monsieur Jacques would be able to see his family members at the other extremity of Europe. Years had to go by before Ginette came into the world as a 'surprise child' after two charming French girls. On his way back, he had sojourned to San Sebastian in the Basque Provinces before proceeding on to Italy to observe the splendid panorama that fascism displayed in Rome. An emotion, difficult to describe, had overwhelmed him, like many people. Was this due to admiration? He couldn't tell. In order to understand it better he had to have a closer look at the situation. This was his philosophy on board the ship which had weighed anchor from Naples and was en route to Istanbul. A storm was brewing whose effects would also be felt in the waters of the Bosporus in due course, which people could not predict at the time. In the meantime there would be wars, peace, deaths, the collapse of countries, and people would be immigrating to unknown destinations without understanding why. Theirs were different lives, lives in different times. For us, for those of us who had stayed behind . . . Well, a gap opened wide between us and those people, regardless of the experiences and accounts that came to light; a gap never to be filled. Now we are busy speaking of a gap we are at a loss to understand, using our own language, in the languages of this world. I wonder whether those that remained behind, in that age can understand our language. The answer to this question was certainly concealed in that breach. Are the words, the words that engendered in us so many lives waiting to be discovered so that we can re-edit what has already be expressed?

You could not snuff out the dark

I wish Marcel Algrante, with whom I could never develop an intimate relationship, knew that I had been keeping guard over that breviary he had made me a gift of in one of the drawers of my cabinet, at a place quite different from the places it is usually kept, in other words, its correct place. Here, a latent attempt at self-exposure can be witnessed once more; extravagant or willfully conspicuous behavior which cannot be repressed and reveals itself all the more in certain relations and snapshots; the same pattern of behavior marked with attempts to reproduce it defying all inclinations to consign it to oblivion . . . with a view to carrying on one's life in the company of our resentments . . . to perpetuating our existence despite our deficiencies . . . The result remains the same, though; one cannot interfere with it, it seems. The child does not want to get lost in the dark, it cannot abide for long in the body of a stranger; it is reluctant to find a shelter within him. On the other hand, the adult, the mature person, cannot do away with that child; he cannot avoid seeing its images in his dreams, nor can he remove it from the apprehensions he could not account for. Thus, we stand exposed to endless questions begging for answers. Would you not be disposed to do for that little child what you would do for others? Would letters you wrote hoping to convey to others the moments and the people you have left behind, as they are reflected on your history, in their echoes and visions not carry express concern? This may have been the effectual cause that had induced me to pen the story of Nesim and Rachael, which holds true also for 'that letter' expressive of compelling evidence . . . even for that letter which enables us to timidly touch that aspect of life which we will never be able to understand and describe properly . . . even though that testimony 'there' be a testimony to be shared and never forgotten. That letter was the only one Monsieur Jacques had succeeded in unearthing among the heaps of letters that his elder brother had left in which he spoke of his life and which was given to me in spite of all concerns. The lines that would inform us of Nesim's experiences in Paris and give us clues about whether his view of Istanbul had been mislaid or simply lost. Life had caused him to meet people who would interpret certain emotions wrongly. He had to endure the consequences of betrayals originated from unreserved confidence invested in other people. In other words, he had learned how to be prudent. Thus, it was possible to look for the real cause of his preference for speaking cursorily about the affective attitude of those letters in this insecurity. However, this letter was different; it had not been written by Nesim; it did not include the exchange of intimate feelings; it looked like a story finished and concluded. The author of the letter was Enrico Weizman, the newspaper seller who had been with Nesim on their death march to the concentration camps. The letter had been mailed in 1945 from Biarritz, addressed to Monsieur Jacques. The account had to be put to paper by someone, even though the words were not sufficient to reflect the actual truth. I believe that the writer, the reader, and the person who had posted it had believed in the veracity of its contents. The same questions had arisen in me as well at a time when I had been hearing the sound of the steps pointed toward death. I wonder if the words, the words to which we could have access, the words that enable us to convey the experiences we had of those camps to other people contributed slowly to our longing fostered in many a text. Would I be able to understand what had been left, abandoned or lost 'there' by the help of words with their equivalents within me? Would those recollections allow us to restore in a new text those experiences in defiance of those witnesses? The experiences had expressed that certain moments could not be narrated in those texts, that the words would fall short of justification. However, I believed that, daring to repeat the same wrongs despite all the restrictions imposed, I had felt that I had to try, or at least observed that I had tried. It appeared that I had to try despite the stares of other people which we could not easily escape, for a story which I believed had not been written yet in the geography of my emotional life, and which had not yet been exhausted. Following these words I could perhaps follow this new voice to those letters that would enliven in me, my own genuine letters . . . Then . . . the time that followed belonged to other hours, other discoveries and silences.

Enrico Weizman had a newspaper stand at Biarritz. He was a confirmed communist who had escaped from Spain in the wake of the defeat of the insurgents. He had his own abode somewhere and a modest family. He was the closest friend of Nesim and Rachael . . . He had been thirty-nine when he was interned. When he returned, his age was irrelevant.

The letter from the concentration camp

Enrico Weizmann's letter seemed to me as though it had come out of space and eternity, despite its accuracy and substantiality. This state of affairs was accompanied by a sense of impermeability. What I had experienced entailed many an interpretation and question; I had conceived this venture during my lengthy studies on the matter; yet, there seemed to be things between the lines that forestalled my march toward those individuals, toward the source. I was realizing once more the necessity of reticence. This is the reason why I contented myself with merely 'showing' the letter, just like Monsieur Jacques. Its contents will find their way into the story, I know. Under the circumstances, I have no other choice but to endure my hopes forever, despite their detriments. I feel bound to pursue the right words even though I may run the risk of straying from the direct path. This path had already been trodden in pursuit of other pasts lost or stolen. Those people, those who had succeeded in returning from there had to wait for years to find a place for themselves, thus struggling against their own lives. Most of them had preferred to march on toward their new countries rather than going back to their homeland, toward new destinies in the new lands they had been heading for. Enrico Weizman had been among those who had been able to come back to his point of departure. He had already lost his homeland, his true fatherland. This had contributed to his endurance of the suffering he had to undergo, to his ability to delineate the borders of his country for himself alone, despite exiles, deaths, and the impossibility of return. In the course of this self-pursuit, the voice of silence, earned in return for a consideration, had to be heard. Despite my cramped condition, I had to listen to this voice between the lines. I had understood that thanks to my words, during my days of slavery that one had to risk new abandonments.

My dear friend,

Through the postcard I had sent you as soon as I got back, I had wanted to inform you that I had arrived here safe and sound. I had not had the opportunity to go into details. I was not ready for this. I'm going to speak to you now about our tragedy that started at 02.00 a.m. January 11th, 1944.

When they came to arrest us as criminals, we had long been asleep. Maria was pregnant with our second child. This I distinctly remember. I realize nonetheless that a good many substantial things which might re-connect me to my place, from which I had been ripped, have been obliterated from my memory. However, not a long time had elapsed in the meantime. Only recently had we been together with our loved ones. We believed that we would open our eyes to another day. When one wants to forget certain things one just does. One forgets them, or thinks that he has forgotten them; even though time appears short to those who live their morning routines. I'm saying all this just to draw your attention to my ignorance of the exact date of her pregnancy. I believe it was her fourth month of pregnancy. Or it might have been her third . . . anyway . . . It is not important any more . . . There is no end to the number of things we have lost in the mist of our past, of our darkness. Yet, we have not learned how to lose . . . because of our resolve. Daniella, my first-born, had done her homework, and was ready for her French test the next morning. Having performed her task, she had gone to bed with a clear conscience. A strange coincidence, she had asked me to tell her the tale of Little Thumb; she had listened to the very end of it (by the way she usually fell asleep before the end of the tale, confident in the protection her storyteller father could offer.) Then I used to caress her hair staring long at her. I recalled other tales I had long forgotten. I promised myself to recall them later and tell them to her one-by-one. I was positive about this, although I had not forgotten what I had gone through in the past and the things that I had to leave behind. "Dad, if I ever get lost in a wood you'll come to my aid, won't you?" she had asked once. "Certainly, dear," I had rejoined, "You'll also rescue my brother who's waiting to be born, won't you?" I had kept silent. This reminded me of the corpses we had to abandon in the wood. They were the children who had strayed and could not find their way back. "Certainly, my dear, your father will find you and rescue you." I had promised myself to keep my children removed from this nightmare. How could I ever guess that the same fate would be knocking on our door so soon after? Difficult to believe, isn't it? You may think that I'm exaggerating a bit, that my imagination is running wild. Not at all! In our tribulations there was no room for imagination. The things we were going through and could not escape were already forcing the boundaries of our imagination. It's true; I had promised Daniella I would come to her aid. What else could a father do? However, this conversation was fated to be our last effectual exchange of words. I was soon to witness how helpless we would be in the face of certain incidents, despite our conviction to the contrary. In fact I was going to lose a precious part of myself that would be ripped from my entrails. It so happened that Liliane had stayed with us over-night. Her mastery of the German language, her mentioning of certain names likely to be influential seemed at first to be of some use. She spoke about her sister's situation, of her pregnancy. Whereupon, they said that they would be taking me solely, 'for the moment,' and would be thinking over the cases of the rest. This was a blessing amid the heaps of grief. I found an opportunity to whisper into my wife's ear to get prepared for a journey with our daughter, to take with her whatever valuables she could find and set off soon. On the way to my destination all that occupied my mind was how they would manage to escape and whether it was at all possible. They at least had a chance to flee this nightmare. However, my joy was not to last for long. Maria had not been quick enough as she thought that they might not return so soon; they found them in the state they had been left. No word could be heard anymore, between the whole lot of us including Maria, Daniella, Nesim, Rachael, Paulette, Anette, Isaac, Lilianne, and myself. We met a short time later in the Bayonne prison. We were intrepid explorers of a land we did not know, or better still, one we did not want to admit was there. We were not in a position to realize what was happening to us. We tried to survive, each one of us in a different fashion, grounding ourselves in our habits and imaginations. Everything was topsy-turvy and we were all curious. Everything had happened so quickly and unexpectedly. It was too late for controversies, interrogations, and cross-examinations. We had been expecting such an onslaught alright, but for some reason or another we had a latent conviction that we could find a way of escape. Spain was not very far, if the worst came to the worst. Personally, this path was far from being secure for me. But, I could manage somehow. "Why did you linger and not set off immediately, remaining with folded arms?" you may ask. No explanation. Routine enslaves one and binds you to insignificant things. You cannot do away with them, with these fatuities; you unconsciously let yourself be enslaved by your habits. Nesim, relying on his Turkish citizenship, believed that they wouldn't touch him. This was a privilege from which his relatives would also benefit. He had his children registered as Turkish citizens at their birth al-though they were born in France. (There might be one exception, however; I was not so sure of Ginette's registered nationality. Anyway her fate would not be the same as ours.) This was quite astonishing for me, an attitude involving contradic-tory elements. She had told me all about her experiences regarding her departure from Istanbul and that she had found the serenity she had been looking for in

Biarritz, stressing that she had not the slightest intention to go back. You must have discussed this subject during your visit here. She must have given you all the details relative to her resoluteness. Yet, I feel as though she had had certain secrets which she kept to herself. She had a sentimental attachment to Istanbul which she did not confess even to herself. She just could not acknowledge it. I felt it. The same attachment I had myself to Teruel in Spain which I was forced to leave and for which I harbored bitter resentment. We took the cities we lived in for our own kingdoms. Although we now and then remembered the fact that we bore in our depths similar sentiments for other cities we had lived in. The city in which he had spent his childhood and had to depart from later was for Nesim a perennial realm, lasting indefinitely and impervious to change. Istanbul, he grew wistful about, excessively sentimental, sometimes feeling an abnormal yearning to return to it. This was a yearning to return not only to a geographical setting or climate but also to an irredeemable past. For him, Istanbul brought to mind the 'Last Ottomans' as well. During those nights when we were hunted by the Gestapo, he had said: "If only we had stayed where we were . . . Comfortably settled in our house overlooking the Golden Horn, we would now be dreaming of a more fascinating country . . . It must be the season of the blue fish now." This was enough to show me how nostalgic he felt about Istanbul and about his losses. Rachael's eyes were wet with tears; her tears also reflected other feelings of hopelessness and resentment. All of us were linked to our past. The blue fish I heard mentioned for the first time by Nesim had become associated for some reason or another with Istanbul. The fact that I still dwell on such an insignificant detail surprises me. On the other hand, I don't want to turn a deaf ear to the call of nature. When I come over, one of the first things that I will be asking from you will be to take me to a fish restaurant. The night within me calls for this . . .

That was the last time that Nesim mentioned Istanbul. His acknowledgment of the New Nation and making it his own must have been due to his attachment to his native country. He was fully aware of the fact that he could not betray it despite all likely developments and changes. Everybody who knew him closely was aware of this. One should not forget, however, that this had a pragmatic side as well. To hold the citizenship of a foreign country in a strange land is always advantageous so long as your economic situation is all right. How come that Nesim, who was well acquainted with all these intricacies and had access to that valuable intelligence according to which Turkish citizens enjoyed privilege had missed this important fact? I was not a fatalist, nor am I at present. My experiences have taught me to have confidence in coincidences. This might suggest you have recourse to your fate naturally. When I recollect those coincidences and unanticipated life choices, I feel like keeping silent; simply to keep silent . . . The incidents that took us to the prison had developed at a dizzying speed . . . Nesim had been arrested four or five days before us. You should have seen the moment he and Rachael encountered each other in the prison. We had all given in to tears. We were in such a plight that any spark could kindle a fire in us. Rachael had clasped Nesim firmly, saying: "I thought I'd never be able to see you again." I was witnessing that love; true love provided the vital force one needed. I had once again borne testimony to a love rarely experienced by a human being. What I have gone through in my life has transformed, eroded, and corrupted lots of things with the exception of this conviction. This conviction I tried to keep intact partly because of my observations at the time. Then I noticed the grief in Nesim's eyes as he stared at his daughters, Paulette and Anette. "I had to entrust Ginette with Madame Manzi. It was the only thing I could do . . . under the circumstances, I could leave only one of our children and I chose the youngest. At least she would be able to outlast us without deeply feeling the bitterness of our experience, by remembering certain incidents, and to start a new life, perhaps. Forgive me," Rachael had said. At these words we were strangely overjoyed. It was a joy nourished by grief, a grief never to be forgotten . . . One of us at least would resolutely be heading for a new life. We were ready to face the adversities now. We knew that we were going to change and how difficult it would be to go back. I had noticed the grateful expression in Nesim's stare toward Rachael. They were no longer able to exchange such looks nor would they be allowed to embrace each other. Paulette, who had also noticed this, had said: "This was our common decision, father." It was not difficult to guess the meaning that this sentence conveyed. Who knows, perhaps Nesim's looks also expressed a regret to have begotten his children in France. Paulette was twenty and Anette sixteen, at the time. Ginette was barely four years old. Only the three of us had experienced regret. I stood near Nesim and Rachael. We were enjoying once again a moment of togetherness which we were reluctant to put into words. The words would follow later . . . We had more than enough time to babble. We were obliged to talk and talk in order that we might cling to life and keep our souls alive. For us, every single detail was important henceforth, details that under normal conditions would be trivial. I would like now to share these details to the extent I can haul them from the store of my memory.

As I have already told you, Nesim had been arrested before us. I hope you'll overlook my repetitions. I cannot help being verbose at times. This is something new with me. I believe this helps me to concentrate on my thoughts. Otherwise I cannot focus if these repetitions that expose my obsessions are kept undisclosed. In the coming years I may reveal the skeletons in my closet, I hope. Let's wait and see, let's keep waiting . . . Nesim had set out for that journey of no return on a Sunday morning. That morning, before he heard the knocking on the door by the 'uninvited guests,' he had got up in a gleeful mood he had not experienced for quite some time: he prepared breakfast, and put on one of his favorite outfits, knotted his tie fastidiously, and polished his shoes. He had then brewed tea in the 'Turkish manner.' This was, by the way, one of the habits Rachael and he had never broken with. In the meantime, he had opened the lid of the orange jam jar he had been keeping for a special occasion, placing it carefully on the table, quite unaware of what was awaiting him and his family. The visitors had come when the household members had gathered around the table taking joy from his merriment. The visitors had acted in the most refined manner; they had asked Nesim to go with them to the headquarters for some insignificant formalities. "Very well," Nesim had said. Although he still felt optimistic about it, he had not neglected to whisper in the ear of Rachael just before leaving: "I think I'm being taken to an unknown destination," adding, "one has to be ready for every contingency; do your best to entrust the children to a member of our family." It was a great responsibility. Rachael was trying to express her hopelessness as she was narrating the incidents to me. Was there still a flicker of hope to return to Istanbul? They began to consider this eventuality when no news came from Nesim since his departure two days previously. Paulette had suggested that everybody had better go on their own and take the path he or she deemed best; they should not attract attention. Anette had said that she would go with her elder sister. Ginette was in her confined world and was not aware of what was happening and what should be expected in the future. Rachael had felt pride mixed with a deep sadness due to their eldest daughter's readiness to confront such adversity. In case they would be obliged to live somewhere else, it appeared that they had sufficiently grown up to consider life as a little game . . . However, all these suggestions seemed unacceptable. She could not be divested from her fixed legacy. Despite her many years in France, she had a different identity, she had preserved in her a different person; she had, actually, lived on a different emotional plain. They had to set out together toward their fated destination. They had begun elaborating on different alternatives; they were planning to travel through Spain, from the free zone perhaps. Conceivably they would be obliged to bribe their passage. She had touched her jewel box in her chamber. Then she had cast a glance at her reflection in the mirror, having a closer look at her wrinkles. Nesim, on the dresser in front of her, was looking at her with a smile. She was realizing that there was no way out, all things considered. New schemes had to be envisaged. On the morning of the third day, their maid, Madame Manzil, had knocked on their door in great perplexity and said that the Gestapo had been patrolling the grounds; intruding on the privacy of people and arresting them at random. An immediate decision had been taken about Madame Manzil's custodianship of Ginette. Rachael communicated Nesim's last wish to her, which she had accepted heartily saying: "Well, of course, people must be helping each other out in such times. Soon nobody will be able to look into the face of his or her fellow being," and added: "However, I can manage only Ginette, since to hide a little girl is easier, after all." She had other problems as well, with regard to the rested space. Her account was certainly correct and plausible. The moment was not propitious to hide oneself behind lies; realities had to be faced; rapid and realistic solutions had to be envisaged. This had facilitated taking that step. Everybody had first lent an ear to their inner feelings. This process had not lasted long. They told Ginette that they had to set out on a long journey in order to bring their father back, while the journey was not suitable for a little girl of that age. They told her that this might take some time, although they would do their best to make it as soon as possible. Madame Manzil's account had been the same. She would be doing her best to protect her and care for her. Rachael had asked Madame Manzil to pray for them. At such moments every one of us had to believe in something.

The next day we were woken at four in the morning and taken like criminals at gunpoint by three soldiers. Daniella, dumbfounded as she was, kept saying that she had to go to school while clasping my hand. She was asking me where we were being taken. I said I hadn't the slightest idea. After so many years I realize that the answer I had given was correct. Anyone who had not had the opportunity to see those places could not fathom them. I had also said to my daughter that all this was part of a game. Somebody was playing a trick on us, or staging a play; yes, a play, since all these could be interpreted as scenes of a play; one which destroyed its actors leaving the remaining scenes without players; scenes in which the children aged before their time, a play they watched with unfocused eyes, a play they were compelled to act in.

Before long we had found ourselves at the platform where freight cars stood behind the train station. They were actually livestock cars. You can guess how they shoved us into them with coarse insults. Each car contained sixty people. Among us were octogenarians and newborn babies. Once filled, the doors were slammed shut and bolts were pushed through; during the two-day journey we had had to answer the call of nature in the car. At the conclusion of the second day we arrived at Drancy. Legal formalities were performed, among others 'cross-examinations.' My situation and the situation of my wife and daughter were clear enough. Our formalities took no time; decisions were made immediately. Notwithstanding our situation we still entertained some hope for Nesim and his family. After all they were Turkish nationals, subjects of a country for which Germans had some affinity. I was aware that it was too late. But hope persisted. Nevertheless, our privileged case was disregarded. To be a Jew meant to be a criminal to the Germans. Nesim's impeccable German dating from his Viennese days might have served some purpose. It was up to your elder brother to decide rather than up to them. It was unacceptable for him to observe the betrayal and ill treatment by a culture he had always admired. He had vowed not to speak German from that moment on; he had buried the language deep within himself. His mastery of the language could serve him as an asset that should not be waived. Everybody tried to discover something to hold onto in those days. This betrayal had enabled him to see the collapse of something in his depths. That was the moment of his death, the moment when he had resigned himself to death. Death, for him, started exactly at the moment in question, at the very moment when silence fell.

Following the interrogation, we, as a collective mass, without distinction of sex or age, were dragged out of the room. Once outside, Paulette, in her pristine innocence, said, remembering her boyfriend: "I hadn't the opportunity to make a call to him and say farewell." All those images are still fresh in my memory. I distinctly remember: life had suddenly come to a standstill. Time had stopped. Our surroundings, the circumstances, the conditions, and the objects by which we were surrounded would vanish into thin air in no time, their image seeming to have been left in another world.

Our sojourn in Drancy lasted four days. I waited in vain for aid from the Turkish consulate; everybody was so helpless.

At the end of the fourth day, we were once again aboard the freight car which took us to Auschwitz; the time of our arrival was 10 p.m, January 23rd. We were hauled down from the car and they allowed us to take a minimum of things we had brought along with us. What followed was the most heartrending scene of our lives. Husband and wives and children were torn asunder without finding the opportunity to say goodbye to each other. We were heading, I believed, for our final destination. Three men, Nesim, Isaac, and I, three men, we had remained behind; just like during our strolls along the beach at Biarritz. The conditions were different, of course. Our feet were engulfed in icy water up to our ankles. It was bitterly cold. It rained cats and dogs. After a while, our feet began aching. We were going to get accustomed to such pains soon. Under the pouring rain and deprived of shelter, we stood there side by side until two in the morning. Then, we were hauled up and dumped in a truck which took us to Morowitz, twenty kilometers from Auschwitz. From there we were hastily unloaded and shoved into a large shed. Having promised that they would be returning them to us, they told us to strip off our garments. With skulls cleanly shaven, we were pushed under an icy shower. There they dispossessed us of our wedding rings, the last 'relic' we kept from the earth, lost along with all our other assets. In Paris, we had been robbed of our valuable effects; under the circumstances the loss of our wedding rings might seem insignificant; yet, we had the impression that we had been disinherited. I can still feel the sharp pain that this had given me. When we came out of the shower, there was no trace of our garments. Stark naked, in cold weather, we were led to a shed and had to cover a rather long distance on foot. Whenever I think of those days, I cannot imagine how we had plucked up the courage to put up with all those tribulations. There must be more than one reason, surely. Moreover, looking for a sufficient cause outside the framework of those encampments may look somewhat absurd. Nevertheless, I still keep asking myself about my place in that setting. This is, by the way, one of the ways I can endure my solitude and abandoned state. A man learns how to coexist with the dead, allowing him to cling to his own life even more strongly. After some time we began to recognize our dead as our most trustworthy companions. Our death reminds us of the days we have lost through deferrals and which we ought to recapture. We found our new garments in the shed: they consisted of a striped cotton jacket, slacks, a beret, and clogs. The setting was complete; we had been acclimatized; we were no longer casual visitors to the place. We were abandoned to starve for hours; then, at three o'clock we were served a black soup that contained a piece of black pork in it. At a moment of starvation pieces of black pork flesh! German gentility! Personally I didn't care. The important thing was to survive. Nothing was more valuable than one's subsistence. I was resolved to be a war veteran; yes, a veteran of war. Moreover, we were so hungry that even that execrable piece of flesh had tasted like a succulent beefsteak. There were other things besides; this was but one of the ways, subtle in deceit, that our executioners took their revenge on us. At present I feel as though I should not overlook this possibility.

The next day we were transported to a quarry; we were given a pickaxe and a shovel; we were supposed to hew huge stones and carry them somewhere. The job required superhuman strength and a capacity for endurance. In addition to a series of illnesses, Nesim had an inguinal hernia. When the overseers took notice of this, he was given a belt; although it was of worn out material, it proved helpful. "Now, here you have a token of human diligence and generosity!" you may say. Yet, when you consider that this was meant to enable him to go on working so that the employer could derive greater benefit from his toil, you start thinking otherwise. Among the things we learned were also the benefits one could derive from contemplating, entertaining suspicions, and thinking *ad absurdum*. Nesim got sick at the end of the eighth day. He was covered with blisters and wounds; he had to be hospitalized. We could not learn of his experiences during the course of his stay at the infirmary; what tribulations he had faced over the course of that one month, who he had communicated with and to what extent; back among us, he hardly uttered a word. He was about to lose contact with reality. He even denied hearing, let alone talking. It didn't take him long to be re-hospitalized. We knew what had happened to him. His hyperglycemia had worsened and begun to impair his faculties. He needed special treatment; but asking for special treatment would be tantamount to a revolt.

For three months, he shuttled between the infirmary and the jobsite. One day an announcement was made according to which the able-bodied and the disabled were to be sorted out. Nesim had to remain among the latter group. He, along with a group of others, were taken away to a place of which we had no idea. We did not expect that the moment of separation would come so quickly. We cast each other furtive glances. Notwithstanding, we tried to behave as though we would meet again. We needed this conviction in order to be able to survive. We were obliged to believe in our self-deceptions.

That was the last time I saw or heard of Nesim. To be precise; I did see him, although in a different guise. Barely a month had elapsed since our separation. I noticed a hernia suspension on one of the inmates in the dormitory; the same that Nesim had worn. At such times you cannot help being inquisitive. We stared at each other for some time. I could not possibly expect him to understand what I was thinking or feeling. I kept quiet. I said nothing, I didn't inquire. He, in turn, was ostensibly struggling for survival, like me or like any one of us, for that matter. I had already got the gist of it. I had parted with Nesim in full consciousness of the fact that we were seeing each other for the last time. Similar partings I would be experiencing in the days that followed. Not only hopes but also our self-deceptions served us in keeping body and soul together.

We remained in this concentration camp up until January 18, 1945. We had heard that the Russian army had been advancing. This must have been the reason for the sudden evacuation from our place on an icy night under a howling blizzard. There was a layer of snow half a meter thick on the ground. It was almost impossible to advance with our clogs. In spite of all the adversities that beset us we marched on and covered a distance of eighty kilometers without stopping for a rest. Those who failed to make headway were machine-gunned. The rest you can imagine. The cold was not the only enemy that confronted us; the rifle butt was like the sword of Damocles. What followed I dare not recall.

Another day and another night . . . and we were at a new camp where we were to stay overnight. The next day we traveled in open freight cars for six days and nights under the severest of conditions toward an unknown destination, at the end of which we found ourselves at Buchenwald. Many people died on the road. We were continually diminishing in number. Whose turn was it next? That was the only question we asked each other. Every now and then one of us was snuffed out like a candle. On an interminable road we were rapidly reduced to the point of almost complete extermination in compliance with their whims. This reduction meant for me a kind of proliferation that connoted escape and deliverance. A considerable number of our traveling companions had abandoned us on the road; I often see them in my dreams, their contours in different guises as though they are still alive through me in the labyrinths of my nightmares.

There, at the least expected moment, I came across my beloved friend Isaac who had disappeared at Morowitz without leaving any trace. It was as though we had not seen each other for ages. We dared not speak about those we had had to leave behind. We hardly put questions to each other. Oblivious to any concept of time, we didn't know how to live or what to live for. Anyway, it would not take long before we were to part again. Isaac was emaciated; he could hardly stand on his feet. It was a miracle that his legs still held him up. I can freely use this word now, when I remember those days. Our survival was a miracle indeed! The coverage of those long distances was a miracle; to be able to forget those we had to leave on the road was a miracle. Our unexpected encounters were miracles. Our touching each other was a miracle. After a few days we were told that we were to set off again. This journey would be different, however; we knew that. This would be a fatal separation. I was seeing Isaac for the last time. Both of us had felt this predicament that we could never escape. Our new journey lasted two days. We had become inured to traveling in open freight cars to destinations unknown. Well, we had ended up at Clavikel, the extermination camp. The burning flesh stank to high heaven. We were told that this camp was not like other camps and that no one could come out alive from it. So was this the end of the long journey? Had we been faced with all those tribulations for nothing? Had all those hopes been entertained in vain? The scarcity of food and the heavy working conditions seemed to justify the intelligence we had received. They told me that I would be receiving my job description soon. I was eventually given the job of shoving gassed bodies into the ovens. I was pressed for time. It was a nightmare I cannot put into words no matter how I try; a nightmare that haunts you even when you are wide awake; innumerable masses of human bodies who had come to this world like any of us, living in different cities, and communicating with different individuals; who had experienced joy and sorrow like any one of us, who had suffered, hoped, striven to survive but ended in a lifeless rigidity. They had possibly come there having traveled long distances like us; they also had had—up until a few months before—tomorrows and pasts and expectations. They had had their weaknesses, regrets, little accounts to settle, and letters planned but deferred to be written. After all those sentiments, struggles to cling to life, they were now ageless, denuded of nationality, name, sex, and vernacular. At first, I had felt as though I had fallen into a nightmare from which I could never awake. The nightmare haunted me day and night; I continued to perform my duty even in my dreams, in contorted images. The only difference being that the bodies suddenly resurrect as I am about to throw them in the furnace while a young woman lasciviously screams: "Young man," she says, "how about pulling me from this inferno!" On the other hand, a small kid cries: "Uncle stoker! How about catching me, eh!" then runs away. Some, once thrown in the furnace burst with laughter, speaking in Spanish, like the Spanish I used to listen to when I was in Teruel; while others exclaim: "Enough of this fire! We are overheated, you brute! We are overstuffed in this hole!" Once I had heard the voice of my mother coming from the furnace. She was chanting one of those psalms she had taught me when I was a child, a psalm I had completely forgotten, one I preferred to forget. I began to chant with her; the strange thing was that I remembered the entire psalm which I thought I had forgotten. Were you to ask me to repeat it now, I doubt if I can remember a single word of it. Having come to the end of her chanting, she had said: "You're growing up, my dear child. Be not afraid. I won't say anything about this to your dad." She must have thought that my father, a confirmed atheist, would be annoyed were he to learn that I had sung this psalm with my mother. However, I had never had any fear of my father in any period of my life. We had always been intimate friends, companions. Such are the nightmares that haunt me. But I have no other choice but to live with it. As I shoved the bodies into the furnace one after another, I kept repeating: "He's dead, and I'm alive! He's dead, and I'm alive!" I was living, I had to live. However, a short while after I became inured to it. When, after 'the work day' I went out into the fresh air, I ceased to smell the burnt flesh. The 'profession of stoker' had become a routine job. I would never have believed it, but there it was! I must confess, however, that this experience of mine was not unsullied, but accompanied with a very important anticipation: I was inured to this execrable job, alright, but I had a gnawing apprehension within me: suppose I came across the body of someone I knew, one of my relatives! This person might well be someone I had left behind in Biarritz, but it could be worse; it might be my wife or my daughter! Nothing was impossible for us anymore. Among the bodies, among the thousands, the hundreds of thousands of bodies, I might well come upon one of mine, i.e. of those I had buried within me. I was reminded of such a possibility by the nightmares faithful to me; those nightmares that ever recurred without giving me any respite. Although the details, images, and conversations change, the fear of encounter lingers at the doorway of that labyrinth of fire. I'm trying to ignore it; what else can I do? I'm averse to describing to you all that I have gone through partly for this reason.

Among the unforgettable experiences of those days I must also mention that some mornings we were obliged to eat rubbish for survival. Food was served on certain days of the week. Sorting out edible rubbish among the heaps of waste material every day just before dawn, believing that it could provide us with enough energy to keep body and soul together, even only for another day, had developed into a habit. One could survive anything except death! Having survived thanks to the energy that the rubbish had provided us with and presenting ourselves to the sight of our employers was the only victory we could dream of. I heard that the living souls waiting their turn to be snuffed out had eaten the livers of their fellow beings, boon companions, for the sake of remaining alive a few hours more. The amateur cannibals were doctors; one time doctors, upon the earth. They were experts in recognizing the edible parts of human flesh and liver apparently outlasted all the other organs of the body. How far this is true or false, I cannot tell. Yet, nothing was impossible there. A man had to be prepared for any contingency imaginable or unimaginable. To be able to find food of some sort was a blessing. Under the circumstances, I think it is high time now that we have to redefine such notions as true or false, right or wrong. Our insights and prescience may guide us in this. As a matter of fact, I had had an unshakable belief in my mind even then. They had also told me that I had to be glad for the sake of the beloved Nesim who had not witnessed this part of our journey. I had felt this satisfaction for others as well. To be glad to witness the death of someone one loved was to be the bearer of a sorrow in another guise. I think I can never explain to you this feeling.

About two months later, we were taken back to Buchenwald. We covered about 100 kilometers in two days, at the end of which a new journey was to begin. The new journey was to last twenty-one days. The food to be served every day would consist of 200 grams of bread and three raw potatoes; ninety-six people were to consume one jerry can of water every three days, of which only the sturdier among us, after brawls, could benefit. At the beginning of the journey, we numbered about five thousand; at the end of the twenty-first day there were only six hundred of us that survived. I had become thin as a rake. My legs hardly supported my skeleton. The name of the camp where we had arrived was Dachau. We knew the name. For the first time I felt that my end had come. "This is the end! This is the end!" I kept repeating to myself, after all that we had endured and suffered. Memories from the past came flooding back to me: visions, human figures, voices, etc. Different localities in my past were fused together which did not follow a chronological order, Teruel, Biarritz, etc. My father, Daniella, and my unborn child, my child who could not enter to the world. The end . . . Sedately I began waiting for my end.

The Americans came to rescue us. I could not believe it. Even now I find it difficult to believe. It was the beginning of May. They took me to a French hospital nearby. I had become infested with lice; I was invaded with fleas. The first thing they did was to disinfect me. The next thing I could not bring myself to believe was the clean, snow-white bed sheets. One and a half years had gone by. For the next ten days I was properly treated before being taken to Constant Island; it was a paradise in the middle of a lake. I weighed forty kilograms. Within six weeks I put on twenty kilos. I was invited for brief interviews by the broadcasting station. My new duty was 'to bear testimony.' They were innumerable, the things I had within me; they were inexhaustible. They were to abide within us forever and ever.

I left Constant on June 21 and arrived in Biarritz on June 28. I had been nurturing the hope of finding the members of my family in this city where so many memories lay buried. I had to see at least one of them, I had to. Yet, silence and desertion reigned. Streets, houses, stones, trees, and the beach . . . the city had undergone a complete transformation; or, at least so it seemed to me. My expectations proved to be unrealistic; there were no encounters, no embraces . . . those had remained in other peoples' movies . . . Unfortunately, no one had come back here, no one that I anticipated to see. Now and then I tried to deceive myself by imagining things. Some may have remained on the Russian side, I said to myself. There, on the Russian front . . . I wonder if I also should have been with them . . . I dreamt of old times. It is evening and we are just out from a hot party, discussing our brighter futures. "We must drink tonight," says Manuel. So we go out to carouse. The taverns are at our command. We make the rounds . . . raising a toast in each of them and nibbling at a piece of something. That was the custom . . . Manuel was killed with a single bullet to his forehead in Teruel. I had heard it whistling . . . to say that I had experienced all this . . . Daniella asks me to recount the war. "Such things are not for the ears of children," I say, "When you get older, I'll tell you all about it, it's a promise." She insists: "Just tell me, let's see if I can understand." Then I start telling her all about it. She listens to it as though I was telling her a fairy tale. I know, little children are not supposed to hear all this. Wars must remain fiction for them.

I cannot find my return particularly appealing when I go over my recent past. I had put up with all the adversities with great fortitude partly in the hope to be able to be reunited with my people; yet, no one seems to be in sight. I can remember that tale "Little Thumb" and think that we couldn't keep our word; the word we had given to our children which we have failed to keep. And now . . . here seems so deserted . . .

Enrico Weizman

The letter ended with these words . . . Each of us was to live our respective stories henceforth . . . our respective stories . . . in our distant bearings and alienations.

Unexpected visitor

Enrico Weizman's failure to find any one of his relatives upon his return to Biarritz was quite natural. Their names on the obituary column published after a couple of years indicated them as missing, 'lost' somewhere during transfers between concentration camps. Marie, Daniella, Nesim, Rachael, Paulette, Anette, Isaac, and Liliane were all on the list. Like many whose paths crossed speaking different languages, entertaining different dreams sunken in the depths of despair heading for the same end. Children not yet born did not figure on those lists, naturally.

The list of the 'missing' . . . a mistake might have been made, why not? There was still a possibility that they might be found alive. Some might have defected to a foreign territory and still be living there beyond another boundary. In order that he might endure those nightmares, he needed to delude himself. No matter what designation you might use for defining a deeply held conviction, you cannot deny the fact that it is a confirmed belief in another space, in another world. Enrico's memory was replete with the remains and ashes of bodies exterminated. The dead haunted him. This was not the first panorama he would behold! He had visited those camps, heard those screams, and witnessed those fears and expectations and was prepared for them, unlike his fellow beings. He distinctly remembered; how could he ever forget? There had been another 'conflict' that had led him to 'encounter' Nesim for a very brief but meaningful period of time. A conflict in another time, risked for the sake of a more correct history, a conflict that had to be remembered always. A conflict that fed upon big dreams, upon the shattering of big dreams; a conflict that the witnesses of those days had to pay a high price for. The days of his childhood in Madrid, the days in which he used to accompany his father, who was a confirmed communist, to party meetings were scenes of paradise. The distant contours of his mother who had shown him some aspects of Judaism and who struggled against heretical attitudes to celebrate the holy days at home came into view somewhere in this setting. Then the frontier days had come . . . the forced escapes and exiles with all their devastating consequences . . . It was then that he had experienced losses, and partings with one's loved ones without finding the opportunity to bid farewell. Enrico Weizman was one of the many Spanish communists who had taken refuge in France during the post-war period. The days when Teruel stank of blood and putrefaction had been indelibly trained into his brain. When he had crossed the border he was conscious that he would not be able to return to his country for a good many years. Everybody had to remain on one side of the conflict; in other words, they had to choose sides. His father had risked his life and remained in his own land. One had to understand him. One had to try to understand him. For, it meant suicide . . . suicide . . . He was endowed with life for the sake of that conviction; a life had been built on that conviction. When defeated . . . when dreams were shattered . . . opting for death should be understandable under the circumstances . . . One ought to understand. At the beginning of his exile, he had prepared himself for the grim news of the expected murder of his parents by fascist militia, of that sensitive woman who preserved her strength by keeping silent and of that man who was to remain faithful to his ideals to the very end. In order to start life afresh and cut off his umbilical chord, he had to rely on the truth of this story. The Eden he had lost somewhere along the way had not yet been sullied by an inferno during those days. In that friendly atmosphere that Nesim and Rachael had created for him in a Spanish-speaking environment, which had created in him the impression that he had finally been united with a family, there was nothing out of the ordinary. Human beings could not do without being loved and there were things that he believed he loved regardless of all likelihoods, true or false. The entire countries might be razed to the ground, the boundaries might undergo changes, but man had to preserve a haven for himself no matter what it might be called. One had to feel the existence of a haven from a distance or in close proximity, regardless of all 'one's connections.' It appears that Enrico had still been seeking that haven even on his return to Biarritz after the loss of so many lives, joys, and hopes. The conditions had changed in the meantime, of course. Meanings attributed to human beings, streets, houses, and

Sundays had all changed. The haven dreamt of was no longer the same. The haven had to enclose new areas in addition to the seas it encircled. The story of refuges, of the desire to take shelter in something with the whole of one's being, of his past, of his seas, was the same story, more or less . . . However, this return to oneself seemed to be valid for everybody who took up the challenge. I must also take into consideration the fact that people like Enrico Weizman had already been witness to so many things and had gone through unending tribulations and so could not easily be threatened by anybody. The world they had wound up at was a privileged one, exposed to all sorts of eventualities; it was a privileged world, but one surrounded by massive walls. In order to have a glimpse of that world, we had no means other than mere words and the meanings we attributed to them. To make headway in the story, I needed to find answers to further questions. I should like to know for instance the extent that the new visitor, who had entered his small and private world at an unexpected moment after two years, had exercised his influence on this approach. This encounter with the unexpected visitor reminded me of the old films of adventure and romance that fired the imagination of so many people. This chapter might also begin with the resurgence of a figure who seemed to have vanished somewhere along the way. A person gradually found his way into other people's bosoms, places reserved for others, and went silently, unconsciously toward a more favored time. This time was necessary for the completion of the story, it was chained to a new story. That new time gave access to a new place. Could one explain away the intrusion of 'that visitor' by a design of fate? The assorted answers to this question might be subjective, everybody being desirous to exhibit some aspect of it. The difference of opinions did not matter, in other words. What was important, however, was that a given person would, under the circumstances, have to wait as a substitute to fill in gaps in the story. The trace of that person had long been lost. He lived unconscious of the fact that a person would be writing his story in his shelter known only to a handful of people. He was unaware of the real meaning of deaths and separations. A young and lonely child; a small child who had had to create their own world . . . However, this would not be enough to connect with the other heroes of the story. The words had been given and received in real time. Those willing might go and seek that design of fate in the place where the words were exchanged.

Recollections of the communist fisherwoman Angela and the catholic doorkeeper Madame Manzil

It was a Saturday morning. Enrico Weizman, fresh and vigorous, decided to go to the market to buy fish.

A perfectly ordinary sentence for those not initiated to things hidden between the lines. Had I not been familiar with certain details of this part of the story, I might, to be frank, read this sentence without dwelling on it. Yet, conditions led me once more to witness certain confidential things, certain incidents.

This was my fate. A fate I had devised. I could not bring myself to close my eyes and forget that I had borne testimony to certain things. However, this role pleased me, to be honest. I was not confined merely to words. There were things that I had been trying to conceal as well as positions I wanted to occupy, objectives that I aspired to, and experiences that I wanted to enjoy. Moments get mixed in my memory because of this, partly, and I don't know with whom and in whom I had exactly invested those moments.

The intelligence that was to help with the reconstruction of my story had returned to its true source after a span of many years. Under the circumstances, I had to reopen my door to errors, nay to imperfections. I could not prevent fantasies from ushering in in this context. Fantasies were more often than not much more fascinating than actual realities; they fostered longevity and sought expression. Therefore I would narrate Enrico Weizman's story by trying to look at it through the angle of what I saw and heard. The pieces that I wanted to patch up had taken me to destinations I had not foreseen. At present, equipped with the limited data I have in hand, I'm heading for those places, in pursuit of other answers.

Starting a new day feeling fresh and vigorous was something excellent of course, although this experience was somewhat related to 'buying fish' or 'going to buy fish'; yet, what was of special significance, which deserved to be dwelt upon, was to go and see Madame Angela rather than buying fish. Enrico was heading for a new story, a story that had to be lived. The story was inviting its old heroes and heroines that actually seemed to have disappeared for the sake of those who had been abandoned during those moments of separation.

Madame Angela was a buxom Mediterranean lady with wide hips and dark eyes, whose gestures gave rise to guffaws when she felt in the mood, a woman who never failed to make a jocular remark to passers-by and whose repartees to people came across as improper innuendoes that were always marked by a saucy freedom and forwardness. She was notorious in the market for her emotional maladjustment to her surroundings and as a person who set about howling over something on the slightest provocation, much as she was skillful, helpful, and of generous temperament. These characteristics of hers had made her a person that everybody loved and respected; a behavior mixed with some diffidence. Different lineaments had been drawn through the encouragement one received from different sources. These experiences were the fragments of different pasts, pasts difficult to relate. But her feelings about Enrico Weizman gained substance when they were shared. These feelings found their meaning through mutual resemblances, common roots, through feelings she tried to keep distant from others. I could understand these feelings. I could understand the reason why his experiences, his losses, and the gains he had made from these losses, the fact that they originated from a past capable of empathizing with other lives lived elsewhere, had drawn them to each other. In the context of these pasts, they seemed to have been drawn to one another. Their spouses had died in the war; both could be said to be strangers to France; both had communist traditions behind them. Her family had emigrated from Naples to Marseilles when Angela was but a young girl. Years, loves, and escapes had finally brought her to this coastal town on the Atlantic Ocean. She had gotten married to the man of her dreams in this town. She had learned to live by a new language. However, all these things had taken place before the war, before she had lost all her relatives. The paths of Enrico Weizman and herself had converged in this town and were destined to share a common fate. They had no other choice. To start a new day with a hearty "hello!" was easy for them. To know how to live—nurturing frail hopes in the face of constant change, wearisome routine, and strings of empty platitudes—called for a certain skill after all. Their topics of conversation were usually the happenings within the body of the party, the articles in *L'Humanité*, fish, and their reflections on the market people. Angela stubbornly believed that her husband had not been killed in the war; she said he had fled the camps and stayed in the country of his comrades. She was almost sure that he had started a new life there. He might pop up at any moment. On the other hand, despite all her expectations and anticipations, she was aware of the fact that she did not and could not love the man she had once believed she could not do without. The war had ended four years ago. The losses and the deaths had corroded the romantic side of her. What was important now was to be able to carry on with the job at hand and look forward. She hadn't had great difficulty in managing her affairs. In other words, she had successfully met the challenge of the 'period of transition' thanks to her past experiences and know-how.

It is reported that Enrico Weizman had mentioned Madame Angela during a 'human mission' to Istanbul while telling of his most important encounters. The eyes of Berti, who told me about this woman years later, toward which nobody could remain impassive, betrayed the pride of being trusted with a secret and were mixed with a sadness I could not account for. A time would come when she would occupy a special place in Enrico Weizman's life as a woman about whom he would be inclined to give a more elaborate account when reverting to his recollections. Berti was one of those who had experienced bitter relationships that could not be put into words or shared. I liked him for this particularity. I too wanted to live, taste, and learn how to experience the bitterness caused by inexpressible relationships in situations where I thought that such affiliations would be neverending, in the proper sense of the word. The source of the grievance lay, I think, in the impossibility of explaining what ought to be explained to the right people. Those people were sometimes unconsciously the heroes of those relationships, as well as their onlookers who took notice of the real meaning behind the stories. There were situations in which time was lived the wrong way . . . situations wasted in the wrong hands, lingering hopes deferrable because of apprehensions . . . The emotion that different words had raised in Berti might have been due to an affect generated by a similar situation. However, in order that I might be able to decipher certain details and measure their proper significance, I needed to gauge this effect better, and to learn how to be patient once more. Those stories, like those people, stood there even though they were not lived as they ought to have been, waiting for their 'real' time to come. "That woman was no ordinary woman. I had felt this, but I couldn't bring myself to ask what I really wanted to ask. A hand, an invisible hand seemed to have forestalled my action . . . " Berti said. What was meant by this was that gap, that sense of imperfection generated by my inability to have access to that untouchable and forbidden zone. One may prefer not to soil, with one's foreign steps, the path leading to that zone in the face of people whom one reveres. This experience seems to refer to a period of hesitancy that looks as though it will never end; an old period of hesitancy that looks as though it *has* no end; a period of hesitancy that holds you immobile, unable to decide which action to take, about whether you should take that step forward or not; its real meaning lies in your past, in another human being to whom you cannot have access. I might well understand this hesitancy. However, when I go over Enrico Weizman's experiences, his attitude toward life, it occurs to me that this concern must be concealing quite another concern lying in the depths of the water.

Enrico Weizman with whom I had lunch at Rumelikavağı was a man who tried to make the best out of every situation he found himself in, who, every now and then, laughed, sometimes without rhyme or reason, who spoke about death as though he was delivering a speech on a meteorological forecast and who recounted assiduously his recollections to anybody willing to listen, anyone without the least moral scruple, save for those he had left behind in the years gone by. Berti and Juliet were also at the table. He had returned to Istanbul, in his own words, as someone who had the "identity of an immigrant who had lost his enthusiasm." This was a somewhat belated and inadequate visit. He knew that I had been working on a very long story. Now and then, it occurs to me that he had provoked in me that moral scruple on purpose. I owed that evening to Juliet who had mentioned the dream I held before dinner. We had had a long talk, setting out from the night in question and making headway toward the war, toward the days of old, toward escape and return. Fragments were getting fitted together. This was an encounter, an extraordinary meeting I yearned for for ages.

True encounters called people to special venues. The moments spent during such encounters were at the same time the most important moments in which you took progressive steps, steps which you believed to be exceptional. What we had discussed that evening at the restaurant would resurrect that sensation in me. On his way to see that fisherwoman, the experience Enrico Weizman had during that encounter, brought time to a standstill. At the least expected moment, the flow of daily events diverted their course in a completely different direction, transforming and affecting many lives. The transformation had occurred in one single moment; it was a moment that opened a new darkness within me. I was to open the door cautiously, full of apprehension. The man toward whom the actors of that meeting made headway was a person who had become the figure in quite a different dream, in quite a different wasteland. Whose future was it then? For whose sake and on whose behalf was one to appropriate those indelible visions of that morning lost in the hazes of war? At that moment and because of that moment a French woman had approached him, whose acquaintance he thought he ought to make, a talkative woman, a woman who seemed not to have lingered long at school desks and who was hardly interested in reading, a woman who freely expressed her philosophical ideas whenever the occasion allowed. She had stopped and asked him if he was Monsieur Weizman, by any chance. She shouldn't be reproached for her daring, since the war had changed everybody. He had observed in that woman, who had achieved mastery in making the best of a bad situation with a hot baguette, a few slices of ham, and a few drops of wine, during the intervals between love-making in order to fill the gap caused by penury; to compensate for a lack of affection, a woman who could not help exteriorizing the effects of this mastery through nervous gestures, with her untimely wrinkles and gesticulations and jargon which might be interpreted as audacious by some. It seemed to him like *déjà-vu*, a moment which had been the subject of many an anecdote, experienced by nearly everybody and often recounted. A person comes from afar, from a distant past, a figure lost in the mists of the past, a person whom you have totally forgotten . . . and you feel a certain touch; a small touch, like in poems, between brackets. Then . . . then it becomes a chip on your shoulder you can never bring yourself to share with others. A pain you would prefer to get rid of. Why did he have to think like that? To protect himself? Maybe. He had told her that he was indeed Monsieur Weizman. The woman had introduced herself with a tremulous voice without trying to disguise her joy. She was Claudine Manzil, the concierge of the apartment that Nesim and Rachael had lived in once upon a time. It was my turn now to get excited. My excitement was due to the potential information that this woman could provide me with. Madame Manzil asked me about Nesim, Rachael, and the children. When all her questions had been answered, she grew silent and said that Ginette was alive and working in a monastery nearby. The incidents at the Bayonne Prison and the words that Rachael had said to Nesim while she held him tight had surged up in his vision. They had not merely embraced each other, it was a gesture of hope, a last hope . . . He had said that they had to go and sit down in a café and talk. They were living a story they could not abandon halfway through as they would have to carry it to the bitter end. Madame Angela had understood and tried to turn a deaf ear to their conversation. Madame Manzil went on relating the rest of the story with bated breath and great enthusiasm. The intonation of her voice, her looks, and the person that she tried to speak of denoted her preparations for this anticipated moment. "To withstand the Gestapo's oppression was impossible, Monsieur. My husband kept on saying that if ever we were caught we would all be done for. We were terrorized." She seemed to remember all the details of the incidents they had witnessed in their small apartment. The dress she wore might well have dated from that period. The war seemed to continue for certain people and showed no signs of ending soon. I had to remain silent and listen. "But there was a human being I had been entrusted with and had to protect. There was a life to be rescued, Monsieur! Not merely because I had given my word to Madame Rachael; but because it was my duty first and foremost. I thought that the best thing to do would be to take this poor girl to the convent where my mother and I often visited. The convent in question was a place I felt attracted to. I had gone there even after my wedding. I also took my own children there. I found peace there; I prayed for long hours and communed with myself. I wasn't in a position to guess what Ginette might end up having to face there with the nuns. Poor Madame Rachael! May she rest in peace! I know she would forgive me having done this for the good of her daughter. I was sure Ginette would find safety there. It was long after I visited the place, in accordance with the stipulation of the nuns. She would grow up there in the midst of a single united family. But I couldn't control my need to see her. So, I went to visit. I had seen Madame Rachael in my dreams. She said to me with the usual smile on her face that she missed Ginette and asked me whether I was taking good care of her. She looked downcast. She said she couldn't come from where she was. When I awoke, the dawn had not yet broken. I waited impatiently for the first rays of sunshine before setting out. First, I had had a talk with Marie-Thérese, the prioress. She had grown old. She addressed me as 'my little girl' like in the old days. She appeared not to believe that I had become an adult like her many other 'little girls.' Well, the war had matured us before our time. She might also have wished to instill in me the peace I had lost elsewhere. I think I'm beginning to ramble. Had my husband been here now he would have said: 'Come on, say what you want to say outright, without having to revert to roundabout expressions, Claudine!' Excuse me, Sir. All I want to communicate to you is what I've experienced. Marie-Thérese did not want me to see Ginette. She said I could have a glimpse of her from a distance. I had no other choice. I had confidence in her. I revered her, had affection for her. I believe she was right. She had glanced at her watch. The hour of service was drawing near. Ginette was soon to pass before us in file with the other nuns. She held me by the hand. We walked through the corridor and hid ourselves from view in a dark corner. They passed before us in formation. I immediately recognized her. She had grown up and changed considerably; but, this did not prevent me from recognizing her. She had the air of Rachael. She shot a glance in our direction which made me shiver, although she could not see us. She must have felt my presence. She looked beautiful; her face had an expression of absolute serenity. Marie-Therese told me that she was loved by everyone in the monastery. She told me she kept asking about her parents, about their whereabouts, and the reason they had deserted her.

"The prioress had apparently taken special care of her until she settled in, telling her that her parents had to set off on a perilous journey. Ginette had her repeat the account of their odyssey every night. Do you know that children want you to repeat the same story over and over again in order that they may believe it? It is a sort of game, in a sense. Every child has a tale; every child must have a tale. The best thing for her was to remember the story of her parents as a tale. The prioress was of the same opinion. She and Ginette had spent marvelous evenings together. Those delightful moments must have rendered the tale even more credible and beautiful. Once, the parents of a little girl had set off on a perilous journey. Ginette had wanted to know why they had not taken her along. Marie-Thérèse had told her that only adults could go on such a journey. So, they had to leave her behind safe and sound. Because they loved her so much! She would understand the meaning of this journey better when she grew up. Whereupon, she had asked her when she would grow up. The answer that the little girl had received to this question, which every little child might ask, had not been so simple. The prioress had realized that her instruction to Ginette should start from a point she deemed to be correct. No one except herself would be in a position to tell her when she would have been considered grown up. Only she would be in a position to decide on her station. Ginette had also asked why they, that is, her parents, had to set out on such a journey, and whether they would ever return. To this, the prioress had answered saying that only God knew when, if ever, they would come back. She had told her that in the monastery everybody loved her and took her as one of the family. Ginette had seen God's power, through the eyes of a child, after this conversation. That was the last of her recurrent questions. She had become introverted and morose yet submissive and industrious at the same time. Had this been a consequence of her resignation or of the creation of an illusory world within her? The prioress could not decide which of these alternatives she should opt for; however she told her that she would always be assisting her with her troubles. Shall I tell you something that seems interesting to me? Barring her creeds, she tried to nurse Ginette as a mother; she, in her turn, received things from the little child. I like to think that this was the case. Ginette was a girl who would make her feel this latent deficiency in herself because of the vows she had taken. Don't ask me how I've come to such a conclusion. There are certain sentiments that cannot be described and should be left as they are. Well . . . that is all I can say about Ginette. And now I run into you, a miracle! I must disclose to you Madame Rachael's last wishes. They were actually Monsieur Nesim's, before he had been exterminated by the Gestapo that morning; well, Monsieur Nesim seems to have told Rachael the following: 'I'm going to an unknown destination. Don't ever give my children to any person other than someone in my family.' Much as I'm reluctant, I should say that we must abide by his words. Their memory forces me to act in this way. I'll tell this to Marie-Thérèse. I know her, she will understand. But you should help me in doing so. Should you wish, Ginette may stay with you for a while. We must tell her that she had a family, a true tangible family. She's got a family in Istanbul, if my mind does not fail me, hasn't she? As far as I know, Monsieur Nesim had a brother. I have a vague recollection of him. The two brothers used to stroll along the beach. He often came to visit them. The good old days! Monsieur Nesim used to sing songs. He sang "La Paloma" most often. "La Paloma," such a romantic song: I didn't understand the words; but whenever I heard it, I felt like crying. You see, I can still remember. The war couldn't snatch what we keep within our souls, our souvenirs. I'm sure the family in Istanbul will welcome Ginette with open arms. This will be difficult however, especially for Ginette. But we're doing this for Monsieur Nesim and above all, for Madame Rachael. Do you see? Madame Rachael had absolute confidence in me in this respect. It may be because those on whom she could rely were diminishing in number. But, believe me, her voice was very sincere when she spoke to me. I distinctly remember her last words. 'Contrary to Nesim's anticipations, I'd been expecting this. I'd been seeing dreams replete with nightmares which I couldn't share with anyone; I woke up more than once in the course of the night. Now I feel somewhat at ease. Whatever will be will be. One thing is certain: this is the end of our lingering. Pray for us. God will hear the voice of each one of us in similar situations. He seems not to hear us these days, I'm well aware, and yet, I know He will hear us. This is a new trial, an ordeal; but we have to withstand it and never loose hope. We are Jacob's people. To know how to carry the burden of being a Jew . . . only this belief can help us stand,' Rachael had said. She had reminded me once more of the days we had spent in Istanbul. She had mentioned the streets where we used to stroll and of her adolescent years. To what extent can one truly recall the past in such moments . . . yet, in her short accounts Istanbul seemed to invade us. Maybe she wanted to impress me on the spur of the moment. I'd forgotten all that had been told to me about those streets I didn't know. However, I distinctly remember the Princes' Islands; the Princes' Islands that are part of Istanbul. Madame Rachael used to take her brother to the islands aboard the ferryboat on beautiful spring days where they roamed all alone. The man had an incurable mental disorder. She felt a genuine sorrow for having left him in Istanbul. 'I wonder if I'll ever be able to see Nesim again where I'll be going, whether we'll be able to return here at all. Would you believe that he hadn't had the opportunity to even taste the orange jam he had been keeping for a special occasion? The morning they came to take him, he had laid the breakfast table and among the things that he had garnished the table with was the orange jam. I was so happy to see him so happy. At that very moment we had heard a knock on the door. Life is so strange, isn't it? Well, you see . . . . I'd prepared myself for all sorts of eventualities . . . Take good care of Ginette; you know my instructions. Sell everything, the household goods, the shop, everything, for Ginette's sake. Supposing that we're released, I don't think we shall ever return home. And even though we might be lucky enough to have the chance, we won't be the same anymore . . . ' She has said this before she left. No, this was not a revolt . . . it was as though she had prepared herself to die . . . " These words, visions, and conversations were all intertwined. Dates, lives, and climates were mingled once again. I really am at a loss as to decide the extent to which these were true, this exchange of words based on expressions uttered by bearers of testimony in different languages, as I've been trying to patch up bits and pieces of information. Where exactly do I happen to be? Where do I come into these conversations? To what extent would I ever be permitted to allow people to partake in these conversations? As I've been in search of answers to these questions throughout the years, I've always been confronted with a dead silence; a complete, dark silence which had forestalled my progress in writing, hindering me from making headway after a given point. The men to whom I put questions remain dumb and mute. They don't realize that they are the unrevealed aspects I try to express in words, discovering that I can elaborate on them through my story. They are actually the images I can see in the mirror, which I strive to reflect and project. This seems to indicate that we are doomed to be self-seeking, always at a crossroads. We are expected to make headway in those words; we ought to advance in defiance of all errors, of the consequences and misunderstandings toward that silence and darkness; to learn how to walk, drawing our strength from the wounds received, from our abandonments and unrequited loves . . . Had those relations, borne throughout the years, not brought us to where we are now? Enrico Weizman, who listened silently and patiently to the soliloquy of Madame Manzil, trying to change the subject, said: "Rachael had met Nesim after that unforgettable morning. The fact that she spoke of having been gathered together in the Bayonne prison to be sent in toto to their death may lead us somewhere. Yet, there is no sense in trying to probe any further. One thing is certain: some lives were doomed to remain a mystery, impossible to be shared. You can bring Ginette to me, of course, whenever you can, Madame. Do not worry; we'll execute the will of Nesim and Rachael. I'll look after her for a while before taking her to her blood relations in Istanbul. Leave the rest to me, and please don't worry anymore." Madame Manzil's smiling face expressed a sad calm. Was this a miracle? Was this expression of serenity on her face, this concealed smile originated from her belief in miracles? From where he sat, staring at the iridescence of the waters of the Bosporus, Enrico said: "You've got a beautiful city: I'm so happy to be back. I wish Monsieur Jacques were with us now." Different times had once more been intertwining, directed toward others. We had been advancing toward our own times, toward the unforgettable voices . . . This was one of the magical sentences; my mind had conjured up Monsieur Jacques' apparition in the background of that old sea journey whose poetry has been indelibly stamped on my memory. We were at one of the seaside restaurants at Kireçburnu . . . It was evening. Monsieur Jacques was gazing at the lights on the Bosporus, like Enrico Weizman, with some misgiving, with a sense of inadequacy. He gave the impression of someone looking at the ethereal space in which he expected to see something inexpressible. It seemed as though that beyond was a place toward which he was making headway. His view had been interrupted by the shape of a huge Russian tanker sailing along the water . . . This image had reminded him of Uncle Kirkor. Monsieur Jacques spoke of the stuffed mussels that Madame Alin, Uncle Kirkor's mother, used to prepare, saying that he would never taste anything better in his life. Actually I was perfectly aware of the spot to where his looks had been directed, of the memories that that Russian tanker had stirred in him. He would have liked to see someone else sitting at the table with whom he would have liked to commune. The tanker was coming from a country that Olga was inextricably connected to. It is true that that country had never been a land where she had lived and breathed, but nonetheless an insignificant token that reminded him of her; a pocket watch and chain, for instance, the memory of a watch, the word of an unpretentious, innocuous master who lived in a state of symbiosis with his own cares that revived a web of memories. The tanker had traversed our sanctuary at our table from which we could not escape. Olga had remained behind a boundary. Those moments were being wasted, lavishly, irresponsibly . . . A time that assumed value years later only after it was lost. Can one say that Enrico Weizman had willingly told that story, reflected in him, of those moments lost at the restaurant at Rumelikavağı? What he had said, what he allowed himself to reveal, had opened up one of the important oaths that led me to this story. As for the things left unsaid, which could find no means of expression . . . one had to learn how to wait patiently in addition to using the power of one's imagination. Sometimes certain details added meanings we had not thought were there. The truth that he had concealed from us during that dinner was one of those realities that would knock belatedly on our door one day. About eight months after that evening, a letter arrived from Biarritz. The letter that bore the signature of a lawyer indicated that Enrico Weizman had passed away after a longstanding terminal illness. His client had faced the bitterness that this ailment had caused with bravery. Everything possible had been done, but there were cases when medicine remained powerless in the face of fate. It appeared that it had been Monsieur Weizman's wish to have his feelings communicated to certain addresses just before his time had come. He had expressed his gratitude to his relatives in Istanbul. Their affection showed that there were still good-willed people in the world. He had bequeathed part of his legacy to a lady by the name of Angela Fromantini with whom he had lived over many years, and another part of it to a young lady named Ginette Ventura. With reference to the latter he hoped that his relatives in Istanbul would be kind enough to extend a helping hand in executing the formalities of her inheritance. This help would signify their last duty to the departed. The letter addressed to Berti was written in a style both official and friendly, and had engendered in me something which was to prove to be the birth of a significant story. I think I was somewhat more experienced now when compared to my formative years. In this odyssey of mine, I had been skirting the coast of my writing over several years with a view to finding out, or rediscovering, the feelings that had guided me throughout my life. Under the circumstances, it seemed practical to force certain probabilities for the sake of the conclusion. Enrico Weizman had an awareness that he was going to die soon during his second visit to Istanbul. Death was somehow unexplainable, undeceivable, and irretrievable . . . As for Monsieur Jacques . . . can it be that he had been intending to disclose something that he had kept secret until then? Who knows? I have always wished to believe in such a probability. For, God gained meaning with such eventualities and anticipations, expressed by short poems. I liked those poems. I even thought that to abide in such poems might have removed some of the hard realities from life.

Black or red

There is no doubt that Enrico Weizman had a desire to find out about Ginette in those days. He had prepared himself for an encounter quite different from what he had experienced during those interminable nights. One had to acknowledge the fact that those long nights belonged to a different time in the past. Everybody who shared his pain and was aware of what he was going through was aware of the actual state of affairs . . . Madame Manzil had brought little Ginette in the evening. She appeared to be a quiet, resolute girl who appeared to have found inner peace. She had begun to talk bluntly without recourse to convoluted phrases. "I've been told that you'd be kind enough to take me under your care," she said. Who had told her this? Could it be Marie Thérèse, the prioress, who had addressed Madame Manzil and Ginette, briefing them about the people charged with her care and whose duty it would be to prepare her for a new path in life? Enrico Weizman could not remain impassive faced with the hidden meaning in this sentence. Ginette had shown up carrying a small bag in her hand that contained a couple of garments and underwear. As a matter of fact her entire *trousseau* had consisted of these items. The bag also contained a figurine of Christ which she had kept with her during the long lonely nights. This was a token that Marie Thérèse, to be precise, the entire monastery, had given as a gift to her. That night, she had spoken no further, but had knelt before that figurine in devotion before falling into a sound and restful sleep.

Just before she left, Madame Manzil had presented an envelope to Enrico Weizman, an old worn-out envelope saying: "Not much has been left from the sale of the available effects, I'm afraid; you know everybody tried to hold on to their possessions and rescue whatever they could. I donated part of the sum obtained to the monastery. I don't think that Madame Rachael would object. However, I've not sold the house; both the house and the shop remain unsold. You'll find the keys in the envelope as well . . . Poor little orphan . . . her life is in your hands from now on, Monsieur. I've done my duty. I feel at ease now . . . I have perfect confidence in you."

Enrico Weizman had gazed at Ginette who was sound asleep, possibly dreaming of the fairy world of children. She had taken from her worn-out bag, whose shabbiness was clear to see, cheap clothing, some underwear, and a figurine of Christ . . . A long path had been trodden, one followed by another long path which promised further hardship . . .

It was summer . . . They had strolled along the beach for several hours collecting seashells. Ginette had mentioned a card game she used to play once upon a time with her father. For the first time she was speaking of her father. They had immediately set out to buy a pack of cards. The name of the game was "Black or Red"? French words were now and then interspersed among the Turkish ones. That was the key of the game. Enrico needed to learn how to play. The game consisted of guessing which of the cards turned facedown was 'red' and which was 'black.' The dealer asked: "Red or black?" After the answer was given it was up to the dealer to check whether it was right or wrong. If the guess was correct, the person who answered was declared the winner, otherwise the dealer won. In this game, like in other similar card games, memory played an important role. But, for little girls, this wasn't so important; the essential thing was the mere act of playing. Such ordinary moments seemed to fill those ineluctable, unforgettable moments. Nesim used to play this game with his daughters. Ginette's memory seemed to bear certain hazy streaks dating from those days. When they used to play this game, she usually sat on her father's knee and when her guesses proved to be correct she was 'reprimanded' by her father who tickled her . . . She suddenly began sobbing during the game. "I've missed him so much," she said, thinking of her father. Both had felt disheartened, in a quandary. Only time would remedy their despair. Such moments would remain the only ones they truly lived in that house. Ginette had understood that she was to abandon a life she would never return to in the future. This was an important fact if the path she had already trodden was to be taken into account. She had given this its due, taking the cost into consideration. Partly for this reason, she would be one of those heroines that would suddenly appear in my story only as she saw fit, partly because I might be able to speak of the new land and about her prospects. Yet, what we were to go through, would divert us on our paths. I wonder if I can assert that I may have left some voices or colors in this person who had exposed to me another aspect of my life. I wonder if I can feel self-confident once more. Can I entertain once again such a belief for 'other' sentences? My concerns and the need to put these questions and to show that I desire to ask them may well conjure up certain details left in the dark, eclipsed by my past. But I'm obliged to confess at this stage that she had made a dignified exit from my story, listening to her own voice and turning a deaf ear to what I had to say, just like she had done when she entered. She would prefer to get lost in the country in which she had been looking for a future. For a long time to come, I would be keeping the trace of her that I had lost. A time would come, however, when, having forgotten a good many details, we would encounter each other in a manner suiting the plot of the story. However, now it was my turn to arrange the encounter wherein I hoped to make headway. Whether the venue was the correct one and whether the time suited the boundaries that my story delineated, I'll be able to formulate a judgment on only after I come to know other people, times, and places . . . trying not to forget the relationships in which I had to leave a part of myself, an integral part of myself. For instance, only now can I patch up the various parts of Ginette's story that I have obtained from different sources. It is only now that the venue has become *my* venue and the time *my* time. The true stories were those awaiting their correct intervals which found their places within us at the least expected moment. They were the ones that awaited their real time which produced secret shoots in other stories. However, for this, details had to be dwelt upon. Ginette's sudden bursting into tears while playing "Black or Red" was significant to me for this reason. The game associated the only true vision of her father that had indelibly entered her imagination. She had to cling firmly, tightly, desperately to this vision in order to be able to lay claim to those days of her youth that had been robbed from her, even though this act might involve false hopes. It was as though this was one of the conditions for her survival . . . one of the conditions, griefs, or prices she had to pay for her survival. Ginette, whom I tried to have a better insight into, who, I was sure, would always be in the background of my story occupying a very special place in it, had been able to support the burden of this life lost to her past. In other words, Ginette had never forgotten anything. I was but a kid when she taught me this game. One should not expect me to appreciate the value of this gift at the time. How could she have made me hear her inner voice? And by the time I realized the importance of this detail I had learned that I could not possibly escape this story. We had remained in each other during that short space of time together with our unforgettable details and yearnings. Time had enabled us to see the happenings around us behind different masks and to learn the differing touches of different individuals. Ginette had undoubtedly had access to the meaning of that short space of time long before me. In time I would be learning that after that evening she never cried in front of people and never tried to enter into the lives of people through her weaknesses. This, I believe, was both her strength and weakness. However, the incidents forced people to revise their concepts of good and evil once more. The efforts to relate oneself to others entailed not only the wounds that one received but also the wounds caused to others. The said efforts were also directed to the discovery of the further meanings of betrayals.

Enrico Weizman had also said that it was only natural for a man to be desirous to share his feelings with people he empathized with and that this course of action was almost inevitable. She had taken someone into her confidence; she felt affection for him. It would take Ginette some time before fully realizing how difficult this was to do. It even involved a virtue; a virtue whose meaning was hidden up until the moment one fully understood one's feelings. Throughout the night that followed that evening they had continued to converse like two intimate friends. Enrico Weizman told her about his past, about the things he had to forsake, trying to give her a few snapshots of his history. Other nights would reveal other experiences. Nesim and Rachael would be witnessing the Spanish concentration camps to experience a new climate of sensations. Those photographs would also find their places in due time. That desire to speak about one's experiences originated in a sense of accountability and a need to create a verbal legacy despite all its disadvantages. Enrico Weizman was well aware of the fact that learning certain bare facts might shatter the feelings of a young girl heading for her adolescent years and create irreparable damage. Yet, what he had gone through had taught him that even ill treatment was a kind of boon. To prepare to face oneself meant in a sense to teach yourself how to settle your accounts with the past and walk on incandescent coals beneath a layer of ashes. What lay beneath the ashes would always be smoldering. Ashes would be tantamount to omissions and glowing coals would continue to smolder. Our soles risked scorching if an unexpected wind suddenly blew, wafting the ashes. That would put us off for a while. However, those were the moments when we had a better insight into ourselves, moments during which we gained a better insight and tried to look upon the photographs hidden within ourselves. We could look for the reasons for our desire to narrate the history of the glances that seemed interminable in these escapes by choosing to hide ourselves behind those stories and visions. Those glances, which screened us from ourselves, were concealed on this path. Those glances were our very being. Those glances were what we had lost, what we had failed to gain; our incapacity to rip ourselves from our voices left in the dark.

The time that had been spent in Biarritz was replete with these feelings and visions. On one of those mornings in which they had been combing the beach and gathering seashells, Ginette had said that she would like to go to Istanbul. She believed that she ought to do something in return for the people who had saved her from death. Enrico Weizman had suddenly felt a sharp pang in his heart; an inexpressible sharp pang he would not share with others. To be frank, he had prepared himself for this separation. What linked him to Ginette was a feeling of attachment whose snapshots could be hidden from view. One could speak of attachments, strong and lasting attachments to the visions one had to leave behind in the past, in the distant past, in defiance of all the bitterness, nightmares, and revolts involved; this also denoted another way of keeping death at bay. Ginette was already a blossoming young girl who had left her childhood behind.

Enrico Weizman had written a different letter to Monsieur Jacques . . . here was the odyssey of a life. The little girl of the family was alive in France; she had been with him for the last two years, during which time she had been trying to recognize the people she had lost and to understand what surrounded her while getting prepared for the journey to Istanbul; to where she was expected. The time had come. She was obliged to prick her ears to the voice of fate. Had he been asked, he would be only too glad to come over to Istanbul, bringing this little girl who had unexpectedly dawned on their lives after having suffered so many deaths. It was a long story. The story could be lived by them on their ground and on their terms. They were not, by the way, obliged in any way to reply or to give credence to the story told, since Ginette was being taken care of by reliable people. The mere knowledge of the event would suffice after all that had transpired.

Ginette's arrival welcomed by the same people on the quay

"We had felt a sudden rush of emotion . . . it was as though a new phase was opening in our life," said Berti as he recalled the atmosphere that the letter had created among the members of the Ventura family in Istanbul. Then he had gone on to say: "Those were difficult days for all of us. We had to be careful of every kurush we spent. We were still enduring the agony of the heavy tax imposed by the government on our wealth and earnings. Our recuperation had not been so easy. The individuals who witnessed those days could never be on the road to recovery; they simply couldn't. At exactly the same time, we were looking forward to the arrival of a relative of ours whose existence we had completely forgotten about. I think we should be justified in thinking that the joining of a new individual to our family, of a European, would create a new problem. My father had difficulty in bearing the heavy burden of a large family. We all depended on him. Myself, Jerry, grandmother, grandfather, Lily . . ." He had to break off. I knew why he could not finish his sentence. The apparition of Olga had surged before him while recording the family members. Olga was known to everybody; she was an integral part of the family, for every family member, although no one dared mention her . . . as is the case with all sudden surges from the darkness of the past toward which a person looks in apprehension. This was a sort of game that everybody indulged himself in preferring to ignore certain realities. What had prevented him from mentioning the name of Olga had been merely his age-old effort to deceive himself. Yet, she had surmounted all obstacles and succeeded in making her presence felt through her tabooed memory. I was to have the same experience elsewhere in my story with other individuals as well. We must have owed to a simple coincidence, to Ginette, our making headway with such a sentence. The continuation of the story depended henceforth on Berti, on the person that he wanted to present to me. The words were to join with mine once more. It was unfortunate that there was no other way to rewind time. "To be honest, we hadn't hesitated for an instant after finishing the letter. Ginette to us was an integral part of our family. We'd spoken of the letter with grandfather as well. They believed that my uncle and his family were somewhere else, in Spain, in other words. We informed him that Ginette was on her way to Istanbul to meet her family and was to stay with us for quite a while. They were overjoyed. They had learned by now that they weren't supposed to ask too many questions on this issue. We told Monsieur Weizman about the situation in Istanbul. He ought to know the white lie we had told about my uncle. We had exchanged letters before this encounter took place. It was May. The entire family set off to welcome her. Even grandma was with us; it seemed that she could not accept the fact that she wouldn't be able to see her. Another couple of years had gone by before she realized the situation. We had arrived at a common understanding through the letters we had been exchanging. To be able to distinguish our guest among the multitude of passengers we were to shout "Ginette! Ginette! Ginette!" in unison. Thus not only would we be able to show ourselves to her, but we would also be able to spot her. Whose strange idea was this? Monsieur Weizman's or Ginette's? We couldn't be sure. However, I expect that Ginette would have liked to be received with three cheers. Moreover, it was practical and would make our encounter easier. Everything went as planned. As the ship docked, we started shouting. Not long after, we saw a little girl with a blue beret wave her hand; she came nearer and nearer as the ship drew alongside the quay. It was a thrilling moment indeed! I remembered what my father said once. Long, long ago, as he was boarding the ship on the same quay, he had made a gesture with his hand as though he wanted to say that that was the end of everything. My father never forgot that moment, never! Well, that man's daughter, after many a long day, unaware of this, had made use of her hands to express a different feeling; as though the hands spoke saying: "Here I am!" I glanced at my father, there were tears in his eyes. He must have remembered the same occasion.

"Monsieur Weizman was, as I expected, a stout and chubby man. Yet, he had a thunderous voice. His manner of squeezing one's hand during a handshake and his piercing looks inspired confidence. My father and he hugged each other like old friends. Yet, as far as I can remember, they had met each other no more than a couple of times in Biarritz. However, it was apparent who they were embracing as they hugged one other.

"We had planned to go home together; but he excused himself, saying that it would be better for Ginette to meet her family alone. On the other hand, he intended to make a short survey of the city. He had said that we shouldn't worry about his board as he was used to fending for himself in strange lands. It would be sufficient for him to be given their address. He would visit them as soon as possible. We could do nothing in the face of his resolute behavior. Ginette seemed to be prepared for such an eventuality. It appeared that what was spoken about had already been discussed beforehand.

"Monsieur Weizman stayed two weeks in Istanbul. He rarely paid us a visit. He took Ginette for a stroll once and accompanied my father somewhere twice. The things intended to be conveyed had most probably been expressed during those strolls.

"Separation had not been easy. A sad parting it was, Monsieur Weizman put his arms around Ginette; they remained immobile for a while without saying a word. Then, smiling, he stared at her and pinched her nose in jest. He had done the same thing many times before, he then entrusted her to our custody. It must have been a secret code between them.

"We had taken Ginette home on the day of her arrival. Aunt Tilda and Uncle Kirkor also had come, Aunt Tilda was intensely curious about our guest. While Uncle Kirkor had intimated that she shouldn't leave my father all alone on such a day. He was so thoughtful. In the meantime, a couple of inquisitive neighbors also had dropped by. Their main purpose was, however, to display their knowledge of the French language. Ginette seemed displeased with this show of affection; she appeared to have been put in a predicament. How different she looked among all those people who had come to see her. This was the moment when I'd felt closest to her. This experience would remain attached to me for years to come. I would be nurturing this feeling for years without knowing the reason why.

"Ginette's initial reaction was one of bafflement; however, the real shock was to be experienced by my mother. Before going to bed, Ginette had placed the tiny statuette of Jesus Christ on her night table and knelt before it. 'I always pray before going to bed,' she had said. My mother had tried to explain away the event by establishing the connection with the training she had received at the convent. My father had tried to calm my mother down with a smile saying: 'Don't worry; it may be somewhat difficult, but I'm sure we can arrange for this in the long run.'

"My mother felt it her moral duty to initiate her into Judaism. As a matter of fact, she was a responsible person by nature and felt it incumbent upon her to convert her to the Jewish creed. She had taken to Ginette as if she were her own daughter, thus satisfying her yearning to have a girl. My father felt a special affection for my mother for this reason.

"Ginette lived with us for ten years. My mother loved her, while she, in turn, remained absolutely devoted to my mother. She had perfect confidence in her. Among the family members she relied on most of all was my mother; in whom she confided her intimate feelings. She never ceased to be an introvert, but her assurance that there was someone near to her in whose bosom she could place her head contributed to her growth. Nobody could deny that there were serious reasons that caused her poor adjustment to her new environment. This was due not only to the fact that she was in a foreign land, but also a different atmosphere; however she did her utmost to fit herself into the milieu. She was the embodiment of tact, and took special care not to put the people she met in a bad humor by her silly questions. Thus, she seemed to be sullen when alone. Could this be a sort of expiation and self-torture? Nobody dared to go near her or disturb her in her isolation. Although she said nothing about it, her looks expressed that she would rather be alone. According to my father, my uncle had been of like character. The latter's similar behavior had caused displeasure in a host of individuals, especially in his mother and his wife. These women had remained devoted to him their entire lives. Ginette's outward appearance was not unlike her mother's, but in her moral makeup she had taken after her father. When one observed her smiling countenance, one approached her with a light heart. Yet, her inner world was closed to everybody. To protect herself against the adversities of the outer world she was in need of such a sanctuary just like everybody else. This had been a way to differentiate herself from her surroundings—which she had been successful in doing. This I knew. She had provided me with clues as to the meaning of her behavior that changed according to the individual with whom she was to be in contact. This was our little secret. During her years at the French *lycée,* she was referred to as "Papillon," we had taken to this more than once in the presence of our common friends and inquisitive relatives. I'd done my best to experience this feeling. I'd never left her alone on such an occasion. Thus we had eventually succeeded in becoming good friends . . . "

There seemed to be a hint of resentment lying dormant for years in his depths. The clock pointed to a different time, to a different story left untold, to an absence preferred to be kept secret . . .

My land belonged to others

'We had eventually succeeded in becoming good friends.' Would this sentence be sufficient to explain the relationship between Berti and Ginette? I think that a new situation was arising which could be interpreted by some as cowardice, by some as nobility, and by others as affection. There are relationships which can be based on a footing without being put into words, cogitated on or inquired into. These are relationships that you keep alive within you, through voices that are made known which you prefer to convey through your addresses. You say to yourself that certain feelings must be kept in the same place and manifested through utterances. The reason is that you must already be aware of the boundary line you have drawn for the sake of your preferences, of the fact that you'll not have access to that forbidden zone, and that daring to do so might break the magic of that relationship. In this game of hide-and-seek between Berti and Ginette in which both sides tried to conceal themselves, it looked as though such a voice guided and colored such a relationship and had been desired to be followed. This self-camouflage revealed that sense of friendship that Berti tried to explain to me, conveying it far beyond hollow platitudes. Certain feelings had to be concealed, certainly; they had to be buried, never to be unearthed again. Certain feelings had to be masked against the call of unexpected emotions and be kept undisclosed in order for them to be kept aloof from those eventualities. I believe I had solved and grasped the nature of this relationship better having brought together and patched up these clues. It looked as though Berti was reluctant to acknowledge defeat and lose Ginette for good, while she dared not hurt Berti. In case the concealed feelings were to come to the fore and the words chanced on found out their ordinary identities in those lives, certain difficulties might be encountered. When one considers this aspect of their relationship, they had succeeded in becoming friends who regarded solidarity and mutual devotion. They had learned how to bear each other on that thin line of demarcation through laconic speech. In fact, this was the most beautiful and meaningful side of their relationship. This attitude seemed to corroborate my understanding of their interpretation of life. Berti had, for instance, borne all his relationships by such apprehensions and concerns. What was inherent in this was the apprehension of losing certain things and being unable to live with the illusions they created. I was familiar with this experience. The relations that couldn't be broken or lived properly had been nurtured from this source, and, consequently the poems had remained uncomposed because of this. When you tried to assess certain relations you had now and then an experience of *déjà-vu*. What remained for you after all the experiences, losses, or gains were but leftovers; appearances made you what you actually were; what distinguished you from others were those beautiful appearances, those unprecedented voices. Berti's story was, in a sense, the history of those who had not been able to cross that boundary, of those who were known by others as outsiders.

Ginette had learned how to turn inward in order to be able to take her own path making sure that others did not notice it when she had crossed the threshold of adulthood. She was the sort of person who had to put on somebody else's garb in another person's land. In order to understand this attitude, one had to recall a detail and take it into consideration. At first sight, women, who were ready to take her under their wing and protect her, seemed to have always been within her reach. All these women had been sincere and honest in their dealings with people. Madame Manzil, Marie Thérese the prioress, and Madame Roza were marching in Indian file. The various lives, the variety of women and the different times involved seemed to point to the fact that certain things had been lived with certain deficiencies. Can it be that what had been looked for and what had actually been lived was in fact quite a different woman? If one considers these deficiencies, one should not be surprised to learn that wherever she went, she felt herself to be a guest. In her past there was neither a tomorrow, nor a past in which she could find shelter. Under the circumstances, putting on an appearance that would suit the wishes of those individuals was a revolt of small stature, reminiscent of heroes and heroines who knew how to bear and endure their anonymities; a revolt that gained a special meaning by a wan and mischievous smile; to be able to head for the correct time, to *her* correct time, gingerly, being less exposed to receive injuries. Her success in being a brilliant student at school and in receiving the love and affection of her teachers, ignorant of being true to life, were but integral parts of this secret revolt. Berti had noticed this choice and had done everything to remain close to Ginette, to protect that feeling which he dared not name. However, to be frank, no one had been able to go as far as Madame Roza. Ginette and Madame Roza communed every night behind closed doors. We could never pick up anything from what they had been discussing. The guess was that Ginette had learned how to go on living through betrayals by the time she had made headway toward her womanhood.

The lost diary

To be able to have confidence in someone despite the attention that they may generate . . . this was undoubtedly one of the experiences that a person might enjoy and succeed in enjoying. However, according to Berti, there was but one single person with whom Ginette had perfect confidence and in whom she could find a shelter; a person who knew how to listen to her better than anybody; it was a person concealed in her diary who tried to survive, in that diary which she had begun to keep ever since her arrival in Istanbul, at a time when she spoke almost to nobody, and was still under the influence of her monastic life. Only Berti had been told about the existence of this diary. It apparently contained indications that would likely bring to the surface the images of a young girl trying to explore and understand womanhood. The idea of keeping a diary had been suggested to her by the prioress. This was one of the right paths to teach her how to live, in addition to how to read and write correctly and have a perfect command of one's language. When the right time came, the footsteps of Monsieur Weizman would also be heard. A long return, a very long return was not very far from Ginette's mind when she was getting ready to start her life in Istanbul, in another country. It was time for her to keep a diary and be its sole possessor. She wanted to record the time in question. The rest could be understood over a course of time and be placed next to other texts. Yet, why had she confided this to Berti from whom she had concealed many a feeling and reality of hers? Was it because she believed he would appreciate her efforts to keep a diary, this peaceful and romantic cousin of hers, or to react against that deep and unutterable passion in order to soothe her conscience? Both alternatives could be argued for in addition to many other probabilities I cannot think of at the moment. Barring the realities toward which these probabilities might lead us, that a secret had been entrusted with him was a fact. This secret would contribute to the preservation of that special unutterable feeling whose importance should never be ignored. Ginette had not been wrong. Her peaceful and romantic traveling companion had proven to be faithful to his vow and borne the secret as he had promised. We, on the other hand, learned this secret long after we had lost track of Ginette in a different land. What had been confided, the confidence that Berti believed in should have remained unbetrayed despite the distance of time and space; but the person whose secret he had been keeping, in defiance of their common experiences and their moments of togetherness, the opportunity to catch it had vanished into thin air. To reveal this secret meant a betrayal for Berti. People that failed to have an insight into the childishness concealed in this experience might well interpret this as puerile behavior. She was a person who had lost much of her valuable time in small details according to some, in commonplace details according to others. Personally, I had sided with those who judged her occupation as dealing in vain with minute details. The origin of my joy in taking part in her games must have been sought in this preference of mine. These were, perhaps, the happiest moments spent keeping track of those people. Berti's gentility in imparting the data relative to the diary of others lay in his search for new confidants in the very act of committing a betrayal. He had told Juliet and I, one night, of this clandestine side of Ginette. This was an extraordinary little gift given to me that night, given with a unique hidden smile, the expectations for its consequences having been known all too well beforehand. However, I was to appreciate the real value of this gift after many long stories. What had been told during that night had opened a new vista in my own long story. This seemed to indicate tardiness in my recalling the fact that a great price had to be paid for embracing the inexhaustible passion of studying time. However, I'm inclined to believe that there was another path one had to take that night. This path, which I could perceive through my intuitive power, lay between Berti and Juliet. It was as though a connection had been re-established with a view to sharing a deep scar from the past. The meaning that was hidden in this sentence enabled me to understand a little better the relationship that this sentence contained. One should also consider the fact that Berti was aware of the meaning of things expressed as well as those left unexpressed. Despite all that he intended to tell us, he had said almost nothing about the contents of the diary in question. As we listened to his narration of those moments we had instinctively sensed that Ginette used to read parts of her diary to him with a view to expressing her feelings indirectly. They had discussed on one of those nights the said diary and the important role it had played in their life. That was the only place that one could face oneself in all one's nakedness, wherein one felt absolutely free, believed oneself to be free and alive. Real interrogations took place and letters could be written there. Then one night they had spoken of those books and their contents and what they had left in them, in their histories. Ginette had then asked the reason why books told of loves mostly in bitter terms, why they failed to show the right path to follow, and wanted to know why her questions had remained unanswered; to which Berti had replied saying that the reader of those books perceived them through the questions they left unanswered. Ginette had continued: "I'm writing about love . . . There was a young girl who wanted to go far up the mountains . . . She wanted to move away, away from her past experiences, from her past, even from herself. Then . . . then she set off one day without informing anyone . . . making headway toward those mountains . . . On her way, she met a wayfarer who had strayed from his path, his original intention being the same as hers. They came to realize that they shared the same objective. But they were suddenly taken by fright rather than joy. Both had had insights into each other's private corners, which they would have preferred to keep confidential; their secret corners concealed what they both wanted to hide. They joined hands to flee, to flee as far as possible. Yet, having covered a given distance, they realized they could do no more. Either they were exhausted or reluctant to see the ultimate destination that the path they had taken would lead them to. Actually, what they refused to see were their own realities. What they had been enjoying was a mere chimera . . . or perhaps they had been aiming at illusions and had been confronted with harsh realities . . . " She stopped for a brief moment. In this narration in which one couldn't fail but see the traces of her own world, one could perceive in her eyes the part she had wanted to reflect from her own private life, when she mentioned "confronted with harsh realities . . . " which Berti had repeated to persuade her to go on, she had grown silent. Who had ceased to speak? What words had prevented her from continuing, who had been the person that had been prevented, why and where? Anyway, even I can keep silent; recalling the individuals out of my reach, inquiring of myself the reason why I try to dodge the meanings that certain words projected on me, thus indulging myself in restructuring the whole thing. It was easy to tell the people for whom Berti had suddenly preferred to keep silent that night. It wasn't so difficult to find new words to explain his experiences. We could listen to that story, comfortably settled in our chairs in our little darkness without having to show ourselves. It may be that what she had been trying to recall had been lying deep in her depths. It was as though we had been drawn closer to each other at that moment . . . remembering, without saying anything and making ourselves scarce, those people that we could no longer set eyes upon, the individuals we could no longer attain. However, this situation might cause a minor emotional breakdown in Juliet likely to remain with her forever. However, she had accepted it as part of their history, the man whom she wanted to be always by her side had remained with Ginette. As I had been musing over these things, suddenly there emerged before me the image of Marcellina . . . At that very moment, I saw a smile covering Juliet's face, a smile I remember having seen somewhere else, a smile laden with affection.

In the meantime, at a critical moment of despair in the course of her story, Ginette had put her arms around Berti and begun sobbing. "Once I had done the same thing; when I was with Enrico. At the time I was playing a game that my father had taught me when I was a little girl. For the first time in my life, I'd felt the pang of separation from my father with whom I could no longer speak. I was a little child; my breasts were budding which confused me; well, I was but a child, as I've said!" Ginette said. This confession was followed by a sudden burst of laughter on both sides. Sobs and laughter were mixed with tears of sorrow and tears of joy. Actually both were crying. Then Ginette had put her arms around Berti's neck once again saying that she would never forget their common experiences and the words they had exchanged. Her breasts were conspicuous through her transparent nightdress. Their cheeks met, then their lips . . . Then . . . well that was all. It was the night when they had felt closest to each other, the night when they wanted to present to each other an unforgettable gift in remembrance of that experience. They happened to be in Ginette's room that night.

Ginette had told Berti that she would soon be setting out on a journey and would try to fly with her own wings as far as those wings would take her. Berti, contrary to the efforts of the family to dissuade her from this venture, hadn't deterred her from this daring action. He knew that a decision had been made after a long deliberation with herself. Then the day of separation came. Ginette had wanted to leave Istanbul by boat. For those who had an idea about journeys and departures, this choice had a meaning of course. It had been raining. The quay had that day borne testimony to a journey toward a new hope. On their way to the boat Ginette had said, staring at the splattering of raindrops against the windscreen: "A fine day for separation . . . just like in the films . . . the films that enable us to experience chimerical imagery . . . It might also be a train station . . . but a quay will do just fine. We have the vast sea before us; loves sunken in seas, parting under the rain. I wish someone would write this story, making sure not to skip this particular detail." Berti had understood what she meant. He had watched the stage plays in which the actors had brought the action to such a juncture. He had kept silent at these words; although he had made a promise to her, a promise he would never forget; a promise to the effect that the said moments should not remain exclusively to two people. He would find an audience at all costs. He would ferret out a spectator. They were alone on the way to the quay; it had been Ginette's choice. This last gift had been a shared wish.

A long Istanbul adventure was drawing to a close, never to be repeated. How different was that woman who was soon to depart from the little girl of days gone by? No one could provide a proper answer to this; as a matter of fact no one should have even tried. Certain questions needed other times to find their answers.

For Ginette to acquire the spectator she desired meant that her memory would not die in Istanbul. To live on, to be able to survive in certain people's visions and words. This was the kind of wish that would have its repercussions in time. You could describe the places where those faces, those rooms, and those words had remained unobliterated to your heart's content.

At the moment of parting, Ginette had put her arms around Berti and said: "Give up choosing the wrong people, and don't let life scare you so much!" Is it possible that she had delayed a step so that her decision might somehow change at the last moment? The answer to this question was never provided by Berti to the best of my knowledge; or perhaps he was just reluctant.

Ginette had preferred to travel to Israel with a small handbag in her identity of an immigrant as though intending to remind certain people of an old story. At the start of her journey the number of personal effects she had wanted to take with her wasn't great. She had never had the opportunity to transport her effects as a hunchback. It looked as though the story was being repeated, gaining some meaning in an inexorable and unavoidable text . . . After the lapse of so many years, traveling once again to an unknown destination . . . The unknown belonged to her . . . it was her temple . . . it was the path that would be taking her to that new land. The unknown was her unknown, hers to the bitter end, at all costs and dues.

That was the last of her; despite all those incidents that had occurred in that house, in those rooms, and, which are more important still, the experiences at the moment of separation, she had not even written a letter, choosing to get lost in her unknown. Could this be interpreted as unfaithfulness? If what had been

done for her was to be taken into consideration, this should be the natural inference. Nevertheless, the family had consented to this new situation as though it
was another part of life. Was this a mere appearance, or one of those games we
had witnessed in many a case elsewhere, played with skill, whose true meaning
was not easily accessible? In the face of her guarded disposition, Madame Roza
had preferred not to say anything and tried to act as though she wasn't offended.
No letter meant good news. One ought to believe that everything was alright.
God always guided those who chose the right path. Ginette knew if she ever ran
into difficulty, to whom she could turn, whose door she could always knock on.
The same hope had also been entertained by Berti who had been waiting that day
patiently . . . I had certain vague recollections; I seemed to hear certain echoes
from our talks. As a matter of fact, she had taught me how to play the "Black or
Red" game. She had taught me how to go and act without mulling over certain
decisions. These steps might be considered insignificant, of course. I remember
one day in particular, hand in hand, we had gone to eat a mouse. Not the animal,
of course, but a chocolate pastry that contained a chestnut in it. What was of
special importance was our discerning palate and the delight we took in it. At
such moments I felt paralyzed and was aghast at the idea of it. My astonishment
had given her much delight. This feeling of hers had aroused a sexual drive in me
which my confusion had soon supressed. One day, as we were walking along the
main street of Beyoğlu, an old woman we had come across had approached us
and said reproachfully: "Arman is very sick," and walked on without waiting for
a reaction. We had continued our walk without any comment. I was no longer
perplexed then. Quite another feeling had overwhelmed me, I felt like crying
because Ginette had been clasping my hand more tightly than ever . . . I was no
longer a small kid . . . I had seen tears in Ginette's eyes.

In which photograph did we figure?

A few tears . . . how many years had gone by since then, how many individuals,
expressions, and betrayals have been left behind? The associations revive in one
the sorrow of days spent and the sense of being caught by oneself. Is this an illusion fed upon lies which induces us to admit that we have left certain places far
away, very far away, yearning to be able to touch those distances? Can it be an
escape; a desire to see them again; a desire to display one's sense of belonging;

an absence carried in a different fashion; an acknowledged deficiency; or the need to feel that we are still above them despite all those indignations? A lot of feelings might find their meanings in such a step, in the things generated by that step. For instance, which door had opened at the right time for the right people and the right lives, which door had remained shut although it ought to have been opened? It had been our intention to tackle such issues during that unexpected meeting in Vienna. Ginette and I stood before one another after so many years . . . It would take some time before we realized how far we had succeeded in taking that walk. The city where we met, where we confronted one another, seemed to be the right city for me to start writing the story of that long journey toward death. If one considered the fact that Nesim had been disappointed and disillusioned following the loss of that country he had in mind to build, the starting point of the story might well be that city. It was the right city; it looked that way anyway. But where did we happen to be in that exact time in the story? In other words, were we at the right place? Were we to lose belief at the said time of encounter we had selected by forcing its very conditions? When we considered the moments, and, what is more important, the man, we intended to leave with each other, we had to be prepared for all sorts of contingencies. As for the poems of those moments . . . they were destined, I think, to remain with us. They, in turn, would be perceived by others in different fashions and with different meanings under the influence of associations and histories, in spite of those words discovered after all those efforts and struggles. We had taken our steps toward our solitudes at the very spot where deafness was heard.

"Would you like to have a cup of coffee? I'll have one myself," said Ginette, and without waiting for an answer she had ordered for us both. I had noticed a change in her French accent. There was nothing wrong with the grammar, but it didn't sound like the French of a native. "Do you think it would be a good idea," I remarked, "won't we be late? Do you have people waiting for you?" What had induced me to talk like this? Was it to show concern for her or simply to show off as though I was interested in her predicament? "Haven't I told you that I'm alone? Moreover, you now look sort of grown up, deserving of a few more hours," she retorted. Under the circumstances, I thought I could allow myself some wider elbowroom. "Considering you've been living separate from your husband for over a year now in a foreign land, your marital relations seem to be flawless!" She had reacted to my ironic remark with composure, with an expression that seemed to intimate that I didn't have an inkling as to the real situation. Then a silence occurred, one of those hushed silences. It was broken by the waiter who had come with our coffee. It was apparent that they knew each other. As he put down the cups on the table he even cracked a joke which she received favorably as she craked a smile. However, as the exchange of wits had taken place in a foreign tongue, I had remained a mere bystander.

"To be frank, I was the promoter of this research trip," she said with a weak smile and voice after the waiter had gone. "I have harmonious relations with the people at the university. Actually, I've escaped. I felt obliged to be devoted to my profession. But, you haven't even asked what my profession is! I'm a psychiatrist, specializing in autistic cases." She was staring at me. Her smile seemed to inquire into whether I knew this or not, an important detail related to this long story. We had caught a moment of stillness, laden with meaning. This was the poem of a simultaneous conveyance of a man left at a different time, for different texts, by way of different images and associations. I was reluctant to show that I had been impressed. Certain recollections and enigmatic settlings of outstanding accounts doomed a man against his will to always hear the voices of those memories claiming that they would never let him go. Enrico Weizman's forgetfulness about that detail relating to the past and his unwillingness to share it with someone else was out of the question. Ginette could not possibly ignore these voices instilled in her. "Your uncle should have lived this long in order to witness this," I said, trying to touch that dark world of memory despite my apprehensions. She had understood and saw that I could not proceed any further. She had wanted to express that joy she had felt in having witnessed my establishment of the correct link, gazing graciously despite the developments and defaults that had occurred in between, at the little child who had once been taken to long walks in the streets of quite another city that had to be abandoned later on. Where was that child now, in whose company was she, in which details had she been lost and to what particular feeling? The possible answers to this question did not matter so much as regards that interval, when the meaning was accessible and more easily grasped. By the way, the child was still alive; so was the little girl who had taken all the challenges that life had presented without any hesitation. Both the child and the little girl, lost in that pollution, were justified in their apprehensions, concerns, and introversion. But, at the moment . . . yes at the moment, to feel that togetherness beyond all boundaries, eventualities remaining beyond the realities seemed to be even more important than all the possible anticipations. Time had once again been obliterated. However, not only was it important to realize that what one wrote was under the influence of what one read, but also what one experienced and learned through experience. Ginette had held my hands again. That was enough. No words or new questions were needed. They were within us; a place we could always have access to. Silence had fallen afterward. The place where my associations would take me was from that point on a place which I could descry from afar and understand only through my feelings, its tongue remaining foreign for me. I was observing the traces of a deep wrench on Ginette's face. "My son was killed in action, two years ago, along with two fellow soldiers," she said suddenly. "The funny thing is that we both had a premonition that this would happen. It was so absurd. He'd never believed in war. He'd always been a conscientious objector. He always occupied the first rank in the mass demonstrations staged against it. Before he had left, he had put his arms around me and squeezed me tightly, saying, 'I wish we loved and understood each other more.' He may have said these words as he was compelled to bear arms, for both of us, in fact . . . I had asked him to forgive me for having been unable to understand him better and for having given birth to him, exposing him to a war he did not believe in. What else could I do? I cannot describe the regret I experienced. While trying to help and give succor to others, doing everything within my power to bring them back to life, I'd been working strenuously day and night without realizing that I'd left those near to me untended. Why? I don't even like to think about it; I'm doing my best to dodge the issue, but I cannot control my dreams and nightmares.

"Do you have any idea how difficult it is to deal with autistic people? You can never convince them to accept anything new. That's the reason why they are attached to you wholeheartedly. You couldn't abandon them even if you wanted to. Under the circumstances, you have no other choice but to forget yourself and what you had been planning to do. I've been in this profession quite some time now; I think I've reached a certain point. Articles appeared in papers about my work. My objective was to see that those suffering returned to life. I wonder if all these efforts would prove to be in vain. After all, those individuals were our very conscience; they are the facets of the world we live in which we refuse to see, which we try to garb in different guises. You may be asking similar questions of yourself. Believe me, I've done so myself. Yet during the therapy, that struggle, that desire for struggle overrules everything and you are hardly conscious of anything else. You believe that you're carrying on the struggle for your own sake and you cling firmly to your past, to your experiences, to your future, to your hopes that contributed to your formation and enabled you to reach the station you happened to be in now. This was another sort of flight, another sort of escape which you were reluctant to admit to. In the origin of this struggle lay the bitterness of those things you had failed to discover and attain. It may be you were trying to show, to prove certain things to certain people with whom you could not settle your account. As you may well see, I can't help trying to find solutions for my problems. I don't know the purpose of all these questions and queries. All that I know is that in our profession, one has to admit the fact that in order to make progress, one ought to learn, in the first place, how to accept oneself as the subject of a case study, and that one may, at any moment, feel the need for help.

"Thus, I've been in the thick of the action and lived to fight on. While engaged in this pursuit, I had neglected those nearest to me unawares. As I was being rewarded by the gratitude of people to whom I'd extended a helping hand, in time, the successes inevitably lost their significance, I hadn't realized that I was being driven away from the creature I had given birth to.

"As for my daughter . . . She resigned herself to a life of devotion and married a man who himself was a devout Jew. She had her skull shaved, put on her wig, and changed her lifestyle. She calls me up very rarely. We have nothing to say to each other anymore. We have become strangers; we belong to worlds wide apart. Now and then, when I go over the incidents in my past I cannot help feeling I am being punished by certain people; an ordinary view without any originality, surely; an attitude that makes me more conspicuous than necessary. Such transitions are undoubtedly experienced everyday everywhere in the world. Yet, when I came to know Enrico I'd learned not to feel any need for religion in order that I might know myself better and lead a freer life. I brought up my children in this discipline. I had a world which I had perfect confidence in . . . But now . . . now that so many lives have gone by . . . I'm here at present, in a city which you will find, I expect, meaningful for my writings, for our writings. Now and then my former patients visit me . . . we bandy words . . . as for those to whom it does not occur to make a call . . . "

I felt confused that I had compelled her to make such a long speech. I felt myself like an intruder who was somewhere I was not supposed to be. I had diverted my stare somewhere else. She must have sensed what I had felt. "You don't have to blame yourself for inciting me to make a confession. I was meaning to tell all this to you anyhow. Had I not done so, the story you are promising yourself to write one day will have loopholes in it. I'll soon vanish; I don't think I can carry this burden all alone when you'll no longer be able to reach me." She was smiling. I had once again felt the beauty of her smile. I had heard Berti's voice. Ginette had learned well enough how to appear according to the whims of her interlocutors. We had exchanged smiles without uttering a word; after which I had to divert my stare once more in another direction, despite Berti and all those old photographs that he bequeathed. "No, this is not a play. There are certain things hidden in that smile, real things desired to be disclosed, to be instilled in me," I said to myself.

"I've another bitter experience which I cannot share with anyone. I feel myself lonelier than ever in the face of all that I have gone through. I never had the privilege of knowing what motherly tenderness was, nor have I had the opportunity to show compassion to my children. What really binds us to this world? Who are we? What ought we do?" she said. "You are reminding me of a scene in a film I never forgot," I replied. "The action took place in Mexico. The woman, after whose name the film was called, had brought a big bouquet of flowers to her lover. The man to whom she was deeply attached was married. The woman was aware of this, and felt that the man she loved had to be kept distant; yet, she found in this relationship certain things she thought to be inexhaustible. The man had tried to explain to her the reason why he had to keep aloof in the face of this passion which had remained on a platonic level. Actually, there was someone else he was in love with. It was somebody who shared his small world and garden; it was a love that people called perverted. The beloved was there, under the arbor in the garden that had the foretaste of the garden of paradise, decorated with trees and flowers, each more splendid than the last, singing a Mexican folksong with a couple of friends, while watching him. There were times when hell was experienced in paradise. Glances had crossed; he had timidly touched different feelings, apprehensions, and resentments. 'My wife killed our child,' the man said. What child was that? To which world did it belong? These were the visions of an earthquake, of an invisible tremor. She had seen the inferno of the man she loved, to whom she had been attached passionately. 'Well, what are we, what should we do?' she asked. And the man said: 'We've got to learn how to make our own way silently, in the company of our own dreams, defeats, and routs without trying to understand them. To make headway silently, in the company of our own dreams. Those lives so significant to us, so unforgettable, lives that we could not dispose of might perhaps be explained tersely through words.'" "As a matter of fact, I personally have tried to act according to that man's advice, to the best of my ability. Everybody who feels the subject of an interrogation sets off and takes this path. It's a pity that mirrors reflect only what is allowed to be exposed. Just like those with whom we dare let join our lives," Ginette chimed in. Her words sounded like a call . . .

This also was a game

Mirrors . . . to be able to undergo the challenge of self-interrogation . . . this had reminded me of the words of a woman who had succeeded in delivering herself from the clutch of the concentration camps. It was evening. She seemed to have left those days behind. She lived in Vienna. She had been married and had children and grandchildren. She was invited from the four corners of the world to tell of her recollections to the best of her remembrance. As a child, she had known the ghetto in Warsaw, the ghetto with all the privations, fears, and despair; she had tasted the bitterness of Auschwitz, from the very first days of the war up until the very last . . . We had had a talk. She spoke of those days as a story lost in the mist of the past. The day she had been rescued, she was, to the best of her memory, fifteen years old. She had been a victim of the typhus epidemic; she had been reduced to thirty-six kilos. She barely remembered her last weeks there. Her mother also lay sick and had to be moved elsewhere for treatment. The authorities had told them that she could go with her mother. Under the circumstances, it was quite natural that she performed the duty incumbent upon her as a daughter. However, these were the values of the ancient world, of a lost world. She had declared, in the presence of everybody, that she would go nowhere, and sent her mother to her grave in cold blood. This was a trick; the same trick had been played on many of her friends. Terminally sick people were moved away in the company of their children only to be shoved into death chambers. She wouldn't fall for such a stupid trick. Everybody was on a quest for survival in those days. I'd looked into the eyes of the woman. They bore the painful traces of the loss of life they had seen in other countries rather than remorse . . . I wanted to know the reason why she reminisced on those moments and felt compelled to speak of them after all these years.

Then I had asked her what she had taken with her while she was being taken to the camp. "My diary," she rejoined, "only my diary. But, right after our arrival in Auschwitz, they had confiscated it. I was only eleven at the time . . . "

These stories prompted one to ask questions of oneself . . . This story I'm trying to tell and share with my readers had reminded me of a little secret that Berti had entrusted to us. It was time, I couldn't help asking Ginette: "How about speaking a little about your diary now?" I blurted out. "When I reached Israel, I destroyed it. I was going to start a new life. My memories and nightmares were enough for me," she answered with a laugh. "You fool! Come, let's go and have a glass of wine somewhere," she said. "We both need it." In reply to her suggestion I said: "As a matter of fact, I'm free tonight. After a few glasses you might have more to say about your experiences, about Enrico, Angela, and Arman. There are so many gaps in your account; many a recollection clogged with the flotsam and jetsam sheltered in the recesses of your brain," I added. "Gaps galore, like in actual life; recollections abandoned there to their destiny which may seem insignificant under normal circumstances, but meaningful enough for us. Such is life, isn't it?" she rejoined. Gaps in recollections are somewhat meaningless . . . That evening was our last spent together. The story didn't allow for another encounter. What had been experienced had gaps and was devoid of sense. That evening . . . that evening I had wanted to tell her about that woman.

All the photographs were jumbled together

That morning Monsieur Jacques woke up at the usual hour; he was ready to meet a new day at the correct time, neither earlier nor later. He cast a glance at the old clock that he kept, in the name of a silent place that deserved to be preserved, placed on the night table by the glass that contained his false teeth. It was six-thirty. Just like the six-thirties of days past; six and thirty . . . There was nothing new in the break of dawn, nothing to worry about . . . nothing that would give cause to bother about . . . Everything seemed to be in a state of peace, as time would have wished it to be. He might try to tell about the feelings, the visions, and the things that sounds and voices aroused so that one might have a clearer insight into the situation they occupied at daybreak. It was certainly possible to speak about these things. Yet, as for experiencing the related emotion, breaking news, touches, the real touches . . . He wandered his gaze on the wardrobe that contained his garments each of which was laden with memories, on the statuette of a naked woman on the dresser, on the photographs, on the armchair he used to sit in, on the jockstrap placed all on its own, and, what is even more important, what was to his left that was destined to remain vacant henceforth. He realized that he still had his nightcap on. "I must've dozed off while I was praying. I'm growing old, already burned out," he said to himself. He had pronounced these words in a somewhat raised, articulated voice as though he was intending to make it heard to others. Yet, the voice he anticipated was someone else's. However, he knew perfectly well that in this den to which he had retired (his ultimate shelter), he couldn't possibly anticipate it. He was paying the cost of a long life of loneliness. Not only had he been far removed from his people, but he was also estranged from certain lives and feelings. From the opening between the curtains crept the beams of a bright and sunny day . . . Years had taught him what to expect from the first beams of morning. May was drawing to an end. The days would be getting fairer and fairer . . . The approach of sunny days created optimistic expectations in him. A simple joy not lost yet. The weather was improving, warming up. This meant a noticeable extenuation of pain in his aching limbs; and the resumption of his morning walks. He would soon be able to remain seated in his armchair on the verandah for many hours up until the sunset. They had already begun turning off the central heating at regulated intervals; the nights were still chilly enough to necessitate the turning on of the central heating. He was retiring to bed long before the other members of the family. And when he woke during the night to answer the call of nature, he put on his dressing gown which he had bought a long time ago in London and with which he would not part on any account. Only in the evenings when he took a shower did he fear he would catch a nasty chill. He might certainly find other solutions to prevent the occurrence of such an eventuality. No one prevented him from having his bath during the warmer hours of the day. Thursdays were his shower days. Moreover, he had found the solution against the danger of catching cold. A small electric heater solved the matter and kept the bathroom warm for hours. He used it also in the summer months. *"Maz vale sudar che sarnudar"* (Better sweat than sneeze). His mother had instilled this axiom into his brain over the course of several years which he had never forgotten. In their house at Halıcıoğlu, he and his elder brother used to wash in a large tub. The room in which the washtub was placed was heated by a gigantic brazier many hours before. That house was much warmer than the present one. Nowadays everything had become practical. Central heating, a water heater, and an electric heater were no longer luxurious items. The days when he got up early in the morning at six-thirty to light the stove appeared to be so distant. Then, he remembered having become an adult with a pretty large family. They had been living in an apartment at Asmalımescit now. But the number of family members was being reduced as the days went by; yet, the rest was united as a whole. The same road they had been treading would also take them to the apartment at Harbiye; the number getting smaller and smaller . . . making sure however, to remain united and procreating. In all the houses whose upkeep had been his responsibility, he had made a point to get up first and heat the living room. It was his paternal duty . . . a paternal duty. When the entire household had gotten up, the sitting room was already warm enough to receive its guests. In the dead of winter, they had to use a portable gas heater . . . yes, the gas heater, where was it now? The last time he had seen it, it was at Berti's. That heater might well be unearthed in order to return to its original place for the sake of the good old days. Actually he revived it in his imagination, being alive as a human being among other objects he had lost and which he would have liked to touch; among his recollections that gas heater also had its place as a person to whom he would have liked to see, talk, and touch . . . At the recorded time, all the family members were there; Madame Roza was there. Jerry had not gone to America. Berti had not turned in upon himself: Kirkor, his mother, and father were all there. Lilica was groping in the world into which she had been brought. What awaited Nesim was certainly beyond all inference. Olga was there; it seemed that she would remain there for-ever . . . for a life she was doomed to live, to share, and to re-discover in which she had an unshakable belief. It was Olga's belief. Actually, the belief that had made Olga what she was . . . How distant they seemed now, all those visions, how they came back with prickings of conscience. He had no one but himself now to commune with about the deliberately interrupted nights, which left him at a loose end. Every one of those nights concealed long stories that had to be told to someone, but to whom? Was that so easy? All those people had gone the way of all flesh, having to leave behind their anticipations and expectations. What had been left behind had to go on living within well-delineated boundaries, penned up between walls in their enslaved state. He could not foresee at the time that such a truncation might take place in their branches. However, he had to admit that he had not been deprived of joy and earthly happiness; he should not be ungrateful. There was also a question for which he could not find an answer; he had failed to figure it out, despite so many years having passed. Which days were those? Which days could he refer to as 'those days'? He had recently started to brood over the relics of the past. The days had become longer it seemed. The days were long . . . even the child who used to listen to himself very intently and planned to write a long story had left for a different tale. Nobody had in fact lent their ears to anyone until the end. Nobody had succeeded in carrying anybody to the bitter end.

He got up from his bed with a smile, his mind crowded by such thoughts, a be-atific smile . . . intending to relive his past experiences . . . Now the first thing he ought to do should be to visit the bathroom. The condition of having difficulty in passing waste from his body had worsened; thus it had become his habit to swallow a pill when he woke up during the night. After all everything had a place, an order, a time . . . and he had never strayed from this principle. He had lived so far accordingly, and there was no reason to change this routine now. To shave every morning as though he was to put in an appearance somewhere of consequence was the *sine qua non* of the commencement of his day. The ritual of shaving should consist of the use of shaving cream, a shaving brush, and a razor. There had been certain inevitable changes, of course, in the meantime. Those were minor things, however, like perfumes and dyes. But the style was the same; there had been no change as regards its safety. Having shaved, he sprinkled his face with *eau de cologne* . . . lavender water, this was the same as ever; he had made a point never to change it. Although Berti used to bring home shaving lotions from his trips abroad, which, no doubt, had a delicious smell, he had neverthe-less preferred to remain devoted to his age-old habits. In the process of rubbing his face with the lavender water, he remembered the tunes he used to hum. How many years was it? No, he couldn't tell. The only thing he knew was that he had ceased to hum those tunes after the death of his mother. Why had he suddenly grown silent? Could it be that he had unconsciously been singing for his mother who was deprived of her sight? Her mother was an early riser like him. When she got up from his bed, she used to settle in her armchair without making her presence felt to others. Everybody believed that she continued to sleep. The truth was different from what people thought; it was lived even for those moments be-decked with sentiments that were hardly describable. It was his mother's habit to brood with closed eye over things she had difficulty remembering; what exactly were the colors at sunset in the Golden Horn? Those carpets? Her dresses, her underwear, her womanhood? Yes, it was her custom in the early hours of the morning to recall the days of her youth, when her eyes were closed to the dawning light. He knew this; this was actually one of their common secrets. They had a room of their own there. The songs he sang were the oldies. The songs used to be sung at Şehzadebaşı, the *fin-de-siecle* cabaret songs and hits of the day. Had he been singing them for his mother, really? This was not impossible; as a matter of fact the bathroom was near her room. It was nice to be able to recall those times. The struggle to get to know oneself was a long process, a struggle without an end. What had led him to recall these souvenirs for the sake of what immortal sentiments? Two days before he had dreamt of his mother. She happened to be with his father; they were smartly dressed; she wore a white dress and a white hat. It was as though they were going to a party. *"Como estas Cakito? De che no veined a vermos? No te eskarinyates ayinda de mozotros"* (How is my little Jacques? Why don't you come to see us? Haven't you missed us yet?) she said. They looked as beautiful as they were in their younger days . . . . He felt a shudder run down his spine . . . he wished to embrace them with all his might, with all his heart . . . He knew that such dreams were dreamt by people of the same age and of the same era. Such scenes might well be inserted into the text of a fiction. If one considers the things he had seen in his lonely hours during his night vigils, one should see nothing out of the ordinary in their unexpected return to his mind. Actually, it had been quite some time now since he felt ready for that moment. "It's only a dream . . . I'd eaten a bit too much that night, I think," he said, dodging the issue and trying to move away from the probability that was invading his whole being; he preferred to carefully approach the moments left for him in this world. It occurred to him to think whether he could sing those old tunes to himself. He was once more in front of a mirror . . . He tried to remember . . . No good . . . words failed him, even the tunes failed him, and the oldies refused to be revived. It was as though all the old songs balked at being brought back to life; it was as though they preferred to remain where they had been left. All the tunes seemed to have been transformed into a medley of songs, or into a single song. This was the song of oblivion. He gave up trying. He had already lost the habit of recalling; he could no longer transfer his innermost thoughts into articulate speech, feelings, and emotions by using his impoverished vocabulary. He had ceased to lose his temper when he could not express what he meant to say using the exact words. Had it been otherwise, he could not go on living with his shortcomings. He had learned where to keep his sense of reality, in a safe and sound place with all its naturalness, abandoned and betrayed as he had been. "I wonder what will be the next thing I shall be unable to recall . . . " he thought. He smiled. He felt a pride which he couldn't communicate to anyone. To attribute his actions to rational and creditable motives without adequate analysis of the true and especially unconscious motives showed that his connection with reality had not been impaired. Certain words he might well forego, certain songs might be recalcitrant . . . One thing was certain: his logic and intelligence were sound enough. He could still read, display anger at hearing the news on the TV, or joy at the storylines of the serials; he could still plan for the coordination of his resources and expenditures. He even took pleasure in being alert enough to supervise his own actions. When he thought: "I wonder what will be the next thing I shall be unable to recall . . . " he must have meant: "I wonder what'll be the next thing we'll be deprived of, and move away from." He was looking at the man within, at the man he was doomed to carry, using a different hold. The things that would reveal themselves to this look should not be underestimated in terms of this loneliness. It appeared that this one-man play would be long lasting, if one considered the script that presented itself to him. One could never tell when this play would come to an end. He was the writer, the stage director, the actor, and the spectator. He was the props, the colors, and the setting as well as the witty lines and the curtain that would come down one day.

Brooding over these things, shuttling to and fro between the past and the present, he directed himself toward the bedroom trying to feel the weight of his steps on the floor. He took off his pajamas and put on his jockstrap. He had expected that a surgical intervention would fix his inguinal hernia and his health would be restored once and for all. However, the hernia on his right side had been superseded by another on his left. It was too late now for another operation. He had to cope with it one way or another. After all, this was a congenital condition. His father had had the same problem, so had Nesim; they had had to handle it under very different circumstances.

He put on his shirt and trousers. He tied up his necktie fastidiously. He put on his shoes using a shoehorn which he had been using for years now, he polished them . . . just like in the days when he used to go to his shop. He put on his vest and buttoned it up. He was ready to depart. He looked at himself once more in the mirror. His suit appeared to be too large. He had lost a few stone and had himself decreased in size. Yet, the suit itself had defied time. "After all, British stuff," he thought. He recalled his experiences in London, that Italian restaurant in the proximity of Marble Arch, the illuminated windows of the department stores. He had also left many an unfulfilled memory with others. He hadn't been able to share some of his days with people he would have liked to commune with. All these reminiscences gave him a very heavy heart. Well, what had been experienced had become part of the past; and what had not been put into action had not been the order of the day. What had been lived might at present be communicated to others. To take shelter in recollections . . . with a view to somehow walking farther and dying less . . . despite all anticipations and the surfeit of well-known delusions that had become love objects . . .

He made for the balcony. He drew the curtains, the French doors, and the shutters. Thus he removed the covering objects that had protected him against the darkness of the night, from the hostile, threatening looks of others. He went out onto the balcony into the open air. He wasn't wrong. The dawn was promising a clear and sunny day. The twittering of birds indicated that the dawn was breaking for others as well. He listened to the birds. At least these chirpings were the same as ever. "It's time that we moved to the island," he thought; it was time to stroll along the waterfront . . . Another winter had gone by. Berti must have seen to the garden; flowers, herbs, and trees needed tending and affection. Formerly, he used to take care of all these. When April arrived, he used to take a gardener with him and go to that house on a warm weekend when the sun had begun to warm up the houses, the rooms, and the garden itself. To tend the flowers was an act as laudable as taking care of a loved human being. The affection one displayed was rewarded; the flowers and the trees were in fact more faithful and generous compared to humans. Violets displayed incomparable colors to the people who took good care of them, the four o'clocks with fragrant yellow, red, or white flowers opened late in the afternoon and the sweet basil fragrance made breakfast a treat. The linden tree pervaded the atmosphere with its unforgettable scent. The plum tree blossomed every year and produced juicy fruits . . . without fail, in contrast to the fruit trees that gave their fruits twice a year. Every year . . . to the best of his remembrance, or so he wanted to believe anyway . . . the plums were small, of a yellow tint but tasty . . . small yellow plums that were the essential ingredient of the fish dish: gaidropsarus mediterraneus . . . Yes, Berti must have tended the garden by now . . . but what if he had failed to do so; one had to be lenient toward him. After all that he had experienced, one should be more tolerant. The disaster that had separated them had in a sense drawn them closer. Berti himself might be unaware of this. Berti had no idea of this new sentiment. Anyway, this wasn't so important. Rejuvenation and restoration of youthful vigor was out of the question now. Getting a new lease on life was a thing of the past; just as they lacked the energy required to tend the garden; the garden of which he could be but a spectator from now on; a spectator trying to distinguish the scents of flowers and fruits . . . through the odor of weeds; weeds of wild growth. He suddenly felt a cool breeze graze his cheeks. "You must be careful not to catch cold; recovery at this age would surely be a problem," he said to himself. It was his own voice that he heard; it was the voice of his solitude and apprehensions. The day was just dawning. He went in. He left the French doors wide open; the room needed fresh air. He had already lain open his bed and the weight of the night to enable them to get rid of their stuffy atmosphere. As he went into the sitting room, he carefully closed the door of the room behind him, the room in which he was to perform his morning prayer . . . The first thing he did in the sitting room was to pull the curtains, then he settled himself in his usual armchair casting a glance outside: the street looked deserted, janitors with their baskets hanging from their arms and a few students were the only *hoi polloi* of the streets; there were also a couple of other people, early risers who seemed to be in a hurry. These were his early risers, with whom he had established a connection of which only he was aware; he saw these early risers rushing every morning at the same hour, in the same street, through the same window. These people had their own lives, their own stories, and their own fates. He didn't know them; he had never addressed them nor would he ever do so in the future. This was his sphere of taboo in a sense. In the street he saw that three women and two men were heading, independently from each other, for seemingly predetermined destinations. One of the women worked in a bank, the other was a nurse. The third was working with a Jewish importer, employed as a secretary and an accountant. One of the men was a silversmith and had a shop in the covered bazaar. He seemed to be well off; he led a life far removed from the ebb and flow of the day without entertaining latent revolutionary impulses, being content with modest weekend diversions. He was married and believed in principles associated with the left.

The other individual was a young practitioner; he was a bachelor and seemed a perfect fit as a candidate for marriage to one of those girls, for instance to that nurse; if only someone had introduced them to each other, of course. It was a pity that everybody followed his own way; their paths never crossing, unfortunately. The precinct of each one of them was delineated within a wound-up time. If, by chance, they happened to be late, it caused worries in him. He had always been an early riser himself, which had made him successful in life.

Having carefully watched his usual figures and making sure that none of them were missed, he allowed himself to retire and perform his morning prayer. The first part of his prayer he performed in Hebrew, which was followed by a prayer in Spanish. The words were the same words. It was the *sine qua non* of the ritual. The part in Spanish was a sort of communion wherein he fancied his God as an all-powerful and reliable protector, as a father. God high above had almost human characteristics and looked as though He was more real. He prayed and graciously asked Him to bless him with a painless death, and Berti, Juliet, Nora, and Jerry with all the happiness possible and the Promised Land as well as with peace the world over. Men had to remember the origin of their essence in order that inhuman, heinous crimes could be put an end to. He did not forget to thank his Protector for having delivered him from the concentration camps. He might, as chance would have it, have settled in France, like his brother; but providence had so desired that he stay in Istanbul, which was a blessing and for which his gratitude could never be expressed enough. He had been a witness to deaths just as he had been to the day's peaceful atmosphere. He did his utmost to make the best of these bright days he had been blessed with now. He prayed for the souls of his beloved, so that God favored them with eternal bliss in paradise and fervently asked Him to be delivered of his soul when the hour came, without too much suffering. He was, at the same time, the Father of Benevolence, yes, of Benevolence. At that moment he felt as though he was mixing up his words, or rather as though he could not recall them. He felt dizzy; having recovered from his momentary giddiness, he had to repeat his wishes . . . The very fact of remembering his people in paradise made his voice tremulous and sound more sonorous while whimpering at the same time. There were so many of them that he had seen off to that place . . . when he thought of them, it occurred to him that he had lived long enough and was already sick of it. But that was providence, which he could not possibly meddle with for fear of a major trespass. When he had concluded, he felt terribly exhausted from having been in the presence of his God, from having supplicated Him with all his might, and from searching for the exact words he should use in his appeal. He became erect and tried to relax a bit, closing his eyes. Mixed apparitions rushed before him. Visions of the past and of the present all mixed in a medley. To dispel them, he opened his eyes. He had to make a point of continuing to cling to the days he actually lived. There were nights in which he could not refrain from moving away from the visions it brought along. Those visions should be enough for him. He gingerly stood up, took off his tallith, kissing it and putting it by the Morning Prayer book which he read every Sabbath. "Une place pour chaque chose et chaque chose a sa place" (Every place has its occupant and every thing has its place) he said. This maxim he had learned from his math teacher, Monsieur Nathan, who initiated to his pupils the secret of a disciplined lifestyle during their last year at the *Alliance*. The school called *Alliance Israelite Universelle* on Yazıcı Street commanded a sea view. The wind blowing from the South was always an event; the strong southern wind caused the cancellation of the boat shuttling services between the coasts of the Bosporus, which made it impossible for Monsieur Nathan, who lived at Kuzguncuk, to cross the Bosporus over to the European side of Istanbul where the school was. Monsieur Nathan was notorious among the students for his harsh strictness, which was the way of living he had adopted. For him, to lead a disciplinary life was tantamount to revering people and above all himself. For him the key to success was discipline. It was his wont to say every now and then during the course of admonishing his students relentlessly that the virtues of discipline were innumerable. During his harangue, he occasionally farted, whereupon he tried to shake the lectern to cause a greater noise than his eruption. The noise muffled the noise to a certain extent, but could not prevent the fetid odor from spreading over the entire classroom. To corroborate the inescapable stench, he announced with a rueful countenance that the students had better open the windows, complaining of the stinking classroom, urging them to breathe some fresh air whenever they could and to play a lot of sport, as it was absolutely necessary for their health. He went on haranguing on the merits of a healthy, long life. These sermons flowed without the smallest rambling. Monsieur Nathan was self-restrained in this matter also, self-disciplined in other words. The adherence to a pattern of behavior characterized by mechanical repetition induced Menahem, who sat by the window next to him on the row, Menahem el de loz maloz eços (Menahem the devil), to immediately open the windows as soon as he saw the oscillation of the lectern which had caused the entire classroom to roar with laughter. He was rewarded for this benevolent act and good deed on his part after a few minutes by a slap on the neck by Monsieur Nathan, whose habit it was to amble amongst his students while discoursing. The slap also caused the whole class to bend over with suppressed laughter. This was followed by Menahem's acting out the role of a student wronged and unjustly treated, saying: "Mais, mais je n'ai fait rien, Monsieur!" (But, I've done nothing, Sir!) And as Monsieur Nathan silently closed the window with a wan smile on his lips, had not failed to retort to Menahem's observation "Une habitude, une simple habitude, *Monsieur*" (Out of pure habit, Sir; simply out of habit, no ill intention, none whatsoever!). In every incident in the school Menahem played a walk-on part. Everyone in the school was predisposed to believe that the culprit of all crimes committed had in some way or another Menahem as an accomplice. Once, during an interrogation by the disciplinary committee of the school for one of the usual offenses committed by Menahem, the glass pane at the entrance of the school was broken by accident and one of the members of the committee in session could not help announcing in a loud voice: "O, Menahem again!" As a matter of fact, it was Menahem himself that had recounted this event to them . . . O those good old days! This *enfant terrible* was to be phenomenally successful in life and become hugely wealthy. Yet, it should be expected that such characters indulge in things far from commendable; actually, his name was mixed up with a case of contraband condoms, followed by a case of murder. His later exploits were to remain a mystery. Traces of each other had been irrecoverably lost from that day on. That was a long time ago. This was one of the phrases he was to repeat frequently. He knew the story of those who were destined to lose each other while treading that long path all too well. People believed they had an insight into the meaning of these phrases and stories, and being convinced of this, thought they were allowed to use them. He had lived; he had been obliged to go on living despite losses, yearnings, and resentments. This may have been the reason why he failed to express his feelings from this very sense of having lived. He had not had the opportunity to set eyes on Menahem ever after, nowhere, nowhere he thought he might. Could it be that he was still alive? Was that boy from the old days the same boy? Who could tell? Everybody had left on in their own path, paying their own modest contribution and receiving a modest reward in return, growing up, aging, and being buried in its insulated silence.

Why deny, he had finally understood the value of Monsieur Nathan's maxim: "Une place pour chaque chose et chaque chose a sa place" as he grew older. This golden rule had been of great service to him in his business life. He could not deny or ignore it. Yet, this rule belonged in a different time, to another aspect of his life, conflicting reactions give rise to discontent and regret. The place was not always the right place, the place to be singled out because it had prevented him from living or letting others live elsewhere. But that was it . . . there was nothing to be done about it . . . a story lived and gone by. His faithfulness to the discipline he had been submitted to, imposed by Monsieur Nathan, had exerted its influence on his laying the breakfast table overnight; which, after all did not require great effort. It consisted of a clean napkin, a plate, a teacup, and the breakfast itself consisting of a couple of pieces of toast, some jam, and cheese, whose butter and salt content was almost nil. Sometimes he took a cup of tisane of linden flowers, at other times a cup of hot milk. Everything had diminished in quantity. He remembered that the jam he had prepared with dried apricots was nearly finished. He ought to make a call and ask Berti to buy roses for him at the Çiçek Pazarı flower market. The prices had lately gone up, it's true, but he could still enjoy this luxury. A kilo of roses would do the job, enough to last for six months. To this end, there would be some activity beforehand in order that he could take his time, the process preceding the jam making at home. These preparations were part of his quiet pleasures. Once the roses were there, they would be taken out of the paper bag with due care to be strewn on a sheet of newspaper previously spread out on the table; whereupon before putting them in boiling water their stems would be clipped with a pair of scissors. The scent of roses would pervade the air. Yes, he would not fail to ask Berti to buy him some roses. It was the season . . . indeed, the season! Formerly he used to prepare the jam together with Madame Roza, He used to sort out the roses and fastidiously clip their stems with the Dunlop scissors he had bought in England. That scissors had gotten lost. A swarthy lean man who used to carry a basket containing roses that dangled from his arm used to pass by when the season was in. I think he was called Salomon. Salomon? No, no, that was the fisherman, who traveled about from one place to another on Fridays selling gaidropsarus mediterraneus, solely in the early hours of the morning. The custom required this. The meals had to be ready by noon. No meals were prepared on the Sabbath. However, even this custom had been abandoned in time. The fish by that name was the preferred dish of the Jews which was eaten accompanied by a ritual. This was known to the fishermen of the area who made their rounds in the Jewish quarters. The fish was cooked and served with yellow plums. The fishermen also sold yellow plums. But they bought from him only fish, which displeased the fishmonger as he made greater profit from the sale of yellow plums. "Esta vez la avramila esta para shuparse los dedos . . . Le dae un poco?" (I've got excellent juicy plums, would you like me to give you some?) was the comment he usually addressed to Madame Roza. The latter's humorous retort was "Nosotros no tenemos menester de tu avramila kazıkçı! Ya tenemos en la ğuerta al karar ke no kerez!" (I have no need for your plums, trickster! We've got plenty in our garden, enough to spare). At times such remarks infuriated Salomon who once had said to Madame Roza: "o se le seko ayinda el arvole?" (Not dried up yet, your plum tree?), to which Madame Roza had rejoined: "No se seko'No se seko! Y tu ke no sekes inşalla paşa' Ayde, kaminos klaros!" (Not yet! Not yet! I wished you remained as perpetually fresh as my plum tree!) Such witty repartees were an everyday affair in those days, although words and expressions differed now and then. This jocular exchange of witticisms contributed to the pleasure derived from nearly every daily activity. At present, caught in life's current, other jokes continued to be cracked to add color to the dullness of daily life; jokes and witticisms would persist forever. "Would they, really?" he suddenly asked to himself in a moment of unexpected skepticism. Then he gave up philosophizing, although his lips continued to move, repeating the same syllables with bated breath: "Jokes to continue to be cracked . . . " The jokes he spoke of were those that had remained fresh for them, jokes that involved those that had silently departed. The feelings harbored there were of the sort experienced in a small world that looked hermetically sealed, in which everybody could see everybody since there was no other alternative . . . By the way, the name of the guy that sold roles leaves was not Salomon; it must have been Mordo . . . oh, no! No! He just couldn't remember it. This wasn't the first time that his memory was failing. He could not help laughing at himself. His laughter indicated that he was now looking at life through a different angle; this was proof of his egocentric predicament. There was no sense in dwelling on the lapses of his memory that had caused his failure to remember the name of the flower man. Eventually, he would also, like many people from the past, be remembered for his trade rather than for his name; for the effects that the syllables of his name would engender rather than their intrinsic entity. Those that had gone through life having experienced those sentiments, and the spirit that their memories and voices had left behind . . . This must have been the interesting thing about the life beyond. Eventually, bargaining with the fisherman and the florist was no sweat! Contention was their art; both knew the real worth of their goods, but to be on the safe side, they took precaution right at the start and named a high price for their produce; they took a special pleasure in haggling; their customers were not unaware of their ways. However, the stage had to go on for the sake of age-old habits. The hucksters drove a hard bargain, but so did the customers. There was, however, a rule for this, like in every other bartering. The limits had to be respected. He distinctly remembered. Madame Allegra, the neighbor opposite, had quoted a price far lower than rock bottom; the vendor, taking this offer as an insult, had countered without the least scruple of being heard by the people around and said: "Tamam . . . ke me trayga el çukal i se lo inchere!" (All right, get me your chamber pot so that I may fill it up!) At this likely reaction on the part of the vendor, Madame Allegra had wished the earth would swallow her up, and, shouted in his face: "You cheeky impudent Jackanapes!" as she slammed the door and went inside. This had caused a general glee among the listeners. They were at home. It was a warm morning in May . . . Rosita was still a small child. She had been staying with them. She had asked what 'Tchukal' meant. Having been told what it was, she had burst into laughter. Rosita was a charming little girl with deep blue eyes . . . O that fate! O the inhabitants of that street . . . they were no more, alas! Among others, Madame Allegra . . . She also had vanished into thin air along with her memoirs. One of her sons was in Milan and was engaged in commercial transactions. Another of her sons was a practicing psychiatrist in Geneva, to the best of my recollection. They rarely wrote to their mother to whom they sent enough money as to enable her to lead a comfortable life. She had a maid by the name of Kader; she happened to be the janitor of an apartment nearby. She came to work at her apartment as a charwoman. One day, after seven years of marriage she had been ousted from her home, accused of barrenness with the intention that she be sent back to her village. Having been deprived of all possessions, save for a bundle that contained all her belongings, she had to take shelter in Madame Allegra's home. She had been left penniless and as she had been illegally wed by an Imam, she could claim nothing from her husband in the eyes of the law. On the other hand, it should be noted that Madame Allegra had been suffering from loneliness. This had been the beginning of their companionship which was to last for years. She was to carry on her odyssey either in that house or at a different place, behind a different door accompanied by different awakenings and slumbers. These two women had different origins and had had to leave a significant part of their lives with different individuals, burying it in their vocabularies. Kader was at an age in which she could easily have been her daughter. Despite their initial conflicts of opinion, they had eventually learned how to lead a symbiotic life. It may be that the link that connected them to each other was their betrayals. He remembered them strolling arm-in-arm in the streets. Kader was to remain in that house for many years afterward. Long after, she had said "yes" to the marriage proposal of Selami Bey, a retired gentleman from the Land Registry, in whose presence everybody in the district showed self-restraint mixed with some sort of diffidence, and moved to another house . . . As a matter of fact he had been instrumental in bringing about this liaison. Selami Bey, with whom he had a passing acquaintance, had had a confession to make to him. It was early morning . . . Selami Bey had told him that for the first time in his life he had felt himself close to a woman. This woman had a striking likeness to a little girl, a traveling companion, a figure from an old story, who used to pass by every morning in front of his window in the arm of a blind man begging in the streets, to the accompaniment of the melancholy songs he sang. She was very little and had sorrowful looks. He had wished to adopt her, but had failed to set eyes on her after that morning. It was high time now his wish should be fulfilled. Selami Bey's voice sounded plaintive but affectionate; it was kindly and soothing, full of yearning. Although he could not make head nor tail of what he had been told, he had inferred that his sentimental attachment to Kader was full of genuine emotion. This partly explained Selami Bey's relinquishing his greeting to certain people on certain evenings. Those were most probably the hours when he recollected the little girl in question. Selami Bey had disclosed to him his secret for the first time. Something hitherto kept secret was being revealed to him. Upon his return home, he had spoken about this incident to Madame Roza. To decide was not so easy. They could not guess the reaction of Kader at such a proposal. To begin with the age gap between her and Selami Bey was enormous, which could not be overlooked. On the other hand, was such a relation to be formed, Madame Allegra would be returning to her former solitude. Nonetheless, Selami Bey's insistence had greatly impressed him. She might, after all, try another individual and lifestyle. It was Madame Roza that had broken the news to Kader. She knew all too well how to behave and act in such delicate matters. Kader could not conceal her astonishment and the tremor in her voice; she had inclined her head toward her breast, and after a moment of silence, she had said with a weak smile, that she had lost the greater part of her youth, that something had died within her years ago, but added that on certain nights she felt the lack of a male companion. Her voice was tremulous as she made this confession; she was hesitant as usual, as though exhausted, as though she wanted to conceal certain things. It may be that she had imagined herself in Selami Bey's arms, experiencing her womanhood. But who could tell that Selami Bey was one of those men who divested himself from his robe before going to bed, putting on merely the trousers of his pajamas and penetrated women by pulling them down. Her power of imagination could not go farther than that. After this important avowal she said to Madame Roza: "My name 'Kader,' meaning 'Fate,' suits me well. Please tell Selami Bey that I'm ready to give my hand to him. I don't expect that he would like to be a father at his age." Her words bore the traces of a deep sorrow, of a deception whose roots lay deep in her entrails in addition to a little latent hope. As she was trying to initiate herself to the idea of marriage, she was looking for someone to partake of her unavowed sense of deficiency which she had been keeping concealed; she had never recovered from the grief she felt for having failed to give birth to a child with her first husband, in her first marriage. She had acknowledged that her womb was a wasteland. She acknowledged the fact that her fate had reserved a barren and arid terrain in her which the lies and deceptions that surrounded her, would never let her explore. Could it be that time had enthralled her in vain? One must note, however, that she had been raised in a tradition according to which barrenness could not be attributed to men. Her state might be due to a lifestyle in which emotions were unnecessarily impaired, nay killed, and lives were extinguished because of absurdities. The victims had unduly paid the cost of their deceptions without being given the chance of self-defense, resignedly, without raising their voices. One wondered who the true victim was under the circumstances. Customs and mores were responsible for the gradual extinction of lives. To provide an answer and suggest a solution would thus be impossible for a long time to come. What actually remained were the concrete incurable wounds that the individuals received. The injuries received but not given voice to . . . for the sake of upholding the traditional lifestyle. A short time after the exchange of these words, Kader and Selami Bey were married in a modest and solemn wedding ceremony.

Kader's witness was Madame Allegra, and Selami Bey's best man had been himself. Following the exchange of formal words, everybody had repaired home. The paths of Madame Allegra and of Kader gradually bifurcated despite the proximity of their living quarters. The same was to happen when they were to move into a new house. Their contact was to grow less frequent as time went by; so did the telephone calls, eventually; their old ways and neighborly relations gradually declined till they ceased altogether for the sake of their private lives, forgetting the bygone days. Although there had been no break in their relations as the *Rosh Hashanah* joined them; actually everybody had lived his own life. Madame Allegra never failed to show up on the first or the second day of the Jewish New Year and brought them her specialty, apple jam with mastic that she prepared with her small hands as though it had been her duty. Apple jam with mastic . . . Everybody was aware of its meaning. Everybody shared in the jam in question that was meant to contribute to the sweet course of the coming year. There was no point in discussing such evident issues as everybody knew it and tried to go on living for the sake of that past. Madame Allegra didn't have to announce beforehand the visit she was going to pay. On the other hand, there were people whose custom it was to gather together at certain homes for the sake of rendering the platitudes of life more meaningful. If so, why had there been a hiatus between the family members which had caused a break in relations? After having shared so many moments, communions, and joint experiences how come that they had succeeded in surviving without having seen and talked to each other. Who, in the meantime, intruded on their privacy? Well . . . that was life after all. Willy-nilly, such things happened. This appeared to be the rule enabling them to cling to their new places. In this whirlwind, in their efforts to make them believe in themselves, the price of those omissions was paid, naturally. Differing languages and climates had never been able to prevent the same people from enjoying the same experiences.

How had he come all the way down to where he found himself? Lately such had been the lapse of days, days of which he proved to be a mere spectator at times. A word, a hazy appearance took him automatically to other lives and instances. There were chance encounters which displeased him on this long and silent path; encounters with people whom he would have preferred to turn a blind eye to, or to address with one or two words. All the same, it was pleasant to return to the old days even though for a brief period. It was nice to be able to talk with those people from beyond like in the olden times. Madame Roza's rose jam would never be consigned to oblivion under any circumstances. It would perpetuate that warmth forever. Nor would her dish of artichokes in olive oil, eaten with relish, whose taste remained on the palate long after it had been savored ever be forgotten. Her stuffed squash with minced meat and caramel sauce, and the kashkarikas prepared with the outer layer of the squash swathed with garlic which had an acrid taste . . . her unforgettable leek stuffed with minced meat whose main ingredient was black pepper . . . her broad bean dish with spinach, her white mastic pudding, and to crown them all off the date pudding with currants she specially prepared for the Passover evenings. Those dishes were the tastes, the odors, the local colors that one took notice of after they were gone, real things with living parts . . . These were of the recorded stories which readers interpreted differently. The preparation of these dishes had caused many a controversy between her mother-in-law and herself, just like in other similar houses intent on being faithful to their tradition. However, in weary resignation she had to submit to her fate with resolution, diffidence, and kindness. This affection was expressed by a warm approach. After all she could not turn a blind eye to the state of her mother-in-law. The atmosphere created by this affectionate voice had brought them to a very special standing despite all the problems they had encountered. It may be that over a course of time they had not been conscious of this journey, the place they had arrived at was a place they could not describe nor define, of which they would never be deprived. Could it be that what had brought them so close to one another was the bitter experience of the man who had gone away never to return? She was reluctant to mull this over at present. Actually, they had made a point never to discuss this issue among the family members. To ignore, to refrain from recalling something was in fact one of the ways to carry about a loved one to the bitter end, blessing him with perennial life. There was no sense anymore in starting again from a new point of departure.

Who had Monsieur Kirkor hidden where?

When Madame Perla, advanced in years, had begun waning, shutting herself up in her room with her multitude of 'chambers' within, it hadn't been for nothing that she, whose personality and looks commanded respect and diffidence and whose reticence inspired fear among her peers, had expressed the wish not to die without informing Madame Roza of the approaching hour, having appreciated the favors and sacrifices that her daughter-in-law had shown her, despite her worsening condition. A smile flickered across her face, expressive of her dejected frame of mind. She had dreadfully missed her mother; as a matter of fact, not only had she missed her, but she missed a lot of other things, a lot of other things besides; Halıcıoğlu, her childhood at Halıcıoğlu . . . she inevitably saw it now through the illusory and deceptive gears of her imagination as seen in the other stories. Those were the days when her father's close friend Monsieur Pardo, whose idols throughout his life had been Voltaire and Rousseau, was teaching French, the days when the Little Officers School, once frequented by Ismet İnönü, had not yet been occupied by the British troops. Years were to pass before that officer was to kill that Jewish girl who had turned him down. They lived in a three-storied house with nineteen rooms overlooking the Golden Horn, whose drawing-room was heated by a huge brazier, where electricity was still nonexistent, where water had to be obtained from a well, where rakis of different flavors were kept in cans; in a three-storied house often visited by acquaintances, wherein everybody lived collectively.

A section of the house was reserved as a workshop whose renown had spread not only to the capital but also to most of the major cities in Europe—Vienna, Budapest, and London for example. Her father was a well-known figure among the carpet dealers and collectors. All spoiled carpets dating from the nineteen century which had been damaged, whether they were at the Covered Bazaar or Tepebaşı, were brought to Avram Efendi to be mended. It hadn't been easy to gain this reputation. Just like other masters in the trade, he had also served as an apprentice for many years in carpet weaving. The years he had to pass in this profession had trained him to become a specialist in the root of the madder plant, used in dyeing carpets, chiefly because of its alizarin content in the form of the glycoside ruberythric acid, which enabled him to capture such unusual colors. Thus he was the sole custodian of a secret lore, which had been entrusted to him by his master, Kemani Kevork Efendi, to whom he had been apprenticed over several years. Their move was a rewarding one, interesting in many respects and worthy to be told. Its pathos wasn't solely down to the fact that Kevork Efendi— who used to train him after business hours as a continuation of their routine job, confessed that the reason for this was not simply compensating for his loneliness, as he naturally was—but because the relationship between master and apprentice was of a strange kind. If one considered the history of such a relationship, of such an order whose color and voice happened to be intrinsic in it, an Armenian master entrusting the secret of the calling to a Jewish apprentice was unheard of; it just wasn't right. It was exactly this soft spot of Kevork Efendi's wherein he felt his overwhelming loneliness. He had two sons who had opted for other professions and refused to continue their father's trade. They had never felt any inclination to learn the trade. Kevork Efendi had been discreet about their whereabouts. Now and then, he used to speak of misalliances, political relations, deaths, and illusions. It was apparent that he preferred to keep certain grievances to himself. Nor had he inquired into these matters, as he had been content with what he had been told. The master-apprentice relationship required the latter's submission to the former's will, after all. How had this apprentice pledged allegiance to Kevork Efendi? This was not very clear; it was shrouded in silence. However, once, only once, had he spoken of his failed relationships. It was reported that his mother had had a beautiful voice which was listened to behind many a window, and that she practiced her zither for hours on end. Yes, for hours on end. This practice had lasted up until her marriage, when she had moved to another window. To cut a long story short, Kevork Efendi had gradually initiated his apprentice into the secrets of his profession over the course of many years, in whose bright future he had complete faith; instructing him how he should devote himself to particular colors of his choice during his practice. Then, after several years had passed, to put on the finishing touch and perform his last duty, he had addressed his probationer, saying: "Time now to turn over a new leaf! You are on your own now; open your own workshop and find out your own colors!" It is said that Kevork Efendi had a large circle of influential acquaintances in the Palace; the consideration he enjoyed enabled him to reach the sultan, Abdülhamid, who had received him on many an occasion and chatted on state affairs as well as his affairs of a female nature . . . This was, however, a widely held belief having no sound foundation or source, his father, based on the accounts of his own father, had fancied the Supreme Ruler as a man of gigantic proportions. Once, he had gone to the gate of the palace to see him get in his coach, he had been disappointed at his diminutive stature. Great indeed was his disappointment! A disappointment he could hardly reconcile with the image he had formed of him in his mind. What was the rationale of this disillusionment? Who had been overwhelmed by this unexpected vision, who had suffered because of it, in whose behalf had this vision had an effect? Where did Kevork Efendi stand in this fallacy? Which fancies had been left unrealized?

The strange visitor from Tabriz and being able to make a loop to the future

It is true that Avram Efendi had not had the opportunity to reach Abdulhamid, but he had made great strides in the path his master had opened for him and turned to good account the art he had entrusted him with. Later on, he could not help dabbling, even though on a superficial level, in politics, with some trepidation, in order not to offend some acquaintances. But this had been a passing whim in him, a transient interest. Despite his relations, he couldn't succeed in taking a place among the grandees; he had a more tangible and perennial aspiration irreconcilable with the path that would lead him to the palace while he had been undergoing changes over the years. He felt it his duty to give that unrivaled art he had overtaken from his master its due, and remain devoted to it, aiming at making a loop from the past to the future by transmitting some colors. Every object wrought in Avram Efendi's workshop had to be a consummate work of art. He distinctly remembered his small shop at Akarçeşme. He had not even turned thirty; he could not possibly have guessed that his lifestyle was to undergo such a radical change at the least expected moment. Nesim had left for Paris in the company of Rachael, thus abandoning Istanbul for a new country that he believed to be more secure. He would never return to Istanbul. He seemed to express his intention to his relatives from the deck of the ship he had boarded as she was weighing anchor and bearing off. He had carried on the carpet trade in that shop at Akarçeşme. He had to deal in something after all. His stepping out was meaningful; it had a subtle meaning that connoted a silent crossover. Having acknowledged certain plain realities, he was impelled by the desire to transmit them to the best of his capabilities. He might fail to be a consummate artist in the end, but he felt it his duty to prove and demonstrate to his master that he could stand his ground. He would stand the test of time and abide among the colors of that world he was resolved not to betray and to which he would remain attached to the best of his ability. His own father had been wary of revealing his secret. There was a shrouded reason for his reticence. He had always expected to be initiated into it by his father and make headway in his company, ever since the moment he had come of age. There were only the three of them. Nesim had gone a step further than him. His father continued to be reluctant to talk. He thought he had figured it out; Nesim would eventually be the inheritor of that secret. But then . . . then the separation had come, the decision regarding the departure without return . . .

Every step taken forward was at the same time a step inward, if considered from this point of view. During those days when the steps had been taken, his father had promised that he would wholeheartedly support him. They had had a talk about his future. They both beamed with delight. They had winning smiles, yet they were tainted with some bitterness; charming and winning alright, but also disarming; smiles open to various interpretations. They approached each other only in this way. In those days, this was how they used to behave toward each other. This had been one of his experiences that he remembered now and then. Certain smiles were of marginal importance and had remained so without change. Certain smiles expressed separations, despairs, and unexpected circumstances, just like touches, some warm, some nurtured by affection in order to survive. One day a strange man had popped into his shop. His manners and glances were disquieting. Under his arm was a rather big parcel, carefully wrapped. He looked anxious as though he had something important to communicate. He spoke in a whisper as though he feared he would be overheard, although there was no one else in the shop at the time. Without revealing his identity, and without being asked how he had found out the address, he wanted to know whether the parcel in question interested him or not. He had tried to keep his composure, making as though he was the self-conscious type, he had made a gesture indicating that he was waiting for his reaction. This proved to be his first trial in the shop.

What had disquieted him was not merely the man's gestures and mysterious behavior. It was as though no sooner he had stepped in than he had sensed something very important that was to leave an indelible imprint on his life. The man had opened the parcel cautiously, casting furtive glances. It was as though an invisible pair of eyes were staring at them; and any moment now they might be overtaken by people rushing in. However, when the parcel was unwrapped, he saw that there might be some justification for the man's restlessness. A seventeenth century Tabriz rug stood unfolded before him; the colors, the designs, and the number of knots easily betrayed its origin. Knowledge, the fruit of years of labor in the art acquired in the darkness of history, had instantly revealed to him that he was in the presence of a consummate piece. The carpet had been divided into three sections, the fourth part was missing. He was flabbergasted. The man asked three thousand lira for it. The sum was pretty considerable in those days.

After a short bargaining, he had paid the sum. Touching the three pieces for the last time, the man said: "You'll never be able to guess why it was split up, the individuals who had walked on it and the mystery of the missing part." He said this in impeccable French, although with an accent. Could it be that he believed that French would be a better means of communicating the gravity of the fact that a relic of high value was being entrusted to the hands of a skilled master? Was there any other language as powerful as French which might have been used to express the seriousness of the trade? Having spoken thus, the man had tucked the money in his pocket and taken a few steps before stopping as though with irresolution, but had immediately after continued his outward journey. It was a momentary vacillation. He might suddenly recoil, declaring he could not part with it. It looked as though he had abandoned one of his vital organs. In that rug bearing the signs of the ravages of time, in every one of the three pieces, the mystery concealed could never been solved by any mortal soul. As he had reached the doorway, the man had murmured, "I shouldn't be here," before stepping out in a rush to join the crowd.

Once alone, he had stared at the rug for quite a while. He felt an emotion which he could not define. An inexpressible emotion . . . Was it delight or fear? What had prompted him to experience this emotion? Could it be his sneaking suspicion that the step he had taken might be wrong? Could it be the lingering effect of the man left behind? He hadn't been able to answer these burning questions; he had had no opportunity to commune with the person within him. All that he could say was that the rug belonged to him henceforward and that the shop was not the same as it had previously been. He had realized that he could not remain sitting there. The day, just another day, uneventful, went by as usual. He could not wait till evening. Having tucked the parcel under his arm, he had repaired home. Upon arrival he saw that his father was not there; in the meantime, he said nothing to his mother about the incident or his experience. He had thought it best to share the piece of news with his father first. For, he alone could empathize with him . . .

When his father arrived, the beams of the setting sun lighted the carpets; it was the end of the workday. The carpets and rugs changed their hues at this hour. He had gingerly opened the parcel without saying a word. His father had tried to focus his eyes on it, trying to read the history recorded in those pieces, experiencing the poem of that touch. However, the silence was broken soon after.

That minute seemed never to come to an end. People who have past experience in waiting know well enough how interminable one minute can seem. "You can leave it to me, now. The day will come when you'll never be able to recognize it. But, mind you, you're not to ask anything in the meantime, understood? You've made a tricky job of this. I wonder how you'll get over this. Yet, if I were you I'd have done the same," said his father staring at the three pieces that had come in so unexpectedly. He had not asked who had brought it to the shop, under what conditions, and the price he had paid for it. The important thing was the restitution of it. What mattered now was the skill he would harness to make it viable beyond all subtle differences and probabilities. He had sneaked it into his private chamber without letting his workers see it. That was the only room under lock and key in a house in which only by his express permission one could enter. From that evening on he developed the custom of taking his usual dose of raki at his workshop, and with some cheese and fruit work till the late hours of the night without having to justify his absence. In rare instances, he called in his skilled worker Ali Burhan Usta, senior master of his workshop, a tight-lipped man reluctant in speech. As a matter of fact, his father had never considered him an ordinary weaver. A relationship had developed between them, a solidarity which involved sharing many a secret of the trade. This privileged position of Ali Burhan Usta had earned him a sort of immunity in the house, if one may say so. No one could say anything to him, or ask the reason of his occasional unannounced absences. He was well aware of his responsibilities; he knew what job awaited him and the times he ought to be present in the workshop. Behind his extensive and recondite knowledge of the role he had been entrusted with this rug lay his age-old experience in the field. He had been present during the process of resuscitations until the early hours of the morning. He used to smoke opium; it had become the *sine qua non* of his life. One day he was found dead, lying on the carpets in the workshop. He had no family; his funeral was arranged by the Imam Hulusi Efendi who used to drop in now and then. His death had left a deep scar on the soul of his master. This was not simply due to the loss of a reliable and skilled worker. Life had showed its absurd aspect once again in the form of a wild-goose chase. He had not had the chance of seeing the *opus magnum* in broad daylight. Part of the warps and wefts in the woven fabric belonged to him. The rug would reach its ultimate destination as his work; although everybody would be aware of this fact, the fate of the silent, reticent, and anonymous creators entombed in a work of art, their touches and patience mixed with untold dreams and souvenirs would remain buried. The actors of the works we scrutinized stared at us from a distance, from an angle we would never be able to spot; it required the power of our imagination in order to appreciate them . . . In those actors were hidden the other words we could not find. They were the multifarious facets of our past, invisible to our sight. We had to take notice of the fact that in order to be able to feel we ought to be aware of the things we had lost.

You were in a sea of silver

Almost a year had gone by. One evening, his father called him to that chamber. A rug of a brand new appearance was spread on the bench. First, he had looked at the restituted work of art as an outsider; words had failed him in expressing his impression. Now he remembered only the beatific smile that had grown radiant, illuminating his entire countenance . . .

They had taken the rug to the shop the next day. His father had asked him only then the particulars of the rug's past. A tight-lipped, reliable man had to be found for its sale. This was not an easy matter. In such cases one could never tell who might tell what to whom. Nevertheless, after such a long professional career, his father would be able to find the right man. As a matter of fact, his imagination conjured up the image of Setrak Efendi; a man well acquainted with the world's carpet market, who knew the process of how rugs and carpets would find the right customer who would be willing to pay the highest cost for a piece of true value. He kept his antique shop near the Pera Palas Hotel where he frequently received foreign customers and showed them valuable rare objects hardly offered to ordinary customers. No sooner had he heard the news, than Setrak Efendi had shown up. Having pulled down the shutters, they had displayed their pride and joy; without any hesitation Setrak Efendi had paid the twelve thousand liras asked for such a piece.

They would not meet again for many years; good days, bad days, days of misery, days of simple joys and serious difficulties ran their courses. Both the workshop and the little shop at Asmalımescit were far away now. A new path had been traced for the family. They had at their new home a few carpets they had snatched from the jaws of the flames, which they had succeeded in transporting to their new lives, to their last days, for ultimate eventualities . . . Setrak Efendi was in no better state. He had transferred the ownership of the shop to two bothers from Kayseri. The rugs had gone their separate ways, to experience their new adventures at different places. Perhaps that was the reason why his links with the past were being severed . . . His hands were trembling; he had developed a lisp; and he kept blinking . . . The alcohol had begun to show its effects; the aftermath of many years of addiction, many years of prolonged abuse . . . Years had dragged many a stranger to places unanticipated and unexpected . . . they had made small talk and spoke of their difficulty in keeping up with the times. The exchange of words between two acquaintances standing in the middle of the street had been restricted naturally. References had been made. It was good to hear that Avram Efendi was still alive and had a fairly optimistic outlook on life; it aroused one's envy. As for the losses he had experienced, the tribulations he had had to face, their encounter under these circumstances; he had better not tell his father about it at all. No, he was not going to tell his father, he promised. He would keep this encounter and what had been exchanged between them to himself. Then he had asked him about the rug. Setrak Efendi had smiled at this inquiry. "It's now in a museum in London," he said with a smile. "In London, in a museum . . . " It was a wry smile, a wan smile which concealed at the same time a kind of pride. The strange thing was that the heroes of this story had desired to exchange secrets. Each secret denoted a different time. This story had been recorded based on the words and secrets they had exchanged. You could feel yourself in the picture if you took the trouble to go over those simple joys and times.

At home, he felt that he could not hold the promise he had made to Setrak Efendi. That evening he had to break the news to his father as a belated newsflash, belated but fresh in meaning despite all the tribulations involved. Then they went on speaking of the past and the good old days. They had no other choice but to cling to what the past had in store for them. "I wish Kevork Efendi saw the acme of perfection his apprentice had attained," said his father. The rug he had resuscitated was now in a museum in London! A handful of people would know it . . . very few people . . . and, who knows, perhaps no one would ever know anything about it in the near or far future. What a transformation and process of resuscitation it had undergone; the very name of Ali Burhan Usta would cease to have an echo, let alone the man from Tabriz and the story of the rug before it had come into the hands of that stranger. The important thing was that the rug was there in a museum. His father's smiling face may have expressed the fact that his pains and patience had been eventually rewarded . . . He had a recurring fancy which he could not put in any particular frame, a recurring fancy that had undergone transformation over several years. Every piece of work that came out of Avram Efendi's workshop was a masterpiece. Every one of those rugs should be considered as a piece of art and should remain so and be remembered as such. It was a dream, a cherished fancy; however, his father had another fancy as well which should not go unnoticed, a dream he had shared with many people, a dream infinitely reproduced. This dream gathered meaning. He clung to life firmly as though he was going to die any moment, he wanted to lead a better life. To live to the bitter end . . . to live in defiance of all obstacles; even though this concern may sound strange to the ears of other people . . . even though this concern may not be appreciated fully by others. His daring ventures and aspirations might seem to the adherents of some judgements to be banal and hardly viable. To live for him was having a little drink, just enough to put him in good spirits and make the best of the opportunity presented, and, last but not least, those little pleasures that women had given him, the casual moments of unassuming love he had experienced with his partners. Between the different attitudes which determined the direction that certain lives were to take, it was not possible to trace the demarcation line between the boundaries. The idea of penning—within predetermined boundaries in the hope of attaining certain realities—those lives and the areas that those lives gave rise to, might turn us into slaves of places unacceptable to us. In human beings, who sheltered within them more than one person, we couldn't always claim the right to declare the reason why particular people differed from their fellow beings and with the people they ended up merging with. Nevertheless, when I think of those dreams, I'm inclined to believe that Avram Efendi contained within him two different personalities, living in symbiosis under the same roof. The first of his reveries seemed to reflect his Eastern character, occupied in weaving a weft from the past into the future, while his second dream, a life-affirming message, had a wider context that comprised leading a life of debauchery in nightclubs and cabarets which reflected his Western character. He had known how to let them coexist in peace with each other. As a matter of fact, both his personalities had wanted to understand the mystery of life, spending efforts to remain faithful to it.

Slight tipsiness and modest partners . . . This was where his mother had stepped on stage in order to support the family. Madame Perla had understood the kind of man she had married and would remain married to. It was the custom of Avram Efendi to get up early in the morning to open the workshop before the arrival of the artisans; putting an order on things that had to be performed on that particular day when they arrived, he gave them the necessary instructions and left the premises. Nobody knew where he went, why he went, and whom he would visit. Now and then he returned and tucked under his arm were a couple of carpets or rugs to be mended, he was sometimes cheerful, which indicated that he had had a good day. He examined what had been performed over the course of the day with great diligence. The real work began only then, the fine art in other words; the touches that followed were his exclusivity . . . The hours he had spent outside were destined to remain undisclosed, so were the evenings he spent in his chamber under lock and key.

In addition to all this, he was a performer in mime. During the evenings, when he returned home gleeful, he used to invite his relatives, artisans, and a couple of neighbors he loved into the well heated hall in his house around a huge brazier and perform the role of a public storyteller and mimic. He had a vague memory of those evenings, evenings during which peals of laughter reached the heavens, evenings when he loved life all the more. Performances were often quite impromptu. He used to make his wife sit on the stairs as he serenaded her, using made up French or Greek words, of which he did not have even a smattering, a broomstick serving as a guitar; he even hatched diatribes with words of his own invention, which he claimed to have received from the classics. Those moments reflected the happy married state of his parents. It had been rumored that this master of secrets, who tried to make the best of his life, had been seen a couple of times at Şehzadebaşı in the company of a certain lady, in those hours during which he absconded without informing anybody of his whereabouts. However, these were but rumors, a widely disseminated belief having no discernible foundation or source. Nobody had dared to investigate the matter any further. As a matter of fact the very name of Şehzadebaşı associated in one the image of those doors that opened to another world. At times, they went to see Minakian Efendi. He also recalled *fin-de-siecle* cabaret singers whose names he could not remember. For the child of those bygone days, what was important were the little incidents on the road to those spectacles rather than the spectacles themselves. Certain details were still fresh in his memory. They used to hire a paddleboat at Halıcıoğlu, a skiff in other words, which took them across to Unkapanı. The skiff was equipped with a lantern. His mother used to spruce herself up; once across, they took a phaeton at Unkapanı which took them to the theater. The same skiff waited for them at the wharf to take them back. The sea was so calm, he remembered, during those hours; they hardly heard the sound that the wide flat blades made on it; the oars that moved in cadence. The sea looked like a sheet of silver during the moonlit nights. They crossed the inlet in silence, gliding on the silver surface. One could see the scintillating lights reflected on the water, those lights that never quit his imagination. He used to lean against his mother's bosom and close his eyes and doze off. The splashing water lulled him to sleep. He knew well in whose soul he was residing during those hours. It seemed that in this feeling of confidence another fear was also concealed. His mother's glances were penetrating enough to discern her field of vision; those glances of which he had kept the memory of expressed understanding and were ready to speak through the silence.

Photographs did not always speak

The penetrating glances of his mother . . . had her eyes got tired in the end and had to close their lids, diving into the depths of the darkness? It was so sad to think of this, after so many years had passed. As far as I can remember, those glances had a tremendous impact on the artisans in the workshop. In this diffident behavior, one might also see reserve and affection, as well as the atmosphere that reigned in that large hall. The major reason for the amity that had developed between Madame Roza and herself over time must have been due to these glances. The friendship and goodwill, especially as characterized by mutual acceptance and toleration of potentially antagonistic points of view, had a common basis built up by self-sacrifice; self-sacrifice and mastery in the art of mutual love and affection. She could not allow herself to be torn asunder from there, from her home, despite Olga's insistence, as she dared not to struggle against those glances. His mother had an innate pragmatic knowledge of life; she dealt with problems in a sensible, practical way instead of following a strict set of pre-established ideas suggested in books. She was illiterate. What she could read, truly read, was the distresses of the ones she loved; the conscious subjective aspects of emotions considered separate from bodily changes. What she could write, truly write, were the impressions she had left or would have liked to leave in others. Under the circumstances, solitude and loneliness might be redefined. Freedom from affectations and its reliability might be redefined and reassessed. The mother was illiterate alright; she had not read a single book in her entire life and had to keep detached from society. This was normal practice at the time for those cooped up in their homes. The *Alliance Israelite* schools had not yet made their entry into Istanbul. There was no Jewish *lycées*. There were devotional colleges where the enrollment of girls was out of the question. The paths for girls led nowhere; the doors for girls remained unopened. There were no other alternatives. It had occurred to him that the success of this woman—who had instructed her sons and the group of people she felt affection for about life, and who had based her life on sound logical premises—might be due to her ignorance, although in no way did she hold arguments in defense of her innocence. However life had also shown her the different aspects of illiteracy, which had taught her to consider other methods, canons and criteria for the validity of thought.

Madame Perla, like all mothers, who had not had the opportunity to go to school, was greatly pleased to witness her sons' receiving an education in a good school. She asked them to repeat their lessons to her although she was in no position to understand what they would be saying. To listen to them calmly gave her pleasure. She had the air of intimating to them that she was being instructed along with them. It was also important for her to inspire them with the warmth of motherly care and attention; it was perhaps an ordinary chapter of a well-known story. All things considered, to enjoy such an experience during the length of one's lifetime was a bonus.

In the mother's establishment of a balance between kindness and authority without giving offense to anybody, as a means of self-defense, her efforts to compensate for her shortcomings had its part to play. The individuals who had failed to perceive this petty detail accused her of arrogance. The person she had married had been impressed by this behavioral trait of hers. Theirs had been a loved-up marriage, a marriage that was marveled at by the community, or so his father had told him. He saw her for the first time in the house of a relative and no sooner had he seen her than he had believed to have found in her a woman with whom he could have a lifelong connection. This may have been an anticipated and premeditated occurrence. As with all love affairs and passions, this was an emotional experience that had been brewing in him for quite a while. In any case, this was a love with all its *desiderata* related to its origins and secret dealings. They had had a small talk. On the eve of that new era, of the approaching new period in history, everybody was feeling emotional. They couldn't ask for more in the midst of the crowd of visitors in the house. Yet, even that small talk had sufficed for his father's setting off in pursuit of that conceited maid. Eventually, customs and mores were strictly abided by; the inquiry carried out regarding the family background and their past life had informed them that this maid, as beautiful as a pearl, led a life of purity and innocence in a house whose doors and windows were closed to the outside world. The family lived in Ortaköy. They were strictly religious people. Following that decisive encounter the family members had paid a visit to that house and the hand of the maid had been asked for, according to the standard formula of tradition. After a few introductory remarks about the weather and the latest news, about the past and the future, and the solemn declaration of intent from both parties, the maid's parents agreed to give their daughter away in marriage, mentioning the key word 'kismet.' They remained betrothed for some time before the marriage was consummated. Everything had thus been in the proper order, immaculate, and innocent. Perla had made a point of being spare with words at the beginning, preferring to listen and understand what Avram said. She could declare that she loved him at first sight only after the consummation of their marriage. That was *de rigueur* at the time. There were still many years to come before Avram was apprenticed to Kevork Efendi. During the period preceding their formal union, Kevork used to cover the distance between Hasköy and Ortaköy on foot in order to pay a visit to Perla, planning on that long walk the workshop he would set up in future. Perla's dowry also had contributed to the opening of this workshop, in addition to the know-how transmitted to him by Kevork Efendi. Following their marriage they lived about two or three years at Ortaköy, moving back to the house at Halıcıoğlu once their business began thriving.

His mother's visits to her birthplace grew less and less frequent. "My family is here from now on" she used to say to justify her exiled state. Nonetheless this attitude that she had adopted, or should we call it disloyalty, appeared to have another facet not openly confessed or avowed. The point in question seemed to conceal a bitter experience she tried to repress. The truth, the real truth never came to the fore. The reason might be the oppression she had suffered at the hands of her parents. His father had heard from somewhere, or made as if he had . . . that his wife was not the daughter of the fanatically religious couple living in Ortaköy. Thus, she had been brought up in the stuffy atmosphere of a cloister; and, in the first flush of her youth, she had been the object of harassment by her father. To what extent had Perla put up a fight against his attacks? Quite possibly, this was mere supposition or rumor, a malicious, nasty, scurrilous rumor whose source was destined to remain a mystery. Anyhow, his father had preferred to give credence to it for some reason or other. Was this subject, a subject which was likely to have serious consequences, one of those that had been discussed at great length and tried to be elucidated upon, or just a casual one? He could never learn. His father had mentioned this rumor in his old age, only on one occasion; long after that fire . . . as though he was referring to an insignificant incident, an unimportant incident or an incident that had, by then, lost all significance. This probability, the abandonment by her original parents and his mother's efforts to cling to her family made the whole affair noteworthy. Nevertheless, certain subjects, subjects related to the past, could not always be made the focus of profound investigation. One was brought to a standstill by unforeseen events. One thing was significant, however; on that day when the maid's hand was asked for, her so-called father, who had been accused of being the cause of the harassment, had showed no resistance whatsoever. In addition to all these adopted attitudes and reactions displayed, what was still more interesting and thought provoking was the sudden departure of the aged parents for Jerusalem, to the Promised Land, a few years after the break-up of their marriage. He had never seen them nor met them. One day, he had found a photograph in a drawer; he had asked his father the identity of the figures in it. He was then told this funny story. The tremulous voice of his father had apparently betrayed that the suspicion was still lingering in his mind about this allegation. They were viewing the people in the photograph from that angle. The picture represented a woman with large breasts and a man with a long white beard. One day, they had suddenly declared that they had reached a ripe old age and that they intended to immigrate to Jerusalem, to the Promised Land, so they could die there. Perla had not been upset by this piece of news. She had tried to put up a listless appearance. Nevertheless, they corresponded afterward for quite a long time, his father serving as secretary. Strange though it was, the reading of letters was a job for a man, while dictation of emotions and sentiments were the women's affair. It was though a tale was being told to them from afar; a tale that suited the flow of time well, suiting their imagination. However, a day came when the letters ceased to arrive. Had that end been experienced in a silence that a different world had brought along? This question had remained unanswered for a while yet. Then, a woman had emerged out of the blue who had introduced herself as a neighbor of that old couple. She said she came with an important piece of news. She looked anxious. She said that her neighbors had disappeared. Upon the arrival of the English, they had departed saying that they were going far, very far away. They gave the impression as though they were fleeing from something, as though they were forced to. That was all. It had been two years since she had last heard of them. His mother had remained unruffled at the news and had been exacting not to hear them mentioned anymore in the house after the visit of that woman. Her composure might be an indication of the fact that the old pair had never been of any consequence in her life. This was another sign indicating another truth. Yet, no one had so far touched, even dared to touch this aspect of the truth. Silence had an indispensable facet that had to be fostered and protected. One would have liked to know the reason of the visit of the woman and the manner by which they had disappeared. Yet no one was inclined to put forth such a suggestion. All that had been learned was the fact that answers had been provided and reproduced in hushed silences in different photographs without finding any verbal expression. Once again, the different photographs happened to be distributed. On the other hand, one wondered if those photographs were genuine. Was this story a true story? It was never made clear. For children, this story remained as a tale from distant lands.

Monsieur Pardo's Thessalonica connection

The house at Halıcıoğlu was a house that had been a witness to many an incident. They were there when the Constitution was declared. Scared to death of the sound of clashing arms, they had taken shelter under the staircase. Those days inspired fear in some, hope in others, and for others still, bloodshed. A deathly silence was to hang over Monsieur Pardo. Because of his connections with Thessalonica, the new dark clouds would cause his father to withdraw to his chamber and live in seclusion under lock and key. Knowledge was tantamount to complicity, to shared confidences, the meaning of which lay buried in the past in a different connection. The exchange of confidences would continue through his correspondence during his sojourn to Cyprus and Haifa to which he had been forced to go. The letters were the cause of a family event. The father perusing the letter in solemnity could not hide his empathy with his friend and exclaimed: "Ah David ah! Pedronado ke te veya no kaliya ke te entreras en estoz eçoz" (O David! God pardon you! You should not get involved in such dealings!); or "Ya te lo habiya diço be Pasha! No eras tu para estoz eços . . . Neğro era sit e kazavaz kon akeya ijika? Bo te suruneyavaz ansina a lo manco . . . El Dyo ke no tome la kavesa de dingunos . . . " (I told you, hadn't I? You're not the man of such affairs . . . You should marry that girl; had you done so you wouldn't be living a life of misery now. May God protect us from insanity!) He had always wanted to know what those letters contained; for his father, they represented table talk; a table talk that connoted a sad, bitter, and long separation hardly communicable. His friends could understand from this the extent of their respective abilities. The letters were read and reread over and over again, the contents of which were disclosed to the people present through murmurs before they were burnt solemnly. This ritual appeared to be the wish of Monsieur Pardo, the man who had never failed to communicate his experience in different lands and realms to his only friend and confidante to whom he had clung after all that had gone on in the meantime. It appeared that the said letters came from someone who never tired of narrating the incidents of his life. One day, another letter was received. Having read it, he had grown motionless for a short time, muttering the words: "O my David! Who would have thought . . . " Leaving the sentence incomplete . . . The rest of the sentence seemed to have been transposed to another place for the sake of secrecy. His father's voice gave the impression as though it sounded in a different tone. A tone that seemed to announce some news not meant to change anybody's life. He had folded the letter and tucked it into his pocket. That had been the last letter ever received from him.

Wife of the Italian ambassador, steps, and other songs

They had been under the same roof during the Balkan War and the occupation. Those were the days of retrogression and of withdrawal. This play had been presented on the stage on more than one occasion, performed by different actors in different settings, with the same disastrous ending. Despite their means of protection they were cowed at the sound of the footsteps of the Bulgarians and of the foreign men-of-war that had cast anchor in the Bosporus, although they enjoyed the privilege of minorities. They had worried when Indian officers had come to see their carpets at the workshop, although they had received many a celebrated foreigner in the past, among others, experts and connoisseurs from Budapest, London, and Sarajevo, and ambassadors, high ranking military *attachés*, generals, and other senior government officials. Their names he could not remember now. All that he remembered was his first sexual awakening at the time. The wife of the Italian ambassador was a striking beauty. The grizzled bun at the nape of her neck, the dark-skinned face with green eyes and the wide hips had remained indelible in his mind's eye. Whenever they met, she used to put her arms around him and let her breasts slightly graze his cheeks. One could not tell if the woman continued to play this innocent sexual trick consciously since she saw him as a kid in bloom. He wasn't sure; but what he was sure of was the deep impression she had left on him. He continued to see her in his dreams on certain nights, stark naked. This made him confused. He was afraid of being caught in the act by that woman. Yet, neither his confusion nor her apprehensions had prevented him from dreaming those wet dreams. She had been the seductress of his life. Her wide hips, small breasts, and sweet smell haunted him. Strange to say, he could no longer remember her name. People vanished in the haze of the past, leaving behind only traces, unforgettable moments; to be able to say to themselves or to others when the occasion presented itself: "I've got something to tell as well . . . " especially moments when they felt lonely and forsaken or dared to prefer to withdraw to their solitude.

Among the celebrated visitors to the workshop was also Liman von Sanders. The days of his visits were special, days to be always remembered. The general spoke in German with his elder brother. It all happened so far in the past. And the men back then appeared so innocent and irreproachable compared to nowadays. Neither Nesim, nor Liman von Sanders, nor anyone else could foresee Germany's treachery and atrocities. Their conversations were so gentlemanly, so unblemished, directed toward a better worldview. Those days had also marked the beginning of his separation from his brother. For instance they had begun occupying separate rooms. The days when they invited the kids of the district to see a movie they put on at home themselves and the emotion they had displayed at the advent of the record player had vanished into the past. The motion picture camera was a simple magic-box operated by hand, projecting the film on the wall, which contributed to the widening of the children's power of imagination.

As for the record player, he could still hear ringing in his ears, the voice of Eftalya for which his father had a fascination . . . Were there also Greek songs among the records? No. They were played later on. Later . . . In other districts other voices were heard, other nights ran into other days . . . O! The days at Halıcıoğlu! Business at Akarçeşme flourished despite circumstances which called for the artist to transform his occupation into a trade. Thus, artistry had begun to move gradually away into the distance; he had never discussed this problem with his father, but it seemed that certain decisions had already been made; now he ought to make a point not to offend him. Everybody had a life of his own which he had to make the best of, to add meaning to, and to try to better. Many years had to go by before one became conscious of the ongoing process. One should take care not to offend anyone in the meantime. One would have to settle accounts at the end both with oneself and with others. However, at long last, there would never be any need for accounts to be settled; for, during those days of expectations, yearnings, and deferments, a disaster would be knocking on the door of the house at Halıcıoğlu . . . a disaster destined to change their lifestyle and their dreams for the future radically. All the incidents of that night had remained as the minutest details in his mind.

To be able to become a comedian

That evening they had paid a visit to Yasef, his father's surrogate nephew. Yasef, who was in dire straits at the time, was in an impoverished state, and needed more than anything else comforting and company. His young wife lay fatally ill; she was losing weight, the cause of which could not be detected. Everybody was sure that her end was near, but no one dared to say such a thing. There were mortal conditions which nobody would be willing to acknowledge; there were houses in which the word death was not permitted to be heard despite glaringly hard facts. The family member who was particularly affected was his father who knew Yasef's past better than anyone. On the way to his nephew's house, he kept repeating every now and then: "Poor unfortunate boy!" unaware of the bad luck that would befall him soon. Outsiders might observe this as an offensive remark coming from a successful man about a relative of his who had failed to rise in the world. However, this feeling originated from remorse, despair, to wit, revolt. His father pronounced these words with heartache, as an uncle hardly to figure in an ordinary story. He bore a special responsibility for this boy. This had to do with a legacy; a valuable legacy whose history went back to an unforgettable separation, from a moment of death; a legacy he tried to keep up with.

Yasef's calling his father "*tio*" (uncle) was odd. For, the age difference between these two men—two relatives, whose paths had crossed by fate, by a painful experience—was four years to be exact. Yasef was four years his father's senior. But life sometimes played tricks on its students. They were cousins actually. Yasef had been orphaned; he was still young when Avram Efendi had begun making headway in his profession. The butter trade had failed; he had seen his partners abandon him, leaving him in the lurch while his fiancé had eloped with one of his partners who had hoodwinked him. There would certainly be no end to the deceptions, but he was cheated in more ways than one. On his deathbed, his father had asked him to promise that he would do his best to assume the responsibility to look after his son to the bitter end; and Avram had made that promise. He had vowed that he would never abandon Yasef to his destiny. He had remained faithful to that promise from that day on and had done everything possible to fulfill it. Having settled all Yasef's outstanding debts, he had, by the good auspices of Madame Perla, arranged his marriage. The girl he had married was the daughter of a family not blessed with this world's riches and she had no dowry; however, her ancestors were from Edirne; and, although they might be considered somewhat provincial compared to the citizens of Istanbul, women from Edirne proved to be good wives and mothers; they were excellent cooks and skillful housewives. Anyhow, these were Madame Perla's reflections. Madame Perla was a connoisseur in such affairs; she hardly ever proved to be wrong in her assessments. No one could call into doubt her conviction that the Thracians came from an impeccable stock. For her, the Thracians were more reliable than those who came from Istanbul. In short, the girl she was going to marry him to was an ideal match. Money was no problem; his father was in easy circumstances and could extend a helping hand to his nephew entrusted to his care. These developments, at a time when life seemed to Yasef to be at an end, pointed to an undreamt of revolution, from that day on he was to make headway trying to look on life from a completely different angle. He had learned by now that he should not disclose his intentions to his acquaintances, except to a restricted tight group. This lack of confidence in others might also be interpreted as a lack of self-reliance. At all events, this rigid attitude had contributed, in his own words, to his peace and growth. These words might certainly be interpreted in a variety of ways. The associations they engendered might suggest to different people the lineaments of a different type of man. At any rate, this fitted well with his view on life. Actually, despite his introversion, he never relinquished his humorous approach to people. In this respect he was almost a copy of his stand-in uncle. Thus far, their philosophies on life converged; this fact could be translated as a strong affinity between them. This *Weltanschauung* had united them in many respects, contributing to the enhancement of their mutual affection. Yet what distinguished them from each other was concealed in this very look on life. To make one's friends laugh at one's jokes was a diversion for his father, meant to create a festive mood, while for Yasef it meant to have the genius of a comedian. To be able to be a comedian . . . yes, this was a way of life for him, the art of living itself. The fact that he answered people who asked him what his occupation was, with the words: "I'm dealing in the butter business" connoted his buttering up of people in a certain sense. At times, when he felt low and out of sorts, Yasef didn't refrain from avowing to his female customers that he also pandered now and then. Was this due to his attempts at womanizing? Was he intending to secretly avenge that woman who had betrayed him? Such questions were to remain unanswered; actually as questions never to be asked at any rate. For, putting such a question demanded entry into another solitude. Yasef was in no position to provide answers to such questions in those days. Like many people reluctant to divulge their secrets, he could not describe the situation he happened to be in. His surroundings, those of his close circle, could not be expected to tell him their opinions on him. His store of funny anecdotes being a horn of plenty, one hardly dared to tell him a new joke. All these attempts were ways to cover up the truth about himself, his nakedness, his need for disguise. As a matter of fact such a diagnosis might well be made for any comedian. To this, another detail should also be added, namely flight, the desire to keep running away which should not escape notice. Yasef had always been a fugitive; he fled from himself in particular. As a matter of fact, this was the reason why his feet never found a foothold anywhere. The fact that monetary dealings had not been his forte might have been due to this behavior. He may well have preferred to appear as someone unaccomplished in the art of dealing in the money markets, as his major inclination lay in daydreaming and stargazing. According to his father, he always looked distracted. He had not had a shop of his own; he underestimated routine work, adherence to a pattern of behavior characterized by mechanical repetition like going every morning to a shop and leaving it in the evening at a pre-established hour was a trouble for him. All through the day he wandered through the streets buttering people up. He had no other aspirations. In the course of his wanderings he gazed at the houses bordering the streets, he imagined the incidents, the tragic scenes that could have or might have taken place behind those closed doors; he fancied himself in those rooms, experiencing many an adventure while carrying on a conversation with the actual dwellers without letting them form an definite impression of him. Through his own voices and silences he had experienced more than once the fact that certain fantasies had a way of covering up certain truths. He had never forgotten the fact that it was due to Avram Efendi that he could carry on his butter trade, that he could sleep and rest by a faithful woman who understood, and tried to understand him and his need to win people over. This was the reason for his addressing him as *"Tio,"* as token of his gratitude. Everybody who took part in this stage play had finally got accustomed to this sense of kinship, even though they had found it odd at the beginning. Yasef's difference was once more acknowledged. In order to befriend him and love him, one had to make this acknowledgment. To acknowledge this dissimilarity and bring reason to bear, to make sacrifices in the name of love and affection was justifiable because of his nobility of heart in the first place. The relationship between the individuals who had known how to live with or without one's losses, and the individuals who had tried to understand those people whose losses had been underlined by such a motivation. Anyhow, what Yasef did was to waste time on both people whom he loved and with people whom he despised. In this play Madame Perla would also take a part with all her heart and assets, and not only would she not find it odd to be addressed as *"Tia"* (Aunt), but would gladly reproach her nephew when need be and accommodate him in her home without ever speaking to him disrespectfully. Those had been Yasef's finest days, days worth remembering . . .

His wife had not only a devoted spouse but also a fervent admirer. He remembered her distinctly. She had the looks of those individuals resigned to their fate. She hadn't even inveighed against her husband's occasional sprees and his coming home tipsy late at night. These silences conveyed unavoidable situations, tolerance, in other words; the carotid artery that catered for the longevity of the marital union. This attitude could not be understood; unless one knew the past you could not evaluate it. Otherwise you couldn't find a room for it in other struggles or realities. You could not view this attitude from a different perspective, in the right frame of mind. That attitude found expression there, along with the return it deserved. While he spoke of the long nights of vigil by his wife's bedside, Yasef had always been conscious of his gratitude to her for her self-sacrifice. Those were the nights when he could not imagine himself as a comedian, when he could not even become a comedian, the nights when he could not act as a comedian. A few days after the family visit, Yasef was to lose her. Not even a tentative diagnosis could be made.

This death, like all untimely deaths, would leave behind gaps and regrets. A death that would justify his father's labelling of Yasef as "an unfortunate boy." Isaac, the child born out of this short-lived wedlock, was only seven or eight. Yasef was going to have a second marriage after a lapse of one year. According to him, there was a very important reason that would justify this new marriage. A home could not survive without a woman, could not breathe properly, and could not create a warm atmosphere. Having expressed this important view, there was no further need for dwelling on details. The details belonged to those who actually enjoyed the experience, who preferred to live. However, in spite of all these facts, the bare truth and the correctness of the decision, Isaac would be reluctant to corroborate with his father's plans and continue to feel sorely for his orphaned state, remaining a mere spectator to his father's connubial life with another woman. From that fatal day on a naughty and unruly child would supplant him. The reaction was not out of the ordinary; it was often observed in similar cases; however, one could not of course turn a blind eye to the fact that it would have deep repercussions later on, as he grew into adulthood; as it was bound to cause the development of an irreverent and hostile attitude toward women. Isaac would never be the same again. The new woman's (Bella) sincere efforts to act as a kind and graceful stepmother, or at least as an elder sister, had had a positive effect only on Yasef and his peers. No one could accuse her of acting as a cruel stepmother, with all its untoward connotations. In her efforts, one might seek a guilt complex because of her advent to the house in the wake of a disaster. Nevertheless, this woman who had taken on the challenge of a new marriage by burying another one in her past would in due time endear herself to everybody and prove to Yasef that life could be enjoyed in its different facets. Nevertheless, all these developments would not prevent Isaac from gradually estranging himself from that home. One day when he was fourteen he left at midnight, leaving on his bed a short note which read: "I'm on my way to find my own life. You may stick to yours." The style adopted sounded like those used in similar cases. Such a style intimated that the absconding child should be expected to arouse in himself wild fantasies over many years never to be fulfilled. Extensive investigations, and searches conducted would avail to nothing as Isaac would have obliterated all the traces he might have left behind, thus proving to everybody how he denied the life that had been offered to him. As a matter of fact, on his frequent visits to their house, Yasef would never fail to mention his lost son in the hope of alleviating his abandonment and making others still more conscious of his bereavement. One day he had asked his father: "Had he be a character in my play, should I cast him alongside the other characters? Had his intention been to become a comedian like me by any chance?" These analogous questions were distinguishable from each other by a flimsy thread which expressed despair as well as another sort of regret which can be summed up with one single question mark. Yasef was asking himself how he had acted wrongly. His father kept silent; that was all he could do. They knew each other well. The answer was inherent in the question. One could not forego reiterations. All things considered, the question had to contain in it its answer as well. This was the period during which Yasef did not play the role of comedian.

Isaac would not be returning for years. He had obliterated all the traces he might have left behind. Nevertheless, they would be receiving some information that he had indulged in dark dealings.

After a lapse of twenty years, Isaac would return home a few months after Bella's elopement with a fishmonger at the end of a long life of matrimony. Bella's justification was also laconic and cruel. She had been flirting with that fishmonger for quite some time . . . the man was young and knew how to make her feel like she was a woman.

Was Isaac's return at such a moment pure coincidence? How come that a person, who had opted to be away from home for so long, could trace his father's abode so successfully in no time? This seemed to prove that he had not estranged himself from him as was generally thought. Actually, to run away, to really run away from home was a figment of one's imagination. Isaac had come back home as a decayed figure with a glassy look. He had not explained where he came from, why he had returned home, what he had been doing abroad and what his plans were for the future. He appeared to have lived longer than the twenty years he had spent in exile.

In this new era, father and son had started to try to understand each other's lives and their respective positions for the first time.

Yasef had introduced long talks with his son, in all their minor details, as a new pastime at his house at Asmalımescit. It had become apparent that despite all well-meaning efforts by both parties, they would never be able to see eye-to-eye after so many years of separate experiences and sacrifices. Their fates had been sealed to different lives. Once they had had a row in the house. Isaac had accused his father of failing to arrange a religious ceremony in commemoration of his mother. His voice was timorous. His eyes were full of tears for the first time. Those who saw that scene had all felt like crying. Not once had Yasef arranged a religious service to pray for the soul of Diamante, for that silent and demure woman who had guided him through life and never betrayed him. But this had nothing to do with a lack of affection or devotion to her. He was one of those people who hardly knew how to look backward, or in other words, to look into the past. From that moment onwards this would be the proper way to mourn. Otherwise he would forever be a comedian. To be a comedian was no easy matter; it meant having the genius to forget, to wit, to focus on living. This was his father's salient trait to which, despite all his past experiences and acquisitions, he was blind. Both had understood after their fight that they could never have a relationship. Not a few days had passed before Isaac had sneaked away for good, without a trace, saying: "I've been all around the world, I've tried my hand at nearly every trade, why not tackle new problems in some new fields." They hadn't even embraced each other while parting. Isaac, commanding a voice deep within him, had whirled about, unbuttoned his shirt and tore off his flannel undershirt in an act of fury. Yasef had grasped what had been left untold and did nothing other than nod his head. This moment was reminiscent of the behavior adopted at funerals. The survivors could not help impressing each other by their display of feelings. In the meantime, they had already lost all they had to lose. It was a moment of separation that they had exchanged, a moment of actual separation . . . as though death had paid a visit to their home. This was their only Jewish moment. They had effectively had a perfect view of each other at that very moment. Yasef had one other reason now for acting like a comedian in the streets; another reason for announcing to people that he had been a master in buttering people up. This profession of his had gained meaning especially in terms of his wish to avenge his abandonment. Brooding over these events, he kept asking himself the reason why there had been no common understanding between father and son throughout their long history. He had never found a convincing answer to his question. In this story there appeared to be a remarkable thing devoid of credibility that prevented people from giving credence to what was told. It wasn't so easy to cast doubt on this separation and resolve to live alone. The best one could do would be to remain content with the knowledge that this had been an act of fate; they were fated to journey on different paths. The fact was that they had been caught at a pass where they thought they would find shelter. To have a better insight into this, one had to inquire into the reasons behind that deep remorse. Speaking of this remorse, Yasef had said that he had done his best to be left alone by his people. Life was averse to comedians, the true comedians; supposing it was not the case, it still didn't pardon them.

Isaac would understand Yasef's justified resentment, a revolt he had been able to display to a few people, only years later, when Jacques came across Isaac in the Karmel market in Tel Aviv, selling stockings. Isaac, whom he had run into quite casually, was a decrepit old man. Engaged in selling the wares displayed on his stand, he could not help combining Turkish words with the Hebrew as he sounded off the items he had for sale. He winced at his own coinages at times and while shouting the Hebrew word "Yarad" (sales), he pronounced it at times as "Yarak" (vulgar Turkish word for penis). At that very moment their eyes had met. After a flicker of an eyelash, he had said, as though they had only seen each other yesterday, despite years of separation: "Well, father Jacques, I must have inherited the art of being a comedian from the old man. I understand him much better now. 'Buttering up' is our profession in life." He had stared with affection at the aged boy. He couldn't bring himself to announce to him that his father had died all alone yearning for his only son . . . They had spoken of insignificant things, of the weather and of the affairs in Turkey. They hadn't dared to ask each other the vital questions; they had observed momentary silences before resuming their casual smalltalk, acting out their distress, and trying to appear as if they were in the best of moods. Well, so far so good! As he moved away, he had heard Isaac hum an old hit. An individual in an open market in Tel Aviv singing a popular song of earlier years, of the days he had spent in Istanbul, as though keeping the memory of those days fresh in his mind. Isaac's song also signified his loneliness and was designed to stress the art of the comedian he had inherited from his father. He had found someone who could understand him and empathize with him. The image of Yasef had emerged before him. He repeated the words: "The art of the comedian is our profession after all!" He smiled; he smiled one his frequent smiles.

Yasef had begun frequenting that house at Asmalımescit after his separation from Isaac. Actually, nobody could foresee when his visits would take place. Yet, the door always stood open to him. Everybody in the family, and a man who considered himself one of the family, knew this. His presence was well received by his mother as well. They sometimes had conversations speaking of the good old days, although they could not remember certain details. Certain dates and incidents had been obliterated from their memories; this gave them the occasion to accuse each other of forgetfulness, nay of softening in the brain. This must have been the best method of sharing the past. Yasef used to tell anecdotes to them. However, what he told them were but the repetition of his old anecdotes which he believed he was telling for the first time. The listeners continued to smile and laugh as they used to as if they were indeed being told to them for the first time. They feigned ignorance and took part in the game. Thus both during his talks with Madame Perla and when he cracked jokes, he found the opportunity to display his skill at being a comedian. This was his swan song . . . Yasef's visit had always been a cause for jubilation for those who lived there. It had occurred to him during one of his visits to declare that he had lived to a ripe old age and that it was high time that he died, but death never came to knock on his door. He no longer mentioned the names of Bella or Diamante . . . However, he occasionally muttered the name of Isaac, apparently he had been dreaming of him at night. Then, one day, in a house at Kurtuluş, he had passed away after having recited lewd jokes to them until the early hours of the morning . . . They happened to find themselves moved from Asmalımescit to Harbiye.

Fire

They had witnessed the time when houses, their houses, had begun gradually dwindling in parallel with the rush of the population to the big cities. It was the time when the settled people of a city saw their gardens expropriated; however, what was taken was not merely the living spaces. Despite the fact that he had suffered all sorts of losses over the course of many years, he felt afraid, now that he was isolated and abandoned, of facing new confiscations. Thus he preferred to lead a static life for the time being. Yasef had also lived with the solitude and loneliness that everybody would sooner or later come to taste. There was no denying that solitude was everybody's eventual and ultimate state. Everybody was fated to experience it in the long run as a representation of the places they used to see and live in more deserted, derelict, and forsaken forms. This was the fate of those who lived a long time.

He had chosen Hasköy cemetery for Yasef. It was not because the burying ground was less expensive there. The soil matched that of the man he had wanted to take by the hand; that is where he was born. He had lost his father there at an early age. It was there he had learned how to put up with poverty, with his mother who used to frequent houses as a charwoman; it was there that he had been forsaken in various ways by women; it was there that he had pondered on Isaac's departure to foreign lands; it was there that he had discovered his skill as a comedian, spending most of his time there. It was there that he had exercised his trade in the butter business before he had moved to that small room in that house in Kurtuluş, and to his little lair of a boarding house where he had stayed cooped up, looking at the city outside as an alien sight. He had had one single means which could link him to the earth, his humor; a sanctuary he could take shelter in from the outside world. That's where he had resolutely continued to live in the company of his lies and self-deceptions.

During his days at Halıcıoğlu nobody could possibly have guessed the sudden rush of people that would come from the provinces to the metropolis. Diamante lay ill, seriously ill. His father had had recourse to all possible and imaginable ways of dealing with her malady; not remaining content with the general practitioner he had even asked Doctor Barbut from the Balat Hospital to come over. Nothing worked; it was a hopeless case. The medicine of the time was helpless to make a diagnosis, let alone remedy the ailment. They were in the presence of an imminent disaster for which nothing could be done. Misfortune seldom arrived alone.

It was a fire that was to befall them; one of the artisans living on the premises had come rushing in panting to inform them of the bad news. His words were disjointed. The old retainer 'Jackie the Lame' had indulged himself in raki cans and had drained their contents until he had fallen unconscious, letting the butt of a smoldering cigarette fall somewhere near some flammable material. This small inadvertence had caused the material to catch fire; there was a sudden flare which eventually burnt down the whole house. The lodgers had rushed out like madmen, with the exception of Jackie; having informed the people around him that it was too late before he had realized the cause of the fire, he had stopped listening to their pleas, informing them that he wished to stay inside. Everybody understood the reason for his insistence. He had opened his eyes in that house, every nook and cranny looked at him with a familiar stare. He was one of those retainers who owed service to the household, he was 'jackie of all trades'; in a sense he led a life in synergy with that house. Nobody dared to meddle in his affairs. All things considered he was the next in line to take on the romantic male lead. All the repairs, maintenance of the garden, tidying of the workshop, were among his chief responsibilities. He performed all these jobs without complaint. Jackie came from Italian stock; a child of a poor Italian family. When asked about the number of cans left it had been his custom to lie. He must have taken stock of his situation and concluded that he had to pay for his crime by sacrificing himself. He had identified himself through that house. He had to perish along with the murder he had committed. He could not come out; there was no out for him anymore. He had destroyed the interior, his own interior.

They had all rushed to the blaze; they couldn't believe their eyes. Bereft of all hope, they had nothing else to do but wring their hands. A large part of the house was in flames; dousing the flames was out of the question. Their prisoners could do nothing but look on. In the darkness of the night the flames shot high in the air, while they were licking round the foot of the stairs. There were so many objects inside, of varying significance and meaning for different people at different times, reproduced with untold reminders. The onlookers stood petrified. They didn't say a word: what was being destroyed was not only the house but also the workshop that had been erected by the collective efforts of many people, a treasure in itself, a depository; it was the mainstay of many an artisan who earned his living there; it was a symbol of hope, which appeared seated on an unshakable foundation. The people of the district had done their best to save whatever they could get their hands on, but all efforts had proved to be in vain. All steps ventured toward the house were steps taken into the void. Those were the days when nothing substantial could be done to fight fire.

His father, who stopped, realizing that the efforts were in vain, kept his cool saying to his cousin Albert Naon who had approached him offering his services, "I believe we have no other chance but to stay with you for a while." The fact that he could extend a helping hand to his wealthy cousin Avram at such short notice, had, mixed with the dejection experienced, a concealed pleasure and pride. There was nothing extraordinary about this. A man, who had been shoved by some fatal unforeseen conditions to an inferior position, was thus avenging his fate in the hope that the future would be more promising. All these feelings were the consequences of the tribulations he had suffered during his life. The figures that had had a part to play in his misadventure were no longer around, yet the aftereffects of the steps he refrained from taking still lingered in his mind. The aftereffects would be slow in parting, if they ever did. Cousin Naon along with his wife Beki said: *"El ke bien se quiere, en poco lugar cave"* (People who love each other can squeeze themselves in a small place), agreeing to show them hospitality in their modest home. They could never forget those days and the warmth of the home. When they had set out in a state of confusion, not knowing what to say, the blaze continued. Their father had said that he wanted to be alone for a while and they had better proceed. Needless to say they had not had a wink of sleep that night. He had also felt an overwhelming desire to have a last glimpse of the house in the early hours of the morning. His father was there, seated on a rock, leaning his chin on his palms with his elbows on his knees. He was still staring at what remained of the fire. When he saw him approach, he had waved him to come near: "Come," he said, "come, sit by me." He couldn't utter a word except "Father . . ." The tremor in his voice was meaningful, of course; it might be the sign of many different emotions. Yet what he wanted to say had been jammed together in one single word, 'father.' He was not prepared for such an eventuality. "Say nothing, my son . . . We've been reduced to nothing . . . But we still have our art . . . we'll recover . . . we're not dead yet," said his father. He seemed to have perceived what he meant to say and had given voice to it. Seated side by side, they remained staring with fixed eyes at the ruins of their house which the day before was a symbol of hope for them with its contents, carpets, and rugs, etc. "Don't worry . . . we'll get back on our feet . . . Difficult times are ahead of us, no doubt. That idiot Jackie is no more alas, reduced to ashes. We might have been the victims of the same fate . . . It's true we can never replace those rare specimens . . . pieces that no weaver can ever weave henceforth . . . Years of labor vanished into thin air . . ." However, he was not incensed . . . He did not seem vexed . . . He was not cursing Jackie the Lame. He seemed to be beyond all worldly cares. He was mourning for his carpets as though they had been human beings; every one of them was a treasure trove of souvenir wraps and wefts; they had been his other family, which he believed to be among the people who would live forever.

I had loved my father superlatively at that moment

Labors, hopes and souvenirs . . . Everybody would realize what that fire had taken away in due time. The door that it had opened would, however, contribute to one having a clearer insight into himself and his fellow beings. They had stepped from their secure world into another in which they felt stripped naked. It was true that they hadn't dared to mention this fact the morning after that fatal night; both knew that the cost of those carpets that had been turned into ashes within a couple of hours was as much as five thousand liras—a considerable fortune back then. A fortune suddenly wiped from the face of the earth, quickly to be followed by a similar disappearance of wealth surprisingly soon after. A smile flickered across his face. In the days that followed, during which he spent his time as a spectator to worldly events, how ridiculous it seemed to witness people in his immediate surroundings looking at their fellow beings with condescension; those who seemed absolutely convinced that their means were indestructible and perennial. If only they knew . . . It suddenly occurred to him that he should com-municate certain facts to them . . . certain simple facts . . . Then he gave up on the idea. They wouldn't understand him anyway. He had remained seated by his father without saying a word. "Look, the pine tree also has burnt down; we lost the chance of sipping our rakis at the foot of it in the evenings." They were trying to evade each other's stare. They were aware of the important role played by that pine tree. Now they were burying many a summer night along with it. Had he such a great weakness for melon those summer nights? Had this been the reason why the two pine trees in the garden of their house at Büyükada had had a special place in his mind? Had this been the reason why he had believed in the soothing effect of the pine trees? They were evading each other's stare; they probably had similar thoughts. That silence that reigned was contrapuntal for this very reason. They kept silent. In order to be able to speak they had preferred to observe the silence. A deathly stillness hung over them. This aided the protection of their jealously from one another. "We can sell the shop at Akarçeşme, father. We've got some money in hand. Don't take it to heart. We'll get back to normal; the carpet trade is a dead end. I've got other ideas," he said following this prolonged silence.

His father, who was busy drawing meaningless figures in the soil with a stick, a relic from the blaze, had raised his head to have one last look at the ruins. "As you wish son . . . " he said. He tried not to display his sense of defeat. He could do nothing else at that moment. However, for those who knew him well these few words meant a lot. This was one of the rare moments when he felt closest to his father; when he loved him most. Those who had been a witness to such relationships knew all too well that such moments were very rare indeed in one's lifetime. The feelings were mutual; they were on the brink of an embrace. But something held them back, pinned them down. People were capable of smothering the emotions that grazed within them. One couldn't easily take the one step toward what was nearest to them. "As you wish son" was an important expression; it pointed to the direction they should take in the wake of the fire; it marked a transitional point . . . That was to be the last night when his father appeared to him in his identity as head of the family. It was now his turn to take over. To be honest, he was not prepared for it. Nevertheless, a change of responsibility brought a certain resolution with it. A necessity led to new discoveries. Actually, all the relationships that gave direction to our lives could not be seen beforehand.

The pictures concealed in the rugs and carpets

Putting the shop at Akarçeşme up for sale had its reasons, both logical and emotional. The fire had dried up the financial source that the sale of carpets supplied. That source included not only the workshop as such but also his father's past and his craft. To witness the shop almost abandoned and unprotected would likely cause great distress to his father and induce him to withdraw from active life. They had to trace a completely new path . . . involving completely new aspirations. Moreover, the revenue available from that shop could never provide for the financial future of the family. Aside from all these considerations, times were changing. People had started to look on life from quite another angle.

They had moved now to a rather spacious apartment at Asmalımescit. It was somewhat smaller than their house, but good enough to contain them.

He had opened a little sundries shop at Yüksekkaldırım. This had brought a new color to their lives, to be precise, colors that might contribute to a transformation in their lives. Those colors would gain meanings in the house once it was inhabited, in the name of days gone by, in different guises and touches. Special moments and emotions would be experienced in a box, with a flower design on the cover, on a certain morning, during the sewing of a button. To sew a button on clothing being worn at the time was considered bad luck by his mother, and she had no problem resorting to prayer if she had to; a childish ritual to some. He who had never forgotten the magic words she used to utter at such moments, had difficulty in remembering them now. "Let me see," he said probing the depths of his memory, "how did it go . . . It must be something like this. 'Ensima de ken kuzğo? . . . Ensima del ijo del rey de Fransiya . . . El ke tenga tuz ansiyas . . . Tu ke tengas su bien' (On whose apparel I'm sewing it? On the son of the King of France . . . Let your troubles be his and his troubles be yours . . .)" That was it! He did remember it, after all! Those were the moments that had remained in his memory from those difficult days. What a funny, playful formula! What part did the son of the King France play in all this? Where had his mother learned it? Was the fact that France had long been divested of its King known to that house? He had also recalled this formula when he had visited the *Palais de Versailles* in the company of Madame Roza. His mother was still alive. He would ask her about it upon his return. "Had what you said come true, you cannot imagine where we would be living now," he would tell her. He couldn't suppress his smile at this moment. When he returned he had done what he had promised himself and asked his mother about that formula. But his mother didn't remember it; a good many souvenirs relating to those days from which she had to alienate herself had been eliminated from her mind. This may have been what people called "the long death." He felt close to that hard fact. One approached, learned to approach it, by stripping himself gradually from his burdens. He understood better now. His mother was not to blame for her forgetfulness.

During the days following the opening of his little shop at Yüksekkaldırım he had lived with that breathtaking Thracian beauty and was full of expectations, experiencing both the tangible and the ethereal. His father had thought a lot of this young girl who had brought with her a new voice. His warm feelings for her had been built up over a very short period because of his intuitive nature. They had shared a yearning that had left permanent traces on their past. Outsiders might think that this affection was due to his father's discovery of the girl whom he had failed to find himself, veiled in Roza. He was partly right in his estimation. His reaction had been ostensibly felt by those of his peer group. His father was one of those people who could not conceal his feelings. Life had not changed him despite all that had been experienced. This relationship assumed a deeper meaning if one remembers the fact that Roza had lost her own father in the old days. She had appeared to be seeking the touch of her own father in her father-in-law. This was a fact they had never openly acknowledged to each other. They had to leave the magic of this fact untouched to the bitter end. This magic was even more important than the real fact; the play was colored by a detail. Yes, a detail; a detail that could be understood and justified when approached with care in their play. The emotion that had found its reflection in Madame Roza's skill in embroidery could not have passed unnoticed by his father. The points worthy of notice had been perceived over a short time. Avram Efendi had given his daughter-in-law a gift that might be considered rather valuable. It was a loom which he himself had designed and constructed with his own hands. As a matter of fact it was a small, simple loom. He was going to teach her how to weave a carpet. This was indeed a gift both for Roza and the other members of the family. Roza was to recognize the place she occupied in the eyes of a man whom she revered and loved; the rest of the family was to observe the fact that Avram Efendi, their father, had not been totally defeated by the fire he had suffered. The mutual cooperation between father and daughter would find its reward in the rugs they collectively produced on that loom. The rugs and carpets they would be manufacturing during their leisure hours for their own home and for the homes of their next-of-kin contained their evasions and fantasies as well as their fate. There had to be a few kilims somewhere dating from that period, which he could not exactly find now. Only Juliet could find them in their cubbyhole, she who knew a good many of his secrets. He was going to ask her to come over one day. It had been quite some time since she had last been seen. Yet, he couldn't blame her for such hiatuses after all she had gone through. He understood her, he could share her feelings, empathize with her; they had seen the different aspects of death; they had become accustomed to it, if one may say so.

Juliet . . . Lovely Juliet, who sometimes appeared to him to be closer than his own sons . . . How interesting it was! Fate had traced an interesting path for the family members. He had entertained for Juliet feelings similar to those that his father had felt for Roza. He had found in Juliet the daughter he had long been seeking, the daughter he sorely missed. However, if one went into details, Juliet was very different from Roza, the daughter that Roza had been to his father. Alongside the close affection she had displayed for him lay an undying vengeance.

Juliet had learned almost the entire story from Berti as soon as she had become a member of the family. In that story, she knew that her father-in-law had done a great injustice to the man who she loved and wanted to share her life with. Juliet's love during those years was primarily directed to show Berti to his father. It had not taken him long to understand the situation. People who adopted similar attitudes to life understood one another. From the very moment of her entry into the family, she had decided to introduce herself as a woman that knew how to adopt this attitude and how to endear herself to him. In time they would understand each other better. A time would come when they would jointly assess the people around them, assigning them particular places in their lives. Juliet was different. Their play was different, different from the innocent and innocuous play staged by Roza and his father.

His father used to get up, spruced up, like in the old days, and open the door to their source of income. He removed the particles of dust that lay around. Kevork Efendi had taught him everything. Then, he lit his cigarette and sipped his coffee waiting for his son. Afterward it was his custom to chat with the neighboring craftsmen. They used to call him 'Father Avram.' His skill in weaving was known to everyone; his being a connoisseur of old carpets was also acknowledged by all. Now and then they came over asking his advice about the value of a Persian carpet of six square meters; they inquired whether he knew any reliable carpet mender and the best way to protect carpets in good condition. His father never refused giving an answer to such questions. As a matter of fact, he liked being the source of such wisdom. Sometimes one could read a sadness in his complexion he could not express in words. One especially noticed this in his lineaments when he harangued for hours over the protection and preservation of rugs and carpets. However, behind that aspect of dejection there lay concealed another thing that could not be put into words. They were well aware of his expertise and connoisseurship, but knew nothing of his art. Nor could he communicate his abandonment. At such moments, he set out on long walks. The Park Hotel at Tokatlıyan was his usual haunt; sometimes he got it into his head to call at the tavern of Aşer, or at the café of Sarı Madam or else at Cumhuriyet Bahçesi. Only Roza knew his whereabouts. "If I fall dead one day in the street, you better know where to look for me," he used to say to Roza. He was haunted by the idea of death in those days. Nevertheless he would continue to outlive that blaze by a good many years, however he would carry his own fire within himself in his own way, to somewhere he would tell to no one.

They held long conversations during which he told of his experiences. A close intimacy had developed between them. Must he have been so removed from life in order to gain this closeness?

Who had Lilica applauded at the window?

The only thing they had taken with them from the house at Halıcıoğlu had been Lilica. Lilica had always been considered as one of the family, despite her strange ways and peculiarities, Lilica had been an elder sister of sorts both to him and his elder brother.

She was an integral part of their lives, a person from whom they could not tear themselves. They couldn't possibly forsake her at the place they had abandoned. They would find a corner to accommodate her in every house they were to move into, a little corner, a modest little corner, a corner that would give one the impression of closeness despite detachment, and inspire in one the joy of living by its very existence. As a matter of fact, this little corner had sheltered the whole family under one roof despite the losses they suffered. What placed her in this corner, and made her feel as though she belonged to it, was her funny manner of expression. Her manner of talking had earned her the epithets 'lunatic' or 'meshugga,' used in reference to her by some people who took pleasure in pointing out the differences of someone out of the ordinary. However, it was plain to see that she used her brain in a fashion different from the other people of her entourage, and that her style aroused laughter in many.

However, those who closely knew this protean woman would likely declare how wrong the assessors who formulated their judgments from a distance had been. Those who had an intimate knowledge of her were aware that she possessed intelligence far above the intelligence of ordinary people. A considerable intelligence difficult to describe but which could only be sensed. Everybody had had a share in the realization of this intelligence. The superiority was concealed in a few details hardly to be ignored. For instance, Lilica, by an unprecedented dexterity, rolled dough so thin and of such unbelievable dimensions that one would almost think it to be partly translucent. The days when she performed this feat were considered 'demonstration days.' She delighted in being the focus of attention and to play the leading role even though it was a brief one. However, this was not the only play in which she acted as a prima donna. The Feast of Lots contributed to the rejoicings, at least for her and her elder brother. On the days in question she prepared currant cakes with walnuts. How he missed the tiny Dedos de Haman (Haman's fingers). The ingredients of these tiny buns of which the dough was prepared at home and which was baked in the oven were pounded walnuts, black currants, plenty of sugar, and cinnamon. Those fingers that had made headway, growing in popularity over the years, occupying a major place in his life not only during his childhood but also in the days when he believed he had grown into an adult; later his wife had also learned how to prepare those buns. Goodwill had once more been shown to people cared for. This was another face of mother-hood. When the appointed time came, in other words on the Feast of Lots, the cakes prepared to commemorate Lilica were as tasty as the originals. There was something missing though. The taste was there, but the ritual had been mislaid somewhere over time; that little ritual that contributed to the taste of the cake. That little ritual that reminded the participant that both the preprandial and the postprandial processes of a well prepared meal were equally important, in terms of the titillation of the palate . . . Madame Roza was well aware of this refinement. She preferred to retire to the background, leaving Lilica in the foreground. Ha-man's fingers . . . How funny and childish it sounded, how certain feelings pe-rennially kept their authenticity. The Feast of Lots, the Jewish festival celebrated on the 14 of Adar and instituted to commemorate the deliverance of the Jews from the machinations of Haman was the occasion during which the fingers had to be munched and munched till they were entirely ground in order to wreak vengeance on the cruel vizier. There was no end to the number of fingers that man had. When Lilica was asked about the multiplicity of the fingers, she used to say: "He's got many fingers. He's so bad!" At times he used to introduce to her the imprecations of the word 'ill-omened,' which she wrongly pronounced, the meaning of which she would learn years later. In time, many other ill-omened in-cidents would occur. The adversities of the time were the evils of an unforgettable shadow play. However, the fact that the word ill-omened signified something bad used to qualify that a person had deserved it.

It may be that Madame Roza had kept alive the fingers of Haman in order to preserve the memory of these petty mischiefs. How about Juliet, had she intended to take part in this play? He must not forget to ask her this. He must not forget. Lately his memory had begun failing him. Not only did he forget past events but also the names of certain loci. What had remained in his possession were his visions which linked him to life, anonymous visions from a different time. Most of these visions that had gained meaning by the associations they gave rise to had remained imprisoned in a place where he could take no one.

Among the souvenirs in the store of his memory was also the time when Lilica washed him as a child. How could he ever forget? He had experienced his first sexual instincts and his first *real* woman on the said occasion. Friday was the day for bathing, after his elder brother, who washed himself, came his turn. As Lilica put it, the water they obtained from the cistern was boiled in large copper boilers on a wood fire. Jackie the Lame was responsible for the transportation of the boiler to the room. His powerful muscles seemed to be ill fitted to his small stature; it was as though all his force had been focused on his biceps. Jackie was never sober. His frequent bouts of coughing and his guttural voice did not deter him from smoking. Seeing him in the grip of such fits, one would think that he was about to keel over. Yet he had no match in heaving the gigantic boilers and carrying them to their destinations. They used to take their bath in large wash-tubs. When he was naughty, Lilica used to chide and threaten him by saying: "I'll wash you with boiling water, you'll see!" realizing that her words had some effect. Nobody could guess what crazy thing she would indulge herself in next. Nobody could guess the weak points when she would lose her temper and cause mischief. For instance, she was frequently caught in the act of laying ambush or of setting booby traps for children in the district who harassed her. Those traps were sophisticated designs, mostly pitfalls. Once she had released a big rat from a paper bag in the midst of a game the children were playing in the street. Throwing stones and hitting people and causing them minor injuries were but ordinary events. In this, equipped with a slingshot, she lay in ambush; she never missed her target. Once, having witnessed the neighbor's dog pissing on the clean bed sheets hung out to dry in the garden, she had sought, and found, the opportunity to punish the culprit with incandescent tongs. Nobody could master her temper. Nobody could see what she saw, nobody could understand her jargon. Her tantrums could never be contained. Otherwise, under normal circumstances, she was an attractive and pretty girl who had endeared herself to her peers; a young girl determined to remain a child faithful to her childish pranks. Her occasional verbalizations and logorrhea accompanied by a smile no longer attracted attention in the streets on her way to shopping. As a matter of fact, these manners of hers added to her charm. The threat "I'll wash you with boiling water" sometimes lingered as a friendly reproof. At such times, she suddenly assumed a maternal and alluring air; she knew how to make the water tepid and saw to it that the towels were spotlessly clean. To observe that the towels smelled pleasantly was the greatest praise one could give her. Upon hearing such remarks she smiled broadly like a young girl and said with a feminine charm "De novyo pasha . . . De novyo ke te laves i yo ke lo!" (I hope you'll have such a bath before your nuptial night, and hope that I'll survive to see you then). This formula was repeated at every instance during the bath process. Otherwise Lilica would feel that purification had not been properly realized. These wishes seemed to be a sort of future-oriented contingency plan aimed at reserving a place for her. Everybody had to try on new garments in order to be able to discover a new color. The funny thing was that when he had taken a shower years later in another house before entering the bridal chamber, he would not remember the said ritual and the wish that accompanied it. What had gone by had been buried the past.

When he celebrated his twelfth birthday and came of age, Lilica ceased to wash him. But a time had come when they were left alone. He had experienced his first erection. Lilica had explained to him the mystery of sex with the following words: "A time will come when your dick will grow and increase in size and become like an eggplant which you will use to penetrate into a girl's pussy; but first you must undergo the bar mitzbah." So saying, she used to rub his penis. He felt a pleasing sensation. He experienced an erection but it did not grow as big as an eggplant. He had to wait, apparently, to see it grow larger. One day he had asked her to describe to him a woman's pussy. Whereupon she had shown him hers, it looked much different from the penis. It was covered with dark hair. Sometimes Lilica also exhibited her breasts and buttocks which were rather voluminous. He had wanted to touch those places that seemed to him sights he had not set eyes on before. She let him touch her breasts solely. These visions were to remain indelibly marked on his memory.

After a few years, his initiation was also made; the feast lasted, just like his elder brother's, for three days and three nights. His father had not failed to invite home an orchestra for the occasion. He had thus been formally initiated by rites and ceremonies into his community, becoming a member of it. His father began instructing him in 'the thing' that Lilica had long before initiated him into. He had been waiting passionately for that moment. His brother had also enlightened him on the issue after a lapse of a few months. However, nothing new had been told, since Lilica had already described it in all its details. He, on the other hand, had had the perceptiveness to listen to what he was being told him without passing remark, believing he should not reveal the secret that she had entrusted to him. As a matter of fact, he felt somewhat proud of his faithfulness to his promise; he had actually felt a desire to tell Lilica about what he had been told by his elder brother. However, she had faded into the distance since the day she had initiated him. Hence he had to wend his way toward another woman. Haphazardly he had to follow this new transformation.

He also remembered her countenance on that night of the conflagration: when the flames had begun licking every corner of the house, filled with an infinite number of keepsakes, she had gone into a mad panic, overwhelmed by an acute attack of fear and anxiety, and, running to and fro aimlessly, had started muttering incomprehensible prayers, before she had finally resolved to sit on a rock in the immediate vicinity of the house, listlessly exposed to the adverse effects of the flames, and began to sob. That house had sheltered her over many years; there were so many things that belonged to her, now consigned to oblivion. He had asked his father once, as a kid, when, from where, and why had this strange girl come under their roof; it was an important question no doubt. According to the answer he received, the members of the household would measure the place they were expected to occupy and their respective stations with reference to her. Nevertheless, the simple answer received was: "A distant relative; child of a very poor family, an orphan . . . " He had sensed that something, some meaningful reality was being held back from him. It seemed that Lilica was for his father a little girl, a child that had been brought to the house, somebody more important than an ordinary relative. He had within him a presentiment that justified this supposition; some concrete fact, left unexpressed and unarticulated so far, had surged from his depths to the surface. It was a sentiment unprofessed, but one that gave away Lilica's indispensability to that house. Yet, that was the uttermost limit beyond which he could not go. After all, she happened to be one of the family . . . one of the family. So were that house and the folk living with her under the same roof; together to the bitter end. By the way, it was rumored that Jackie the Lame and her had had some clandestine affair. Let others say what they will, let them call her 'lunatic' or 'nitwit,' she was an attractive girl with big breasts, wide hips, long, fair hair, hazel eyes, and alabaster skin. However, neither at the time, nor later on, had they run into any compelling evidence to that effect. Nobody could be able to guess her age correctly. His father had been reticent about it like in every other matter. His statements had been conflicting. She had left everybody guessing. Lilica had been an integral part of the house because of her originalities and mysteries.

When they had decided to move to Asmalımecsit in the days that followed the fire, his father said: "We must have Lilica with us. She would be at a loss otherwise." This was a request; a request expressed somewhat diffidently for the sake of their communal life and days gone by; the request of someone who had been compelled to hand over the function of 'head of the family' at the least expected moment. He had felt somewhat piqued . . . Anyhow, there was nothing to worry about, since any other alternative was out of question. He knew perfectly well that Lilica could not go on living all alone, torn from the family, that she could find shelter nowhere and that no stranger would be willing to give it to her. Aside from all these concerns, she had made herself a special room in his heart, of which his father had no idea; this fact was to remain a secret.

I believe Lilica had a history of her own, different from every member of the family.

She had had some difficulty in getting accustomed to her new abode, which had no garden or cistern; she couldn't experience the smell of the sea; the apartment had no large shaded or spacious rooms. These scarcities had been felt by everybody in actual fact; but for her, it was a bit different as she had no secluded corner in this new apartment; she would have to live exposed henceforward. She had no other choice but to get used to the new circumstances. She would eventually make a room for herself, although there remained traces of a latent revolt buried in her despite the resignation and submission to her fate. She had lately developed a new habit: having finished her chores, she settled by the window of the living room and looked out at the street outside, at that well delineated narrow space, and kept muttering incomprehensible words, sometimes breaking into a wide applause until she felt exhausted; was she applauding someone outside or inside herself, it was impossible to determine. No one could identify the person she applauded. The first reaction of those who saw her had been disgruntlement but they tried not to let her take cognizance of it. His mother admonished her at times with such remarks as "Ayde! Ya basta loka!!" (Enough now! Silly fool!) or "Estate keda, bova arastada!" (Easy now, come on, cool it!), but to no avail. Despite occasional outbursts of temper, his mother had always been kind to her and that gave her the impression of a safe haven. There had been times when she broke down and began sobbing after long applauses. At such moments, his mother kept a low profile, trying to calm her down by gently coaxing her and saying soothing words like: "Ya eskapo hanumika, ya escapo . . . Ayde, va lavate la kara I ve a komer kon mozotros!" (Come, come; easy now! there's a good girl! Come on, go and splash some water on your face and come to sit at the table with us!) These words calmed her down, she was soothed to hear that she would be eating with the entire household at the same table; she suddenly assumed the air of a little girl pardoned for her offense. His mother brought about this radical change in her; no one else could do it. However, in time, such an occurrence became a daily habit and everybody got accustomed to it. Different histories were being recorded through different touches, different voices, and different experiences.

Lilica was to have a long life. She would bear witness to many a death in the house. During her life, she would have the opportunity to applaud many a final exit through her introversion and unexpressed latent storms. Among those who had passed away, the loss of Nesim, Rachael, and their daughter was to be very hard for her. She had been among those who had felt these losses deeply and tried to find a room for them in herself; details difficult to explain and to which no one could simply plaster over. At such times, she used to sit by the window singing a song; or rather humming a tune to be precise; it was one of the songs she used to sing when she was busy washing him. Those times were known only to the two of them. Had Nesim been alive now, he would be the third person sharing the secret; the real meaning of the song had been disclosed by her only at the time. They had spoken of death only within the context of that song. The song mentioned a sea of milk, of milk alone.

The confessions of consul Fahri Bey

To the extent their power of imagination and their recollections allowed, everybody in his or her way had lived the experiences that the loss of Nesim, Rachael, and their daughter had given rise to, while the family was still living in the house at Asmalımescit. Theirs had been very different from other deaths. They had their witnesses and photographs at various places. The reason for the survival of these deaths must have been found in the photographs concealing their forms and voices. (He could never forget his experiences at that house at Salacak. How had he spotted that house? Why had he been so insistent on returning to that house after so many years, conscious of the fact that it would open up a scarred wound? It was certainly not so easy to share with people the memories of such a distant past. But man always wanted to acquire as much knowledge as possible about the people he loved, for whom he had felt special affection, whose place could never be filled. To acquire as much knowledge as possible, even though what he could glean brought along with it new pains and heartaches.)

Isidor had spoken about that elderly retired consul with some diffidence. Isidor was one of his true friends whom he paid occasional visits to enjoy the bracing sea breeze. The number of his acquaintances was great. His main line of business was the paper trade; but in actual fact he was a handyman; he settled the problems of people with the police in no time, the municipality, and the utilities. How come that he had known and endeared himself to all these people, what sort of relationships had he cultivated with them? Isidor never revealed. That was the rule of the game. Nobody could hazard a guess about who would lend an ear to whom. He also knew the story. It would be useful to appeal to him and hear what he had to say and have an insight into another aspect of the reality if possible. He had desired to prove to himself once again how attached he was to his acquaintances. To make headway toward that house meant striding in its direction; it also signified purposefully treading the path that led to the individual, to the hero, in a sense, concealed within him.

He would always bear in mind what he had heard from consul Fahri Bey; his words had given birth to his ghosts once more.

"I remember having saved a multitude of people. Difficult days they were. We had become accustomed to subsist in depths of misery and in the midst of massacres. I knew your elder brother. I'd been acquainted with him during a visit myself and my wife had paid to Biarritz. He had a shop, 'Les bas Nisso' it was called. We had heard of it quite by chance as we had been shopping elsewhere. He was nicknamed 'Le petit Turc.' We were curious to know more about him. We went to the address indicated; there he was in person. He welcomed us with great diligence and warmth. Then, he returned our visit in Paris when business took him there. We had a long talk. Developments were making us restless. The far-sighted had begun predicting the imminence of war. The approaching war portended far greater bloodshed than the first one and was pregnant with dreadful disasters.

Yet, we had to face the fact that the turn of events were beyond our control. I distinctly remember. For the first time in my life, I'd seriously begun considering and brooding over what we called fate. Up until then, it had been my conviction that man was the maker of his own fate. I was perfectly convinced of it. But when faced with the hard facts . . . that was my philosophy on life. The fancy of your brother had conjured up a world, much different from the dystopia looming ahead . . . What was looming ahead did not tarry in showing up. We were in a position to save him up until the end of 1943. They had to decide to go back to Turkey or defect to another country on surer ground. I'd warned him. He relied on his German connections. He was prepossessing. The German language and culture were the *sine qua non* of his life. We had no inkling of the touchy situation reigning in the zones of death. We did, however, receive gloomy news that leaked out now and then; but frankly, we couldn't imagine the extent of the abject horrors committed by the enemy. Perhaps, we were reluctant to believe them. How can I ever forget those terrible days . . . how strange . . . Your brother had an unshakable belief in his immunity. He was wrong. Those German 'friends' refused to extend him a helping hand. Everybody was in dread of the possible evil that might be looming ahead. We had all lost self-reliance. Everybody tried to save his own skin, hoping for the best on scanty evidence. We were all despondent. To cut a long story short, they were taken away exactly ten days after December 31, 1943. Just ten days . . . imagine! Years have gone by; like my peers I'm confusing certain details. I believe my memory is beginning to fail me. Whenever the said day, that specific time comes to my mind, I prefer to believe that my notes and warnings had surely not reached him. I don't know why, really, I don't. Am I trying to ease my conscience? Am I trying to find an excuse for my shortcoming? I don't know . . . It may be self-justification perhaps . . .

"It isn't altogether impossible; my notes may not have reached your brother; we were in the middle of a war, after all. Regardless we have to give those days their due. How else can one interpret the whole thing as listlessness? But believe me, I'd done my best to divert the paths that would lead to a fatal end.

"I'd been informed that in the group heading for the Drancy prison there were people that I knew, your brother being among them; I handed over a list to the concerned. I realized that life sometimes hung by a thread; I realized my impotence and the hidden aspects of men. To the men in the Indian file ready to set out for the land of the departed spirits; a German had begun calling out the names of the individuals I had picked out; they were the last Turks I had been able to reach. Every name called out meant a saved life. One had to witness and experience that scene: Albert, Isaac, Suzanne, and Nesim. I was on the point of making it. I was firmly convinced, until the moment when something unexpected happened. A man I didn't know came forward reporting to be Nesim Ventura. They had collected the identity papers; there was nothing to be done under the circumstances. I couldn't step in and try to prove the false identity of the man. Everything was hanging by a thread. Any intervention on my part might endanger the lives of others. The Germans now and then connived at certain cases within diplomatic niceties, but one should also consider that there was a war going on. The people enjoying some authority might get it into their heads to send the greatest number possible to death. I couldn't ignore the fact that in front of him stood a man struggling for his life, a man, you see? How could I send him to death now when he thought he was on the brink of salvation? What carried weight for me at the moment was to save as many lives as possible. I had to find the most relevant solution to the problem that confronted me. Time ran at a dizzying speed. You should have seen the passion for life his eyes expressed. We had eventually arranged their journey back to Turkey. The rest did not interest us so much. Unfortunately, I didn't see Nesim afterward. Their sojourn at Drarcy had been brief; they had been transferred elsewhere; to Auschwitz, I believe . . . it was only a guess, we'd never been able to know the true state of affairs," said Fahri Bey.

This account had lingered in him for years never losing its pathos. Was this an account that Fahri Bey had concocted making a point not to recall bare facts, hiding behind certain visions or was it a true story, an old legend lived and shared of which he remained faithful to every detail? Did life depend on such simple and meaningless relationships? The fact that a delay of ten days had sufficed for the appropriation of somebody else's identity in order to survive . . . This visit had enabled him to fill in certain missing parts of the story. Nesim, according to Enrico Weizman's account, was not the type of man who would be resigned to his fate in Auschwitz, a man who would have snubbed the alleged ten day delay. "Had he been aware that his fate would not have been sealed, if he had been conscious that an inaccuracy had played a trick on him . . . that he would be driven to his grave by a simple mistaken identity . . . " he thought. Nevertheless, he might have felt some gratification at the fact that this had escaped Nesim's notice and that he had failed to take stock of this aspect of affairs. One should not forget also that one preferred to ignore certain facts sometimes. At all events, he had more than one reason to rise up against his fate, against the adversities he had fallen victim to. He wondered where that nondescript man might have gone. He mulled over the possibilities "It may well be that we have come across him somewhere in this long life, in this odd life, who knows," he thought. He smiled. In order to be able to hear his own voice, he raised it while smiling again. He believed in coincidences, but such an encounter seemed to him a bit too far-fetched. Furthermore, when one took into consideration the remaining facts of life that lent meaning to certain things, the man who had usurped Nesim's place was not so important. For instance, there was another viable fact in Enrico Weizman's account. "If you can find a way to escape, please tell my brother in Istanbul that I've missed the days when we used to invite the guys of the district to our home at Halıcıoğlu to watch movies. I dreamt of those days last night; I tried to recall the films we showed, but I couldn't. The only thing that I remembered was the event itself. How distant all those things seem to me now," Nesim was reported to have said to his last companion. Distant as they were in fact, they seemed to belong to another world, those moments and experiences. Everything seemed to have melted away; all those lives projected on the screen . . . what had remained behind . . . yes what had remained behind were but scattered memories.

Letters from Spain

Not only the childhood days, but also the days that followed Nesim's death seemed to be very far removed. Separation had once again been on the cards; separation that gained meaning through their plays; separation that had come to knock on their door once more. He hadn't disclosed the news of those deaths to his parents, disguising and putting them in a different picture frame. According to the story he had concocted, Nesim had immigrated to Spain with his family. They had been confronted with certain bureaucratic formalities when taking up residence there. Apparently it would take some time before they would eventually be settled. What was needed was patience. Not to despair, but wait . . . Life was no more as it used to be, everything did not run as smoothly as before. Men had to put up with the aftereffects of the war and try to heal the wounds they had received during it. Actually the war was still going on. For the moment all he could do was write letters. They had to be satisfied with the letters they would be receiving. This was their fate. Nesim's letters from Spain would henceforward arrive intermittently. He would be the author of the letters no doubt. He would write and read them. He would make comments after reading them, together with his father. His father would be giving advice to Nesim and in the correspondence exchanged the counsel offered was to be duly commented upon. This 'mystery play' had to be perpetuated *ad libitum*. There was no end to what had been concocted in the letters. Paulette had got married, she was happy, and the son she had brought into the world had been circumcised, although with some difficulty. Rachael gave French lessons and Nesim, German lessons. They were getting back on their feet; soon, they would be on a much better footing. If they knew that those in Istanbul took care of themselves, they would be more than happy.

Had those in Istanbul really been satisfied with this piece of news? He put on his thinking cap once again and asked himself the same question, only to leave it unanswered like before. Had they, his parents, understood that Nesim had actually died? He couldn't tell . . . He would never be able to, in fact. For he himself had been a part of the lie he had concocted. The funny thing was that he had begun deriving a sort of pleasure from this diversion. He was convinced, however, that they had surely perceived the truth, that the lifestyle he had described to them seemed illusory. They knew the truth; a truth that had been the necessary consequence of the correspondence exchanged; a truth that was to remain unmentioned. In the meantime, everybody that had played a part in this play had tried to act it out without daring to confront the reality, like in the case of those, who, tight-lipped, endured their fate. The house was well aware of this evasion from reality, of this attitude toward life. The reason for the continuation of the game played and listening to their contents should have been sought in this evasion, to be precise, in this traditional evasiveness. In order to be able to endure the death of Nesim, Rachael, and their daughters, they had to cling to this concocted story. This illusion had facilitated their lifestyle. Under the circumstances, the fact that the frequency of letters had gradually decreased alongside the lengthening of the silence, after Ginette's arrival in Istanbul should not arouse any suspicion. The affection, which had failed to be invested until then, had now found a foothold in Ginette, to whom the tender attachments of the family members had been directed. Nesim, before he himself set sail toward Istanbul, had, as a forerunner, sent his youngest daughter. The family had to get acquainted with its own members who were dispersed. This was not so difficult for those who were bent upon perpetuating this lie. Thus, Ginette also had been cast in the play that was being enacted. There was no denying the fact that she had played her role impeccably. Once she had said that she had made a fool of the murderers who had been instrumental in inducing her to choose another lifestyle, by giving her parents imaginary and illusory parts in a scheme she had invented. This had made him love Ginette all the more and made them much closer to each other. Being able to endure, and while enduring, to be able to contrive new paths. He believed that he had tried many a path in this direction. Men had found what they had been seeking on these paths and felt strength in what they had to go through. These oaths contained their contours, their lies, as well as their shortcomings they would take along on the journey toward death. Now that he was far removed from those places, from his peers who no longer saw him as in the old days, he understood his situation better. One lived by the struggles one waged and the courage or the cowardice one displayed both in his own eyes and in the eyes of his fellows. To know all this was a source of self-complacency despite all that had been experienced—the yearnings, the shame. Life was perhaps a much simpler game than one sometimes believed. However, it wasn't so easy to take stock of the real situation and acknowledge one's limitations. One could not bring oneself to face the reality of the fact that one would never be able to divulge all his secrets unless one first experienced over and over again the resentments which followed defeats and mistakes. Only you existed in those resentments . . . only you and your past . . . which you shunned and refrained from understanding. This may have been the reason for your keeping silent.

The voice in the sideboard

All things considered, there might be more than one reason for the impossibility of properly communicating to a fellow being what may remain hidden in unforgettable moments, or in other words, those things that even words fail to express despite the knowledge one has acquired about life at a great price. What is intended to be conveyed had not been limited only to the resentments and injuries received, but it was something else, a 'spot' that made man feel powerless. That dream had been responsible for his inability to suppress this reality. The dream in question was one that his father had dreamt one night during the atrocities and mass murders. The image of this dream kept recurring despite the amount of time that passed; it was an obsession that haunted him, reminding him of that facet of life that cannot and could not be put into words. As he told his dream, his father seemed to have returned to his childhood in a distant land. Nesim had slipped into that large sideboard at home. He looked despondent, restless, and anxious. "What are you doing there, son?" asked his father, "come out!" "Let me alone, go away father, go away . . . It's very hot in here and it stinks. Sorry I cannot come out, I cannot, come, shut the door!" was Nesim's answer. He was petrified to hear this; he hadn't been able to help his son. Nesim looked wretched and desolate. The dream of his father had made an appalling impression on him. One took stock of the fact that those near to you found the necessary means to communicate their experiences of pain and death through different dimensions. It wasn't so easy to establish connections between experiences occurring in different places and at different times. If one pondered the event, what one deduced after careful, measured consideration was that the dream of his father had coincided with Nesim's ordeal, with his death and murder. It was difficult to explain how certain visions entered our life. One was led to believe *per force* in the existence of a different, very different clime. Those days had been lived by everybody through inquiries lost in the haze of the past and by the dreams of an uncertain future. There, a host of words had been hidden heavy with many an emotion which could not be carried at the time, or preserved for a distant, very distant future.

As he turned over those past events in his mind, he concluded that his mother had proved to be more realistic and brave than his father. His mother used to whimper in a corner as silently as possible, not letting others hear her cries. She had simply listened to what had been told about Nesim without comment. Not even a question. Not a single remark . . . to keep silent, to bury one within oneself, within one's nightmares, not to tell anyone her feelings or experiences . . . these had been her wealth of alternatives. Keeping silent and letting oneself be buried in one's nightmares . . . This had been her game. She had experienced that deep sorrow, that painful reality that her motherly intuition had perceived without sharing it with anyone, denying all sympathy and empathy. She would be carrying on this play patiently for years to come. This was for her a duty, in a way. A duty performed by lending her ears to her beloved and bestowing her looks on the eyes of the people she gazed at. How come her looks had made an indelible impression on him, as he frequently saw them in his mind's eye and desired to transmit them to others? What true meaning had those looks concealed? Why had he had to repeat himself over and over again in desiring to share them with others?

Monsieur Bussac should not marry

Madame Perla's eyes that saw what there was to be seen and what should not be seen thus closed to the light forever. Would she become a mere spectator of what her imagination had in store for her?

When had this event taken place exactly? He couldn't tell for sure; how could he recapture the past by returning to it? He had to acknowledge the fact that another loss had occurred. To the best of his memory, Menderes was in power at the time. Radical changes were under way, in the hope that a new era was being heralded. Renewal of hopes . . . glimmers of hope for a transformation . . . This change in power had especially pleased those who led a life similar to his. Those who had to suffer the consequences of the unjust measures imposed by İsmet Pasha were justified in their hatred for him. As he listened to the news on the radio, Kirkor used to say: "Father Antenna foaming at the mouth again!" Kirkor used to refer to him at the time as "Father Antenna," or "Father Battery," or as "Dümbüllü" . . . Those were the days . . . in spite of all that had happened . . .

Kirkor had suffered many tribulations, hardships, and betrayals up until that point. His frequent remark: "Let bygones be bygones! Provided we live that long!" that epitomized his indignation in the face of all the adversities, gratified him. In this silent vociferation, one could sense a revolt against the incarceration of his smothered feelings. Actually, in spite of all his hopes and unwillingness to accept defeat, Kirkor had not been able to live that long; many an encounter, settlements of accounts, and little victories he expected had not been fulfilled in his lifetime. Now, as for himself and the things he had left behind . . . He could view his past experiences through a different frame. He could see what he had experienced through another window without being detected. This made his loneliness more bearable and meaningful. Memories could, at times, knock on the doors of new and unexpected moments. This was the other aspect of abandonment . . . The vanity of having gone through those experiences was mixed with this sentiment. The vanity of having survived those days, of having lived through them despite adversities, of having succeeded in remaining alive . . . just like the feelings that a man would harbor for having an impressive record of achievement and failure at the same time, both of which were borne with equal equanimity. He had known how to recover after every defeat and considered this struggle for survival as human fate. The sundries shop at Yüksekkaldırım had not been a success. He had to close it and deal in a multitude of odd jobs. For instance, he had been involved in the supply of tens of thousands of red and white electric bulbs used on the tenth anniversary of the declaration of the Republic. He had opened a small workshop where he fabricated rubber soles, but being inexperienced in this field, he had been swindled, engulfed in debts and gone bankrupt in no time. As a sales representative employed by the French coal and gas company, he had patrolled the streets of the neighborhood of Beyoğlu, Taksim, Tarlabası, and Sirkeci selling water-heaters to barbershops, dentists, and venereal disease specialists. In addition to his regular pay, he used to get considerable financial incentive for each product sold. He had crept into the good graces of Monsieur Bussac, the general manager. A close friendship had developed between them. Monsieur Bussac lived alone. He was in his fifties at the time. When they sat over a cup of coffee with medium sugar in the evenings, he used to tell him about his past in his own country. He had an old mother living at Belleville in Paris. He had had employment in a variety of cities in a variety of countries, like Cairo, Indochina, Algiers . . . and most recently in Istanbul. He had married three times, divorcing his wives in due course while getting curtailed. "Hence the last thing I would do would be to marry again," he used to say every now and then. He always returned. He was always smartly dressed. He made warm compliments to the two boys of the house. It was an affection that seemed to express deep-seated emotion; it was an affection that the little gifts he used to bring in whenever he came to visit could not contain. Could it be that he had had no child from all three women he had married, had this been seen by him as the greatest error of his life? No one could tell, then . . . then a day came when the coal and gas company was nationalized along with many others. The French people and the staff of other companies would be heading abroad. However, he had lingered for a while in Istanbul, during which time his visits to his house had become even more frequent. At long last, one evening he had announced that he would have to leave this country where he had spent ten years of his life, whose sea and fish would be lost to him, as he had found a job in Senegal. Their cordial friendship had been carried on by correspondence; a few lines sufficed for both of them to keep informed of the latest news. Such relations had opened new paths at different times of their life. Then, in a letter, he had informed him that he had married an African woman considerably younger than himself. His wife was expecting a baby. He wanted to experience this emotion before he died. He sounded happy, although a little bit restless. He could not foretell if he could live long enough in order to be able to give a good education to his child. In spite of everything, he felt elated to be able to see his line propagated. He was asking the meaning of hope; he was trying to explore its extent, and to find out the line of distinction between hope and deception; the result of his findings would have brought him to the ultimate question for which he would try to find an answer. Had this question already been asked? Had its answer ever been found? Beyond that border, there abided absolute silence, darkness without a glimmer of light. That was it for Monsieur Bussac's letters. He would be hearing nothing from him anymore. His successive letters would be returned without having been opened with the stamp: "Could not be delivered at the address indicated." It occurred to him that this might have been devised by Monsieur Bussac on purpose as a way of leaving a positive impression on the minds of those he had left behind on the brink of his departure. In the long run, everybody passed away having followed his own path in life, their prostrations, experiences, and the wrong impressions he may have left behind without ever being able to explain to people how they had actually differed from them. Everybody went the way of all flesh, vanished in his own way, or found certain things within him without being able to communicate them to a third person . . . most of the time having fallen a long way behind, conscious of his delay. Everybody lived up to one's horizon. What remained behind was what one would have seen. Many a place might remind one of that falsehood. For, there was a price to pay in order to be able to experience, to really experience that emotion. Deceptions and lies assumed new meanings through Monsieur Bussac's silence.

Where are your corpses?

The days he spent in the coal and gas company were unforgettable, not to mention pleasurable because of his intimacy with Monsieur Bussac. To be frank, those days also concealed a new line of hope in addition to newly protected memories. He had found the wherewithal to contribute to his recovery, the settlement of his outstanding debts, and, what is still more important, the ability to scrape together the last of his savings. Putting aside some money was the result of his economy rather than of him receiving a handsome salary. They had not had enough means to set aside a sum for the replacement of the linoleum of their floor, nor could they afford to pay the rent for a flat on the island for the summer season. With a view to reducing waste, they made a point to go to the Cumhuriyet joint just before the show started so that they should not be obliged to consume drinks while waiting for it to start; they preferred to take a streetcar rather than hire a taxi, and took care not to switch on the electricity as long as they could do without it in the drawing-room. This was the sate of their economy at the time; a snapshot of the dearth experienced. One thing had to be acknowledged, however, acknowledged and stated openly. He had been able to approach that little fantasy entertained over many years with cautious and silent steps, toward that desired inner experience, making sure that others may not perceive them. He had opened a little shop at Sultanhamam to sell clothes. He had the necessary experience for this; now that the state, extent, duration, and result of his practical knowledge was satisfactory, he was sure he would succeed this time. Nevertheless, life played some unexpected tricks on him. These facts found their justification several years later. A second enlistment was on the way. Life was thrown into turmoil; one felt the serious consequences of the war which had been waged for quite some time now; in the face of an imminent entry into war the State had decided to call to arms some twenty-thousand privates from among the minority population, gathering them in a camp for a possible mobilization of forces. It was a time when all sorts of rumors were spread in all sorts of languages and in all sorts of manners. It was rumored that Nazi Germany might make huge inroads into Turkey any moment now. Ismet Pasha followed a wise policy, to be frank; he discussed the current affairs with Churchill and the Americans on different wavelengths, and did everything to keep detached from the ongoing hostilities. The rumor ran that a secret contract had been signed with the Germans and that a bakery had been set up at Sütlüce amongst other preparations for war. Could this calling to arms be a part of that scheme? It was true, the minorities in question contained Armenians and Greeks as well. Yet, they may have had recourse to this scheme as a sort of subterfuge to handle the situation with kid gloves. The boundaries of fear might stretch very far in this atmosphere of uncertainty and apprehension. The whole mass of conscripts faced with such an unforeseen event had felt a gloomy foreboding that something was going to go wrong. However, this was not exclusive to the Jews, for among the orthodox Greeks there was also a general apocalyptic expectation. This mere supposition might be a debatable subject. But when what had happened was considered, one could not help thinking that this recruitment might be an omen or anticipatory sign of some looming disaster. The Armenians also felt panicky; they were heading inland toward the Anatolian provinces; the majority of this mass migration was dispatched to Yozgat.

Their first experiences had supported their worst fears. They were initially in their civilian clothes. Nobody knew what would happen next. When they had arrived in Yozgat, there were, among the indigenous people, those who had met them with imprecations, screaming: "Down with the infidels!" But General Fevzi Çakmak, realizing the threat that these people might present, had them clothed in military uniforms. Thus, under difficult conditions, their security had been assured. A spark that might trigger a conflagration was thus to remain ineffective since no one of sound mind would attack the military. This had alleviated the generally tense atmosphere. They could not be told apart now from other military personnel. They had no other choice but to resign themselves to their fate. This would be their motto henceforth: to get accustomed to their new mode of life. This was another sort of resistance or way of clinging to life; they knew it. They had done this based on what they had learned from the past. They remembered that they should keep silent and turn inward. Nevertheless, this belief or introversion had fallen short of solving the problems in levels. The unsolved mystery about the future, having no idea about the possible end of this conscription, trying to figure out all the scenarios was enough to take them to the borders of anxiety. There was a sergeant who went around the training field during the muster roll, muttering: "Where are the bodies? Are you still alive?" Or cried during training: "Forget about Istanbul and your wives! We are to go there! Not you!" He said once they had given orders: "Jews, Armenians, and Greeks shall be split into groups!" This rumor had created unrest, especially among the Armenians, some trying to work their way into other groups. Once more they had felt the breeze of fear on their necks. They were in the province of Yozgat. There were times when one single word sufficed to generate panic. Nonetheless, the rumors proved to be groundless in the long run. The groupings of conscripts were eventually arranged for their dispatch in different directions in equal proportions. They were in a better position now to gauge their situation. They were first dispatched to Çanakkale and then to Pendik. Pendik was not within the boundaries of Istanbul at the time. It was not a place for the sort of men they were, in any case. Actually, they had begun arranging amusements among themselves. They were on good terms with the commander of the company. He himself had been given the charge of the distribution of mess. Under the prevailing conditions, this meant an influential position not to be underestimated. This had some influence on the captain who had, in return, developed confidence in him. He even benefited from this privilege, enjoying the freedom to make decisions on his own. He had ended up having the full confidence of the captain who had finally given up his patrolling and supervising duty.

Those days did not seem so bad to him now. What had differed had been the time and the place . . . One might also say that those days seemed now to fall under the term "those were the days . . . "

The time he had spent in arms had been seven months to be exact. He had come home on leave to celebrate New Year's Eve with his family. Actually, parting with his captain had been an almost heartrending experience. His service in the army would continue . . . Soon he would be transferred somewhere off the beaten track to where his companion from Istanbul would never be seen. They had recognized once more the indispensability of living at places removed from each other despite the common experiences and interests that had developed between them. However, they had learned how to have confidence in their fellow beings; they had learned that regardless of their respective origins, two individuals, conscious of the different places they were destined to be dispatched, had taught each other when they first met, to get to know each other and how to establish a bridge between themselves. It had not been so easy however . . . Life did not always smile on human beings.

Taxes and Muammer Bey's bow tie

The days following his return from the army actually seemed to be a continuation of military service. His parents and Lilica were still alive. The children were growing up. He had to have confidence in the days to come, in his aspirations directed toward greater gains. He had desired to firmly believe in this, despite his being one of the minority of which he had been made conscious. This meant that he had to feel the burden of the responsibility of the entire family and of their lives.

Under the circumstances, he couldn't keep the pot boiling, that is maintaining the shop at Sultanhamam as easily as before; yet, it made sense to hold on to that belief in the face of the existing difficulties. Obstacles would be overcome step by step. The shop would attract its clientele in due time. New furniture, new features, and the streets would be regained gradually. Nonetheless, while everything was about to go smoothly, the tax on wealth and earnings leveled was to open the door to a completely new life. The tax charged for him was thirty thousand liras; this sum was not considerable in comparison to the sums levied on others. Yet, his financial means could not afford such an amount. He had invested all his means in the job, the guarantee of his future. He might have been somewhat rash in doing so, ill advised, perhaps. But the step could not be retraced. Moreover what he had left behind had taught him how to experience loss.

Succor was offered by Muammer Bey. He had inherited a fortune; a person having cultivated and refined tastes, who hardly knew the quantity of his assets and was inclined to squander his money; he was the scion of an old established family whose roots extended to Egypt. He was in his sixties at the time. His elegant and fancy suits bought in the fashionable shops abroad or exquisitely tailored at home by prominent dressmakers along with his refined manners gave the impression of a retired ambassador who once had occupied important offices abroad. However, this was a mere image of a man who inspired his peers with such an impression. Actually, he was a man of leisure; he had chosen this lifestyle as his profession. He had never had employment in his life. He harbored the conviction that work was an impediment to decent living. It was his custom to have his breakfasts at the Pera Palas hotel, he called on his tenants at Sultanhamam and Yeşildirek to receive the rents when due, which were districts for which he felt an instinctive dislike, where he discussed the political situation with a couple of friends before finally retiring to his lair. In the evenings, he went to Beyoğlu to have a light dinner. He had a frugal meal and drank rather heavily. He had special companions for such occasions, special recollections and solitudes. He never mentioned these people to others. Regardless of the time of day and of his particular outfit, he never failed to wear a bow tie. The bow tie epitomized his view on life; it was a symbol of his own terms. Nobody had ventured to solve the mystery of this symbol. Everybody had preferred to contribute to the solution of this mystery with his own interpretations and fantasies. It may be that these fantasies reflected a butterfly whose passion it was to perch successively on flowers, a carefree butterfly who tried to do what they couldn't. Years had to go by before he could come up with this interpretation.

Muammer Bey used to shut himself up among his books in his extensive library that contained ancient works; he had a great interest in ancient manuscripts and calligraphy. He used to take down notes written in Ottoman Turkish characters. Actually, the men of his age had been perpetuating their old custom of writing. One could not possibly give up one's old established habits. Muammer Bey was the landlord of the little shop at Sultanhamam. He had shown him his calligraphic exercises; they looked to be the work of a master calligrapher.

The tax on wealth had deeply affected Muammer Bey. He had immediately gone to his aid and extended him a loan of thirty thousand, saying: "It's our duty to share the burden of our fellow beings." He would never forget this generosity, in other words, this human solidarity. Two years of intensive work had enabled him to pay back his debt. Had Muammer Bey not extended him a helping hand, he would not be able to relive his past experiences in old age. There had been such people in his life; people who had guided him on the narrow paths, invisible to many, and who had made him look on life with equanimity in defiance of all outward circumstances.

An era was over. In this period when people felt despair, indignation, and wrath, which were tried to be suppressed, İsmet Pasha had proved to be the ugly face of the State which had to be shunned and dreaded. Was this unilateral attitude an injustice or his *Weltanschauung*? The immediate victims of this policy were not in a position to provide an answer to this question. A sense of having been the victim of a betrayal had penetrated into their souls. In order to forget this, one should hold out for other generations and aspirations.

Talks on the road into the night

Could the mutual attraction between black and white be truly interpreted as fate, as many people claim? In those moments full of hope that induced people to cling to life, to put up courageously with all sorts of adversities believed to have been left behind, this argument had come to the fore once more. One morning, when he got up, his mother told him she had begun seeing everything about her as though through a cloud of smoke. The doctor they consulted heralded the onset of a new era; that was something quite unexpected. No measure could remedy what was fatally determined. Death was out of the question; the fact was that she was going blind. His mother had accepted the onset of this new situation with weary resignation. She had retired to her room and preferred to commune with her past life; with the souvenirs and experiences she recalled in order to be able to listen better to her inner voice which she could not easily transmit to others. That should have been the only explanation; how otherwise could one interpret her leaving her chamber only to gobble down a few morsels of food and hardly speaking with her husband with whom she had shared so many years of her life?

The diagnosis had proved to be true. One morning, his mother woke up to a darkness that was to last for the remainder of her days. "I'll get used to it," she said simply. As a matter of fact, she had done; she had gotten used to it, or appeared to have done so, at least. She was to live with this condition for another fifteen years, during which time she would turn inward more and more. Seated in her armchair, she would retreat into silence, in bouts of depression. She would feel herself nearer to certain fears that certain spells might have given rise to. These were but natural, understandable, and explainable retreats. However, she would not be totally absorbed in self-centered thought as she would attain a desired object or end, accomplish what she attempted and intended, she would hold onto life to a certain extent, and continue the trends of new days with new touches, feeling new colors. She had taken the challenge of fate and stood up to it, knowing how to coexist with and endure its injustices.

Everybody had expressed his or her sorrow in their own way. Everybody had felt the necessity to revise his or her relations with Madame Perla under the circumstances. Lilica had felt that she had lost her mainstay; she had had an unshakable belief that the strongest and most reliable woman in her life would shelter her under her wings till the end of her life. This conviction of hers was her only alternative. Madame Roza had tried once again to divest her from her identity as the alien spinster of the family. As for his father, it was the period during which he would, in conjunction with his wife, revise their past and evaluate their achievements and failures, and for him it was time to assume a paternal duty with a new responsibility. From that day on they felt closer to each other. It was as though everybody had attempted to pay Madame Perla the cost of what had been acquired in the past with a true piece of themselves. Throughout the first nights, mother and son would sit for long hours talking of the days they had spent at Halıcıoğlu. He asked her to tell him about past incidents as she patiently narrated them to the best of her recollection, trying to recall all the details. These details were indispensable for both of them in order to build up a new world of confidence through legend.

Madame Perla now and then had long talks with her husband. She was inclined, however, to listen rather than to speak; the latter spoke to her about daily events, kept her informed of the developments in the outside world. They had had their legends in the past; legends rediscovered, taking different steps toward them. They lived in separate rooms; they were like two close friends under the same roof. This separation was his mother's choice. It seemed that it was for her a preparation for the world to which she wanted to devote herself. Both reality and dream had their equal share in that world. She had become accustomed to finding her way in the house by gingerly groping along; throughout the twenty-four hours during which darkness surrounded her, she was able to manage on her own. These ways of hers they could understand; ways quite different from the road of solitude they could never approach. Certain mornings he observed bruises on his mother's forehead or arms. When he asked her about them, she simply said: "Don't bother! The clumsy age!" or "I bumped against the door." The causes were all too evident. Madame Perla, who influenced people by her demeanor and attractive figure, banged her head and arms here and there during her sleepless night walks. At such moments tears rushed to his eyes; he would have liked to embrace her and kiss her. He had not taken that huge, little step at the time. The reason? Brooding on the answer to this question created in him a sense that everything seemed to have been settled. When the time came, he had already become inured to it. He had given up asking questions and probing into issues of which he had had surfeit knowledge. He knew that she gingerly wandered on certain nights in the corridors and rooms when everybody was fast asleep, touching the objects around her, especially the old ones, while holding conversations most probably with the Madame Perlas of yore in an incomprehensible language. When he woke up in the middle of the night to answer nature's call, he had had the opportunity to see her. He knew that he had to be careful not to make any noise and leave her to manage on her own. Quite probably, they were her brightest hours, when she felt she most existed.

His father had begun feeling attached even more closely to his Perla, to his dear pearl, after she had lost her sight despite the fact that he and she lived in separate chambers and in separate nights. At first sight one might think that there was nothing noteworthy in this relationship. The emotions insidiously built on regrets in certain individuals were certainly known by others living in other houses. Pangs of conscience were mixed with a fear of death at such times. One should also take into consideration that, in addition to these concrete truths, he bewailed the loss of Nesim. At such times he could go to the remotest corner of the earth with his wife, to the moments of which no one had an inkling. His father, during this time of bereavement, had the mentality of a person who had failed to bring anything to light. A darkness was being experienced through different words and glances . . . a darkness trying to be conveyed by new touches . . . a darkness trying to be clarified and explained with new touches . . . a darkness that created in a person the sense of being shoved aside, of being far removed from those districts and streets. This connoted holding the hand of a person, feeling the need to do so. Attaining the truth, the real truth from outside was not possible. Betrayals were experienced and kept alive on account of the ignorance and invisibility of those boundaries. Those betrayals were the extension of the impossibility of exiting from that region . . . Those betrayals were the result of another silence. Those betrayals meant solitudes from which there was no escape.

Who were you able to kill in those silences?

Avram Efendi had rather belatedly noticed his flight with Madame Perla. He had noticed that that woman was able to give him other things as well, as she was staring through that unexpected darkness. All the same, she was not the woman he once knew, the only traveling companion with whom he once had shared his gambols, who had kept him company during their silent strolls hand in hand; he, as the master of his past had experienced many other flights throughout his life when the free play of creative imagination affected his perception, enabling him to feel at home in his illusory world of colors and shapes. The hours he spent at the café in Sarımadam with Monsieur Moise almost every morning, sipping their freshly brewed tea, talking about the past and the present, could also be considered as his hours of flight. These were their favorite pastimes, which they were reluctant to be deprived of, a valuable gift presented to one another. However, if the connotations of a real gift are to be taken into consideration, one should mention the exchange of lottery tickets, a token of their reciprocity. Here we had the stage play of two small children. The day when the draw took place was the greatest event of their otherwise dull routine. This stage play repeated every month on predetermined days was colored by the same heightened expectations; the particularly interesting thing about this was that none of the draws had lived up to their expectations except for occasional small prizes won in defiance of the heroes' insistent and persistent efforts. Neither of them had a chance of giving the first prize to his companion. However, their pursuit of the prize conjured up excellent images: what they were especially after was not the money they would be getting had the result proved to be in their favor, but the very act of winning something; the demonstration of having achieved a goal. The money they might receive would remain unspent, as they had neither the power, nor the avidity, nor the passion for extravagance. They were conscious of this fact, of this cold reality. What was more essential, the cost of dreaming or the cost of playing? They had learned at last; or they had a justification now for believing in the acquirement of knowledge. The years that had been spent at those places with those men had not been for nothing.

He had often seen them conversing at that café. They lapsed into silence now and then, not failing to make signs to the women around with gesticulations and the raising of eyebrows with ogles and grimaces just like boys that had newly come of age. Those were the moments when they unconsciously awoke the child within themselves. Both had need for small conquests. Their discussions seemed to be confined to their shortened future save for their comments on daily events, their fiancés, their youth in Paris, Edith Piaf and the tax that had changed their lives. Monsieur Moise must have often referred to his days of exile at Aşkale. Some of the exiled saw their dreams stolen along with their riches. As for the account his father might be conveying; it was a long story, a very long one . . . He himself was a part of it, and could not get rid of it. Certain people would remain forever bound to certain places. This story was not his exclusively, he knew that. But to know it did not necessarily imply one's taking stock of reality all the more as time went by. This was not enough to cover up that sense of defeat.

Before he went out, he used to give his father some pocket money. Those were the days during which nobody was willing to go back to Halıcıoğlu. His father spent this money to cover his expenditure at the café and bought candies for his grandchildren. The price of the lottery tickets also was defrayed from this money. His father asked him for extra money to be able to cover the expenses of a friend.

A petty lie repeated with the same intention lent meaning to those moments; a lie that might remind one of an old children's tale. Actually both knew the reason why the extra money was asked for. What caused that lie was the desire to gulp down a few shots in one of the old haunts, to enable Avram Baba to get a little nearer to Avram Efendi in his imagination. The performance took place to the extent the circumstances and expectations allowed. He used to favor him with one lira, giving him fair warning at the same time: "Promise that you won't buy yourself a drink!" His father retorted: "It's a promise. Anyhow my heart is weak, you know that." Promises were made only to be broken. This performance nourished at the same time a concern he kept deep within himself. The reason why he insisted that his aged father refrain from drinking was due to his concern about his being a victim of an accident in the street. It was his turn now to feel anxious for his father. Formerly his father had the apprehension whenever he went out; Jacques wouldn't be able to come back. However, during those days when the play went on, he had grown inured to this sentiment like he was to many others. The fear of death had begun creeping in his body.

A few more years would go by during which other bodies would be consumed by other hours. At the close of day his father came home drunk confessing that he drank a bit more than necessary, but he could not help it for some reason. He said that he had run into Isaac Saporta, whom he had not seen for years. Isaac looked crushed under a host of burdens he seemed he could no longer bear; he was fed up with life. They had preferred to exchange a few words seated rather than standing. He was the one that had suggested the idea. After all, he happened to have been once the master of Isaac. He had witnessed his father making a mess not only of a great many incidents but also of many lives. He did remember Isaac Saporta. He had been among the workers at Halıcıoğlu. He had carried on his trade after the fire and had established new business relations thanks to his past connections, managing to climb to a certain summit. He had always acknowledged his debt to his master, Avram Efendi, and openly declared to his staff that he owed his achievements and talents to his apprenticeship at the workshop. This was certainly a humanistic gratitude; a gratitude not everybody was ready to acknowledge. They had only heard of such expressions of gratitude from others. One also had to know that they should be prepared for the worst and that hearing similar expressions, or a lack thereof to that effect had its own rationalized justification. Having already learned to look at the incidents of his life from such an angle, he blamed no one. Isaac Saporta had made his choice, which was far removed from theirs. The reason for this might be found in the life of poverty he had experienced in his childhood and youth. He might understand better his reluctance in exposing to the view of others, to whom he felt grateful, the scenes of his impoverished years which had decided his future. Yet, despite this dodging, he couldn't avoid being the victim of the tax on wealth. They had heard that in order to be able to pay the tax, he had been obliged to sell the carpets he had under his charge at a price much lower than their actual worth. Those were the days when vultures swarmed and flew lower to the ground. Isaac had been able to settle his debts, but as far as one was informed he had not been able to recover and had died peacefully in his corner by the side of his last family. When they were informed of his death by coincidence, two years had already elapsed. Everybody had a distance according to which he lived and was intended to live. In other words, his father could not possibly have met Isaac Saporta. In consideration of this hard fact, it was interesting to hear him concoct such a story. What was even more interesting was that in the late evening hours when his father had returned home more drunk and exhausted than ever and sat down in an armchair with a face that betrayed astonishment, being unconscious of his surroundings, the fact was that he had died a short while afterward without imparting his imminent death to anybody. Everybody happened to be in a different corner at home. As far as he could remember, Roza happened to be in the kitchen. He himself occupied the balcony, filling the coal bucket with a view to pouring some more coals into the stove. His mother, seated on her bed, was presumably combing her long white hair before sitting down for dinner. Lilica was most probably busy applauding someone in her place by the window. The children were lost to themselves. A noise was heard that was followed by Lilica's scream: "Padre! Padre!" She rushed toward the balcony. They had all at once made a dash toward the drawing-room. His father lay stretched by the armchair as though he wanted to say something. He had on a white suit, a cream silk shirt, a white silk necktie, white socks, and white shoes. Everything had occurred in such a short space of time. His mother, having wandered her bland gaze over the onlookers, had announced the death of her husband, saying: "I'm sorry!" And after a short silence, continued: "Good for you Avram! The last straw!" and without asking anyone's help she had silently retired to her chamber. They could never learn what or who she had dreamt of during those initial hours. All that they knew was that she had not shed a single tear for the only man in her life, or, if she ever did, she had not exposed it to anyone's gaze. Had this been the only emotion her sightless eyes could exhibit? This attitude might have been regarded as odd, straining one's credulity. Her ranting at her husband's corpse might be considered strange as well. However, with some effort, one could perceive that behind that reaction lay concealed a deep love. In this reaction was also hidden the defiance of a proud woman, contrary to the expectations of individuals who preferred to join in the opinion of the majority by choosing to evaluate the events from outside exclusively, based on her resignation to her fate and reluctance to expostulate about her husband's doings. His mother had deeply loved this man with all his pros and cons who had tried to live by groping around in life so that he might live somewhat better. The burial of her affection for him following the loss of her sight implied a great refinement and beauty. She had, as a woman in need of others to survive in that period of her life, refrained from letting her husband be exclusively devoted to her. An affection gained greater meaning mostly through true sacrifices and meaningful silences. She had lived in her solitude, her real solitude, confined to a lair and a glance. This solitude, like all other true solitudes, was a solitude bound to remain unexplained. A long silence endured with patience, protected by reserve. It was a silence that gained meaning by the fact that a man who had discovered many a nicety in details and colors inaccessible to others, had failed to see this meaningful truth that the woman wished to give him in acknowledgment of this introversion to that altered situation that this unfortunate transformation had given rise to. Her withdrawal was not suggestive of any indignation, any misunderstanding, and was particularly devoid of all efforts to force others to listen to the voice of their consciences. Their frequent long *tête-à-têtes* were irrefutable proofs. Madame Perla's anxiety was due to her husband's inability to see through the real meaning of this passion. In their mutual affection, something had always been absent. Her mother's rare mentioning of Avram Efendi after his death might be explained by his wish to carry on with this performance for insistence. After their separation, she had remembered her husband only on special occasions. These moments remained far removed from those poetical moments that a song from the radio or the smell of an old dish might associate in the mind. The moments when she felt the absence of her spouse were ordinary ones that nobody would pay any attention to, like when her eyes were fixed on the tassels of the carpet or the slamming of a door. These were the last scenes of her life in which she was acting solo. In this performance that gave the impression that it had been wisely devised, Madame Perla remembered her soulmate not at such times or moments that almost everybody expected her to recall, but at moments nobody would have suspected or consider opportune. Can it be that in this attitude there might have been, in addition, the wish to express once more her meaningful attachment, the wish to enjoy her revenge on his escapades and betrayals? This might well be the case! Actually, what contributed to the pleasures of life were those little plays and details to which only a select number of people might make inroads toward.

Madame Perla's show did not end here, if one thought about the extension of life somewhere else. As a matter of fact, she had willingly assumed the charge, during those days, of trimming the tassels of the carpets. No one else among the household was allowed to appropriate this duty of hers. The job exerted some influence on the person involved if certain connections were to be taken into consideration. However, the proper execution of the job was *de rigueur*, suiting the demands of the existing circumstances. The same concern for perfectionism had been displayed in laying the table, in the lacework, and in the paring of the string beans. This woman, whose beauty had been the object of much praise, seemed to have desired to attach herself to that life whose sight had been barred by those chains she herself had found through her own efforts. This silent struggle had occurred both in the house at Asmalımescit and at Harbiye. One must not fail to mention the fact that she had had sunny days as well in those houses. When they had moved into the house, to the apartment, I mean, at Harbiye, they had seen good days. They were now occupying a brand new modern flat with central heating which their relatives in the surroundings of Tünel and Kuledibi were to envy. Berti was getting ready to set out for Cambridge. Olga was to remain somewhere untouchable, inaccessible to everybody. Madame Roza was at home; she would create the impression of being a long incarcerated victim. Lilica was dead. Jerry was growing: however, he would grow into adulthood in another land. The shop at Sultanhamam was growing in size; it had become one of the fashionable boutiques of the district. Whenever he became conscious of the fact that his father would not be able to see how prosperous he had become, he felt sad, a sadness mixed with some pride he preferred to keep secret to himself which he knew he could share with anyone else. He had covered such a long distance since the day of the fire . . . They had no house there anymore, the streets had remained deserted. The new inhabitants of the district nourished other fantasies;

the old riches and the old rooms were no more, alas. One had to admit the fact that truths just like lives were liable to change. One might say that despite his occasional and inevitable nostalgic feelings for his past experiences and the things he had left behind, the conditions of the present day were considerably better. The basic emotions underwent no changes though, despite outward appearances. In the new houses were the same expectations, the same old customs, the same mores continued to thrive. For instance, one of the most important rules in commercial life was to honor one's debts. One day as they were talking about checks and bonds, his father had told him that notes and IOUs were for honest people. In fact, even a promise was good enough; it meant acknowledgment, respect for one's dreams. On the other hand, for dishonest people those notes would be worthless. This conviction had had a perennial character. In this regard, he had lived up to the established order. One of the prerequisites of the established order was to have one's lunch everyday at exactly a quarter past twelve. Another such force of habit was not to order meals from outside. He had his metal containers brought from home used as a meal pail. The job of selecting the menu from the leftovers of the preceding night to be stuffed into the pails, which were patiently carried everyday to the office for the sake of perpetuating the business, was Madame Roza's strict responsibility. This was repeated every morning, every noon, and every evening, having been arranged in the most perfect manner. Years had to go by before he realized this reality after having gone through other solitudes and separations, and, what were still more important, isolations. Every morning meant another return. The experience of such an emotion was quite probably due to Madame Roza's personality. As a matter of fact, the affection closely felt was the consequence of the contribution of this personality. Affection was a kind of bondage under the circumstances; a bondage whose boundaries could not be delineated, and were often experienced in ignorance because of this lack of definition. On the other hand, this bondage, experienced naturally, had its traits that made a man happy just because there was nowhere else to go. Had it not been so, how could one explain those happy little moments? Before the Sabbath the dishes were already prepared; the courses changing according to the season, constantly being recycled; it being understood that they abided in that hearth. The smell of a stew, the ingredients of which were meant to be used in combination with other food would pervade the house, combined with the odor of fried or roasted eggplant. He used to heat his meals himself on a stove in the shop. He never neglected to put his napkin on the table with great care, filling his glass with water, and occasionally inviting Kirkor to partake in the chow. Those were the days marked by Madame Roza. She knew which dishes he preferred and made a point of cooking them and putting an additional pail in his bag. Those were the moments, every minute of which had been duly benefited from. They had remained attached to their memories, habits, traditions, and little happinesses more than anybody and had perceived each other's pros and cons during their long partnership in that shop. The proper performance of addressing a single word to each other was the *sine qua non* of their combined operation. On the first day of the New Year it was their habit to come to the shop early and strike a pomegranate against the counter in order to see their crimson seeds disperse to the accompaniment of their own prayers so that they might have a prosperous year. Then they had a cup of coffee and spoke about the duties awaiting them. After which they went back to their house. This New Year ritual was not theirs exclusively, of course; the ritual had been ingrained in the constitution of their fellow beings. However, everybody believed their moments, their experiences to be more valuable than their neighbors despite the resemblances. What made the rituals different were exactly these petty details, the requisite aspects of them. They made a point of seeing to it that no stranger took part in their gathering. They happened to be the inherent heroes of the ritual. The pomegranate seeds dispersed on the floor were swept with a broom that they considered to be among the jewel of the shop, making a wish for many happy returns. They were to see their wish fulfilled over the course of many years to come.

Days had been spent enjoying such happy moments in addition to experiencing fears and indignations needing to be hidden. Arguments and disputes were an integral part of life; these were inevitable and served in a sense to understand life better. The imposition of taxes and the revolutions had been consigned to the past. Having made a modest fortune, he had, in conformity with the rule to this effect, bought Madame Roza in succession: a fur coat, a mink overcoat, and a diamond ring from Master Dikran, his jeweler friend at the covered bazaar. They had not failed to take trips to Rome, Milan, Paris, London, Vienna, Athens, Geneva, Barcelona, and Palma de Majorca. He himself had also made business trips to London and Geneva. They hadn't missed the opportunity to visit their relatives in Israel. These visits differed from their tourist trips in that they did not have to look for a hotel or cover the boarding and lodging expenses. Instead, they used to take with them such items as salt bonito, sausage flavored with garlic, beef smoked and dried in the sun, thin sheets of dough, and white cheese. The tourists had to buy such food locally before bringing it to their point of departure. All these things from a country far in the distance were to compensate for the cost of free lodging. However this wasn't a simple barter. It was a question of reviving a forgotten aftertaste. The expectation that certain places could never be consigned to oblivion had once more been on the agenda. Such experiences could not be felt in other cities; they had had proof of this. In other cities, they had followed their friends' recommendations and put up at modest and fairly comfortable hotels. The rest involved shopping, the proof of their being abroad which they showed off.

Olga, who had expressed her disapproval and indignation through such gestures and behavior, had not reacted by word of mouth. In her silence there seemed to have been concealed a struggle related to the preservation of her pride and to a better understanding of her femininity. This struggle was directed to the defense of her pride to the bitter end and to the refusal to make use of her despair as a shield, in full consciousness of the fact that man was destined to remain alone sooner or later . . . even though such an attitude frequently opened the door to solitude. Right here he had to come to a standstill. He knew it, he knew . . . In his actual solitude, at a time when he had no one who would shelter him, he realized that he could not be pretentious, that he could cover that long distance only through little steps. Despite the fact that he had missed Olga, he had to pass the weekend with his family, as he couldn't dare do otherwise. They often went to the Hotel Tarabya for their five o'clock tea. Sometimes they were joined by friends. In summer, they used to call at the summer house after their tea session at the Stavropulos', their neighbors. Monsieur Stavropulos, a short while after the death of his first wife, 'fat Filiça,' at quite a young age—an islander who had no merit other than being an excellent cook—had married a young widow by the name of Afro, an attractive woman having the potential to seduce the majority of men in her circle by her liveliness, charming smile, and looks. This followed the death of her first husband, who used to give French courses at the Lycée Zografyon. Mihali, who had led an extremely sober life during his first marriage and earned the name of 'the miser,' had, after his second marriage, been frivolous with his money just to show that he was far wealthier than what people thought him to be. By the way, Afro had brought her sister Sophie along to the house with her. Their joint life seemed to be a happy one.

The trip to Tarabya was made by a community taxi which was later on re-placed by a car they had purchased. The car in question was a *Desoto*, a trendy vehicle according to the day's fashion which they made use of only on weekends. He had stuck to his custom of traveling to and from his office by taxi. Repeating to himself over and over again that life required the endurance of hard times, he waited in line for several hours on rainy winter days and sunny summer days with complete resignation. To be anxious about what the future would bring de-spite past acquisitions demanded a considerable command of one's doubt. Yet, as time went by, even these visions had undergone transformation and passed on to another history. Berti had traveled to the shop with a black *Humber* he had bought from a retired senior officer who had been in the employ of the British Consulate. Times were changing just like in the flow of fiction, of film, and in song. He used to give him a lift. They hardly spoke while on the road. They hardly spoke at all.

If only I could find rose petals

A pair of eyes, the eyes of an outsider, could, from a distance, descry only little departures in lives earned gradually. The same eyes could also see another aspect of the impossibility of moving on. Those eyes were looking from a distance; they had opted to keep their distance, or saw the incidents, inclinations, and the things one preferred to have always before him from a distance. In order to derive a true satisfaction required a *Weltanschauung* which could be obtained only from expe-rience. This was another sort of mastery . . . another sort of skill . . . a skill which he could not help perpetuating with suspicion and regret, despite the encourag-ing glances of his friends at times of no return and solitude. He was conscious of those times. The things he had left behind and those acquisitions believed to have been enjoyed were amenable for discussion, arousing deficiencies and emotions that seemed to have been suspended or sunken into oblivion. Those emotions had effectively been lived and were to be lived. However, he had another mastery which had marked a turning point in his life, that served his enjoyment of cer-tain hours of his life with a feeling of genuine pride; this mastery was such that those who knew those hours or who were out in the open did not feel capable of discussing it and had to remain content with simply watching. In the eyes of the people with whom he shared those hours, he was known to be a master of bezique. Every Sunday afternoon he and his friends gathered in a given house to sit for a card game. The real aim was to come together, to fool away the time, not to feel lonely, and instead to feel that one belonged to a community. Those who had adopted this lifestyle knew this emotion all too well. They could speak to each other during those meetings around the table of their experiences and their daring actions. The emotion of collective life was experienced differently, of course, according to the person involved. Actually, what was experienced there were the experiences which they mutually found in each other and could magnify. This was partly responsible for the lingering of his renown as a master. It was as though he had established a whole kingdom that was reluctant to make a show of itself. A small kingdom that was beyond the reach of a simple game; a kingdom that might at times remind each other of the fact that one or two touches might sometimes conceal a deeper meaning. Those Sundays had made those years more meaningful and colorful. The absence of those Sundays, that absence one could hardly explain to anyone or speak about to anyone, was compensated by these little victories. Everything had undergone change, the companions, the community, the houses, the streets, the dishes, and the manner of serving them had all changed, except for the little joy of the gathering and the superiority of bezique. Their living space had dwindled, and ended up confining each of them to a single room. Some of his acquaintances had passed away. He didn't know who remained and where were those who had survived, and with which emotions. All that he knew was that he had not played cards for years. Those who could still remember his skill would now be very distant and stood in his mind only through their virtual images. He understood his abandonment better at such times and that the days lived were actually the days of other people. This was another facet of death.

After the purchase of the car, their trips to the Bosporus had become more frequent. Before paying a visit to a friend, it had become their custom to have their lunch at a restaurant by the seaside or to consume that delightful flaky pastry with plenty of powdered sugar sprinkled on it and to have a cup or two of brewed tea served in their car by the sea at that renowned pastry shop in Büyükdere. These actions added meaning to their behavior. The entire family had to congregate and exhibit their presence to the fellow human beings they encountered there. Those little scenes came back to his imagination now despite the white lies and deceptions veiled in the unsoiled colors. He had missed those places so much. Could he tell Berti about this yearning of his? If only they could go there, to the seaside on a Sunday morning . . . he could no longer eat the flaky pastry as he was not allowed to; he could, though, perhaps taste a morsel or two, and have a cup of weak tea, failing which, flower tea. The important thing was to be able to inhale that bracing sea air. He knew that much had changed there as well; he had seen on the TV that in place of old houses new ones had been built and that certain streets had been widened. However, he had learned how to behave in the presence of radical changes and absences. He would still go to the seaside all the same, to roam the streets that had superseded the old ones and make as if he could not perceive them in their true colors. He would make as if he did not see what he ought to have seen. As a matter of fact, he had acted in this same way through the many instances of his disappointments and delusions. To ignore the whole thing, perhaps that was the best thing to do. The years had taught him how to wear such a countenance. Moreover here was another street, another road . . . and he might live there by his own sea in other people's worlds. He might try to protect his own world or build it up among those of others. This story was his story.

The walls were the walls of all of us

To cope with certain heartaches by just ignoring them, keeping them within one's breast, or at least not showing them to others had a meaning of course. It was as though there was an original emotion concealed beyond all resentment and indignation likely to shed some light on a private past, not always easily accessible to anyone. One could live more at ease perhaps in that corner believing all the while that no pain was insurmountable. Monsieur Jacques, the person I had known, effectively entertained this belief. One could also learn how to live with wounds unscarred, despite all the victories achieved in the meantime. When I ruminate over that long story which I'm intending to write one day, based on what he has left in me, I feel inclined to think that I can approach him more closely. In that story, I think, I must make a few more steps forward. To be bold enough to take a few more steps forward means renewing his hopes. However, before taking such steps, I feel inclined to inquire of myself whether I have the right to intrude in someone's life, when it occurs to me to revise what I'm intending to disclose. I had felt the same concern elsewhere as well. There were people that crowded my imagination, whose lives I intended to narrate for the sake of that long story I'm purporting to recount. Those were people who had given me their precious photographs, people who had inspired in me the fictions I had made up; people who had seen me both as a spectator and as a hero who would at least have a part to play in the story. To delineate the boundaries was my responsibility. The walls were once more my own. On the other hand, I was aware that I would never be able to thoroughly understand those people. That was to do with the method one would adopt and the manner by which one approached an individual. One morning, as I woke up, it occurred to me to visualize Monsieur Jacques as though he had penetrated my soul even in his moments of absolute solitude, and, based on his own accounts as well as on the accounts of others, I had tried to tell his story. I found myself in a labyrinth that led backward. In order to persuade myself in the first place that certain emotions were better described in this way, I had, at first, ignored those problems that were related to time and interior monologues. My own interpretations might well lead me to fatal errors; yet, in all consciousness of my situation, I took the challenge and on I proceeded. I felt obliged to convey this man who had made me a gift of so many things in life. I know that this seems to be a self-indulgence which denotes, like all self-indulgences, a self-preservation. Now, after all that I have gone through, I ask myself once more whether I had the right to gain ground in that field. I might, of course, find some justification in defending myself, saying that I had seen what I had seen from my own angle. I can even go so far as to assert that his life had exposed itself to me only somewhat in certain aspects. Here again, I sensed that there was in me a desire to find some shelter in these flights, in the escapes from both others and myself. Thus the words and the probable interior monologues were being resuscitated. Could I try to probe into the origin of these escapes? Could I find out in whom or in what I was trying to find shelter? And would I be able to disclose what I had found and give voice to it? These questions have never found their answers. Perhaps I don't propose to find any answer to them. The emotion that that screen of fantasy provides me with satisfies my expectations . . . This repetition and reiteration does not upset me anymore. For, we are lured by our errors which we nourish with our truths, or by our truths which exhibit voracity for our errors, not only in our factual experiences but in our world of imagination as well. When we try to convey a person to his fellow being, the person we want to be lurks behind. That is why I have qualms about my unconscious personal involvement in the story of Monsieur Jacques I am writing. What else could I do? To have recourse to the accounts of other witnesses and make use of a reported speech would be an alternative . . . I might, for instance, move away and keep a comfortable distance from him and try in my own darkness, taking into consideration my own weaknesses, where nobody would see me, to assume the role of a new spectator. I'm conscious of the fact that this was one of the ways that would likely enable me to understand a person, i.e. using different languages. But then, had I ventured to do so, I would have run the risk of moving away from the sincerity which I resolutely intended to preserve. I just couldn't allow my people to be expressed in other languages. That was the reason I had decided to make headway toward that place in the company of all my wrongs. That was the place where I might run into people whom I wanted to obliterate from my life. I had reached that boundary from which there was no return. Man never feels satisfied, he always wants to take another step forward, another and another . . . having it in mind to forget the steps he has taken not too long ago, or the steps where he had first made his strides in order to delay his return to the man he now cannot find as he had left him, the man he can no longer see. Another step, just another step forward . . . This explains why that story keeps making headway within me despite the lapse of such a long time. That is why that vision haunts me every now and then; it haunts me at present with an increased number of words and multiplied details. Monsieur Jacques, in his house, confined to his last chamber, removed from everyone, during the lonely hours he spent all alone, tried to understand his life and his people through journeying back in time. He ruminates, he smiles, he buries himself in bottomless silences. He broods and becomes an actor in his own stage play. Personally, I'm trying to understand him in my capacity as a witness to many a turn of events in the hope of getting nearer to him. The real responsibility gains value through the emotions that this testimony gives rise to. To bear testimony means to be responsible. I might have delayed in deciding on my role in the play, but I had succeeded in the end. I simply wanted to watch and listen to what was being spoken and multiply it through my own words. This was a short play, ideal for listening. Years would go by and emotions would find their places. We knew it; we had tried to express it clearly, by our looks, gestures, and touches, although words might remain insufficient. This was a short play for listeners. In a world where the number of listeners or of people willing to listen kept on dwindling, everybody needed to talk, and there were all sorts of facts needing to be discussed. We were living in a world wherein it was the desire of the listeners to listen only for their own sake. This was another facet of the story that tried to conceal itself . . . one of the facets of the story that kept calling me against the likelihood of losing me altogether. This may have been a reason for my delusion of having been called by those witnesses . . . My story had been written for 'that place,' 'in them,' which I had never given up seeking. Monsieur Jacques was one of those heroes in this present text. In those days there appeared to be a time when relaxing was as important as listening. My testimony also implied the fear of plunging into solitude—the gradual construction of loneliness. The visions I have of him confirm this impression.

We had to break our conversation for very special reasons. One day I encountered him in front of the French Consulate. He had under his arm books he had borrowed from the library of the Consulate. He looked old, far more aged than when I had last seen him. How many years had lapsed? Four, five, seven, perhaps? I don't want to recall. He looked offended by my lack of concern for him all those years. I'd told him I had had to travel abroad and had to stay there for several years. He had nodded his head. Life brought to us different people and taught us to experience different moments. He had said he devoted the majority of his remaining time to reading. He had worn himself out. He hardly called at the shop. Everything was in a state of collapse anyway, waning; just like in certain houses and lives. That shop had provided the livelihood of many souls, kept them united . . . He must be thankful now to possess a house, a house that nobody dared touch, the house, the last witness of his loneliness. It's true that he had another house in Büyükda, but he rarely went there anymore . . . What had been lived there belonged to another time. He lived there all alone. Nobody knocked on his door anymore. However, he had learned how to remain content with what he had. He got up early in the morning. He had his breakfast for which he laid the table the night before. To live in his new world in the company of his old things contributed to his passing the time more easily. The old things represented expectations, regrets, voices, and scents, naturally. The old things were Madame Roza, little Olga, and little Lilica . . . they were Kirkor, Niko, and his parents; the streets that led him to those houses and rooms . . . the things that had sunken into oblivion . . . the things which were still fresh in his mind. I knew all these things, of course. Life had brought those people to me too. These were individuals whose stories I might one day have the courage to narrate. I'd told him about this, about this fantasy of mine. He had smiled. We both knew that this story could be written in a completely different time . . . It was a spring day . . . just a couple of days to go before the advent of Passover. Those who had been staying at Berti's would join the rest of the survivors. I might go. We could come together for the sake of our crowded days. If only I could get some rose petals from somewhere. He had told this to Berti as well; but he was absent minded, he had become more abstract lately. This was understandable; it had not been so easy to put up with what he had to endure . . . . To cut a long story short, I might pass by the Flower Market after all. Provided I remember. He had missed that scent so much. It was the season, the season the roses would be in bloom. Then he had glanced at his old silver pocket watch hanging by its chain. We knew the story of that watch. There were tears in my eyes. I had looked at him with a deep affection I can never describe. I think he had noticed it. We had a past, a past that included our joint existence, in different places and cities but essentially at the same place, a past that we had reflected on telling the same story. "Those ships had passed us by . . . " he said at that moment . . . Those ships had passed us by . . . We were strolling along the main street of Beyoğlu . . . once upon a time . . . along the main street . . . Those ships had passed us by . . . A couple of eyes were fixed on us . . . A couple of misty eyes, their pupils smiling . . . We were once more at the spot where the stories recycled.

Can you watch that star?

I had paid a visit to Berti long after the time of that short story, whose meaning was stressed by the memories those vessels had aroused in us, of those vessels that we had missed, of which we were simple spectators. I had recalled the rose petals as I happened to pass by the Flower Market long after their season, feeling once more that sense of delay. I had thought of another season. "That will be for the new season," I said to myself. However, whether there would be another season or not could not be determined. Another spring and another summer . . . Would Monsieur Jacques be able to express his modest yearning once more in another season, while getting prepared for the summer? I could not tell. All that I knew was that all my heroes who had figured and breathed in the present story were aging in their respective corners along with their different resentments. Berti himself had passed the allotted span; the shop seemed to him a long way off. Those values had been exploited by those emotions. Our talk had not lasted long. He spoke of his intention to close the shop and turn his assets into cash with the least possible loss. His neighbors from Konya showed some desire to purchase it, but they had quoted a price much lower than its actual value. Notwithstanding, he would still give in as he had no other choice. He distracted himself, putting off his acceptance. That was the only thing he could do. The day belonged to others from that point on. He was certainly not the first person who pronounced those words and tried to interpret his ventures from a similar angle. The story was an old one. There were those who would replace others, this would go on perennially. What was important was to be able to understand, to know and to discover the identities of those 'others,' of those that seemed to be others, and to be able to identify them accordingly. The emotion inspired in one the image of a question lurking behind a blind alley, a question that might not so easily be put forth the next time. The absence of Olga, Uncle Kirkor, Niko, and Arab the Negro was deeply felt. This was an absence felt by us all . . . Berti also felt this absence . . . He had understood that certain objects breathed only with their possessors to assume some meaning. His father may have decided to keep remote from the shop he valued so much. Now and then he dropped in and talked at great length with Juliet. Juliet used to call him up every morning at an appointed time to hear his voice and his wishes, if he had any. There! He had once again been shoved aside. The foreground was occupied by Juliet. However, no offense was meant in this; it was only a sardonic and derisive remark; a longstanding sardonic remark that only those who knew Berti could notice. What changed in this song, left unsung, was this silent stare. He had been able to reach that boundary during those days, in those separate solitudes. In the meantime, his father, having reserved a place for the death of Jerry, had devoted himself to religious practices. He used to borrow books on the philosophy of religion from the vast library that a friend of his had converted from a synagogue. Juliet saw this gratification from his own thoughts and feelings as a natural consequence of his approaching the great beyond. This demise was one way that old dreams contributed to its interpretation. I had understood this reality even better the last time I had gone to see him. He seemed much older than the Monsieur Jacques I had encountered in front of the French Consulate, notwithstanding the fact that only six moths had elapsed . . . only six months . . . He had taken me to task for failing to show up at their house during the Passover, as such returns might not be possible in the future. I had certainly not expressed my feelings about the fact that I had refrained from paying a visit to them lest I experience that undisguised debacle. There had been so many voices and visions there . . .

During our interview, he had read me a few chapters from the book he had been reading, the latest one. What was written in the Talmud or in some books of philosophy he could understand only now at his advanced age.

"I've just purchased a lottery ticket, for the first time in my life. 'When God throws, the dice are loaded,' as the Greek proverb goes. Suppose I win, I'll be able to leave a pretty legacy for my family. My father had spent his life saying, 'Perhaps next time!' I think I've missed much, very much," he said as he saw me off. His wish had been to leave something for his family before he departed . . . despite the fact that he knew that his children had remained somewhere far away and disappeared from the face of the earth. It was interesting to nurture such a feeling without ever losing hope. In that long road, one needed, in addition to one's realities, fantasies and delusions.

As I recall all this now, I cannot help but feel remorseful about my failure to attend his funeral because of my delay in receiving the news of his death. What had endeared us to each other? What sort of a cell had I locked myself in that had impeded me from receiving the news of his death? It will take me some time, I know, before I'll be in a position to provide an answer to this question. I need some time. After I realize how to proceed on unreservedly . . . I might, on a whim, convey my answer to the people of my choosing perhaps, to my own people. There's no harm! I would thus be able to reach them on all accounts. I would prove to myself that I had made it, sooner or later. Yet, I'll never be able to suppress my regret for having been absent at his funeral. These doubts will never quit me and will surely break through when the occasion presents itself; doubts that I will never be able to give utterance to or share with others. What he had bequeathed to me there were certain realities which assumed meaning mixed with wry joys, resentments, sorrows, renewable hopes, and efforts to cling to other human beings. I'll never forget those moments that transmitted those people to me, and instilled certain feelings in me that I gradually became aware of as I grew up.

The news of Monsieur Jacques' death was communicated to me by Juliet on a sunny winter day. We had run into one another by chance close to the French Consulate. She wore black. I must say that my belief in meaningful coincidences was once more confirmed. As I looked inquiringly, she bluntly said: "We lost our father!" She was smiling; she said that this hadn't been a surprise and explained that they had learned to live with death. I noticed that the wrinkles under her eyes had grown deeper and more pronounced. I was at a loss to find the right words. As though she had understood my feelings, she had patted me on my shoulder with such feminine sympathy. She seemed to have set out on a new journey, one steeped in sorrow. She still made the effort to keep smiling. "I understood that you hadn't heard. Otherwise you would have done your utmost to come over. You knew him well; he hated ostentation. We gave just a small note in the obituary column; had he known of it he would have been reluctant to see it printed. Very few people attended the funeral; you know the usual cousins and relatives, a few old acquaintances from the market and a couple of individuals we didn't know . . . You had obliterated all traces of yourself; we thought about trying to find you but we didn't know where to begin. We felt sure you would be there had you been informed. Just before he breathed his last breath, he asked what time it was. It was five-thirty. I gave him his old pocket watch on the night table. He cast a glance at it; then he said he wanted to sleep . . . These were his last words. In three days' time it'll be one month and I'll no longer wear mourning clothes," she said. We were silent; we were familiar with such short and dead silences. Our speechlessness was, in a sense, the continuation of our conversations we had to break off at certain intervals in the past. I asked how Berti was. "The shop has been closed," she answered; "he stays indoors . . . Sometimes he goes out to see an old colleague. He's got plans for the future. 'How about immigrating to Mexico city?' he said only the other day. He said he had old friends there; they would help him settle in and find him a job. As though it would be easy for him to work at his age . . . We're obliged to draw on the fund; the prospects seem to be grim. By the way, I began giving English lessons; just in case, you know . . . And please, do show up more often; you see how scaled down we've become, don't you? We've been dispersed all over the earth . . . to learn something more of life. But, please find a way to drop in now and then. We're always at the same place and we're resolved to remain there. We'll talk as much as you please, no more, no less . . . Berti has always been friendly with you, you know, don't you? When he speaks with you, he feels happy . . . you know," she said.

No, this would not be our last encounter. In spite of our different outlooks on life, they were the rare people in whom I could trust in many respects, at which some people might look skeptically. We were linked to each other by a deep-rooted, ineffaceable affection despite the distance that separated us. The fact remains, however, that a rupture in our relations has occurred; who can tell what the future holds? We feel a sense of distance from each other. This distance . . . Perhaps it will serve us to understand each other better some day . . . Distance without ever forgetting that our connection will continue at different places, though farther and farther away . . . just to remind me more poignantly that Nora's call within me has never lost its meaning . . . farther and farther away . . . For the sake of the past we have mislaid. When I brood over them, I want to believe even more firmly in the fact that when we watch the stars at night in heaven we are sure that our gaze will unite on the same star. A star is twinkling there for all our losses; a star is shining there for all our solitudes . . . even though that star is there due to the rapid changes in the brightness of that celestial boby and the turbulence in the earth's atmosphere . . . even though this illusion reminds us of other delays.

The rest involves but a few steps . . . just a few . . . I know now that I can also exist steeped in the night.

EPILOGUE
OR
FAREWELL LETTER

Istanbul, June 1999

Dearest,

When I was six, death had, for the first time in my life, shown itself on the countenance of my great grandmother, who had had to live on a great many streets in Istanbul with her misty eyes closed to the daylight. What would be the point of looking through quite another obscurity at a very old tale, after having been acquainted with the crimson of the sea at sunset? How come that emotion had been conveyed through that obscurity? Toward whom had those steps been taken through that emotion whose voices and sounds were left unshared? During my first attempts at making headway in my story I had had no answer to these questions. As a matter of fact, even today I'm not able to, despite so many words, deal with returns or deaths. Actually everybody lived in his own darkness according to his own way with his own voices and touches.

One morning, in March, we awoke to see that snow had covered everything. Snow fell more heavily in those days. In those houses, which had already begun making preparations, the residents looked unable to decide whether the coal (which had been supplied in modest quantity) would be sufficient to heat up the rooms till the commencement of spring. Portable gas stoves might have been made use of to warm up the air, no doubt. But the heat that the coal stove emitted was a different heat altogether. Everybody was aware of this. An individual coming from outside and entering a heated room went immediately to warm his hands, holding them up to the stove. People smelled the odor of the scorched orange grinds that were usually placed on the stove cover; people should not be made to feel the absence of that warmth.

Don't think that I'm longing for those times, despite the strong passion we have for returning to that lost world of our childhood. Yet, I've preserved that very special story of Madame Perla relating to one of the houses heated by a stove that dictated itself to me in drips and drabs. The reason why I want to bring back those days, heated by the coal stove, must be uncovered in this little story. Had there been, I wondered, other ways, alien to me, of finding shelter in that climate? I think I'll find the true answer to this question when I'll be able to unfold myself once more in front of that mirror. However, the very question I put to myself seems to indicate that certain things have been absent in me, which I will not and cannot define. My great grandmother had tried to cling to life over the course of the last five years before her death, sapping the energy she needed, relying on this warmth, which might seem senseless to many; an old tale, the touch of a sightless woman. I can say nothing more from my present position. The place I now occupy leads me only to this coast, to this coast of solitude. What I've been able to channel from the past to the present requires me to rediscover, to reconstruct in a sense, that time I had lived with my wrongs, inquiries, and despairs that I find no difficulty in recalling or interpreting. At least I want to believe that I find no difficulty in recalling or interpreting them. Like every other child, I also had my tales concealed, hidden somewhere within me. How can I forget that room? How can I ever forget the story blowing up within me through the songs that made the room what it actually was? No, I haven't forgotten. I ought not to forget so that I might rediscover myself. In order to be able to attain a sense of reality in my tale, I had to remember to live it so that I might tell it like those other tales without getting tired or running out of things to say. I couldn't forget, I couldn't . . . This was also the fate of those in search of new lands, of those who had to look for new lands. The real realm of strangers was perhaps their only story because of this fact; the train and bus stations were instrumental in establishing bridges between quays and cities that concealed unwritten poems for this very reason. Certain silences had been kept alive thanks to the voices and sounds which could not be carried across boarders and which remained within oneself, detached from certain people. This may have been the reason why my great grandmother, conscious of the fact that her speechlessness was her shield, her only castle whose indestructibility she was sure of, had lived using the Spanish language as her vernacular, as her tool of thinking and feeling. The streets were alien to her. She was not familiar with the Turkish language. The language of the city in which she as born, lived, and whose light she had seen, had never had any appeal to her. As a matter of fact, no one would be able to tell exactly what language was spoken in the city during those days. She had awoke blind one day in the wake of a long lasting disease she had not deserved and which my grandfather was reluctant to name, only to lie down in another bed to sleep and wake no more. Her life to outsiders was plain and simple. As the years went by, I would be able to see the concealment of an individual who had spent great efforts to understand and convey to others the different aspects of the struggle for life behind this simplicity, behind that ordinary tale, in order that I might believe in this truth I would have to take certain steps forward; or at least I would have to try to do so. I think that the fact she said nothing to anybody before departing seems meaningful for some reason or another when I think on the experiences I had to go through thereafter.

I was not allowed to go into that room, into that last room; but my elder sister who had been instrumental in acquainting me with many boundaries, had let me step over that threshold. This was, to the best of my knowledge, our first complicity. We had opened the door making sure that nobody heard us. Over her body was spread a sheet, whose color had faded from concealing many labyrinths from many bodies. As she lifted it lightly she said, "she is fast asleep now." She was right. A profound, silent and innocent sleep it was. A sleep that showed that the essential things that people desired to express were much simpler than they were thought to be. Death and sleep seemed to have been cast in the same mold. Yet, the sleep of death was much colder than I had imagined, somewhat colder, whiter and more silent. Whenever this image recurs in my mind, I ask myself for whom we try to keep our individual past alive, which we carry over to other relationships we cannot break with? I wonder whether it had been our words which seemed to hold us united and that gave birth to our solitudes. I would be feeling the same experience at other times and in the face of other deaths as well. The death of my paternal grandmother that I would witness years later would remind me of that same sleep for instance. The death of my grandmother meant my breaking with one of the vernaculars of my warm childhood days, with Spanish, in other words; while the death of my great grandmother was my breaking with those tales whose value I would appreciate whenever I intended to go back to those places. It had slowly given birth to those continental islets in a never-ending continuity. The things I had left behind seem to me now as though they are tales of a distant realm. I think I can now hear better than ever those voices, maybe because I've distanced myself from those tales. I feel myself nearer to those voices and scents and can see better what lies were concealed behind those appearances. In those appearances I rediscover myself in a form that is alien and forgotten to me. After all, we had coexisted with tales, hadn't we? In tales we had loved, tales in which we were born and died . . . tales without end . . . without ever knowing the origin of the past . . . We used to tell tales to each other . . . tales . . . in order to see the past through our inner soul, through our inner window. It hadn't occurred to us then that we might get lost in those tales, that we might be estranged from the people nearest to us.

(. . .) In the mornings that followed the nights I spent suffering from asthma attacks that seemed interminable, I was obliged to pay a visit to that house that was an integral part of the ritual that our tales necessitated. A time would come when I'd realize that the things I had discovered had gotten me closer, without my being conscious of it, to another long text written in a different climate. I couldn't possibly expect my great grandmother to take an interest in the truth, in this aspect of the truth. Her fate involved being fitted into a tiny story known to hardly anyone. In order to make headway in that tale, one had to experience the visions and the words that that language required from us. My hero used to move his hands back and forth holding cloves in his palm, making circular motions above my head and chanting an invocatory prayer with a tremulous voice whose origin has always been a mystery to me, in order to ward evil souls away from me. The cloves were then thrown in the stove in order to keep out the cold of the night. From today's vantage point, we happened to inhabit a house haunted at night by cold shadows and sounds, and during the day pestered with deficiencies and things that are untouchable. At times I heard barely aubidle creaks . . . a few creaks . . . so that I could imagine that the spell might take effect and restore some semblance of order. I liked the cloves for their permeating odor which I tried to find in poetry. I was writing time, my time, slowly, silently, getting nearer and nearer to the emotion that that house had inspired in me. I was to be acquainted with them in that place, with those who led a life like theirs, with those that had been compelled to lead a life like theirs, who experienced many different deaths in many different ways and who carried many different emotions through many different times.

The odor of cloves creates other memories in me when I ruminate over these things. I remember that the atmosphere of the synagogue that my maternal grandfather used to take me to was permeated with the essence of cloves. An ancient silver burner, reminiscent of a big perforated lemon or artichoke, associated in me the maces of old containing cloves that were swung to and fro; the burning of incense took place after a short incantation. This must have been thanksgiving for God's creation of perfume. Those moments were the most pleasant moments of the ritual. All prayers have been indelibly inculcated in my brain and have survived to this day, probably thanks to that perfume. This was an eleventh hour prayer; a prayer that lingers in my mind, a prayer I'd like to carry about with me forever. I cannot remember the contours of the people in the background. The only thing I remember is the radiance reflected on the faces of the congregation during the Sabbath. The devout passed the remaining time either in the houses of their relatives or in their own homes. For my part, if it was summer, I used to go to the Caddebostanı beach for a swim, and, in winter, my recreational interest dragged me to a movie theater. That was the time when the sea of Istanbul had not yet been polluted; the beaches were still populated by a host of people, a time that seems very distant today. Some preferred to hire a special cabin with a key, which was a way of displaying one's privileged position in society, instead of changing in the cabins which allowed any one person to change in succession. The difference was obvious; those who had paid for a special cabin used to come out with only their towels while those who changed in the public cabins had to take their clothes with them to the beach. Those cabins would in time create other associations in me; associations related to the passionate moments of our adolescence; in those cabins illicit love scenes were a frequent occurrence. All these things were all the more pleasant during the days when the south wind didn't blow. The south wind brought ashore watermelons, grapes, algae, and jelly-fishes whose origin was a mystery. No weather forecast could, at the time, predict the changes. We used to be beachcombers along those shores . . . on the shores of our childhood . . . with our little steps . . . in our solitudes . . . with all our secret passions pregnant with the sadness that they aroused in us at any moment. This is the way the door to old stories is opened. Having gone through different individuals and tried new faces, your stories turn you back to your losses that are more easily stowed. In this way you can bring yourself to live the words you liked the most, words which are never-ending in your city, which can continue to exist in at least a few people through visions nurtured by those words. In this way you can ask yourself the reason for one's belief, firm belief in certain people, in certain things to the bitter end, without any fear of your past or the shadows you left behind. For whom had you been experiencing that passionate love, why and for the sake of which worlds? Those little squabbles at home, would they be considered worthwhile to be contemplated and inquired upon by other people once the contenders had vanished into thin air? When one ponders on the probable answers to such questions, be it myself or others, it really does not matter under what circumstances, where and when I was born and raised in Istanbul. We might, off-hand, speak of the demeanor of a child, of a witness, trying to solve the mystery of the world within him, having recourse to new languages. Under the circumstances, there is no sense in brooding over in which schools I had studied, which of my toys I had lost in which of my dreams. Every one of those individuals has gone away to a destination detached from his fellow beings', every one of those individuals spent years hoping, experiencing, and yearning; hopes, experiences and yearnings different from those of his fellow beings; every one of those individuals has vanished in the distance. When I look back in the light of what I can descry, I realize that many lives are wasted, what could be lived at present was being put off to the next day; that certain regrets are rendered meaningful by silence and that fears guide experiences. One thing I know, however, is the meaning of preferring to dissolve, by appropriating certain people with certain personas. I have not tried to understand or to explain in vain, looking back at my past, the history one could not put into words, the moments in which you were reluctant to face yourself and chase away the voices you preferred to forget in the shadows of the past, of the nightmares you wanted to get rid of despite your hopelessness in taking into consideration all sorts of repetitions. What I tried to put into words were those moments during which I kept walking back and forth in my room, from one corner to the other covering long distances, making myself believe that I had been walking on an interminable road—those recurrent nightmares. You feel that something is loosened in your legs during those long walks. You feel you are being followed in the silence of the night. To lie in that room is tantamount to hallucinating. The occupant of that room was a child who had confined himself there, who tried to speak about the green almond eaten in the shell although he had never tasted it in his life. The green almonds belonged to another spring. The clock indicated another time. This might have been the most proper and reliable way of patiently feeding that waiting and dreaming, that certain people could come before others in the proper sense of the word, after a lapse of many years. At the head of my bed was a weeping woman whose face, whose real face I was not able to see . . . My dream would not come to an end . . . I would try to change that dream by putting it on paper and hiding myself behind words of my choice for which I had a predilection and affection.

Everybody has a story which he takes to be lost, which he tries to collect bits and pieces of for the sake of the preservation of his life. To have lived several years in the company of individuals that seemed alien, to have studied in schools one has disdained and to have toiled day and night in disagreeable jobs, to have been fancying that one feels exiled where one lives, imagining the ideal jobs awaiting one somewhere else day and night . . . all these things . . . do they imply efforts to return sooner or later to one's own small world? I do not know. Either I don't know, or I prefer not to know, and confine myself within the boundaries of a single answer. Yet, I should like to think that the very act of asking this question brings me to that human being I have been looking for all these years and never given up the hope of finding him. To return, to return after a series of departures means to desire to enter a new room unvisited until that point. One wonders what sort of a room one penetrates after so many years. Who will be facing you in that room as your step into it? Beyond the boundary, you are alone, whether you like it or not. At such moments, beyond the boundary you hear your own voice . . . It is time you touched it with your hand . . . you have to touch that face. Other people's geography has brought you gradually to those regrets and deep scars, the story of which you can tell only to yourself. When I consider all those questions and returns I find myself asking where exactly I happen to be in the midst of those little victories and those defeats I always tried to hide and cover up, in the midst of the fantasies bordering my imagination and of my realities, of 'that family' that I'm trying to reconstruct with what I could gather from other families. At such times, I feel dejected; it is meaninglessness, an abandonment which I could share with no one. I find myself once more at a crossroads. I'm faced with a dilemma: either to beat it, consigning to the body of an ordinary human being all the variations, associations and absurdities within me, or to continue on the road of that old story in search of new words. I have always wanted to describe this hesitancy; perhaps I will be carrying this hesitancy around with me till the end of my days . . . even though I am aware that certain emotions will never be able to find the places reserved for them and even though I cannot ignore this fact. I must say I've been obsessed by the idea of describing those human beings for many years. My dreams might have had the objective of describing those brief moments of love making, of reviving those true moments, of finding that brief span of happiness. For that brief span of happiness likely to associate in one those brief moments of joy. That story whose end was far from being predictable had a magic spell; it was as important to live the story as it was to tell it. This long story must have had a share of my desire to be seen as a volunteer exile on an island where I would narrate my recollections to a native, from my own island, inspired by the author of a work I can never forget, during those days when I used to shuttle with clumsy steps between unrealized dreams. I had many reasons for reproducing my delusions and illusions. This small dream inspired me with the idea of arranging a meeting in which the individuals whose writings I wanted to share would come together on my island for that very purpose. For that island reminded one not only of exile and thralldom, but also of the exigency of collective life. That island had been the selected venue where people would come together, a locale where a wish to remain separated, to be protected, to share a privacy might be realized to the extent the prevailing circumstances allowed. They might be inclined to act out once more the personas they would never symbolize. It was necessary to postpone the retaliations to an unknown date, and to forget the relations that secretly stole from certain people the possibility of contributing to the incidents that had occurred. However, as I made headway in the story I realized that this dream, this meeting, would never become reality. Everybody was lost in their own respective solitudes. Everybody was in his own exile. Everybody had a smile that he or she would not be able to express and would have preferred to keep to themselves. Platitudes meant that everything was alright, like in all climates. Walls had to be raised. Walls would always be raised; otherwise, I couldn't explain our being dragged to new islands of solitude when we wanted to live, truly live, for a very brief period of time with our fellow beings. The deafness we had to experience in the places we thought we had to visit. We had to ask once again where, in whom, and when we had lost the keys to that adventure . . . We had been called there sometimes by a look or by a word . . . only a look or a word. In order to understand and decide, which is more important, which defeats we had suffered in consequence of which dreams, we had to live our true losses . . .

(. . .) Did that time include my experiences during which I had been newly acquainted with the walls of my primary school or those moments when I had to show up in my green pinafore rather unwillingly at the flag ceremony on

Saturdays? Is it hovering over my memory at present? The brilliant students were rewarded with the privilege of carrying the flagstaff. I personally had that privilege once. But I could tell no one my distress for having to carry that heavy burden with my puny body in the presence of that crowd, it seemed appalling to me then; the so-called reward had been a punishment. In holding the flagstaff I was helped by mistress Türkân, whose smiling face and full breasts are still in my memory and whom my mother had sympathized with on account of her short-lived, unhappy marriage. Those were the mornings when smiles drew me toward a warmth whose real source I could never find. My failing to compensate for the coldness of the school despite my affection for mistress Türkân might perhaps be explained by my remoteness from that source. I was making head-way toward a nightmare. The sound of cutlery coming from the refectory and the loud laughter of my fellow students heralded a fear I could not define. I was on the brink of turning inward. I well remember my diffidence in failing to ask permission of mistress Türkan for answering nature's call during the class and the consequent incontinence and the distress felt in remaining in that condition till my return home might have been due to this. Moreover I wasn't used to the old style toilets without a bowl. The hole on which one crouched was so large that I had dreamt of children just like me falling into it; the children who could not pull themselves up despite their best efforts. Adults haunted that place, but they didn't see or hear me. Only one had turned his gaze toward me and looked at me with a broad smile and appalling eyes. I had tried to shout but without success. He was smiling; he seemed to know that I could not shout or make myself heard. That speechlessness and that silence, were they really the darkest alleys of those nightmares?

(. . .) Dreams or things left behind somewhere as though in a dream . . . I wonder in which of my writings I had tried to announce that odor, an odor that can never be forgotten, one which gave life to a city. I can remember, for instance, the smell of chocolate coming from the *Nestle* chocolate factory which pervaded the air of my primary school next to the *Bomonti* brewery, spreading as far as the house of my grandmother. The streets breathed a different atmosphere at those hours. I was to visit the origin of that odor one day in the company of my grand-father. The enormous cauldrons where chocolate was made are still in my mem-ory. A man by the name of Master Yorgo, a man of very old aspect, perhaps due to his hoary hair, had tasted the confection and said something to the apprentices around him. I had wanted to taste it as well. "No, Sir," he said, "the chocolate is not ready yet." Before leaving the plant we had been given bars of chocolate as a gift, the same bars of chocolate available in the market. Master Yorgo knew my grandfather from the time of his military service. There was a longstanding connection between them, a connection that could not be soiled by equivocations. Everybody had had to climb his own ladder to professional perfection. For me, the magic lay in the mystery that that confection in the cauldron contained. By the way, the smell of meals in the process of being prepared had appealed to me as much as their tastes and flavors. Those smells associated in me the places to which I could not have access. This may have been the reason why certain people had occupied those houses in my imagination.

In this outlandishness there lay concealed the traces of what I had experienced during those midday meals on Fridays at school. As the mealtime approached, I began waiting impatiently for my grandmother who brought me in lidded meal containers of hot meatballs and fried potatoes, the taste of which is still lingering on my palate. On one of those Fridays there had been a heavy snowfall. We were in the refectory. The meal had been distributed. I felt uneasy. This restlessness had prevented me from laughing at the clowning of Selahattin, my bosom friend at the time, who drank his soup emitting a hissing sound disregarding the admonition of his teachers and its being splattered about, when he had grown up he had taken to climbing mountains after having failed to realize the Demirkazık climb during the winter sports months following the marriage of an alpinist he was infatuated with to another alpinist, both of whom finally opened a little shop at Mercan. My grandmother had arrived in the middle of the meal service. I can still remember her distinctly as she came down the stairs with a smile on her lips. She had made it in spite of the blizzard outside. Yet, the icy soles had made her fall and she had to descend the staircase at a more rapid pace than otherwise foreseen, on her buttocks. Uncle Dursun had rushed to her aid; he gave a helping hand to everybody and was often reproached not only by our headmistress or other teachers, but also by certain parents, for his awkward manners although he did all the handiwork in the school. He fixed the malfunctioning electrical gadgets, kindled the stoves, plumbed the sinks, stayed overnight in the school, and befriended the boys by his mimicry of animals. No harm was done. "Your packed lunch! Your packed lunch!" cried my fellow students in hoots of laughter. Selahattin had a gift of keeping cool; and being furious at his school fellows for their guffaws, he had thrown forks and spoons at them; for which he was sent to stand in the corner on a single leg for half an hour by mistress Müzeyyen, nicknamed 'the ramrod,' in doing so setting a record hard to break.

However, that was the last of the meals brought to school. I had asked my grandmother to stop. In those days I could still imagine the possibility of getting lost in others and behaving like other people. In the long run, I would realize how fascinating the dream I had been chasing was despite all the disappointments. When one considers those disappointments, one cannot help concluding that the school was a *locus criminis*, full of sound and fury, signifying nothing.

A long time thereafter, I tried to remind my grandmother of those days. She was an aged and senile woman lying in bed silently in one of the shabby old rooms of the French hospital. She had had a sudden obstruction of a blood vessel by an embolus; not only did she suffer from amnesia, but she had also lost her faculty of recognizing people. It was my only night of vigil at her bedside. She had nodded with a smile as though she understood what I had been saying. Had she really? I doubt it. It may be that she had visions of her past life that she could not share with me. Time-honored visions she couldn't communicate, visions whose witnesses had disappeared without exception, and consequently without possible testimony from someone. I wouldn't have the pleasure of secretly sneaking her the food the doctor had prohibited anymore due to her high blood pressure. Those days heralded the end of my boyish aiding and abetting. One day she had ceased to utter a word and remained in that state for days. I cannot exactly say when we actually parted.

(. . .) Now and then on Saturdays at noon my grandparents came to fetch me and took me to their house where I passed the weekend. In their place, I would be carrying the yearning for a true home to other rooms during the years to come. This yearning would continue in other houses, with other people, and would be penned in the company of other visions and words; to be transformed into other people in other rooms. It was there that I had listened to the hits of the day, on singles . . . my first singles. I want to believe that I will one day go back to the songs of those days and write about them. Certain songs are unforgettable. Even though certain songs meet with others and flow together they remain one's favorites all the same.

(. . .) As the days, months, and years went by my visits to my parents were to become more frequent. The days spent at school would one day come to an end and the indignations that enriched different recollections and lent meaning to them in Şişli would bring about my departure on a new journey. My learning how to drink soda pop direct from the bottle was one of the first signs of growing up in the eyes of those individuals who lived a peripheral life to mine. Those were the people who asked children the multiplication table as proof of their having become adults, as well as to confirm their own expectations. For me, one of the most important manifestations of having grown up was one's endeavor to act as though one had already become a big boy in that secretly confined space. One had to learn how to act with different people and how to abandon who at what time. This was the only way of preserving the child within you perennially. That eternal child had to be kept intact. That child should have you, yourself, as the only interlocutor. You could hear this voice in many old texts. That voice had emerged through different people disguised by different words. That voice had vanished into thin air along with those people at different periods of history and those deaths manifested through different verbal expressions. The reason for your apprehension of being unable to convey to another person your experiences as you would have liked might be due to that difference or your desire to cling to its protection. A price has to be paid for this, of course. You have to suffer losses. Separations are imminent. You have got to acquiesce to returns. A moment comes when you feel like coming to a standstill, a standstill that is premeditated. Then you begin keeping close track of yourself; this will take up all your time. You will embrace an individual you are attached to who had settled within you and whom you had not seen for quite a while, for instance in front of a movie theater, and as you are experiencing the warmth of that embrace in all its nakedness, who do you think would be that person or thing that you are embracing . . . on those Sundays when none of your worries are given voice to, when one's feeling low, those who go to have a lunch in a restaurant, accompanied by their respective anxieties and desolations cannot confess even to themselves what importance those family deaths have? What sort of families are they in which no questions are asked properly? And if they are ever asked, none of them receives a proper and frank answer, who considers the climax of early ejaculation into questionable women of easy virtue, or who is unconsciously buggered with simple tricks? These are some of the problems found in this city in which I live, which I try to understand, and which is moving away from me apace. Amongst other issues, I must also quote the case of individuals who cannot properly live in their homes because of their outer concerns, who go on package tours in order to pack their experiences in their luggage, who give serious cause for concern about cars that consume less and less oil, who sit in tasteless dinner sets, and who believe themselves to have been informed of the goings on by the headlines of newspapers. At such times, I leave everybody where they belong. I leave everybody in his own reality in order to find myself. The flights that ripped me gradually from those people were the same old flights seen the world over. According to those books that are supposed to be guides for our lifestyle, the said flights have their special designation. We happen to be under the umbrella of knowledge accumulated and stored. Must I make headway toward a rain without paying any attention to what I may run into under these circumstances? Must I remember once more that to live one's emotions, to venture to live them is much more difficult than to narrate their story? Certain defeats had certainly killed certain things within us. Certain defeats had most probably made it possible to proceed on toward new defeats. But was there any other way to believe in one's past, to hear one's footsteps or to feel oneself continuously in the midst of that squabble?

(. . .) Now that I've reached a state in which I may be able to share those lives carried by regret, not omitting to interrogate myself, the reason for my supposition that we live mostly by our fantasies may result from our acknowledgment of defeat after a given stopover along the way, or from our consideration of the fact that we do not take it as a defeat, or from our simple conviction in stories. I had returned to the inexhaustible pack of lies without end. I must have been prepared for certain things at least. These returns and deceptions can foster the belief in writing and make it defendable. We cannot deny the existence of one-man shows in the various scenes shifting to other backgrounds during a death play. There, one can remember those little seclusions, those shadows and the long road that leads to solitude. That road is your road, that country is your country, that time is your time. You may come across certain people with certain procurements in the tales you assembled over the course of those years you let pass you by; those years parade in front of you as though not experienced because of your fear of the demolition of those shelters or those years which you were content to merely observe and in certain cases exhaust through deferment; those years you have tried to fit into a couple of words, visions, and objects. With the acquisitions of those years, you dream of announcing with all your heart to certain people that you have become resolved not to return. They are the things you saw during your different lives which you could not understand. They are your impossibilities of return. They are your regrets, your deficiencies, and your dilemmas. You must have learned by now that you should not and cannot leave a person in a very distant place after all the losses suffered. No one has remained or will ever remain at a time or place where one cannot relive the past. In the play you have acted with closed eyes, you feel carved within your depths scars marked as wrinkles. Then you ask yourself who were those people who had raised those walls around you. For whom had those photographs of happy moments been shot? Who had those walls hid and spared from whom?

(. . .) Such questions are undoubtedly asked in many cities throughout the world, in their streets, beyond the walls that bar entry for certain people to a history they are in pursuit of, the history of their own 'old city.' Whose ghetto was it, for whom had it become a forbidden zone, under what name and in which languages and during what times had those fears and estrangement been experienced? Whether we like it or not the history of Milan, Warsaw, and Budapest, in the background of their reflections in us, open the door to many a story that had been acted in those ghettos. However, it seems as though, in addition to all this, there are people waiting for us far beyond those visions. One cannot help asking whether there may be people who have preferred to remain in those ghettos among the architects and foremen of those walls. Had those walls not been erected, the history written would have been much different of course. The history would have been written, blending different colors with different days. Such hesitancy begins with those emotions of fear and alienation, in that sense of failure, in a place where you cannot meet with other people whose presence you are aware of. This hesitancy lends breath to other songs which you still find difficult to sing. You must know that the walls, once demolished, continue to soar afterward. One is inclined to ask who had been the possessors of those walls henceforth. To whom did those walls belong? To those who had been set aside, or to those who had been willing to be set aside? Everybody created his own ghetto and lived there until the end. Everybody unconsciously incarcerated himself in his own ghetto. Those stories had for this reason brought me to that boundary from whose bourns no traveler has returned. This was also the boundary wherein I inquired of myself the credibility of what I beheld, heard, and told; if the things I had dreamt of might have actually occurred or not. Nevertheless, I had to make that step forward which would take me to the other side of that boundary in order that I might be able to understand myself better. That was the reason why

I went back to those streets that I could never exhaust in the background of that district and that story. Everybody had walls that remained far beyond that history. Everybody needed to display to somebody else his experiences and had to have them confirmed by them. Everybody was his own slave and victim in the long run. For instance, my pencils whose lead frequently broke, my perfumed rubbers, and my compass which I never used as well as the smell of that floor polish were all there. There, in addition to what I had abandoned and the things that I had moved away from was that epileptic beggar who always stood in the same corner, whose smile gave me a fright; and Madame Vera who went around with her greasy and disheveled hair in rags despite her wealth; apartments; the hoard; and the taxi driver 'Kemaletting the Crazy,' an enthusiastic devotee of the Feriköy football club, who invited his clients sporadically to a tavern to have a mug of beer; Aleko, the communist newspaperman who never ceased to heap the Party of Justice with faint praise; the Pinocchio Gatenyo with the bulbous nose; the 'fake plumber' stinking of alcohol throughout the day; Monsieur Oscar, 'the asthmatic carpenter' who died of a stroke when he was about to complete a colossal kitchen cabinet for a client unknown to us, while sipping at his raki, working till the late hours in his small shop over many years; Münip Bey who, having opened his window on summer nights, used to play the song Tereddüt (Hesitancy) on his lute; the grocer 'Bekir the Kurd,' the 'Swindler'; 'Talat the Silent' who starched and ironed clothes without speaking to anyone; 'Aslan the Sodomite,' the maker of quilts who used to hire boy apprentices with gnarled hands; Uncle Selahattin 'the pedophile opinion dealer', notorious for his absent-mindedness and who frequently gave us colored pencils and crepe paper as a gift; Madame Alice the gossip whom I always imagined naked as she kept telling me that when I grew up I would pay a visit to her shop to buy slips and bras for my sweethearts; and last but not least 'Kemal the Dwarf,' the assistant pharmacist who used to give hypodermic injections to his clients and who harangued willing listeners, imparting them with his 'vast knowledge' of poisons, and who never failed to divest himself from his impeccable costume of a tie and white pinafore and who had ended up poisoning himself . . . When I remembered the images of these people I considered myself justified in having a profound belief in dreams, in fantasies and in new stories. This may have been the reason why that house had always welcomed me. That is why I tried to make headway for years and years in the story of that street and apartment with the hope of having a better insight into myself and into those lives. My walk would not come to an end. I lived my fantasies leisurely, as I learned how to abandon my words and 'kill' them. I wonder which of my unredeemable qualities had I given to those individuals that I tried to describe and comprehend in this long text, to which individuals had I sought within me; in my attempts at unmasking the identity behind which I had hidden myself? In a world what is there to lose, there are the issues pregnant with other meanings, the mirrors to reflect our new locations, windmills, all the sexual fantasies presented with all their illusions and all the other aspects of war as shown on the TV, with anonymous torturers all around us who are not exposed to the sight of the viewers. Everybody dies despite his dreams, especially for himself, in his own chamber; because your place in that long adventure is determined by those hopes that you have conveyed to others, or, what is still more important, by the hopes you were able to communicate to others. What cannot be expressed or is not desired to be expressed is, I think, that spot where truth and falsehood converge and which you cannot help seeing in the long run. In that spot which you would not be willing to share with others, you are hiding the truth which you are reluctant to approach, the truth which you are reluctant to consider at length, to analyze or to understand it. I had loved the poem found in those rooms that the sun had failed to illuminate properly, especially at such moments, these moments of silence. Those rooms also concealed the history of a contentment with certain things, little things which a person might enliven by referring to them under various names and associations. Those rooms were the spaces with which you established links between you and your personal effects, they were the drinks which you always deferred to a third person, the books you had not found the opportunity to read, your garden which you had failed to tend, your sea where you could not swim, and perhaps your house which you could not renovate. But the history of your contentment with these things had remained in calendars covered by a thick layer of dust, called for by other voices and other mornings. Those hotel rooms you visited on weekends, more often than not in the company of others, had not been nurtured with those flowerpots for no reason. Those telephone calls had not aroused new hopes in vain. Objects concealed other objects simultaneously.

(. . .) In those things, those yearnings and wry joys we could not always share with others we became viable, as well as discovering a beautiful little poem or at least having dreamt of such a discovery. I had let myself penetrate the story, having been encouraged by these things on one of those days when I felt the entire text within me. Long long ago, I happened to be by the seaside in that café or in the tea garden, as it is preferred to be called nowadays. The summer was drawing to a close. I was hoping that what I saw, what I could see, would be able to dictate to me a sentence untouched up to this point, despite the old emotion that the summers aroused in me and whose stories I had been able to write. Fishermen were returning with their catch. It was the season of bonitos. Casting a glance on the bonitos lying scattered on the waterfront before taking their place in the chests, I had said to myself: "they are lean yet; at least one month to go before they get fat; all the same I must buy a couple on my way back home; why not fry them instead of having to roast them in the oven; I'll add salted onions dressed with olive oil and lemon and . . ." It was early yet for a Saturday morning for those who wanted to dispel the stress of the weekend and bask in the melancholy of Sunday evening and for the arrival of entire working-class families with blank expressions to watch the beauty of the sea passing platitudinous comments . . . On one of the tables sat an elderly gentleman with his face turned toward the sea. A feeling difficult to describe had drawn me to him. I had perched on a chair next to his table. "I knew you'd come," he said. "I knew you'd come" was a sentence I had also read in other stories which had always given me a shudder, a sentence whose associations I couldn't ignore. With a faint smile he looked at me as though he had heard the voice in my head. "It's my habit to come here quite often at this hour of the morning. Quite often, so long as my health permits. I couldn't quit this corner despite all I've lost . . . I'd been waiting for you . . ." he said. I approached his face. I understood the reason for my shudder. The person I was facing was my exact double, my exact future replica. His smile must have been due to his apprehension at my realization. The smile was reminiscent of my unforgettable dreams. "Certain encounters have no explanation, despite all the words you rely on and in which you take shelter, you just cannot explain them," he said. "Just like in those stories . . . a stranger meets you and says to you during one of your visits somewhere I knew you'd be coming," I replied. "Just like in some stories . . . you have nearly come to the end of this long one. At least you happen to be somewhere which you believe to be near the end; you are somewhere where you intend to leave certain things awhile to be rid of them," he said. "I know, however, that certain relationship will continue in others, in some way or another," I said. "You're right there . . . but when relationships are lived as they should be, when all debts are paid, different words are used," he said. "One must know how to emerge from the egg, pupa, or chrysalis," I retorted. He remained silent, staring into the distance. "I might figure you are at the very beginning of this story," I added. This sentence was used to find a place for this piece of writing in my story which I realized more and more everyday that I would never be able to complete and to which now and then I wanted to take up once more with fresh enthusiasm. I was now in a position to tell all about it. Many a book for which I felt an attraction began with a little call. I distinctly remembered; that time was my own once more. The words were once again the words I tried to bring together, the words that would contribute to my new expectations. A letter, a note, or an unanticipated voice . . . Every preparation gains meaning by a journey to a completely new man, to a world of emotions, of probability. Who knows what one is going to meet on the road, who has called us from there, from the place from which we have received an invitation, what hopes or failures we are to run across. Bags are packed, suits are made ready; this is one of the questions begged, which figures in poems. One is puzzled to decide what he should take with him before setting out. Books, perfumes, objects, hallucinations, words . . . which of these things should one take on the journey? What exactly, since there will be no return. What exactly, since there will be no dawn anymore for such a hope? The spell has been cast. You can carry the sense of death more freely for this very reason. I had the opportunity to cast another glance at the letter left in my postbox. Both the address and the hour of assembly had clearly been stated. I was at the outset of a journey I had been looking forward to for a good many years from which I could put off no longer. The journey I was invited to undertake was to be a long and interminable one. I had arrived in the venue long before the stated hour; it was a restaurant far removed from all the known texts, a restaurant that concealed in it many details of the past. I looked about. The first thing I noticed was the profound silence that reigned there; it was a complete, hushed, and deathly silence . . . an introversion . . . Some of the tables were occupied by clients that exchanged words among themselves without turning their heads to look around. They seemed to be in a distant world of their own. A dim light illumined them. As I got used to the general atmosphere, I realized that these people were the figures in 'that story.' They seemed to speak openly about things. They hadn't noticed me. I was absent, as though I had not come there at all. I had thought that I had to consider and try to understand my extraneousness and the place that my estrangement had brought me to. Under the circumstances, I might keep silent, I might shut up and wait and use my sight once again. There sat an elderly gentleman. The fact that if one stood stationary and abided in a state of immutability over many years, this resulting expectancy would present versatility. I gingerly advanced toward him. It was as though I knew him better than anyone, better than anyone that I had set eyes on up until that point. My diffidence might have caused my flight at any moment. I had felt once more the presence of the man within me. He had smiled: "I was the one who invited you; I knew you would come," he said, "sooner or later . . . regardless of whether you'd try to evade and resist the urge to turn and run." Suddenly I saw the sound of my fright. He was my old age, the future that lay ahead. "All right," I said, "but I haven't completed my story yet. The story I wanted to live to the bitter end has not yet ended . . . " He inclined his head to his breast, evading my stare and said: "I know well enough that it has not. As a matter of fact, certain stories never come to an end; for some people stories never end . . . " Relations with some people never end . . . some stories never end. To whom were these words referring; for whom were they meant; for which lack of communication; who had been ignored; for which last sentence were they aimed? Both of us kept our eyes from each other. During the whole length of the conversation our looks would no longer meet. "Beginnings or last steps . . . There seems to be little difference between them, very little difference; a difference created by a single sentence, a sentence that everybody would have liked to appropriate, everybody would attribute meaning according to his own idiosyncrasies. For, sooner or later everybody returns to the spot where the journey started. One realizes in time that walking means making headway toward your God. That is why one likes to live stories. Certain stories are exhausted within you by an interior dialogue," he said. "I want to believe that what we are experiencing here is real and that it will, like all other dreams, be given life in my writing, like many similar dreams I tried to describe," I said. "There are dreams you can never describe," he said. Whereupon I asked him where I was supposed to place this encounter in my writing, in the name of which dream, and the reason why he had invited me there. He smiled and stared at me at length for the first time. "You haven't understood yet, have you? Just look around. They were your heroes, the figures you described, tried to describe in your other stories," he said. "But," I retorted, "it seems to me that I'm seeing them for the first time here; none of them address me." He kept smiling. "Now, how about a new story?" he

asked. I directed my look to the door. "You are looking in the right direction
. . . again . . . even though we may not meet . . . again . . . for that writing . . .
earmarked . . . the price being paid." The sun had begun to make its warmth felt
on that morning café. We had to keep silent, only for a brief moment, at this
very spot of the story that I had not completed, of the story I had dared to commence. Our conversation had been interrupted by a silence which could be fitted in an ancient photograph laden with emotions and shortcomings, a photograph not suitable to be shared. "This story should come to an end with a different hero at a different place . . . " I said every now and then during the whole
course of our silence. To this end, I had wanted to tell the last part to someone
at least, to an individual who would really listen to me . . . "There was a woman,"
I said, "who had forsaken me for a painter and had gone to live on the Aegean
coast . . . she was to return to me many years later, at the least expected moment
. . . at a time when I had succeeded in acclimatizing to myself and giving myself
over to myself . . . to run into each other years later in Şisle, on the shoreline; we
were to walk on the sand with bare feet in order to feel our weight pressing in
the sand . . . with bare feet, hand in hand . . . a last walk . . . a last walk or the first
true walk of our lives. Perhaps only then would we be able to tell the stories we
had left behind . . . only then could we be telling each other our stories and tales
. . . in order to die in our dreams, in our last dreams as individuals who have
known true touches," I said. He retorted, "but who told you that our story has
come to an end? We'll have to try to bring together the pieces by having recourse
to other people, to other voices and languages. We can no longer stop. Nevertheless, it's still too early to see the figures in that café, or to live that walk along
the shore . . . For the moment I can offer you the seashells of another shore . . .
the seashells of another shore . . . as a small clue . . . "

We remained sitting for a while before he stood up slowly, having been convinced that he had had his share of conversation. I made as though I was going
to make a comment. He stopped short, pointing to somewhere on the opposite
coast, to the sea or to the shore . . . as though he was implying that he could not
set out on that journey with me. He might have gone to that place which I believe
I'll reach one day. For the moment I was to stay where I was, on the last coast I
could descry . . .

(. . .) Now we are once again alone with our fantasies, our stories which we
cannot share with others . . . there once again . . . at the spot we deserve . . . we

had loved each other for a flight we had been nurturing and for which we had been waiting to take for a good many years . . . for a flight . . . because flights fitted loves . . . flights fitted loves . . . we had desired to believe firmly in this legend of flight; but were we ever able to attain the meaning that lay within us of this flight? Now once again we are eating, making love, and dying with that which we had taken shelter from. Love, love that we sublimated, got transformed into a homicide after the trespass of a given boundary. After all love meant dying in somebody's arms, didn't it? Love was a play of loneliness with a different name, wasn't it? Love consisted of a few photographs, leftovers from those old deceptions which we had lived absentmindedly in our rooms, in our rooms alone, alien to others, distant from them, did it not? Had we not brought to these homicides barbed wires and minefields meant to protect us, considering our values and the assumption that nakedness was shameful? Under the circumstances how and by which representations can we ever convey to others what we are going through within the confines of these boundaries? The city was replete with stories unknown to others, which could not be lived by outsiders. Our brains had been stuffed with knowledge that made true knowledge inaccessible.

All that had been experienced might be explained perhaps by our inability to transform ourselves into chrysalides, by the pain such a failure involved. Does this little death not explain also the deafness and the sense of abandonment? Was that deafness and sense of abandonment a gift given to us because of our striving to live a long life? When I think about all of this I see before me millions of chrysalides . . . when I think about all this . . . I want to become immoral . . .

Yes, immoral, to be immoral in order not to disappoint the expectations of those who bestowed to us those monumental constructions and extensive knowledge. To be immoral, to know how to to be immoral . . . in order to finally discover my own morality, to discover myself in another morality . . . According to those with such expectations, there is no sense in what is being told here, anyhow. The heroes of those stories fell in love in those worlds, in those lives, in the same way for the same fantasies and illusions. The heroes in those stories could betray each other or themselves by following the same path, they felt remorse for having answered the calls of the same road or abiding in the same lie. Every human being had his own unforgettable photographs, streets, and little shops. If so, why on earth did I want to tell all this? There is no one answer to this question. Perhaps, I just wanted to speak about myself, about those colors, about the histories and stories that those languages have left with us. I don't know to what extent I have been successful in this, taking into account my expectations and efforts. Frankly I don't know. The only thing I know now is that I will not go back there for quite some time; I don't want to. At present I'm thinking of one of those typical, ordinary beaches which I'll never cease to speak about . . . typical, ordinary, a place that everybody will experience . . . I may light a cigarette . . . I can walk into the sea naked . . . I can return to that human being with those words despite all that has occurred in the meantime . . . I can return to that person with those words . . . "Tell me," I can say to him, "tell me once again . . . once again, tell me . . . once again. Tell me for the sake of that place, time, and individual . . . for the sake of that country, for our country . . . tell me another story I can believe in; a story, true, real, without adornments. Tell me, tell me, tell me . . . "

MARIO LEVI was born in 1957 in Istanbul. He graduated from Istanbul University's Faculty of Literature with a degree in French language and literature in 1980. In addition to being a writer, Levi has worked as a French teacher, an importer, a journalist, a radio programmer, and a copywriter. *Istanbul Was a Fairy Tale* is his first novel to be translated into English.

ENDER GÜROL was born in 1931 and pursued his studies at the English and French Philology Departments of Istanbul University. A prolific translator into Turkish, he has over a hundred books to his credit, including titles by Bertrand Russell, Charles Dickens, Ernest Hemingway, and Carl Jung. His translations into English include *The Time Regulation Institute* by Ahmet Hamdi Tanpınar.

PETROS ABATZOGLOU, *What Does Mrs. Freeman Want?*

MICHAL AJVAZ, *The Golden Age.*
The Other City.

PIERRE ALBERT-BIROT, *Grabinoulor.*

YUZ ALESHKOVSKY, *Kangaroo.*

FELIPE ALFAU, *Chromos.*
Locos.

JOÃO ALMINO, *The Book of Emotions.*

IVAN ÂNGELO, *The Celebration.*
The Tower of Glass.

DAVID ANTIN, *Talking.*

ANTÓNIO LOBO ANTUNES, *Knowledge of Hell.*
The Splendor of Portugal.

ALAIN ARIAS-MISSON, *Theatre of Incest.*

IFTIKHAR ARIF AND WAQAS KHWAJA, EDS.,
Modern Poetry of Pakistan.

JOHN ASHBERY AND JAMES SCHUYLER,
A Nest of Ninnies.

ROBERT ASHLEY, *Perfect Lives.*

GABRIELA AVIGUR-ROTEM, *Heatwave and Crazy Birds.*

HEIMRAD BÄCKER, *transcript.*

DJUNA BARNES, *Ladies Almanack.*
Ryder.

JOHN BARTH, *LETTERS.*
Sabbatical.

DONALD BARTHELME, *The King.*
Paradise.

SVETISLAV BASARA, *Chinese Letter.*

MIQUEL BAUÇÀ, *The Siege in the Room.*

RENÉ BELLETTO, *Dying.*

MAREK BIEŃCZYK, *Transparency.*

MARK BINELLI, *Sacco and Vanzetti Must Die!*

ANDREI BITOV, *Pushkin House.*

ANDREJ BLATNIK, *You Do Understand.*

LOUIS PAUL BOON, *Chapel Road.*
My Little War.
Summer in Termuren.

ROGER BOYLAN, *Killoyle.*

IGNÁCIO DE LOYOLA BRANDÃO,
Anonymous Celebrity.
The Good-Bye Angel.
Teeth under the Sun.
Zero.

BONNIE BREMSER, *Troia: Mexican Memoirs.*

CHRISTINE BROOKE-ROSE, *Amalgamemnon.*

BRIGID BROPHY, *In Transit.*

MEREDITH BROSNAN, *Mr. Dynamite.*

GERALD L. BRUNS, *Modern Poetry and the Idea of Language.*

EVGENY BUNIMOVICH AND J. KATES, EDS.,
Contemporary Russian Poetry: An Anthology.

GABRIELLE BURTON, *Heartbreak Hotel.*

MICHEL BUTOR, *Degrees.*
Mobile.
Portrait of the Artist as a Young Ape.

G. CABRERA INFANTE, *Infante's Inferno.*
Three Trapped Tigers.

JULIETA CAMPOS,
The Fear of Losing Eurydice.

ANNE CARSON, *Eros the Bittersweet.*

ORLY CASTEL-BLOOM, *Dolly City.*

CAMILO JOSÉ CELA, *Christ versus Arizona.*
The Family of Pascual Duarte.
The Hive.

LOUIS-FERDINAND CÉLINE, *Castle to Castle.*
Conversations with Professor Y.
London Bridge.

Normance.
North.
Rigadoon.

MARIE CHAIX, *The Laurels of Lake Constance.*

HUGO CHARTERIS, *The Tide Is Right.*

JEROME CHARYN, *The Tar Baby.*

ERIC CHEVILLARD, *Demolishing Nisard.*

LUIS CHITARRONI, *The No Variations.*

MARC CHOLODENKO, *Mordechai Schamz.*

JOSHUA COHEN, *Witz.*

EMILY HOLMES COLEMAN, *The Shutter of Snow.*

ROBERT COOVER, *A Night at the Movies.*

STANLEY CRAWFORD, *Log of the S.S. The Mrs Unguentine.*
Some Instructions to My Wife.

ROBERT CREELEY, *Collected Prose.*

RENÉ CREVEL, *Putting My Foot in It.*

RALPH CUSACK, *Cadenza.*

SUSAN DAITCH, *L.C.*
Storytown.

NICHOLAS DELBANCO, *The Count of Concord.*
Sherbrookes.

NIGEL DENNIS, *Cards of Identity.*

PETER DIMOCK, *A Short Rhetoric for Leaving the Family.*

ARIEL DORFMAN, *Konfidenz.*

COLEMAN DOWELL,
The Houses of Children.
Island People.
Too Much Flesh and Jabez.

ARKADII DRAGOMOSHCHENKO, *Dust.*

RIKKI DUCORNET, *The Complete Butcher's Tales.*
The Fountains of Neptune.
The Jade Cabinet.
The One Marvelous Thing.
Phosphor in Dreamland.
The Stain.
The Word "Desire."

WILLIAM EASTLAKE, *The Bamboo Bed.*
Castle Keep.
Lyric of the Circle Heart.

JEAN ECHENOZ, *Chopin's Move.*

STANLEY ELKIN, *A Bad Man.*
Boswell: A Modern Comedy.
Criers and Kibitzers, Kibitzers and Criers.
The Dick Gibson Show.
The Franchiser.
George Mills.
The Living End.
The MacGuffin.
The Magic Kingdom.
Mrs. Ted Bliss.
The Rabbi of Lud.
Van Gogh's Room at Arles.

FRANÇOIS EMMANUEL, *Invitation to a Voyage.*

ANNIE ERNAUX, *Cleaned Out.*

SALVADOR ESPRIU, *Ariadne in the Grotesque Labyrinth.*

LAUREN FAIRBANKS, *Muzzle Thyself.*
Sister Carrie.

LESLIE A. FIEDLER, *Love and Death in the American Novel.*

JUAN FILLOY, *Faction.*
Op Oloop.

ANDY FITCH, *Pop Poetics.*

GUSTAVE FLAUBERT, *Bouvard and Pécuchet.*

KASS FLEISHER, *Talking out of School.*

SELECTED DALKEY ARCHIVE TITLES

FORD MADOX FORD,
  The March of Literature.
JON FOSSE, *Aliss at the Fire.*
  Melancholy.
MAX FRISCH, *I'm Not Stiller.*
  Man in the Holocene.
CARLOS FUENTES, *Christopher Unborn.*
  Distant Relations.
  Terra Nostra.
  Vlad.
  Where the Air Is Clear.
TAKEHIKO FUKUNAGA, *Flowers of Grass.*
WILLIAM GADDIS, *J R.*
  The Recognitions.
JANICE GALLOWAY, *Foreign Parts.*
  The Trick Is to Keep Breathing.
WILLIAM H. GASS, *Cartesian Sonata*
    and Other Novellas.
  Finding a Form.
  A Temple of Texts.
  The Tunnel.
  Willie Masters' Lonesome Wife.
GÉRARD GAVARRY, *Hoppla! 1 2 3.*
  Making a Novel.
ETIENNE GILSON,
  The Arts of the Beautiful.
  Forms and Substances in the Arts.
C. S. GISCOMBE, *Giscome Road.*
  Here.
  Prairie Style.
DOUGLAS GLOVER, *Bad News of the Heart.*
  The Enamoured Knight.
WITOLD GOMBROWICZ,
  A Kind of Testament.
PAULO EMÍLIO SALES GOMES, *P's Three*
    Women.
KAREN ELIZABETH GORDON, *The Red Shoes.*
GEORGI GOSPODINOV, *Natural Novel.*
JUAN GOYTISOLO, *Count Julian.*
  Exiled from Almost Everywhere.
  Juan the Landless.
  Makbara.
  Marks of Identity.
PATRICK GRAINVILLE, *The Cave of Heaven.*
HENRY GREEN, *Back.*
  Blindness.
  Concluding.
  Doting.
  Nothing.
JACK GREEN, *Fire the Bastards!*
JIŘÍ GRUŠA, *The Questionnaire.*
GABRIEL GUDDING,
  Rhode Island Notebook.
MELA HARTWIG, *Am I a Redundant*
    Human Being?
JOHN HAWKES, *The Passion Artist.*
  Whistlejacket.
ELIZABETH HEIGHWAY, ED., *Best of*
    Contemporary Fiction from Georgia.
ALEKSANDAR HEMON, ED.,
  Best European Fiction.
AIDAN HIGGINS, *Balcony of Europe.*
  A Bestiary.
  Blind Man's Bluff
  Bornholm Night-Ferry.
  Darkling Plain: Texts for the Air.
  Flotsam and Jetsam.
  Langrishe, Go Down.
  Scenes from a Receding Past.
  Windy Arbours.
KEIZO HINO, *Isle of Dreams.*
KAZUSHI HOSAKA, *Plainsong.*

ALDOUS HUXLEY, *Antic Hay.*
  Crome Yellow.
  Point Counter Point.
  Those Barren Leaves.
  Time Must Have a Stop.
NAOYUKI II, *The Shadow of a Blue Cat.*
MIKHAIL IOSSEL AND JEFF PARKER, EDS.,
  Amerika: Russian Writers View the
    United States.
DRAGO JANČAR, *The Galley Slave.*
GERT JONKE, *The Distant Sound.*
  Geometric Regional Novel.
  Homage to Czerny.
  The System of Vienna.
JACQUES JOUET, *Mountain R.*
  Savage.
  Upstaged.
CHARLES JULIET, *Conversations with*
    Samuel Beckett and Bram van
    Velde.
MIEKO KANAI, *The Word Book.*
YORAM KANIUK, *Life on Sandpaper.*
HUGH KENNER, *The Counterfeiters.*
  Flaubert, Joyce and Beckett:
    The Stoic Comedians.
  Joyce's Voices.
DANILO KIŠ, *The Attic.*
  Garden, Ashes.
  The Lute and the Scars
  Psalm 44.
  A Tomb for Boris Davidovich.
ANITA KONKKA, *A Fool's Paradise.*
GEORGE KONRÁD, *The City Builder.*
TADEUSZ KONWICKI, *A Minor Apocalypse.*
  The Polish Complex.
MENIS KOUMANDAREAS, *Koula.*
ELAINE KRAF, *The Princess of 72nd Street.*
JIM KRUSOE, *Iceland.*
AYŞE KULIN, *Farewell: A Mansion in*
    Occupied Istanbul.
EWA KURYLUK, *Century 21.*
EMILIO LASCANO TEGUI, *On Elegance*
    While Sleeping.
ERIC LAURRENT, *Do Not Touch.*
HERVÉ LE TELLIER, *The Sextine Chapel.*
  A Thousand Pearls (for a Thousand
    Pennies)
VIOLETTE LEDUC, *La Bâtarde.*
EDOUARD LEVÉ, *Autoportrait.*
  Suicide.
MARIO LEVI, *Istanbul Was a Fairy Tale.*
SUZANNE JILL LEVINE, *The Subversive*
    Scribe: Translating Latin
    American Fiction.
DEBORAH LEVY, *Billy and Girl.*
  Pillow Talk in Europe and Other
    Places.
JOSÉ LEZAMA LIMA, *Paradiso.*
ROSA LIKSOM, *Dark Paradise.*
OSMAN LINS, *Avalovara.*
  The Queen of the Prisons of Greece.
ALF MAC LOCHLAINN,
  The Corpus in the Library.
  Out of Focus.
RON LOEWINSOHN, *Magnetic Field(s).*
MINA LOY, *Stories and Essays of Mina Loy.*
BRIAN LYNCH, *The Winner of Sorrow.*
D. KEITH MANO, *Take Five.*
MICHELINE AHARONIAN MARCOM,
  The Mirror in the Well.
BEN MARCUS,
  The Age of Wire and String.

FOR A FULL LIST OF PUBLICATIONS, VISIT:
www.dalkeyarchive.com

SELECTED DALKEY ARCHIVE TITLES

The Princess Hoppy.
Some Thing Black.
LEON S. ROUDIEZ, *French Fiction Revisited.*
RAYMOND ROUSSEL, *Impressions of Africa.*
VEDRANA RUDAN, *Night.*
STIG SÆTERBAKKEN, *Siamese.*
LYDIE SALVAYRE, *The Company of Ghosts.*
   Everyday Life.
   The Lecture.
   Portrait of the Writer as a
      Domesticated Animal.
   The Power of Flies.
LUIS RAFAEL SÁNCHEZ,
   Macho Camacho's Beat.
SEVERO SARDUY, *Cobra & Maitreya.*
NATHALIE SARRAUTE,
   Do You Hear Them?
   Martereau.
   The Planetarium.
ARNO SCHMIDT, *Collected Novellas.*
   Collected Stories.
   Nobodaddy's Children.
   Two Novels.
ASAF SCHURR, *Motti.*
CHRISTINE SCHUTT, *Nightwork.*
GAIL SCOTT, *My Paris.*
DAMION SEARLS, *What We Were Doing*
   and Where We Were Going.
JUNE AKERS SEESE,
   Is This What Other Women Feel Too?
   What Waiting Really Means.
BERNARD SHARE, *Inish.*
   Transit.
AURELIE SHEEHAN, *Jack Kerouac Is Pregnant.*
VIKTOR SHKLOVSKY, *Bowstring.*
   Knight's Move.
   A Sentimental Journey:
      Memoirs 1917–1922.
   Energy of Delusion: A Book on Plot.
   Literature and Cinematography.
   Theory of Prose.
   Third Factory.
   Zoo, or Letters Not about Love.
CLAUDE SIMON, *The Invitation.*
PIERRE SINIAC, *The Collaborators.*
KJERSTI A. SKOMSVOLD, *The Faster I Walk,*
   the Smaller I Am.
JOSEF ŠKVORECKÝ, *The Engineer of*
   Human Souls.
GILBERT SORRENTINO,
   Aberration of Starlight.
   Blue Pastoral.
   Crystal Vision.
   Imaginative Qualities of Actual
   · *Things.*
   Mulligan Stew.
   Pack of Lies.
   Red the Fiend.
   The Sky Changes.
   Something Said.
   Splendide-Hôtel.
   Steelwork.
   Under the Shadow.
W. M. SPACKMAN, *The Complete Fiction.*
ANDRZEJ STASIUK, *Dukla.*
   Fado.
GERTRUDE STEIN, *Lucy Church Amiably.*
   The Making of Americans.
   A Novel of Thank You.
LARS SVENDSEN, *A Philosophy of Evil.*
PIOTR SZEWC, *Annihilation.*
GONÇALO M. TAVARES, *Jerusalem.*

Joseph Walser's Machine.
Learning to Pray in the Age of
   Technique.
LUCIAN DAN TEODOROVICI,
   Our Circus Presents . . .
NIKANOR TERATOLOGEN, *Assisted Living.*
STEFAN THEMERSON, *Hobson's Island.*
   The Mystery of the Sardine.
   Tom Harris.
TAEKO TOMIOKA, *Building Waves.*
JOHN TOOMEY, *Sleepwalker.*
JEAN-PHILIPPE TOUSSAINT, *The Bathroom.*
   Camera.
   Monsieur.
   Reticence.
   Running Away.
   Self-Portrait Abroad.
   Television.
   The Truth about Marie.
DUMITRU TSEPENEAG, *Hotel Europa.*
   The Necessary Marriage.
   Pigeon Post.
   Vain Art of the Fugue.
ESTHER TUSQUETS, *Stranded.*
DUBRAVKA UGRESIC, *Lend Me Your Character.*
   Thank You for Not Reading.
TOR ULVEN, *Replacement.*
MATI UNT, *Brecht at Night.*
   Diary of a Blood Donor.
   Things in the Night.
ÁLVARO URIBE AND OLIVIA SEARS, EDS.,
   Best of Contemporary Mexican Fiction.
ELOY URROZ, *Friction.*
   The Obstacles.
LUISA VALENZUELA, *Dark Desires and*
   the Others.
   He Who Searches.
MARJA-LIISA VARTIO, *The Parson's Widow.*
PAUL VERHAEGHEN, *Omega Minor.*
AGLAJA VETERANYI, *Why the Child Is*
   Cooking in the Polenta.
BORIS VIAN, *Heartsnatcher.*
LLORENÇ VILLALONGA, *The Dolls' Room.*
TOOMAS VINT, *An Unending Landscape.*
ORNELA VORPSI, *The Country Where No*
   One Ever Dies.
AUSTRYN WAINHOUSE, *Hedyphagetica.*
PAUL WEST, *Words for a Deaf Daughter*
   & Gala.
CURTIS WHITE, *America's Magic Mountain.*
   The Idea of Home.
   Memories of My Father Watching TV.
   Monstrous Possibility: An Invitation
      to Literary Politics.
   Requiem.
DIANE WILLIAMS, *Excitability:*
   Selected Stories.
   Romancer Erector.
DOUGLAS WOOLF, *Wall to Wall.*
   Ya! & John-Juan.
JAY WRIGHT, *Polynomials and Pollen.*
   The Presentable Art of Reading
   Absence.
PHILIP WYLIE, *Generation of Vipers.*
MARGUERITE YOUNG, *Angel in the Forest.*
   Miss MacIntosh, My Darling.
REYOUNG, *Unbabbling.*
VLADO ŽABOT, *The Succubus.*
ZORAN ŽIVKOVIĆ, *Hidden Camera.*
LOUIS ZUKOFSKY, *Collected Fiction.*
VITOMIL ZUPAN, *Minuet for Guitar.*
SCOTT ZWIREN, *God Head.*